DRAGON BLESSED

BLEEDING REALMS

THE COMPLETE SERIES

NINA WALKER

ADDISON & GRAY PRESS
WWW.NINAWALKERBOOKS.COM

Copyright © 2020 by Nina Walker

All rights reserved. No part of this publication may be reproduced, distributed, or transmitted in any form or by any means, including photocopying, recording, or other electronic or mechanical methods, without the prior written permission of the publisher, except in the case of brief quotations embodied in critical reviews and certain other noncommercial uses permitted by copyright law.

ISBN: 978-1-950093-17-5

Published by Addison & Gray Press, LLC.

This is a work of fiction. Names, characters, businesses, places, events, locales, and incidents are either the products of the author's imagination or used in a fictitious manner. Any resemblance to actual persons, living or dead, or actual events is purely coincidental and not intended by the author or publisher.

Cover design by Artscandare
Interior design by We Got You Covered Book Design

*For Travis,
the boy who taught me how to write love stories.*

CROWN OF DRAGONS

NOT QUITE EIGHTEEN YEARS AGO

THE CHILD WAS BORN WITH two colored eyes: muddy earth and summer sky. The dragon clans believed her a gift from the Gods, a blessing bestowed on the new generation and a promise of royal strength. He thought it superstitious nonsense, another way the unholy beasts justified their elemental blasphemy.

He traveled under the cloak of night, pushing his fatigue to the breaking point— he had to move fast. Once the child and mother were deemed healthy enough to travel, they'd be relocated to the castle, and if that happened before he got to her, he'd miss his chance.

The village smelled of filth, of cattle and moody winter and crops gone sour. He curled his lip, slipping between long shadows and past the sentries without trouble, breaking into the hovel and finding her fast asleep. She was a tiny thing, pink cheeked and bowed lipped, with a wisp of raven hair. Some might say she was innocent. Pure. He knew better.

He scowled at the sleeping parents and the child tucked between them, imagining ways he could execute all three—end them while he still had the chance. But no, another Dragon Blessed daughter would be born with heterochromia to take this one's place. That baby might be born of better circumstances. Unreachable.

This one was right here. It had to be her.

The spell was nothing save for a few quick utterances. But he still had to procure the blood. So he cast the second spell, the one that would leave all three inhabitants lost in slumber until sunrise. Their breathing relaxed into the magic and the night grew impossibly quiet. He raised the bed sheet and found the child's foot. It was as small as a baby bird and blushing velvet to the touch. He felt no remorse as he pricked her heel and drained the blood. He let it run, much of it sopping onto the sheets, until his vial was filled. With a flick of his long finger, he erased the mess and wiped her clean.

Tomorrow, the trio would wake, fully rested and surprised at their good fortune. Tomorrow, he would take the blood to its intended target and cast the final spell. He held the warm vial as he would a precious gem and smiled for the first time in weeks. One day, this blood would prove to be the killing blow against the dragon clans, ending their reign—ending them. It really was a shame the baby had to be born with two colored eyes.

She never had a chance.

ONE
HAZEL

A WOMAN WITH A BUTCHER knife sticking out of her back is pulling my hair. At least, she's trying to. She hasn't quite figured out that I can't actually feel her, so she's gone from the polite ask, to the shoulder tap, to full-on hair pulling.

It's a new low, even for me.

I shift away, biting back an annoyed growl, and attempt to focus on the classroom whiteboard where Dr. Peters is scrawling something about Aristotle. I blink, hoping to tune out this obnoxious lady who's now flashing images of her medicine cabinet at me like she's going to die if I don't help, and I'm seriously about ready to punch her in her dead, pasty face.

Not that it's even possible. But seriously!

"You okay?" Macy whispers from the seat next to mine.

I sink into the padded chair and refocus on the lecture hall as I nod, hoping she'll forgive whatever horrible nonverbals are morphing my expression at the moment. Macy is kind and cool and pretty, and dang it if I don't want her to be my friend.

Yup. I've turned into *that girl*.

It's only been a week since I started my freshman year of college, and I've already managed to join what's turning out to be our dorm's "in crowd." Don't ask me for tips. Considering that I graduated a year early from high school over what Mom so lovingly calls "The Regina George Situation", I don't have any tips.

I moved into my dorm last Sunday, only one day before classes started, because I didn't want to be noticed. I didn't have visions of grandeur, of being tossed a frisbee my first day by my future husband or something equally moronic. Quite the opposite. I was awkwardly trying to blend in with my oversized hoodie from the sales rack at Target, my dirty blonde hair pulled back into a ponytail, wearing the barest of makeup (no contouring here), and hiding behind my nerdy and totally fake black-rimmed glasses. Which, by the way, I love—I'm proud to call myself a nerd.

I shouldn't have stood out, and I definitely shouldn't have made friends effortlessly. But did that stop the other girls living in my dorm from sticking to me like white on rice? No. No, it did not. And so far the "Mean Girls" group in our dorm is turning out to be the opposite of mean. They're like the glittery unicorn group of girly friends I'd always dreamed of having but only thought existed in cheesy made-for-TV movies. Who even knew pretty and popular *and kind* was possible at our age? But Mom promised college would be different, and so far, she wasn't lying.

The dead lady is still hovering right in my eyeline, distracting me from whatever's going on up front with Doctor Peters. It's pretty clear that she was a drug addict and she's going through some major withdrawals. I don't quite understand how that works considering she no longer has a body, and I feel bad for her—I do. But I'm *also* trying to focus on Peters as he goes over the origins of anthropology, and she's making herself rather difficult to ignore. I catch my other new friend Cora's raised eyebrows from across the room, and she points to her phone before turning back to the lecture. Discreetly, I check mine to find her text.

Wanna study for Friday's quiz together at lunch? My treat ;)

I smirk. The dining hall is included in our dorm fees, so it's not like Cora's going to treat me to anything other than the pleasure of her company. I quickly text her back. **Sure. So generous of you ;)**

I'm lucky this class has my two newest besties in it. Okay, they are the only true friends I've made so far, but still, it's best friend status at this point with the three of us. We've spent nearly all our time together over the last few days since we met. I wish all my classes had them, but no, that's not how college works. We just caught a break with Anthropology. Yay for General Education, or something like that.

Cora waggles her eyebrows with a cheeky grin when she reads my reply, and I'm hit with this surreal feeling of imposter syndrome. I'm suddenly cool, aren't I? How is that possible? It won't last and I hate that I care. This stint at popularity is a total farce that hasn't done a thing to change how I feel inside. I still feel out of place. I still have anxiety every single second I'm around these "normals" because deep down I know these people won't understand me and will probably mock me once they figure out my secret. Because they *will* figure it out. Given time, everyone does. Try as I might, I can't help my freak flag from flying high and following me wherever I go.

Actually, *they* follow me wherever I go. *They're* my stupid freak flag.

But I can't very well go around telling my new friends the truth about them, can I? I can't just announce, "I see dead people," like some kind of female Haley Joel Osment. The kid was a loner in that movie for a reason. And yeah, I guess these days it's cool to be weird and different, but not *that* weird and different. It would be one thing if I read tarot cards and wore a pretty rose quartz on a dainty chain around my neck; that would be passable. That might work.

Talking to the air? No. Definitely not okay to be babbling into the empty aisle, all like, "Oh, hey crazy lady, get off me! And spoiler alert, you're actually one of the dead people. I'll just send you on your way. Go be with Jesus!"

Can I do that right now? Hell to the no.

So that's why I'm about ready to spontaneously combust right here in this padded seat. I should be paying attention to the anthropology lecture. Peters is a campus favorite for a reason, and I actually really like this class if our first lecture was anything to go by.

But there are a lot of dead people hanging around campus. I purposely chose a small liberal arts college in a backwater West Virginian town so that spirits wouldn't bombard me like they do in big cities. Lucky for me, I don't see ancient ghosts, so I wasn't worried about the Civil War history here. It's the recently dead who appear to me. And as it turns out, Hayden College has its fair share. They seriously won't leave me alone now that they've realized I can see them. Even though I'm not talking to them or acknowledging them whatsoever, they sure aren't scared to bombard me.

It's like this: I can see the spirit realm. The ghosties sense that about me and send images to my mind. Sometimes it's moments from their lives, or people they love, regrets they have, but usually, it's random objects that make no difference to me. It rarely makes sense. But they do it all the time regardless of whether I'm busy—like right now, in the middle of class. And oh goodie, I'm supposed to be answering a question.

"Umm, sorry, Dr. Peters, what was the question?" I ask, voice cracking. My face burns as everyone in the classroom, living and dead, turns on me. It's a smallish lecture hall, but all fifty seats are filled. Lucky me.

Peters raises a bushy eyebrow, notices the phone tucked in my palm, and turns to another student. "Mr. Ashton, perhaps you could enlighten us?" The heavy gazes of my classmates turn from me to someone sitting in the back, and I let out a stilted breath. That could have gone better.

A brief silence is followed by a deep silky voice dripping in exasperation. He has a slight accent that for the life of me I can't place. "Anthropology comes from the Greek words anthropos, meaning human, and logos, meaning logic. That's an easy question, Dr. Peters. If people would listen instead of being glued to their phones, perhaps we could all move on to the more interesting bits."

A few students snicker. Shame washes over me, along with that awful feeling of being the butt of the joke. I can't believe he called me out like that! And it's not like I didn't know the answer. I just didn't hear the question because of this crack-baby ghosty hovering over me—who by the way, is still on my case, sending image after image of prescription medicine bottles. The shame burns up quickly, consumed by anger as I grit my teeth. I continue to tune out the dead lady's hysterics and turn back to glare at the know-it-all in the last row.

I'm stunned at what I find. An icy chill creeps over my body.

Whoever he is, he's glaring right back, his expression venomous, and with eyes so dark, I swear they're black. It's unsettling to the point of making my pulse race. He sees me looking but he doesn't turn away. A jolt of electricity shoots up my spine. His jaw is clenched tight, accentuating the sharp lines of his cheeks and the fullness of his pink lips. I take him in, this man with a face made of daydreams and nightmares. He's the kind of attractive meant for Photoshop and glossy magazine ads, not real life. And from his brazenness, I'd guess the good looks come with a crap load of arrogance. Gross. Also, total eye-roll.

The marker squeaks against the whiteboard as Peters continues the lecture, bringing the class back to focus.

But I don't turn back. Not yet. Instead, I sneer at the guy who's still openly staring at me with complete and utter disdain. Like, I'm sorry, but what does he want? He's probably used to women fawning over him, but I refuse to be so predictable and lame. I also don't want to be the first of us to break eye contact. It's as if we're playing a game of cat and mouse, but guess what? Cats are my favorite animals. I have two back home. Plus, I have claws. So back off!

Okay, I don't really have claws. I bite the crap out of my nails if we're being honest. But what I'm trying to say is I'm the cat in this scenario—I'm the winner.

He tilts his head, curls his lip, and averts his gaze.

Ha! I knew I was awesome!

Satisfied, I whip back around and resume my attempts to pay attention. I'm here to learn, dang it! The back of my neck heats all throughout the lecture, like a laser beam is being directed right at me. It's even more distracting than the ghosts all up in my business. But I don't turn around again. Not because I'm afraid of the jerk in the back, but because I don't want to give him the satisfaction of knowing he's bothering me. For whatever reason, the hatred between us is instant and mutual. I smile. It's a nice distraction for a haunted girl.

And lo and behold, a half hour later I find him waiting for me after class.

"Mr. Ashton" leans against the wall in the hallway and the moment he sees me, he pushes off it, stalking toward me like a lion about to attack an innocent baby gazelle. Yeah, I am well aware I just went from awesome feline warrior goddess to a baby gazelle.

"What are you doing here?" he demands, the accusatory tone slamming right through me.

I stop, Cora and Macy at my side. All three of us seem to be momentarily blinded by both his attractiveness and that continued brazenness. I blink rapidly, downright baffled by this behavior. It was one thing to challenge me in class, but to wait for me afterward so he can yell at me? Who does that? It only takes a second for that stunned feeling to evaporate into one of indignation.

"Back off," I snap, stepping forward in challenge. I almost can't believe my fearlessness. I've always been so afraid of the bullies, so ashamed of my curse, my self-esteem weakened by something I couldn't change no matter how hard I tried. I let the kids at my old school walk all over me to the point of graduating early and running away. But not today. Not with him. Something about this feels oddly different.

I glare up into his face, voice tight, "I don't even know you."

He scoffs and shakes his head, pointing at me until his index finger pushes against my shoulder. "Don't play dumb. I know what you are."

My whole body lights up with recognition, but not in a good way. I step back, nerves rushing through me like electric currents. He knows *what* I am? He knows I'm a medium? How?

"Don't touch her!" Cora bursts forward, her voice an angry growl. She's the kind of person I wouldn't want to mess with, but he doesn't even give her a second glance.

"This is my territory," he says, leaning in closer, hateful eyes trapping me in.

My inner voice is screaming at me to run far, far away. But something else inside me, something base and primal, wants to destroy him, to tear him limb from limb. Who does he think he is?

Our classmates have begun to form around the two of us, mixed expressions of shock and outrage and curiosity and even delight glued to their prying faces. But nobody intervenes. Go figure.

"Your territory?" I question with a laugh. "What is this, Westside Story? Like I said, I don't even know you. And don't you ever lay a hand on me again."

He pauses for a second, looking me up and down like I'm half diseased, like I smell bad or something. Do I smell bad? I quickly inhale and catch his scent; it's campfire and spice and oddly intoxicating. He's dressed in the kind of laid-back black t-shirt and jeans that cost a fortune to look like he doesn't care about his wardrobe. Typical. I'm wearing butter-soft black leggings and an oversized Gryffindor hoodie. And proud of it! His nostrils flare and that "could cut glass" jaw tenses again.

The moment stretches out between us, taut as a wire. Nobody moves. Nobody speaks. I suddenly grow hot. A ghostly gurgle of water streams across the floor, pooling at our feet an inch thick. I look down and stare, panic rushing through me. *Not now!* It seeps into my high top sneakers. Nobody else sees it. Nobody feels it. Dread sweeps over me. Where did it come from?

"Pack your things and get the hell out of this town," he hisses under his breath, the venom in his tone meant to sting. I blink up at him, out of my element. Then he pushes past me, his broad shoulders nearly knocking me to the tiled floor, into the ghostly water that only I can see.

I'm speechless.

Macy rushes to steady me, her face pale and her wide eyes twinkling with worry. "Are you okay, Hazel? What was that about?"

"I don't know," I croak, confused as ever. Blood rushes to my cheeks as my adrenaline begins to fade, and I realize that everyone is staring at me. Why is this crap always happening? Seriously, I cannot handle another bully, especially one that *looks like that*. Good Lord, he's sexy and scary and I don't even know what to do with this situation.

Cora slides her ebony arm through mine, tugging me close. The water sloshes around my ankles and I refuse to look at it for too long, to search for whatever spirit is doing this to me. Cora's a physically affectionate person in general, and something about her vanilla perfume and warm skin relaxes me a fraction. I can get through this. With friends like her, I'll be okay.

"Dang girl," she sighs dramatically. "What on earth did you do to piss off Dean Ashton?"

TWO
KHALI

I FLY AHEAD OF OWEN, dipping close enough to crest the water and fling an icy spray into his face. If he were in his human form, he wouldn't cough or cry out, he'd laugh. And then he would send it right back. But in his dragon form, he relishes the water. A loud splash echoes throughout the darkness and the flapping of our wings goes from two sets, to one. He must have gone under, his water elemental magic eager for a ride. I push harder, flying as fast as I can, sticking to the air. While I have an affinity for all four elements, air is my favorite. I'll need the advantage if I'm to beat him to the outer wall.

A torrent of water shoots up, and I crash straight into it. It's quick to twist around my body, dragging me down into the murky lake. Water floods my throat and dulls my senses, and I instantly draw on my water elemental. The magic springs to life, giving my dragon self new life underwater. I thought it was dark above, but below the surface, it's black as ink. Fear clamps down on me, despite my efforts to push it away.

Where are you, Owen Hydros Brightcaster!? I yell at him through our telepathic link. *I am going to murder you! You know I hate going under, especially at night. It's creepy down here.* But it's not only creepy, it's filled with terrible memories that I'd rather not revisit. Ever.

I'm met with a sly laugh. *Don't be such a baby!*

I'm almost a grown woman, you twit, I challenge. I don't even bother to search for him down here. Our jet-black hides camouflage too well in the watery darkness. I tug at my fire elemental, just enough to warm my limbs so I can swim faster to the surface.

Oh, believe me, he replies with that same laughing tone, *everyone has noticed.* His words ring through our link and send my heart skittering.

If I could blush in my dragon form, I would. Not because he and I have anything between us other than a deep friendship, but because there's no hiding the way my body has blossomed. I'm beginning to resemble my mother, who wears her curves like a badge of honor. I could never be like that, walking around court like a prize to be won.

Even though that's *exactly* what I am.

The moment I crest the lake to greet the late summer air, my fear washes away with the water. I hate going down there, night *or* day, and my dragon side doesn't like it much either. Everytime I do, logic vanishes and the animal within demands I get out before the merfolk sense us. Not that Owen and I couldn't fight them off. He's not the least bit afraid of sea monsters, but I'd rather not face those particular demons ever again. As a child, they used me to get what they wanted from the dragon royals, and I'll never be able to let that watery experience go. No matter how hard I try, the trauma follows me.

The familiar shapes of our towering castle home and the surrounding village rise like hands in the distance. The village spreads out over the landscape for miles with a looming stone wall circling the entire thing. The sun has yet to break the horizon, thank the Gods. Owen and I have to be back in our beds before morning, with no one the wiser to our midnight escapade. I stretch my wings to their absolute fullest and push every muscle to maximum effort. I can almost taste my forthcoming victory.

Once a week, for the last year, Prince Owen and I have snuck out at night to race around the territory and practice our magic. The sentries and guards don't mind him, he could walk right on through the gates if he wanted. Princes can do almost whatever they want. *Almost.* It's my presence that requires our secrecy. I've gotten caught out here before and the reprimands cost me dearly. But if he were caught *with* me? There are some things even princes cannot overcome. And yet Owen insists. He's my best friend at court and understands how much I crave to fly. He risks everything to give me the chance.

I love him for it. It's because of his friendship that I'm here, wind rushing off my scales, night shrouding my dragon form, the thrill of the chase nipping at the tip of my wings.

This is the happiest time of my week. Always.

Owen swoops up next to me, and having left his beloved lake behind, he's faster than ever. Sometimes I wish he'd let me win, but I know he won't. He's far too competitive. And I wouldn't be satisfied if he did. I could use one of my other elements to delay him, just as he did with the wall of water, but I don't. I never do. It wouldn't seem fair to use the wind or earth or fire when he cannot. I'm just as competitive as he is and a level playing field is half the fun. So we stick to water and flight.

He's inches from gaining the lead and the outer city wall is closer now, Stonesheart's Castle rising beyond it. The first one of us to land along the edge and shift back to human form wins. We advance, neck and neck, our wings slapping the wind, until he presses ahead. I quickly veer to the right and knock into him, hoping to jar him off course, but he's bigger than me and it proves futile. Something foreign ripples through me, pulling me down, like weights clinging to my scales. I baulk, confused, tumbling to the rocky ground. Did I just lose my power? No. Not possible. I quickly push the thought away.

Owen circles back, landing next to me with a thud. We shift back, our clothes half drenched. My long hair is a matted mess down my back that will be its own cruel punishment come morning, but still worth it.

"Are you okay?" Owen asks, crouching down next to me. "What happened?"

My breath catches in my throat. I bite back the worry and force a smile onto my face. "One of these days, I'm going to beat you."

"I have no doubt." He winks. His eyes are the brightest blue, even at night. It's impossible not to stare. But there's still something unsettled in his gaze. He's also worried about me, but he lets it go for now.

We sneak back into the castle through one of the many underground passageways. It's musty and cramped. The floor is worn dirt and the damp stone walls are so low we have to crawl in some spots. There are a few places where we travel close to public spaces. We take extra care to go slow here, and even still, every sound sets us on edge. But we're also used to it and, as far as we know, we're the only ones who've found this particular passageway.

We take this risk week after week, knowing that if we get caught together, he'll bear the brunt of our punishment. I'm selfish for it. I know that. For a prince to be caught sneaking around with me is prohibited, and if caught, he—or any one of his brothers—would be given a very public and very painful lashing. But its effect wouldn't be lasting, wouldn't be life or death, and perhaps that's why we tempt fate.

No. It's my kiss that is deadly. Should *anyone* be caught kissing me, they're to be sent into immediate exile. And should they foolishly try to return? Executed. Owen has never kissed me, and I pray he doesn't. Because two years ago, his older brother did, and we haven't seen him since.

"LADY KHALI. PLEASE, HOLD STILL," my ladies maid, Faros, says with a great deal of exasperation as she tugs my corset's strings. I catch her eye in the gilded mirror and shoot her a chagrined smile, but I do what she asks, wincing as she finishes tightening, dressing, and primping me for the day. Faros has been with me for as long as I can remember. I consider her my second mother, though she's much kinder than my real mother who took to court life like a knife to venison, cutting her way to the top.

"Does it have to be Friday already?" I complain. "Let's just skip right to Saturday so I can rest."

The missed sleep from last night weighs heavily on my limbs. That and the pressing worry about what happened. I've never once struggled with my dragon form like that. It was as if one second she and I were together, and the next, we were separated into two different beings. The thought of it leaves me hollow.

Faros clicks her tongue. "You have to give all the princes equal time. You know the law."

I frown. "Yes, I do."

Some of us choose our fate. Most do not. But in my seventeen years, I've come to realize that we all have control over what we believe. Our lives may not be ours to mold, but our thoughts are ours to own. Do the Gods have their hands in our lives at every moment, continually directing us on a course of their choosing? Or is fortune left to chance, left to ambitious men and women, willing to take what they want?

Or perhaps it's both.

I was placed here by the Gods. My past, present, and future are clay between their fingers. There was a time when I rebelled against my fate, but I've since accepted the truth. And *that* acceptance was my choice. My *one* choice. My path was bestowed on me the day I sparked life in my mother's womb, and, from the moment my eyes fluttered opened as an infant, it was known that I would be the next queen. My status from commoner to royal has never been questioned.

No, the question was, and still is, this: which of the four princes is to be my husband?

I brush my hands along my robin's egg blue bodice, admiring the crushed velvet. Velvet is my favorite fabric, even in summer, and it makes me smile. There's little I get to choose, but this dress is one.

Still, I sigh, returning to the truth of the day ahead. "But why does Bram have to be so boring? He never wants to do anything I want to do. It's all study, study, study with him."

"You would do well to read a book every once in a while."

I fake a gasp of outrage. "I read!"

"Only to satisfy your tutors. I'm talking about taking a real interest in your responsibilities."

I roll my eyes, even though I'm not surprised. This kind of advice is constant. Ask anyone, and they'd tell me to be grateful, to embrace what I've been given. "You sound just like Mother."

"Oh hush," she replies with a twitching smile, breaking her orderly façade.

As if her timing couldn't be any more impeccable, my mother sweeps into my room. Her chestnut hair is neatly done atop her head in a sort of silly bird's nest design and her dress is perfectly pressed silver silk against her tanned skin. She's beautiful and cunning, and I steel myself for whatever she has come to demand of me.

"Tonight is an important night for you," she says coolly, her eyes landing on me like I've already begun to argue.

I roll my eyes. "Aren't they all? You know, I'm tiring of all this fanfare at my expense."

She looks at me like I've gone insane, gathering her thoughts. "Then I'll make this quick. I've come to encourage your courtship with Silas," Mother says. She glides across the room to stand in front of me, placing cool hands on my shoulders and peering into my eyes. "Silas will take good care of you *and* this kingdom when the time comes. You should be nicer to him and stop paying so much attention to the childish twin."

I shrug her off me. "Owen is my best friend, and why does it matter who I pay attention to? The king will choose my mate anyway."

"It matters because people talk. So you'll give Silas extra attention tonight. Do it for your family."

I fake a smile, but inside I'm boiling. "As you wish, Mother." I want to argue with her, but it's so much easier to give in to her demands.

Not for the first time, I wish my father wasn't gone so often. She never does this kind of thing in his presence. He's too protective of me, and she's too enamoured of him. He's the kind of person who brings out the best qualities in all of us. I miss him terribly, like an emptiness is in my heart and only he can fill it up.

She raises a perfect eyebrow and then leaves me to Faros without another word. The second she's gone, I groan and Faros shrugs, a look of regret passing over her eyes. There's no point in talking about it. These are the kinds of conversations I've been having with my mother for years. She only has a place in this castle because of me and she's desperate to make sure that everything I do stays in her control so that *she* can keep things the way she likes them.

Faros ushers me to the hallway as if the previous scene never happened. I wish she'd stand up for me, but I forgive her for not quite understanding me, because I love her, and at least she doesn't try to control me. It's like that with the people I call my family. With Father and Mother and Faros—even when they try to put me into the tightest of places, even when it hurts me to contort to their ideas for my future, my forgiveness is automatic. Perhaps that's foolish, or perhaps that's normal when it comes to family.

Faros stays close as we walk down to Bram's chambers on the other end of Stoneshearth's Castle. The staff step out of our way as we pass. Courtesans smile and offer cheerful greetings. Around us, the stone floors and walls are polished to gleaming gray. Giant arched windows line the long hallways, letting in rivers of golden light, brightening the glittering dust particles suspended in midair. Beyond the windows, countless dragons swoop and swirl in the distance. Some of our dragon army is practicing, their training drills sending a pang of pure want through my body. I long to be out there instead of cooped up in here, but I know that will never happen.

It doesn't take long until I find myself standing outside of Bram's door. I release a breath and knock against the oak. I hope he doesn't answer. I know he will.

Every day it's a different prince, except for Saturdays, which belong to me, and Sundays which belong to the Gods. Prince Owen is my best friend, and we always have loads of fun together, joking and lounging around with our pals. Prince Silas is witty and intense. He likes to play chess and talk about war strategy. Sometimes we'll go for strolls in the hedge maze, which I quite enjoy. He's fairly easy to talk to, but he doesn't have many friends; he's too critical, too barbed. Nobody stays close for long, nobody wants to get cut. And there's something about him that scares me, something about the way he sees the world, like it's another one of his chess boards. Everything can be won or lost.

But it's Bram whom I struggle to connect with the most. He's as dull as a butter knife. All he cares for are his books and tutors. Whenever I spend the day with him, we barely speak, let alone leave the musky library attached to his chambers. I suppose that's to be expected of someone who isn't Dragon Blessed. It's not his fault, really.

In a matter of seconds, he opens the door, nods once, and goes back to his desk.

"Your majesty." I bow and Faros and I stride into his chambers. All the princes have their own studies and sitting rooms for our meetings, and when we're together, we're never to be alone. At least not until one is crowned King and I'm married off.

Bram's sitting room is dark, with thick curtains drawn over the window, dripping candles burning in the candelabras, and stacks of books piled on every available surface. True to form, he doesn't even bother to look up from whatever he's studying today. I eye the tome in his lap, catching sight of the name of our greatest enemy: The Sovereign Occultists. I shudder and swallow down the instant burst of fear. The warlocks are terrible in every possible way and, worst of all, they want to eradicate elemental magic. The dragon race is top of their list.

I drop into the closest chair. It smells like dust. Faros shoots me a pointed look and I sit up straight, resting my hands on my knees and smiling meekly.

"Do you have any novels in here?" I pick up a book about the Jeweled Forest and toss it aside. Geography is no fun for someone who's never allowed to go anywhere. Not that I'd go *there*, not from the way people talk about it like it's sure to lead to a gruesome death.

"Like what kind of novels?" He doesn't look up.

"Action and adventure," I respond. "Romance, too, of course."

That gets Bram's attention. He peers up at me with mossy eyes like I'm one of the puzzling science experiments dissected in his books. "No," he clips.

I roll my eyes and reach for the nearest history text, absentmindedly thumbing through the worn pages. Neither of us wants me here. There's no way Bram will be named King and we both know it. A Non-Blessed prince has never been king. But the law requires us to spend this time together and so we suffer through it.

A photograph in the text catches my eyes and I gasp.

Bram jumps forward, ripping the book from my hands. "You can't have that," he snaps. But my heart is racing so fast I hardly care what he has to say about it.

"That's not our history," I challenge, "that's from the other realm." My mind reaches back to what I saw. A city of glass buildings towering into the sky like giants, glinting in the sun. I've never seen anything like that here, but I've heard stories of the non-magical realm where people aren't dragons or wizards or seers, but are instead slaves to technology. I don't quite understand what that word "technology" means, but I've had good enough sense not to ask. Whatever it is, it's not for our realm. "Are you allowed to have that?"

Bram's eyes level on mine. "Yes," he says plainly. I don't believe him. But I don't press him on it either. He sighs with exasperation and stands, rummaging through books for a while, until he drops a novel into my lap.

The title says, *A Midsummer Night's Dream*.

"What's this?" I ask, running my fingers along the spine. It's smoother than any book I've ever seen before and glossy in the sunlight. It doesn't seem to belong with the rest of the books in his library.

His eyes dart to Faros, but she says nothing. She sits in the back of the room, busying herself with her needlepoint work, feigning that she's giving us privacy. She's not. But even then, she can be trusted.

He swallows hard and levels his gaze back on me. Something foreign shoots up my spine and I sit up taller. "It's a play. Just read it," he finally says. "You'll like it." Then he settles back into his own text.

I've nothing better to do so I begin reading. The words are lyrical and somewhat difficult to understand, but I soon find myself drawn in, laughing through the tale of mischievous fairies and unrequited love. It's the first time today I'm able to stop thinking about what happened last night with my wayward magic. Finally, after a few hours of nothing but comedy playing out in my mind and my occasional laugh to break the silence, Bram speaks. It catches me so off guard that I jump in my seat.

"Pardon me, what was that you asked?" I close the book but hold a finger between the pages. I don't want to lose my place!

His gaze pins me down. "I said, I'd like to talk to you about what happened with my brother."

My heart jumps and my eyes dart to where Faros sits in her chair along the edge of the room. But she's just as startled and can't help me. "Which brother?"

He raises a dark eyebrow, calling my bluff. His voice is dry as sand, "Who else but the one you got exiled?"

Tears warm my eyes. My lips press together. I knew this day would come eventually, but now that it's here, I can't remember all the lies I'd so carefully prepared.

THREE

HAZEL

THE COMFORTING AROMA OF COFFEE wafts from The Roasted Bean and wraps me up like a warm blanket. I sigh and breathe it in, my eyes darting to the shiny glass door. When I notice the "help wanted" sign, I smile at my good fortune. I worked at a coffee and bubble tea shop back home in Ohio, so this place is a perfect fit. Fighting down the sudden flutter of nerves, I pull open the door and stroll into the upscale coffee shop. *I am a girl on a mission. I am a confident goddess. I am the best candidate for the job and they'd be crazy not to hire me.*

Help wanted? Coming right up!

For a girl like me, receiving a full ride scholarship was a complete godsend. Growing up with a single mother, we never had a lot of money. Not that I noticed it too much. Mom works ridiculously hard as an emergency room nurse and has always made it a point to provide for me in every way that two parents would have. But when it came to paying for college, my options were limited to student loans or scholarships. I earned good grades, and I even graduated a year early from high school, but I wasn't "Miss Valedictorian/Debate Captain" or anything like that. Not to make excuses, but having spirits in my face at all hours was rather distracting, not to mention the bullying that went on in my Ohio hometown kept me from being much of a joiner.

So when all was said and done and it came time to apply to colleges, I assumed scholarships were out of the question. I applied to all the best schools located in small towns that I could find. The day a thick letter from Hayden College landed in my mailbox, I opened it up and my world opened up with it.

The craziest thing about it was that I didn't even think I would get in to this school. It's ranked high and the class sizes are small. And now I'm here with a scholarship? I sometimes wonder if the admissions office made a mistake, but it's not like I'm going to ask. Anyway, if I keep a full schedule and my grades above a 3.5 average, my room and board will continue to be paid through four years of undergrad. All I need is a part-time job to pay for extra expenses and save up for vet school. Easy enough.

There's not a line at the counter this late in the afternoon which makes me a tad nervous. I guess it's now or never. I quickly catch the eye of the barista, a young guy with white-blonde hair pulled back into a man-bun and bright cobalt eyes, and wave a friendly hello.

"Don't I know you?" He grins, and my stomach does a weird flip-flop. He has dimples. Honest to God, all American boy, swoon-worthy dimples. Those might make up for the man-bun situation—not my favorite look.

"Umm, I think so?" I bite my lip, smoothing my hands along my frayed jeans, trying to place him because yeah, he actually does look familiar.

"You're in my organic chemistry lab." He leans over the edge of the counter, hooking me in with his gaze. Okay, yup, I remember him now. He looks even better in his black barista apron than his chem lab jacket, by which I mean, he's freaking hot.

College has turned me into a total boy-crazy lunatic—that much has become alarmingly clear over the last week. I swear, everywhere I go I'm checking out all the new hotties. It can't be helped.

"Landon, right?" I ask, then immediately redden. I remembered his name and now he's going to think I'm a stalker chick or something.

His grin grows even larger. "That's me. And you are?"

"Here to apply for the job."

He gives me a quick once-over with those startling blue eyes of his and I'm not even going to pretend that I'm breathing properly. Oh sweet baby Jesus, if working here means I get to flirt with this cute guy, then please Lord, give me the job. Don't I deserve this?

"Right, let me grab an application. You can fill it out now. I'll give it to the owners myself and put in a good word for you." Landon winks and holds a hand over the corner of his delicious mouth as if to let me in on a secret. "I'm a local. I've been working here for years. This is my family's business."

I smile, the bundle of nerves unraveling inside me like a tangled ball of yarn. He slides the application across the counter, and I snatch it up. If he has any say in who his parents hire, then today just might be my lucky day.

"Thanks," I squeak out.

"So you're a freshman, right? I'm sure I would've seen you before, otherwise."

I nod sheepishly.

"But you're in an upper level chem lab with me, that's pretty impressive."

"Thanks." Is that all I can manage to say to him? Thanks?

"You're welcome. You must be pretty smart, what with those cute glasses and all. What's your major?"

I automatically reach up to touch the black frames of my fake glasses. Would he think I was smart if I told them they're fake? "Umm—biology. I want to go to vet school." That's better, at least that was a complete sentence.

He smiles and little wrinkles spring up around his eyes and I nearly melt right then and there. I don't even care that he used the most obvious question ever of "what's your major" to flirt with me.

"That's awesome. Good for you. Well." He nods to the application and raises an eyebrow. "I'll look forward to working with you, Freshman."

Oh my gosh! He gave me a nickname. Never mind that he didn't ask for my real name. Never mind that he probably uses that name on all the new girls. I smile back and say something awkward about looking forward to it too, the whole time my face growing scarlet by the second. If only all the guys on campus were as sweet as Landon, this place would be heaven.

The altercation with Dean Ashton has been following me around since yesterday like an ugly cloud hanging over this whole "college experience," and I don't know how to shake the feeling that Dean's not going to let this thing go between us, whatever *it* is. Cora seems to be in the know about everything on this campus and she claims he's the mysterious, bad boy that all the girls want and all the guys want to be. Talk about a total cliché. This isn't some bad 90's movie that's so bad it's also so good. If Dean's really that cool of a dude, then why he is so bent out of shape about me?

Pushing the thought away, I settle into a sleek leather booth and get to work, my mind still spinning at the possibilities of Landon. Back in high school, I never dated. Not that I didn't want to, but I wasn't part of the crowd—any crowd—and nobody ever asked me. People thought I was weird. They stared. And laughed. And besides, I took extra classes so I could finish up early, choosing to spend my time on that goal rather than finding some pimply teenager to date.

The application itself is pretty standard: normal questions about previous employment, available hours, references and whatnot. But I find myself getting distracted. Not by Landon who's looking pretty good behind the counter if I do say so myself—and I do, not by the bell that chimes every time someone enters the coffee shop, and not even by the group of rowdy college kids in the next booth.

No, it's the dead girl sitting in the booth across from me that's the source of interruption.

Seriously, why is this always happening? I can feel her sitting there, staring at me. But I don't look up. My pen scrawls across the application, filling in the information, all the while, a prinkling sense of foreboding creeps up my spine like a needle pulling thread. I can't help it anymore. I look up. My pen drops to the table and rolls to the ground with a clatter.

I know her.

Terror grips me tight and I press myself back into the bench seat. I just met this girl at our dorm welcome activity four days ago while she was alive and well. And now here she is, sitting across from me, dead. A ring of blue blooms around her mouth in a way that usually means death by drowning. Her black hair hangs around her face, dripping wet, exponentially adding to her creepiness factor. And her eyes are so bloodred that I can't tell what color they were in life except for the fact that when I met her, I thought she had the most gorgeous green eyes I'd ever seen. I'd been momentarily jealous, annoyed that mine were a boring hazel to match my name.

Drowned Girl opens her mouth to speak, which I know is impossible. Water rushes out in a gagging torrent. It looks just like the water from the hallway earlier. She's been following me.

I jump up, about ready to scream.

"Oh, heck no," I mutter, adrenaline racing through every vein. I do not want to deal with this, not today, not right now. She stares after me through watery eyes as I gather up my application and shove it haphazardly into my trendy jean backpack. I zip it up so quickly that I take off a bit of the paper on the corner. Dang it all!

"Is everything okay?" Landon calls after me as I scurry toward the exit.

Oh, crap, I'm not acting normal, am I? I slow and turn around, giving him a 1000-watt smile. I probably look like a lunatic. Of course, since I'm the only one who can see dead people, this kind of thing happens a lot.

"Everything is great," I sputter. "Thanks, Landon. I actually have to go, but I'll bring the application back tomorrow." Even as I speak, I can hear the places where my voice sounds high-pitched and dare I say it? Spooked. Landon's expression is questioning but luckily a new customer walks in and pulls his attention off of me. The dead girl is still gargling from the booth, still trying to speak, still spitting water all over the place.

I can't do this.

I don't spook easily. I've seen enough ghosts to make my life a living horror show, so what's one more. But this girl, *this girl* is a different story. She was alive four days ago! I met her, her name starts with a K or C or something. She lives on my floor and has already declared a major in Elementary Education and wants to be a freaking Kindergarten teacher. And now? Now she's one of the ever-present ghosts haunting me.

Tears prick at my eyes and I push my way out the door and onto the street. I try to breathe. I try to calm down. I can't.

What happened to her? She clearly drowned, but how? This West Virginian town of Westinbrook is small, a college town centered in the Smoky Mountains. With only fifteen thousand residents, a third of them being college kids, there isn't much to do here to get yourself *killed* unless it involves drinking oneself to death.

My mind races to any known water sources in the area. There are neighboring forests dotted with lakes, but students have been in school all week. We haven't even made it to the first weekend when the parties are known to kick off. What was she doing out at a lake? Swimming to cool off or something? Or maybe it happened in a pool on campus somewhere. Maybe something crazy went down in the dormroom shower? Visions of the shower scene from the old movie *Psycho* pop up in my head and I shudder. I am officially freaking out!

I turn back to make sure she's not following me.

And she totally is. Awesome.

Water pours off her, an unholy sight reserved only for my cursed eyes. Every time she opens her mouth, I'm met with more of the water. It's not real. It belongs to another dimension: the spirit world. But it's terrifying and horrible and I can't take it. A pang of guilt shoots through me. I should try to help her. She's probably so much more afraid than I am; she might not even know what's happened to her yet. Even though I'm standing in daylight in the center of Main Street, what choice do I have but to try to help?

"What happened?" I croak, looking the ghost-girl up and down. Maybe she can send me images and I can piece this together.

I'm met with no response besides an open mouth and more gurgling water.

"Okay, I know you're scared or whatever but you're literally going to give me a heart attack. You have no idea how freaky this is," I reply in a rush. I haven't engaged with a ghost since arriving on campus and I had vowed not to. That lasted less than a week. Big surprise.

The problem was the few times I've tried to help one of them, I've tended to create more harm than good. Their family and friends never wanted to hear what I had to say. They didn't believe me, called me crazy, a crook, blasphemous, and even once, the devil's child. Not to mention, helping one ghost always means more would show up to pester me.

Turns out, everybody wants something, even dead people.

Mom knows all about my problem—or curse, as I call it. She calls it a gift, which would be downright laughable if it were funny. No joke, we've spent years and years trying to make the ghosts go away, but nothing ever works. Not therapy. Not pharmaceuticals. Not support groups. Not random blog articles with advice about how to cleanse under the full moon.

Nothing.

We've also tried to embrace it. Maybe if I learned how to control the ability, I could pick and choose what I had to deal with. Yeah, all that did was attract more ghosts than before. Scary ones. Nowadays, they are everywhere. All the time. I largely ignore them and try to live a normal life. It's not easy…

But this poor girl! I can't seem to help myself from speaking to her again.

She and I could have been friends. We're not that different. If she's dead, isn't it possible I could be in her place right now? We live on the same floor and have things in common. She wanted to help innocent baby humans. I want to help innocent baby animals. Practically the same thing, right?

"What do you need?" I press, stepping closer.

Her face slackens, and she points a thin index finger off into the nebulous distance.

"I'm not sure what that means," I continue, staring back down the street. The area is lined with cute restaurants, shops, businesses, and a few clothing boutiques for tourists. With the swell of Smoky Mountains as a backdrop and the trees lining the sidewalks, it could be a postcard.

Someone giggles from behind, and I turn to find the same group of college kids who'd been in the coffee shop. They're not laughing with each other anymore. They're looking at me like I'm a crazy person. Maybe I am. Either way, I've become the joke. Embarrassment prickles over my entire body and I grin sheepishly, my eyes probably bugging out of my head. One by one, the group averts their gazes and rush past me.

"I'm sorry," I say, speaking low to the drowned ghosty girl once I'm sure we're alone again. "I don't know what you want and I don't know how to help you, but you're dead. If you see a light or a tunnel or something, my advice is to go to it."

She gapes at me, mouth open like a fish, bloodshot eyes wide and terrified.

Did she not know she was dead? Bile rises in my throat. There's nothing I can do, so with a stab of guilt, I turn from her and hurry away, back in the direction of campus. Of one thing I'm certain—I really need to get a grip on my ghost problem if this college thing is going to work out. I sure hope I don't end up in the loony-bin one day. I say it as a joke to myself and to Mom all the time, but I actually mean it. It's my worst fear. Some days it feels inevitable that my future will involve padded rooms and straitjackets.

"I can help you," a woman steps out from a shadowy storefront. I squeak and stumble, nearly jumping out of my own skin.

I hold up a hand. "Holy Hannah, you scared the bejesus out of me!"

Her smile is playful, her pale blue eyes framed by deep wrinkles and twinkling in their intensity. Her white hair is dreadlocked and even though she's clearly pushing old age, the look works well for her. A knobby finger points up to the name scrolled across the building: The Flowering Chakra.

"Oh, no thanks." I stop her right there, my heart sinking.

"I think you and I could help each other, actually."

Her tone is genuine, but I quickly shake my head and continue on my way. I want to look back, want to give this lady a shot, whatever she's offering, but I know better. Believe me when I say, I've been there and done that. Nothing and nobody can help me, especially not the metaphysical crackpots of the world. Most of them claim to see spirits too, and while that may be true for some, it's never close to what I experience on the daily when it comes to the spirit realm.

These people always think they know, always think they can help me.

They can't.

"Come back," she calls out, her voice as thick as slow-churned butter, and I want to believe her so badly it hurts. It's the familiar ache of old disappointments all lined up in a row, and I hate it. "Come back, soon, my dear. I really do know how to help someone like you."

I shake my head. If only it were that easy.

Four

KHALI

THE ENTIRE DRAGON KINGDOM IS waiting for my eighteenth birthday. Sometimes it feels as if the whole world is waiting for me to come of age so I can be married off. The pressure of every passing day adds another drop of anxiety to an already boisterous ocean. I only have four months left, and Bram isn't making this easier. Sometimes, I think I'll drown underneath the weight.

I narrow my eyes at him. Inside, I'm that ocean storm, but outside, I'm a calm surface. Practiced. Perfect.

"You've had two years to question me about your brother's exile and yet you never said a single word," I quip. "Why the sudden interest?"

"It isn't sudden," he replies casually. "I never believed he would have engaged in an inappropriate relationship with you."

Guilt racks my body and I sit up straighter. "Well, he did and it's over."

"So I've heard."

He eyes Faros for a long second, as if measuring how much she can be trusted. As my chaperone and ladies maid, she's with me nearly all of the time and has been for years. She knows almost everything about me. But even *she* doesn't know the specifics of how and why I got the oldest prince exiled.

"There's nothing you can say in front of me that you can't say in front of Faros," I retort. "She is family. I trust her with my life."

"How lucky for you to trust family so implicitly," he says dryly. "But I wonder if she values the princes' lives above yours. We still don't know who told my father about your alleged tryst with my brother two years ago."

Faros raises her hand to her mouth. "I would never do such a thing." Her tone is shocked, and I believe her.

"Get to the point, Bram," I snap. "Whatever you want to say, say it. This conversation is growing tiresome."

His eyes lock me down. He's never held my gaze for so long and it's unnerving. I haven't had the opportunity to measure how green his eyes are until now. They remind me of a rainy spring that won't seem to end. He runs a hand along his jaw, considering. "What would you do to get my brother back?"

Dark mistrust and bright hope battle through my veins. "Don't speak of the impossible," I reply. "He's gone. And if he returns, he'll be killed."

"Maybe..."

"No, not maybe. It's a fact."

"Before he left, he said he had initiated the kiss. But I find that odd. What I'm trying to figure out is if he *actually* liked you back, because it was painfully obvious how much you wanted him. I believe you kissed him, and I want to know why he didn't just say that."

"You don't know what you're talking about!" I lean back into the padding of my chair, wishing it could swallow me whole. Blood rushes to my cheeks, but I refuse to break eye contact, even if I'm powerless to hide my shame.

"I think I do." He leans back as well, studying me. "I know you had harbored a secret crush on my brother for years, but he never returned your advances as far as I could tell. And yet, he never denied kissing you, something forbidden, something he knew would get him sent into exile. Why would he cover for your blunder? Did he *want* to leave the kingdom?"

My throat turns to ice, freezing the words within.

"He was the most powerful of the princes," Bram continues. "He loved it here, excelled at court politics and would have been a formidable leader and war hero. Besides that, everyone knew he was my father's favorite. He was destined to be crowned our next King."

"Perhaps." My voice is steady but my nerves are a riot.

"And *you* would have been his queen. You would have gotten the prince you desired since your girlhood."

That part is true, but I swallow my response.

"But the two of you ruined it. I want to know what happened and why."

"I am not speaking to you on this matter. It's none of your business." I gather my dress while still holding onto *A Midsummer Night's Dream* and stand, rushing toward the door. Guilt nips at my heels, but I promised more than just myself that I wouldn't tell anyone and I won't break that promise, especially not for someone as frustrating and sure of himself as Bram.

"Now you only have three brothers left to vie for your bed, but of course you and I both know I'm about as likely to be crowned king as a horse," Bram calls after me. "So why keep secrets from me, Khali Elliot?"

Faros stands at my side but I don't dare to look at her. My shaking hands press against the cool wood of the door. Outside, children's laughter echoes down the corridor. Careless and free.

"I'm suddenly not feeling well," I say over my shoulder. "I apologize, but our meeting must be cut short. I hope to see you at the ball tomorrow night, Your Highness." I end the conversation and burst into the hallway, my heart hammering against my ribcage.

"Do save me a dance!" Bram's mocking words reverberate through the open door. Faros slams it shut.

I growl and grind my foot into the stone floor. My dragon raises her head within me, eager to take out the frustration in our favorite way, but I can't shift without permission. And I *never* have permission. My dragon may be the reason I'm here, but she's just as caged as I am.

Faros and I hurry back to my chambers and all the while, Bram's words ravage my thoughts. He was right about too many things. I did have a crush on his older brother and I do have a secret about what happened that night. Just thinking about how it unfolded sends my heart twisting and my jaw clenching so tight that pain shoots through the bone and into my teeth. I take a steadying breath and count to ten. Just because Bram's a keen observer and the smartest of the princes doesn't mean I'll ever confess the truth. Not to him. Not to anyone.

THE CLAWING FINGERS OF THE corset dig into my skin. I straighten my spine like a puppet on a string, but it doesn't help the pain. I take a breath, double check that my gown is in immaculate condition, and slip into the ballroom. Tumultuous thoughts of what could have been slip in with me. Drat! I haven't been able to stop thinking about Bram's accusations since he laid them out yesterday. This party had better be a good one.

My gaze travels over the members of the Court, and I click my tongue. The disparity of wealth among Blessed and Non-Blessed families is becoming more and more noticeable, from the degree of fine clothing, to the level of desperation behind masked expressions. Had I not been born with my peculiar set of eyes, I wouldn't even be here. I'd most likely be starving in the backwater village on the edge of nowhere. We may have all descended from dragons, but not everyone in the Kingdom of Drakenon is actually Dragon Blessed and can shift. Furthermore, it's only my two colored eyes that clued others into my elemental powers, that marked me as something *more*.

"Princess, there you are." Silas appears, dipping in close. His voice is as smooth as the black silk tie around his neck. "I've been looking for you. I wanted to get the first dance."

I smile calmly and he takes me into his sturdy arms, twirling me around the ballroom in a familiar waltz. I'm reminded of growing up with the brothers and learning this exact dance during our hours upon hours of painstaking lessons. Silas didn't enjoy dancing then, but he certainly seems to be enjoying himself now. Everyone watches us. He watches me. Is it because my birthday is approaching that his indigo eyes glow with pride? And with something else—something hard to place. Confidence, perhaps? No, not confidence. Determination.

King Titus and Queen Brysta preside over the party in their raised thrones but seem to care little for the guests below. The monarchs draw in the most ambitious among us. Several Dukes and Duchesses flit around the pair like moths to the flame, keeping the royal pair busy with flattery and politics. My mother is among the group, of course. She hasn't looked my way yet but I know she will soon. Her dark tresses are piled on her head in complete perfection. It's only a matter of time before she glides over to remind me of our earlier conversation about Silas. At that thought, he tugs me in closer.

"You look radiant tonight," he says, his gaze running over my face and then landing playfully on my own. "I'll never get over how beautiful and unique your eyes are, Khali. Truly extraordinary."

Wow. I'm used to his flattery but he's really going for it tonight.

I scoff and raise a brow. "Your mother has the same eyes. It's not *that* unique."

He shakes his head. "But they are. I love my mother, but you, you are vastly different from her." His eyes flick to my lips and I glare and stiffen.

"You know the rules," I say sharply. "You know them better than anyone."

He only smiles. It's all a game. Silas is far too ambitious to be tempted to kiss me now. I can only assume it's the other way around. He wants to be the one to tempt me, wants me to want him. Ultimately, the King will decide which one of the brothers I'm to wed after I turn eighteen, but it will be easier to convince his father if the court is talking of how much I longed for his lips during the Autumn Equinox ball. I stiffen, because while I consider Silas a friend, I'm not charmed by his ambition. And while I do find him attractive, it's the kind of attractiveness that comes with a bite.

"May I cut in?" Owen's cheerful voice is that of pure salvation. He swoops in before Silas can argue otherwise and steers the two of us in the opposite direction. I give Silas an apologetic look as I go, but inside, I feel nothing but pure relief. Silas keeps his mouth in a thin line, his eyes zeroed in, his jaw tight. He never looks away.

"Thank you," I whisper to Owen.

Owen just laughs, his glorious blue eyes brightening. He never takes any of this seriously. It's all a big game to him, too. But he's not playing to win; he's playing to enjoy himself. Between him and his two brothers, I'd rather marry Owen in a heartbeat. He is my best friend, afterall. Though deep down, I know it will be Silas. The Court loves Silas. His father dotes on him. Silas's ambition is unmatched, and because of that, he's best suited for the job of future king. My stomach clenches into a ball of nails knowing what that will mean for me.

"How many here do you think can shift?" I ask, trying to take my mind off of Owen's twin. We turn to take in the guests. The ballroom is packed fuller than normal for one of these parties. They flutter around like desperate moths to a flame, each one seeking to be part of the light. But it's the ones who are Dragon Blessed who were born to burn brightest. I wonder if some of them are part of the dragon army I saw training earlier. What would I give to be one of them?

Owen shrugs, running a confident hand along his suit jacket. "Maybe half."

I bite my lip and nod. That's what I thought, too. To be a dragon and not permitted to shift openly, like myself, is a cruel way to live. Does Queen Brysta hate it as much as I do? Does she long to break free and fly, to be her true self? If she does, she's never shown it in my presence. Maybe it would have been better to have been born without the ability to shift, like Bram.

"Do you ever find it strange that we're called the Blessed because we're simply the ones who can shift into dragon form?"

Owen shoots me an odd look. "Well, it's a blessing to the kingdom, isn't it? Dragons can do incredible damage to any invading armies. It's why we've stood strong for as long as we have."

"I guess so," I say. What I don't say, is that I don't feel so blessed. The closer I get to my birthday, the closer I get to having a husband thrust upon me and the less fortunate I feel. My job here is to become queen and produce elemental Dragon Blessed heirs. I'm lucky to have all four elements. Rare. So rare, they can't risk losing me.

I think of how *easy* it would be to fall in love with him when I glance up at Owen's deep blue eyes that fit his ability so well. Prince Owen Hydros Brightcaster. His element is water and his personality is as fluid, even if he is my rock. Like water, he can be gentle and calm, or wild and unpredictable, and underneath the surface, his personality runs deep.

Prince Silas Skylen Brightcaster is Owen's twin, though the two don't match in any way. Silas possesses the elemental magic of sky and is a formidable warrior. Not only can he cause the winds to blow so hard that they lift entire buildings, he can conjure storms and wield lightning to strike his opponents dead where they stand. I haven't seen it with my own eyes, but I've heard the stories brought back from the battlefield over the years. And I've seen what his father can do, how his moods direct the weather around the castle. A chill skitters down my spine.

I peer around the room for Bram but I doubt he's here. He rarely comes to these things, and nobody cares. He probably wasn't serious about dancing with me, thank the Gods. Bram doesn't dance. In fact, he doesn't do much of anything besides study and scowl and study some more. But Prince Bram Oaken Brightcaster never shifted, so nobody bothers him about dancing at these things, or even attending. Had the magic not skipped him, he would've been able to manipulate earth. He could have caused the ground to shake and rise, could have caused entire crops to flourish or crumble and die. And he would be here at this ball with his brothers, asking for his turn to dance with the future queen. I find it strange that Bram's eyes are still bright emerald to match his element, like his brothers' eyes match their own gifts. Sometimes that's what happens, though. Sometimes, entire families can be dragon shifters, their bloodlines thick as chainmail, save for one lone outcast, one weak link.

Life isn't always kind.

But I don't feel too bad for Bram. He's still a Brightcaster Prince and still enjoys the luxuries that come with the title. All that freedom with none of the responsibility. No, I don't feel bad for him at all.

"What is going on in that pretty little head of yours?" Owen asks. We've stopped dancing and have found ourselves outside on the terrace. The cool night washes over me, softening my dark mood. We lean side by side against the balcony, inches apart. Music and party guests float in and out. The night is a blanket of darkness and stars, our lands reaching far, far beyond what I can see. My future kingdom.

An endless prison.

I turn to Owen and search his concerned expression, looking for a sign of some sort of go-ahead. Should I tell him about Bram's questioning? As my closest friend, surely he'd understand. But then again, what if it made him question me further? Question our friendship? In the end, I make up nonsense about a tiff with my mother and we fall into companionable silence. He accepts my story without question. Lady Alivia Elliot and I are always at odds and my father is rarely around to buffer our spats.

Pesky thoughts creep back into my mind—the consuming ones about the eldest royal brother, the man we never speak of. His eyes were so different from any of his younger brothers. They were black as coal, which makes sense considering he was the strongest fire elemental dragon in generations and more dangerous than all of his brothers combined. He would have been the king we all needed, the one who would've ensured Drakenon's safety and prosperity for generations.

I peer over the glittering city into the dark horizon and wonder where he is, knowing he's utterly unreachable. Maybe even dead. It's my fault. Because of me, Dean Ashton Brightcaster will never be the king of anything.

FIVE
HAZEL

CORA AND MACY'S HIGH-HEELS clack on the sidewalk as we head across campus toward the first party of our college careers. Their bare arms are laced through mine, which is actually quite appropriate considering how badly I'm struggling to walk in this dress and the accompanying high heels. Is it luck that Cora and I are both a size seven shoe and I could borrow a pair from her, or that Macy and I are both a size six dress? They would say yes. I would not.

In fact, I'm convinced the weird wobble my legs are doing is making it look like I have to pee. In my defense, I'm not used to high heels or the suffocating fit of the dress, even if the bright white fabric looks great against my leftover summer tan. I keep telling myself to suck it up—it's just for one night. It's my own fault. I was super nervous about the party so I went against my better judgment and gave into peer-pressure.

"You look hot." Cora slaps my hand away from where I'm tugging at the short hemline. "Seriously, stop worrying about it, Hazel."

"You two are bad influences," I shoot back.

"Oh, you know you love it," Macy interjects. "Doesn't it feel a little good? Whenever I'm sad I go shopping and curl my hair and go out on the town. It makes such a difference!"

I raise an eyebrow. "No. I can't say I've ever done that." My voice is deadpan and something about that makes my friends bust up laughing.

Truth be told, I don't have *anything* like this outfit in my closet, and now that I know how impractical it is, I don't plan to go shopping anytime soon.

Doesn't matter how sad I might get. I just hope Cora is wrong and this isn't the standard attire at these things, because if that's the case, then I'm screwed for all future parties.

"Should we establish a code word?" Macy grins, changing the subject. Her curtain of perfect strawberry hair flashes under the street lights. If she wasn't so freaking nice, I'd hate her. "You know, if one of us needs to get away from a creeper or something."

Cora laughs, pointing a sharp finger at Macy, her silvery bracelets jingling together. "Just tell the guy to back the hell off, and if he doesn't then he can deal with me." She flexes her bicep and waggles her eyebrows in that endearing way she does.

Macy rolls her eyes. "The point of a code word is to get out of a sticky situation without causing a scene."

"That's so sad, though, right?" Cora protests. "We shouldn't have to have a code word. Men should be respectful. And actually, if something does happen, if someone does make a woman uncomfortable, she *should* cause a scene instead of always trying to be polite."

I study Cora for a second, taking in her smooth chocolatey eyes and the way she's narrowing them at Macy. She's way more passionate about this than I first thought, but why shouldn't she be? Everything she's saying makes a lot of sense. "You're right, Cora." I nod. "I am going to do a better job at that."

My thoughts flash to the drowned ghost girl from yesterday. Maybe what happened to her wasn't an accident. Maybe if she'd made a scene, she'd still be alive. Either way, I haven't seen her since The Roasted Bean and I hope I don't have to again, especially now that I've been refreshed on her name.

Katherine.

Not Katie. Not Kat. Katherine. I remember her saying it.

Her school I.D. picture appeared all over campus this morning on "missing persons" leaflets. I know better. She may be missing, but she's more than that. And I've been debating all day about going to the police with a tip to go look for her body near open water sources. But I can't. It would make me a person of interest. They'd never believe the truth. Who would? Even I can't believe it sometimes.

As if sensing my thoughts about Katherine, Macy speaks up, "I wonder what happened to that girl. I hope she's okay."

"She's probably dead," Cora says, her voice going dark.

"Don't say that!" Macy gasps.

"Well, if they don't find her within seventy-two hours then her chances drop down to like 1% of survival or something crazy like that. It's already been three days. I'm sorry but that girl is as good as gone. Don't you watch any cop shows?"

"You're seriously freaking me out." Macy squeezes in closer. "None of us go outside at night alone, okay?"

"Deal," I say. But that's all I say. I keep my mouth shut about Katherine even though the backs of my arms are stinging with all the little raised hairs, even though my conscious is begging me to do something more, even though I might be able to help her family recover the body.

"This is it." Cora stops, guiding us toward the white-pillared house looming up ahead. Lanterns light the porch and the front of the house where huge Greek letters are hung. It's a surreal sight. Even from here, the stench of booze and bad decisions wafts through the night. Going to frat parties is what normal people my age do in the movies. This isn't what I do.

Well, I guess it is now.

When we walk into the Alpha Sigma fraternity house, the first thing I notice is the awful smell. The second is the noise.

The place reeks of old beer and too many sweaty bodies, and the offensive rap music blasting through the place is worse than nails on a chalkboard. *Not my thing.* I scrunch up my nose, already eager to leave this party and never look back. I'm sure it'll be overrated. But from the looks on Macy and Cora's faces, leaving already is not going to happen. Macy's blue eyes are wide and glittering with excitement, and Cora's got a knowing smirk on her face, her gaze fixed on some lucky schmuck across the room.

"I'll see you two later. It looks like I've got myself a date," she says, her silky voice dripping with confidence.

She pushes her way through the crowd of college kids, taller than most of them, even the guys. Her bare ebony shoulders and head of thin black braids bob above the sea of students. She's cool in a way that I could only dream of, and I'm suddenly filled with gratitude, and confusion, that of all the people she picked to be her first friend at college, she picked me.

I raise my eyebrows at Macy, curious if she knows where Cora is off to, but Macy only shrugs.

"Let's get a drink," she suggests warmly, grabbing my hand and tugging me toward the kitchen.

I've never drunk any alcohol before and still haven't decided *for sure* if I want to when the red cup lands in my hand. It's not legal. I'm only seventeen so I have years to go. Logically, I should say no. But this is college and it's not like most of the people here are twenty-one. And this is part of the whole coming-of-age experience, is it not? I eye the foamy substance wearily but the weight of my insecurities hits me hard and before I can make a choice one way or the other, I'm drinking.

The taste is not good. Not even close to good. It warms me right up and before I know it, I'm reaching for the keg and helping myself to more. Macy does the same and then we head toward the dance floor, a tad wobbly, but ten times more courageous than when we first walked in here.

My defenses are down, and the music pulses louder but it's not so annoying anymore. My body moves with the throng of people, and I'm not the totally awkward dancer I thought I was—I might even be good at this. I find myself laughing and enjoying myself as one song fades into the next and sweat glistens my skin and maybe this dress isn't such a bad thing after all and where did Macy go? She was just right here. Oh hey, is that Landon? I should go dance with *him*.

But just as quickly as I see him, Landon disappears into the crowd. I blink, dread prickling through me, as the crowd itself shifts, the college kids overcome by transparent shapes, gray and colorless, ghosts appearing out of thin air, approaching me, surrounding me. I stand frozen in my heels, my knees turning into elastic.

That's when the spirits attack.

Maybe attack isn't the right word, but it sure feels that way. They bombard me with images flashing one after the next after the next. People laughing and fighting and tucking their children into bed. A car screeching. Someone lying on a beach, watching the surf as it crashes against the sand. Another running, headphones tucked into his ears, his breath heavy. Someone dropping a dish, the white porcelain splintering and scattering across a wood floor. A woman screams.

They're all kinds: all ethnicities, all ages, with all manner of death bleeding out on their ethereal forms. I don't know where to look or how to block them out, even a little bit. They press down on me, their thoughts louder, my heart pounding harder. Somehow, I've opened myself to a flood of these images and they just keep pouring in. They're from a contemporary time; I've never seen a ghost older than a few decades, at least. It's the one shred of silver lining here. But even then, they won't stop their attack on my senses. They're relentless.

The thing about spirits is they don't care as much about the living world as you'd think. They have no issues walking right through us, squatting in our homes, or scaring the bejesus out of us. And as it seems, they have no problem crashing a college party to get to me. They don't care that I'm trying to have a good time, trying to be normal, *to blend in*. In fact, something about the alcohol in my system has made me defenseless.

But they know it. Oh boy, do they know it.

And I can't seem to get control back. My head is spinning, and their lives are flashing before my eyes in one giant lurch of movement. I push my palms over my ears and squeeze my eyes closed, not that it helps. I need to get out of here. I stumble forward but there are too many people on the dance floor. They're caging me in, bodies pressing me back. I gasp, tears springing to my eyes. There's something seriously wrong with me, the alcohol has hit me way harder than I anticipated. Am I drunk? This is not fun. My balance is crap. I'm sinking to my knees, hot tears ruining my mascara, when two male hands steady me.

Landon? I smile weakly, despite the terrible situation I've put myself in.

My eyes flutter open, expecting to find my favorite cobalt blue gaze, but what I get are two dark as coal eyes, angry, with a tiny flickering line of orange-red around the pupils. So, not Landon then.

"You! What are you doing here?" I sputter at *the* Dean Ashton. The words are thick on my tongue, like I'm trying to swallow peanut butter. Something about that image of peanut butter stuck in my mouth is the funniest thing ever and I can't suppress the giggles. What the heck is wrong with me? How is anything funny right now? I'm a mix of terror and laughter and I don't even know what to do with myself.

"I should be asking you the same thing," he growls back, lifting me to my feet. The high heels suddenly feel three times higher than they were earlier tonight and I fall, my ankle twisting, but he catches me in time. "I'm taking you back to the dorm," he sneers.

I want to snap back, to tell him to leave me alone, but instead I mutter, "They're everywhere, please make them stop," and I turn away from the barrage of spirits still throwing their problems at me with such ferocity I can't tune them out. My head is ringing. The noise of their stories is growing, and I can't make out what Dean says next over all the racket. My face presses flush against his rock-like chest, and I close my eyes again, trying to ward off a spirit-induced migraine.

He expertly maneuvers me through the crowd and before I know it we're outside in the cool air, the noise fading away, and he's plopping me into a shiny black car like I'm a bag of bricks. "If you puke on my leather seats, I swear I'll make you clean it up yourself. I don't care how drunk you are."

Okay, rude much? The door slams and I squeeze my eyes shut.

A few minutes and a gloriously quiet car ride later, I'm blinking them open and we're parked in front of the freshman dorm. My headache has cleared a little, and the alcohol has worn off enough for me to know I'm in a car with someone who's not only much bigger than me, but who hates my guts. The feeling is mutual. I almost can't believe I got myself into this situation but then again, knowing me, nothing is out of the realm of possibility.

"Why did you help me?" I ask, braving a glance at the man who challenged me in class, accosted me in the hallway, and has now saved me from a terrible situation.

His grip on the steering wheel is so tight that his knuckles are stark white. His face is forward, the same profile, same chiseled features and clenched jaw. His anger is a pulse, a heart beating so wildly that it circulates the emotion through the car, and I swear I can feel his body heat. But no, that must be the beer playing tricks on me. Never again!

"I'm not helping you," he says. "I'm helping myself. First of all, I've already told you that this is my territory, and whoever you are, you need to leave before I force you to leave. Second of all, what were you thinking, drinking that disgusting human alcohol? Are you trying to get yourself killed? Are you trying to expose yourself? To expose me?"

I have no idea what he's talking about.

"I have no idea what you're talking about." I want to laugh at the way it comes out as an echo to my thought, and I would, except I think he'll probably kill me if I do. I laugh anyway.

He whips around, his glare deepening into two black coals. The car grows even hotter, prickling against my skin. My mouth slams shut. So, maybe not in my imagination? What is going on? I peel away from his gaze to fumble with the controls on the dash, looking for the AC and the heat button. Both are off.

He slaps my hand away. "I don't believe you," he snaps. "Did someone send you to spy on me? Which clan are you?"

My head spins again. A prickling of exhaustion hits me and all I want to do is crawl into my bed and sleep this horrible feeling off. Good heavens. If this is what alcohol does to people, why does anyone drink it?

"Thanks for the ride," I grumble, wishing I had the energy to deal with whatever this guy is going on about. My words are a bit slurred as I continue, "Seriously, I don't know what you're talking about and you're being a total jerk and I'm just trying to get an education here. I can drink whatever I want. I'm a big girl."

This time, *he* laughs. "How old are you? Aren't you a freshman?"

Yeah right, like I'm about to tell him I'm still seventeen. I point, my index finger jabbing at him with each word, "I'm done with this conversation, Mr. Ashton."

I wrench open the door, peel myself off the leather seat, and wobble to the entrance of the freshman dorm building. When his fancy-pants car peels out of the parking lot, I don't look back, and I'm a teeny-bit proud of myself for that. It's a small consolation. I'm developing a headache, my stomach churns, and worst of all, the spirits are back! They don't travel with me inside cars, but they aren't bound by a body the way we are, so it's easy for them to pop up just about anywhere. The creepers follow me inside, still demanding things of me with all their life stories. I've never had so many of them come at once. Ever. There's got to be at least fifty of them.

I can't take it—not for another second!

By some miracle, I make it to the second floor and stumble into my small room with enough time to text Cora and Macy that I'm home safe, put on my noise-cancelling headphones *with* music on, rip off the awful high-heels, and crash into my pile of blankets.

As I'm drifting off to sleep, the annoyingly handsome image of Dean Ashton's face floats across my mind, taking center stage above all the others. And those startling black eyes, they pin me down—those black, knowing irises with a ring of orangey-red around the pupils. Now that my head is clearing, I have a chance to think about what his eyes remind me of…

Fire.

But no, I must have imagined the fire in his eyes. But I didn't imagine the heat in the car and he did say something totally weird about drinking "human alcohol". Like, what other kind could there be? And what's with all this talk of territories or the accusations about spying and exposing him? Even as I'm drifting into the reprieve of sleep, even as the numbness in my limbs starts to melt into the warmth of blankets, one thought roots itself into my mind.

Dean Ashton has a secret and it has something to do with me.

SIX
KHALI

I EYE THE BLOODRED DRAKENON wine in my chalice but don't drink. Nobody pays me any mind. They've already filled themselves with several rounds of wine, not to mention the delicious meal of roasted pheasant with its mountain of trimmings. I sigh and try to listen to the inane conversation going on around me, but I'm itching for this evening to end.

Midnight can't come fast enough.

All week, as I tended to my responsibilities, my skin crawled with the need to escape the castle, to fly into the void and let my dragon breathe free. I rarely get the opportunity to be my best self unless it's during my weekly secret rendezvous with Owen. Afterall, I wasn't brought here to fly. That's a fact King Titus has made clear to me many times over the years.

So it's every Thursday night after the prominent families of court dine together, gorging on fine food and drinking themselves into oblivion, that Owen and I risk our futures and sneak away using the underground network of tunnels hidden beneath the castle. Tonight should be no different.

The court grows boisterous and sloppy as the hours-long meal nears its completion. Queen Brysta looks as if she's about ready to fall asleep at the table, but my mother, The Lady Alivia, is sitting next to her and chatting cheerily as if she doesn't notice the Queen's boredom. I look just like my mother except for our eyes. Nearly every time we're together, someone points that out, much to my annoyance.

All the ladies are dressed in elegant gowns of silk and velvet, jewels dripping from their necks, and I'm no exception. Everyone dresses their best for these gatherings, the royal family especially. The Queen's emerald tiara glitters in the candlelight, weighing her down even further. I see myself in that image and have to look away.

"No," King Titus grunts, his fist pounding on the table and clattering the dishes. "We have to focus on our borders first, let the other kingdoms fend for themselves. We especially don't owe the *Fae* anything." He says Fae like it's a dirty word.

"Quite right, Father," Silas agrees with whoever happens to be the most powerful in the room, as usual.

Next to him, Bram rolls his eyes and I still, a little shocked. I almost want to laugh but I don't dare!

Silas and the King have been engaged in hearty conversation all night, going on about our greatest enemies, an army of warlocks who call themselves The Sovereign Occultists. The more those two drink, the less sense they make as they try to piece together war strategy. The King's round cheeks grow rosier as he slurps more wine, a stream of it running down his chin without notice. He is the older, and fatter, version of Silas.

"We can't come to anyone's rescue right now," Silas continues. "Nor is that our duty. We must keep our borders strong and our armies numerous, as we've been doing. Should they dare attempt to brave the wards and cross into our territory, we'll be ready for them."

It's the same old story we've been hearing for *years*.

Owen catches my pained expression from across the table and waggles his eyebrows until I *do* giggle. This kind of behavior is exactly why he and I picked Thursday nights as our weekly midnight flight. It's easy to slip away unnoticed once the meal is complete and when those who would care about our whereabouts are either busy sleeping off their hangovers or sleeping with each other. Plus, by the end of these nights, I'd do just about anything to get away from the castle.

A servant dressed in black pads over, presenting a silver plate of steaming blueberry pie. The aroma is tart and sweet and perfect but my mouth doesn't water. I feign enjoyment as I pick at it, but inside, I'm a bundle of nerves, waiting to be excused—waiting for a few hours of peace. I set down my fork and tuck my arms in close to my bodice. The vast room has grown chilly and outside the rain smatters against the stone walls and glass window panes. It won't stop Owen and I tonight. He lives for water and I can navigate any element with ease.

"Owen," the King's voice breaks through the chatter. "What are your thoughts on all of this?"

I expect Owen to shrug or offer up a joke. I suspect his family does too, because we all look surprised at his answer.

"The Occultists have taken over our entire realm save for our kingdom." Owen's face changes, turning serious. His blue eyes deepening, his gaze hardening. A blonde curl drops across his forehead as he leans in. "It's only a matter of time before they make another move on us."

"Well, I could have told you that," Silas scoffs. "They want our lands. They want to destroy us."

"But it's not just our lands that they want," Owen replies. "Nor do I truly believe they wish to destroy all the Dragon Blessed, not when they need us."

"What else could they want?" The King asks, growing just as serious as his sons. The room quiets and curiosities are piqued. Rain pitters against the windows.

"The human realm," Owen offers.

His answer is met with a spattering of laughter.

"What could they possibly want with a useless realm where the magic is so stifled?" Silas challenges. And it's true. In the human realm, nobody's magic is strong. Many lose it entirely. It's considered a terrible punishment to be sent there. But...

"It makes sense," I cut in, my voice rising as I realize what Owen means by all this. All eyes turn on me, a mix of puzzlement and irritation. Women aren't supposed to talk politics around here. "As far as we know, only the Dragon Blessed can move between the realms, *but* is it possible we could take an Occultist with us? They are born of magic. Sure, they lack our same elemental magic, but that doesn't mean it would be impossible. Maybe they could use us to somehow boost their spells."

Throughout our realm there are hidden ley lines where portals meet. Those with elemental blood can use these portals to travel between this magical realm and the human one. But it's rare anyone does—nobody has good reason to leave. But maybe the Occultists feel divinely called to travel to the non-magic realm for some reason or another. Those wizards are known to be crazy, afterall. Owen could be right.

"They're thirsty to extend their rule and enforce their religion on others," Bram adds nonchalantly, speaking for the first time all night. He's so quiet and easily overlooked, that people often forget he's there.

His interjection quiets the room even further. Bram might not get a lot of respect when it comes to magic, but everyone knows that when it comes to logic, he's the smartest person in the room. He leans forward, his elbows resting on the table. "I've been considering this for a while, and I have to say I agree. Why wouldn't the Occultists want to take over the human realm? It's the next logical step, assuming they can get to us first. They'll need the Dragon Blessed to get them through the portals, but I do think it's possible that ruling the human realm as well as this one could be their end goal."

Because Bram isn't Dragon Blessed, he isn't always taken seriously. Dragons don't shift until reaching the age of puberty, around twelve or thirteen years old. And even then we don't exhibit any elementals right away. Those take time to develop, if they're going to develop at all, which they don't for most shifters. I was no exception to waiting. It wasn't easy to be patient, to wait for my first shift, for the powers that followed. But in time, everything happened. It happened for Dean, for Silas and Owen, too.

But it never happened for Bram.

Because of that, not everyone took him seriously. But the King has always been smarter than to underestimate his son. The King looks at each of us now, from one to the next, to the next, until his eyes finally land on me. They match Owen's, the son with his legacy element. And he smiles broadly, a light seeming to go off in his mind. "Princess Khali, I didn't realize what a good team you and Owen make together. Perhaps I'll need to rethink my plans for your birthday?"

My heart leaps, and I nearly choke on my breath. Do I dare to hope it could be true? It's not that I dislike Silas—who is turning so scarlet, his eyes are bulging from his head—it's that Owen is my best friend. I truly believe our relationship could one day shift to love, but if not, life wouldn't be bad with him as my husband. Once king, he would let me fly whenever I wanted, would do anything to give me a life of happiness.

"Owen might be the perfect king to your queen," Queen Brysta speaks up, fully awake now and with a happy twinkle in her eye. She rarely offers an opinion, rarely speaks at all. She's my opposite in that way and my jaw drops at her admission.

My mother kicks at me under the table and I close my mouth and smile meekly. Mother has always said love is not in the cards for me, that I was dealt a much better hand. Silas is her choice to play that hand best. But is it so wrong to want both love and respect? I clear my throat and gather my courage, laying those cards out on the table for everyone to see.

"I think so, too."

EVERYTHING HAS CHANGED.

That night, after Owen and I spend a glorious hour racing around the countryside, we shift back into our human forms and face each other. We stand next to the lake's edge, and I try to ignore the bubbling fear I always have around water. I step away from it's black surface and look at my best friend.

We can't wait a moment longer—we have to figure this out. The rain has stopped but the air isn't clear; nothing is clear. Things between us are murkier than ever. Water drips down his face in long rivulets. His clothes are soaked, his blonde shaggy hair matted to his cheeks. I'm also soaked to the bone, but I don't feel an ounce of cold. All I feel is the change—the change between us.

He feels it, too.

Even in the darkness, I can see it in his crystalline gaze. The way he looks at me now is entirely different, like he's seeing me for the first time. But is it for the better? I can't read him well enough right now to say. And that is the part that kills me. I've always been able to read Owen before. What if this is the moment where he rejects me?

His eyes flick to my lips.

I take a step back. No. We can't risk it. Especially now that there's a chance for us.

I clear my throat. "I hope that was okay," I say awkwardly. "What I said tonight. About us."

He exhales and turns away, peering into the night, running a hand through his wet hair. I want so badly to ask him what he's thinking, but I don't say a word. We stand side by side, a few feet from the lake's edge. The landscape is smooth, a line of gray on black, save for the crest of the castle wall two miles behind us. The clouds obscure the stars and moon, darkening everything more than normal. The air is thick with humidity, the ground beneath our boots sticky with clopping mud.

"I never wanted to be king," he admits quietly. "My whole life, I wanted it to be Dean, and then when he left, Silas." He tilts his head toward me and smiles. "You know me. I've always wanted to be free, to travel, to be my own man. Being king comes with so much responsibility."

So he's rejecting me after all. I'm met with mixed emotions. Sadness for myself, but love for my friend. I can understand his need for freedom. I want that for him, too.

"If you don't want it," I say, swallowing the lump in my throat. "I would never force it on you. Only one of us has to bear that responsibility. And Silas will make a fine king."

"I'm not finished," Owen says, smiling again. "I never wanted to be king. But I've *always* wanted you."

I blink, my heart skipping.

"I can't have one without the other," he continues, inching closer, "but I never thought I would get either, so I didn't even try to get you, and I certainly didn't try to get the throne."

"Oh." It's all I can manage. But I smile, too. Ultimately, I want my friend to be happy. I want what's best for him, even if sadness sweeps through me at the thought.

"I want to kiss you right now, but I won't. I won't risk it even though it's killing me. I won't risk it, because even though we're alone now, once I start, I know there will be no possible way I could stop and we *will* get caught." He reaches out and takes a lock of my hair between his fingers, twisting it. "So I'll wait… and I'll start trying."

This time, my smile is real.

Thunder cracks across the landscape. Lightning flashes through the darkness, brightening everything for the briefest of moments. Owen and I jump apart and search the sky. My nerves tangle into knotted fear, recognizing the storm for what it is: magic. A massive black dragon appears between the clouds and swoops down, landing feet away from us with practiced grace. The air around him crackles with electricity as Silas shifts into his human form. He's dressed head to toe in black, blending with the night, but there's hatred on his face and *that* stands out.

"There you two are," he sneers. "I thought I might find you out here."

Neither of us speak.

He steps closer, the hem of his long black cape brushing the mud. "Oh, you didn't think I knew about your little Thursday night illegal activities, did you?"

Owen raises his hands. "It's not what it looks like, it's just for fun."

"I thought it was just for fun." He turns on Owen, pointing a long finger. "I overlooked it because I care about both of you and I trusted you to be an honorable man. But I can't overlook it anymore, now can I?"

"What do you mean?" I challenge, widening my stance. "You're not going to turn us in, are you?"

Silas ignores me, stalking toward his twin. "You just couldn't let me have it, could you? You saw that I was going to be given the throne and you had to get in the way, even though everyone knows I'm the best man for the job."

"It's not like that," Owen replies, his voice growing dark, but Silas doesn't care, he moves in close anyway, rage rolling off him in waves.

I expect that at any minute, they'll fight. Brother on brother. It will be a wild mess of crunching bones and flying limbs and hurled insults, and it could take a turn for the worse, with Silas drawing on his air elemental and Owen his water. But I've seen the brothers fight before. First as boyish children, then as sparring young adults, and it's nothing I can't break apart with my magic if it comes to that.

What I don't expect is the knife.

Silas draws it from his pocket so quickly I nearly miss it. He rushes forward, slicing the blade straight across his brother's throat in one quick motion. Zero hesitation. I gasp, disbelieving. This isn't real. But it is. *It is.* Silas cut Owen wide open, the blood pouring from the wound too fast to comprehend.

Owen's eyes are wide as saucers as he crumples to the mud.

I scream, shock slamming through my body, and charge forward. I have to save Owen. Somehow. I have to help. Have to stop Silas. Have to do something!

Silas jumps out of my way and I fall into the mud, grasping Owen's lifeless body in my arms. He's still warm, but he's not there anymore. His eyes are vacant. There's too much blood. His soul has been sliced from his body and I can't believe this. This can't be happening. This can't be real.

"What did you do?" I cry up at Silas. The rain has started again, heavier than before. This time, I feel the chill, feel it right past my bones and down into my very soul. "You killed him!"

Silas takes a step back, his eyes round and still. At first I think he's realized what he's done, regretful. But then his eyes thin and he glares at me through thick lashes. "Did I?" he spits back. "No elemental powers were used here. Anyone could have slit his throat had they caught him by surprise."

"What?" I sputter through hot tears mixing with the rain.

"My brother shouldn't have been so stupid as to sneak out here at night. And what with our enemies out to get us? Terribly careless. Senseless tragedy. This could start a war."

He's going to deny what he did? I swallow back bile as the realization sinks in. He's not only going to deny that he murdered his brother, but use it to feed his political aspirations. He pretends that all he wants is to protect our borders to keep his father happy. But it's Silas. Of course, he wants more.

"How could you? You're a monster!" I choke out.

"How could *I*?" He shakes his head, his eyes filled with certainty. "No. How could *he*? How could my own brother betray me? How could he suck you into his clutches like that when he *knew* I was going to be crowned? I did what I had to do for the betterment of this kingdom and for *your* own safety, Khali. In time, you'll see I had no choice. He made me do it."

I pull Owen's limp body into my lap. My tears run cold and loathing consumes my every word. "You'll never be king. I'll tell everyone what you've done here tonight, Silas. You have murdered a royal—your own brother. You will be executed for this."

"Nobody will believe you," he sneers. "I have an airtight alibi already in place at this very moment. And actually, I'm certain everyone will blame you for Owen's unfortunate death if you present lies about me. Once they discover he was out here with you, so you could fly around like a couple of lovesick idiots, ignoring the danger, ignoring the *law*, they'll know it was your fault my brother was killed."

"Murdered," I spit back. I don't want to believe one foul word, don't want to listen to his murderous mouth utter another lie. But a small part of me wonders if he could be right. Will they blame me? Should I blame myself?

We never should have come out here. Never.

I glare up at Silas, the weight of my bad choices a million pounds on my heart. "No matter what happens, mark my words, you will *never* be my husband."

He smirks. "I'm all you have left, sweetheart. Four more months, and you're mine."

I shake my head.

"And one more thing," he adds. "If you tell anyone about this, mark *my* words, everyone you love will end up like Owen."

I'm going to be sick. I always knew he was intense, but never did I imagine he was capable of something like *this*.

He smiles mockingly, blows me a kiss, then shifts back into his dragon form.

I don't watch him go.

I can barely see through the tears. Violent sobs take over my body as I hold my friend for the last time. Owen's face is so pale now, it's almost white. His dead eyes are open, lifeless, peering into the afterlife beyond. Water drips down his cheeks. Not tears. Rain. Rain that will never wash away this moment or the terrible way his brother stole everything from us.

SEVEN
HAZEL

I HOLD THE FINISHED APPLICATION for The Roasted Bean in my hand as I walk down Main Street—a girl on a mission. I'll turn it in, get the job, and that will be that. I should smile, but I can't. All I can feel is sadness. Behind me, Kathrine's ghost follows in my footsteps. She's been tailing me all day and my heart is broken for her. There's nothing I can do. She keeps sending me images from her life, but they're just random, and none seem to have anything to do with what happened to her. I don't know what I can do to help her or erase the guilt I feel.

At least for now, Cora, Macy, and I have made a pact not to go anywhere alone, unless it's out in public. I haven't told them about my curse, they don't know what I know, but at this point, they're not the only ones who believe Kathrine is dead.

The smell of coffee leads me to my destination, but just before I get there, something stops me cold in my tracks, like cement has been poured around my boots. I stare across the street at The Flowering Chakra shop. The store sign's script is purple and flowy with the "o" in "flower" shaped like a daisy. It's actually pretty cute. The place has a welcoming energy about it that's undeniable.

It kind of pisses me off.

It pisses me off because it pulls me in like a magnet and before I know it, I'm crossing the quaint little street. I stand right in front of the cute red brick shop, my nose pressed to the front window. Hoping to see what? I don't know. An answer to everything, maybe. As if that'll happen. Katherine stands with me.

Inside are several rows of glass cases filled with jewelry and crystals of all shapes, sizes, and colors. Geometric art pieces made from a variety of metals hang from the ceiling, twirling gently. Two large distressed wooden tables stand centered in the airy space with a variety of trinkets expertly laid across the top. A row of matching bookshelves lines the back of the shop. I expected clutter. But this is organized. Loved.

The door swings open. "Well, are you coming inside or what?"

I scrunch my nose and take in the older lady from last week, the same one I swore I would avoid because I can only assume she's out to scam me. Her eyes glitter like sapphires as she smiles knowingly. I don't want her metaphysical mumbo-jumbo or whatever it is she's offering, but then again, why am I standing here?

"Come." She reaches out to embrace my hand. Her skin is soft and thin, cold and wrinkled with age, but her touch is oddly relaxing. "We have so much to discuss."

She leads me inside, flipping the open sign on the glass door to CLOSED and locking it behind us. My natural guardedness is screaming to get the heck out of dodge, but curiosity keeps me from that.

"Is that really necessary?" I ask, folding my arms over my chest. "I don't plan to stay long."

She shrugs the question off and leads me to the back of the shop to a dark purple door. "Reading In Session" is written across it in bold letters. She pulls it open and inside is a pale lavender box of a room with a couch, two puffy chairs, a little black card table, and one window covered with a bamboo shade.

I'm struck with a feeling that's not quite déjà vu but close enough. I've been in rooms similar to this one before and the experiences never ended well. I can't go through more pain of false hope, and I'm struck with cold-feet and take a step back. What was I thinking, coming here?

"Sit down, dear," the woman continues in a calming but firm tone. "I promise I don't bite." She winks and then spins around, sitting down and watching me with that same knowing smile from before. "My name is Helen Marnie but I've gone by Harmony for sixty-seven years and don't plan to stop. I'm a woman hellbent on making this earth a better place to live in and when I said I could help you, I meant it. In order for that to happen, *you* have to be willing to at least sit your butt down in that chair there and hear me out."

I bite my lip. Something brought me here, didn't it? I don't know if it was fate or if I even believe in fate, but all I can think is I ought to at least give this woman a shot. What's the worst that can happen? I can't imagine anything could be worse than the incident on Friday night, what with those spirits hounding me until freaking *Dean Ashton* had to save me. Even if she makes things harder for me in some way, nothing could be worse than that.

I release a deep breath and settle into the center of the cushy brown chair across from her. "All right, Harmony." I say her name awkwardly, part of me wanting to laugh at the "Helen Marnie" of it all. "How is it exactly that you can help me? Do you even know what's wrong with me?"

"Of course I know what's wrong, but it doesn't have to be considered wrong. It's all a matter of perspective."

"Okay…"

"You have eyes for the spirit realm and you don't know how to manage it. Not that I blame you. It can be a particularly challenging gift."

I gape at her. I didn't expect her to hit the nail on the head on her first try. How did she know?

She raises an eyebrow. "How did I know?" Her question mirrors my thought, leaving a trail of goosebumps over my body. "If I told you, I'm not sure you'd believe me. What's your name, by the way? Are you ready to tell me?"

I sit up a little taller and clear my throat. "I'm Hazel and I'm a haunted girl. But I think you already knew that. So whether or not I'm going to believe you… how about you try me."

"Well then," she quips back. "I like a girl with some sass. Okay, what do you want to know?"

"How did you figure out my problem so quickly? Do you see them too?"

The silence spreads between us as she studies me with a knowing gleam in her watery eyes. The mood shifts like afternoon shadows, growing more serious.

"All right then, Hazel, I'll tell you about me. No, I don't see the spirit world. What I can see are the paths."

I blink. "Ehh, the what now?"

She leans forward. "When I meet people, I see many paths laid out in front of them, those future possibilities that could play out in their lives. When I saw you, many possibilities spiraled out in front of you, all involving the future of your spiritual gift. In one of those futures, I was helping you manage it and you were thriving."

I blink at her. I have no words.

"And that's how I know you're going to agree to work here and not at The Roasted Bean."

I suck in a breath, catching the musty scent of sage mixed with sweet lavender. Part of me wants to latch on to this woman, to make her spill everything that might or might not happen to me. The other part of me wants to run far, far away. She's probably a crook. She's probably bad news. But then why the interest in me? How did she know my secret with only one chance look? I try to picture myself working here. But I can't. It feels too… confrontational. Too real.

"Even if you are the real deal, I'm sorry, but I can't work here," I say, my walls growing thick. "No offense, but this isn't really my kind of place."

She laughs. It's a joyful sound and it catches me off guard. "Hazel, my dear, no offense to you but this is exactly your kind of place. And as for what you'd do, I thought that was obvious. You'll do readings for the shop."

I raise an eyebrow. "And by readings, you mean?"

"I'll keep to psychic readings, and you'll do the mediumship readings."

Now it's my turn to laugh. "You're crazy! I can't do that."

"And why not?"

"Because if I open myself up to the spirits, they won't leave me alone." Even as I say it, that long-held hope flares to life. Maybe this lady is the answer to controlling my problem. *But what if she's not*, my mind reels, *and she makes everything worse?*

She nods and a white dreadlock falls over her bony shoulder. Understanding shines in her eyes. Empathy, too. "And are there any spirits in here right now?" she asks kindly. "Go ahead, look around."

I blink, realization practically slapping me across the face. Kathrine didn't follow me inside the shop. In fact, none of the spirits did. Something a lot like hope spreads over my entire body. "Wait, how did you do that? Where did they go?"

"I can teach you how to create dedicated safe spaces where only invited spirits can enter. And I can help you protect your person when you're out and about so that they don't bother you as much. And in return, you can work for me. How much does that coffee place pay, anyway?"

"The application said $10 an hour plus tips, which are probably pretty decent. They needed someone for ten to fifteen hours a week."

"You can work *here* ten to fifteen hours a week instead. I'll pay you the $10 an hour when you're on the sales floor but give you half commission for any readings you book. That's $50 an hour right into your pocket for those. Plus, I'll teach you anything I can to help you manage your gift, because, Hazel"—her eyes grow soft, shifting from business woman back to compassionate matriarch—"it *is* a gift. You're going to do great things with it."

"I just want to do normal things, to *be* a normal girl." I'm overcome by the words and everything they hold.

"Oh posh! No you don't! Normal is for the birds. You have a big, big life ahead. It's coming for you whether you're ready or not, so you might as well get ready."

I close my eyes for a lingering minute, breathing in the quietness of the room, the solitude of this space. No spirits. No ghosts. It's downright glorious. I can't believe what I'm about to agree to, but then again, how could I not? My eyes pop open and I extend my right hand. "Harmony, I can't believe I'm saying this, but you have a deal."

THE NEXT FEW WEEKS FLY by in a blur of classes, work, friends, and studying. Needless to say, I don't touch another alcoholic beverage, nor do I plan to. But thanks to Harmony, this college thing is going better than I ever hoped for. I've made my dorm room a ghost-free zone with large black obsidian stones strategically placed in the four corners. Now they can't come in unless I invite them. Hahaha, suckers! That's never going to happen!

My classes are going splendidly well because I finally have a quiet place to study. I've started recording every lecture just in case I get too distracted while in class, but my new obsidian necklace has lessened a lot of the spirit realm's noise and images. Life is flipping fantastic. Who knew the black stones could be so powerful at blocking the spirits?

Landon and I have been flirting during organic chemistry labs on Tuesdays and Thursdays, and I always stop by his work on the way into mine. I'm certain he's going to ask me out on a real date soon—he asked for my number this afternoon. And even the perpetually grumpy Dean Ashton has inexplicably decided to leave me alone. Guess he gave up on the territorial stuff? The man doesn't even *look* at me anymore. In fact, I'm pretty sure he's avoiding me. Not that I care. Sure, I still want to uncover his big bad secret, but every time I allow my mind to go there, I end up shutting that nonsense down. The possible explanations are too… weird. Which says a lot coming from me.

I finish ringing up a chatty customer, when my phone vibrates in my back pocket. Once the customer has left the store and the place is again empty, I slip my phone out and find a waiting text from Landon.

Hi, Gorgeous. How's work going? Caffeine wearing off yet?

I smile and bite my lip. Ya, I know it's a stupid pick-up line, but him calling me gorgeous sends a flutter of butterflies scurrying through my chest anyway. Sometimes I am *such* a girly girl.

I type back.

Starting to, but working here is interesting enough to keep me awake. :) How are you?

His reply comes in almost immediately.

Still wish you would've applied here instead. And I'm doing good. It's dead here right now. So bored.

…

The three dots on the phone blink for a second before another one of his texts pops up.

I'm lonely. Wish you could keep me company.

The butterflies are having an all-out war in my chest now, and I'm considering asking Harmony if I can take my break when she comes bounding in from her back office with the kind of cheeky grin that makes her look twenty years younger. Oh, no. This can't be good.

"Guess what I just did?" She rushes to put her arm around my shoulders. She smells of her usual sage—not my favorite scent in the world. I hold back a cough, my eyes instantly watering. The stuff sells here by the boatload, so it comes with the territory, but I swear I'm allergic or something.

"What?" I grit my teeth and smile.

"I just booked your first reading! Your customer will be here in five minutes."

I blink at her, my heart stopping and then furiously catching up to the fear. I knew this was coming. She's been preparing me on what to do and putting feelers out with her regulars. But I'm not ready.

"You *are* ready, Hazel." She lets me go and glides through the store, arms outstretched like this is some kind of "world is your oyster" moment. "Remember what we talked about?" Her watery blue eyes travel up and down me. "You let the customer sit and you invite any spirits of the light to join them and then take it from there. Let them ask questions. Tell them what you see and hear. Simple. The hour will go by in a flash. And if anything weird or uncomfortable happens in there, you're allowed to end the session early."

I gulp and nod, forcing my expression to relax. "I'm going to be cool as a cucumber, even if more than five minutes notice would have been nice."

Harmony only laughs and busies herself with one of the displays. I guess the $50 commission will have to make up for this sudden attack on my nervous system. Harmony's been saying that it's only a matter of time before I'm completely booked for these "psychic medium readings" and not able to work on the sales floor anymore. If that happens, I'll be earning several hundred dollars a week. Maybe even $750 a week if I can work up to the full fifteen sessions. That number is staggering for a girl who grew up in a single parent household and needed a scholarship to be able to attend college without going into serious debt. It's the kind of money that could go a long way in getting me through veterinary school one day. It's true what they say, vet school is just as costly as medical school without the fancy BMW waiting ten years down the line. Sigh…

Okay, I can do this. It's a great opportunity.

The door opens and the little bell chimes. My whole body lights up with nervous energy.

Nevermind, I can't do this!

I take a steadying breath, once again clearing my face of fear, and look up to find my first customer, a fake smile frozen on my lips. He strides into the shop like he owns the place, like he knows exactly how this day is going to go for him and it's going to go *super well*. His scruffy dark hair is curled around his ears and somehow, my own hands twitch, my treacherous fingers wanting to frolic through those silky waves.

What is wrong with me?

My eyes travel down the curve of his arms to where his hands are pushed into the pockets of his jeans. The man is sporting a leather jacket that oozes so much sexiness, it's completely unfair. I can only pull off the nerdy girl look. Not the "hot librarian fantasy nerd" version. Just the regular one. But it's his dark eyes, those two black depths, no longer lit by fire, that send an icy shiver over my entire body. The shiver battles with the nerves already there!

He's no longer the man who knows exactly how this day is going to go, in fact, his expression is saying quite the opposite. But that doesn't make sense! Dean Ashton is scowling at me, eyes blazen, lip curled, jaw tight, and all I can think is that now would be a good time to quit my new job.

EIGHT
KHALI

WITH EACH PASSING HOUR, I shift from chilling numbness to staggering grief. Every small action seems like a mountain of overwhelm that I don't care to climb. I can't eat. I can't sleep. Mourning has left every muscle aching and even that isn't enough to push away the turmoil. And the worst part is that my thoughts of Owen are tainted with guilt for having put him in that vulnerable position in the first place. We shouldn't have gone out alone unprotected. And we never should have trusted his brother. I always knew Silas wanted to be king, but how could we have underestimated him?

Because after two weeks of hell, I'm beginning to think Silas is going to get away with what he did. He's the only Dragon Blessed heir left. He'll get the crown by default.

I stare up at my stone ceiling and force myself to replay what happened; all the tears dried up days ago. Parts of it are hazy. I still don't know how long it took the guards to find me with Owen's body. After Silas threatened me and left, I stayed. I stayed and I held my best friend's body in my arms, sobbing until the rain stopped, the sunrise bled over the horizon and they found us.

I was a babbling mess and they were quick to take me into custody, locking me in my chambers. And I've been here ever since. Every time Faros comes in with a meal or to help me bathe or dress, I plead with her to send King Titus and Queen Brysta to come speak with me. They need to know what happened. Why don't they come? But Faros says they've refused to see me and forbidden anyone but her to come in here. I haven't even received a visit from my mother.

At this point, I'm waiting for my death.

Because why else would Owen's parents refuse to talk to me if they didn't believe I was responsible for their son's murder? If I could just explain what happened, warn them about Silas, then they could punish Silas and protect Bram. He might not have magic, but that doesn't mean Silas won't find a reason to end his life too. Besides, perhaps the King and Queen could find it in their hearts to bring Dean back from exile. Surely they could override the law? What good is being a monarch if you can't do that? If they knew the truth, they'd have to agree that anything would be better than Silas getting away with murdering his twin.

I drift into sleep, exhaustion taking over like a spring mud, thick, heavy, and bitter cold. I sink into it, letting it take me. Anything is better than to be left alone with my thoughts.

Sometime later, I wake to find my mother sitting at the end of the small bed. Her hair and makeup are done perfectly. She wears a black mourning dress. Her eyes are red but she doesn't look sad. She looks angry.

"What did you do?" she spits out.

I don't have the energy to entertain her right now. I roll over, pressing my face against the cool stone wall. It smells of winter.

"Khali Elliot, you *will* talk to me." She grabs hold of my leg. "What happened? What did you do to Owen?"

I shift to glare up at her, yanking my leg away. "Maybe you should ask your buddy, Silas, about what he did to his twin?" I hiss.

Her eyes widen. Her body stills. I can see her mind is racing as she puts it all together. I don't know what I expect from her. Shock? Sadness? Anger?

I get none of these. Instead, I find fear on her face.

"Silas must have been provoked," she says calmly.

"No!" I snap. "Silas killed Owen in cold blood."

"Shh—" she jumps forward and slams her hand over my mouth. "Don't you ever speak those words again. That's treason."

I want to laugh. To cry. To bite out every angry word I have for her. I do none of those things. She stands, brushing out her skirt, and leaves without a backwards glance.

She doesn't come to visit me again.

And all I can think about is how much I miss my father. I miss him with every fiber of my being, but he never comes through that locked door, despite how many times I plead with the Gods. He's still gone from Court, I'm sure. If he were back in our suite at the castle, he would have noticed my absence and upon discovering what had happened to me, demanded an audience. But his missions for the king are so secretive that his travel locations and lengths are left to my imagination. I never have any idea when he'll return and this latest absence is no different.

What use is thinking about it? It only adds to the pain I already have to live with.

The days spread into nights and back again, until finally someone comes through that door who isn't Faros. He enters alone, dressed in his own version of the black mourning clothes. His eyes are rimmed in red with long shadows under each and the stubble on his cheeks is days old. For a moment, he looks so much like Owen that it kills me all over again.

"King Titus." I scramble from my bed and curtsey. "I'm so glad you finally came to hear what I have to say." Genuine gratitude blooms within. "Thank you."

He closes the door with a thud and strides forward, holding up a hand. "I didn't come here to hear what you have to say."

That gratitude is plucked away in a second. "But Silas—"

"Stop," he commands. "I do not wish to hear it from your mouth and I forbid you from ever speaking of what Silas did, do you understand?"

My throat goes dry as sand and I blink in surprise. "You already know?" I wonder if my mother told him but I can scarcely believe it possible she'd be so bold.

"Yes," he says evenly. "Brysta and I know what Silas did to Owen."

"Then you have arrested him? Where is he?"

He shakes his head and narrows his eyes, stalking in close. The man towers over me, and a prickle of intimidation claws across my flesh. The laugh lines around his eyes and mouth no longer look welcoming. Something tells me this meeting isn't going to go how it should.

"Owen is gone," he says calmly. "There is nothing anyone can do about that fact. Silas is the only heir left that could possibly take the throne. You will never speak of what he did to Owen, do you understand me? Owen was murdered by an unknown assassin. That's it."

His words push at my wound, twisting the knife Silas put there to begin with. "What about Bram? What about Dean?" My voice rises in disgust and anger.

"You are forbidden to speak that name," he roars, meeting my volume with his own demands. "He is in exile and to bring him back would be to void the treaty of the dragon clans. It will *not* be done."

"Well, Bram is still alive," I challenge. "Why can't he be king? At least he isn't a cold-blooded murderer!"

"Bram is useless!" King Titus scoffs. "He can never be king!"

I stumble backward until the back of my knees hit the edge of the unmade bed and I stare up at the King, seeing his true self for the first time. He has always been intense, powerful, with an air of superiority that leaves other men cowering, but the boiling anger in his tone is so startling, this demand so terrible, that the breath is ripped from my lungs. Tears prick at my eyes, and I clench my hands into fists. I'm not upset for being yelled at, though it tilted me off my axis. I'm horrified by the unjust way Silas's treason is being treated. He really is going to get away with this, and his parents, the ones who should want to avenge Owen, are going to make sure of it.

"How can you do this to Owen? He was your son, too!" I'm crying now. I can't help the burning tears that splash down my cheeks but I can't be bothered to wipe them away or feel weak in front of this man. I'm a roiling mess of emotions and the elemental powers within are demanding to break free. I hold them down because I know there's nothing I can do with them, not in here, not with *him*. This isn't right. This isn't fair. This is sick.

"Silas will be the next king." He glares, speaking softly now. "There is nothing anyone can do about that. Not you. Not me. Not my wife. Not anyone. If what Silas did comes out and he is punished for his crime, the clans will rebel and we will lose our royal line to another dragon family."

I nod, giving in, because what else am I to do? But I'm already running through all possible options in my mind, trying to stay strong. All I can think is while the Brightcaster family will lose everything, I won't. I'll be forced into a loveless marriage with some other son of some other noble family, but at least I won't have to take Silas as my husband. The Gods offered me as Drakenon's queen but I'm not bound to *this* family. I'm bound to whoever takes the throne. If I marry another, at least I won't have to lie about what happened to Owen, to live my life at Silas's side, to go to bed with him and give him elemental dragon children. The thought of a marriage to Silas leaves my stomach twisting with disgust. I can't do it. I won't.

"Fine," I lie, meeting King Titus's eyes. "I won't say anything. I'll keep your secret and go along with Silas as the next king, but you have to do something for me."

He smiles ruefully, his eyes narrowing into stormy slits. "Oh, darling, this isn't a negotiation. In fact, I came here to tell you that should you betray my trust, your parents will pay for your folly."

My hands shake. I hold them against my chest, feeling the breath leave my body. "What are you talking about?" But I already know. Like father, like son.

He tilts his head. "It's a pity. I never wanted it to be like this. I like your parents. They've been friends of mine ever since you were an infant and we brought the three of you to live here."

"Just tell me what you've done," I snap.

"Your father is fortunate enough to have the privilege of traveling the kingdom on my behalf. Should you betray me, Princess Khali, I can promise you that you won't ever see your father alive again."

Can he do that? Neither of my parents are Dragon Blessed. How would they defend themselves against this wicked man?

"And not only will your father die, but your mother will be ruined. I know all her secrets. Lest you forget, Lady Alivia is quite the court politician. She's made errors over the years in her climb to the top, and I know of each and every one of those errors. If you break my trust, Khali, I will make certain your mother is the joke of the entire kingdom. It won't matter who takes the throne, she'll be the outcast." His air elemental crackles behind his stormy eyes, a promise of what's possible.

My mother probably does have terrible secrets. She and I don't even get along, surely he knows that? But then again, I'm not cruel. I don't want her to be unhappy, and as much as she and I butt heads, she's usually the only family I have around. I would never want to see her ruined, but is that enough to stop me from avenging my best friend and keeping his murderer off the throne? My father's possible death is King Titus's best play and I don't know how to use it to my advantage.

"And if that isn't enough," he continues, catching on to my thought process, "well, I can always have your mother killed as well. Gods know she has enough enemies. And what about that maid you love so dearly? She's a cousin to your mother, is she not? She could easily be taken down with the rest of them."

"You're sick." I shake my head, the extent of the betrayal sinking in deep. "You would do that to your own friends? To innocent people? My family has been completely loyal to your family since day one. They moved me here, didn't they? I've heard stories of other future queens being hidden away, but not my parents. They came forward the moment I opened my eyes. And since that day they've encouraged me to embrace the role I am to play, even during those moments when I didn't want it."

He leans in close, his eyes shining, and I catch the faintest scent of Drakenon wine on his breath. "You may possess all the elements, Khali. You may be used to the incredible power flowing in your veins, but you have no idea the kind of *royal* power you're dealing with. The Brightcaster family has held this throne for over a century and you will *not* cross us."

My mind races through my options but I don't see that I have anything tangible. He's right. Even if I do stage a coup, he will still extend his power long enough to hurt or kill the ones I love. Silas going to prison won't mean he'll automatically lose his throne, but it will mean he will have years to torture me until it's time for him to step down and give up the line to the next strongest clan.

"Owen is gone," he says, his voice catching. Deep-rooted pain crosses his features. "It never should have happened. But it did."

I won't let it change me. "How dare you grieve Owen," I sneer. "He deserved better!"

The slap comes fast, charged with electricity. The pain blossoms on my cheek and I fall to the bed.

The King continues as if nothing happened. "After we started questioning the events, Silas came to Brysta and me to confess his sins. He is remorseful over what happened. He lost his temper and things got out of hand. *He's sorry. We all are.* But he can't take it back and we can't lose our royal line over this one mistake. So we won't."

I rub my cheek and sit up, contemplating my lack of options moving forward.

"Do we have a deal?" he asks. It doesn't sound like a question.

"I don't see how you are giving me a choice," I finally relent bitterly. "But King Titus." I meet his gaze square in the eye. "You raised a murderer. I was there that night and I can promise you, it wasn't an accident. It was a planned murder and Silas had zero hesitation or remorse before or after the event."

His face pales but he says nothing.

"You had better watch your back, because Silas wants your throne and the only one left standing in his way is *you*."

"He wouldn't—"

"He murdered his twin brother," I say between gritted teeth. "He would. You're a fool to protect him."

NINE
HAZEL

"SHE'S THE MEDIUM?" DEAN ASKS, gaping at Harmony like she's gone and lost her mind.

"Best there is," Harmony replies, shuffling forward to wrap Dean in a loving, familiar hug—as if he were her favorite son. But I know for a fact Harmony never got married or had children. It's too bad, she would have been great at family life. But then again, what she's doing is pretty great, too.

I'm standing behind the register, my hands balled at my sides, my breath caught in my chest. I'm a mixed bag of shock, defensiveness, and a heck of a lot of confusion. I thought Dean knew what I was. He certainly acted like he knew exactly what I was when we first met and that my presence was this massive affront to him and his "territory." I assumed he had a problem with mediums or perhaps he was something similar. I don't know.

None of this is making any sense.

Then another thought comes to my mind so quickly and I can't help myself from blurting it out. "*You're* a regular *here*?" I let out a laugh, then try to cover it up with a fake cough as they both turn on me.

Harmony's lips purse, and I know I should feel utterly terrible that she's hurt by the comment but *come on*. I hold up my hands in defense. "I'm sorry. He just doesn't seem like the type of guy to frequent The Flowering Chakra, that's all."

Dean glares, folding his arms over his chest. He towers over Harmony, all muscle and petulance. "You don't know anything about me."

I almost want to laugh again but I hold it in for Harmony's sake. I mean, he's not wrong, except I know that he's a cocky prick. Even when he drove me home that Friday night a few weeks ago, he could have redeemed himself and been a gentlemen about it but he chose not to be. And in Anthropology, he totally has a superiority complex, acting like he's the smartest guy in the class.

I meet his challenging stare with my own. This is my work and my town now, too. So the way I see it, he's in *my* territory. I tilt my head, realization dawning on me. Are his cheeks turning pink? Because I think they are and it is totally making my day. Who knew the big man on campus would turn out to be a patron of the metaphysical arts? This is too good. Cora and Macy are going to love this. Would it be mean to make fun of him behind his back? I'm not normally that kind of person but something about Dean Ashton makes it too easy.

"So if you two are ready," Harmony says, clearing her throat and attempting to clear the air, "we can start the reading."

I step back, shaking my head vehemently. "No way," I blurt at the same time Dean says, "I've changed my mind."

Harmony's head bobs between us, her gray eyebrows knit together. "Why on earth not?"

"Are you kidding me?" I laugh, sounding crazed. "This guy's been a total jerk-face to me from the moment I met him."

"Jerk-face?" He questions my choice of words like I'm a child. "How old are you?"

I ignore the question even though I'm burning up with the implication. I shrug at Harmony. "I'm sorry, Boss, but there is no way I'm going into a room with him to do… *that*."

Okay, did that sound bad? Because I'm pretty sure I made it sound like my readings come with "extras". His eyes flicker to mine, and he snarls like he just smelled raw sewage. My cheeks burn even hotter with utter embarrassment.

Harmony is unfazed. "I'm *so* sorry, Dean. I didn't know you two knew each other. I'm wondering why I didn't see that?" Her voice trails off and she looks at us for a minute, humming to herself. I clear my throat and it snaps her out of it.

"Anyway, Dean," she continues. "If you'd like me to give you a reading instead, I'd be happy to help. I don't have the same gift as Hazel but perhaps I can still help."

His lips are a thin line, and he shakes his head. "No, I don't need a reading from anyone today. I'll grab a few things and be out of *Hazel's* way." He says my name like it's the same raw sewage he smelled earlier. But how is that fair when he's the one who's been awful to me? Besides, I have a right to turn any client away that makes me uncomfortable. That was the agreement.

The shop is filled with crystals, books, herbs, and all sorts of metaphysical paraphernalia. I can't pretend that my curiosity isn't piqued. What "few things" would *he* need?

Dean turns his back on me and meticulously picks out three of the sage smudge sticks from a nearby wicker basket, and then he approaches the register, tossing them onto the wooden tabletop for me to ring up. My eyes travel from the sage on the counter to his eyes, my lips slightly parting in a smirk. He glares again.

I'm sorry, but I can't help it. Dean Ashton smudges? Okay, this is getting weird. What kind of college guy uses a smudge stick, let alone knows what it is? The bundles of dried sage leaves are tied together with twine and even have a few sprigs of dried lavender mixed in. People light them up and then use the smoke to get rid of bad energy in their homes and funky stuff like that. But they smell pretty gross so even I don't use them *and I work here*!

Harmony clears her throat again. "Hazel, can you please ring up our customer?"

"Of course." I plaster a smile on my lips and get busy.

As I scan his items, Dean casually slips a piece of folded up paper from his back pocket and hands it to Harmony.

She unfolds it and her face pales. "Another one?"

"Second one in as many weeks," he replies grimly. "I don't know what to make of it."

I lean over the counter to get a better look. Is that nosy? Sure. But I don't care. And the second I see the Missing Persons flyer, my breath catches.

Harmony turns to me. "Have you seen this one?" She slides the black and white image of the girl to me. I know what she means. Not, have I seen her in person. But have I seen her dead. Her name is Alexandria Burk, she's 17, one of the students at the high school. Her smile radiates from her round face. She wears a cheerleading outfit, ribbons tied up in a high ponytail.

"I've never seen her," I say. But I wonder, if I took off my obsidian necklace, would she come to me? Is she dead like the other ones?

Harmony puts her hand on mine. "Good," she says, "but watch for her. Let us know if she comes to you."

I swallow hard and nod. Then I finish up the transaction. "That will be twelve dollars and forty cents." He hands me his card then turns back to Harmony.

Through all of this, Dean hasn't acknowledged me in the slightest. He's no longer angry or shocked or questioning. He's indifferent. He treats me like he'd treat any other clerk he didn't have a history with. His attitude is aloof and when we're done, he turns away without saying goodbye or acknowledging me. *Not even a smug retort? No glare? Nothing? Where's the Dean I know and hate?* It bothers me. And the fact that it bothers me, *really* bothers me.

The second he walks out from the store, Harmony spins around and raises an eyebrow.

"Really, Hazel? You hate him? Why? *What was that?*"

"Okay, I can see that you're less than happy."

Her mouth is slack, her eyes two bulging marbles, and her face is nearly the same shade of pink as the watermelon tourmaline crystals in the locked display case behind her.

"I'm sorry," I continue, feeling like the totally ungrateful brat she must think I am. But what was it that Cora said? If a guy is a jerk to a girl, she should be allowed to make a scene instead of always having to be polite. And Harmony did say I didn't have to finish a session if I was uncomfortable. This is kind of the same thing as far as I am concerned.

But I don't want to fight with her or sound ungrateful. I like Harmony. I like this job. I take a deep breath and hope that I can make her understand.

"I promise I can explain. Thing is, Dean accosted me the first moment he met me. We have a class together and basically, we don't get along. I have no idea why he hates me, but he does. He hates my guts. Neither of us would want to spend an hour together in that room."

She nods slowly and runs her hands over her face. "I've never been so embarrassed. Dean is one of my favorite customers. He's such a good boy."

I somehow doubt this is the most embarrassing moment of her entire life, and the idea of Dean as a "good boy" is questionable, but I take a deep breath, knowing I didn't handle myself very well and I need to fix this. Not that I want to, but Harmony has changed my life, and I hate to see her so disappointed in me. My stomach hurts just thinking about it. "I'm truly sorry. I will go and apologize to him right now if that helps." Maybe a bit reluctantly, but I'll do it for her. "I'm still not going to be able to do the reading for him though. Is that okay?"

She mimics my deep breath and her zen-like state returns. Her expression has cleared of the earlier torment, and she's back to the woman I've grown to know and love over the last few weeks. "I guess that will have to be okay."

She points to the door with a flick of her wrist. "Go before he's gone. He drives an unnecessary sports car. It's black. You can't miss it."

"Oh, I know all about that car," I mutter to myself, skipping through the store and out the door. Truth be told, the car is hot. Dean is hotter.

It's all so annoying and I've decided not to be effected like other girls.

The world outside has that shadowy late afternoon filter that hits a few hours before sunset. It's colder than it's been all month, and I wish I'd thought to grab my sweater. I'm only in a thin black t-shirt and blue jeans. I wrap my arms in close to my chest, and glance down both ends of the sidewalk to search for Dean or his "unnecessary" car. Main Street is gorgeous, sprawling before me like a storybook. A few of the leaves are starting to change color, but it's pretty void of people at the moment.

As far as I can tell he's not here, nor is his car parked on the street. I hurry past a few storefronts to the side parking lot at the end of the block. There are more spots there and I'm betting if he's one of Harmony's regulars, he knows all about them, especially if he likes to keep his visits to her establishment discreet. I mean, the man must have some pride, right? He has a reputation to protect. Since I've worked there, The Flowering Chakra hasn't had many college-aged patrons, certainly none that were male—until Dean.

Sure enough, I round the corner just as he's getting into his car.

Part of me wants to turn back and pretend I didn't catch him in time, but I can't disappoint Harmony. Nor would I want to lie to her. I've already embarrassed her and she's been nothing but good to me. Even if I don't want to do a reading for Dean, I still want to do them for her other customers. I want to learn. I need that kind of $50 an hour money and I want to prove to her that she made the right choice in hiring me.

I swallow my pride and stride up to the car, tapping on the driver's side window. It's tinted to complete darkness—like a celebrities car or something. Typical. It rolls down and Dean is there, his expression unreadable. Again, I'm struck by his almost inhuman beauty. I sort of hate him for it, but that's not what I'm here for. I sigh.

"I'm sorry about what happened back there," I say in a rush. "I wouldn't ever want to upset Harmony and even though you and I don't get along, I hope you won't take it out on her."

He blinks at me for a few moments as the quiet stretches between us. His fingers flex around the steering wheel and he leans back in his leather seat. "How hard was that for you to say?"

"Umm—pretty hard."

"I thought so." He laughs bitterly. "But I would never take it out on Harmony. It's you that I hate. Not her."

I scoff at him and step back. Is he serious? "Hate is a pretty strong word there, buddy. What possible reason could you have to hate me?" I can't help but ask the same question that's been driving me crazy. I've never done anything to him. He doesn't know me. How could he say he hates me? It's utterly ridiculous and doesn't make any sense.

He pins me with that smokey gaze, and I'm reminded of what I saw in those eyes that Friday night. This man has secrets. "It's clear to me that you're hellbent on pretending that you don't know the reason for my disdain, so if that's the way you're going to play it, it's better we don't talk and you stay out of my way."

Well, okay then...

He rolls up the window and the car purrs to life. I turn and scurry back to the sidewalk, more than ready to be finished with this conversation and be done with Dean Ashton.

As I'm about to round the corner, something swoops in on me. Something monstrous, black, and of the spirit world. But it's nothing like any spirit I've experienced before now. It swoops again, closer, and I'm knocked to the ground, landing hard on my back. White-hot pain shoots through my hips and elbows. I cry out, more surprised than anything. I scramble back until I'm pressing against the brick building. Blood whooshes through my ears, and I can hardly breathe.

Images flash through my mind so quickly I can't grab onto a single one.

Images of castles and courtiers and a girl with two different colored eyes. I blink until the images are gone.

The creature settles to the ground in front of me, huge and terrifying. My heart basically stops—I can't believe what I'm seeing. And yet, it's clear as day, clear as if it were flesh and blood and fire and smoke. It's a ... dragon.

A freaking *spirit dragon* has come to visit.

TEN

KHALI

THE FUNERAL PYRE GLOWS AMBER against the yawning gray sky, a solemn dance of flame and smoke. It's been hours since it was first lit and still I've held my tears at bay, watching the pyre burn and burn and burn. What started as an inferno, hungrily consuming Owen's cloth-wrapped body, has since dwindled to a pile of fiery coals. I stand on the crunchy grass, my velvet black dress gripping my torso, the suffocating corset underneath holding me up. The matching black cape hoods my face and hides me from the barrage of unwanted stares.

Once they cool, Owen's ashes will be split in two. Half will be taken to the sea that's nearly one hundred miles away as tribute to his water elemental, and the other half will be laid to rest in the castle cemetery alongside his ancestors. Perhaps then, his soul will be free.

But I'll still be here, a prisoner to fate. Here, without him.

It's only fourteen weeks until my birthday when I'll be forced into an engagement with Silas, and soon after, forced into his bed. The Gods will bind me to him forever. He will be my jailer, locking me to his side again and again with each child. The cruelty of it leaves my mouth tasting of soot that no amount of water will wash away.

A thick gust of smoke blows in my direction, swatting my cape from my head. The smoke burns my eyes and throat until I finally look away from the pyre. That's when I notice most of the funeral party has left, returning to the warmth of the castle—the warmth of life. I can't bare to join them. I can't will myself to move from this place until there's nothing of the wood left, and even then, I don't know that I can leave. Because I'll have to face them.

"My daughter." Lady Alivia's voice is smooth as pearls as she appears at my side. "It's time to be done here. Come, let's share a pot of your favorite tea together. Lavender?"

I don't answer her, but I take in her perfectly made-up face, expertly covering her few wrinkles, and the long dark curls styled to add to her youthful appearance, but it's the twinge of triumph shining behind her amber eyes that tell me all I need to know of my mother's true beauty. This funeral is not too sorrowful of an affair for her, not when Silas is next in line for king and whatever he's promised her will come to fruition. I look away bitterly, longing for my father. *He* would understand.

"The depth of your heartache will not do you any favors," she tries again, more forcefully this time. "People will question your relationship with the water brother if you continue on in this manner."

"Let them," I challenge through clenched teeth. "Owen was my best friend. I don't care if my grief is too strong for you or anyone else."

"But *Silas* is to be your husband now," she interjects.

"Do not speak to me of Silas again," I snap. "You got your wish. Whatever he has promised you is yours. There is no need to gloat. Now leave me to my heartache and let me grieve in peace."

She folds her arms over her chest, peering at me like I'm nothing but a petulant child, but she relents with a wistful sigh. "Very well. I will see you at the dinner tonight. I trust you to behave."

As she leaves, I don't dignify her with another word or glance. When did she go from being my loving mother, looking out for my needs, to being simply another person looking to use me for personal gain? She has no idea how lucky she is that I care about her life and reputation enough to protect her against the King's threats. Anger towards her and everyone else who has wronged me and Owen grows stronger. The dragon within rages to be let free, to take revenge, starting with Silas himself. But I cannot give in. *Not yet*. All I can do is stand here and watch the coals fade to white.

Hours later, I change into a different mourning dress of head-to-toe black, this one comprised of hideous piles of lace that itch with each movement. I'm sitting next to what is left of the Brightcaster family, trying not to break my "deal" with King Titus. I can't even look at the man without wanting to scream and scratch out his eyes. Nor Silas. And Queen Brysta, her tear-stained cheeks mean little to me. She's an accomplice in all of this too. The one with more elemental power than any of them, but who stood back and let it all happen.

Bram is quiet and withdrawn, watching the members at our table like he would one of his experiments, green eyes alight with questions. That's how he is, always in the background, nose in a book, but somehow, always keenly aware of what's going on around him. Today there is no book, and his eyes keep darting to me and then to his other family members. His earthy brown hair is more messy than usual, like he's been running his hands through it over and over.

Does he know what happened to Owen? Would he go along with his parents' wishes and cover for Silas? He is smart enough to figure it out on his own but suddenly, I have the urge to tell him. Even so, he may already know. He may be just as terrible as the rest of them. The thought of it stings like ice. I want to believe the best of Bram, need to believe he's the last good one left. But I don't know that I can.

Queen Brysta is seated to my right, the King at the head of the table next to her, the two brothers across from us. Everyone dressed in black seems like a slap to Owen's memory. I glare at the brothers. Save for their height, the two look nothing alike. Silas is fair-skinned and white blonde, polished, confident and oozing with lust for power and glory. If I thought he was open about his wishes to be king before, this is ten times worse. And Bram? Bram couldn't care less about power and glory. His unkempt chestnut hair flops haphazardly in front of his observant eyes, his shoulders hunched over in exhaustion. Down our long table and the ones adjacent, the rest of the party dines. This is not a night of wine and raunchy behavior. The conversations are muffled. The energy is tense. And eyes are shifty.

I do not speak to a single person. I fear I'll proclaim the truth and ignite Titus's threats against my family. I do not care to pretend that I want to be here as I've done every day previous to this one. I've always done my duty, gotten in line and smiled through the pain. I had resolved to go along with my predetermined future years ago, believing that my feelings didn't matter more than the betterment of the kingdom. All that mattered was what the Gods wanted and they wanted me Queen. That was it.

Well, I don't care about my fate anymore.

What have the Gods ever done for me? What did they do for Owen?

Nothing.

I'm done with this. I don't want to be a queen. I don't want to play this part or try to fit in with these people. This role is wicked and it makes me ill to play it. What is power and glory without loyalty and love? These people don't understand anything of either and the whole lot can rot in hell for all I care.

The crowd is a sea of richly embroidered dresses and tunics, many belonging to desperate or scheming faces. People who would do anything to get on the throne, so why must I prevent them? There are hundreds of Lord's daughters and thousands of untitled peasant girls living within Drakenon's borders who would kill to be sitting in my seat, so why didn't the Gods give this burden to one of them?

I catch Bram's gaze across the table and his eyes narrow. He is always curious, but tonight he is filled to the brim with unanswered questions. Those eyes lock me in, intense and demanding. Then he flicks them to Silas so quickly, that I almost miss it. But I don't and the question is there. Bram returns his stare to me, willing me to answer through our eye contact alone. I can't know for certain what he's asking, but I'm no fool. Bram is wondering if Silas had something to do with Owen's death. Indecision rocks me. I shouldn't do it; it risks too much. Let Bram figure it out for himself.

He stares at me. And I stare back. *You know the truth*, I direct my thoughts to him, knowing he can't hear me. Only in dragon form could he and that's impossible for him, but still, I shout the words inside my mind. *You know who your family is! You know what they're capable of! Don't be fooled! Silas killed Owen!*

He's waiting, waiting for me to indicate the truth. I look away.

Nobody else notices me, it seems. King Titus and Queen Brysta are occupied with Silas, the trio of serpents speaking in low tones, and none the wiser to Bram or myself. I let out my own sorrowful breath and return to spreading a heap of mashed potatoes around on my plate, uninterested in eating a single bite. In the presence of all these people, in my regular seat at this table, without Owen here, it forces the weight of his death onto my shoulders. I doubt I'll ever live without this pain. It might lighten with time, but it will never be completely lifted from me, nor would I want it to.

I'm so sorry, Owen. You didn't deserve this.

King Titus fists his silver goblet and stands, a splash of cranberry colored wine dripping onto his meaty hand. The room falls into silence and the guests turn toward their leader. If only they knew. I eye some of the more prominent members of the Drakenon Court, noting their fleeting looks of sadness and sympathy, but also the distrust in their eyes and the unanswered questions held on their tongues. Maybe they don't know the full extent of it, but they have to suspect. Titus was right to assume some would make a play for his throne should it be revealed that Silas committed an unforgivable crime, and there are no other Dragon Blessed heirs. I smile. Maybe I won't have to say a thing; maybe the Brightcasters will dig their own graves.

"I want to thank you all for coming to mourn the death and celebrate the life of my son, Prince Owen Hydros Brightcaster of Drakenon," Titus says. "He was a gifted young man with a promising future." Tears spring to his eyes, and I bite the fleshy inside of my cheek, holding back a torrent of angry words. "Our family is distraught over what happened. We are still in shock that we lost our gifted, humorous, beloved son. He had a vivacious taste for adventure, a cunning mind for battle, a generous heart for leadership, and the kind of water elemental power that outshined his peers. We loved him and he will be greatly missed." He raises his goblet high. "To Owen, may your adventures continue in the next life and may the Gods guide you."

"To Owen," the court echoes. I join in, even though it guts me.

The King doesn't sit. He shifts his stance and continues, "Now, as you may have already heard, my son was murdered in cold blood." A few gasp but most are quiet. Word travels fast around here and surely they all spent the two-week mourning period spreading rumors. "No elemental magic was found, nor any traces of the death being the result of a dragon attack."

His eyes harden as whispers erupt. They were not expecting this, it seems. Something about that makes me gleeful. Bram isn't the only one who suspected foul play here.

"It could have been someone in this court," the King says louder, his booming voice quieting the whispers. "But more likely, it was an enemy assassin or a foreign spy. But no matter what, I can assure you we will not rest until Owen's murderer is caught and his death is avenged."

What he really means is he won't rest until he can pin it on someone believable, and most likely someone who would suit his plans. I can't help but glare.

"Our investigation started the moment he was found with Princess Khali," he continues, as more whispering ensues. "She did not see what happened. She discovered him after he was already gone and I would kindly ask that you do not question her any further. She's been through enough, poor thing." Every eye in the room is trained on me and my face is practically in flames. Titus's patronizing tone makes me want to scream.

"Until we have answers," the King goes on, his face growing softer, kinder, "we must protect the family we have left. Silas and Khali, will you please stand?"

Icy dread pours over my body as I rise on shaky legs. I knew this was going to happen, everyone did. But it seems knowing something is coming and actually experiencing it are two very different things. My stomach rolls over in protest and tears prick at the corners of my eyes. I force myself to smile and the action physically hurts my heart, like a knife is running right through its center.

This isn't fair! I wasn't supposed to get engaged until my eighteenth birthday. That's how it works. That's how it was for Queen Brysta, and Queen Isabel before that. A ring and vow on the eighteenth birthday, followed by six months of engagement. Then the marriage and all that comes with it.

Titus smiles, charm reeling us in. "I am pleased to announce that Silas has proposed to our kingdom's elemental princess and Khali has graciously accepted."

The crowd claps along and a few even go so far as to cheer. My mother winks at me like I'm the luckiest girl in the world. My breath is lodge in my throat, my vision narrowing. Silas stands and saunters around the table to my side, wrapping an arm around my shoulder and softly kissing my cheek. He's laying his claim. I don't breathe. I don't speak. I don't move an inch.

"Normally we would expect a longer engagement," Titus says, "but given everything that has happened, my wife and I feel the Gods wish this union to start the day Khali comes of age. The pair will be married on December the fifthteenth, on Khali's eighteenth birthday."

I want to rip away from Silas and demand justice. Instead, I blink back hot tears and smile through the pain. Maybe I will look like the picture of happiness instead of rage. If the members of court suspect my true feelings, they don't dare show it.

Either that or they don't care. And why would they? Arranged marriages happen all the time in Drakenon. I'm no different. And I'll be queen, the second highest position in the kingdom. Nobody will have an ounce of pity for me. But just because the position is ranked so high, doesn't mean anything to me. I see the way Queen Brysta acts and her complete lack of power. She's caged just as I am—just as I'll always be.

A clang reverberates throughout the dining hall. The massive oak doors burst open. Everyone turns toward the noise, guards and warriors unsheathing their swords. A man stumbles into the room, his dark hair ruffled, his eyes wild and afraid.

"Father?" I gasp, breaking free of Silas and rushing toward him. "Are you all right?"

Dirt stains his rumpled clothing, and it's as if he sees right through me, right through all of us. He can't focus on one person or one thing. *Has he been struck mad?*

I reach him, my hands gripping his. They are ice cold. "What's wrong, Father?" He does not hear me.

My mother pushes her way to us, her dress billowing out behind her. "What happened?" Her voice cracks. There's shrillness there, a fear in her voice I've never heard before.

He shakes his head over and over, as if a demon has possessed him. "There was a spell," he finally speaks, his voice garbled and frantic. "There was a spell. She's not safe. She's not safe. She will die!"

"Who's not safe, Father?" I beg him, pulling him closer. My mother is right there with me, urging him to relax. His wayward gaze finally locks on mine. His pupils are blown, black covering the entire iris. But he must see me because his face crumples and he breaks into gasping sobs. I squeeze his hands tighter. I'm so shocked I don't even move. I have no words. I've never seen my father cry. Not once.

"You," he says. "You're not safe!"

Me? That can't be right. "I'm right here," I say, bringing his hands to my face. "See? I'm fine."

"No! No! No!"

"What are you saying?" my mother pleads. "Calm down and explain yourself."

We're both holding him now, and I'm filled with hardened terror. The spectators surround us, the royals at the front of the pack. But nobody knows how to make this behavior stop or what to do with a man who's lost his mind. He has been a respected member of court for years. He is known for his level head and calm demeanor. This isn't like him.

He coughs and blood spurts from his mouth, black as tar. It sprinkles across my face and down my bodice. "Father!" I scream, my voice sounding far away—not my own.

His eyes begin to shift again, the earlier presence of madness before he could speak sweeping over. Finally, they land on me. Fear takes hold between its clawed talons.

"You're going to die!" He grinds out before his eyes roll back and he collapses to the floor.

ELEVEN
HAZEL

NO. THIS CAN'T BE HAPPENING. I'm losing my mind. I must be, because this kind of thing only exists in storybooks and make-believe. *Dragons aren't real.* They're just not! My body is alive with tingling horror, and my injured elbows are screaming out in protest, and my pounding heart is about to escape through my chest… and I can't do this, I can't do this, I can't do this.

I press my palms tight against my eyes and stand on legs of elastic. Little gasping breaths slip from my lips, one following the next and the next. They're supposed to be slow and steady, supposed to calm me down, to shore me up, but my lungs aren't cooperating.

It's okay. I'll open my eyes, and that dragon, or whatever it was, will be gone. It will all be a figment of an overactive and over-caffeinated imagination. That's all. I remove one hand and start with the left eye, slowly opening it.

Bad idea.

The dragon is still there. It's at least twice my height, towering over me and seething hot air out of its gruesome mouth. Its eyes are like a blue ocean rimmed in blood, its body like tar, its scales like that of a venomous snake. It sits on hind legs, outstretched claws as long and thick as scythes. The creature stands, growing even more massive, and I scream.

I take off, running back down the side of the building toward the street, my feet slamming against the pavement. I'm not fast enough. Part of my brain is reminding me it's a spirit which means it's already dead. It can't hurt me. But the other part of me is stuck on the whole "run for your life" option. Because what if it *can* hurt me? I comb through my recent memory as my breath pumps in and out and legs push forward.

Did the dragon physically knock me over at first or did I fall from shock and fear? I don't know. But I don't want to wait around and find out.

I probably look like a raving lunatic running down this street but I don't care. There are a few living people, several more dead ones, all with startled expressions locked on me as I sprint down the sidewalk. My necklace bounces against my neck. It's there, but it doesn't seem to be doing its job well enough.

Harmony. She'll know what to do. She'll be able to help.

A car screeches to a stop just up ahead—a black shiny one that sends my nerves into an all-out frenzy. Dean tears himself from the driver's side and rushes toward me. His black hair flops in front of one eye, giving him a rare frazzled look. His jaw is tense and his mouth is set in a line.

"What did you see?" he demands.

When I move to get past him, he grabs my elbow. I screech in protest but he hangs on.

"Tell me, Hazel," he presses. "What spooked you? What's there?"

I shake my head. No way I'm telling him anything.

"I have to go!" I try to push past him but his grip is iron tight.

He tugs me toward his car and throws open the passenger side. "Get in. We need to talk."

"No. I need to find Harmony. I need—"

"Absolutely not! You can't tell her and risk exposure! I'm still not sure if she can be trusted."

I've been looking past him, toward the Flowering Chakra and my getaway plan. But his final words shake me from that haze and I whip around. What is he talking about? Harmony already knows all about my gift. He's obviously aware of that. Of course, she's trustworthy.

"Seriously, get in." His eyes bore into mine, more intense than I've ever seen them before, and the fire dancing around his pupils has returned. A sharp breath catches in my throat. So it *was* real… It's so small, it's almost unnoticeable. But I do notice and it both chills and burns me. It's wild and unnatural and I should run far, far away.

But I get in the car.

TWENTY MINUTES LATER, AFTER A silent car ride and a chance for my nerves to settle, Dean parks us in the middle of nowhere. There are fat pines and about a million trees alive with the colors of autumn, but that's it. We're alone out here. My nervous energy comes racing back. Katherine is dead and now there's another missing girl to think about. I shouldn't be so careless.

"Are you going to murder me out here or something, because I'm pretty sure a bunch of people saw me get into this car so it's not like you'll get way with it," I ramble, my words may sound like a joke, but I'm only half-kidding. I don't really *know* Dean.

"Come on," Dean orders before stepping out of the vehicle and slamming his door.

I slip my phone from my pocket and check it, planning to send a message to Cora and Macy with my whereabouts, in case Dean really is a crazy murderer. It's a no-go. I don't have any service. Fantastic. But hey, at least the location services are on so if the cops need to search for me they'll have a place to start.

I huff out a breath, trying to keep calm, and open my door.

"What did you see?" Dean asks again. His voice crawls through the clearing, and I glance back to the empty stretch of one-lane highway.

When I don't immediately answer, he stomps around the side of the car to stand toe-to-toe with me. He's so close I can smell the campfire and spicy aroma that is distinctly his and distinctly intoxicating. His eyes bore into mine, coal black and no longer dancing with flames. My prickly nerves relax a fraction, and I remind myself that no, he didn't bring me out here to murder me—he brought me out here because he wants to know what I saw.

And I want to know what he's hiding.

"Why should I tell you?" I ask, genuinely curious. Because what good does it do me to tell him what I saw? "Are you going to help me or something?"

And do I even need help? *Hazel, you saw a dragon. You clearly need help.*

He rocks back on his heels instead of answering my question. "You're a medium, right? So you see the spirit realm?"

I nod once. I thought we'd already established this. I thought he knew that about me all along. This situation is getting weirder by the second.

"Who's your father?" he asks sharply.

The question is so unexpected, it's like a slap to the face. Not that I care about the "sperm donor" but because I don't like to think about the missing part of my life too much. I look away into the distant trees and frown. "I don't see how that has anything to do with you."

"It has everything to do with me," he barks out.

I whip around on him, both intrigued and annoyed. "Why? Why is the identity of my father any of your business? What could it possibly have to do with you?"

More importantly, what isn't he telling me?

His jaw is tight but once again, he doesn't answer my question or react to my anger with anything other than his own calculated hatred. I can see it in his eyes, see how much he despises me. And now it might have something to do with the "sperm donor"? Dean's not the only one who can ask questions here. He's left me confused and it's a tangled feeling I need to unravel.

I fold my arms over my chest, widening my stance. The earthy smell of the autumn forest brushes past us on the wind, whipping my hair behind me. "I don't know who my father is, okay? He was a one-night stand and my mom never got his name." I narrow my eyes on Dean. "Why do you want to know about him?"

His gaze is hooded and he thinks for a minute. "Who's your mother?"

I scoff. "You're going to dodge my questions but keep asking more of your own? No, I don't think so."

Apparently, he doesn't care what I have to say. "Where does she live?" he continues, his expression intense. "What does she do for a living? Is she… normal?"

I roll my eyes. This is getting ridiculous. "She's an ER nurse in Ohio and she's a wonderful person and perfectly normal except for her terrible taste in men. Okay? The end." I lean against the car before shifting closer to him. "The way I see it, if you want answers from me, I should be able to get answers from you."

He raises an eyebrow. "When you see the spirit realm, what does it look like?"

Okay, maybe not.

I exhale and rub the goosebumps on my arms. It's colder now than it was earlier, and it was chilly before. More shivers run over my skin and I rub at my arms even harder. I really don't want to answer, to play victim to his interrogation or whatever this is but I find myself spilling the truth anyway, "I see spirits. Usually the people who have recently died. They don't talk but they show me images from their lives. It usually doesn't make a lot of sense."

"That's it? Just people?"

I pause. That was it. Until today.

"Did you see something that wasn't human today?" he presses, guessing—or maybe it's not a guess. Maybe he knows. Maybe it's part of *his* secret. Nervous energy spreads through me at the thought.

Somehow he's even closer now, and he slowly reaches out and grips me above my wrists. He runs his hands delicately up my arms, warming me up. I hold my breath, the nerves now firing like crazy. His hands are so hot and wonderfully smooth and they remind me of warm summer days and of a time before things got complicated.

I nod once.

"Was it an animal?" He's inches from me now. So close that I can see flecks of gold in his eyes, can smell the spearmint on his breath.

Should I tell him? I don't want to tell him and I do want to tell him at the same time. Before I can catch myself, I'm speaking, "I guess you could say that," I whisper.

His eyebrows furrow together. "Did it show you anything? Any images?" I notice that he doesn't acknowledge *what* it was, only speaks as if he already knows. But surely, if I said, Dragon, he'd laugh at me.

"Hazel." He shifts closer. "Did it show you images?"

I blink and nod.

"It's okay to tell me."

"It was black... the creature," I say, my voice low. "It showed me a castle and several people but it focused on one girl in particular. I think she might be in trouble. I think it wanted me to help her."

"What did she look like?"

"She had two colored eyes. One blue. One brown."

He cusses and rears back, ripping the moment in two. "Khali."

I'm stunned. "Who's Khali?"

He shakes his head. "I have to go. Do you have a driver's license?"

I look around, confused. What just happened? "Yes… go where?"

He reaches into his pocket and pulls out his keys. Frantic, he removes the black key fob and presses it firmly into my palm. "Drive yourself back to the shop," he demands, his words quick and decisive. "I'll pick up the key from Harmony later."

I gape at him. "What? Where could you possibly go all the way out here?"

But he doesn't answer me, doesn't even seem to care that he brought me out here in the first place. He takes off running into the forest of all places. There's nothing out here but trees. Where could he possibly be going? Any traces of the man are gone within seconds and I'm still standing here, still bracing myself against the cold and the sudden loss of his heat.

TWELVE

KHALI

THE COURT PHYSICIAN LEANS OVER my father one last time; the wrinkles around his eyes deepen in examination. He stands to offer his conclusion. "Lord Paul Elliot has been hexed."

Mother gasps, and dread spreads through me like boiling liquid. I was worried it might be something like this. I don't know too much about magic, but I know if he's been hexed, it probably was done by a dangerous hand. He's lucky to be alive, to have made it back to us, but I don't know how much time he has left. Tears spring to my eyes and I grasp his feverish hand.

I can't lose you too, Dad. I plead to his sleeping body and to the Gods, wherever they may be. *Please, don't die.*

"Are you certain?" King Titus stands back from us, keeping his distance. A crease forms between his bushy eyebrows, but something else flickers in his gaze too: something suspiciously like acceptance. He must have been worrying about the same thing. Did he know this was going to happen?

"There is no other explanation for the way his symptoms are presenting," the physician says. "This isn't an illness. This is dark magic."

I place my hand on my father's sleeping back, rubbing small circles as I hold back tears. He's warm again. Sweat beads his ashen skin and wets his white linen shirt. He rolls over, mumbling incoherently, and the black stubble on his chin brushes against my hand. Since his arrival in the banquet hall and subsequent collapse, he hasn't woken. Not once. It's been four days, and Mother and I have stayed by his side, alternating shifts when one of us grows too tired. His temperature has spiked and plummeted a dozen times. He is going to waste away in front of our eyes.

"Who would hex him?" My mind races through the possibilities but I don't know where to start. Witchcraft is a forbidden art in Drakenon and punishable by death. As far as I know, the craft has been eradicated from our kingdom. We have dragon shifters and elemental magic but nothing like witchcraft. That is an entirely different beast that was slain long ago when the Brightcasters took the throne, saving us all from those who'd want us dead.

Oftentimes, our dragon ancestors were slain as ritual sacrifices for magical purposes. The idea of it sends a terrified shiver down my spine. The Brightcasters may have their own levels of evil, but at least they're nothing like the Occultists, who worship demons.

"Could he have left the Drakenon border?" the physician asks, his eyes bouncing from each of us in the room.

"He travels around the kingdom," Mom says defensively. She's even more of a mess than I am. "He is exposed to all sorts of people, but he isn't foolish enough to leave the borders."

The physician nods sympathetically but I catch a twinge of guilt from King Titus. His eyes are shifty, like he can't look at any one of us for long. It's his biggest tell. I've known these people for as long as I can remember and I know when they're hiding something. And he's *definitely* hiding something important.

"Did you send him beyond the borders?" The accusation leaves my lips before I can think it through.

"Khali!" Mother chastises, but her eyes tell a different story. She wants answers as much as I do.

"Of course not," King Titus says automatically.

I don't believe him but I hold my tongue.

Nobody leaves the borders unless in exile or to spy. We obviously aren't privy to who the King's spies are, lest they be compromised. Drakenon sits on the eastern edge of a larger, very contentious continent called Eridas. The other kingdoms consist of witches, fae, elves, mages and all manner of wiley beasts. They constantly vie for power over each other; bloodshed and broken treaties and entire family lines murdered are the norm. But not the dragon clans. Our borders have been warded by elemental magic for three centuries and only those with dragon lineage can enter. We keep to ourselves, protected from outside invaders. It's inside the border that we have to worry about threats, but the clans have been at peace for one hundred years under the Brightcaster's reign.

So why would my father leave the kingdom?

Several things click into place at once. "Is my father a spy?" I turn back to the King, my heart hammering. When he doesn't immediately reply, I have my answer. "He is, isn't he? He hasn't just been traveling around the kingdom for you, he's been crossing the border into enemy territory at your request."

"No," Mother says. "Paul wouldn't take that risk. He promised me."

"Tell us," I beg the King in a raspy whisper. Tears break free and run down my cheeks, two hot trails of pain and sadness. "Please, you know what I've done for your family, what I am doing for you now. I deserve the truth."

Titus stills, his shoulders softening, and turns to the physician. "Would you please leave us for a few minutes?"

The man, pale as a ghost, takes no time scurrying out of the room. It's just the four of us now. If I wanted, I could shift into my dragon form and assassinate the king where he stands. It's the only thought I've had in days that gives me a moment of relief.

"It's complicated." The King lets out a slow breath, finally stepping further into the room and approaching my father. "But yes, Paul has been crossing the border for me."

Anger burns deep, ripping its way out to the surface. "How could you ask him to do that?" I seethe. "You know the risks! My father considers you one of his closest friends."

He ignores me, and I'm over it. I'm over the lies, over the choices others have made that have hurt me. The Brightcaster clan may be beloved and powerful, but they have cost me too much.

"Is he going to make it?" Mother asks, tears shining in her eyes. For as much as she and I oppose one another, we've always had the same soft spot for Father. He's the only thing that keeps us together.

"We've seen this a few times before with our spies," Titus says. "I'm afraid he won't die but he won't wake, either. He'll be stuck in this torment."

The room is silent as we all stare at my father.

"For how long?" Mother asks.

"Until we end his misery."

Mom and I both shoot him deadly glares, outrage burning us up. As if that is an appropriate answer. How dare he even consider it?

"No," she snaps.

My voice is shrill, "How do we cure him?" My elements are rising underneath my skin, especially the fire. I will not let *anyone* hurt my father. I will kill them first!

Once again, his silence tells me all I need to know and the anger only doubles. Titus doesn't have a way to help my father. Would it be more cruel to leave him like this? Should we end his suffering? Those are the unspoken words that die on my lips because I do not have the strength to consider it.

"You have to do something," I challenge. "You have to at least try to help him."

"Of course I will do everything I can to help your father," the King states matter-of-factly. "But for now I must take my leave. I assure you both"—he levels his gaze on my mother and I—"we will keep searching for a way to break this hex."

Again, I don't believe a word that falls from his mouth.

"Wait," I call out as his hand rests on the doorknob. He didn't bring any guards with him today, stupid man. He should know better than to underestimate me. Again, I'm tempted by the idea of assassination. "You never told us why you were sending him over the border. Don't we deserve to know what was so important to risk his life?"

He turns back and clenches his jaw, his kingly stature returning to his broad shoulders. "It's classified," he snaps, leaving us with more questions than answers.

I hate him.

THERE'S A STORM OF EMOTIONS raging inside, destroying my heart, but hopelessness is perhaps the worst of them. All I want is for things to return to what they once were. For Owen to be alive and for us to be on our way to starting a life together. For my mother to carry on with her courtly intrigues instead of hovering over my father like a ghost. And for my father to be safe, whole, and healthy once more. But magic doesn't work like that, at least not mine. I have no means to change my past, and my future has spun so far out of my control, I can scarcely recognize it.

It's all hopeless.

I walk down the corridor alone, a rarity for me, but I couldn't stand to be in that room for a second longer. The night fell hours ago, and the castle has since grown quiet. I need to change and bathe, to gather my thoughts, sleep for a while, and then I'll return to my parents, and Mother and I can brainstorm ideas for Father's healing.

I'm hardly ever alone. The sensation is a little nerve-wracking, but also freeing. I usually have Lady Faros to attend me or one of my semi-friends from court to chirp in my ear as I go from one duty to the next. I call them semi-friends because they don't really care about me, they only care about what I can do for them. They're nowhere to be found these days.

Since Owen's death and Father's subsequent illness, I haven't been available for socializing, and they haven't been available for consoling. And I saw no need for Faros to stand around aimlessly while Mother and I tend to Father during this time, so I dismissed her until further notice. She didn't want to leave me. I didn't really want her to leave me either. But I did it anyway. Nothing is how it was. King Titus never sent any of his guards to watch me, foolish as he is; he must have decided I wasn't a threat or in any danger. Why would I be in danger when the murderers around here all need me alive?

I'm almost to my chambers when a faint giggle drifts through the corridor. That's a sound that isn't so strange around this massive castle, considering so many live here. I ignore it, as I always do. What do I care for affairs and romantic secrets? It's always been beneath me.

A man's voice whispers darkly and cackles. I stop. Apprehension crawls over my skin. I know that voice. I should leave. Whatever this is—and I'm sure I already know—is none of my business, but I tiptoe toward the hushed voices anyway. Around this corner lies a darkened alcove, one of the many that rarely get decent light during the day, and at night, are used for their shadows. I'm certain that's where this couple is, and if it were anyone else, I would ignore them and move on.

But that damned voice…

The woman giggles again and then she lets out a deep sigh. The man mumbles and groans hungrily. I hold my breath, not quite believing I'm going to follow their promiscuous noises. But it's not like anyone else is forbidden from the act of kissing before marriage as I am. I peer around the alcove, straining against the wall of darkness, wondering if perhaps I should announce myself. My eyes adjust, and I see them for myself.

Against the far end of the alcove, two figures press together. The man towers over his partner as his hands greedily rove up and down her body. So not *just* kissing. I gasp, stepping back as the pair breaks apart. It's exactly who I thought. Silas. Silas and… not a woman… but a girl by the innocent looks of her.

The girl smirks at me, her wide eyes twinkling as she runs her hand possessively along his arm. I try to place her. Her clothing is disheveled, the bodice of her mauve dress far too loose and her pink rouge smeared across her cheek. She doesn't seem to care, but rather wears her appearance as a badge.

"Come to watch or did you want to join in?" Silas grins, turning toward me.

"Do you have no shame?" I snap, disgusted.

He shrugs and the girl laughs. I recognize her as a Duke's daughter but I can't remember which nor can I recall her name. She's at least two years younger than my seventeen, maybe three, and certainly not of age to be behaving this way with a man of nineteen. This kind of behavior may be normal around here, but not for a girl so young.

"Oh, Khali," Silas says. "If you could see your face right now. You really thought I was saving myself for you, didn't you?"

I bite my tongue, holding back the hate I'm dying to speak. Of course I knew there was a double standard when it came to me and the princes, but it's never been thrown in my face before tonight. I've heard whispers, seen flirtations now and then, but I assumed it was all harmless. This is so callous, I don't even know what to think.

He sighs, tucking the girl closer to him but making no attempt to leave. "My father is an anomaly, did you know that? He's chosen to stay monogamous with my mother, the darling man. But most kings before him kept courtesans and I intend to do the same. Gods know you're not going to come to my bed without force." He runs his tongue along his lips. "We'll both learn to appreciate my playthings to keep me company."

The girl smacks him but then runs her hand through his hair and roughly pulls herself closer to him. He laughs and returns to kissing her hungrily. "Let's go to my room," he says, loud enough for me to hear. "I need to get you back into my bed before I take you right here."

She giggles. "Would here be so bad? We might enjoy it."

"If you insist," he replies excitedly, lifting her skirt like he's done it countless times.

Bile rises in my stomach.

My entire body is alive with shock and disgust, and I stumble away, hurrying back to my chambers. I slam the door behind me and lean against it for strength, struggling to catch my breath. I can't. I run to the bathing chamber to empty what little contents I have in my stomach. It takes several minutes to calm the ache before I can return to my bed and rest.

Silas is my *fiancé* and yet he's carrying on like it means nothing. And that foolish girl is far too young to have already turned herself into his mistress. He's taking advantage of her and she's a willing participant. How long has he been carrying on like this? Do her parents know? Are they encouraging it?

I'm a fool to have thought I knew anything about the Brightcaster family and their moral character. A guilty thought comes to my mind, a thought that says I'm just like that girl. I'm also a willing participant in all of this, even if I tell myself I'm not happy about it. I'm here, aren't I? I'm engaged to that vile creature, am I not?

My mind runs and runs into the early morning hours, sleep too far away to grasp.

Is Silas carrying on with other women besides this one? I don't know the answer but I do know that Silas choosing to be in that alcove by my chambers wasn't an accident. He wanted me to catch them. He wanted me to see that while I may become his queen, he will still carry on however he wishes. That *he* is the one with the power and always will be.

I'm nothing but a prize to be won, unwrapped, used, and then cast aside.

My chest heaves up and down, and I clench my fists so tightly that I draw blood. I'm not hurt—I'm livid. And no matter how much power Silas thinks he has over me, I won't stand by and let him continue to flaunt his power. One way or another, I'm going to end Silas Brightcaster. But first, I have to save myself.

THIRTEEN
HAZEL

THREE DAYS AFTER THE INCIDENT with Dean, Katherine Donahue's body is pulled from a nearby lake.

The police called a press conference and announced their suspicions comfirmed of foul play, opening it up as a murder investigation. That was yesterday and now her death is all anyone can talk about. That, and the fact that two other college girls have gone missing over the last two years: Tessa Smith and Charlene Connelly. Both brand new college freshmen when they disappeared, just like Katherine. But their bodies were never found. It's not lost on anybody that there's a connection. The pattern is unmistakable.

And now that there's a high school senior missing as well, everyone is on edge.

"I didn't know any of this when I picked Hayden College," Macy complains as the three of us walk to our Anthropology class Wednesday morning. "Had I known, I would've gone somewhere else. I mean, I was waitlisted at Vanderbilt. I should have pursued that more."

"I didn't know either," I complain, looking around the beautifully landscaped campus. It's everything pictured from the brochures, with its sprawling manicured lawns and red-bricked buildings. "It's not like these missing girls showed up in a Google search for Hayden College." Once again I'm struck by the fact that I not only got into this place, but I received a full scholarship. It was the only scholarship I got and I applied to a lot of schools that weren't as highly ranked as this one.

What if it wasn't an accident? What if someone wanted me here for a specific reason that has nothing to do with academics? An icy shiver runs down my spine. *No way. Don't be ridiculous.*

"Well, the world is going to know all about this creepy school now!" Macy says, smoothing out her glossy strawberry hair. As if it could get any smoother, it's always perfect.

Cora rolls her eyes bitterly. "Girls our age go missing all the time. Especially women of color and especially women on tribal lands. The amount who just up and disappear is disgusting. And do most of these women get any sort of news coverage or fanfare?"

I shake my head, hating the answer as I say it, "They don't."

"That's right," Cora continues. "They don't. But this is different. This is a possible serial killer targeting beautiful *caucasian* girls. It's bound to get national attention if it hasn't already."

We continue discussing the unfairness of news coverage giving preferential treatment, all the while goosebumps spread over my body. This is so creepy. No, it's more than that. This whole situation is downright terrifying. But at least I haven't seen any more of these girls' ghosts. Just Katherine. But since meeting Harmony, even Katherine has disappeared. I make a mental note to thank Harmony again. The woman may be an oddball but she certainly knows her stuff. I don't feel haunted anymore. I still see ghosts now and again, but thanks to the little black beads of obsidian around my neck, they can't send me images unless I allow it.

Well, except if they're spirits of the dragon variety.

Then, apparently, they can send me all sorts of images without my permission. I shiver to think of that monstrous creature lurking around here, and the striking girl with the mismatched eyes also returns to my memory, followed by the castle and the way they were all dressed like it was medieval times. The things I saw that didn't make any sense… and the frantic, fearful energy surrounding it all. Dean seemed to understand it, even if I didn't. It's all been running through my mind on a loop for days.

I still haven't seen Dean since he ran off like a crazy person. I was tempted to keep the car and force him to come find me so he could explain his behavior, but I chickened out and returned his car to the parking lot near The Flowering

Chakra like he'd ordered. I gave Harmony his keys and that was that. His car got picked up between my shifts and come Monday morning, he didn't show up to class.

Just as we're about to go inside our building, someone taps me on the shoulder. I turn to find Landon and dare I say it? I become giddy with excitement.

"Hey there," Landon says, smiling his big goofy smile at me. Perhaps he's excited to see me too. "I haven't seen you in The Roasted Bean in a while. Are you getting your caffeine fix somewhere else?"

I laugh and give him a hug. He's warm and smells of coffee and cologne. "Hey, yourself. I haven't seen you in The Flowering Chakra in a while. Getting your crystal fix somewhere else?" I tease.

"You know it!"

Cora and Macy exchange a knowing look and raise their eyebrows at me.

"No, truthfully, I've been trying to lay off caffeine for a while. I haven't been sleeping well, what with everything going on."

He nods. "Ya, it's pretty crazy."

The silence between us grows awkward as we think about the missing girls.

"Well, I better let you go," he says, running a hand through his blonde hair. It's not in its usual manbun and he kinda reminds me of a guy on the cover of a romance novel. "Just wanted to say hello. I'll see you in lab later, ya?"

"Absolutely." I grin as he leaves and Cora and Macy pull me into our building, both gushing about how cute he is and asking when I'm going to make a move on him. I don't know what to say to that, I've never made a move on anyone, but I can feel the smile pressing against my cheeks and the blood warming my face.

If he doesn't make a move, then I guess I'll have to learn how.

We stroll into the lecture hall with its theater style seating and my eyes dart to the last row where Dean's usually camped out. I ignore the quick pang of disappointment when I don't find him. Why do I care? I'm being ridiculous. I shake off the weirdness of my fascination with Dean and I turn toward the front of the room where I like to sit.

There he is.

He's lounging in one of the chairs like he owns the place. He raises a dark eyebrow at me before looking away, shifting his weight toward the pretty girl sitting next to him. She says something, and he laughs that wicked laugh and he's flirting and I hate it.

Wait, what? Ugh! Stop it, Hazel!

But he's in the front row. He's right next to the seat I've been in all semester and *that* can't be a coincidence. He must want to talk to me again.

Being the grown up I am, I slide into the empty chair next to him, Cora and Macy filling in the rest of the row. This is my spot after all. I don't need to avoid Dean. My girls both shoot me odd looks but all I do is shrug at them. I mean, let's be honest, it's not like I have a clue what I'm doing sitting next to Dean Ashton either. They *know* I hate the man. I'm just not sure if I know it anymore.

He finishes up with "Pretty Girl" and turns towards me. The way he looks at me, it's like I'm the only one in the lecture hall. Like he doesn't hear or see the other chatting students. It's unnerving. I'm caught in his black eyes and his intensity and his campfire woodsy scent, realizing with clarity what it is he smells like.

When I was growing up, I'd spend one glorious week at Y-Camp each summer. I loved every minute of it, from the camp songs, to the horse rides, the canoes, the hikes, the swimming, the temporary friends and heart-stopping crushes. All of it. And without fail, every single summer, there would be a night that the campfire would get rained out. We'd be sitting around it, doing our skits, or singing songs, maybe building the perfect s'more, when the thunder would roll in and the rain would spill from above. Nature would come together, blanketing everything in this wondrous scent of burning wood and thick raindrops and fresh air and perfect, perfect summer night. And everything inside of me would buzz from being alive.

That's exactly what Dean Ashton smells like… and oh my Lord, I've totally got a crush on him. *Shoot! How did that happen?*

A wistful feeling comes over me. I miss that time at camp more than I realized. Those are some of my only memories of being myself and having fun with other kids who didn't make fun of me. It was easy to fit in at camp because everyone was a little bit different. Maybe that's what college is like, too? And maybe that's why I like it here so much.

"Can we talk after class?" Dean asks, his focus still steady and solely on me. One ebony lock of hair curls around his cheek and his eyes narrow into a hooded gaze. "Alone."

Oh, boy...

I bite my lip, considering if "talking alone" with him is a good idea. But who am I kidding? Of course I'm going to say yes. Hot or not, I have a lot of questions for the man. I need to know if what I saw was real. I need to know what he has to do with it. I need to know who that girl with the heterochromic eyes is and why she matters to him. And I also need to put this ridiculous crush aside because he is *so not right for me.*

"Please?" His voice drops an octave, and his thick black lashes flutter closed for the briefest of seconds and I can't seem to pull my gaze away from him and sweet baby Jesus, *I'm in trouble...*

"Sure." I swallow hard. He looks at me for a long second, as if sensing the effect he's having on me, then turns away to talk to "Pretty Girl" again. My heart drops into my butt. Gosh, dang it, why am I so bad at this?!

Doctor Peters clears his throat, starting the lecture and ending the embarrassing moment. Bless him. I do my best to take notes and stay attentive over the next ninety minutes but Dean is too close. I can't stop thinking about this newfound discovery of my crush, or feeling the heat of his body against my side.

I thought I hated him. I really did. Actually, I'm pretty sure I still do.

But I'm obviously *attracted* and I can't help but want to spend time alone with him, to unravel whatever it is between us. Because despite the sheer anger he seems to bring out in me, he also draws me in with the mystery, intensity, and challenge.

How messed up is that? Maybe I should get my head checked.

I DON'T KNOW WHAT I expected but this wasn't it. Naive little ol' me figured we'd go chat in the hallway or at least *somewhere* on campus, probably to yell at each other—like usual. But instead of any of that, Dean is leading me across the street to the posh neighborhood adjacent to this part of campus. He doesn't utter a word as fallen leaves crunch beneath our shoes and the earlier chill is thawed beneath the mid-morning sun.

My limbs grow hot under my cherry-red peacoat, especially with the long sleeved t-shirt I've got on underneath. Dean could be one of those aerobics speed-walking ladies at this pace. He's three steps ahead and being a socially awkward weirdo.

"Could you slow down?" I ask in a huff.

He doesn't slow down. And this, this kind of thing right here, is indicative of why I should abandon any crush on Dean Ashton. His black suede boots continue forward. I peer down at my white Converse, wondering if the little blue constellations I drew on them are childish.

We turn onto a tree-lined street with houses that are at least a century old, all beautifully refurbished with immaculate curb appeal. There are plenty of rental houses around campus where many of the upperclassmen live, but this area is most definitely not home to college-aged renters. Of course it would be home to Dean.

"I'm right here," he mutters, turning up the drive of a darling red brick cottage.

Ivy sweeps across one side where it meets with the sloping roof. The house fits right in with its neighbors. It even has a turret. A turret! Once again, Dean has surprised me. This time, I know better than to laugh and piss him off. The guy buys sage and is a frequent visitor to The Flowering Chakra, after all. It's a sensitive subject.

He leads me to the massive four-car garage and quickly keys in a code before I can catch sight of a number sequence. Not that I was snooping. Okay, I totally was. The garage door opens, revealing his fancy black car in one spot next to a shiny bullet bike. The rest of the garage is a home gym, complete with giant tires and those huge ropes guys like to throw around.

I just learned three things about Dean. Number one, he likes to workout alone. In fact, I rarely see him with anyone, so he must like to do most things alone. Number two, he apparently has a deathwish, because he has a bullet bike and those things are terrifying. And three, he's much wealthier than I'd originally guessed.

"This is your house?" I ask the stupid question, but seriously, what kind of college kid lives like this? I mean, isn't living off ramen noodles and five dollar pizzas some kind of right-of-passage? Maybe he lives with his parents. He must.

He doesn't bother to answer as we walk into his house. I have to consciously keep my jaw from dropping once we get inside. If the outside belongs in *Town & Country Magazine*, the inside belongs in *Modern Home Magazine*. It's all clean lines and chrome, concrete and wood finishes, stark white against caramel brown and slate black. It's gorgeous in a way that makes me feel separated from it, like I don't belong. I'm too cozy and relaxed for a place like this.

"So, your parents are loaded, huh?" My mouth gets away with me *again* and heat spreads across my cheeks. "I'm sorry, that was a rude thing to say."

He shoots me an unreadable glance, still not saying a word, and goes to the kitchen, pouring us both tall glasses of ice water. I follow his lead and take off my backpack and coat, setting them on the nearest chair.

"I live alone," he finally says. "I bought it when I moved here for school."

He bought it? Again, I'm left with more questions than answers when it comes to Dean.

He downs his glass of water in one go and then fills it up again, drinking more. And then he does it again. The guy must be the poster-boy for water or something, either that or the gallon challenge. Mom would love that. She's always harping on at me to drink more water and ditch the soda, as if that will ever happen. Dr. Pepper for life! I miss her. We talk on the phone almost daily but only for a few minutes each time. There's not much to say now that our lives are in two separate states.

"So what did you want to talk to me about?" I ask. I'm supposed to meet Cora and Macy for lunch in an hour and I have an English Literature class this afternoon that I still haven't finished the reading for, but I don't say any of those things. I just wait. Because I'm pretty sure I know exactly what he wants to talk about and it's exactly what I want to talk about.

The spirit dragon!

He puts both of our empty glasses in the sink and comes to stand across the kitchen island from me. His fingertips press down against the sleek countertop and he gazes at me with a questioning glint. I'm not sure what happened to the air in here but my lungs aren't cooperating fully. "About Friday... I wanted to apologize for my appalling behavior and running off as I did. I shouldn't have left you so vulnerable."

Ummm, what just happened? I never thought I'd see the day. "Why do you suddenly care? I thought you hated me." I tilt my head at him, looking for a crack in his exterior. I don't find one.

His jaw tenses as he considers. "I don't hate you, Hazel. I hate that you're *here*. You're not supposed to be here if I'm here but I don't want to leave, either."

Again, what just happened? He doesn't want to leave either? "We've been through this before, Dean. This whole, 'you're not making sense' and this thing is getting old."

He holds up a hand. "But I've come to realize that you aren't lying and you truly don't know what you are."

I know what I am. He knows what I am. I narrow my eyes, trying to figure this out. "Yeah, about that, what on God's green earth are you even talking about?"

He continues as if I didn't interrupt with a really important question, "I've also accepted that you're not going to drop out of school on my account. And I'm not going to leave because you're here. Especially not when you have certain talents that could be useful to me. So I want to call a truce."

I can't help it. I laugh. "I have certain talents, do I? You're talking about the whole psychic medium thing, am I correct? So, suddenly, I'm of interest to you and you're going to be nice to me when you were a total asshat to me before? I don't think so."

He lets out a slow breath and walks around the counter, moving toward me with the same kind of intensity as always, like a predator hungry for his next meal. This time, I won't let him scare me. And he should, I know that. I feel it deep in my bones. He's the predator. I'm the prey. But maybe I like it. And maybe he does, too. His eyes flicker over my body, over my folded arms and the jut of my hips, before lingering on my lips and then finally resting at my eye level. A shudder runs through me. It's annoying, what one look can unravel inside.

"You've always been of interest to me," he says. "Since the first moment I saw you and you didn't see me. Do you know it took you three days to notice me? That doesn't happen often."

"Wow, Dean. How fascinating," I deadpan. "Are you always this arrogant?"

His smile is wicked. "Comes with the territory."

It sure does.

"So I was wondering if you would help me?" He steps closer. "I need to know more about what you saw the other night. Anything at all."

I consider it. I actually do. He runs a fingertip along the edge of the counter, coming to a stop when it hits my elbow, but he doesn't move his hand. "And if possible," he continues, "I'd like you to do a reading for me. Tell me what spirits you see surrounding me. Try to communicate with them. I'd be happy to pay for your services."

"A reading here or at the shop?" My breath stalls and my eyes search his, looking for the catch. Because there has to be a catch.

"Here. Not to cut Harmony out or anything, but now that I know what you are capable of, we have to be incredibly discreet."

"You don't trust Harmony?"

He tilts his head. "I don't trust anyone."

I look around the kitchen some more, taking in how barren it is. It's perfectly clean, perfectly normal looking, but something tells me he doesn't have people here often, if ever. So why me? He must trust me to some degree to let me into his home, and yet he's a closed book.

Part of me wants to give in, to say yes. But the other part can't ignore the red flags. This guy has been a jerk from day one. He threatened me the first day I met him and has constantly argued with me ever since. And then, after a terrifying ordeal, he convinced me to get in his car, took me out to the middle of nowhere, and left me.

Besides, women have gone missing and a girl was found dead. There is a serial killer still on the loose and here I am, the smart one who decided it was a good idea to come into this house alone with him, without telling anyone where I was even going. What if Dean is the murderer? I don't want it to be him and I don't *feel* like it is, but who really knows. Fact is, I *don't* know.

There are too many mysteries when it comes to this man.

"I don't feel good about it," I say at last. I press my fingers against the white countertop. It's ice cold to the touch and just as smooth. "It's not about the money. I mean, good for you and all, congrats on being rich or whatever, but I don't want your money." I'm rambling but I can't seem to stop. "Truth is, you scare me and this whole situation scares me."

"And why is that?" he whispers, coming to stand mere inches from me.

I give in. "I know what I saw. I saw you with fire in your eyes, twice. I felt the intense heat when you got angry that night after the party and it wasn't the alcohol and it wasn't normal. And what I saw on Friday, the spirit that came to me. I can't even say it out loud, it's too crazy."

"Not crazy," he mutters, licking his lips.

For a second, I can't breathe. "If it's not crazy, then *you* say it."

He says nothing.

Silence stretches between us until I speak up again, "Dean, if you want my help, you'd better be willing to shed some light on all of this and answer my questions."

"I can't do that." He steps back, adding to the secrets already between us.

"Are you kidding me?" I scoff, walking around the kitchen island. I need to put some distance between us so I can think clearly. "You want me to help you but you won't do anything for me in return?"

"I said I would pay you."

I fold my arms over my chest. "And I said I don't want your money."

He glares, his jaw clicking. "But I thought you needed money. Why else would you be working at The Flowering Chakra? You're a scholarship kid. You don't have a dad in your life. You must need financial help."

Outrage grips me, tearing me up from inside out. There is something about his pitying look that makes me want to burn this pretentious house with all it's glossy, unloved surfaces, to the ground. "Who even says something like that?"

I grab my stuff off the chair and push past him, heading for the front door.

"Wait," he follows. "That came out wrong. I'm sorry."

"No, you're not. Just leave me alone." I make it to the front door and open it, all in two seconds flat, storming outside. A pattering of booted footsteps follows behind. Dean actually has the audacity to follow me? I shake my head. Unbelievable!

"You don't understand. I need you to help me. You have to."

"No," I shoot back, keeping my eyes straight ahead. "I don't!"

"You can't say no to me," he growls, reaching out and grabbing my arm. Burning heat presses against my long-sleeved shirt and I yelp, jumping back. My eyes don't want to believe what I'm seeing but there's no denying it. There's a hole in my shirt sleeve, singed around the corners. The pungent smell of burned fabric wafts through the air between us.

I whip around. This time it's my turn to make demands.

"Explain this!" I point to the black mark against the white cotton. He looks, but he doesn't say anything. "Explain why your eyes have fire in them right now," I continue. "Explain why your body heat raises when you're angry, or why you just burned a hole through my shirt. Explain why I saw the spirit of a dragon when I was with you on Friday and why you act like I have something to do with all of this. Tell me everything, Dean, or don't ask for my help."

He shakes his head, pained. "I can't."

"It's always been just me and my mom," I say, my voice cracking. "For me, letting other people in is super hard. And I get that, I get that you don't want to let me in."

His eyes search mine, but he doesn't say anything.

"I get it, because I'm the exact same way." I pull my arms into my jacket, covering the singed material. "I can't let you in on my secrets without you returning the favor. I'm sorry, but this is how this works for me."

He grimaces. "It's too risky for me to answer your questions."

Does he think he's the only one who has risks involved here? The disappointment is heavy, but I know what I have to do. I step back onto the sidewalk, my voice calm and my resolve strong. Maybe I'll regret this, but right now, I'm fresh out of options.

"I'm sorry, but I can't help you."

Fourteen

KHALI

I HOLD MY FATHER'S LIMP hand in mine. He's no longer feverish. He's cold. I don't know which is worse. Mother lays next to him, pressed against this back. She's asleep and her face is swollen with grief. Her dark hair is a tangle around her head. I've never seen her look so unkempt. It's unnerving. She won't say it, but I can tell she's starting to give up hope. How much longer can we go on like this? Someone has to do something.

And yet, nobody seems to be doing much of anything.

After my run in with Silas the other night, I've noticed more and more guards following me around. He must be keeping a closer eye on me. That, or King Titus decided to consider my father's words before as a real threat.

It all races back to me, the horror of it, the confusion, the terrible moment my father said I was going to die before succumbing to the hex. At first I didn't want to think on those words, but now that several days have passed, I can think of little else. If my father is right, and I'm in trouble, I need to know why. I want to know what I can do to stop it. But the Brightcaster cage is tightening around me each day, and if I don't get out soon, I fear I'll never find the answer.

"Alivia," I say. She doesn't stir. I say it again, just to double check that my mother is truly sleeping. There's no response, not even a flicker. Satisfied, I pull the pack I stashed out from underneath the bed along with the thick velvet cape, slipping them on. I go to the infirmary window and crawl out onto the ledge. If I fall, I'll shift and fly, so I know not to be afraid. But logic does little to calm my racing heart.

I only need to climb one floor down to get where I'm heading. My fingers grip the stone but it's harder to hold onto than I'd anticipated. In some places, I'm holding on with the tips of my fingers and the edge of my boots, nothing else. I keep my breath steady and force myself to move, climbing down inch by inch until I find the glass window pane.

I breathe out a sigh of relief. It's still unlocked, just as I'd left it.

I slowly push it open with my foot and stand on the window's edge, then slip silently inside. This part of the library is as empty at night as it usually is during the day. Tucked back in the corner with nothing but musty old books, people rarely venture back here. I'm quick to find the passageway hidden behind one of the shelves. I'm betting my life that nobody else knows this is here.

Once inside, I'm careful to keep my breath steady as blood thunders through my ears. My shaky fingers trail along the cold wall, urging me down a narrow set of stone steps. My vision strains in the pitch-black darkness. I've memorized every nook and cranny of this castle so this should be easy. At least, that's what I keep telling myself. But it doesn't mean I'm not terrified. I count out ten paces until I reach my target, and thankfully, the torch is right where Owen and I last left it. I draw on my fire elemental and light the flame. It will be enough to get me out of here.

There are mazes of secret passageways between Stonehearth's walls, and Owen and I had spent most of our adolescence searching them out. Some are meant for the servants, some for the royals, but when we found this one, it was so filled with dust from disuse, we considered it ours. Now it's just mine. I swallow the lump in my throat and hurry along the path, careful to keep my footsteps quiet. What if others know about this passageway? It's unlikely, but possible. They could look for me here. They could be looking for me right now.

Around the castle are two thick walls I'll be able to go right under. One wraps around the castle itself and the other protects the village. I could fly over the walls, but that was how I got caught sneaking out a few years ago. It's not an option. I'll sneak through this passageway to where it exits near a pile of rocks next to the lake. Once I'm far enough away, I'll shift and my black dragon scales will camouflage me against the inky night. I'll fly far away from this place and begin my search. I won't return until I've found a cure for my father.

I pray that right now, the King assumes I'm still tending to Father's bedside as I've done all week. My mother is sleeping, but even when she wakes up, she'll still be a mess. She won't think to look for me right away.

I hear a scraping sounds behind me, like a boot catching against the edge of the wall. I stop mid-step. Gooseflesh prickles over my body. It could be an echo, or something from the other side of the wall, but I can't risk it.

I run.

I'm careful to keep my footsteps light and quiet. The fire of the torch lights the way, and I can only hope that if someone is following, they don't have the same advantage. After a few heart-pounding minutes, I approach the break in the path. The left passage leads to back into the castle and the right path will take me to freedom. I go right.

I make it to the first wall in record time. One floor above, the castle guards patrol. As far as I know, there is no exit down here. They know the tunnels, as that's their job. But they don't know this one, because if they did, Owen and I would have seen them down here at least once.

The stone of the outer wall is different than the stone of the castle. It's thicker, blacker, and burrowed deep into the earth. I press my hand to its slightly damp surface, imagining it to be as old as the Gods themselves. Then I crouch low, to where the passageway will allow me to crawl out. From there I'll be able to follow an underground tunnel beneath the city.

My hand doesn't hit dirt, it hits rock. I pull it back, stunned. *There is no more tunnel.* It's caved in. I curse, tears instantly welling up. Desperation claws its way in, decimating my hope, as I try to think of a plan. I could use my earth elemental to get through the rocks, but it will be felt by those above, or it might cave in the rest of the tunnel. How did this happen? The King or Silas must have known this was the passage Owen and I had been using and closed it in. What am I going to do now? I have no other way out. I kick the wall and grit my teeth in frustration, wiping at my eyes.

Footsteps tap down the passageway behind me and I freeze, quickly snuffing out the fire. I pray it's not Silas. I don't want to be alone with him. He scares me, sure, but at this point I'm more afraid of what I'll do to him. If I have the chance, I'll kill him. I know I can—at least, my dragon can. But I don't want to be a murderer, even if he deserves to die. I don't want him to take away another shred of my innocence.

"Khali?" a deep honeyed voice whispers. "It's okay. I'm not here to hurt you or turn you in."

"Bram?" I cry out, a little shocked, and scoot back out to stand. Magic travels through my hand, and I light the torch again, and sure enough, it's Prince Bram before me. His green eyes shine gold against the fire's glow, and they're filled with so much emotion, I have to step back. He's dressed head to toe in black, blending him into the darkness behind.

"You're running away, aren't you?" he asks. It's not an accusation but an observation. I see no point in lying so I nod.

"Why?" he questions further. "To get out of marrying my brother?"

"Silas is a monster," I reply, my voice sharp. "He murdered Owen. You need to watch your back around him. He'll kill you too if he feels threatened."

Bram twists his lips, thinking hard. He doesn't seem surprised. Sorrow flits across his features but so does acceptance. "You saw him kill Owen? You're sure it was him?"

He deserves to know the truth. "Not only am I sure, but your parents know it, too. They're blackmailing me to keep it all a secret."

Brams sighs. "I was afraid of that."

"You suspected?" I whisper, accusation rising. "Are you part of it, too?"

"My parents are very protective of the Brightcaster legacy," he says, his voice thick with disdain. "But I would never do something like that. Don't you know me better than that?"

I scoff. "I hardly know you at all."

"We've grown up together."

"Yes," I say. "But you've barely said more than two words to me at once."

He's quiet. It's not like he can argue with me. All those times we were forced to spend time together, he largely ignored me. And I him. The accusations he shot at me about Dean a few weeks ago were the only real conversation we'd ever had.

"If you run away," he says, "you won't be able to help your father."

I don't know if I can trust him. I want to.

"That's exactly why I'm running away," I say. What else can I do but admit the truth? I'm at a dead-end and I'm not going to hurt Bram. "I'll come back when I have figured out the cure to break the hex. I left a note hidden in my chambers indicating as much. Faros will find it. Only once I cure my father will I willingly become queen."

What I don't tell him is that I have no intention of letting my king be Silas. I no longer care about King Titus's threats against my parents. Somehow, I'll find a way to protect them in all of this. I expect Bram to argue with me, to try to convince me to return, but he smiles like I've impressed him.

"Fair enough."

I turn back to my ruined exit. "But I might have to resort to going back up to my chambers and flying away. My exit was destroyed."

He kneels down and eyes the area with a frown. "So it is. But flying out of here will never work. You'll be seen instantly. You won't get far."

I sigh, because I know he's right. "Do you have any other ideas?"

His eyes shine in the darkness, the cunning intelligence I've seen there a million times sparking within. "I know another way out," he says, "and I'll show you if you do something for me."

Of course his good news would come paired with a price. He is a Brightcaster, afterall. "What do you want?" My voice is guarded. The tunnel grows quiet. The scent of rock and dirt and smoke fill in the space between us.

"I want you to take me with you."

I shift back, shaking my head. "Are you serious? Why would you want to leave?"

"I have reason to suspect your father was crossing the border."

I shrug. "I already know that."

"But do you know where he was going? Do you know why? Do you have any leads at all? Because I do."

He's got me there and he knows it.

"Go on."

"I believe he's been visiting my brother Dean to make sure he's okay in his new life."

My eyes widen. "Do you know where Dean is?"

He's quiet for a moment, eyeing me as if calculating how much he can trust me. "I think he's in the human realm," he says matter-of-factly. "And I believe your father has been using the ley lines in the neighboring elfin kingdom to travel to Dean."

This is news to me. I can't even utter a coherent response. I would have never guessed this. Dean wasn't supposed to go to the human realm. He was supposed to be exiled into the larger continent to fend for himself and never to return to Drakenon again. But the human realm would be the safest place for him, even if slowly losing his magic would be torture.

"I wouldn't have put it past my father to have somehow helped Dean sneak into the human realm, not only as a favor to your parents, but because he loved Dean as much as we all did," I say quietly.

Bram nods, but doesn't say a word.

"I have no way to know if any of this is true," I grumble, wishing this were easier. The memory of that night when I kissed him trickles to my mind and I can't lie to myself anymore, Dean took the fall for me and willingly left. He almost seemed *resolved* to leave, like some kind of martyr. Why would he have done that if there wasn't something else going on beyond my comprehension?

"We can't know for sure if that's what happened given our limited information," Bram says, "but you're running out of options. And it gives you a tangible lead. We can go there together and find out if Dean knows what happened to your father."

I swallow, wanting to argue, but knowing I will not.

"Fine," I say. "Lead the way."

He nods once and turns. I notice the pack slung over his shoulders. So he assumed I would say yes? Or he just planned for the best? I have something similar on my back, it's not like I can blame him for preparing. A sudden suspicion leaves me cold. Could Bram have been the one to block this passageway, essentially forcing me to go along with his plan? He's smart enough to have thought out all of this. And if there's anyone who spends a lot of time in our musty library, it's him.

I don't have time to question him and nor do I want him to know my suspicions. So I keep my mouth shut and follow as he hurries back the way we came. He takes the left fork in the passageway, the one that leads back around to the castle's center, and navigates us through the labyrinth of passageways with more expertise than Owen or I ever had. How much about Bram have I underestimated?

Soon we make it past the first wall, under the city, and out past the outer wall.

I step into the cool air and let it fill my lungs like a healing balm. I could leave Bram here. I could break my word and forget him. But I can't help but think he might be onto something with his hypothesis. He knows more about the world outside Drakenon than anyone I know, what with his nose constantly in a book. If anyone can help me solve this mystery, it's him.

We begin our journey by foot, careful to avoid detection. The castle is surrounded by vast fields and the miles-wide lake which I would do anything to avoid. Further away to the east is the sea. In the other direction are the mountains and plains. The kingdom stretches for thousands of miles, filled with our villages and people. Those families who are Dragon Blessed are the ones most likely to live in the capital city or close to it. The further out someone lives, means the less magic they'll have. Of course, I was the exception to that.

But my family and I were moved from our home and brought here. Stoneshearth's castle, the surrounding city, and the fields beyond are all I've ever known. With each step I take away from it, I'm met with both apprehension and relief. The Brightcaster family may have dominion over all I can see, but soon I will leave this behind where my life is no longer theirs to claim. Once I return, I'll save my father, and then I'll tell everyone the truth about Owen. Silas will pay for his crime, the Brightcasters won't have a Dragon Blessed heir, and I'll be free of their family for good.

FIFTEEN
HAZEL

I'M WALKING THROUGH CAMPUS THE following afternoon after leaving Dean standing there on that sidewalk, preoccupied with my busy mind, when I spot Landon and stop short. *The boy looks good.* He's lounging in one of the grassy areas with his friends, the sun lighting up his white blonde hair like a halo. I wish my hair did that. Mine is what we call "dirty," which is such a terrible but accurate description for the shade caught between two colors. At least I bothered to style it in loose curls today. His looks so good that I don't even mind how it's tied up in a manbun.

It's an unseasonably warm day for October and probably one of the last we're going to get for the year, so everyone is soaking it up. The women are in shorts and skirts, nobody has a coat, and apparently, some of the men have decided shirts are optional.

Landon and all his friends have their shirts off, and even from here, I can spot the dewy sweat on his tanned and muscled torso. I can also spot the myriad of girls making eyes at the half-naked dudes all lined up in a row. It seems none of us ladies are exempt from staring, not that I'm complaining. A bright yellow frisbee lays a few feet from their crew.

Feeling brave, I smile and walk over, picking up the plastic disc. "Are you guys practicing for your competitive frisbee league, or what's going on here?"

The four guys laugh up at me but my eyes are locked on Landon's. I can't help it. His dimples are showing and those baby blues are sparkling like crazy in this light, which is good because I don't want to get distracted by those abs. But my eyes flick down to ogle them anyway. He catches me looking and my stomach flips. Whoops!

"Freshman." He practically purrs my nickname. "Have a seat. Come meet my boys. Boys, meet *the* Hazel Forrester."

I hand him the frisbee and plop myself down on the grass next to Landon. He reaches in for a side hug. He's so attractive that I don't even mind the sweat, which is kind of gross. He introduces me to his friends, Tim, Garret, and some guy they've nicknamed Howdy.

"They're in my fraternity," Landon explains happily. "Tim's the president. Garret is a ladies man. And Howdy's the fun drunk."

I nod and smile and try not to look judgy even though I totally might be judging them right now—Landon made it so easy introducing them that way. The three guys shake my hand and turn back to their conversation.

"And what does that make you?" I ask flirtatiously.

"I'm the serious one," he says. And then we both burst out laughing. If there's one thing I know about Landon, it's that he likes to keep things light.

We lay back on our elbows, gazing up at the expanse of clear blue sky.

"When is your next class?" he asks, scooting closer.

I close my eyes, letting the moment settle over me like a warm hug. "Actually, I'm done with classes for the day." I open my eyes and grin at Landon.

"Very interesting. So am I," he replies, his eyes lingering on my lips. My heart jumps to the point of heart attack status because I'm pretty sure we're going to make out soon!

"But I have to work in an hour," I add, a little disappointed.

He pouts, and I roll my eyes playfully. Landon and I have been flirting—mostly through text—for weeks now but we haven't gone on an official date. He hasn't asked. Maybe he won't.

I've seen him be as flirty with other girls in our Chemistry class. And the one time I went to his frat house for that party, he was dancing in the middle of a *circle* of sorority girls. He didn't even notice I was there. This chemistry between us is likely a result of his personality, having nothing to do with him actually wanting to date me. And as cute as he is, I'm young and inexperienced. I won't turn eighteen until Christmas break and if he knew that fact about me, he'd probably run for the hills, or at least wait until January to ask me out.

Besides, I don't want to "get experienced" with some guy who only sees me as a booty call or a side chick anyway.

I have a feeling that's how most fraternity guys work around here.

I sit up, brushing the grass from my clothes. "Well, I just wanted to say hello but I'd better get going. I've got to get changed before heading in to work."

I stand and he jumps to his feet, wrapping me in a hug.

"Go out with me?" The request is confident.

I still, my whole body rooted to the spot.

"Like on a date?" I sputter.

He laughs and releases me, stepping back slightly. I must look startled because he laughs again. "Of course it's a date. I really like you, Fresh. When are you free for dinner?"

I don't want to sound too eager, but I totally am. "I don't work on Saturday or Sunday night."

"Sunday is great," he says, one of his dimples popping in his cheek. "I'll pick you up outside of the freshman dorm at seven." He catches me in another tight hug and as he lets me go, I spot his friends laughing at us over his shoulder. I'm not even a little bit embarrassed. Because I, Hazel Forrester, have a date with Landon Freemount, one of the hottest guys I've ever met in real life. Not as hot as Dean Ashton, but we're not going there. Not today, Satan!

I practically skip back to my dorm to get ready for work.

"HEY, THERE BIG GUY," I say, reaching out my hand. "Are you okay? Where's your home?"

The dog appears to be a stray. It's black scruffy fur is matted and it's skinnier than it should be for its hulking size. The poor baby was digging through some trash when I found it.

"C'mere, boy," I say, walking closer. "I can help you."

He takes a tentative step forward, looking at me with big watery eyes, when he tenses. He barks, the sound echoing through the alleyway, before skittering off.

Disappointed, I resolve to look for him again after work. He could use some love and there's nothing I'd rather do than help him.

Something prickles along the back of my neck, a rush of grasping awareness. I freeze, listening intently, and the feeling only grows.

Someone is following me.

Not someone of the dead variety. I'm used to that. No, whoever this is, they are very much human and very much *alive*. I keep my head still but my eyes dart from side to side, taking in the alleyway, the red brick buildings on either side, searching for signs that I'm not alone. I will someone to come out of one of the back doors or to turn down the alley from Main Street, but nobody does. I fumble to get my phone out of my pocket and quicken my steps, gathering the nerve to look behind me.

There's nobody there.

Nobody that I can see, anyway. But they *are* there. I know they are. I want to release the breath caged in my chest, want to relax. But I can't. Because I can still feel them. The awareness is like a boa constrictor, wrapping itself around me, disabling my ability to reason. Glass scatters across the concrete behind me and I turn around.

This time, I see him.

He's tall, over six feet, wearing dark jeans and a black windbreaker that's zipped all the way to his chin. He's sporting a gray ball cap that hoods his turned-down face. I can't get a good enough look to gather more, to get an age or coloring or anything identifying. I'm stuck in static indecision, wondering what I should do next. Am I being paranoid? Something dark and ethereal flashes above him and I squint, unsure what kind of spirit I'm looking at.

He pauses for a second, and then runs toward me.

It happens so fast, the feelings and thoughts that jolt through my mind. Part of me wants to be logical, wants to assume the best, that this man isn't a threat. But the bigger part of me knows all the way to my marrow, to my atoms, and the space in between, that he wants to hurt me. That he's already chosen to hurt me. That if I don't get away right now, he will succeed.

I whip around and run. Blood rushes through my ears, the soundtrack of panic.

Why did I come this way? How could I have been so naive? At night, after closing up the shop, I always walk along Main Street back to campus. It only takes a few extra minutes and from there I can follow the populated and well-lit walkway down the main part of campus back to my dormitory. There are always people around. I'm never alone. Never afraid.

I usually take this route during the day as well. And yet, today, of all days, I didn't. What was I thinking? Girls have gone missing. There's a killer on the loose! I never should have ventured off anywhere this remote, even if it is the middle of the afternoon. But it's a good shortcut and after flirting with Landon earlier, my mind became a flighty moth of a thing and before long, I was running late. I hate being late. So I took the shortcut.

Maybe today the long way would have saved my life.

The thought drips in panic and I run even faster. But his soft footsteps are closer, his breath a steady cadence growing near. And he isn't slowing down.

Neither am I.

It's only a few more buildings until I'll be out in the open. I'm almost there. I can get there. I have to. I keep fumbling with my phone but it's a useless weight. I don't have the ability to run for my life and use it at the same time. So I grip it, hang on for dear life, and push my body harder.

I'm frantic, praying for someone to see me.

"Help!" I yell, my voice high and reaching. I don't know if anyone heard. If they did, they don't come.

The footsteps behind me don't slow.

Something catches and scrapes. "Shit," the man mutters in a low, growly tone.

I glance back. He's lying on the ground but he's quick to scramble to his feet. I take off again, running at full speed for Main Street. It probably takes thirty seconds but it feels like a millennia, like I'm in a thickening dream and I can't wake up. Once I stumble onto the sidewalk, I brave a look back.

The man is gone.

The adrenaline is still electric in my veins and my lungs are on fire, but he's gone. He's gone. Tears prick at my eyes and I can't get my breath to slow. I hurry to The Flowering Chakra, trying to make sense of what happened. Wanting to pretend it wasn't real. Wanting to cry.

As I'm about to enter the shop, I look around one last time to make sure the man isn't still following me. My phone clatters to the pavement and I yelp.

The spirit dragon is perched on the roof across the street. The sunlight shines right through it, almost to the point that it's absorbed by the creature, like the ghost is a black hole for energy and light. It's ghastly and hulking with reptilian eyes that pin me down, watchful and intelligent. Their blue sheen stands apart from the black, unsettling my defenses.

The dragon is quick. It stands, unfurling two massive wings. They span ten feet on either side, a monument of power. And then it jumps, diving down first and then flying in a swooping arc, disappearing down the same alleyway I just came from. Is it simply a coincidence or is the dragon going after my attacker?

I don't follow. I'm never going back there again.

"Are you okay?" a gravelly voice asks, and I nearly jump out of my skin. It's Dean. "What's going on? What happened?"

He towers over me, his bare arms crossed over his white t-shirt. His eyes dart around before zeroing in on me. I don't know what to say, and when I do open my mouth, nothing but a frantic gargle comes out.

"Did you see the dragon again?" A long strand of black hair falls in front of his coal eyes as he stares me down.

I blink, trying to process what just happened, my heart still racing.

"Hazel! Where did it go?"

His forceful tone snaps me from my trance and I point toward the direction of the alleyway. Dean takes off running, charging around the corner and disappearing from sight.

SIXTEEN
KHALI

BRAM IS AS QUIET AND observant, as per usual. And even now, with so much happening that we could talk about, he hardly utters a word. I don't mind. I don't have anything to say to him either.

We've spent a few hurried hours on foot, but we can't continue this way. As soon as we're discovered to be missing, the King will send his army after us. I've seen them training. I know how fast they are, how skilled. There's little time to waste.

"We need to move faster," I say, my voice carrying over the flat landscape. Even through my velvet cape, a chill brushes along my spine. It doesn't help that my long black dress still leaves an opening for the chill to nip at my legs. "I feel so exposed out here."

"Agreed." His voice is soft.

I let out a breath, scarcely believing what I'm about to offer. "If I change into my dragon form, you can ride on my back."

He stops abruptly, his eyes shining under the moonlight. "Are you sure?"

That's one of the things about dragon shifters: under no circumstances do we carry *anyone* on our backs. We're not pack animals. We have pride and to be forced to carry someone is considered shameful. Some even say it's an affront to the Gods, though I'm not sure they care about us as much as we think they do. I've certainly never carried anyone nor has Bram climbed on a dragon's hide—they'd probably take his head off for such a gross offense.

"I don't see any other way." I run my cold fingers along my long braid and tuck it over one shoulder, trying to come up with the right words so I don't further embarrass myself. "If we don't take to the skies while it's still dark, we're not going to cover enough ground. The second your father discovers that we're missing, there will be dragons flying in all directions to find us. We need to take advantage of our early start while we still can."

What I don't add is that if they find us together, Bram will be in more danger than myself. Dean was exiled for a single kiss. What would they do to Bram for running away with their future queen? Without my magic, there is no guarantee the next line of royal children will be elementals. And what's he going to do when we return to the castle? I'm sure he has some sort of plan, but I don't ask him. Not yet, anyway.

I try to meet his eyes but he's looking down at the space between us, considering my offer. His gaze is hooded, hiding his thoughts from me. I don't try to figure them out. I've never been able to figure out the puzzle that is Bram Brightcaster, but then again, I haven't made much effort when it comes to him.

"Well, what do you think?" I ask, my voice catching. He'd better not make me beg because I'd rather leave him out here to fend for himself. "I'm fine doing whatever we need to do to make this work, just as long as we stay away from the water."

He nods. "I remember what the merfolk did to you. I'm sorry you had to go through that."

"Don't." I hold up a hand and push away the memories. "I don't want to talk about it."

He nods and looks away, then points. "Let's fly south but we'll have to take cover during the day. We should be able to make it to the Jeweled Forest before morning. Once we're in there, we can travel by foot and nobody will be able to see us from the sky. No water involved."

The Jeweled Forest? My stomach twists into a knot.

It's a brilliant idea, of course, but even if I don't know very much about the place, I do know it's dangerous and forbidden. I'm momentarily struck with gratitude for Bram and all his studies to have thought of such a great idea. I wouldn't have known where to go to hide along my journey to the border had I gone alone.

I walk a few paces away from him and shift. Turning into my truest self always feels like salvation, like slipping into a hot bath or taking off a too-tight corset. The magic's work is quick. The glimmer rises from within, growing around me in an orb of shimmery air. Then in a blink, the human part of me, and everything I'm wearing, vanishes and my dragon form appears.

My black hide gleams, and I stretch my wings out wide. The hum of elemental magic is stronger when I'm in this form and it calls to me as naturally as breathing. I hear the grass moving beneath my feet and the wind whispers an ancient song as it rushes past my ears.

There's something else there, too. Something… unwelcome. It nags at the magic, trying to weaken it. Like a physical sprain on my elements. I fight back, pushing it down, until it goes. Worry trickles across my hide but I push that aside, too. I'll deal with it later.

I crouch down and Bram doesn't hesitate. He climbs on my long back in between my wings. Once I'm sure he's secure, I launch off the ground. My wings pump and carry us up, up, up. If Bram is afraid, I don't sense it. His heart rate doesn't speed and his body doesn't tense. It's strange that he's probably never had this experience before. He doesn't know what it is like to fly. Not for the first time, I feel bad for him. He grips me tighter as I press forward, flying south toward the Jeweled Forest.

The hours pass by in a blur of thoughts and the constant flapping of my wings. I'm faster than most dragons, but carrying Bram slows me down slightly. He might not know the difference, but I can't stop worrying. This will be a disadvantage to us but there's nothing we can do.

I grow tired but I don't allow myself to slow. Finally, the sun crests over the horizon and relief washes over me. Not far off, a forest sparkles like a rainfall of diamonds fell onto the trees and stuck to their branches. I dive low for our destination, grateful we made it in time, but also a little worried that this place is as dangerous as I've heard. I fly over the tops of the towering trees until the light is too much; it bounces off the jewels and blinds me. I force myself to keep from shielding my eyes as I bring us to a clearing and land. Bram jumps off my back and I shift back to my human self.

"Are you doing okay?" Bram asks. "You're not too tired? We covered a lot of ground."

I'm too distracted to answer. "It's so much more beautiful than I imagined." My voice is wistful as I stare at the enchanted landscape. Seeing it from above was nothing compared to standing among its brilliance. The trees don't grow leaves here. They grow the most beautiful of jewels. They range in every color and shape, from red rubies, to white diamonds, to bright green emeralds and everything in between. I step forward, my fingers reaching out to touch a sparkling blue sapphire. It's mesmerizing. The size of an apple. If only I could have it...

"Don't!" Bram slaps my hand away.

I gasp and turn on him, rubbing the injury. "What was that for?"

"Did you not pay attention to your geography tutor at all?" he challenges, exasperated. "Anyone who takes a stone from this forest will be cursed to sleep for a thousand years."

I blink. "I guess I *might* have heard that." In all honesty, I am certain I did during some lesson or another, and I'm also certain I didn't pay attention as Bram has pointed out. I swallow my pride. "Thanks for looking out for me."

It makes sense. Nothing so incredible as this would still be here if it didn't have this kind of protection. There are enough people in the kingdom who would exploit it, if not just for the riches, then for the ability to ease their load, for the ability to fill their childrens' bellies every night.

The Brightcaster royals have a treasury of jewels, but *nothing* compared to some of these. If they could have taken them, they would have. They take everything they want, and damn the consequences to anyone they have to trample over in the process.

My eyes travel from gemstone to gemstone. Some are bigger than my head. This place isn't natural and it's not meant for me. The gemstones don't call out to my earth elemental, not even a little. I didn't notice at first, I was too drawn in by the sheer beauty of them. How could I have missed something so important? The realization makes me nervous.

"Let's get going," Bram says. "When you're tired, let me know. We can rest and I'll take first look out."

We walk until the sun is high in the sky but we don't move nearly as quickly as I'd have liked. We're too scared to touch any of the jewels with our hands. I'll have to make up for this delay once the night falls by flying us again. The forest is thick, which also doesn't aid our speed. And it is eerily silent. Save for the crunching our boots make as we navigate through the trees, there's no other noise. We don't even come across any animals. No water, either. It's as if the trees here are surviving on magic alone.

Perhaps they are.

My eyelids grow heavy and after catching me trying to cover a yawn, Bram insists we take a break. We find the tallest tree and settle beneath its generous canopy of glittering branches. The forest floor is littered with gems so we use our boots to clear a space, careful not to touch anything with our bare hands. I lay my thick, black cape out and curl on top of its velvety surface in a tight ball. Bram sits on a tree stump and turns away. My breathing slows and within a few minutes of closing my eyes, my mind drifts off to sleep.

SOMEONE SHAKES ME GENTLY, TWO steady hands of sunlight. Bram's hands. I blink to the setting sun and to him leaning over me. In an hour or two, it will be dark enough for us to fly. Red rims his eyes, brightening the green. He mumbles something about not letting him sleep too long and then he lays down, using his pack for a pillow and falls asleep almost instantly. I'll let him sleep until the second the sky is black, and then we're getting out of here.

I relax with my back to the wide trunk and root around in my pack, pulling out the block of cheese wrapped in beeswax cloth, one of the apples, and the heavy waterskin. I started gathering supplies the day after I ran into Silas in the hallway. It was then I knew, I was leaving. Luckily, I don't have to ration the water because of my water elemental. Should I need more water, it will be easy to gather by calling it to me. But I only eat enough food to barely satisfy the hollow ache in my stomach. Food might be harder to find in the coming days.

"Khali…" a male voice sing-songs in tickling whispers. I whip around to Bram, but he's still fast asleep, his breathing steady and messy hair blowing slightly in the wind.

I still myself and listen hard, but several minutes pass by in silence. Maybe it was in my mind, a response to exhaustion.

"Khali," the voice whispers again, louder this time, and also seemingly from farther away. This is definitely not in my head and it reminds me of a voice I know as well as my own. But no. How could that be possible?

I hold my breath and listen harder, my heart wild in my chest.

"It's me," the voice says. "It's Owen."

I blink in disbelief. Could it be? My ears are playing tricks on me. Surely, that's all this is. I ignore it and busy myself with repacking my items, tucking the rest of the cheese at the bottom. The second I finish with the pack and everything falls back into silence, the voice is there again.

"Khali, come here. Come talk to me." It does sound like him.

This can't be real. And I can't move from my spot.

And there is that part of my mind, that logical part, which knows it's all a trick and I should wake Bram. We should leave this forest, sunset or no. Because something about this forest is utterly wrong. But that part of my mind fades to the other part, the part that is desperate to talk to Owen, pulled in by the enchantment like a moth to the flame.

I stand as quietly as I can.

I'll just go see what this is and come right back. Maybe Owen is speaking to me from beyond the grave. I've heard stories of the Gods allowing it. It's not impossible.

I leave my pack and cape where they are and creep through the forest toward the direction of the voice. The glittering gems don't entice me but I'm still aware of them and avoid them, even though they shine brightest in the setting sun. They have little hold over me compared to Owen. He coaxes me forward like nothing else would.

"This way," he says, his voice a feathery whisper on the wind. "That's right. Just over here. You're close."

I speed to match the thudding of my heartbeats. The more I walk, the more the need to find Owen overpowers me, pulling me forward. Soon it is the only thing that matters and I'm running.

"You're almost here," his voice says in that teasing, happy way of his. I smile. I've missed him so much.

My boot catches on a fallen tree and I stumble, going down hard. My momentum carries me over the rest of a hill and I'm rolling, branches and stones pummeling my exposed skin. I squeeze my eyes shut and tuck my arms in against the pain, fisting my hands against my chest. It all happens so fast. I'm spinning and then I'm not. I blink, the beginnings of winking sun momentarily blinding my vision. I find myself on flat earth and sit up with a groan to glare at the hill that I just tumbled down.

"Owen?" I ask, rubbing the side of my head. I pull my fingers away to find blood and wince. "Where are you?"

"Over here," the voice replies.

Once again, I'm confused if I'm hearing it in my head or aloud. But does it matter? It's Owen! "Over where?"

"Don't you see me?" the voice continues. "Look up. I'm right here."

I search the forest and then I see… something.

"Is that you?"

"Yes," he says, breathy. Eager.

"Why are you lying like that?" I rush forward to my friend. He's lying on his front, his face buried in the dusty ground. And he's dressed funny, not in his normal princely attire, but in aged clothing that's practically rotting off his body. But his hair is that same dusty blonde curly mess and his skin is the tanned honey I know so well.

I kneel at his side and roll him toward me. "Owen?"

I yelp. The man that stares up at me isn't Owen. Before my eyes, his hair turns to orangish copper, and his face changes to that of an older man's. His brown eyes are glassy, vacant. But his skin is warm, his cheeks pink. A light breath of exhaled air tickles my arm.

"Who are you?" I growl.

Gripped in his hands are piles of gemstones and then I know.

I stumble away, scurrying across the dirt floor on my hands and knees until I can manage to stand.

"Where are you going?" the voice calls after me. It still sounds like Owen but I know that it is all an illusion. I don't know if it's the man somehow doing this, or the forest, but I'm not going to stay and find out.

"Khali, come back," the voice laughs. "It's not so bad here. You might like it."

Tears burn my eyes and I glance around the clearing. Horror overpowers me at what I find. There are *more* people here. At least ten more. And all are lost to a cursed slumber with shining gemstones clenched in their hands. The trees grow around them and over them as if they don't exist.

I need to get out of here.

I run back, trying to find the way I came in, fighting with the hem of my dress, climbing the hill, holding my hands in tight, fighting the barrage of panic. I'm almost to the top when I see a woman. She's flat on her back with a peaceful expression on her sleeping face. Her eyes are closed, and her raven hair curls around her in perfect symmetry. She looks to be young, my age. But her dress is of a style from centuries ago. Her bowed lips and cheeks are painted cherry red. Straight through the center of her stomach, a silvery sapling grows, encrusted with spiky rubies.

It's not magic that the trees feed on. It's not the elements. It's blood.

I scream.

SEVENTEEN
HAZEL

"YOU LOOK LIKE YOU JUST saw a ghost," Harmony says the moment I step into the shop.

I point at her. "So. Not. Funny." But I'm shaking, and even though I want to sound like my happy-go-lucky self, my voice doesn't come out even a little bit playful. The tone is akin to a strangled kitten. Not cute.

She wiggles her gray eyebrows but stops short when I shuffle closer. "No, really, you don't look right, Hazel. Are you okay? What happened?"

I swallow, not quite sure how to put it into words. "Someone followed me," I finally choke out. "He chased me down that back alleyway between Main and Crestmont."

Her eyes widen into milky-blue saucers and she closes the distance, wrapping me in a motherly hug. I sink into her, tears springing instantly.

"I can't believe I didn't see that coming," she mutters. "I'm *so* sorry. Paths can change so quickly, I don't always see these things in time. But I'm *so* glad you're okay. I don't want to think about what would have happened if you'd never showed up for your shift today."

"Neither do I."

She takes my hand in her weathered palm and leads me to the little back room where we do the readings. "I'm going to call the police. They can come take your statement in here."

I want to say no, want to put this whole thing behind me and pretend it wasn't real, that it didn't happen. But I also want the police to catch this guy, whoever he is, because he's still out there and it's very possible that he's the creep responsible for the missing women. He could come back for me. But why? What's the pattern? What am I missing? What am I forgetting? I can feel the truth nagging at me, so close to coming into focus, but I can't see it yet.

"I didn't get a good look at him," I mutter hopelessly, falling into the soft brown couch and sinking into its homey caress. I can finally breathe again, but it doesn't help. I can't stop shaking. I sit on my hands.

"That's okay. We still need to report it."

An hour later, the police have come and gone. I told them everything I could. Of course, I left out the encounter with the spirit dragon—or any spirits—because I'm not a moron. The police were eager to write down every bit of info like it could be the missing puzzle piece. And maybe it could be. The head detective, a stout, balding man with a wiry mustache, left me his card in case I remember anything else or run into trouble. I hold the flimsy cardstock between my fingers, staring at the black ink: Detective Sanders. I quickly type the number into my phone, saving it to my contacts, then shove both items into my pocket.

The surreal terror of the afternoon has started to fade into the quiet of newly minted evening. I don't know when I stopped shaking but I'm calm now. And exhausted. My eyelids are anchors but I'm terrified that if I close them and sink into sleep, I'll end up reimagining the incident over and over again, unable to escape it.

Harmony pops her head into the back room, looking me up and down with pity. And I hate it. A fresh anger burns bright against my ribcage. How dare this guy take something away from me? I don't want to spend the rest of my life looking over my shoulder, let alone the rest of the school year. And the worst part is, there's nothing I can do about it. He was going to hurt me. No question about it. And if he was so brazen in broad daylight, who else has he hurt? What else has he gotten away with?

"I'll be giving you a ride home after work from now on," Harmony says matter-of-factly, snapping me from my torrent of angry thoughts. "Even if you're working the shop alone, I'll come back at closing and take you back to your dorm. And we have cameras here. Keep that detective's number on speed dial."

"You hired me to make your life easier."

She tilts her head. "So what? I don't want you out walking in the dark, at least not until they catch that man. Okay?"

I nod once. "Okay," I say, but in my head I'm thinking about the possibility of them not catching that man, or anyone. That whoever chased me today, and whoever hurt those girls, will get away free and clear. Free to live their sick life. Cora, the true crime-obsessed girl that she is, informed me and Macy that a third of the murders in the United States go unsolved. So that's a fun statistic to keep in my back pocket right about now.

I stare at the lavender wall, studying the way the plaster underneath creates the faintest pebbly pattern. The anger from moments before has been eaten by an emptiness, a hollowness that scares me. I spring up and brush myself off. "Enough of that," I say. "I'm not going to wallow in what happened or feel sorry for myself. It's over. I'm lucky to be here. And I'm not going to think about that creep anymore or let him stop me from living my life."

"Oh, honey," Harmony sighs. "I think we should close up early tonight—"

"No!" I cut her off so abruptly that she jumps. "I want to stay busy. I need it. Give me something to do, please. Let's just go on, business as usual."

She wrings her hands together. Her dreadlocks are piled on top of her head, like a basket of wiry snakes, but her eyes are kind and her rosemary and sage scent is a familiar balm to my emotional wounds.

"Are you absolutely sure?" she asks carefully.

"I'm absolutely, infinitely, utterly sure. Please, I need this. I need to work."

Harmony stares for a long second before her eyes become hazy, like she's seeing right through me. Probably to my "paths". Her eyes stay like that long enough for me to get nervous. But then they clear and she nods, relaxing into an easy smile.

"Yes," she says. "I have a new client who's interested in a reading. She's from out of town and called in last night. She'd like to meet you. And I think it will be okay. Despite what happened today, I see it as a positive path for you to take."

"Let's do it," I say, pushing down any lingering feelings of fear or worry. Time to move forward.

"I haven't met her in person yet," she continues. "So I don't know any specifics as to how the reading will go because I can only see her paths if I can get close. I see it going well for you, but I don't—"

"It will be fine," I cut her off like I have all the confidence in the world. I think back to Dean, and how I refused to work with him and what a disaster that whole experience was. But that was last week and that was different. Since then, I've done three readings for Harmony's best clients. Each one was just as she said it would be. Easy and natural. All I had to do was go into that quiet room with them, invite any spirits of the light to join us, and tell the clients what images I saw.

I couldn't always make sense of what the images meant, but that wasn't my job and nobody seemed to mind. The clients knew what to make of the images that came into my mind. And by the end of the hour-long session, all three clients left in tears. They would smile and thank me for a job well done and head over to the cash register to pay. It felt good. It felt like I was turning my curse into a gift, into a future, like Mom always said I could.

Maybe doing it again today will soften the empty feeling in my gut.

THIRTY MINUTES LATER, THE CLIENT arrives. She's polished and put together in the kind of "high-gloss" way that doesn't fit into an earthy place like The Flowering Chakra. But then again, Dean didn't fit in here either. I've learned not to jump to conclusions about who needs this woo-woo stuff. Everyone probably needs some version of it. Not that half of the population would even consider it. But then again, people can be full of surprises.

Surprises and secrets.

The client tiptoes into the shop like she's not meant to be here and is desperate not to touch anything, like the crystals might reach out and bite her. When her manicured fingers smooth out a sheath of crimson hair, a massive diamond ring catches the light. Her high heels click-clack on the wood floors.

I blink at her, worry sweeping wide. Will she believe a word I say?

Harmony greets her with a smile but after a few moments, she shakes her head and puts her hand on the woman's shoulder. "Are you sure you want to do this? It might be harder on you than you realize."

"What?" the woman sputters. "Of course! I came all this way. I've been on standby to meet Hazel."

"No," Harmony continues. "I've changed my mind. Hazel had a bit of a scare today. She isn't in the right frame of mind to do this reading."

All my senses are alive, trying to figure out why there's a sudden change in Harmony. Her tone is protective, so it must have something to do with getting a look at this woman's future paths. But it doesn't matter. I want to do the reading. I want to be distracted, even if I'm not in the right frame of mind.

I hurry over to intervene. "I can do it," I assure them both, offering a pleasant, and totally fake, smile.

The woman's eyes soften when she takes me in, and Harmony looks like a ripened tomato, her face has grown so red. She keeps shaking her head. I know this is Harmony's shop, this is her thing, and I need to trust her. But right now, I don't care. I must take my mind off that alleyway and what could have happened if that man hadn't tripped.

"Right this way," I say brightly and lead the woman back into the lavender room. Before Harmony can stop us, I close the door. Now it's just me and this woman and the unknown of whatever's next.

If this lady were an animal, she'd be one of those million dollar race horses. Everything about her is power and money and winning at life. And her eyes are alight with so much gratitude for me that I don't know what to do with it. I don't want to let her down. I gesture for her to have a seat so we can get started.

"What's your name?" I ask, settling into my chair.

"Evangeline Connelly." She has a slight southern accent and there's an alarm in the back of my mind. Like I should know that name. Do I? I eye her again, but I've never seen her before today.

"I now invite any spirits, angels, or guides of the light to enter the room with me and Evangeline Connelly." I unclasp my obsidian necklace and place it on the side table.

They come. They materialize, surrounding her on all sides. Ancestors, and what I've figured out are guides by they way they glow like a nightlight is lit from within. And then there are the angels. She has two. They stand on either side of the room, stoic and massive.

I've seen all this stuff since I was a child. But the angels don't always show themselves, so when they do, it's hard not to stare. They look exactly like they're depicted in the Bible. Gigantic wings and warrior-like garb and massive energy. But they never say anything to me. They don't show me images. They don't interact. Ever. I'm sure they're here for a reason, but I can't say what that reason is. All I know is they're not *my* angels, they're hers.

It's the spirits, the ghosts of those who've lived here before, that I can connect with, that can send me the images. And it's one of them in particular that I now gape at.

Charlene Connelly.

She was that freshman girl who went missing two years ago. She looks exactly like the photos that popped up in the news over the weekend. They never found her body. Now I know why.

I look down at my hands. They're shaking again.

"Do you see her?" Evangeline Connelly asks gently, breaking the tension. "Do you see my daughter? Is she dead?" Her voice is laced with the kind of deep unresolved sadness that reaches into my soul and rips it wide open.

I don't want to be the one to tell her. But I have to.

I take a deep breath and meet her eyes. They're hopeful. They're broken. They're two years of living without knowing what happened to her daughter.

"Please, just tell me. I need to know. Is she dead?"

"Yes. I'm sorry."

She nods, the pain seeming to settle in deep, but also, some other emotion right along with it. Something I can't quite name yet. "Is she okay?"

I look over the woman's shoulder to where her daughter hovers. Oftentimes I see the spirits caught in between this life and whatever comes next. I don't know where they go. They don't either, I don't think. They seem to be stuck here, trapped by the things that happened to them on Earth.

But not always.

Sometimes they come through from a far off place that I *can't* see, traveling to come to me. Sometimes they're happier than anyone walking this earth. And as for Charlene, her smile is genuine and she glows with the light of pure, unfiltered joy. And when I look at her, I don't see the pain, or the horror of what happened to her, or a young woman who had her life stolen away. I wish I could somehow allow Charlene's mother to see her this way.

"Yes, she's okay," I say. "Sometimes what I see is... disturbing. But with your daughter, all I see is her happiness. She's smiling. She's full of love. She's at peace."

Tears fall from Evangeline Connolly's eyes. Moisture instantly pools in mine, too.

"Do you know what happened to her?" she asks, so hopeful and needy.

I was afraid of this. I almost don't want to know what happened to this girl. I'm afraid of what I'll see. But I do ask because I must. For Evangeline's sake, but for mine too. Mine and every other young woman at Hayden College. I look up at the peaceful spirit hovering over her mother and ask the question that can only have a terrible answer.

I meet Charlene's gaze. "What happened to you? Will you show me?"

But she doesn't show me anything of her death. No water, like with Katherine's ghost. No death or screaming or terror, like with so many others. Instead, her spirit shows me a memory, a memory she wants me to share with her mother.

"She's seven years old," I begin. "Charlene is in first grade and she doesn't want to go to school because the other girls have become friends and have left her out. You and Dad don't let her stay home. Nobody is allowed to stay home from school unless they're sick. Not her two older brothers, either. It's the rule."

Evangeline nods along, mesmerized by the story, as if she's seeing it all again in real time.

"But on the drive to the elementary school, just as Charlene is about to burst into tears in the back seat, you look at her through the rearview mirror and you tell her that it's a girl's date day. Then you turn away from the school and the two of you spend the day shopping at the mall and go to the movie theater to see *The Emperor's New Groove*."

"She loved that movie," Evangeline says, tears streaming down her face. I hand her the box of tissues and she dabs at her makeup gingerly.

"She loved it because *you* made it special. After that day, the two of you kept the girl's date day a secret, a secret that became a yearly tradition. Once a year, you would ditch school and work and do the same thing, go shopping and then eat a bunch of candy and popcorn while watching a matinee."

Evangeline is ugly crying now. There's no other way to describe it. And I probably am too. This was not what I expected would happen when I saw Charlene's spirit. But I couldn't stop the tears even if I tried. It's not fair, what happened. She died with her whole life ahead of her.

"Thank you," Evangeline finally whispers.

"I don't know what happened to your daughter and she doesn't want to show me. Sometimes they do, sometimes they don't."

Her lower lip trembles. "I guess I can accept that."

"But I do know that her soul is at rest now. She's happy. And she wants you to move on and be happy, too. And she wants to thank you for being the best mother she ever could have asked for."

Evangeline wipes at her tears and nods. A smile cracks her face, a real one, this time. Not the fake glossiness from before. A peaceful feeling settles over the room and she stands, reaching for my hand, pulling me into an embrace.

"You remind me of her, you know?" she says against my ear. "Something about your eyes. They sparkle the same way hers did. And you're a helper. You care about people. She did, too. She wanted to be a doctor, cure cancer, save the world."

"She still cares about people. She cares about you."

"Thank you." Her hug tightens.

"You're welcome."

She steps back and gazes deep into my eyes. "Be careful out there."

"I will," I whisper.

She nods once but she's not convinced. "I'm leaving this town tomorrow and I'm never coming back. But you don't get to leave. You have years of school, but can you feel it?"

"Feel what?"

"There's something dark about this place. Something that killed my daughter."

My breath catches and fear builds up inside me like an incoming storm. I nod because I know what she's saying is the truth. There's something terrible happening in this town and for some unknown reason, it's only getting worse.

When I walk her outside, I forget to bring my necklace. I realize the loss of its weight around my neck the same moment Evangeline's warning is confirmed. Not only is Kathrine's spirit hovering over the sidewalk, ghostly water dripping down into a supernatural puddle, but so are the other women. Tessa is there, the girl who went missing last year. And the high school cheerleader. She breaks the pattern. She wasn't in college, she was only seventeen.

She wears her fitted white and red uniform, a large W embroidered over her chest, for Westinbrook High. Her long ice-blonde hair hangs plastered against her face, her mouth gaunt, her eyes bloodshot. All three spirits shoot images at me at once, images of their lives, of their lost hopes and dreams, and worst of all, of drowning, of water filling their lungs until their consciousness washed away. It takes over my vision, cold and final.

    I don't stick around. I sprint back to the reading room and slap the necklace around my neck, falling onto the couch with choking breaths, as if I'm the one drowning.

EIGHTEEN
KHALI

"BRAM!" I SCREAM AND THEN force myself to be silent. I'm afraid to listen, afraid the cursed forest will mess with me again and confuse me with its ghost whispers. But I can't leave Bram here. I can't do this alone.

I stumble forward, battling wild emotions and wicked branches. The sun has almost set. My lungs burn against shaky sobs and my vision blurs behind a veil of tears. Where is he? I need to get out of here. I can't stay another second, especially not once darkness falls. My heart pounds and my hands shake and the trees press in around me. I need to shift and fly away.

"Bram, w-where are you." My voice catches and more tears erupt. I was never much for crying but ever since Owen's death and my father being hexed, I can't seem to stop.

More voices call out to me. Are they the voices of the dead? Are they linked to the trees, part of the enchantment of the forest itself? My elementals roar to life under my skin and I welcome them, tucking them close to my heart like a security measure. Panic races through me when I realize they're dimmed again, just as they've been on and off over the last few weeks.

What is happening to me? Am I losing my powers? As I get closer to my eighteenth birthday, I should be growing stronger, not weaker. I choke out a sob.

"Khali!" Bram yells.

I search for him, praying he's real.

"Bram?" I call louder. "I'm over here!"

And then he appears, fear etched into his face. Sweat beads across his brow and his eyes are frantic as they search me out. My sobs continue, but now in relief. What would I have done if I was all alone out here? Would I have taken one of the jewels and been cursed to the same fate as all those sleeping people? I stumble over the brush and send the Gods a silent prayer that I'm still standing. Bram's warm arms wrap around me, pulling me in close.

"Khali," he says, his voice hoarse. "It's okay. I've got you."

He tucks my body against his. The plane of his chin brushes the top of my head, and I turn my face into the hollow of his neck.

"It's okay," he says, over and over as I continue to cry.

I'm surrounded by scents of oak and cherries and comforting earth. He smells of life. The magic may have skipped him, but in this way, it clung to him. I've never been held like this before. A prickle of calm runs through me and I rub away the tears, feeling a bit foolish but also grateful. Then I untangle myself and tell him what happened.

He's quiet as he takes it all in, glancing around the sparkling forest of gems with a sour expression. It's not too far away that those bodies lie, twisted beneath the forest's grip. The sun has almost set, and in a few minutes we can leave. But I can't talk to him telepathically through the dragon link so we need to talk about this now.

"Why do you think that happened?" I ask.

His green eyes flash, and he runs a worn thumb along his lower lip as he thinks. "You're the most powerful Dragon Blessed on the continent. This forest won't be the only dangerous thing attracted to that. I knew the forest was enchanted but I didn't know it could speak to someone's mind. There are no documented cases of this happening in the history texts, probably because anyone who wakes up after a thousand years spent here has probably lost their mind. It could be that many who wake up here are trapped in the trees."

I blink, horrified. To be trapped within these monstrous trees? A soul should be free after death. How can something so beautiful be so misleading?

He clears his throat. "I'm so sorry, Khali. I shouldn't have—"

"It's not your fault," I quip.

His lips press into a flat line, jaw popping. A lock of chestnut hair brushes his cheek and shines golden in the sunset. The planes of his face are cut almost as sharply as the gems surrounding us. He suddenly looks much older than I remembered. He almost looks like Dean and that makes my heart ache.

"Come on," I say. "Let's get out of here. How much farther do we have?"

He searches the last bits of coral sky flashing through the jeweled canopy. "We're close. Maybe a few hours flight," he says. "But we need to be careful. No doubt the army is out in force searching for us."

We start to walk back to our spot under the tree where we left our packs.

"That's true, but once we cross the border, they won't follow us," I say confidently. We'll be faced with other issues, but at least this one will be over and done with for now. Keeping inside our borders is part of why the Brightcasters' have been so supported in their reign. The kings might have had their spies over the years but the wards keep our enemies from coming in and we don't risk leaving. Save for the merfolk, who tend to keep to themselves, our people are the only ones inhabiting this land.

"They won't risk the army and weaken the wards, not for my sake."

"I wouldn't be so sure about that," Bram laments. "Do you forget how important you are to this kingdom? To my family?"

I bite my lip and look away. I've heard this kind of talk my entire life. I don't need to hear it now, not when my mission is so important. Father is counting on me. And besides, it's not like I won't be back. I still have to take down Silas!

I rub my boot into the dirt and fight the thought, the wish, to never come back.

"We just need to leave," I say. "Now."

He studies me carefully and then continues walking. "After we cross the border, we will be in Fae territory. You know what to expect?"

"I think I do."

"You need to be prepared for anything. The Fae are immortal beings comprised of different races of faeries and elves and the like. They can be killed but their ageless existence has made them extra cunning and equally dangerous, especially the High Fae" He sounds like he's reading from a textbook. He sounds like the Bram I know, not this new one full of adventure.

"But their magic is elemental, like mine, so shouldn't they be similar?"

He twists his mouth, thinking for a while, before speaking. "We don't know the full extent of what they can do. They had their own secretive courts and kings until the Sovereign Occultists conquered them, killing off all the royal lines in one swoop. There are barely any High Fae elves left as far as I know."

I bite my lip. That could be our kingdom next if we're not careful.

"We're heading into unknown territory, occupied by the most ruthless empire ever to rule in Eridas, so we need to be careful. Anything could happen."

His words leave me hollow and I suck in a breath, trying to fill myself back up. Even though I want to take to the sky right now, we need to have this conversation first.

"You're right. I didn't know all the rules to this wicked forest and I won't make that mistake twice. So remind me of what I might need to know."

"You can eat the food and drink the wine," he says, "but since my blood isn't magicked, I can't. And if we come across anyone, we do not want to make enemies, but we absolutely can't make any deals. Their magic is far more binding than ours. If we make a deal and we break it, it could kill us."

We fall silent, letting that truth settle over us.

"They can't tell lies, though," I add, remembering that part. I always thought that would be odd, but also useful for a court such as ours. "That's to our advantage."

"But they can tell half-truths," he says. "They are shifty. Don't trust any of them."

I gulp. "Okay. And you know where the ley line to get to Dean is?"

"I have a pretty good idea," he says, but he doesn't add more and I don't press him. If anyone can find it, it's Bram.

I'm not sure what to expect. Ley lines can't be seen, they can only be felt. Three realms sit on top of each other but operate independently: the magic, the spirit, and the non-magic. The ley lines are energetic lines connecting significant places and sometimes where they cross, the energy is magnified so much that those with elemental magic can move between the realms. It would make sense that when Dean was exiled, my father helped him cross through to the human world where he would be able to live in safety. My father doesn't have dragon magic, so he couldn't cross into the human world alone; Dean would have had to have helped him as well.

There *are* a few advantages to being nonmagical in this world, mainly that magical beings can't sense the nonmagical, nor do magical beings really care to be bothered by those without magic. Maybe that's why King Titus sent him.

The thought of crossing realms gives me pause. I remember Owen's words at dinner the night he was killed, finding the hole in his ideas. "Why would the Occultists need us to cross if they've conquered the Fae? Couldn't they have crossed into the human realm with Fae magic?"

"I've been wondering the same thing," he says. "And I'm afraid I only have a flimsy theory. They must have tried, but they might need all of us. Why else would they be moving from kingdom to kingdom, conquering every magical race?"

The thought hardens my stomach. "We can't get caught," I whisper.

"No," he replies. "We can't."

His theory solidifies why King Titus would be using my nonmagical father to cross into Fae territory instead of one of the Dragon Blessed. My father, the bravest man I know, would have agreed.

I need to draw on his strength now. I need to be like him.

I hold Bram's gaze for another long moment, taking in the intensity of his green eyes until I can't handle another second and look away. We've reached the place where we rested, our packs untouched and waiting for us. I wrap the cloak around my chilled body and drape my pack over my shoulder, Bram's too, then shift into my dragon form. When I shift, the clothes and packs disappear and shift with me, held to me by some unseen force.

Bram isn't shy this time as he climbs onto my back.

I'VE NEVER SEEN THE BORDER before. I've heard the stories, seen artists' depictions, but as we get closer, my heart speeds in anticipation. I didn't expect to be able to *feel it*. Even from here, miles away, the energy buzzes through me and pulls me closer, like gravity. The magic of the wards are the same magic of my four elementals, but I've never heard of this happening to anyone else. I long to ask Bram but I cannot in this form and we can't stop.

Firelight twinkles in the distance. A nearby village. I'm careful to steer clear. Since there are less villages and people this close to the border, I'm able to fly low, but those lights leave me uneasy. With the wards' energy crackling through me, I feel safer down here, more grounded. I want to be as close to my land for as long as possible. I want to turn back. To stop. To keep going. I want everything and nothing and the riot is maddening.

Finally, the border rises up in front of us, an iridescent wall of fog reaching too high to fly over. The warring energies settle into one smooth thought: I cannot pass through.

But I must.

I land us in a field of grass, a dozen paces from the wall. Bram jumps off my back, and I return to my human form.

He must see the fear in my eyes because he takes my hand.

It would be so easy to turn back. I'm safe here. I matter here. I'm going to be the next Queen and even if Silas ends up as my husband, I could live a semi-happy life. My people need me. They need me to bring them more elemental royal heirs; for it's only the elemental magic that keeps these wards strong. Dragon Blessed is not enough on its own. If that magic was lost, the wards would fall and we would be thrust into war. If the Occultists conquered everyone else, what would make us so different?

I swallow my fear and think of my father, lying in his deathbed. I think of Dean, living a new life because of my choices. I think of Bram, who has come so far and risked everything to help me. These thoughts, they urge me forward.

I squeeze Bram's fingers tight. "Let's go."

Together, we walk through the fog and into an uncertain future.

NINETEEN

HAZEL

"I CAN'T BELIEVE YOU'RE DOING this," I mutter to myself. Just yesterday I was chased down an alleyway and giving a statement to the police. And today? Today, I'm skipping anthropology class to go sneak around Dean Ashton's house.

Alone.

Because he knows something about that dragon spirit, the same spirit I saw go after my would-be attacker, the spirit he was desperate to find. There's a connection. I don't believe Dean is the murderer, my instincts tell me not to fear him, but there's more going on than meets the eye and if he won't tell me, I'm going to figure it out myself.

I don't meet Cora and Macy at the dining hall to eat breakfast before class like we've been doing all semester. Instead, as I leave the dorm building, I text Macy a quick excuse and veer in the opposite direction, tugged toward Dean's neighborhood. The gray sweep of clouds and gusty autumn wind add a wintery bite to the air, sharpening my senses.

Nobody seems to notice me in the midst of their morning hustle once I'm walking down the suburban streets. Sleep-rumpled parents are busy ushering bright-eyed children onto overheated school busses. Commuters pull out of garages, strapped into shiny vehicles, already tuned in to their favorite radio stations and podcasts. It doesn't take long to locate Dean's house, but I walk right past the brick cottage and wait much further down the street until the man himself comes through the front door, locking it behind him. He doesn't see me or even look my way as he heads toward class.

A couple of minutes after he's gone, I stroll back to the house, keeping an eye on the neighborhood. The morning rush has come and gone in a mad dash and once again, the street is empty. No cars. No kids. No parents. But it might not last. I need to be quick.

I saunter up his driveway like I'm a regular guest of Dean's and go for the garage. I don't know the code to get inside, but there's a gate along the white vinyl fence that's my target. If there's a padlock, I'm screwed. But sweet mercy, there's nothing but a latch. I slide it up and open the gate just enough to slip into the backyard. This guy must not be too worried about security if he doesn't even lock his gate. I wonder why not? That in and of itself comes with its own suspicions.

It's as well kept back here as it is out front. No surprises there. I hurry past the aging trees, heavy with their dying leaves, my shoes crunching on the yellowing October grass. My lungs inhale steadying breaths, the brisk scent of the morning filling me up. The back porch is covered. None of the back neighbors will be able to see what I'm about to do, thank God.

I try the sliding door first but it's locked, as expected. I go for the adjoining window next and press my face against the large pane of glass, eyeing the modern living room and kitchen inside. I don't see signs of a security system anywhere, no cameras or monitors or anything. Is it really worth it? Breaking and entering is a crime. I could get caught. If I do, what will happen to me? Will Dean press charges? Will I get expelled from school? All my dreams of vet school and a career helping animals heal could be washed away.

Hopefully, Dean was telling the truth when he said he lives alone.

I palm a nearby rock before I can talk myself out of what I'm about to do and throw it squarely at the window. It crashes through, the glass splintering and falling to chaos. The wind is almost enough to drown out the noise. Not quite. I pray nobody heard it but me. Adrenaline storms through my veins. My nerves kick into overdrive.

I can't believe I'm doing this! I am acting like a crazy person right now!

There's no turning back. It's time to find out why Dean knows about the spirit dragon, what his fiery eyes mean, why he was so horrible and territorial when he first met me, and most importantly, why these things have anything to do with me.

I pull my hood over my ponytail and hug my arms in close. The beloved burgundy Gryffindor hoodie is all I have to protect myself as I shimmy my arm through the hole I made, trying to avoid the sharded glass, to unlock the window and pry it open. I swear, if I accidentally cut this hoodie, I'm going to cry.

I look around, taking in the clean lines and spotless decor. If I was hiding something in this house, where would I hide it? Heck, *what* would I even be hiding? I start with the kitchen drawers, tearing through them in a mad dash, but find nothing but perfectly organized cooking utensils. Dean is a clean freak. And he cooks. Who knew? But spatulas and measuring cups definitely aren't what I came here for.

I release a puff of air and go for the stairs. Considering this place isn't massive and the main floor is designed for open living, Dean's bedroom must be upstairs. There's bound to be something in there that will help me make sense of it all. With him in class, I should have a full hour to look, but I don't want to dawdle. The faster I'm out of here, the better.

The stairs are one of the only things left inside the house that have been restored with the original design. They're dark hardwood and narrow, polished and quant. I'm hurrying up them when I notice a tingle at the nape of my neck. Almost like the beginnings of a sunburn. I grip the railing and take another step, brushing it off as nothing and continue climbing.

But then all at once, it grows and heats, spreading around my neck like a burning noose, reaching up and over my head, pouring down my limbs like lava.

I drop to my knees.

All thoughts fall from my mind except for the need to make it stop, but I can't. I'm immobilized. I'm unable to do anything but lie on the stairs and pull at my clothing with fumbling fingers. *I'm burning up.* I'm being seared alive from the inside out.

Suddenly, I can't move anymore.

Somewhere in the recesses of my mind, I hear the screeches of agonized screaming. It's animalistic. And then I realize where those primal sounds are coming from—me. Tears pour down my face, the salt streaming into my mouth. I'm coughing in between my panicked screams. The burning is relentless. I try to climb back down the stairs, but it's all too slow. Nothing is working. I'm not moving.

And none of it makes sense because there's no actual fire. My skin isn't blistering. To my eyes, nothing is happening. And yet, all my other senses are firing and the pain goes on and on. I'm sealed in place, sealed right in the middle of a hell that stretches on for eternity.

My vision blurs and my eyes flutter shut. I'm lost to the agony, ready to surrender to death. That's better than this. Anything is better than this endless torture.

"Hazel!" The voice is far away, a figment of my imagination, a ghost on the wind or the beginnings of a dream.

But then arms are lifting me, dragging me further up the stairs. I keep screaming. I can't stop. I can't think. I'm nothing. Nothing but pain.

A door slams open and metal clicks against metal and the sound of falling water penetrates my mind. My eyes pop open just as I'm being thrown into a cold shower.

Blissfully, mercifully, the heat is washed away. It melts off of me as quickly as it came, and I lie on the shower floor like a newborn baby, grasping at life. I'm traumatized and born again, and reality sinks back into my consciousness.

"Hazel!" The voice shouts again and this time there's no hiding from it, I know it's real—he's real.

I look up at Dean through the pummeling water. The glass shower door is open and he's standing, fully clothed at its entrance, glaring down at me. I'm also fully clothed, drenched from head to toe, but I can't get enough of the water.

I close my eyes again. The cold is pure bliss.

"Oh no, you don't!" He shuts off the water. "What the hell are you doing breaking into my house?"

Well, I guess it's time for me to face this. I blink and peel myself off the tiled floor to stand. All the burning pain from before has gone. I run my hands over my body, my eyes trailing down, looking for proof of what I endured. But there isn't a mark on me. Water drips down my face. My long hair is matted to my head and shoulders. Somewhere in all that, I lost my ponytail. My hoodie and jeans weigh a ton, and my tennis shoes are filled with water.

But I'm alive. It wasn't real. How is that possible? I don't even have a headache.

I'm not even tired. There's literally no trace of what just happened.

"I should call the cops on your ass right now," Dean continues, so fuming mad that his hands are clenched and once again, his eyes are ringed with sparks of dancing fire. "You have some explaining to do."

I fold my arms over my chest and glare right back. "Actually, Dean," my voice cracks, so hoarse from all the screaming. "I think it's *you* who has some explaining to do."

Because what in the world just happened to me?

He rocks back on his feet, his jaw tense, as he holds my gaze. The air between us crackles, neither one of us willing to give in to the other's demands. The tension grows taught until he finally turns on his heel and storms out, slamming the bathroom door behind him.

But he's not getting off that easy. I ignore the wet clothes and the thought that he could be calling the police at this very moment and go after him.

"Dean Ashton," I yell, storming into the hallway. "Don't run away from me. We need to talk, buddy!" I go from room-to-room, bursting from door-to-door, tracking water everywhere, but don't find him straight away, and that bothers me even more. "You've been weird since the day I met you, Dean. Don't even try to deny it. I'm tired of all these unexplainable things happening whenever you're near."

I locate the master bedroom and push my way inside, continuing my tirade. "What is going on? You want my help? Well, it's like I said, you need to help me understand this."

It smells like him in here and I stop, letting water pool onto the hardwood. The bed is perfectly made, the corners of the slate gray bedding tucked in tight. The walls are eggshell white and the furnishings a mix of light and dark grays. There aren't any photographs or really anything personal in here. The rest of the house is the same way, but I figured he'd have something in here that spoke of his past. But it's like walking into a museum for minimalist design.

If it weren't for the faint woodsy scent that is distinctly Dean's, I wouldn't have any way to know this was his bedroom, let alone his home.

"Did you have to drip all over my floor?" He steps from the door on the far end of the room, which I presume leads to the closet or bathroom. "You already owe me a new window."

The sunlight streams in through the opened curtains, lighting him from behind so that his expression is in shadows. I glance down to where I'm leaving a puddle on the dark floor. These floors are old and restored; I'm sure they've been through worse. But hey, he was the one who threw me in the shower and then left before explaining himself.

"Give me a towel"—I shrug—"and I'll clean it up while you explain to me what's going on."

He sighs ruefully, raking a hand through his disheveled hair. He returns back through the door for a second, holding a fluffy white towel and a pile of clothes that he promptly throws onto his bed. Our gazes collide and his is still hard as steel, but something has shifted the tides of our tumultuous relationship. There's a gleam of defeat somewhere in those blackened eyes, a gleam that sends a shiver of triumph through me.

"Hazel, you are so damn annoying."

I smirk and stick out my tongue.

He walks past me. "Get yourself cleaned up so we can discuss this like grown ups." And then he's gone.

TWENTY
KHALI

THE FOG DOESN'T WANT ME to pass through to the other side. Its magic yanks at my emotions, demanding my elements to keep me in Drakenon. I'm powerless to refuse. All I can see is a thick cloud of gray. The iridescent shine must have only coated the outside because in here, everything is void of color. My body shakes and Bram's hand tightens around mine.

"I don't think I can do this," I say between gritted teeth. I am speaking to Bram. I am speaking to nothing. I am nothing if I leave Drakenon.

"Yes, you can," he urges, his tone doubtless. "Don't you dare let go of me, Khali."

But letting go? It's all that matters.

The need to rip away from him and run back is so strong that I can hardly think of anything else. Bram must sense what is about to happen because his arms wrap around my torso and he lifts me off the ground completely. I shriek. I want to fight him, want to hurt him for this. And I could. I am powerful. He wouldn't stand a chance against me. I could burn him to cinders or drown him with his own saliva. I could call upon the winds to suffocate him or raise up the earth to bury him alive. Well, truthfully, I don't know if I can do these from actual experience, but I can feel the power within me, just waiting to be unleashed.

He rushes us through the last of the fog, bringing us out the other side. My malice evaporates into gratitude. Thank the Gods for Bram. If it wasn't for his lack of magic, if it wasn't for his quick wit, I never would've made it out of Drakenon.

"Thank you," I whisper softly. He's holding me so close that my lips brush against his warm neck as I speak. We both still and then he sets me down carefully. I take his hand again and squeeze. "No matter what happens," I say, "we stick together from here on out."

"Deal." He squeezes back. He looks different to me, somehow. And the same. And my stomach does a little squeeze.

Then we turn and stare, wide-eyed, into a new kind of danger.

The elementals connecting within me feel the same as our kingdom, but the horizon is much different. Where we have fields of grass that roll into mountains, this area is flat and covered in a thick, mossy forest that is both unfamiliar and unnerving. It's darker here at night than in our home. And while there doesn't seem to be anybody around, that doesn't stop the sensation that we're being watched from washing over me like a July breeze. Something about the warm temperature feels off.

"Why is it so hot here?" I ask. I remove my cape and stuff it into my pack. "It's late enough in the year that it shouldn't feel like mid summer." Or maybe we came much further south than I realized.

"The magic is different," Bram answers. "The seasons take on a life of their own in Fae territory."

I'm not quite sure what that means but I think it's something to do with the way the Fae Courts operated before the Occultists conquered. A flying insect of glowing white hovers near my left ear, buzzing louder than the bugs back home. I swat it away. The air is thick with water and it settles on me like a second skin. Owen would have loved that. The shadows are long and unmoving underneath a sky animated with winking stars.

"There is no moon tonight." I peer up and sigh, not sure if that's a good or a bad thing.

"Come on," Bram says, pointing toward an indent in the forest. "There's a road."

"Aren't we going to fly?" Fear sparks in my voice. The thought of walking into that unknown forest makes my skin crawl. The trees are different here than in Drakenon. More alive, somehow.

"There are no dragons here," he says. "Who knows who, or what, will see you if you shift. We can't risk it."

"But won't they know me by my eyes?"

"Not until morning," he says.

I swallow and nod, stepping through the tangled grass toward the direction of the road. Bram pulls up his hood as well. We need to blend in and travel unnoticed for as long as we can—he's right about walking.

"How far do we have to get to the ley line?" I ask as we hike side by side through the waist-high grass, my palms brushing along the wispy tips. I breathe in the sweet, leafy scent, and try to relax.

"To travel between the realms, one would need to find where the lines intersect in both our world and the human one. I only know of a few places that could be. The land takes on energy in significant places."

"Like at churches?" I ask, thinking of the centuries old chapels back home and the reverence they hold inside their walls.

"Could be," he says, "but it would have to be a place where people have been going to worship for centuries if it was a church."

I bite my lip. The Occultists are also religious but I've never heard that of the Fae. They worship the earth, the elements, the seasons and stars. I don't think they have actual churches like we do.

We're at the edge of the forest now; the thick line of trees feels like a threshold into a new life. I don't want to go in, my senses rioting at the very idea of it. We stop and look at each other, and I sense the same worry on him, even in the darkness. Either way, neither of us wants to continue this conversation in there which is probably for the best.

"I have been looking into this ever since Dean left," he admits. "When he was banished, I lost my mind and demanded my parents intervene."

"I remember you two were close." My eyes were always on beautiful Dean, barely noticing little Bram in the background, but he *was* there.

He nods. "You always had Owen, Silas did his own thing, but Dean and I, we got each other. I don't know how to explain it."

I hold my tongue, not wanting to say the wrong thing.

"My mother promised he was going to be okay, swore that they had a plan for him. She wouldn't give me details, but she said he was going somewhere that nobody from the other courts could get to him. Where else could that be but in the human realm?"

The unfairness of it hits me harder than ever, that something as small as a kiss with me could lead to a man being banished from his kingdom. The dragon clans agreed long ago that it was the best way to keep things fair for princes before one would be chosen as king. Do the Brightcasters really have so many enemies within their own court that they couldn't change things for Dean?

"I'm sorry," I whisper. "I'm sorry you lost your brothers because of me." I'm not just talking about Dean. Owen's face floats to my memory and my heart hurts.

He reaches out and squeezes my hand for a moment. "You didn't choose to be born with all that magic, just as I didn't choose to be born without any."

I think on what he said about Dean being taken to the human realm, where he'd be safer. It *was* strange when Dean left. His parents followed the law without question, but they didn't mourn him either. Not as I expected. They acted like nothing just ripped their family apart by the seams. They acted like Dean's future wasn't their concern anymore, loyal to Drakenon only. Maybe this is why.

"It makes sense," I agree.

He stops, dropping his pack and rummaging in it. He pulls out a map, worn with use and marked up by what is, most likely, his own hand. Of course, he would have a map, because who doesn't carry a map with them when running away? Oh wait, that would be me. He looks at it for just a few seconds before rolling it back up and returning it to its place in his bag.

"We're on the right track."

"Where are we going?"

"There's a place not far from here where a human battle occurred during a civil war. It was many years ago in their realm, but it was brutal. Brothers killed brothers." His voice grows hoarse, and I can't help but wonder if he's thinking of Silas and Owen. "They said the land was stained red with rivers of blood. Anyway, that kind of energy doesn't just fade away. It gets absorbed, especially if what happened is what was recorded. The humans have since created monuments to the battle. That alone will hold the energy over the years."

"And the Fae?" I ask.

"That area just so happens to be the same place the Fae has had their Summer Solstice rituals for centuries before they were taken over by the Occultists."

A place like that with so much energy in one spot could create a fold in the ley line and a place where an elemental like Dean could slip through. The realms are layered on top of each other. We all share the same planet even though we walk different planes.

"How far?"

"A few days by foot," he says. "Faster if we can get horses but I'm not sure I trust Fae animals."

I study the mossy black forest. The road is narrow and surrounded on all sides by trees with monstrous qualities in the darkness. "What do we do once we get there?"

He doesn't say anything at first, so I turn and study him just as I studied our surroundings. He swallows hard. "That's the thing I don't have an answer for," he says reluctantly, "but if your father could travel through the realms to visit Dean, I'm certain you'll be able to do the same."

I frown. "But what about you?"

"I'm not sure if I'll be able to come or not," he says. He sounds so brave, so certain that this is the right thing to do, but how can he face all of this without worry for his well being? He came with me because he wanted to see his brother, but what if Bram can't get out of the Fae realm? What happens when we have to go back home? What if he has to go without me, won't they send him into exile as well? Could the Brightcaster princes dwindle down to only one? Bram coming with me suddenly doesn't make sense. The questions build upon another like bricks.

"Why are you here?" I press. "Seriously, why are you taking this risk?"

He cocks his head, his eyes unreadable in the shadowy darkness. "I thought it was rather obvious."

My chest warms. I let out a breath and look away, putting the questions away for another time. I rummage around in my pack, find my waterskin, and take a quick drink and then pass it to Bram. I also find the last of my food and hand that over to him as well.

"What's all this for?"

"I can get more food and water," I say, "You take the rest of mine. You need it more than I do."

His smile is barely there. I can't tell if he's grateful or embarrassed or something else entirely, but it doesn't matter. We're in this together and if he's going to look out for me, I'm going to do the same for him. Hopefully there's enough magic in my veins for the both of us to survive this place and travel to the human realm.

"Come on," I say, leading the way. It's time to put the bordering wall of thick fog behind us and head into the canopy of trees.

Save for the occasional glowing insect with their buzzing wings and our boots trudging across the rocky dirt road, the first few hours are met with silence. I find that worrisome, but what can I do but stay alert? The smells are more vibrant here, more earthy and alive. The magic feels stronger, too. In Drakenon the magic is mostly reserved for the Dragon Blessed. Sure, we have the merfolk and the occasional enchanted relic or forest, but the elemental powers stay inside the bloodlines of a select few families. The only randomness of our magic is which baby girl, with all four elementals, will be born to the newest generation.

But here? Here it's different. It's as if the land itself, the trees, the thin blades of grass and the pebbles embedded into the earth each have their own kind of magic. Is this where the Fae creatures get their power? Perhaps it's not passed down through bloodlines but rather offered up from the land itself. I wonder if Bram can sense it too but I don't dare ask.

The morning sun begins to rise, turning the sky a blue that will soon transform to pink. It lights up the forest, transforming it from menacing to enchanting. But I know not to trust what I see. Looks can be deceiving.

"Hello, good sir." A woman's cheerful voice echoes up ahead and we freeze.

She appears from between two trees, slipping through their opening as fluid as water running down a brook. Dressed in nothing but a sheer white dress, her nakedness is on display. I try not to allow a horrified reaction to show on my face because this is truly shocking. Are all the Fae like this? Her long raven hair trails to her feet in luminescent waves. Her mouth and cheeks are perfectly rosy, her smile seductive, her golden eyes latched onto Bram.

"Can you help me?" she asks sweetly. "I seem to have gotten lost."

Bram's eyes are shifty, his cheeks flaming. "Um…" He mutters a few incoherent words.

"I'm sorry," I offer, stepping in front of him, "but we are in a hurry." I can sense the magic about her. And the menace.

The woman ignores me, never looking my way. But is she a woman? Something about her doesn't feel human. She's certainly not like us and she doesn't have the pointed ears of higher Fae. So who is she? *What* is she? My muscles pinch with tension.

Outstretching a dainty hand toward Bram, she speaks again, "Please, young man. I need your help. If you'll just escort me home then I'll be safe."

"I thought you said you were lost," I deadpan.

Bram's eyes are on her now, both unfocused and focused. A glossy shine has fallen over the green of his irises, the black pupils narrow with intent on this woman.

"Bram?" I whisper. "Are you okay?"

He lifts his own hand toward hers.

"Don't touch her," I growl, pulling him back. The woman hisses at me, giving me an enraged glare. Her pretty eyes turn deep purple and inky lines of scarlet bulge in her face.

Something shoots through the air with a snap and slams into her shoulder, knocking her down. She howls, rips the arrow with blue feathers from her skin, and scampers back into the trees. As she turns away, I flinch. Her backside is nothing but hollow blackness, a void.

"What was that thing?" I wonder aloud as I look around for the source of the arrow.

A man drops silently from the canopy of trees, landing like a cat a few feet from where I block Bram.

"That was a huldra," the man says, looping toward us on silent feet. He raises a sly eyebrow, the color of spun gold. "Cousin to the siren. She and her sisters lure men to their deaths."

I gulp, terrified of what could have happened to Bram. I know of the siren, though I've yet to encounter one, but not the huldra.

The man skulks closer, his movements as feline as some of his features. I study this new threat and widen my stance. He is tall and thin, with a beautiful face of high-cut cheekbones and cat-like blue eyes. Even his pupils are long slits. Dressed in finely stitched clothing, his golden hair tied back, his pointy ears framing his perfect face. A large bow with a quiver of thin arrows hangs over his shoulder.

Bram places a gentle hand on my arm and eases me back to him, the glamour having lifted from his eyes. "I know of the huldra," he says slowly, "but that one caught me off guard."

"You can't look them directly in the eyes," the man says, his own eyes sparkling with mischief. "I'm Terek." He extends his hand to me. "But don't worry, Princess, I'm not going to bite you." He winks. "Unless, of course, biting is your thing."

I freeze. *Princess*. He must know me by my eyes. Of course he does. The Drakenon tradition has lasted ages.

Bram and I exchange a guarded look, unsure of how to proceed. He is an elf, meaning he's one of the High Fae still alive. Someone was bound to recognize me. But the elves used to rule this territory and if anyone can help us navigate it, it's them. Or they could just as easily be our demise. Before the Occultists, the elves were our greatest enemies. This one not only knows my identity, but he intervened and saved Bram's life.

What does he want?

"I'm Prince Bram of Drakenon," Bram says, surprising me by shrugging off his earlier hostility and shaking Terek's hand. "And you're correct in assuming this is our Princess."

I quickly run through the list of rules Bram and I talked about before walking through the border fog. We aren't to make any deals but we also aren't to make any enemies with the Higher Fae, and we certainly can't be caught by the Sovereign Occultists. I eye Terek. I can't trust him, but I decide to try, to see where this could lead us.

He may be powerful, but so am I.

I pull off my hood, shaking out my mane of dark hair. Then I bring the most dazzling smile to my lips and take his hand. His nails are long and pointed, like a cat's. I don't let it bother me. "Hello, Terek," I say, all confidence. "It's a pleasure to meet you." I glance around the forest, assessing its beauty like it's a part of him, like I'm a guest in his home. "I think, perhaps, you and I have something in common."

"And what is that, Princess?"

I hold his gaze with mine. "We share a common enemy."

TWENTY-ONE

HAZEL

I TAKE MY SWEET TIME getting ready because it will piss Dean off—which is an added bonus for me—but also because I'm nervous. Deep down, I know that whatever is about to happen could change the course of my life. But this is what I wanted. I came here, came to him. I broke in. I did this. And I am not going to chicken out now.

So I pad into his ensuite bathroom and sneak a look into the closet at the back. As far as I can tell, there's nothing out of the ordinary. Just a chest of drawers and two rows of hanging clothes. His closet is boring compared to mine, which Cora has lovingly named The Land of Misfit Toys. I snoop in the drawers as well, but it's just underwear and pajamas and workout gear. Since when did I become the creeper who goes through someone's underwear drawer? But more importantly, what kind of person doesn't have a single nostalgic item hidden in said drawer? Or in his closet, for that matter? Heck, I brought my favorite stuffed animal to college with me—a floppy rabbit that's seen better days—a blanket Mom made with pictures of us printed on the fabric, and a stack of ratty old t-shirts that mean the world to me because of the memories attached to them. I'll never part with my oversized middle school band t-shirt, thank you very much.

As far as I can tell, Dean has nothing cool like that. Not one single thing.

I grumble and go back into the bathroom to undress, toweling myself off, and slip into the dry clothes he offered. The black sweatpants and cotton v-neck are super soft and way too big for me but they are clean and comfy and melt away my defenses. They smell like the same lavender fabric softener my mom is obsessed with, which makes me chuckle. I roll my eyes because of course, Dean uses this stuff. I fish my phone from my wet pants pocket, figuring I'm going to need to stick it in a bag of rice and pray for mercy. But miraculously, the phone is still alive. I shoot Mom a quick "I love you" text and then pull up the message waiting for me. It's from Cora.

You're sick, huh? This illness wouldn't happen to have anything to do with why Dean took off ten minutes into class like a bat out of hell?

Maybe, I type back.

What's going on with you two? Her reply is almost instant. **Are you hooking up and trying to keep it a secret? Cuz you can't keep that shit from me!!!**

I snort and text her again. **Not hooking up with Dean or anyone. But I am with him right now, actually. If something bad happens to me, you know who to blame ;)**

She replies right away. **Don't even joke about that…**

Well… I'm not really joking. BUT I'm fine.

You better be! What the heck?

Don't worry. I'll see you later. XOXO

You have to tell me EVERYTHING.

I drop the phone into the pocket of the sweatpants and run the towel over to the floor, mopping up the mess. I head out into the bedroom and then the hallway, cleaning up the trail of water that leads into the other bathroom where Dean threw me into the freaking shower! That experience was definitely not a *steamy* one to remember, dang it.

I hang the towel on the bathroom door and hurry downstairs, ready to face whatever is next with a mask of confidence.

I find Dean in the family room. He's already swept up the glass and is busy taping up a flap of cardboard over the broken window. The wind outside isn't helping matters. It keeps blowing the board into his face and while part of me feels tremendous guilt, the other part wants to point and laugh. Maybe take a video. Post it to YouTube. Start a channel. Strike it rich. *Anything is possible, right Mom?*

But I'm going to be a grown up about this. So I hurry over and help him finish the job, neither of us saying a word to the other.

When it's finished, he steps back and turns on me with an annoyed groan. His eyes have settled back to their unreadable charcoal gray and he runs a hand along the stubble on his chin.

"You really want to know why that happened?" He nods to the stairs, his mouth pressing into a grimace.

"I have to know." But my palms are sweating and my hair is cold against my cheeks and suddenly, I'm not so sure of anything except that I probably shouldn't have ever come here today. A smarter girl would have left it alone.

"First of all, you're not as stealthy as you think you are," Dean says, raising an eyebrow. "I have a silent alarm in here. *And* I have three hidden cameras set to monitor the outside of the house. I knew you were here the minute you walked into my backyard and one of them alerted me on my phone."

Blood rushes to my cheeks. Well, that's not embarrassing or anything…

"And what about the burning?" I ask. "How is that possible? Because nothing was really happening but my brain thought it was. I felt it. It was…" my voice catches, "horrible."

"That was my ward doing its job."

"Ward?" I'm stuck on that word, like a *real* muggle would be. Holy crap! "So what are you, like some kind of warlock? Are you a wizard, Harry?" I make my best attempt at the Hagrid voice but inside I'm reeling.

"Who's Harry?" he asks, a worry line appearing between his eyebrows.

I blink at him. Has he been living under a rock? The poor, poor deprived man. But I can't get into Harry Potter with him now. This whole wizard thing wasn't what I was expecting. I don't even want to say what I was expecting considering it had to do with dragons, shifters, trainers or something even more impossible. I guess the wizard thing makes sense if really I stop and think about it logically. Magic is a better explanation for what happened to me on those stairs than temporary insanity, which, let's be honest, that isn't out of the realm of possibility. I do see dead people. Not quite magic. But close.

"I'm not a warlock," he says, with a slight sneer. "But I can cast a fire ward with my elemental, given what I am."

I bite my lip. I have to ask the question. I have to know. "What are you?"

"Are you sure you can handle this? You're positive you want to know?" His eyes are glued on mine and there's a vulnerability there I've never seen before with Dean. My heart skips and I nod.

"I can show you right here, considering you've just about figured it out on your own," he says. "But you have to swear never to tell another soul. Not your friends, not your family, not even Harmony. And you have to swear to help me because I need your help. I need you to do that mediumship reading for me."

Again, I nod. This is what I wanted all along.

He points to a chair tucked into the far end of the living room. "You'd better take a seat for this. Keep in mind, it's not going to be as impressive as if I were at home."

Ummm… okay?

I stride over to the chair on shaky legs and plop down. My hands are shaking, too. I squeeze them together in my lap and take a deep breath. Whatever he is, I'll deal with it.

Dean stands in the middle of the room for a long minute, staring at me, as if considering his decision. The black sleeves of his shirt are rolled up to his elbows, his tanned skin popping against the fabric. His dark eyes glow with intensity and his perfectly disheveled hair falls around his cheekbones. *It's hot. I have to admit.* Finally, he exhales and rolls his broad shoulders back.

And then, he transforms.

One second, he's Dean, dressed in that standard attire of dark washed jeans and a snug cotton top, smirking in that exasperating way of his. The next second, there's a glimmer of light and shadow, almost like what happens right before a spirit appears. And then, standing before me is something no longer a man, no longer a human. And it's no spirit, either.

It's a dragon.

A flesh and blood, living and breathing, real-life dragon.

It's so large that it has to crouch so it doesn't hit the ceiling. It looks so much like the spirit dragon that I almost believe that's what I'm seeing. Except that creature is of another realm and this one is most definitely part of this world. It's black and scaled like the other, but where that spirit dragon has blue eyes, this one's are orange and red, swirling like fire.

"Dean?" I whisper.

The dragon nods its head.

His head. *Dean's head!*

Somehow, I'm not afraid. And I know that's crazy. I should be terrified, not believe my eyes. I should run for my life, hide away, never come back here. But instead, I stand and walk forward, my hand outstretched. His wings are wrapped in on himself and his claws look like they could kill me with one swipe, but I continue until I'm close enough to touch. As I'm about to press my finger to the scaly skin, he shifts again.

And it's Dean standing before me, dressed exactly as before.

I pull my hand back.

"So now you know," he says, narrowing his eyes. "And like I said, you can't tell another soul. If you do, you'll be putting innocent people in danger. And I'll have to silence you."

I gulp. "Is that a threat?"

He smirks but I know he's serious. "You bet."

"I won't tell. Besides, nobody would believe me if I did."

"Don't be so sure of that, Hazel. There's a lot to this world you don't understand."

I let out a breath, trying to open my mind to what he's saying. "What does any of this have to do with me? Why did you tell me to get off your territory?"

"I'm sorry about that." He moves to the couch and I sit on the other end. "When I first met you, I felt that you were different, too. I thought you were here to spy on me."

"Why would I do that?"

"It's complicated."

"Try me."

"Let's just say, this place isn't exactly my natural habitat. Where I come from, is much, much different. But I *have* to be here. I can't go home. So I've made myself comfortable and I don't want to leave. If the wrong people find me here, I will have to leave."

"You thought I could be one of the wrong people."

"I did," he replies. "Now I realize you know very little about your gifts or lineage. You could be dangerous to me. But for now, it's probably the other way around."

"Gee—thanks," I scoff, but inside my curiosity is piqued. And also, I'm a little bit freaked out. I don't think I'm ready to ask him about my *lineage* because this is too much to process right now. And then I blurt out the next part before I can think like a logical person, "Did you have something to do with those missing girls?"

"Of course not!" His entire body tenses. "I'm a dragon shifter. Not a monster."

"Glad to hear they're not the same thing." I raise my hands in surrender.

"Not at all," he retorts.

"Because I saw that dragon spirit again yesterday after almost being attacked."

"I know."

"Yeah. I know you know. I remember. So why did you go after it?"

Dean's body is a coiled spring, tension tight and ready to explode. "The dragon must be here for me. He has to be one of my kind who's passed on and I need to know what he wants with me, especially after he sent you a vision of Khali in trouble. It's why I wanted to do that reading. I can't see him like you can. I can't talk to him. Only you can do that."

We fall into silence for a moment.

"Hazel, if you see him again, you must call me."

"I've only seen the dragon twice," I mutter with a shrug.

"Not the dragon. The dragon won't hurt you," he presses. "I'm talking about the man who tried to attack you. Do you feel safe? You can't go around by yourself anymore. He might be targeting you."

My heart rate picks up as the PTSD washes over me. And to think, it could happen again. It could end much worse. But if Dean's right, *why* is he targeting me? There has to be a reason.

"I know," I grumble, disheartened. "You don't need to remind me."

"Apparently, I do." He reaches out and takes my hand in his. Warmth floods my body. "I need you safe."

Dean is a dragon shifter. He's not even human. But he's the least of my worries, it seems. Because even he doesn't know who tried to attack me and I believe him when he says he had nothing to do with the missing women. If Dean isn't the one out to get me, if he's not the enemy, then who is?

TWENTY-TWO
KHALI

"WHEREVER YOU TWO ARE GOING," Terek says with a conspiratorial grin, "I'm coming along for the ride." He flits a hand about the air nonchalantly but, with those nails filed into clawlike points, I have to force myself not to jump back. "It's been so *boring* around here lately," he whines. "I'm in dire need for an adventure."

"But we just met," Bram interjects. "Why should we bring you along for anything?"

"I saved your life," Terek's reply is smooth but full of metal. "That means you owe me a debt."

Silence stretches between the three of us because like it or not, Terek makes a good point. The Fae are notorious for this kind of trickery, and we can't afford to argue ourselves into a worse position. And if this man's mind is anything to match the feline features of his appearance, it is going to be hard to best him. I'll play along with his game—for now.

"We don't need a tagalong," Bram continues, his voice hardening into accusation.

"It's fine," I interject and elbow Bram in the ribcage. "But we're not telling you where we're going or why. You're just going to have to trust *us*."

Terek grins, and a long, thin tail wraps around his body, dancing between us. I try not to stare, not wanting to appear rude, even though it's one of the strangest things I've ever seen. "Oh, darling," he says, "I don't trust anybody but myself, and even *that* is questionable at times."

Bram grumbles but there's nothing more to be said about the matter. I trudge forward and the three of us set off, an odd trio if ever there was one. Terek seems to be a mix between cat, man, and elf, and he's a ball of energy, constantly moving, graceful but wild. He loops through the trees, and a few times hisses at threats unseen to us. Bram and I try not to stare but it's hard not to watch him, especially with the strange hissing. I knew the Fae often took on animalistic qualities, but this is beyond what I'd ever imagined. It's a little terrifying. Was he always like this? Or did something happen to him? Terek might tell me if I asked. And Bram might already know. But I don't ask.

After what feels like hours of traversing along the quiet road, Terek finally speaks, "So how far is this mystery location?"

I clear my throat. "A couple of days walk." Maybe that will put him off.

"Wonderful," he says, happily. "Just so long as we aren't going to Highburne. It's such a dreadful place these days. I'd rather swallow thorns than step foot there."

Curiosity gets the better of me. "Why is that?" Of course, I think I already know. Highburne is where the Occultists have set up residence. They're known for their brutality. I can't imagine it's a joyful place for any of the Fae.

Terek pulls a bow from his quiver and twirls it around his wrist like a baton. "Oh, you already know why Highburne can burn, Dragon Princess. Common enemy and all that."

"Have you been there?"

He stops abruptly, causing Bram and me to stop, too. The forest is quiet, but not the kind of quiet of predators nearby. Then again, what would I know of it? I widen my stance and pull my elements to the surface where they sizzle just under my fingertips, ready to fight. Should I need to shift as well, my dragon is ready.

The forest grows deathly silent, holding its breath.

Terek is quick. He strings the arrow into the bow, points up into the canopy of green, and shoots. Seconds later, a flutter of movement is followed by the arrow fumbling back to the earth with a dull thud. A large bird, much like a hawk, lies bloodied and dead at our feet, the arrow centered through its heart. My nerves slowly uncoil. This is not what I was expecting.

"Lunch." Terek practically purrs, picking it up. I almost expect him to bite into the raw meat by the way he's looking at the fowl, as if it's the tastiest treat he's ever seen. But luckily, he doesn't. "Shall we stop soon?" he asks, eyeing me and Bram with utter delight. "The Princess can conjure up a fire for us and I can cook this beauty to perfection in no time." He licks his lips and I'm stuck on the fact that he knows I can conjure fire. He must know about my abilities.

Bram and I must appear to be shocked speechless because Terek grins savagely.

"Come," he says, veering off to the side of the tree-lined dirt road. "I know of an excellent spot for a picnic. We ought to get off the road for a while anyway. We're nearing a village and the merchants will be on the road soon. Best not let anybody else see you two." He winks. "Not everyone would be as kind as myself."

"That remains to be seen," Bram grumbles but if Terek hears, he doesn't react. I elbow Bram yet again and he widens his eyes at me, his mouth set in a determined line. He doesn't trust Terek. He knows too much about the Fae to trust any of them, I suppose. And I get it, I do, but I also want to survive this place. So far, Terek has proved useful.

The cat-like elf leads us down a path so thin and overgrown, it must be the kind of trail made by deer hooves and not meant for larger human feet. Unease washes over me. This time, it's Bram's turn to elbow me in the ribcage. I shrug and keep going because I don't know what else to do other than to follow Terek farther into the forest.

"Seriously, what have you gotten us into?" Bram whispers from where he walks close behind. His breath is feathery warm on my neck. His accusations feel like barbs. "What's the plan, here?"

"I don't know," I bite back, annoyed. "But will you relax for two seconds, please?"

"I'm trying to keep us alive."

"Yeah, so am I."

Bram huffs but doesn't say another word but I feel his glare hot on my back.

Terek leads us deeper and deeper into the forest until we come upon a clearing. We walk into its center and he motions around us with the widest grin. "You're welcome," he says.

Above us, the sun hangs high in a swath of azure sky. Below us, the grass lies soft as crushed green velvet. All around the edges of the clearing are the same mossy trees, but also, tall flowers of every color and shape. I breathe in long and deep, letting the floral aroma carry me away. For the first time in weeks, my body melts with relaxation.

"It's so beautiful." I'm breathless. Enchanted. And definitely cautious, but that feeling seems to be fading on the breeze.

"What is this place?" Bram asks. "And those flowers," he points a curious finger, "what are they called? I think I've seen them depicted before in one of my books." He seems to be shuffling through the encyclopedia of information in his head and for once, unable to locate the answer. I don't know if that's a bad thing but it makes me giggle.

"What are you laughing about?" Bram's voice is teasing in return.

Bram catches my hand and pulls me to him. I laugh again. My palm spreads open against the flat plane of his chest. He's so much more manly than I realized. He's grown up.

"I can feel your heartbeat," I say softly. But I don't find the speed at which it's pounding to be funny. Neither of us are laughing anymore.

We're standing so close now, closer than *ever*. The floral aroma of jasmine and lilac, rose and juniper, and so many others I can't name, marry into the scent of the wonderfully warm earthy scent of Bram. I gulp, a shudder running through my body. When did he get so tall? When did he fill out like his brothers? How did I not see this before?

He shifts closer, his eyes leveled on my face. It takes courage, but I find it within me to look up and meet his gaze. They are ablaze with a galaxy of sparks, layered with depth. They brighten in intensity as I stare, matching the green surrounding us. I can't seem to focus on anything but those two bewitching eyes.

His hands circle my waist, drawing me in so we're not just standing close anymore, but our bodies are flushed together. Then he runs his smooth hands, ever so slowly, up my arms to cradle my face. The feeling is complete bliss, sending shockwaves over my skin. His thumb brushes a loose strand of hair from my cheek, lingering for much too long. My eyes flash to his cherry lips, so full and inviting.

What would it feel like to kiss those lips?

I don't have to wait to find out. He presses them to mine with that perfect intensity that is unique only to Bram. His is the kind of focus that takes souls, and he takes mine without caution. I surrender, closing my eyes and opening my mouth and my every emotion to him. I never knew a kiss could be like this. I never knew *anything* could be like this. My heart burns in my chest, my every sense tuned into Bram, to the feel of his muscles under my hands, his scent in my nose, his taste in my mouth. If I am lost in him, then I don't want to be found.

Terek's insidious laugh breaks us apart. "Wow, that was quite the response!"

Bram shuffles back from me, his cheeks splotchy and eyes shiny with the impact of what just happened. I exhale, lifting my hand to my swollen lips.

"What the hell was that?" Bram growls, turning on Terek.

"Don't blame me." Terek holds his hands up in surrender but his expression drips in satisfaction. "Blame them!" He points to the tall flowers. A breeze rushes through the clearing, sending a few of them swaying and more of their otherworldly floral aroma into the air.

"What do you mean?" I ask, trying to make sense of it. My heart is a wild beast in my chest, and even though I know better, all I want is to crawl back into Bram's arms and surrender.

Terek's grin is wicked. "This isn't Drakenon, Princess. How am I to know that you and your little prince would react so strongly to the flowers? They *are* magic, you know. Everything in this land is here for a reason."

I don't have a reply to that. I don't even know what I *could* say. Was the kiss real? Was it the result of the flowers and nothing else? I want so badly to know but I can't go there, can't think it. Because either way, that kiss with Bram can *never* be repeated.

"Nobody can know about this," Bram says in a rush. "It could be dangerous to us both and anyway, it wasn't our fault. We didn't mean it."

I hold my breath. He's right, surely. But I can't speak.

Terek smiles at us like we're his best friends. I take in his pink lips, slightly pointed teeth, and the thick golden hair framing his face. Somehow, I highly doubt that we're anything close to friends, especially after he brought us into this meadow. He's playing a game of cat and mouse. At first I thought he had a reason for toying with us, but now I wonder if he wasn't lying before, and if the elf actually is just bored.

Actually, I know he wasn't lying. Elves can't lie.

"Consider this already forgotten, please?" I ask through my most charming smile. I've had seventeen years to perfect my fake smile, but I wonder how many years Terek has had to perfect his. He could be centuries old, for all I know.

He holds up the bloody dead fowl and waggles his blond eyebrows. "Who's hungry?" When we don't answer, he clarifies with a teasing laugh. "Hungry for *food*, I mean."

I want to sink into a puddle of embarrassment right then and there. Once again, Terek laughs at our expense. He never agrees to keep our secret. Of course he doesn't. He can't. *That* probably *would* be a lie, afterall.

"Welcome to Fae territory, where we trade in lust and traffic in secrets."

TWENTY-THREE
HAZEL

"I SHOWED YOU MINE," DEAN says. "Now it's your turn."

My cheeks flush and I clear my throat. "I'm assuming you want me to do that reading for you now?"

He raises an eyebrow. "That would be correct."

"Right now?"

"It's only fair."

I have so many questions for him but I know those will have to wait, so I start how I always start, by inviting only the spirits of the light into our space. As I speak, embarrassment twists in my gut. I feel so weird doing this in front of Dean but then again, if he thinks I'm weird, then he'd be one to talk. He's a dragon shifter, for crying out loud! That, my friends, is the opposite of normal. I've never met someone who's stranger than me, and as much as I hate to admit it, I like this new revelation. I like him. And I shouldn't. I should be focusing on my feelings for Landon. He's the kind of person that will keep me sane. He's what I should want. He ticks all the right boxes… I think. At least, I'm pretty sure he ticks off the "normal" boxes.

As Dean and I wait for the spirits to reveal themselves, I run my index finger along my obsidian necklace. I know I need to remove it. I always keep it on, even when I'm showering or working out. The only times I remove it is when I'm doing readings at The Flowering Chakra, so I can allow the spirits to fully come in. For some reason, I'm too afraid to do that now. The little circular stones lay warm against my skin, a protection.

Dean's secret scares me, but it also draws me to him. Maybe I should take off the necklace.

"Anything?" he asks, his eyebrows drawing together in concentration. This is important to him.

I bite my lip, knowing I'm about to disappoint him. I mumble, "No, there's nothing coming through yet."

My heart is racing. *Take off the necklace!*

I'm so used to him getting angry at me that I expect anger to be his immediate reaction. But it's not. Frustration and sadness filter across his face, even as he holds his composure. Then his eyes dart to where I'm playing with the obsidian necklace and an idea sparks.

"Maybe you should take that off," he says, nodding toward the necklace like he can read my thoughts. "Those are protection stones, right?"

"Right." I sit back, revealing my own vulnerability. "Truth is, I'm afraid if I take it off, the unwanted spirits will come. You're different than other clients. What will happen? And anyway, both times the dragon spirit came through, I had this on. I don't think the stones protect against that spirit, just other ones."

He lets out a breath, laying it all out there. "Please, Hazel. I need your help. I'm the only dragon shifter here. Something happened and I had to leave my home. I can never go back."

There's a vulnerability in his dark eyes I haven't seen before. I want to help, I do. But to take off my necklace?

"Who's Khali?" I ask. Her name has been rolling around in my brain since the moment he spoke it. To say it aloud almost feels like I'm admitting to the crush I've developed for the guy, because I'm illogically jealous of a girl I've never met.

"She was my friend and the reason I had to leave." He frowns and rakes a hand through his hair. "I've been worried about her ever since that dragon sent you her image. I need to know more because I can't go back. Was the dragon her or someone else? That night I left you with my car, I was trying to get more information, but I couldn't get anything. I have no idea what's going on back home and it's killing me."

Is he being purposely vague about this? Probably. Is he in love with this Khali girl? It sounds like it. I don't blame him. I saw her, she's drop-dead gorgeous. They match in so many ways. They would be perfect for each other. And that thought makes my heart pound even more.

"Okay," I say and before I can second guess myself, I unclasp the necklace. It drops into my hands, and I ignore the icy fear creeping up my spine as I set it on the nearby coffee table.

And then all at once, I'm surrounded. The spirits come from all directions, but it's one that sends a terrified gasp to my lips.

Katherine.

She's still dripping wet. She's still gagging on the water, her hair stuck to her face, her eyes vacant and bloodshot. She's still trying to speak to me, even though I know it won't work. She seems to realize it too, because suddenly, she rushes at me and grabs hold of my arms.

I know it's not real, know she can't actually touch me or hurt me, but I scream anyway. And then everything goes black. I fall back against the couch, my eyes fluttering shut, as the images wash over me, one after the other, so fast they consume me until I am her and she is me and I can't get away.

IT'S THE FIRST DAY OF *classes. There's not much to it, no real assignments yet, so when I see the flyer for the party at the fraternity house, I decide to go. Maybe there will be some sorority girls there and I can get a jump on recruitment week. I dress up in a black silk blouse, tight ripped jeans, and black heels. I don't want to go overboard but I still want to look good, so this seems like the perfect compromise. I don't know any girls in my dorm yet, but I should be fine to go alone. Greek row isn't far from here. And I'm sure I'll make friends when I get there. I wasn't all too good at making friends as a kid but I have improved and these days, it's easy for me to strike up conversations with strangers.*

And that's exactly what happens.

When I arrive at the party, I make polite small talk with the girls and flirt with the guys. It's really fun! There's this one guy in particular that catches my eye the moment I see him. Honest to God, it's like time stops when our eyes meet. And he walks right to me and introduces himself. He's the fraternity president but he seems so serious and smart, too. I like that about him. Plus, he's really cute. We dance and hang out for a while, but he never makes a move which makes me like him even more. He's respectful and that's what I look for in a guy.

It gets late and soon the party empties. I'm getting tired and have a 7 a.m. yoga class planned. It will only be a ten minute walk back to the dorms, five if I hurry. My new friend says he wants to walk me home but I know if he does, he'll kiss me. I can tell just by looking at him. And I want to keep him waiting. Not too long, of course. But I don't want to give him the wrong impression about me. So I leave alone, sticking to the lighted paths as I walk back. A few students mill about, but I mostly ignore them.

I'm still thinking about him, a huge smile plastered across my face, when it happens. It's so fast. Footsteps rush and someone grabs me from behind. They push me to the concrete and my face hits it first. Pain explodes along my jaw. A hand quickly locks over my mouth and another hand wraps around my waist. I try to scream, but I can't get much sound out. I can taste blood on my tongue. And the skin of this stranger's hand.

Terror pours through my every cell as I'm lifted and blindfolded. I'm kicking and arching and desperate to get away, but whoever this is, he's so much bigger than me. And I can't see a thing. For the briefest of seconds, the pressing hand lets go of my mouth. I scream. But something is stuffed into my mouth and then duct tape is pressed on top of that. Tears stream down my face. My heart pounds out of my chest.

This can't be happening. This can't be real!

I'm carried away. Thrown into the trunk of a car. Just as he's shutting me in, I catch sight of his eyes. They're black—dead black—like his pupils have blown all the way to the edges, covering any trace of white. I can't understand it. I've never seen anything like that before. It's evil. Pure evil.

The rest? It's forgotten. A stain on my memory. When I wake up, I don't have a body. I'm a spirit, floating over a lake, confused, angry, and panicked. And there's nothing I can do about it. I stick around for a while, until I finally get the nerve to roam the nearby town where I was supposed to spend the best years of my life. I go back to the lake and I watch as they pull my body from it days later.

And still, there's nothing I can do. I'm stuck in a loop of the terror. It's all I can think about. The images consume me. I don't know what I'm supposed to do next. I don't know where to go. I don't know who murdered me or why or what those black eyes meant.

"HAZEL!" HANDS ARE WRAPPING SOMETHING around my neck and a voice is yelling my name over and over again. I cough and wake up. My face is wet. I wipe away tears with shaking hands, hands that I can't control. I don't think. I just crawl into Dean's lap and sob.

"What happened, Hazel? What did you see?" He runs a warm hand over my hair. My mind is blank. Everything is numb. I don't even want to think about it. I can't go back there. I'm so cold, like I'd been the one stuck at the bottom of the lake. Dean's inner fire is the only thing I can cling to for warmth.

"Did you see Khali again? Is she okay?"

Reality settles over me, and I crawl off him to sit back on my end of the couch. Dean is so eager, and I hate to disappoint him, but I am never taking the necklace off again around him. He must have put it back on when I was in the middle of that horrid experience, because it's once again secured around my neck. I grip at it like it's my lifeline to sanity. Which at this point, it basically is. When I took it off at The Flowering Chakra, I never got any sort of reaction like this.

"I'm sorry," I say between ragged breaths. "I didn't see anything of Khali or dragons."

"Then what did you see?" he asks, confused.

I don't want to say it. My eyes well up again, and the memory is so alive in my mind that I can't shut it off, but I force the words out anyway, "I saw that freshman girl who died the first week of school. No, I didn't just see her, I was her. I felt it all. She went to a party and walked home alone. While she was walking, she was attacked from behind. The man"—the tears are heavy now—"he bound and gagged her and then put her in his car. She never saw or heard him. And then she was dead, her body thrown into that horrible lake."

All color has washed from Dean's face as he stares at me. "You said you were chased in broad daylight yesterday? Do you think it could have been the same guy?"

I want to say no. But I can't help but wonder if this is part of why Katherine keeps coming to me. "It could be. This guy had black eyes and I couldn't see my attacker's eyes."

"What do you mean?"

"I mean that his pupils were completely blown, like he was on drugs or something. But it was more than that. The black covered all whites of his eyes, too. That's not possible, right? Could it have something to do with magic? Or your dragons?"

"I'm taking you home," Dean says. "You've had enough stress for one day. We can worry about my stuff later. Besides, you have a class this afternoon to get to and so do I. Midterms are coming up next week so I just want you to worry about staying safe and I'll worry about finding this guy." There's something more he's not adding and I think it has to do with the blacked-out eyes and my questions. I want to scream at him, to demand he tell me what he knows. But I don't because I'm afraid of what I might hear.

My voice sounds hollow and far away when I say thanks and stand. I doubt I'll be going to any more classes today.

"Wait, don't you want me to try again? Try to find out who that dragon is?"

He shakes his head. "Not right now. I can't do that to you again." He points to my necklace. "Keep that thing on."

Dean drives me to my dorm. It's not far, but I'm still shaky and he insists. He doesn't tell me anything more about himself. Just before I get out of the car, I asked if there were more dragon shifters like him. I've been wanting to ask him about it since the second he shifted for me.

"Yes. But they are not here in this human realm. Like I said, I'm the only one."

Human realm? I'm not sure what that means exactly, but just the thought of other realms makes me shiver.

I want to see him shift again, want to know more about him and the shifters. I want to know what he thinks about the black eyes. I want to know everything, but it feels like as soon as I get one question answered, a dozen more pop up. I realize that I'm basically living in my very own young adult novel at this point, and I need to find out what's going to happen next. But it's true that midterms are coming up and Dean and I both need to study. Not to mention, I need to get those horrible images scrubbed from my mind. Katherine wants me to help her, but I don't know how I possibly can. I don't know who attacked her. I don't know how to send her to the next life. I don't know anything.

I STAND IN MY DORM room, staring at myself in the mirror, failing to drudge up the motivation needed to get my butt to my afternoon class, when a knock sounds on my door.

"Open up, Hazel." Cora's voice filters in from the other side of the wood. "I know you're in there. I can see your shadow."

"I'm worried about you," Macy adds in a softer voice.

"And I'm wanting the dirt on what happened with Dean." Cora laughs.

I pad to the door and open it. I don't know what I'll say to them. They'd never understand if I told them everything. Besides, there's so much about me that I've kept from them. I've been so fearful that if I told them the truth about what I can do, they wouldn't want to be friends with me anymore. That's always what I experienced back home in Ohio. They know I work at The Flowering Chakra, but they don't know I do anything besides stock shelves and ring up customers. If I tell them the truth, will they still love me?

The second they see me, they must know something is wrong, because they rush in and hug me on both sides. I sink into them, trying not to cry.

"Oh, hon, it's okay," Cora mumbles into my hair. Her vanilla scent wraps around me.

"What happened?" Macy asks gently.

I step away and close the door, ushering them to sit on my bed. My room is a tiny box but at least it's private. The bathroom and showers are shared and down the hallway. All that's in here is a tiny closet and a chest of drawers, a twin bed, and a desk. But I've decorated what I can in my favorite colors, forest green and lilac. And being in the familiar environment settles me enough to tell them the truth.

I leave out Dean's secret, of course, but I tell them all about my gift and about Katherine. I explain what happened today, that I sneaked into Dean's place but didn't find anything. That he caught me on his security camera and confronted me. But that after we talked, I trust him and I don't think he's responsible for the missing girls. I tell them about how I took off my obsidian necklace and got flooded with images, and how Katherine came to me and showed me what happened to her.

By the end, their jaws are practically on the floor.

But they don't mock me or doubt me. They don't leave or laugh. They believe me. And that alone makes me love them even more than I already do. I've always wanted friends like this. Now that they're mine, I'm terrified I'll lose them. So I take a deep breath and tell them all about almost being attacked yesterday. Macy starts crying. Cora cusses and stomps her foot.

They get it. They understand why the fear is so real for me.

I beg them not to go to any more frat parties, not to go *anywhere* alone, and to be extra careful. When they agree, it's my turn to start crying. Again! It feels good not to have to keep this to myself anymore, to have more people to share my burdens with. But somehow, even with the cathartic crying and the confessions, I still don't feel any better. Because somehow, I know this is far from over.

"Hazel, we have something to tell you," Cora says. She looks as if she's about to cry.

"What is it?" I ask. When they hesitate, I fold my arms and raise my eyebrows. "Just tell me. I can take it."

Cora and Macy exchange a worried look but then Cora finishes her thought anyway, "Another one of the freshman girls went missing yesterday. They already found her body. She was murdered."

The world crashes in around me and my breath is knocked out of me. This is number five in two years, but these deaths are occurring at a much faster rate and whoever is killing people isn't afraid to keep acting. I pull my friends into a tight hug, the three of us a tangle of limbs and shaky fear. How much longer until it's one of us?

TWENTY-FOUR
KHALI

"TRAVELING WITH YOU IS PROVING to be an education at our expense." Bram glares at Terek.

"That's an interesting way to put it," Terek retorts coolly, "because it seems to me that you rather enjoyed kissing your pretty, pretty Princess."

"Enough," I cut in sharply. "We don't have time for this. Let's eat and get back on our way."

I expect them to argue, but Bram looks away and Terek busies himself with defeathering the bird. Bronzy feathers go flying, and I try not to gag at the sight of it. I occupy myself with starting a small campfire for Terek to cook on, all the while avoiding Bram's loaded gaze. I don't have to be in my dragon form to access my power so I draw on the spark of life within me, pulling it forward and creating a slow burning flame in the palm of my hand.

"That's not something you see every day," Terek remarks gleefully.

I shrug and light the kindling and wood, and ten minutes later, lunch is ready.

Terek waves the cooked bird around like a trophy. "You're welcome!"

"And I can trust it's safe to eat that?" I raise an eyebrow.

"This is absolutely safe," Terek purrs. "I wouldn't lie to you."

Ha! More like he *can't* lie to me.

I lay out my cape again, sitting on the black velvet. The poor cape is starting to look tattered. The juices run over my fingers and it smells like heaven compared to what I've been eating the last few days. I take a bite and groan, it's so good. Terek also found some purple berries to round off the meal so I plop a couple of those in my mouth. They are sweet as sugar and stain my fingers and lips. I don't bother with the canteen since I gave it to Bram. All I have to do to get water is draw it out from the petals of nearby flowers with my water elemental. Little watery balls float to me, landing gently on my tongue.

"Such a show off," Terek teases, but from the way his eyes stay fastened on me, I can tell he's fiercely intrigued. Maybe it's foolish to let him see my magic in action, but Bram needs that canteen of water more than I do. Bram, of course, doesn't eat the elf's food. He sticks to the provisions we brought from home.

We finish and clean up, and I try not to look at the flowers or breathe them in too deeply. My heart still feels like it's a feather floating on the breeze. We set off again and this time Terek leads us along a forest path that he promises will veer us around the village so we won't have any run-ins there. It adds an extra hour onto our journey, but according to Bram, we're going in the right direction, so neither of us offers any complaints.

All the while, the feel of Bram's lips lingers on mine, an imprint, a tattoo that won't go away, devouring my every thought. His scent lingers with me, too, even though he's not walking close enough for that to be why it follows me. We don't look at each other, don't make eye contact. It's too strange, everything between us has changed and I don't know what to do about that. Questions whirl around in my brain, a cyclone of them that are better left unanswered. Bram can't be caught kissing me *ever again*. And besides, it's not like that. I don't have romantic feelings towards him and he isn't interested, either.

Terek's odd feline tendencies continue as we travel, and I can't help but wonder if they have something to do with the Occultists. Fae shouldn't act like this. They might be born with some animalistic features, but their behavior has always been reported as being just as human as the dragon shifters. As I'm considering how to ask Terek about it, he crouches and growls, pulling out his bow.

The fire burns under my palms. In the space of a breath, I'm ready to fight.

"There, there, little kitty cat," a silvery voice whispers from behind the thick trees. "I'm not here to hurt you, as much as I would enjoy it."

Terek hisses, primed to release his arrow.

"You are a hard one to track." The man attached to the voice steps out from hiding. "But I would expect nothing less."

I immediately recognize him as a Sovereign Occultist from the heavy crimson robe with black embroidered symbols that hangs off his thin frame. His face is ageless and white as porcelain. And his eyes, they glow red as freshly spilled blood. His appearance blends right in with everything I've heard of the powerful cult of warlocks that have terrorized Eridas. I've never seen one in person and never wanted to. Needle-like terror prickles over my body. Their magic is unlike mine, but just as powerful if not more so. Where I draw from the elements of nature, the occultists deal in black magic, ancient oaths, and blood sacrifice.

"And I see you brought some friends." He sounds pleased. Pale, long fingers remove his hood, revealing his sickly smile. He could be my age, or middle aged, or he could be a thousand years old, there's no way to tell. The warlock's features drip in agelessness and eternal damnation. His red eyes travel from me, to Bram, and back again.

"Leave them out of this," Terek snarls as he loosens the arrow. It shoots straight at the man, swift as a heartbeat, but with only a flick of the Occultist's eyes, the arrow turns at a ninety degree angle and embeds into the trunk of a tree.

"Uh, uh, uh," the man chastises. "Do that again, Catboy, and I will turn your little arrows back on you."

"Your quarrel is with Terek, not with us," Bram speaks up, his voice strong but cordial. "Please, let my friend and I pass and we will be on our way."

Terek shoots Bram a hurt glare, and once again, the Occultist smiles that sickly sweet grin. A long row of perfectly white, square teeth glint in the afternoon sun. He looks so human, almost normal. A chill runs through my bones. Something isn't right about him. I can sense an evil darkness radiating from him and I don't know what to do. I call on my magic, bringing it under my surface, should I need to use it.

"I would be remiss if I didn't introduce myself to a Prince of Drakenon," the devilish man says, drawing the words out like a sharp dagger across a soft throat. His eyes land on me. "And to Khali, the future queen of Drakenon."

We fall into silence, the pressure building.

It was one thing to be recognized by a Fae, but by an Occultist? This won't end well.

"Then again," he says, gliding forward, his height seeming to grow. "I have met Khali once before." Those bloodied eyes lock me in. "Not that you would remember." My mind is whirling, trying to grasp what this could mean. "You were an infant." A cruel shadow passes over his eyes. "And I spelled you to sleep through it. Tell me, Princess, have you noticed anything strange happening to your magic recently?"

I suck in a breath, memories of my magic failing me coming to mind. Is it possible I've met this horrid creature before? And if so, what does it have to do with my magic? I let the possibility of it settle in. A strange sense of déjà vu and a keen awareness that I can't quite place takes over. Deep in my bones, I know he speaks the truth.

"I must say," the man laughs, "this is quite a fortuitous meeting. I've been tracking young Terek here for weeks. I was rather annoyed with him for escaping me the first time but now I can't say that I'm anything but delighted with how things have turned out."

Terek pounces.

"Run," he yells, as his claws rake across the Occultist's face, who immediately throws him off with a roar.

Bram and I explode into an all-out sprint. My dragon ignites and I welcome her forward, shifting in an instant. Bram jumps onto my back, his grip tight. Good thing, too, because I have to fly straight up through the canopy of branches.

"Head south," he calls into my ear against the rush of wind, "as fast as you can. Look for the part of the forest where there are many lakes. That's where we're going."

My wings lift us higher and higher. The road cuts into the thick forest below, though it is peppered by the occasional village or estate, and most of the land is a picture of wild green. Adrenaline runs through my body, and my dragon gains speed. I have to get us out of here. As far as I know, the Occultist can't fly, but he also can't be far behind, not with his level of magic. If we're caught, we'll never make it to the human realm, let alone back to Drakenon.

A wall of dominant energy slams into me with such force that the air is knocked from my lungs. Bram's hold on my back disappears. I whip around, horrified as his body pinwheels toward death. We're high enough that there's no way he can survive a fall like this, his body would explode on impact. I race after him, pushing every muscle in my body to the max. But it's not fast enough.

The trees grow closer. There's no time left. I can't lose him, too.

I draw on my elementals, bringing a giant gust of wind up underneath Bram. It wraps around him, slowing him enough to break the fall. Relief is quick. I fly toward him but another wall of invisible energy blocks my path. I slam against it with a thud and fall. A screaming pain pummels through my right wing. I tumble into the trees, branches attacking, while desperately holding onto my dragon form. I'm stronger this way, my scales creating a thick hide of armor.

As soon as I land, I pick myself back up and search for Bram, pulling on my wind elemental. The sky darkens. My storm.

Bram! I call out through the dragon link, but it proves fruitless. He can't hear me. He never will in this form. I'm desperate to find him but he's no longer in the area where he landed.

Thunder claps echo through the air. Rain starts to fall in needling pelts. I welcome it, urging my elements on. I can see clearly through it, can control it. The Occultist won't have the same luxury. I breathe in deep through my nostrils, trying to catch Bram's scent. But I made a critical mistake by calling the storm in too quickly and the water has washed away all smells.

I rip through the trees, charging back to where I left Terek and the Occultist. Somehow, I'm sure that warlock has Bram. Fire burns hot in my veins. Smoke rises from my nostrils, mixing with the mist from the rain. Where are they?

I no longer care about drawing attention to myself, no longer care about this forest or what threats lay within it or beyond. All I can think of is Bram. He risked everything by coming with me on this journey. I can't let him down. I can't be responsible for another Brightcaster's death.

I make it back to the road, the rain pounding harder, turning the dirt into slippery mud. A cry sounds from further down and I charge toward it.

A flash of red magic pulses and I scream. The Occultist is standing next to Bram but Bram can't move. He's been put under a spell. Even though nothing binds him, it's as if invisible ropes tie him up. His eyes bulge with the effort to break free.

I want to call out to him, but I can't in this form, and I don't dare change back into my more vulnerable human body. I growl, readying myself to send a plume of fire at the man, but he beats me to it. He pulls Bram to him, using him as a human shield.

"Come with me willingly," the Occultist says, "or come with me by force."

"Don't trust him!" Bram yells. The Occultist sneers and employs more of his invisible force to squeeze Bram, who cries out in pain. But Bram grits his teeth and continues, "Go! Go, like I told you."

"Come with me, Dragon Princess," the Occultist continues, "Or pay the price."

The elements are demanding to be let free, to destroy this man, but I know that's impossible with Bram in his clutches.

"Go!" Bram cries again. "Save your father. Come for me later."

I'm immobile between the two choices, but the elements continue to build. The rain pelts down harder, the wind blows into a wild hurricane, fire rises around me. The earth shakes.

"Have it your way," the Occultist snaps, howling overtop the noise but it's so loud, I can barely hear a thing. "You'll be coming to me soon enough anyway, whether or not I had your useless prince. Tick, tock, Princess, you're almost eighteen."

Confusion and fear whirl within. A tree cracks and plummets to the road. Lightning flashes through the sky, a clawed reckoning. The Occultist lifts his hand and twists it in an intricate pattern. A glittering symbol hangs in the air for the briefest of moments before vanishing to smoke. Seconds later, both he and Bram disappear.

TWENTY-FIVE
HAZEL

THE WEEKEND COMES FAST AND thank God for that. Each minute is filled with studying for midterms, shoving junk food into my face, and avoiding the gloomy weather. Before I know it, Sunday morning sweeps in and my focus turns to my date with Landon tonight. When he texted to confirm, I replied with a happy "yes" but I couldn't help but notice a little pang of regret. My thoughts have been consumed with Dean. Everything about him is dangerous and wrong, but I can't help myself from wanting more. And being with him, it makes me feel alive in a way I've never experienced. And now Landon doesn't compare. Another thing I can't help. Nor can he.

It's not his fault that he's normal. It's not my fault I'm not.

"Are you sure you want to go on this date?" Cora asks.

"How are you so good at reading me?" I laugh.

We're walking back to the dorm after having a giant breakfast at the dining hall. The bagel and cream cheese I ate at the end of our meal sits like a rock in my stomach and I'm already regretting my life choices. Why don't I love grapefruit and plain Greek yogurt like Macy? It would be so great to crave only healthy food and know when to stop. But in my defense, I secretly think the woman is lying when she says she *loves* all the healthy foods she eats. Who loves kale? Nobody. It's all lies.

"You've been a distracted mess ever since your confession to us," Cora continues, "and I'm sorry, but I don't think your most recent distraction has anything to do with Landon."

"Agreed!" Macy pipes in.

I sigh. They're right. The wind is chillier than normal and it suddenly rushes at us, wrapping us in an icy cold grip. Macy squeals and we take off, running for the dorm. After a couple of hellish minutes, we tumble inside. I'm breathing way too heavy for a seventeen year old. I probably should start working out more often. And eat kale.

"Landon will be good for you." Macy grins. Her hair is piled on top of her head in the kind of messy bun that looks sexy. When I try to do that, I look like a toddler. "Don't stress. Just have fun tonight. I'll help you get ready."

Flashbacks to the white minidress and high heels on that first Friday pop up and I grimace. "Umm, I don't know if I want to go and if I do decide to go, I'm not sure I'll need help getting ready."

"You're really going to cancel on Landon?"

I twist my lips as I think it through. We do have chemistry and he's a fun guy, for my first ever date, Landon's a good choice. "I guess not," I sigh. "He's harmless. I just don't know if I'm interested in him anymore."

"Because of Dean?"

I nod, equally hating and loving how the man has gotten under my skin.

"Well, if anything, the date will just make Dean jealous," Macy says happily. "I'll make sure Deany finds out about it tomorrow." She winks. "No worries, Girl, I got your back."

Cora laughs. "That's actually not a bad idea. Guys like what they can't have."

"So come on, then." Macy cocks her head to the side and studies me. "You have the prettiest coloring. Your hair is amazing but you always wear it up in a ponytail. If you let me curl it, you'll look like Goldilocks."

I gape at her, horrified. "And this is a good thing?"

She laughs again. "*And* I'll do your makeup so it enhances your natural beauty but isn't too much."

We make it to our doors and I continue to think on her offer. My door is the first. Macy's is across from mine, and Cora's is at the end of the hall next to the bathroom. Macy is so earnest and her big blue eyes are so hopeful that I finally relent. "Okay, you can do my hair. But don't get here before five. I need to study between nap sessions."

"You mean nap between study sessions," Cora interjects.

"Yup!" I laugh and unlock my door, slipping inside.

Macy giggles and Cora yells, "If she gets to do your hair and makeup, I get to pick out your clothes!"

I don't answer. I close the door and lean against it with an amused groan. What have I gotten myself into? I should have learned the first time I agreed to be their human puppet.

Once I'm in my room, I crash on my bed. I haven't been sleeping well at night lately and the naps are starting to catch up with me. But at this point, there's nothing I can do about it. If I'm going to be Goldilocks, I need my beauty rest. Wait, that's Sleeping Beauty. Well, same difference.

My phone rings, and I pull it from my pocket to see my mom's smiling face light up the screen. I answer, lying back on my downy pillows.

"Hey, Mom. What's up?"

"Hi, Sweetie." Her voice is clear through the line. "I just wanted to check on you since the incident. How are you doing? Are you safe? Are you sure you don't want to come home?"

I sigh. I knew this would happen. I told the police that I didn't want to call her, but they insisted because I'm still a minor. Mom lost her mind when she found out and has been worrying nonstop since, calling and texting day and night. She's even offered to bring me home and work out an independent study with the school so I can leave before the semester ends. It's only a matter of time before she asks me to transfer to a different school.

"I'm fine," I assure her. "Seriously. It was a wrong place, wrong time, sorta thing and I promise I'm being more careful now."

My mind races back to breaking into Dean's place and guilt prickles hot. I'm such a liar. But I am not lying when I say I am going to be more careful now.

"You know how I feel about it, Hazel. I'm your mom. Of course, I'm worried."

"I know, but can we talk about something else. Please? I'm doing the best I can."

"Okay—"

"What's new with you?"

The line goes quiet for a moment and then her tone changes to its normal cadence. "Nothing new here. What about you? How is your weekend going? Are you feeling ready for your midterms next week?"

I sigh and roll over. "Not ready yet, but I will be. My first one isn't until Wednesday. We get two days of a reading period so there's no classes tomorrow or Tuesday. Good thing, because I need it."

"Well, that's nice. You'll be able to get a lot of work done."

"Yup."

"And you're sure you're liking this college?"

My smile is real and *that* feels *so freaking amazing*. "I actually really like it here. My job pays well and is actually pretty fun. My boss is helpful, as you already know. My classes are super interesting. I absolutely love my new friends." And Dean is here…

Really, Hazel? Stop thinking about Dean! Landon. Think about Landon. Dean isn't right for you. He's a dragon shifter for crying out loud. Besides, he's obviously in love with that Khali girl. And Landon actually asked you out on a date. Did Dean ask you out? No. No, he did not.

Mom's been saying something but I'm so caught in my own thoughts. Oops. "Sorry, Mom. Could you repeat that?"

Her voice is patient. She's used to me getting distracted. Until recently, it was the spirits that caused it. "I was just wondering if there are any boys you're interested in. Have you met anyone?"

I burst out laughing. What is it with everyone reading my mind lately! "I dunno. Maybe. I do have a date tonight, so I'll call you in the morning and let you know if it was a bust."

"Well, that's great. Have a good time and don't put up with anything less than you deserve, Hazel. You're such a special girl." Her voice is back to being all concerned and motherly, and for a second, I wonder what it would be like to have a dad. How would he react to me going on a date? My heart squeezes because I'll never know and it's best not to think about it. That's how I've always coped with being fatherless in the past. But ever since Dean mentioned me not knowing my lineage, it's been on my mind.

I have to ask.

"Mom, I know we haven't talked about this very much, but was my father disrespectful to you? Is that why you never let him come around?"

The line goes silent and, for a moment, I wonder if the call dropped. But then she lets out a slow breath. "You haven't asked about your father in years." Her voice is even. "Are you sure you want to start now?"

"I'm ready to hear the truth. What happened? It's okay, Mom," I say, "I can take it."

Because I'm pretty sure the reason we haven't talked about it much is because whoever he was, he wanted my mom, but he *didn't* want me. I think she's been protecting me by staying quiet about him. And I love her for it. But what if my father is the reason I'm the way I am? What if learning my history could help me now that I've embraced this mediumship stuff?

She lets out another long breath. "The truth is I didn't know much about your father. He was a one-night stand. I didn't even know his real name."

"What!" I sit up so fast blood rushes from my brain and starts blossoming along the sides of my vision. Shock gives way to laughter. "Oh my gosh, Mom! I never knew you had it in you."

"It was a one-time thing and it never happened again!" Her defensive tone is playful.

"I have to admit, this wasn't what I was expecting." And I am a little disappointed. Not in her, because everyone makes mistakes and I love my mom. Besides, if it weren't for that encounter, I wouldn't be here. So who am I to judge?

No, I'm disappointed because if she doesn't know his name, then it's official. I'll never meet my father. Part of me always wondered if maybe I would. I even assumed it would happen eventually. That one day he would show up and I would have the chance to get to know him, or at the very least, to tell him off for being a deadbeat.

"Can you tell me about him?" I ask gently. "What do you remember?"

Her voice softens, and I can hear the smile on her lips, "He was gorgeous. Tall and broad and really something to look at. You get your stunning blonde hair from him, though your hazel eyes are all mine. He was this mystery I wanted to solve. He had this tortured soul and once I saw him, I couldn't look away."

Well, damn. "Where did you meet?"

She clicks her tongue. "I met him at a bar, actually." She sounds embarrassed but not ashamed, which is good. It means I can laugh at her without feeling like a total brat. And I do! "You know me, Hazel. I'm always trying to heal every broken person I meet. It's who I am."

"No kidding." I'm still laughing, but silently this time.

"And this guy had something about him that was just so sad, but also magnetic. I struck up a conversation with him because I had to, it was like I was being pulled to him by some unseen force."

Okay, that's weird. My mind races and I want to ask Dean if magic could have been a factor that night.

"It wasn't like me at all, and I don't know how to explain it," she continues. "But I had to meet him and see what was behind his sad eyes. We had a few drinks. He came back to my apartment. We were both a little drunk. I was a brand new nurse back then, you know. I didn't have much but he didn't care. He was kind to me. One thing led to another…"

"Okay, yeah, I get it. You don't need to go into details."

"Well, the next morning, I woke up and he was gone. No note. Nothing. I never saw him again."

I lie back down on the bed and stare at the white ceiling. "That's kind of depressing, Mom."

"It was," she agrees. The smile in her voice is gone, and my heart hurts for her. "I barely knew him but I wanted to know more. I really did. He said his name was Jack but I could tell he wasn't being honest about that so I introduced myself as Jill." She laughs. "I was sad to see him go, but you know what? It brought me you. So I could never regret it."

"Aww, Mommy!"

She laughs. "I'm being serious! Hazel, you're the best thing that's ever happened to me. I love you so much. And I miss you. You're so far away. I worry…"

"I miss you, too."

An hour later, after talking about everything and nothing, we finally end the call. I'm no longer tired so I get back to studying. But I'm distracted again. Lost in the revelation of Mom's one-night stand and if there was more going on there than she realized, by the looming date tonight, and still, by the thoughts of Dean and what he is and what it could mean for me.

I skip lunch, opting to snack on the junk food I have in my room and end up crashing into a sugar coma by mid afternoon. I'm pulled from my nap when Cora and Macy come knocking.

"It's time to get ready for your date, Goldilocks!"

I'm basically their Barbie doll over the next two hours. Cora styles me in a white knit sweater that's *the* softest thing ever. It's like butter on my skin and I never want to take it off. When I tell her I'll fight her for it, she rolls her eyes and rummages through my chest of drawers. She pairs the light gray top with my black skinny jeans. Finally, she makes me wear her suede ankle boots. The heels are only a couple inches high and the zippers on the side stabilize my ankles.

"These are the type of heels I can do." I grin and strut around the small dorm room, feeling like a million bucks. Something about the comfortable heels give me an extra boost of confidence.

Macy comes at me with a lipstick wand. "This stuff will stay in place all night." She winks. "Which is perfect for when he kisses you."

I stop, my stomach tight. "You think he's going to kiss me?"

Cora waggles her eyebrows. "Oh girl, you two have been flirting for weeks. I know he's going to kiss you."

Okay. I'll just deal with it when it comes. Maybe I'll want him to kiss me and it will be magical. Maybe I'll turn and run away screaming into the night. Guess we'll find out! What nobody here knows is that I've never kissed anyone before. It's a secret I keep to myself. But in my defense, nobody has wanted to kiss me! It's not like I had a choice. I've had many crushes over the years and would have happily kissed them all.

Macy slides the sticky burgundy wand across my lips. I press them together to smooth it out and then let the lipstick dry. She messes with a few of the already perfect curls she's slaved over, stopping for a second to touch my obsidian necklace. They know all about it now, so even if it doesn't look good with this outfit, neither would dare to remove it or make a negative comment.

Cora rifles through my closet and pulls out my red peacoat. "Wear this one," she says. "Dresses the look up a bit. Makes you stand out. Not that you don't already stand out, because you totally do. You're a babe."

I blush and slide into the coat, hug and thank them both, then tuck my keys and phone into my pocket. Ready or not, it's time for my first ever date. It only took until I was a freshman in college to get asked out, dang it! If only it were a date with a certain someone…

As I walk down the dorm hallway toward the stairs to the parking lot, I decide to give Landon a chance. I *really* liked him earlier in the week when I agreed to go, and I can get back to that feeling if it's the right thing. He's a great guy. He's cute and he makes me laugh. With everything going on lately, I need someone who can make me laugh.

It's settled. If he tries to kiss me, I'll kiss him back. I'm positive that one kiss from him will have me forgetting I ever even met Dean Ashton.

Ha! Yeah, like that's possible.

TWENTY-SIX

KHALI

I DON'T FLY SOUTH. I need answers, and if anyone has answers, it's that damned Fae elf.

Back in my human form, I stalk down the road like a confident predator, no longer caring who, *or what*, has seen me. I'm certain my magicked storm was witnessed from miles away. Drawing on my elements as I did would have certainly scared off anyone, or anything, that wanted a piece of me. At least, that's the silly lie I tell myself. I know it's foolish to stay, but I'm desperate to get my friend back. I need *him* to get us into the human realm so we can find Dean and ask him about my father's hex.

It doesn't take long to find the nearby village Terek spoke of. If he was lurking around this area when he found Bram and I, and was so adamant we went around it, then chances are he knows somebody living here. Maybe whoever that is, can help me find him, and from there, maybe I can help Bram, because I can't leave him with that horrid Occultist. Who knows what that creature would do to him. Maybe I can rescue Bram before going for Dean, or more likely, relay some kind of message back to Drakenon. Either way, I have to do something.

I don't know what I expected of the Fae village, but I thank the Gods it appears to be elfin and relatively normal. Elves, I can handle. It's the other forest creatures, the nymphs and huldras and such that I don't want to deal with right now. I don't know a lot about them, but if they're anything like the terrible merfolk that populate the lake near Stonehearth's Castle, I don't want the opportunity to find out.

The village is designed much like a typical village back in Drakenon. Most of the homes are meager but liveable, comprised of heavy stone and thatched roofs. Others are built of solid brick and mortar, and a few of the largest aren't ordinary homes but lovely, sprawling estates, laid out with whitewashed walls, dark wooden roofs, and massive lawns with abundant greenery.

I walk right through the center of town, my senses open to anything that might assist me. This place smells of summer evening sunshine and newly budding florals, of yeasty bread rising and sweet tea melting. I search for anyone who might have answers, but the second anyone here spots me, they scatter away. Much like Terek with his feline tendencies, all the elves are animalistic in their features and movements. A pinkish woman, who resembles a tall bird, loops into a doorway and slams the door shut. A child with a crop of yellow hair and ram's horns scampers around a corner. He's on all fours, tufts of fur peeking out from under worn clothes. I frown, wondering again what kind of spell the Occultists used on these people?

Movement from a nearby window catches my eye and I stop. A woman blinks from behind a thin pane of glass. Her eyes are the largest I've ever seen, open saucers of soft brown. I head in her direction, hoping she'll talk to me. Her home is one of the larger ones and well kept, with a bounteous flower garden out front. Before I can knock on her front door, she opens it.

"Come in," she whispers. "Quickly, please."

I hold my breath as I step over the threshold. She appears to be quite young, perhaps no older than myself, but I know better than to assume her age. Elves are immortal. They can be killed, of course, but otherwise, they don't age once they reach maturity. This one is tall and willow thin with skin of beautiful smooth caramel. Little white furred patches perfectly frame her angular face and accent her large, doey eyes. Trademark elven ears poke through long white-blonde curls. She's gorgeous, the fusion of a deer and an elf woman, and from the way she keeps her distance from me, just as skittish. But it seems she's willing to talk, so I smile brightly.

"Thank you," I say.

"Come." Her voice is hasty. "We don't have much time."

I follow her into the parlor with walls of polished river rock. The worn ornate rugs and threadbare furniture are perfectly arranged to feel as welcoming as the woman's startling eyes. This is the kind of place that used to have a staff, but now, its halls feel void of what was once bustling with life. It's as if she's the only one left and she's trying to keep up with appearances in case everyone comes back one day.

"I'm Khali," I say, reaching out a hand. She eyes it wearily and doesn't shake it, but motions for me to have a seat on an emerald green lounger instead. "I'm looking for an elf named Terek. Do you know him?"

She pauses, and then slowly sits down, still not offering a word.

"Please," I continue, urgency rising up in my voice, "my friend is in trouble and I think Terek might know how to help me find him."

"Terek needs to take care of himself right now," the woman snaps.

Worry floods my system. Worry, and anger. That Occultist was tracking Terek. He led the warlock right to us. I have a right to seek him out!

"What's your name?" I ask sweetly, trying to keep the anger inside.

"Does that matter?" Her expression is grim. "I could die just for talking to you, let alone bringing you into my home, when I should be turning you into the Occultists as they'd wish. Many of my kind have died for much less than opening their door to an outsider. Like I said, let's make this quick, then please, leave here and never come back."

An overwhelming hurt consumes me. I never asked for any of this. If she'd just give me a chance to explain, she'd know that. "I'm not dangerous. I won't hurt you. I'm looking for allies."

"But you are dangerous! You don't understand," she continues in a rush. "It's not safe for us if you're here. You'll lead unwanted visitors into our village who will stir up trouble. We have barely survived as it is, and only from obedience to the Sovereign Occultists." As she says the name of their cult, her face falls into anger, but her voice holds steady.

"So do you know where they could have taken my friend?" I lean forward.

She nibbles at her lip, considering. "There's nothing you can do for your friend," she says. "I'm sorry. They take any creatures they find back to the capital city so they can properly spell them, just as they have with all of us. The more powerful of us or the ones with royal blood, they usually just kill them."

My breath catches and I choke on my words, not wanting to ask about the spells, not wanting to *know* about the murders. Maybe this is what happened to my father. Perhaps he was captured and spelled, but he got away somehow.

"I have to ask," I say. "Are the Occultist's spells why you're all so…" My voice trails off, not sure how to proceed without causing harm.

"Yes," she says, understanding. "The spell they've used on my people has stifled our magic and is turning us into the animals that we once resembled."

It makes sense considering what I've seen today, but it's still hard to imagine what that must be like for this once proud race of magical beings.

"It takes some time," she continues on sourly, "and if we behave, they will release the spell from some of us, or lessen it so it's not as fast. Not many have had that good fortune. The ones who do, well, they're usually the worst of the traitors to our kind."

"I'm so sorry," I say. An entire kingdom, an entire species, will be lost if this doesn't stop. Not only did they kill off all the royal lines, but the Occultists conquered the people and are slowly destroying their minds and bodies. If they can do this to the elves, a formidable, strong, and magical people that have been in this land for centuries, what could they do to the dragon shifters? Are we strong enough to fight them? Are we prepared for this?

"Thank you for answering my questions," I say. "Where is the capital? What's it called?"

She shakes her head violently. "No, you cannot go there. You won't stand a chance."

"I'm the most powerful dragon in Drakenon," I say simply. "I have to try."

She reaches out and takes my hands in hers. The edge of her right hand is rough, having already begun its transformation into a hoof. I swallow hard.

"Don't go there," she continues. "You must go back to Drakenon and convince your armies to help us. We have no other hope. The Occultists have taken over the rest of Eridas. They've killed off so many. If they continue this way, you will have no allies to help you when they come for your kingdom, too."

I don't have the heart to tell her that the Brightcasters would never agree to help. They care about protecting their own hides and nobody else. That's how it's always been. But with that thought, I wonder how they've reacted to my leaving. To Bram, a prince, being gone as well. They might not need him, but they need me. It won't be until I die that another with my power will be born, and by the time she's eighteen and of age for marriage and childbearing, it could be too late for the dragons, especially the ruling family.

My mind flits back to what that Occultist said about my birthday. He claimed to have met me before, to have spelled me. He said that I would be coming to find him once I turned eighteen. Could it be true? A hurried sense of unease washes over me.

A deep rumbling growl sounds from outside the walls, followed by a hoarse roar that can only mean one thing. I jump up and rush to the window. Outside the house, a black dragon lands, the wind whipping around him. I scurry back from the window.

"Hide," I whisper and stalk toward the door.

The dragon must have shifted back into human form, because a voice shouts my name. A voice I know well. A voice I wish I could never hear again.

"Khali," Silas yells. "I know you're here! Come out before I storm this village to the ground."

When he says storm, he literally means it. Silas could use the weather to take down entire buildings. And as an air elemental, had he been in the area, he would have recognized my magic the moment I used air earlier to try to save Bram. There's no point in hiding. I know what Silas is capable of. He doesn't care about this village. He only cares for himself.

I gather my courage, square my shoulders, and stride through the front door.

"Didn't you get my note?" I say, raising a confident eyebrow. "I didn't want to be followed. But of course, you've never been one to care about my wishes, now have you, Silas?"

Silas turns to me with a haughty glare. He's not alone but that doesn't surprise me one bit. He has a party of at least ten other Dragon Blessed shifters with him and maybe even more hiding somewhere. They're all armed with long swords for their human forms. They have spent all of their lives training for and engaging in battle and the cockiness is hard on their faces as they look at me. I glare right back, my magic raging in a cyclone of elements beneath my skin.

"Fiancé." Silas stalks forward. "You did not have permission to leave, not then, not now, not ever."

"I have to help my father," I spit. "There was no other way. Now go back to Drakenon before you get yourselves killed. I'll be back as soon as I find the cure for my father's curse."

"Your father is a lost cause!"

Anger ripples through me. I hold my stance. "*You* are a lost cause."

"Where's Bram?" Silas asks, his lip curling. "My brother will have to answer for his sins."

I laugh at that. "Don't you dare speak of answering for sins, Silas. Or did you already forget what happened to your twin?"

The men surrounding Silas bristle, a few questioning eyes turning in his direction, but he plays his part well, a confused expression masking his true self.

"Bram was taken by the Occultists," I snap, getting right to the point. "So if you don't mind, I'm going to go get him and be on my way."

"No," he presses, "you're coming home with me."

"I'll return when I'm good and ready!"

I don't hesitate. I shift into my dragon, letting her roll over me like a blanket of power, and lift my wings into the sky. Silas and the men also shift with the cracking of bones and the cries of battle, readying themselves to chase me. But there was only one dragon faster than me and Silas killed him. As my wings pump and I zip over the landscape, I deflect the headwind Silas tries to thrust at me. I push the wind back at them, and summon a torrent of prickling rain. Again, just underneath my hide, I can feel something chasing at my magic, something trying to drain it away. I push it down but it exhausts me. I fear I'm running out of time.

My heart pumps and my thoughts zero in on my next step toward saving my father. I don't know where Terek is and I don't know where the capital is and I can't find the Occultist and Bram without those two things. Now that Silas is on my tail, I can't stay in this kingdom for much longer. The only person left who might be able to help me save not only my father, but now Bram, is Dean Brightcaster. The first prince. My first kiss. My first love.

And so, I fly south alone.

TWENTY-SEVEN

HAZEL

"DO YOU HAVE ROOM FOR dessert tonight? Our tiramisu is delicious." The waiter offers a little black menu, and Landon shoots me a questioning smile.

I shake my head. "I'm way too full to eat more." Plus, I'd feel bad to add to the bill. This place isn't cheap. I was a bit surprised Landon picked it, given that he's a college student and I know where the guy works.

"Just the check, thanks," Landon says and the waiter leaves us to our conversation.

The Italian restaurant is tucked around the corner from Main Street, between a dry cleaners and a karate studio. Inside the owners have kept everything high end, with black tablecloths and crystal glassware, low lighting and authentic Italian decor. There are only a few other parties dining here tonight, giving the place an even more romantic ambiance. It's the perfect date restaurant. The food was amazing. The company was even better.

So why do I feel so guilty? Oh, probably because I know I shouldn't have come on this date in the first place.

A candle's long flame flickers in the center of the table. The fire reminds me of all the unanswered questions I want to ask Dean, questions about where he comes from, questions about what he meant when he asked me about my father. My mind is so full of these questions that it's difficult to focus on anything else. Landon doesn't seem to notice, or if he does, he never indicates anything is off. The guy is as happy-go-lucky as they come.

A few minutes later, Landon helps me back into my coat. On our way out he holds my hand, threading our fingers together, and leads me to his gigantic white truck. He smells like coffee mixed with spicy citrus cologne. It's quite nice. But it doesn't stir me in the same way a certain someone's woodsy fire and rain scent does.

I have to use the foot rail to climb into his truck. He gives me a little boost and as I slide into the seat, I catch his blue eyes staring. They are bright and clear and stunning. But they aren't mysterious. They don't draw me in and hold me suspended. They don't shift from fire to coal.

He smiles that big goofy smile of his. "What are you thinking?"

"Nothing," I say, because I don't have a fair answer to give him.

I study his dimples for a second. I've always loved dimples. Who doesn't? Landon's smile comes easy. I don't have to work for it, and even though I tell myself that's a great quality in a man, I picture the smile I've only witnessed a couple of times. A smile so rare, it's like catching a shooting star on a moonless night.

But no matter how hard I try, I can't stop comparing Landon to Dean. Poor guy.

"Should we head out?" Landon asks. "I want to show you something."

I nod, and he closes the door, running around to his side of the truck. He jumps into the driver's seat, still smiling, and another wave of guilt pummels through me. He doesn't deserve this. I'm leading him on and I should ask to go home. I should tell him I just want to be friends and be honest about my feelings.

But he's so happy and I can't bring myself to wreck that. I'll talk to him about this tomorrow. No need to ruin tonight for him. And besides, I'm totally curious about what he wants to show me. He's lived here his entire life and probably knows all the best spots.

"So why veterinary school?" he asks, sounding genuinely curious. He's not just making small talk to pass the time while we drive.

"I love animals."

"So do I, but you can always have pets. Why not go become a doctor instead? You'll make a lot more money."

I shove down the rising annoyance. "Why does everyone always assume money is the end-all-be-all to happiness?"

"You got me there," he laughs.

"What about you?" I challenge. "What's your plan after graduating? Are *you* going to try for medical school?"

"Umm, yup." His tone is so self-deprecating that I can't help but laugh.

"What can I say?" he relents. "I want to make money. I could lie and act all noble about it but the truth is, I want to pick whatever medical specialty will pay me the most amount of money for the least amount of work. I'm not going to be one of those doctors who's on call all the time."

"So what kind of doctor are you going to be? Because my mom's an ER nurse, and last I checked, everyone who works at her hospital is always busy."

"True." He nods. "But I'll figure it out. I'll get good grades and then find some fancy practice where they'll let me work four days a week and golf on the weekends and all that shit."

He's serious about this plan. Hey, at least the man is being honest. I don't know whether to find it annoying or to keep laughing. "Too bad you aren't getting a huge inheritance, Landon, because you'd be really good at that lifestyle. You could have your own TV show!"

He nods, playing into the joke. "I'm still praying some long lost uncle will turn up dead somewhere. If med school doesn't work out, I'll marry rich and become a kept man." He turns and waggles his eyebrows at me. "But you'd have to be the mistress," he jokes. "You can take care of the stables."

We laugh about it for a few minutes as we drive along the two-lane highway. The last time I was here, Dean drove down one lane like a maniac and then left me to drive back the other way all by myself. I rub the bad memory from my mind and focus on Landon again. He slows and turns off onto a tiny dirt road. The path is so hidden, I'd have never guessed it was there in the first place. The truck bounces up and down on the road, the headlights revealing a thick pine forest on either side. I hold my breath and try not to squeeze my hands into fists. My heart picks up the further we get from the main road.

"Where are you taking me?" I finally ask, but my voice is drained of courage and it comes out a little too high.

"Don't you worry, little lady," he assures me with a smile. "You're going to love it." His hands are tight vices on the steering wheel as we continue down the dirt road. "Everyone loves it," he adds.

"Everyone?" I twist my lips, wondering what he means by that, and okay, now I really *am* getting annoyed with the guy.

He grins but doesn't say anything more. So is this where he takes all his dates or something like that? Is it some designated make-out spot outside of town? I'm a bit confused and trying to let that confusion overpower the fear under the surface, because anything is better than giving into that. I've learned that fear can be all consuming, and I don't want to go there. I want to be calm. Want to trust. I know Landon. He's my friend. He wouldn't do anything to me. So I shouldn't jump to any conclusions.

But what if I'm wrong?

My mind races all the way until we turn off the dirt road onto another one. The second road is even more remote than the first. It's so dark at this time of night, the headlights are bright white against the trees. They press against both sides of the truck, and I'm beginning to wonder if we're going to make it when the road opens up into a huge clearing ahead.

No, not a clearing. A lake.

My stomach drops and Katherine comes to mind. The headlights glitter on the water as Landon stops the truck and backs it around until the rear of the pickup is facing the lake. He jumps out and I do the same, my boots crunching into the long grass. He opens the tailgate, hopping up to sit on the metal frame. He pats the space next to him and reaches out a steady hand.

I swallow hard and take it, trying to force images of Katherine and dead girls from my mind. He pulls me up and slides in close, putting his arm around me. It's cold tonight but not frigid, and between my coat and his arm, I'm plenty warm. I don't feel warm, though. I'm chilled to the bone. I try to breathe slowly, to relax, to tell myself I'm perfectly safe. Now that the truck's lights are extinguished, the wide open sky fills with far-away stars. My eyes adjust more and more with each passing second, until I can see those same stars above reflecting off the lake's surface. That sight does calm me a little.

"It's beautiful."

"It really is." He leans in closer. "I've been coming here since I was a kid. In the summertime, it's the best swimming spot. But it's also one of my favorite places to come when I want to be alone."

My thoughts cloud over and I'm right back to where I was. "It's not the lake they pulled that girl's body from, is it?" Katherine's memories hover closer than ever now that we're here. It could be the exact same place, it looks like it to me. But in the dark, I can't tell for sure.

"God, I hope not," he says. "But I don't think so. There are hundreds of lakes in the surrounding areas, so odds are, it wasn't. They're lucky they found her at all."

I can't shake my thoughts of her, and I automatically run my finger along my obsidian necklace where it's tucked under the edge of my coat. I'm so glad I have it, so grateful that I met Harmony and got the help I needed to manage my curse. I can't imagine still having Katherine's ghost following me everywhere, and now the cheerleader girl, too? It's terrifying.

The memories Katherine thrust upon me will never leave. Because while I'm used to spirits sending me awful images, I've never had a spirit get so close and show me so much. I've never had one be able to put the images in my mind so clearly, as if I were living them right along with her. No, not with her, but *as* her. And I can't help but think that she wants more than just my help. Maybe… maybe she wanted to warn me.

"What's wrong?" Landon asks.

"Nothing," I squeak. What's wrong? The alarm bells are blazing! I shouldn't be here. I'm pretty sure this *is* the same lake, I recognize the shoreline.

Landon rubs my arm. He's closer now, his body pressed up next to mine. My face prickles. If I don't say something now, he's going to kiss me. Wasn't it just hours ago that I planned to let him?

Well, I've changed my mind.

When I wasn't in this moment, it was so easy to imagine our kiss. But now I'm here, I don't want it to happen. There are too many things that make it wrong. My feelings for Dean are too strong. My worries about Katherine won't let me go. And this lake… it should be romantic, but it's freaking me out. Because all I can see when I look at it is what it was like for Katherine to see her body pulled from the water.

"Landon, I appreciate—"

His lips take mine. Hard. It's so fast, it throws my defenses off guard and I don't know how to react. I've never done this before. My mind is a racing mess and I'm frozen, numb to his touch. He must take that as a good sign because he wraps his other arm around me and pulls me closer, opening my mouth with his. His tongue is warm and wet and I'm suddenly distracted by how gross this whole thing is. *This* is kissing? This is what all the fuss is about? Are you kidding me? It's so… slobbery!

My thoughts are rolling around like marbles in my head. He lets out a low moan and shifts his weight, overpowering me. He presses me back onto the bed of the truck. The metal is sharp against my hips, painful against the back of my head.

Okay, I'm done!

"Ouch," I cry out, my hands pushing back against his chest. "Wait. Landon, hold on."

He doesn't wait.

He spreads his body over mine, driving me even harder into the cold metal. His hands are frantic now, traveling over me without reservation or care. He reaches for the buttons of my coat, moving his mouth to my neck.

"Landon," I try again, louder, screaming. "You're hurting me. Stop!"

But he doesn't stop. It's as if he doesn't even hear me. Each one of my senses blast into overdrive. I balk against the cold air when he rips open my coat, his scratchy fingers going for my sweater next. He presses his fingers into my stomach and I kick out.

"Stop!" I yell as loud as I can this time, and it echoes over the lake. "Landon, what are you doing? Get off!"

His hands are everywhere. His breath is garlic and hot and so, so wrong. His heat contradicts the cold, jarring and unapologetic. Half my mind is focusing on fighting him but he easily overpowers me with each move. The other half of my mind is observing everything from above, shocked that this is happening. Disbelieving. Floating away.

Landon doesn't stop. He doesn't utter a single word as I beg and scratch and scream and cry. He grips both my wrists and forces them above my head. He locks them in one large hand and squeezes tight. With his free hand, he rips Cora's white sweater right down the middle, exposing my nude bra and heaving stomach. Tears burn my vision. I can't see the stars anymore.

How is this real?

Landon's eyes glisten black as soot to match the darkness as they assess me for a long second, the black has spread to cover the whites of his eyes. *Just like the man who killed Katherine.* How is it even possible? Then he's back on me, his hot mouth nips at my neck before crashing to my mouth again, splitting my lip. I cry out with the pain. His hand travels over my skin, greedy and unrelenting. He is so heavy. He is a million pounds. He is stone and I am dust. I taste the coppery blood in my mouth and try not to gag. He probably tastes it, too. It does nothing to stop him. In fact, it encourages him.

His free hand travels to my neck and he grabs onto the obsidian necklace, pulling. It's too tight against my neck, so tight, that I cough, lost for breath. Terror flows through me, stinging and hot. But then the necklace breaks free and I gasp for air. The circular beads spill out over the bed of the truck, clattering like pebbles and rolling away.

His hand releases my neck and heads south, and I scream even louder. His mouth kisses along my jaw, oblivious to my fear. What is going on? I don't understand how he could do this. I don't understand how I could have missed this in him. I blink up into the darkness.

We're not alone.

A spirit hovers over our bodies. Dressed in a wispy black cape, I can't see the spirit's face except for two glowing red eyes. Evil reverberates from its floating form. It's an evil so dark, it sucks any light from its surroundings. Something about it is familiar. I've seen it once before. Its outstretched arm is reaching right *into* Landon, holding on tight, *controlling him.*

My screams pierce the night.

Landon's head snaps up. His eyes aren't those of the predator anymore, they're not black. They are those of the prey and they're his normal blue. There's something frightened behind them, something trapped and animalistic. But his body doesn't seem to connect when his widened eyes return to black and he bears back down on me.

I finally understand. Whatever this *thing* is, it's possessing Landon. It's forcing him to do this. He doesn't want to hurt me. But we're both powerless to stop it. This isn't right. This shouldn't be happening. The spirits don't have power over us. In all my years, I've never known of a spirit who could. But this isn't a normal human spirit. This is otherworldly and I remember where I've seen it before. I caught just a glimpse of this thing hanging over the man in the alleyway who tried to attack me.

Is this the thing responsible for all the dead girls over the last two years?

The creature and I lock gazes and it feels as if its red glowing eyes are peering into my soul, judging, assessing, deciding my fate.

Judge, jury, and executioner.

Landon's hands wrap around my neck and squeeze.

TWENTY-EIGHT

KHALI

WHEN I WAS SEVEN YEARS old, I almost died. I was playing by the lake with the princes when I saw something pretty, glittering in the water. Innocent as I was, I stomped through the bank to investigate. That's when a slimy hand wrapped around my ankle and pulled me under, sharp claws digging into my flesh. My screams echoed over the surface for barely a second before cold water rushed my lungs.

I had no power then, no way to fight back or defend myself. The fear was so suffocating, that even to this day, I hate the water. I didn't know it then, but the merfolk had kidnapped me with no intention of actually killing me. At least, that's what I've been told in the years since. I'm not so sure about that. I think had they not gotten what they'd set out for, I'd be dead. They used me as a bargaining tool to manipulate the Brightcaster family into a truce, allowing them more dominion over Drakenon water. I'm still unsure of the details surrounding my release, but I do know they magicked me to breathe underwater and held me down there in the freezing darkness for two days while they negotiated with the royals.

I've never been the same since. After that experience, my childhood innocence was lost to that murky darkness. No matter how anyone tried to explain it, I knew from then on that my life wasn't like others, that for as long as I lived, there would be people willing to use my suffering for their gain.

As I fly, gaining distance from Silas, I'm grateful for what I've been through. Because of it, I was afraid, and I trained in secret whenever I could as a way to try to make that fear go away. And as I got older, I began on my weekly excursions with Owen, stealing away into the darkness to see what was possible. I did what I could, used what I had, and now I'm a faster, stronger dragon because of it.

Now it's my turn to use what I am to my advantage.

The cloudless sunset has turned the sky to a swash of coral. I can't let the coming darkness stop me, I have to keep going. I have to fly faster. With worries for Bram centered in my mind, I peer down at the lakes below and muster the courage to fly lower. The sun is gone but my vision in this form allows me to see in the dark. I search the area, trying to match what I'm seeing with Bram's description of where the ley lines meet. I don't know for sure, but I think I've found it.

If this is the area Bram spoke of, then somewhere down there is the very spot where I can draw on my earthly magic to cross from this realm into the next. If only I knew where that spot was! I hate that I'm alone in this. I'm amazed that it only took a few days alone with Bram for my heart to care so much about him, about his well being and his safety. I'd give anything to have him with me now, to be doing this together. I hope Silas cares enough about his brother to try to help him, but I know that thought is nothing more than hope. Dean's all I have left. If he doesn't know how to help my father and how to save Bram, all of this will be for nothing.

I land next to the largest of the lakes and shift back into my human form. My dragon is my comfort zone, but she's also terrifying to anyone who might be lurking around here with answers. Hunger and thirst roll through my belly but I ignore the ache, looking around for signs of life instead. My vision isn't nearly as strong now, and the darkness of night is expanding by the second. There's nothing here but silent trees and still water and an undercurrent of Fae magic. I release a panicked breath. I don't know what to do.

What did Bram say? Ley lines are energetic lines that connect places of significance, and when lines from our realm cross over with lines from the human realm, then it creates a passageway for those with elemental magic to cross through. But it can't just be elemental magic, because my father isn't an elemental and he's been visiting Dean. Unless Dean helped him through? Or maybe another creature with elemental magic did it?

I have so many questions, a few theories, but no real way to test any of it. I chastise myself for not questioning Bram more on these things while I had the chance! I was foolish to let that opportunity pass me by.

My eyes strain against the darkness, looking for some kind of indication as to where these ancient Fae rituals took place, but there's nothing out of the ordinary. It looks like the same Fae forest from before, with its thick trees and magicked air. The panic swells up again. I take a long, slow breath to settle my nerves and close my eyes.

The ley lines are all about energy staying with the land. Perhaps if I focus, I'll be able to feel it myself. Each of my elementals has a unique imprint, a different sort of current to the magic. Earth is a grounding power. Water is fluidity, and air is light. Fire is the hardest to explain, but it's like a wild calm. And I feel each of those within me now. But they're not what I'm looking for, so I shift past them in search of something unfamiliar.

At first, there's nothing.

But I keep myself fixed in place, exhaling softly, my eyes shut, and imagine I'm like the trees that grow here. Tall and strong, deeply rooted, interconnected, and observant. Patient.

A pulse of ethereal energy flashes through me, soft as a whisper. I welcome it, letting it come again and again, until I'm sure it's real and not my imagination. My eyes open and my feet lead me toward the source of the energy. I walk along the edge of the large lake. It's almost as big as the one in front of Stoneshearth, but I won't let that stop me. The darkness spreads over the water like a black mirror, hiding whatever lurks in its depths. With each step, the energy rises more and more. Hope surges, and I run, careful to stay light on my feet, to keep quiet. But I've got to move. Too much is riding on my success.

Suddenly, the energy stops.

I skid to a halt and look around, searching for what, I don't know. There's no indication that this is where I cross through. I'm still in the Fae forest. I groan and clench my hands into fists, stalking through the area. A glimmer of something, that's what I need. But there's no glimmer, no signs. There's nothing.

I force myself to relax and allow the unfamiliar energy to wash over me once again. It's stronger here than it ever was, but again, it pulls me in a direction. Not around the lake, but toward it.

I hesitate. Fear rushes me, the memories of my time trapped underwater heady and suffocating. But I don't have time to hesitate. I don't have the luxury of fear. I walk forward until I'm right at the lake's edge. The energy continues to draw me in, and I step into the water. It's cool but not icy. It feels like summer rain, and it welcomes me forward. I take another step. And then another. All the while, my breath pumps to and from my lungs, faster and faster.

Are there merfolk in this water, too? Something worse? What hidden darkness lies beneath the surface of the water? I remember what it felt like to have that clammy hand wrap around my ankle as a child. It's a thought that flashes through my mind every time I'm near the water. If it happened again, would I survive this time?

Tears prick my eyes. I'm shaking so bad, the water ripples around me.

"Another one," a voice hisses from the water.

I scramble from the lake, landing with a thud on the shoreline.

"Who's there?"

A head pokes out of the surface. She doesn't look like the merfolk from my childhood nightmares; she's much more beautiful than that. Her skin is moon white and sparkling, her eyes are onyx glitter.

"The real question," she says, rising further from the water, "is who are you?"

I swallow. There is no point in trying to deceive her. "I'm Khali, future Queen of Drakenon."

She tilts her head. "I thought so," she says, coolly. "Have you come to see your prince who lives on the other side?"

"The other side of what?" I ask. Hope swells in my chest.

"The other side of my lake." She lifts a hand and motions a finger toward me. "Come, I'll show you. But I must warn you, if I help you, you'll owe me a debt."

Terror rakes through me because debt is exactly what Bram warned about. *Bram… he needs me.* I stand and step into the water. She's the only lead I've got.

"Fine," I say. "A debt equal to this one."

"How well can you swim?" she asks, her lips curving into a cool smile.

I call on my water elemental and ready myself for the task ahead. She dives under. Against my better judgment, I trust her, and dive under as well. The fear of this being a trap, of becoming subjected to the things that lurk down here, is more real than ever. But I have to be brave, and so, I swim.

The creature is fast, her fins giving her the advantage. But I'm fast, too. And my water elemental allows me to not only breathe under here, but to use the water as a tool for speed. It pushes me forward, past kelp, through the darkness, deeper and deeper and deeper still.

She leads me straight to the bottom of the lake. The energy down here is so strong, it crushes me on all sides, heavier than ever. I try to scream, to struggle, to break free, but it's like fate is pulling me under without my consent. My vision blurs from black to the brightest white. Someone calls my name and my heart leaps with recognition, but it all happens so fast that I lose all thought. I'm spinning. I'm lost. The deep dark returns.

The energy pushes me to my breaking point. And then, it washes away.

The woman leading me is gone too.

The water is no longer that of summer, that of Fae. It's icy cold.

I swim back to the surface, desperate to be free, my legs kicking with unchecked ferocity. The moment my head breaks the surface, I breathe in the cold air, letting it fill my lungs with its freeing salvation. My eyes blink open, my vision settling, and I know. I know what has happened. I know where I am. I can feel it in the change of temperature, can see it in the landscape. But most of all, I can sense it in the way my magic has lost some of its breath. The elementals dancing within are but a wisp of what they normally are. I've passed through the ley lines. I've crossed over from one realm to the next. I blink the water from my eyes, my vision fixed on the dark shoreline.

TWENTY-NINE
HAZEL

MY THROAT BURNS AS LANDON pushes the last ounce of oxygen from my lungs. My vision is nothing but a black tunnel. Stars wink along the edges. And Landon. He is centered in the darkness. It sweeps over me. Fast. Too fast. I claw at his hands and wrists, drawing blood. I snag a long strand of his hair and rip it from his scalp. I kick out and knee him with all the energy I have left. He's unmovable. He's made of stone. Unfeeling. Unshaken. Above him, the robed spirit has taken control, those two red eyes glowing luminous.

I'm going to die.

My limbs grow weak. The panic settles beneath a haze of acceptance, like a single feather floating on the wind. There is nothing more I can do. I have no fight left. My eyelids flutter and just before they close, something darts through the black, something I've seen before. I try to hold onto the image, to place it, to understand what it is, but my memories are drowning in death.

My life doesn't flash behind my eyes. Nothing does.

Landon's hands loosen ... then release. I cough and roll onto my side, gasping for air. The oxygen burns hot as salvation, filling my lungs with fire. My head swims for the surface. Blood races through each vein as my pulse quickens. It feels like a millennia until I'm brought back to awareness. I scramble against the truck bed, scooting away from Landon.

It's dark and hard to make out everything that's going on, but even from here I see his expression transform from dazed to horrified. He stares at his hands like they aren't his own. His mouth opens and closes in stunned silence. His chest rises and falls, faster and faster. Then he looks up and catches my gaze. I cower farther away from him.

"I'm so sorry, Hazel," he whispers, his voice raw with emotion. "I don't understand what came over me. I didn't mean—"

But I can't. I can't do this right now. I race over the edge of the truck, landing on my hands and knees in the long, scratchy grass. It's half dead from the approaching winter and stinks of mildew and mud. I scramble to my feet, ready to run, but movement over the lake catches my attention.

Above the still lake's surface, two spirits hover.

The cloaked demon, who moments before was using Landon to choke me, circles the large spirit dragon. It's the very same creature I saw twice before, the black dragon with the cobalt eyes. I stare in shock for the space of a heartbeat. And then, they attack. Their forms fly at each other over the water, but nothing reflects below them. Nothing but the stars. Nothing but the darkness.

I glance at Landon. "Do you see them?" I choke the words out as I point.

He turns and frowns, shaking his head. He doesn't see anything. My heart sinks but I'm not surprised. This sight isn't meant for regular human eyes.

"Hazel, I'm so sorry," he continues, rubbing bloodied palms into his hair. Most of it has fallen out of its bun, the blonde streaked with liquid red. "Please, forgive me. I would never—"

I hold up my hand and cut him off. "Not right now."

The spirits battle. The dragon roars and charges, flying through the air, long claws outstretched and teeth bared, but the black cloaked spirit is otherworldly in its movements. It disappears into wispy smoke before the dragon can touch it. Then it materializes again at the right moment. This time, it's right behind the dragon, its claw-like hand reaching out. As far as I can tell, it doesn't carry any weapons. But it doesn't need to. Its skeletal hands are the weapon. Whatever the cloaked demon touches is brought into the darkness. The dragon is no exception. It arches and cries out, flying away and then twisting back to continue the fight.

I've never seen anything like it, or anything like *them*. Human spirits are in their own kind of void. They don't touch each other. They don't touch us. But these two things have so much more freedom. I'm reminded of that first encounter with the spirit dragon, when it had knocked me down but I'd talked myself out of that being a real possibility. I had told myself I fell out of surprise. Now I know the truth. These spirits, whatever they are, and wherever they're from, I don't know, but I do know this: they can touch each other—they can touch us.

And apparently, some can make humans do horrible things.

I swallow hard, realizing the implications of this new development. Maybe the supposed serial killer isn't one human man. Maybe it's actually this *thing* using whoever it can get its deadly hands on, using multiple men to murder young girls.

The two spirits continue to fight until the dragon is bested a second time, weakening further and skidding against the water. It cries out, a sound that sends a shiver of fear down my spine. It's losing. It won't be long until the dragon flees or is killed. How does a spirit dragon die? I don't know. And I don't want to know. Because once it's gone, Landon and I will be helpless once again.

"Get out of here," I yell at Landon.

"What are you talking about?" He jumps out of the truck bed and approaches me carefully. "I think you're in shock."

"Landon, listen to me. You need to get in your truck and go. Go, before it comes back for you!"

His face is ashen under the starlight, dazed and disbelieving. The dragon cries out in pain again, a sound Landon can't hear. If only I could explain! But I can't do anything about it. There isn't time. I don't wait to see if he follows my instructions. I take off for the trees. I have to hide from Landon and this creature. I have to get to safety before I become like Katherine and those other girls, before I end up as another lifeless corpse at the bottom of the lake.

I'm caged in by the heady scent of pine and blood, of night air and cold fear. I breathe hard even though I don't want to make a sound. Tree branches scratch at my bare arms and torso. I'm only in my bra, skinny jeans, and Cora's suede boots. The heels sink into the mud and catch on the rocks, slowing me down. The cold licks at my skin, but does little to penetrate past the terror that has become a heat all of its own. I push further into the forest, climbing over fallen trunks and through thick weeds.

After a few minutes, I stop to catch my breath and listen. The silence is eerie. It doesn't belong out here. There should be something to fill the quiet. Birds.

Squirrels. Larger animals—I'd even take one of the normal ghosts. But there's nothing. No wind. No cries from the spirit dragon. And no truck engine, either.

My insides squirm. Sweat drips down the back of my neck. It's so silent, I can hear my heart beating. And all I can think is that Landon didn't take my advice. There's no truck pulling away. He didn't leave. Oh God, why didn't he leave?

"Hazel!" His voice breaks through the silence. "Where are you?"

I can't trust him. Not with that thing around. And I don't dare move. He could be possessed again. In fact, I'd bet my life on it.

"I know you're out there!" he yells again, his voice closer this time. "I just want to help you."

His tone rings false, but I'm frozen to the spot. It's too quiet out here and if I move, he'll hear me. If that thing is using him again, he will be immune to pain. He'll be so much faster than me. I'll never get away. Hiding is my only option. Inch by inch, I sink to the forest floor and crouch low. Something hard presses against my hip bone and hope swells. My phone!

I fish it from the front pocket of my jeans and make sure to switch the button on the side to silent. Then I cover the screen with one hand and press the "wake up" button with the other. A picture of Macy and Cora's smiling faces light up the backdrop. I'm quick to turn the brightness down, tears burning my eyes as I look at my friends. If I don't get out of here, I'll never see them again.

What if they come looking for me? They could be next.

I hurry to find the contacts and scroll for Detective Sanders' information. When his name comes across the screen, I let out a small sigh. I push the contact and pray.

Nothing happens.

I only have one bar of service out here. I grit my teeth and look around helplessly. How am I going to get service without being seen?

"Come out, come out, wherever you are." Landon's sing-song voice cackles through the night. He's getting closer and closer. He might find me. Maybe I should run. But if I can get this call to connect, I might be okay. And then I realize that even if I make the call, it's not like I can *talk* to the detective without alerting Landon and the creature to my location.

A tear drops loose, splashing against my cheek. I have to try a different tactic. I type in a quick text to the detective, giving my name, what I know about my location, and that I'm in trouble and need the police right away. I press send and watch helplessly as my phone struggles to connect to service. The text doesn't send. I shake the phone in my hand, more tears falling.

"Where are you?" Landon's tone has turned dark and guttural, nothing like his true self. "When I find you, I'm going to teach you about respect."

The hot tears trail down my cheeks and neck unchecked. My breath catches in my chest as it rises and falls in little gasps. My arms are covered in cuts and goosebumps. And I can't move. I know it's true, that the dragon is gone and whatever that thing was is back in Landon. Because there is no way the Landon I know would ever say anything like that to me. Those have got to be the demon's words.

But why me? Is it just bad timing? Bad luck? Were we in the wrong place at the wrong time? Or am I being hunted by the creature for a specific reason? I think back to the black spirit finding me in the alleyway and can't help but wonder if that wasn't a coincidence.

I release a small breath and grab onto what little courage I have left. I press send on my text again and slowly stand, reaching my hand into the air and praying to whatever is up there, to please save me. Please, let the service connect. Please, let the detective see it right away.

"There you are!" Landon snarls. His force knocks me to the forest floor, and the phone skids loose from my hand. He stalks over to where it's lit up in the darkness and scowls. "You won't be needing this anymore."

He stomps on the screen. It cracks and goes dark.

He comes for me, yanks my shivering body up to his and twists my arms behind my back. I yelp, the pain white-hot.

"Landon don't," I plead. "I know you're in there. I know this isn't you. You don't have to do this."

He brings his mouth right up against my ear. The voice that comes out is not his. Not his at all. It's scratchy and putrid, thick with death and heavy with decay. "For two long years, I've been searching for someone like you. Oh, Hazel, you are exactly what they need."

He's been searching for someone like me? What does that mean? Who are *they*?

I slam my head back into Landon's face, feeling his nose crunch under my skull. It doesn't seem to hurt him. He cackles again and squeezes tighter. The sound omitting from his mouth is still not Landon's. It's nothing like his sweet, carefree, happy laugh. The demon is in total control now.

"Don't fight back," he snarls. "Or I will do much worse. You will not have known true pain until you receive it from me."

He lifts me up and squeezes those strong arms around me like a vice, carrying me from the forest and back to the lake. I scream for help the entire time, twist and kick out, try anything I can, but it's useless. Landon's strength is that of ten men with this demon in charge. I'll never break free.

"You are a disgusting girl," the creature spits angrily. "But soon you will be nothing at all."

Oh, God. I don't like the sound of that. I keep trying to claw my way out of Landon's arms, but it's impossible. We approach the edge of the lake.

"It's time to start the ritual." This time, the voice smiles.

THIRTY
KHALI

A DEAFENING SCREAM SLICES THROUGH the night, and I whip around in the water, searching for the source of the noise. A woman's voice cries out again, sobbing, and then goes silent. I should stay away from trouble, should be looking out for myself and my mission in coming here, but I can't stop myself. That merwoman brought me here for a reason. This can't be a coincidence.

I swim in the direction of the sound as quietly as possible. The icy water seeps deep down inside, all the way to the marrow, but I push through the pain with each stroke of my arms and legs. Something base and instinctual has risen within me, screaming that I must get to that woman. I must help her.

My magic isn't the same in this place. It's still there, but it's like it's been softened, muted down. The water elemental barely makes a difference in my speed through the water, and the fire elemental is nowhere to be found in this terrible coldness. Perhaps it's the shock. Perhaps it's the need to get to the woman outweighing the need to figure out what's wrong with my magic. But more likely, it's this human realm. Things aren't the same here.

It's been called the non-magical realm for a reason, and while I can access some of my magic here, it's not nearly the same. I can't imagine what it would be like to stay here long term. It's terrible. Is this what Dean has to live with on a daily basis? Is this what it's like to be Bram, only worse? I hate to think about it, and try to focus on the present moment over the questions.

The Fae kingdom had the sticky warmth of summer to it, even in the late autumn. But here, even though it's technically the same area, it's less autumn and much more biting winter. It's drier and colder. There is no mistaking that this place isn't meant for magic.

So with that in mind, I suck in a breath and quietly approach the shore. The woman is still crying, her voice growing more muffled and strained by the second. There's something about her that pulls me to her, like a string, like I must help her, no matter what.

I emerge from the water, going for the closest cropping of trees for cover. Even the trees are different here. Heartier pine trees made for all seasons like what we have in Drakenon. They are special, but still lacking in the enchanting hum of the Fae forest. I don't know if that's a good thing or a bad thing.

I crouch low, my clothing, velvet cape, and bag all soaked through and weighing me down. I carefully dispose of the bag and cape and sneak through the trees, moving closer to the crying until I find the source, until I find them. The hem of my dress drags in the dirt. My boots are squishy with water.

The woman is not alone.

I can hardly make her out in the darkness, but she's there, lying on the shore, a large man kneeling beside her. I inch closer, my vision straining to take it all in. She's young, hardly any older than myself. Her blonde hair is matted around her face, wet with water and blood. Her face is wild and afraid, eyes staring into night. Covered in blood, she's nearly dead.

The man next to her is also young. Dressed only from the waist down, his muscled back glints in the darkness and is covered in a layer of sweat. His long blonde hair glistens with blood in the moonlight. He leans over her, muttering some kind of incantation. It's not a language I understand, but something in me tingles with recognition. This isn't a human language; it sounds like something that could be from Eridas.

How many creatures can use this ley line portal to travel between realms?

The idea of great and terrible beasts roaming this human forest sends me to my knees. Can I really do this? Can I really help? But I don't have time to think about the what-ifs, not with this horror scene playing out only a few yards in front of me.

I move in even closer, unable to look away. The man has something in his hand. A stick? Bile rises in my throat as I realize what he's doing with it.

Crouched over her, holding her down with his weight, he's got the girl's shirt up and is carving something into her abdomen with the end of the stick, like it's a knife, and not wood. She writhes and screams, begging him to stop, but he's not the least bit deterred. And no matter how much she fights him, no matter when she pulls his hair, when she lashes out at him, drawing blood, he is utterly unmoved.

Anger grabs on tight. I can't sit here and watch this mutilation.

Bringing whatever of my powers I can to the surface, I shift into my dragon, the trees around me cracking with the force, and I charge.

I slam into the man, throwing him off the girl with all the strength my dragon holds. He flies across the grassy meadow, arcing high, and then lands in a heap of limbs on the shoreline. It doesn't stop him. His body shakes and rumbles, and changes. I growl, because that doesn't make sense. Slowly, he stands, blood pouring, bones broken and cracked. But still, he stands. And a dark form steps away from his body. The broken man collapses in a pile of death, his eyes wide and vacant, shining in the reflection of the lake.

"He's dead." I shift back to human and give my assurances to the bloodied girl. But I don't look at her, not when my gaze is stuck on the dark form that has emerged from the human man. Because it wasn't my imagination. It was real.

I've seen it before. Not in person, of course, only the spirit elemental would allow that, but in many textbooks growing up. Everyone knows of the reapers. They are the spirits tasked to take magical souls from one realm to the next life. What is it doing *here*? And how am I able to see it?

It glides toward me, and I blink, still hoping this isn't real. It can't be. But it is.

The girl groans at my feet, her sobs weakening by the second. She's losing too much blood. I kneel and scoop her up. I don't know how to explain it, but something primal is drawing me to her. I can't leave her here, not with that thing. I have to save her.

"We need to get out of here," I say, hoping she'll be able to help me do that. But her face is snow-white and the life within her eyes is fading fast. I shift her weight so I can carry her. She cries out, then whispers a name. I go still.

"Dean," she says his name again. "I thought you were Dean." Her head lulls to one side. She passed out.

The reaper knocks into us, sending us crashing to the ground.

Not only is the reaper real, it's materialized from the spirit realm and into a physical being. Horror prickles through my entire body. How can this be? It leans over me, the hood covering its unknown face. Only two red eyes glow from within the inky darkness. It reminds me of the Sovereign Occultists, but it's so much worse. Where an Occultist looks like a normal human, this thing is skeletal and putrid and *death*.

"There are two of you," it hisses gleefully. "My master will be so pleased with me."

Then it pounces. Claws dig into my leg, and it yanks me across the mud and rocks, back toward the girl I dropped.

The reaper grabs her too, dragging us toward the water. I kick out but its strength is incredible, built up by something much darker and stronger than magic alone. I scream and call my dragon to me, transforming to my truest form, catching the reaper off guard. I release my full power, snapping at it with my teeth and claws, drawing on the flicker of fire elemental burning within me now that I'm out of the cold. I let that fly loose, too.

The creature screeches, howling in pain, but it goes for the girl, still dragging her into the water. She's passed out, and if he pulls her under completely, she'll drown.

I block him, pushing him out of the way again. He flies across the meadow as the boy did, and stands just the same. From behind him, something massive and black appears. I recognize the dragon the second he comes into focus. It's Dean.

We don't hesitate. We charge. The reaper meets me halfway, wrapping its cold hands into my hide and pushing some kind of unknown magic into me. It's cold as ice, and carries the scent of death with it. It sinks me to my knees, the pain racking through me, all the way to the tips of my wings. I cry out, death fast approaching, but I can't give up yet. I refuse to go out like this.

Dean pushes him off and the reaper lets out a guttural moan.

I call on my magic once again and this time, find more fire there. It burns within me like a newly stoked furnace, and I release it into the reaper's empty hole of a face. Dean stands at my side, joining me. We don't let up. The fire flows from our roaring mouths as the creature falls to its knees. It screeches and burns and burns and burns to ash.

After a few minutes, after I'm sure there's nothing left, I stifle the flames with the water elemental, bringing everything to a muddy, ashen mess. I manipulate the lake, rolling a wave over the pile of ash, washing it all away.

Dean is with the girl, kneeling at her side once again. I shift and join him and run my hands over her, checking her injuries. His face is drained of color, taking in the blood and the symbol carved into her stomach.

"Are you still here?" I ask, gently slapping her cheek. She doesn't wake up.

Her chest is no longer moving.

"She has a pulse," Dean says.

I let out a panicked breath. "Thank the Gods she's still alive. How can we save her?"

"We have to get her to the hospital."

I peer at him. I don't know what this word means.

"We have a lot to talk about," he says. "Firstly, why you're here. I felt your dragon come through the portal and I came straight away, but there's no time. Hazel needs us."

I'm exhausted, drained from using magic, and I can't imagine shifting again to take her to the hospital place. This kind of exhaustion never happens back home. I don't know how Dean manages it. We stumble toward a road. That's good. It's a start.

A high-pitched screech sounds through the still night. Red and blue lights flash against the trees. I freeze and dig my feet into the earth, expecting to battle with another terrible creature. What will it be this time? I don't know if I can survive any more of this, my magic is so diminished.

"We can't be here," Dean says. He lays Hazel on the side of the road, guilt lighting every plane of his face.

"Come on," he says, and sprints toward the tree line.

My legs don't seem to want to work, I'm too mesmerized by what I'm seeing. Something shiny and fast bounds down the road toward me, coming to a halt as blinding bright lights of red and blue shine in my face. Is it an animal? A beast of some kind?

The *thing* opens and a man jumps out and runs toward me, arms stretched out and holding some kind of black contraption in his hands.

"Is she alive?" he calls out gruffly.

I nod, deciding it best to answer honestly. "But she won't be for much longer.

She needs the hospital."

Another one of the flashing light beasts bursts from around the corner. It blares so loudly through the night that I have to cover my ears.

"Who did this to her?" the man asks, staring horrified at the girl's mutilated stomach. He drops to his knees next to her. "Did you do this?"

Do I answer? Do I tell him about the reaper? "No," I reply, beginning to shake. I should run, go find Dean, get away from here.

"Did you see who did it?"

I swallow, my knees growing weak. "Something evil did this," I say and point back to the shore. "But it's dead, now. I killed it."

THIRTY-ONE
HAZEL

I AM FILLED WITH LEAD. My arms and legs are sinking into quicksand and I couldn't move even if I wanted to. I try to pry my eyelids open but they're a million pounds. I groan, awareness seeping into the fogginess of my mind.

"Hazel?" The voice is far away. "Honey, are you awake?"

"Mom!" My eyes finally flutter open, bright lights glaring down. I groan again, but relief floods my system. "What happened?" My voice is hoarse and my throat is raw. "Where am I?" I try to sit up but a searing pain shoots across my abdomen and I'm forced back. And then I remember, I remember what he did to my stomach and I burst into tears.

"Oh, honey, it's going to be okay." Mom is right there, but she might as well be a million miles away, the emotions are a wild storm. I squeeze my eyes shut against the overwhelming onslaught.

"Let me get the light," a second voice says, moments before the lights adjust to a dimmer setting.

The pain and tears and fear and emotions keep coming, one after another, until finally, it washes away enough for me to open my eyes once again. I look around, taking in the tiny hospital room. I'm hooked to all kinds of machines, little sticky tabs stuck all over my body, and a needle taped down and pressing into a vein in my left hand. Everything hurts.

"Where's Landon?" I gasp, his name clings to my worst memory in a way that makes it hard to say it. But I can't blame him entirely, can I? I saw what happened. He was possessed. He was hurting me but not of his own will. There was so much blood, but he couldn't stop. *It* wouldn't let him.

"It's okay." Mom leans over and grasps my right hand between hers, squeezing it tight. "Landon is dead. He can't harm you anymore."

"How?" Tears spring to my eyes. Landon didn't deserve to die.

"Your friend saved you." Mom nods toward someone standing by the door, shadowed by the drawn curtain around my bed. The mystery girl steps into the light with a little wave.

"Hi," she says.

My eyes go wide. I know her, but I can hardly call her my friend. I've never met her before.

"Khali." I swallow hard, putting the gorgeous face to the unique name. "*You* saved me?"

She bites her lip and smiles sheepishly. She's as beautiful as she was in the images the dragon spirit sent me. Her long, wavy, dark brown hair shines perfectly, even under the fluorescents. Her eyes are large, wide set, and absolutely stunning, one of ocean blue, the other of rich soil.

She saved my life?

I try to remember her there that night, but after that thing possessed Landon and he started to carve into my stomach with nothing but a sharpened stick, the pain and blood and shock of it all became too much and I blacked out. My breathing speeds up just thinking about it and the little beeping on the machine races to match.

"It's okay," Mom says, running a hand gently down my hair and cupping my cheek. Tears rim her reddened eyes as she holds my gaze steady. "He can't ever touch you again."

I shake my head. "But it wasn't Landon. He wouldn't do that."

A line deepens between Mom's eyes. "Oh, honey, you don't have to protect him. He's gone."

"I'm not worried about *him*." Tears spring to my eyes and fear pummels my bruised body. "It's that *thing*. It's still out there."

Khali steps forward gracefully, her posture perfect and her voice soft as cotton. She's dressed in normal human clothing that's nothing like the medieval stuff I saw in the visions. It fits her perfectly but she seems about as comfortable in the jeans and t-shirt as I am in high-heels. "May Hazel and I speak alone for a few minutes? I think I can help her feel better about what happened if I tell her what I did."

"I don't know if that's a good idea," Mom says, but I nod vigorously, and so she stands to leave. "All right. I'll go tell the nurse you're awake."

As soon as she's out the door, Khali perches on the edge of the bed and tells me the truth of what happened without hesitating. "Your friend was possessed by a reaper."

I swallow hard. "Like a grim reaper?" It almost seems laughable had I not been there to witness it for myself. "But I never saw a scythe." The word seems silly saying it aloud but then again, I'm past the point of the supernatural being anything remotely silly or fake.

She shrugs. "He was using Landon to perform some kind of ritual on you, I think because you have magic, and he needed someone in this realm with magic to get it to work."

"I don't have magic," I challenge. Even as I say it, the words ring false.

She raises an eyebrow, but doesn't press the issue. "Anyway," she continues, "I believe it completed the ritual because it took total possession of your friend." She pauses for a second, as if weighing how this is affecting me.

"Please," I say, "I need to know everything. I can handle it."

"It was using a language I've only heard used by the Occultists. I don't know what it means. But in the end, it killed Landon, hurt you, and took on a physical form."

My eyes go wide. "Physical? Like you and me?"

She nods. "Reapers aren't supposed to be able to do that. They're creatures meant for the spirit realm only."

Horror crashes over me and I struggle to sit up again. I have to get out of here. I have to do something to warn people about this. "It's alive? It's just walking around out there?"

"No," she says flatly. "I killed it."

I fall back against the pillow and let out a shuddering breath. "You can kill a reaper?" I question. "How does that work? Doesn't it just go back to the spirit realm?"

She sighs, rubbing a hand along her shoulder. "It must be possible to kill it because I certainly did," she says, "but as far as I know, a reaper has never done anything like this before. So truthfully, I don't know if it simply returned to the spirit realm, but I don't think it's in the human realm anymore. This kind of reaper isn't meant for humans. They're for the supernaturals, like me. It shouldn't have ever been here in the first place."

So why was it here?

All this talk of realms and spirits is making my head hurt. I reach for the necklace around my neck, and then remember it's gone. But no, that can't be right, because it's strung around my neck the same as it always is. But Landon broke it.

"Your friend brought that over a few hours ago," she says. "A lady with white hair? She insisted you needed it and your mom agreed. They had to fight the doctors about it but they won. What's it for, anyway?"

I sigh in relief, running a finger over the little balls of cool stone. I don't think I'm ready to trust this Khali girl with my secrets just yet, but as I look at her, I can't help but sense we're connected somehow. We're cut from the same cloth, even if she is a magical dragon shifter and I'm... well, I don't know what I am. I thought I would hate her, considering the man I'm falling for is clearly already in love with her, but I don't hate her. Not even a little bit. She feels too familiar, too much like family.

"Hazel," Dean's gruff voice calls into the room as the door opens a crack. "Can I come in, please?" My heart explodes, the monitor picking it up. Khali raises an eyebrow and I could die. "I've been worried sick about you," he continues from behind the slightly ajar door. "I'm so glad you're okay. If Khali hadn't gotten there in time, you wouldn't have made it."

Geez, I didn't know he cared so much.

"Sure, come in," I say, squeezing my eyes tight. I can't see the look on his face when he finds Khali here. I don't think my heart can bear it.

The door opens and shuts, and the room fades to silence.

"Khali," he whispers. "You're here too. I've been looking for you. What happened to you? Why didn't you come with me?"

I can't stand it anymore and open my eyes. Khali smiles and goes to him, wrapping him in a tight hug. "I've missed you," she murmurs. "We have a lot to talk about. I really need your help."

I wish I knew what they were talking about.

As if sensing my feelings, Khali pulls away from Dean and speaks, "Dean came and helped me finish the reaper off. When those people came to help you, he left but I stayed."

"People?"

"The police," Dean offers. "You shouldn't have stayed, Khali. You don't understand how human police think."

I swallow hard, still stuck on the fact that Dean was there last night, too.

He's still staring at his friend and I'm sinking into my bed like I don't even belong in my own hospital room. "Khali, what happened to you? Why would you risk coming here?" He takes her hands in his.

"Drakenon needs your help." Pain wells up in her eyes. "Bram needs you. The Occultists have him. And your brother, Owen…" Her voice catches.

"I already know," he whispers in a dark tone, gaze flicking to me. "Owen is dead, isn't he?"

Realization hits me then. *Owen* is the spirit dragon with the blue eyes. He was here to find Dean, to relay a message about helping Khali. My mind goes back to that place, to that moment Landon was choking me, and I remember how Owen's dragon appeared again and fought the reaper long enough for me to get away the first time. But something must have happened to him after that because he disappeared. I swallow hard. I can't bear to say a word about it now. They've already lost him once, they don't need to know the rest.

"Knock knock," the doctor says as he comes through the door. "How are you feeling, Hazel? Doing all right?"

Dean and Khali press themselves into the corner of the room, whispering quietly among themselves, their eyes still trained on me. Two residents, a nurse, and Mom all shuffle into the room. It's filled to the brim now and everyone's looking at me like I'm a broken piece of china they're trying to meticulously reassemble with tweezers and super glue.

The doctor launches into a myriad of questions, all of which I do my best to answer. He tells me my wounds will take a few months to heal but the plastic surgery department did a great job fixing me right up and not to worry. He then goes into a psychiatric referral and says I'll need PTSD therapy soon.

It's all too much to handle. I'm pretty sure he knows what he's doing if he thinks I'm going to need a phyciatrist. Dang, my life is crazy!

"When can I get out of here?" I ask, my voice pleading. "I want to forget this ever happened and get back to my classes and my *life*."

He answers to Mom. "I think she's going to need at least another few days of observation but it's up to you if you want to start the discharge process sooner."

"Why is it up to her?" I challenge, angry that I'm not being listened to. "It's my body. I should get a say here, too."

He frowns. "I'm sorry," he says, "but since you're a minor for two more months, it's up to your mother."

"December sixteenth isn't that far away," I snap. "I'm not a child. I'm in college, living on my own. I think I'm smart enough to make my own decisions."

"It's okay," Mom steps in, her face soft and her hands up. "Why don't Dr. Saunders and I step outside to discuss the details of discharging you as soon as is safely possible, okay, Hazel?"

I let out a frustrated breath but nod because I know I'm overreacting a little here. She and the rest of the medical staff leave the room. I shut my eyes tight, embarrassed at my outburst, and then I turn to my friends in the corner.

"What are you looking at?" I question. They're staring at me like I've grown a second head or something. Okay, maybe the painkillers are wearing off because I'm starting to get annoyed with them, too. I'm grumpy to the max but who can blame me? The skin on my stomach feels like it's been set on fire, and I'm ready to be alone to sulk in peace and quiet.

"When did you say your birthday was?" Dean asks.

"December sixteenth," I reply. Great, I didn't want anyone to know.

"And you're seventeen right now?" Khali's eyes are round saucers and her mouth is shaped in a cute little "O".

I frown. Okay, this is getting weird. "Yes. Why the sudden interest?"

Khali steps forward, wringing her hands. "I'm seventeen and my birthday is the sixteenth of December," she says. "We were born on the same day."

I shrug. "So, we're birthday buddies. That's cool but it's a coincidence that happens all the time."

She turns to Dean. "An Occultist said he put a spell on me when I was a baby. He mentioned my eighteenth birthday. And I feel this strange magical connection to Hazel, it's hard to explain, but it's undeniable. When she was hurt, I knew I had to save her. And when you ran away from the police, I couldn't leave her. Physically couldn't move. That can't be a coincidence, can it?"

They stare at each other for a long beat before turning back to me. The dancing fire has returned to Dean's coal eyes, and Khali's are just as magical, sparkling with her thoughts. But no, she's reading way too much into this. Our birthdays matching has to be a coincidence. I'm obviously *not* a dragon shifter. I'm human. And I'm not like them, I'm not special except for this annoying "seeing spirits" business, but that's nothing to do with them and tons of humans claim to have that ability.

"Hazel is a psychic medium," Dean says slowly. "Could it be something more than that? Could she be part of the spell, too?"

"It's possible," Khali replies, her voice growing soft and her eyes watering with something I can't quite place. Fear? Love? She approaches me again and sits on the edge of the bed, this time taking my free hand into hers. When she does, I yelp. The connection between us grew from a spark to an electrical current. It's a charge that I've never felt before. Is this magic? And maybe it is the result of a spell, but it's undeniable. I don't know what to do with this news.

She swallows hard. "You can see the spirit realm?"

I nod.

She considers this, her ethereal eyes pinning me down with her turning mind. "Hazel, I think you might be more than just a medium. I think you might have elemental magic."

Dean is frozen behind her, looking down at me like he's never seen me before. Elemental magic? I'm not sure what that is but it doesn't sound real. It sounds like it's made from a storybook. Then again, my whole life these last few months has been like that. Like I said before, it's like I'm turning into the heroine of some cheesy teen novel!

"Dean's elemental is fire," she says. "I'm all four—fire, water, earth, and air." She lets out a breath and smiles gently. "And you, my friend, are spirit. You possess the rarest element of all. One so rare, it hasn't been seen for over a century."

I burst out laughing. "No, sorry," I say, "that's ridiculous. It can't be true."

"You saw the spirit dragon," she says, "and the reaper, both creatures from the supernatural realm. I don't think you'd have been able to do that if you were a regular human medium."

That shuts me up. I look to Dean. "You think this is real? You think I have some kind of spirit elemental? Something from *your* realm?"

He stands tall, all brooding eyes and hands shoved into his jeans pockets, but he nods.

Khali continues, "I think you and I are linked somehow. There's something else the Occultist said." She talks of this "Occultist" person like I should have a clue about him, but I do know one thing, whatever he is or it is, it can't be good. "He told me that when I turned eighteen, I'd be coming to him, begging for his help." Our eyes are locked and dread settles in deep. "I think we're connected, as part of a spell." Her voice catches. "And I'm not sure what it means, but I think we're both in deep trouble because of it. Have you noticed anything strange happening to you in the last few months?"

I burst out laughing, a reaction to the shock and the morphine and the fear.

"I'll take that as a yes?"

I swallow hard and stifle the laughs, nodding. I don't want to believe her, but believing her feels inevitable just the same. The reaper might be gone for now, unable to terrorize innocent women while he looked for someone with ties to magic, but he *was* here. And what happened to me is confirmation enough. Khali speaks the truth. There *is* something wrong with me. I think I've always known it, have always *hated* it. There's something magical going on with my ability, something reaching far beyond what is normal for a medium, and even if I didn't choose it, it's mine to own.

"My abilities have been stronger than ever, but they've also felt out of control, like I'm attracting unwanted spirits," I say, building as much courage into my voice as possible. I feel like a fraud. "So I guess you and I have two months to break the spell."

Her hand squeezes tighter around mine. "Two months to break the spell, save my friends and family, and stop Silas from enslaving me as his wife."

I blink, surprised and trying to take it all in. All of this *and* I have to get through my first semester. What have I gotten myself into this time?

KINGDOM OF SPIRITS

PROLOGUE

THE BOY'S BACK ARCHED, BENDING like a sapling in a cyclone. His screams released in an incoherent mess, caught between gnashing teeth and bloodied lips. It's possible he would have been heard for miles if they weren't buried so deep underground, so deep that the air reeked of sulfur and whispered of sacrifice. The man dropped his hands, his inner frustration popping like the freshly lit torch on the nearby wall. He sneered as the boy writhed atop the stone altar like a wounded animal.

The spell—it wasn't working.

He'd been trying for days with the prince. Days and days. And for what? Nothing. He ought to kill the pathetic creature and be done with it. Move on to more important matters than a false prince.

His hand reached for the dagger strapped against his side, his fingers twitching along the blade, yearning to slide it through the boy's neck and let the life drain free.

No.

No, his master had forbidden it. His master was wise, and certainly more restrained than he when the need arose, plotting the long-term gains with an eye toward the future. His master was sure—if this boy could be spelled correctly, he'd go from useless, to a weapon they could wield against Drakenon. And then finally, the warlocks could lay claim to what was righteously theirs.

The problem wasn't the spell itself, though. It wasn't his abilities as a warlock, either. No, those were unmatched by any Sovereign Occultist, except for his master. The problem was the counterfeit prince. The boy seemed to be stuck between the places where magic could work: not quite human, not quite dragon, not quite anything of value!

He stalked in close, leaning down mere inches from the boy.

His brown hair was plastered to his face. Strings of sweat and blood and dirt marred his pale skin. He smelled like he hadn't bathed in weeks, and his glossy eyes shone in the flicker of the torch light, emerald green and alive. Alive, but barely there, rimmed in red, and begging for death.

"Please," the boy whispered, his voice cracking. "Please, stop. I'll do anything." He coughed, blood splattering in a sickly arc across the stone. "Just stop." Another cough. This time, flecks of blood stuck to the warlock's face, hot and sticky and sinful.

The warlock stood, wiping away the unclean blood, running his palms down his robes, only to start the spell again. He spoke the ancient language in hushed reverence until a burst of magic shot from his hands, black tendrils enveloping the boy, forcing every cell within him to respond to the magic's demands. Once again, the boy screamed and begged and cried for life, for death, for anything but this. The warlock pinched his mouth, his eyes narrowing, pushing more magic in, in, in. He had a job to do. No, not just a job. He had a mission, a calling much bigger than himself—bigger even than his master.

God wanted this. God.

And if He wanted it, then it must be done. If it took ages, if it drove them both to madness, if it came with unfathomable darkness, or endless pain, he didn't care. He would find a way. God had placed this boy in his hands, had offered him up as a gift, a key to a locked door, and it was only a matter of time before all was revealed. One day, everything would come together for the greater good—every sacrifice would be given its worth.

The boy's screams echoed down the cavern, lost to the mountain of soil and rock and centuries of death surrounding them. The warlock continued, letting the prince's pain bolster his resolve. He knew he was making the right choice.

This was God's plan.

ONE
HAZEL

I SHOULDN'T BE HERE. I shouldn't even be alive. But I am. Miraculously. And now I'm standing outside of Dean's house without an invitation and feeling like a total weirdo. A ball of nerves tumbles around in my stomach, because I'm stuck wondering what's going to happen to me next. Also, I think I might puke. So *that's* cute.

My right arm tingles as I press my shiny, new iPhone to my ear, listening to Mom's pleas for me to come home and finish out the semester as an independent study. Given everything I've been through, Hayden College has offered to let me choose what I want to do for the rest of the academic year without repercussions to my GPA or scholarship. I can withdraw and come back later, I can finish my current classes at home, or I can stay here with everybody else.

"I'm not giving up," I say into the phone for what feels like the billionth time. On the other end, the line goes silent. "I promise, Mom," I continue. "I'm fine now. Landon is dead. I know it's only been a few days, but yes, I *still* want to stay on campus."

As I'm filled with thoughts of Landon, my throat dries up like the Sahara Desert and guilt squeezes my core. *Poor Landon.* He had no control over what happened to him and now he's been blamed for murders that weren't his fault. Mom knows all about my abilities with the spirits, but I didn't dare tell her the truth of how I ended up in that hospital. Like almost everyone else, she thinks Landon was a deranged serial killer. If she knew a supernatural grim reaper had crossed into the human realm and was controlling men to murder young girls, and that the terrifying creature tried to sacrifice me for reasons that are still murky, she'd probably have a heart attack. And rightfully so. This whole thing is crazy.

Mom lets out a long sigh. "I just hate that I wasn't there to stop it. And I hate that you're so far away."

It's only been twenty-four hours since she flew home and I refused to go with her. But I'm not leaving and I can't explain all the reasons, even if I already miss her and the comfort her presence brings. Sometimes, "adulting" is harder than I thought it would be.

"I know, Mom," I say, needing to end this call before I give in and find myself on a flight back to Ohio, "but I don't want to talk about it anymore. I'm fine now. I'm safe. It's over and I'm going to move on with my life. Besides, I'll be coming home soon for Thanksgiving and then winter break." I swipe the toe of my boot along the cobbled driveway and suppress a shiver. It's extra cold out today.

"You promise to talk to the school counseling services? Call them right away?"

"Yes." I let out a huff of pent up energy. Will I call them? Doubtful. Because what could I possibly say to a therapist that wouldn't end with me locked up in a padded room? This supernatural craziness is far beyond the run-of-the-mill patient and no therapist will believe a word of the truth. And I know myself. I'd somehow get my story all mixed up if I tried to stick to what the police were told. At least being a minor allowed my name and image to be withheld from the nosey reporters. I don't know what I'd do if everyone on campus knew about what happened with Landon.

A minute later, Mom and I say our goodbyes, and I pretend that I didn't just lie to the woman who loves me more than anyone on planet Earth.

I slide my phone into my coat, suck on my bottom lip for a hot minute, and stare up at the brick cottage—Dean's house. It's still cute as a button, with its slanted roof and adorable curb appeal. The ivy crawling up one wall is officially hibernating; most of the leaves have fallen since autumn surrendered to winter. A trickle of sweat drips down the back of my neck, making me doubly cold. Ew, I hate the cold. Why didn't I get a scholarship to Florida? California? Or even better—Hawaii? I can picture it now, me on a beach with a lei around my neck, a coconut drink in my hand, and a cute surfer boy to crush on.

But then again, somehow I *know* that Khali chick is right and we're connected. We were drawn to find each other, fated in some strange way. And if I wasn't here in this small town of Westinbrook, West Virginia, I wouldn't have met Macy and Cora. And I wouldn't know Dean.

One thought of him and I'm blushing. My crush has gotten out of control, and now it's turning desperate because the dragon princess has shown up. Khali is gorgeous times a million, a perfect match for Dean. I'm glad she's here, considering she saved my life, but seriously, I can't compete with *that*. I'm not even going to try.

A cold breeze sweeps a strand of my dirty blonde hair from my ponytail and I brush it behind my ear. I can't keep procrastinating this or I'll never be able to focus enough to actually study or live a normal life. I need to march up there, knock on the door, and talk to him and Khali about what I should expect from here on out.

Do I move? Nope. I just stand here, freezing my butt off like the little chicken I am.

I haven't heard from them since they left me in the hospital. They didn't give me any more details about what's been going on, either. It's been three days and I haven't seen or heard from them at all. No calls. Nothing.

Radio silence.

Gosh, I'm being so annoying, just standing here! I force myself forward, practically running up the narrow front walk, and knock on the front door. I also push the doorbell. Twice. It chimes inside the house and I step back, waiting for footsteps—footsteps that don't come.

They're not home.

I groan and begin trudging back the way I came, just as Dean's sporty black car rolls into the driveway. From behind the sheen of glass, I spot Khali sitting in the passenger seat. She waves and smiles, her friendly grin breaking down a fraction of my worry. Dean's face is rigid and motionless, that unreadable mask he tends to wear firmly in place. And once again, I'm uneasy.

They pull into the garage and jump out of the car, coming to meet me on the front lawn. Despite the cold, he doesn't invite me inside, and something about that makes me sad. His muscles move easily underneath the thin heather gray sweater and tight dark jeans as he walks my way, and I have to blink several times to keep myself from staring like a kid in a candy shop. Why does he have to be so hot?

"What's wrong?" Dean asks, getting right to the point. He's standing so close to Khali, I'm convinced he's protecting her from me or something, which seems a little weird considering she's a powerful dragon shifter. Or maybe they're a couple now and he wants to be close to her like I want to be close to him.

My heart twists and I clear my throat. "Nothing is wrong, it's just, I haven't heard from you guys and I wanted to know what's going to happen next."

Khali opens her mouth but Dean beats her to it.

"Nothing is going to happen next," he grumbles. "Khali and I are going to take care of things and you're going to return to your normal life."

Khali flashes him a heated look, her face set in a guarded expression. Does she agree with him? Little sparks of magic dance behind her one brown and one blue eyes.

I shake my head. "Are you serious? But you said Khali and I are connected somehow. Aren't we supposed to figure that out? Aren't I supposed to help you? You might need me."

Dean's sigh is long and arduous, like I'm a pest that won't go away. It's one more form of rejection to add to the pile when it comes to this boy. I'm so emotional lately, I can't help the tears that spring to my eyes. *Dang it!*

"I should go," I snap, quick to anger before they can tell he's hurt my feelings. "If you don't want me here, then fine. Whatever!" I turn and stomp away. I don't have time for this crap. I should be focusing on my studies. I need to remember why I'm here, to ace my Biology degree and get into a vet school. I have plans. I don't have to help them with their weird dragon stuff. I'd prefer to spend my life with furbabies, anyway.

Even as I think it, I know it's not entirely true. And I know that, like them, I'm also different. I don't exactly fit into the regular world, which is probably why I want to be a vet in the first place. Animals are so much better than people.

"No, wait," Khali finally speaks, her voice solid. "What if she's right?"

I keep walking. I can't get away from Dean fast enough. But Khali catches up to me, grabbing my arm, and something inside of me erupts. It's like floodgates opening, or a high-watt lightbulb bursting to life. Energy floods me—insane, amazing, crazy, powerful energy!

Khali stumbles back, her unusual eyes wide and her head shaking in disbelief. Her dark caramel curls blow across her forehead, a few strands catching in her mouth.

As quick as the powerful energy was there, it's gone. And I don't know what to make of it either. Khali and I stare at each other, our mouths opening and closing like fish out of water.

"What just happened?" I croak. "You felt that too, right?"

She doesn't answer. In fact, her expression turns frantic.

"I'll be right back," she says, her voice no longer solid, but weak, and then she runs inside. To see that fearsome warrior princess—the kind of badass girl perfect for movies or anime—*run away* from little old me is downright confusing.

"What did you do to her?" Dean's voice drips in accusation.

I scoff. Unbelievable! "I didn't do anything. And P.S., I thought you and I were friends. I guess I was wrong."

It's my turn to take off. Does he follow me? No. He goes after Khali, as I expected. And it feels just as bad as I thought it would. No, it feels *worse*. Rejection is a twisting knife in my heart that won't stop turning and I'm tired of putting myself in this position. I wanted to talk to them about everything that's happened to me, not to get warped by my stupid crush.

My insides are a complete mess from all the emotions and the strange energy that shot through my body when Khali touched me. All I want is to get back to my dorm room and process this encounter in privacy. Scratch that—I need a good Netflix binge with Cora and Macy. I wonder if the newest season of our favorite comedy is up, the one about the snooty family who loses their fortune and ends up living in a backwater town. I could use a few belly-laughs right about now.

Hello there, girly, a raspy voice calls out.

I stop midstep, icy fear covering my entire body. Goosebumps race across my flesh as my fingers automatically jump to the obsidian necklace heavy on my neck, making sure it's still there. It is, of course. So why isn't it working?

Can you help a poor fellow out or are you too selfish to care about anyone but yourself?

I can feel the spirit hovering to my right but I don't dare look directly at him. He's a human spirit with a frenzied darkness swirling around him. The people who hurt other people during their lives and end up dead and milling about? Yeah. *This* is what they look like. They carry a dark energy with them that's unmistakeable. It's terrifying and turns my stomach into a knot, but I've always ignored them. This is the first time an evil spirit has been able to talk directly to me, and what's worse, it's as if he knows I can hear him. He knows I can talk back.

I start walking again, pretending I don't know that he's there.

Blood pumps through my veins like boiling water. The spirit follows me. I hurry along the quaint neighborhood street, careful to keep my head down.

What's your thing? the spirit asks, his demanding voice adding fuel to my fear. He sounds so arrogant, so in charge and used to getting his way. *What do you like? Maybe I can help you and you can help me. We could come to an agreement.*

I don't know how to make this thing go away. My hands are shaking. My vision is blurred by tears.

I know you can hear me, he sing-songs. *You're just too selfish to listen. Well, you better watch out, girly. I'll make you listen!*

"You can't touch me," I snap, finally turning on him. He's dressed in a fancy business suit, looking like he was a highly successful man in his life, the kind of man used to taking whatever it is he wants without apology. The darkness that surrounds him is thick as oily smoke, and I know that whatever he did during his life, it was not good. Not at all.

I bet you're self-righteous. He comes in close, looking me dead in the eyes. His are practically black. Evil. I don't know what comes over me, but I stare back, glaring and sending as much defiance in his direction as I can. He can't touch me. He can't make me do anything.

You think you know how biology works. You think my needs are wrong? They aren't wrong. They're completely natural. You have no idea how self-righteous you all sound when you tell me what to do with my body, who to be with, what's allowed. As if we don't just make up our own rules as we go along, anyway!

"Get away from me," I snap, interrupting his diatribe. "You aren't going to get what you want from me. Ever."

Or perhaps I will.

"You don't want to mess with me." I stand my ground. "I know how to cast you to Hell."

It's a total bluff but thank heavens it works. His eyes narrow and then in a roar, he leaves.

Just as he goes, he flashes an image into my mind and my entire body reacts, my stomach cramping until I have to stumble over to the bushes and vomit. Everything convulses with the shock of what happened. My eyes and throat burn. That man, he was a very bad person. He showed me what he did during his lifetime. Not only that, he wants me to help him hurt more people, some of them children. Even in death, he's sick and twisted. Addicted. Wrong.

I sit on the sidewalk, my legs useless jelly, my stomach rotten, and I burst into tears.

My abilities, they aren't getting better. They're not under control. They're only getting worse. If that vile ghost can talk to me and send me those horrible images, what's next?

After a few minutes, I calm myself, remembering exactly where I am—on the side of the street, squatting in Dean's picturesque neighborhood. It's late evening and starting to get dark. I look around, grateful there's nobody out here but me. That won't last. If I don't get moving, someone is going to stumble upon me and ask if I need help. Either that, or they'll call the police. That's the last thing I need right now.

I stand on wobbly legs and force myself to keep walking. This time, I don't turn toward campus but toward Main Street, heading for The Flowering Chakra. I have to talk to Harmony. I need help, and if Dean and Khali aren't going to give a crap about me, I know she will. My mind races, my thoughts a tangled mess that begin to unwind as I hurry. I know that evil spirit left, but I can't help but think he's going to come back. And if not him, maybe another one? Maybe one that's even more awful? If Harmony doesn't have the answers to help me, I'll have to find someone who does. The thought strikes me like a punch to the gut. I need to know where I come from to know why I'm the way that I am. There's a good chance I'm going to have to track down my sperm donor of a father.

TWO
KHALI

THE HUMAN REALM IS NOTHING like I expected. It's much, much worse.

After touching Hazel and experiencing my magic's reaction, I raced straight through Dean's house and to the privacy of his backyard, dropped to my knees, and dug my fingers into the cool grass until I found a layer of dirt. And then I stayed. I don't know how long I've been out here, but it feels like ages with every second stretching into a desperate eternity. Why is this realm so damaging to my magic? I saw Dean in his dragon form the night I arrived here. He's been living here for a few years and he can still shift. I've been here for a few days and I doubt I could stay shifted in this place for very long. My dragon feels like she's about to be put into a deep sleep.

Dean stands waiting underneath the porch, his presence quiet and protecting, as if he senses not to interrupt but knows I don't want to be alone, either. He's a good man, strong, solid and sure, and being around him again highlights the emotions battling inside me. I'm weak and confused and so many other things, quickly switching from one feeling to the next.

The sun is setting, bathing everything in a pretty blue-gold light. It's getting colder by the minute which is distracting. I'll have to give up soon. But that might feel like giving up on my magic entirely, and if there's anything I've learned about myself these past few weeks, it's that I don't give up. I can't. I won't.

I stay in my spot on the cold grass, focusing, relaxing, staying present with who I am and what I can do. Finally, it's there—praise the Gods! It's a little speck, a tiny seed breaking open after a long winter. It begins to grow, slow but persistent. My beloved earth elemental returns to me. It's like liquid sunshine being poured over my entire being and I've never been so grateful for the element. I smile with pure relief and sit back. My hands are covered in green stains and clumpy brown dirt, fingernails caked under the edges, but I don't care.

I get up and shake out my legs, finally meeting Dean's worried gaze.

"Are you okay?" He stands immobile, seemingly immune to the cold. I would be too if I had pulled on my fire elemental, but I didn't want to risk using it while I searched for my missing earth magic.

I nod. "I'm okay." Even as I say it, it feels like a lie.

"Want to talk about it?"

I nod again and point toward the glass door. "Yes, but let's go inside and get warmed up."

He raises an eyebrow. He knows what I'm capable of, that I shouldn't have to worry about the cold for the same reasons he doesn't have to. "We have a lot to talk about."

Once we're inside, I busy myself with scrubbing my hands clean under the faucet and he starts up a pot of tea. I know it's called a faucet because I asked him when I first saw it. Just like many things in this realm, they're brand new to me. Technology is fascinating, I'll admit, but I still wouldn't trade it for the thrill of magic and the unblemished countryside of Drakenon. It's times like these where I long to fly and fly until I can't think of another worried thought.

Dean moves around me, pulling mugs from the cupboard and tea packets from the food pantry—the tea packets are another new convenience for me. I'm still a little off-centered at his house, bewildered by the white and dark smooth surfaces and the sleek, comfortable lifestyle he lives here. Everything about it is the opposite of the castle, or anything in the realm of Eridas for that matter. *I miss home.*

"I know this mortal world can be jarring, what with our magic being so diminished as it is," he says, leading me to the couch and handing me a cup of steaming tea. "It's nothing like being at Stoneshearth. I'm sure you miss it."

It's as if he read my mind even though I know that's not possible. It's nice that he understands and that he probably misses it, too. I'm less alone and that is worth his company.

I take a deep inhalation of the lavender scented liquid and bring my lips to the edge of the hot mug, allowing some of the tea to warm me from the inside out. It tastes as it smells, and I close my eyes for a second, breathing it in. Then I set the mug on the side table and face Dean.

"It's not just that," I say carefully. "There's been something happening to me over the last few months. I didn't want to face it for what it was, but I can no longer pretend it isn't real."

A line forms between his dark eyebrows and he also puts his mug down, shifting closer. "What's wrong?"

There's no point in dragging this out any longer. "I think I'm losing my magic." My voice is shaking but I'm still relieved to speak this aloud. "It's been little moments," I continue. "Small lapses in magic where one second it's there and the next it's gone. Not weak, not dormant, but *gone*. Has it ever been that way for you?"

He shakes his head. "Mine is weaker, and sometimes uncontrollable, but it's always been there."

"That's what I expected to happen when I came here," I continue. "I've heard the stories about this realm and thought it would be the same for me, that my magic would slowly dwindle the longer I stayed. But it's been happening so much faster than that. And the only difference I can think of is that I was immediately drawn to Hazel when I got here, and truthfully, I still am. Are you drawn to her, too?"

His jaw tightens, his gaze holding fast to the floor. "I don't know how to answer that. Hazel is ... something to me. I'm not sure what, yet."

I suspect he harbors romantic feelings towards her that he doesn't want to acknowledge. Is it because I'm here that he won't say? Because of who I am to him that he's afraid to care about her? I leave that conversation for a later time. I'm not ready for it either.

"Well, I can feel the connection between Hazel and me. Like I said, I think with our birthdays being the same, there's no coincidence there. Here's the other thing. The few times I've touched her, I've felt my magic react. Every single time. I didn't put it all together until earlier when I grabbed her arm and it happened again. It suddenly became obvious." I swallow hard and search his coal-like eyes, hoping he'll know what to do.

"React how?"

"Not well. This last time, my earth magic disappeared. You saw that it wasn't gone for a few seconds or minutes, it took much longer to get it back. How long was I outside?"

"Two hours." He frowns as he digests this information, conflicted emotions flickering across his tanned face. "We need to continue to keep you two away from each other," he says. "At least until we figure out what's going on." This has been his idea from the beginning, to keep her out of things. I don't like it because I wonder if I'm going to need her, but now that my magic isn't responding well to her, I'm scared of what it could mean.

"I hate to agree, but I don't know what else to do." I lean back and find my mug again, taking a drink and letting the warmth calm me. I check that my four elementals are intact, and I find them easily. Once again I wonder if Hazel isn't only a human medium, but if she's mixed blood, part of our realm too, and if her abilities are linked to spirit magic. They must be! It's the only explanation that makes sense as to why she's seen supernaturals on the other side, especially the reaper. And Owen. Just thinking of him makes my eyes water. More than missing home, I miss *him*.

"Are you okay?" Dean immediately slides closer and wraps a protective arm around my shoulders.

"I miss Owen," I breathe softly, letting myself admit the truth of my feelings. "He was my best friend. I loved him. It seemed like we might get to end up together on the throne. And even your parents started to be open to the idea of it. Silas couldn't handle seeing someone else taking what he felt belonged to him."

Dean freezes, and I wonder what he's feeling, what he's thinking. "I miss Owen too. I can't believe my brother would do that to him, but I do believe you. It makes me sick." His eyes take on a haunted gleam and I wonder how he'd react if he'd seen the things I saw that night.

Hatred for Silas eats me alive and I have to grit my teeth to keep from spewing out all the pent up feelings for that vile princeling. I need to change the subject before the tears start and I'm unable to stop them. "Anyway, back to Hazel." I sigh. "I can't help but think we're going to need each other at some point. Logically, I want to stay away from her, but it's like instinctively I can't."

He places two warm palms on my shoulders and looks me square in the eyes. "No. You can't risk losing more of your magic, especially while you're here where it's already weakened. Let me take care of Hazel. You have enough to worry about."

"What do you mean when you say take care of Hazel?" I raise an eyebrow.

"I will make sure she doesn't get hurt." The tiniest bit of color blooms on his cheeks and now I know for sure he has feelings for her. He must. But it's strange. I'm happy for him and I'm also scared for myself. I thought my girlhood feelings for Dean would come racing back when I saw him again, but so far, they haven't. Maybe I'm too distracted by everything that's happened. Or maybe we weren't meant to be together in the first place. Or perhaps, feelings don't matter and only what's best for Drakenon does.

Now I'm starting to sound like my mother.

"I've only been in this realm for a few days but I already feel like I'm wasting time," I grumble, thinking about the people who need me right now. "I've got to *do* something."

Since arriving, Dean and I have had a lot to talk about, mainly trying to come up with an actual plan to save my father and his brother, but so far, we have nothing. I don't know what to do. Not only that, but Dean's been cagey and still hasn't told me *why* he willingly came here, because I'm pretty sure he did. He and I both know what happened the night he was exiled from Drakenon, but it's like he doesn't want to speak of it, like it's all a big secret, even from me.

I stand and pace the room. Frantic energy races up and down my limbs the more I realize the position I've gotten myself into by coming here. Bram has been kidnapped by an Occultist. I'm engaged to a murderer who wants to use me to make him elemental children, and my father is still lying in his deathbed, hexed and unresponsive. He could already gone. No. I can't imagine a scenario where he's not alive. I have to stay strong.

"Why are you really here, Dean?" I turn to face him. "That night, *I* kissed you, not the other way around. You could have at least defended yourself, but you didn't even try. You willingly took the fall for me and left." I snap my fingers. "Just like that."

He doesn't say anything, just stares at me and swallows hard, before picking up the empty mugs and taking them into the kitchen. I follow close behind, frustrated.

"Tell me why you're in this realm instead of back in Drakenon. Maybe it can help me. Maybe it can help your *brother*. Think about it, Dean. Bram is completely defenseless and at the hands of the Occultists."

He gently places the mugs in the sink and hangs his head. "That's not my fault," he finally speaks. "Bram shouldn't have left the castle. He knew the risks."

"If Bram didn't leave with me, I'd never have made it here," I huff. "What aren't you telling me?"

But he doesn't say anything beyond, "I can't say." And then he grabs his car keys and heads for the door. "I have a class tonight. I'll see you later." Two seconds later, the door slams and he's gone.

I'm dumbstruck, still trying to catch my breath, fingers opening and closing with heated magic; I'm so mad. What in the world just happened?

I hate his car. Riding in that metal contraption is unnerving. I've had to do it a few times and every time I want to jump out of it and fly away. But right now, I'd jump right in if I could catch up to him. I rush outside to do just that and watch as it speeds down the road. Anger builds. I came all this way to get his help—Bram needs him, my father needs him, his kingdom needs him—and he runs away from me? He exits mid-conversation when I risked everything to come here and get his help?

I don't think so!

It's time I test my shifting abilities again.

MY BLACK HIDE BLENDS INTO the inky darkness. My inner-dragon feels strange, like she's lethargic. But she's eager to please and together we work as one cohesive unit, tracking Dean's car, our wings bouncing on the air current, our senses attuned to the night. The city lights twinkle below as if the stars spilled out of the sky and fell to the earth. It's a unique beauty unlike anything I've seen in Eridas, but something about it also feels wrong, like admiring it would make me a traitor to my realm and diminish my magic even more.

Dean wasn't lying about his destination. I expected his car to drive a great distance, but he only drove it to the other side of his school. I hover from a distance, landing on the roof of a nearby building, and will my dragon body to be as quiet and camouflaged as possible. I also hope Dean doesn't sense me nearby, or if he does, he assumes I'm still at his house. We all have that ability to sense others of our kind but Dean's talent for it is stronger than most.

Nobody is around when he slides from the driver's seat and walks toward a nearby building, going inside like he's done it a million times before. I fly down into the extra shadowy space between the buildings and shift back into my human form. I'm dressed to match the other human women here, with tight blue pants called jeans and a black flowy top called a blouse. We don't dress anything like this at home and I have to admit, I love these clothes. This is so much better than wearing heavy dresses all the time. My limbs move freely as I stealthily charge into the building after Dean.

I don't understand technology, but it doesn't take a genius to realize that this place is filled with it. The main hallway is well-lit and empty. It reminds me of Dean's home, with its white walls and gray floors. On either side of the hallway are doors with glass windows. I peer into a few, seeing rows and rows of what Dean told me are computers. The strange-looking boxes don't make any sense to me, but he said computers run the world here. They must be important. Some of the rooms have long tables with all sorts of glass vials, like a modern-world apothecary, and others are filled with all sorts of metal and tools. The only thing I can liken it to is a blacksmith's shop, but even that doesn't explain it properly.

Most of the rooms are empty, though a few have people working in them. I keep going, noticing how eerily quiet it is. Somehow I doubt Dean is here for a class. There doesn't seem to be many people in the building, let alone enough for a class. Dean took me with him earlier today to sit in on one of his classes so I could experience his world. I was both overwhelmed and energized by the buzz of the students, the people everywhere, the air of learning. All that seems to be gone now.

Where are you, Dean?

That's when I spot him. I quickly slink back from the window, take a deep breath, and then look again. His back is to me, and he's working in one of the blacksmith-type rooms. I squint, trying to see what he's doing, and my heart hammers. He's using his magic. Wait. No. He wouldn't. Yes. He is! He's using his magic! It looks like he's trying to fuse something together with a ball of fire in his hands. What is he thinking? It's so risky; he could get caught by a regular mortal. In fact, it's only a matter of time until he does if he keeps this behavior up.

I burst through the door, unable to stop myself from yelling at him. "Are you insane?"

He stills, his back moving up and down as he takes a deep breath, and then turns on me. "I hoped you'd follow me," he says, voice laced with relief. "I swore to my mother that I would not tell *anyone* what I was doing unless they already knew. Now that you've seen me in action, now that you know, I can finally tell you what's been going on and why I'm here."

I blink, bewildered, and look around. In front of him are little tiles that almost glitter under the lighting. Some appear to be melted.

"What's going on? What are those?"

His eyes flash to the door for the briefest of seconds, as if double checking we're alone.

"These are microchips," he says. The word means nothing to me. He goes on. "I have independent study labs set up in here nearly every night when nobody else is around so I can do my work. I don't normally blast them with fire, but hey, I had to get your attention."

"I don't understand." I fold my arms over my chest and continue to stare, confused as ever.

He swallows hard. "I came to this realm on purpose. My parents knew because I had been asking them to let me go for a long time. They didn't want me to leave." An embarrassed expression crosses his features and he can barely look at me. "I needed to make it look like I was exiled from Drakenon so that I could come here without them stopping me and without others questioning my motives." He gives me a sheepish look. "I knew you had feelings for me, so I used them to my advantage. I'm sorry."

My throat goes dry and it all comes back to me. The way I'd pined for him for years, and the way he'd ignored me until one magical night, he'd flirted with me mercilessly. I couldn't help myself—I'd kissed him. And it was wonderful. My first kiss! And suddenly, it was as if everyone knew about the kiss, knew he'd broken the treaty. The next day, he was gone. Just like that. It had all happened so fast and I'd lived with daily guilt over it ever since. Guilt, and questions, because he'd never put up a fight.

I don't know what comes over me, but I stride up to him and punch him straight in the gut.

He grimaces and doubles over. "I deserved that," he says in a grunt. My hand aches but I don't care. That felt too good to regret.

"Do you have any idea the guilt I've lived with? All this time I thought I'd ruined your life. You *used* me!"

He inches closer, reaching out an arm like he wants to hug me but is also wary of another punch.

I pull back. "Don't touch me."

"I'm sorry," he says again. "Truly, I never meant to hurt you."

"All so you could run away from your people, your kingdom, your *destiny*, to study these human devices? This is ridiculous, no wonder your parents didn't want you to go."

"No." His eyes are wide, growing fiery with the intensity of his passion for this. "You don't understand. It wasn't because I wanted to leave home, it was because I wanted to save it." Silence stretches between us as I try to take that in. The room itself is a contrast of stark surfaces, just like me and Dean, apparently. "The Occultists had taken over the entire Fae Kingdoms," he continues. "The capital city of Highburne had fallen and nobody thought they'd ever be able to conquer the fae, *but they did*. Don't you see? It's only a matter of time before they do the same thing to Drakenon. I knew that and everyone else seemed so casual about it, like it was impossible, like we'd never lose to them. I couldn't get my father or his advisors to listen to me, so I left. I'm here to find a way to defeat our enemies before it's too late."

"And how are you supposed to do that here?" I scoff. "This mortal realm is devoid of strong magic." Sure, we can still use our magic in the beginning, but it's not nearly what it is back home. And over time, our magic will fade to nothing. How could he think coming here was a good idea?

"Technology," he says simply.

I frown. "Technology doesn't work in our realm. You know that. Everybody knows that. Sure, we don't get taught a lot about this realm, but we all got taught that much."

"But what if technology did work?" he whispers. He steps closer, his eyes sparkling and alive in a way I haven't seen since arriving here. He really believes in what he's talking about. "The kind of technology they have here is extraordinary."

"More extraordinary than magic?" I ask, skeptically.

"Sometimes," he responds. "And sometimes more deadly, too. If I can get my plan to work, I can save Bram and your father. I can save everyone."

You can't save Owen, I think. *It's too late for him.*

"And if it doesn't work?"

That sparkle in his eyes dulls. "It has to work. What other options do we have to fight the Occultists? You've seen one of the warlocks, but Khali, there are *thousands* of them in their cult. If they conquer Drakenon, the rest of Eridas will fall. We'll all be helpless, and many of us, especially anyone with royal blood, will be hunted down and executed."

I bite my lip, knowing I have to say more. My memories race back to the conversations Bram and I had, to the theories talked about over dinner at the castle. I have to tell Dean. As much as he deserves my silence right now, my kingdom deserves so much more. "Not just Eridas," I say. "We believe that once the Occultists conquer our realm, they won't stop there."

He sighs, his lips forming into a tight line. "I always suspected it. Are you sure?"

I nod. "They want to find a way to get through the portals. They're coming for this realm next."

THREE
HAZEL

HARMONY IS ABOUT TO CLOSE up shop when I find her. One look at me and her misty blue eyes well up with the kind of concern I was searching for in the wrong people. Everything I've been through hits me all at once and I find myself bursting into tears. *Again.*

Nobody is here but us so she immediately locks up The Flowering Chakra, leads me to the back room, and wraps me in her grandmotherly arms. "What's wrong, Honey?"

I have no one to talk to about this. I don't want to scare Cora and Macy away from me. Even though they know the basics of my curse, what if they didn't believe the rest? They'd probably think I was crazy. Or what if they do believe, but decide I'm too much of a risk to be around? Mom can't know the truth because she'll make me come home. Dean and Khali are freezing me out. Harmony is all I have. So when I open my mouth to speak, my story comes tumbling out before I can stop myself.

I'm careful not to mention anything about the dragon shifters since that's not my secret to tell, but I do explain how the reaper controlled Landon to try to perform a ritual on me and ended up killing my friend in the process. As I speak, her knobby hands cover her mouth and her aged eyes fill with tears, but she stays silent while I finish up with my current problem.

"Somehow, I've opened myself up to more spirits than ever before," I say, a chill taking over my entire body as I think about it. "It's gotten really, really bad."

"Bad how?" Her eyebrows knit together, accentuating her wrinkles.

So I tell her about the horrible spirit who'd just *spoken* to me and sent me grim images, images that I'll never be able to scrape from my mind. Goosebumps race up and down my arms and my stomach feels like it's filled with rocks. "Can you help me?" I run my fingertips along the obsidian necklace, wishing things could go back to the way they were a few weeks ago. "Is there anything more I can do to keep these unwanted ghosts out?"

Her eyes go hazy, and I know she's doing her woo-woo thing where she looks at a person's future paths in order to give them advice. She's previously told me that these paths were always changing and that she didn't always see every possibility, but she could see enough to help someone make a decision when standing at a crossroads. I think it's a great gift, even if it has its flaws. I would take her gift over mine any day of the week. I'd much rather sit down with a client and talk to them about which direction to take in their life as opposed to helping them connect with a deceased loved one.

"I hate to say it," she says, her eyes clearing, "but I think we need to stop the readings you're doing here until we can figure out how to control this. I see this getting worse before it gets better."

I suck in a breath. Getting worse? Fun times—not.

An overwhelming feeling of defeat hovers over me like a dark cloud and I lean back into the puffy, brown couch and stare at the lavender wall. Outside, the sun has almost set despite the early hour, the signal to my body that it's time for my yearly dose of seasonal depression.

"You'll have to go back to working on the sales floor," Harmony says, her voice soft. "I'm sorry. I know you want extra money for grad school."

"Thank you, but you're right." My voice sounds as defeated as I feel. Truth is, I don't know how I can live this way. Vet school is the last thing on my mind right now. If this is the beginning of the dark spirits getting more and more access to me, they'll ruin my life. I'm sad to let the easy money go, but I'm also terrified of willingly opening myself up to the spirit realm any more than I already have. What will come through next time? And if I'm with a client when it happens again, how will I handle them *and* an evil presence? No way I can take that on.

"Anything else I can do in the meantime?" I take in a deep breath and force the fear to leave my body. I need to be strong.

"There is one thing I could show you," she says slowly. "And I've seen that you're open to it, but…" Her voice trails off and her eyes go hazy again so I give her a moment until they clear. "Yes, good," she finally says. "You can be trusted."

My heartbeats scatter. Trusted? Of course I can be trusted!

"Come," she says, "we don't have much time. The spell needs to happen within the first hour of moonlight for it to be most potent."

Umm, what now? Spell? Is she a witch?

Okay, I know she's a little bit of an oddball but I didn't know that she does things under the moonlight. Sure, a *lot* of her customers claim to be witches, but their version of witchcraft seems to be more about positive thinking and manifestation than about actual spells. I guess they're "witches" in their own way, but something about Harmony's energy is eons beyond what a regular human could attempt with witchcraft. Had anyone else suggested a spell, I probably wouldn't agree to go along with it. But I trust Harmony. Even if I am beginning to realize there's something supernatural about her.

We hit the lights, lock up, and hurry to her car. It's a cute little robin egg blue Volkswagen Beetle that's seen better days but I immediately love it. It's so her. We stay silent as she drives, the car's heater working overtime and smelling faintly of decades old dust and fresh clary sage. After a few minutes of comfortable silence, she pulls into an empty parking lot and stops in front of the *last* place I want to be: a cemetery. That same fear once again prickles up and down my arms and I have to take a bunch of short breaths to keep from freaking the freak out. I hate cemeteries. Are they crawling with spirits? Actually, no. Spirits tend to go to the places they were familiar with, and not many people spend a lot of time hanging out in cemeteries while they're alive, but cemeteries remind me too much of my curse so I avoid them whenever possible.

"It's okay." Harmony touches my arm and her warmth immediately settles my nerves. "You're going to do great."

"I guess we'll see about that," I sigh.

The gates to the cemetery are closed and I think this is my chance to get out of here, but then Harmony produces a key. She unlocks the gate as if she's done this many, many times before and inside we go. This place is one of the old civil war cemeteries they have all over this part of the country. It's more of a relic and tourist's spot than an actual functioning cemetery.

"How did you get your hands on a key?"

She chuckles. "I have friends."

"Okay, so do I, but none of my friends can lend me keys to cool, albeit a bit creepy, places."

She chuckles again and we fall into our regular companionable silence.

As we walk, my eyes adjust to the night. The sky is clear, but it's cold, winter is almost upon us and the air smells like it might snow. There aren't any clouds and since it's so clear out, sound travels freely. Not that there's much sound here besides our footsteps on the cold, crunchy grass. Everything is blanketed in eerie silence. We hike for a while, going deeper and deeper, until we finally stop in a clearing of trees. There are old and sunken headstones all around us. Above, the moon shines down, washing everything in an icy blue light. It's not a full moon, like I would imagine is necessary for spell-work based off of the way The Flowering Charka's customers talk. It's just a regular half moon up there, waxing or waning, I have no clue.

Harmony turns to me. She's dressed in her typical flowy clothes but has added a massive black knit cardigan overtop. It has a hood, which she's pulled over her head of white dreadlocks, and something about this style is incredibly creepy but also super cool. Her eyes and skin shine pale in the moonlight. I mean, she's got to be a witch right? Just look at her!

"You are spirit energy," Harmony says, breaking my train of thought. I stare, hanging on her every word. "You possess the *very rare* fifth elemental."

I hold my breath, swallowing the truth down like a rock in my throat. She's confirmed the things Khali had said about me, but I still don't really know what that means, or if I want it to be true. Since I don't want to bring up Khali or other realms right now, I opt for a simpler question instead. "Does that mean I don't belong here?"

She smiles and her eyes twinkle in the moonlight. There's love there, I know it. Somehow she and I are bonded. The unease I've been feeling vanishes and I know, intuitively, that I'm in good hands. Harmony is safe.

"The spirit realm is so vast, so multifaceted, and you are a bridge between it and other places," she says. "Yes, you belong here. Just as you belong in…

other places… and other realms."

My heart races, blood whooshing through my ears. I knew it! Harmony has to be some kind of supernatural. There's no other explanation for her knowing about the other realms.

"My gift is linked to both the spirit element and the earth element," she continues. "I can siphon off a bit of my earth to help you stay grounded here. It won't stop the spirits from coming to you, but it will make *you* more in control of what they can and cannot do, it will make you the one in the driver's seat, so to speak. Not them."

"You would do that for me?" Hope is a beautiful thing and it fills me to the brim.

She nods. "I won't do it for anyone else because it takes such a toll on my own energy," she says. "But I've seen your possible paths and I've seen what you might one day do for all of us. We need you."

"Who's we?"

She doesn't respond.

"The supernaturals?"

A small smile plays along her lips but nothing more. I know it's possible she could be from the darkness, perhaps tied to the reapers in some way, but that's a thought I don't entertain for long. She has helped me so many times and my heart has only felt good things from her. If she's a supernatural, she's one of the good ones. Of that much, I'm certain.

Without another word, she clasps her hands over mine and begins chanting in a language I've never heard before. It's guttural and thick, rich, *earthy*, like the element she claimed to be lending to me. My breathing relaxes and I try not to squeeze every muscle tight. The wind picks up, the leaves lying on the ground swirl around us in a cyclone. They clatter together, their sound reminding me of faint windchimes. The moon seems to shine brighter. I can't see them, but I swear roots made of energy are growing out of my feet, like a tree taking strong hold in its earthen home. Harmony's chants grow stronger and louder. Then all at once, she stops. The leaves flying around us fall to the ground.

I breathe the moment in, and she's right. I do feel different—more confident. It reminds me of when Khali touched me and I was zapped with all that energy for a moment. Only this is different, it's controlled. And it stays. I look up at

Harmony, smiling for the first time in what feels like forever. "Thank you."

"You're welcome, Dear Hazel." Her voice is quiet as a whisper. Then her eyes flutter shut as she goes limp. I catch her reed-thin body just as she passes out.

I CURL UP UNDER MY butter-soft comforter as my body practically melts into the mattress. Tonight was intense. Harmony woke up a couple seconds after losing consciousness and needed to sit down for a while. She assured me she was fine, that she was physically drained after performing the spell and she'd be able to regain her strength soon. I hope she wasn't lying to keep me from feeling guilty. Either way, I do feel bad about it so thank God the spell worked. Sure, it's only been a few hours but I feel so much better now, like I woke from the greatest sleep of my life. I am relaxed and energized at the same time. Not only that, the spirits are back to ignoring me. If I take off my necklace, I bet that won't be the case, so I'm keeping the thing on. I already have her phone number, but Harmony added her home address to her contact details on my phone and said to come straight away if I encountered any problems. She's awesome, but luckily I feel amazing!

There's a light knock on the door. I check my phone. It's 10:50 at night. Only Cora or Macy would be knocking this late and I'm more than happy to have a visitor. My friends have been as worried about me as Mom so it's no wonder they've been checking on me constantly. I don't bother to put on my fuzzy pink robe as I pad over to the door, wearing only the long sleep shirt that barely covers my bum. It's pretty cute, with a cartoon moose eating s'mores and the words "s'more sleep please" written across the top. Mom got it for me as a white elephant gift last Christmas but little did she know I would love it, so the joke's on her.

"You better come bearing gifts in the form of salted dark chocolate," I say as I swing the door open. Only it's not Cora standing on the other side. And it's not Macy. It's Dean.

His lips quirk and his hooded gaze travels up and down my body. "No chocolate, sorry."

Except when those eyes land on mine, I can't help but notice they're close enough to salted dark chocolate—all melty and addictive. Yum. My mouth waters and my cheeks burn. "What are you doing here?" I ask. "How did you get into this building?" He doesn't have access.

He shrugs. "Someone let me in."

"Of course they did," I grumble, trying to sound mad. I should be mad that he's here, mad at him for being a jerk earlier, but the butterflies in my stomach are saying something else.

"Can I come in?" he asks. "We need to talk." Gone is his earlier attitude of exclusion towards me and I don't get it. I pull the door open wider and invite him in. Once inside, I *do* wrap myself in my fuzzy robe, like it's protective armor against his manly charms. Yeah, like I'm going to fight off a sexy, fire breathing dragon shifter with the magical power of comfort. The thought makes me laugh.

"What's so funny?" He raises an eyebrow.

"It's private." I roll my eyes.

He smiles for real and something about that sends those butterflies in my stomach onto a total roller-coaster ride. Goodness me, that is a beautiful smile. He turns to study my room, taking in the nerdy shrine that it is. My bedding is a pretty forest green with lilac accents which is normal enough, but there's no ignoring the many fandom posters, enlarged book quotes, and silly pictures of my friends plastered all over the walls. Hey, at least I don't have cheesy cat posters, I'm leaving those magnificent things for my future veterinary clinic.

"You're in a good mood tonight," he says.

"Well, my good mood is no thanks to you." I fold my arms over my chest and straighten my spine, like the empowered female that I am. Either that, or the earth magic is more potent than I thought because I feel amazing.

"I guess I deserved that."

"Well, in case you forgot, you pushed me away, not the other way around. And now, here you are at eleven at night, so what do you want?"

"I need to explain." He looks pained, like this conversation is hard for him. Oh, please!

"Yes, you do," I say. "You wanted my help. You told me your big secret. I helped you. I got hurt. Landon is dead. Khali saved me. She thinks I have spirit magic and that we're linked. So much happened and now you're suddenly freezing me out? It's crap, Dean."

He steps closer. "It's not like that."

I scoff. "Then what's it like?"

"You and Khali are connected somehow, right? We're not sure how or why yet, but it's there. Do you feel it?"

"I definitely feel it. It's exactly why I came to your house earlier tonight."

A lock of raven hair falls into his eyes, casting them in shadow. "The thing is," he continues, "you need to stay away from Khali."

My heart sinks, and a swell of embarrassment rises to the surface. "And why is that?"

He swallows and stills, his eyes shifting away, like he doesn't want to tell me but knows he has to. Is he ashamed of me? "When you're around her, her powers have ... *problems*. It's almost like you siphon the elements away from her or something."

I want to laugh, want to tell him he's wrong, but somehow I know he's not. "My powers have been more pronounced lately, especially after seeing her, and tonight after I left your house," I swallow down the lump in my throat, "something happened."

His face drains of color. "What happened?"

I look away, the thoughts heavy in my mind. "I don't want to talk about it."

"Are you okay?" He reaches out and takes my hand in his, and I swear I could spontaneously combust. But his priority is Khali, not me. He's here on her behalf, after all, not mine. I pull my hand away.

"I am now."

"Are you sure you don't want to tell me what happened?"

I let out a breath. "The spirits have been bad lately, that's all. Harmony is helping me sort it out."

He frowns.

"I trust her," I add.

He steps back. "I'm glad you have her then."

"Me too."

The silence stretches between us as he holds my gaze. It feels like he wants to say something so I ask, "What is it?"

He breaks eye contact and the tension is lost. "Khali and I have some work to do together and I need her to be strong. So if you could stay away from her, from us, that would be ideal."

The oxygen is sucked from the room.

He continues, backtracking, "But if you need help with anything, you call me and I'll come straight away. We just have to leave Khali out of it."

I smirk. "I don't have your phone number, Dean."

He still doesn't look at me when he walks over to my desk, finds a pen and paper, and scrawls his number across it. "Save this in your phone," he says. "If you need anything, call me. I'll come."

Somehow, I sort of doubt that.

"Are you sure there's not something more you want to tell me?" he asks, meeting my gaze again.

I consider it. But what would I say? That a spirit practically attacked me tonight? That Harmony and I took a little trip to the cemetery to perform a grounding spell, using earth energy to help counteract the spirit energy? Or maybe he wants me to explain in detail why his preference to be around Khali instead of me hurts so much? Hurts for more reasons than one…

No thanks. I'd rather eat overcooked spaghetti.

"No," I say simply, looking him in the eyes again. He's staring back with such intensity that I can hardly breathe. Oh, and there's that little ring of fire dancing around the irises again, which doesn't make sense because he's not angry right now. I don't bother asking him about it. He probably wouldn't tell me anyway. "You should leave. Khali needs you, right?" I shrug and hold my emotions back. "Shouldn't keep your girl waiting."

His gorgeous lips open like he's going to say something more but then he pushes them closed. He's completely still for a beat too long, and I'm struck with the thought that he's going to step *toward* me instead of away. And then what? Hug me? Kiss me? The butterflies in my chest are ecstatic at the thought of either.

But he doesn't do any of those things. He leaves, exactly as I asked.

FOUR

KHALI

THE MORNING SUN STREAMS THROUGH the curtains, casting the room in a yellow hue. Little flecks of gold particles drift on invisible currents, an image that reminds me of home. My chest tightens. I roll back under the fluffy covers in Dean's guest bed and close my eyes. If only the castle were still a home for me, I'd give anything to be back in my own chambers. But as hard as it is to accept, I know my life will never go back to the way it was before Owen died. Every day I stay here is another day I waste when I could be actively trying to save my father and rescue Bram from the Occultists. That is assuming they're still alive.

Dean has gone to his classes for the day so the house is still and silent. After our discussion last night, I understand his decisions better, but I'm skeptical whether his plan will work. He's at Hayden College studying engineering, technology, and computer science—vocations that don't exist in Eridas or make much sense to me. I also asked why Bram didn't take his place considering Bram would have been better suited to come here instead of his eldest brother. Dean claimed he chose not to consult Bram because he didn't know if Bram could pass through the ley line portal, nor was he sure if Bram understood magic enough to do the job.

I held my tongue on that point. I believe Bram could have handled it. In fact, I know he could have. They don't give him the credit he deserves simply because he doesn't have the same magic. Even though nobody will admit it, the prejudice against the non-magic folk is so prevalent in Drakenon that even family members don't realize they're treating one of their own as "less than".

Dean chose Hayden College specifically because of the ley line portal nearby and the classes available. He said he first tried getting the technology to work by smuggling it through the portal into the Fae Kingdom for his meetings with my father, but their attempts proved fruitless. The technology was always rendered useless during the process. The thing I can't get out of my head is that my father was part of this plan. He traveled through dangerous territory to meet Dean on the other side of the portal—multiple times!

I groan and peel myself off the bed, my muscles aching for no apparent reason, and head to the bathroom. The little room is as strange as it is miraculous. When Dean first showed me the basics of how it worked, I almost couldn't believe it. It's only been a few days but I can't imagine going back to the old ways. I use the self-cleaning chamber pot—the toilet—and then step into the shower, letting the instant hot water cleanse me of my aches. The rain equivalent of cleaning is so much faster than drawing a bath, and before long I'm drying off and dressing in the traditional mortal clothing Dean provided. It too is very strange and miraculous.

My dragon is weary. I need to find a safe place to shift so I can test my elements and make sure my magic stays sharp. I slip into my new shiny lace up boots and matching black puffy coat before heading outside into the blustery wind and too-bright sun. My cheeks burn with the cold but my fire elemental is barely a flicker this morning. I try to pull it closer to the surface, to stoke the flame within, but it doesn't change enough to do much. My heart speeds and my breath catches, little beads of sweat forming around my hairline. Why does this keep happening to me? I've plaited my hair down my back but it's still wet, now to the point of freezing, and I'm not used to this level of discomfort.

Maybe I should go back to Dean's house.

I look around, no longer on Dean's street but on a neighboring one with what appears to be mortal shops and a myriad of taverns. Fine clothing is displayed behind large windows and the enchanting aromas of the various foods are unlike anything I've experienced back home. The street is busy but the people here don't seem to notice me as they hurry to get out of the cold. I catch the scent of sugary pastries—and something else. My stomach yawns to life. I don't have currency for this realm, and Dean has plenty of food back at his house, but I follow my nose into the little cafe anyway. The Roasted Bean is warm and the smells are strong, odd, foreign... and intoxicating. My mouth waters as I study the massive menu listed on the back wall, trying to make sense of it but having no clue what anything means besides the tea selections, of which there are many.

I walk toward the front table with a shy smile. There's a chance I can talk my way into a taste, right?

"Hello! There's a line," a young woman's voice calls sharply, and I turn to find a girl staring at me with a heated glare. She's right. There is a queue of people waiting and now they're all looking at me like I've grown a second head.

"Right," I respond quickly, "of course, yes. I apologize."

The girl huffs and whips her head away. I move to the back of the room and wonder what I should do. I'm not used to paying for things, standing in queues, or being glared at by everyone in the room. Being born so highly beloved in Drakenon came with privileges I took for granted.

"She's the type of girl that gives us millennials a bad name," she says loudly to another girl and the two cackle at my expense. Her friend says something about how she bets I order something called the avocado toast, which sets them off into even more laughter. I don't know what any of it means but a raw sense of shame prickles through me and suddenly, all I want to do is to get back to Dean's place.

Actually, no, I don't want that. I want to go home. I need to return to Eridas. Dean isn't going to figure out how to magic his technology anytime soon and I have people counting on me to save them *now*.

I slip past the bystanders and rush toward the door.

"Excuse me," a deep rumbly voice says, "we've been looking for you."

I ignore it and reach for the door handle but a large hand stops me, his calloused fingers spread wide against the glass. I turn to find a familiar face—the man who helped me get Hazel to the hospital. The guard. No, not that. What do they call one of those here? Police officer.

Dean told me to stay away from them. In fact, he told me not to go anywhere without him. Guess I should have listened.

"Hello again," I say sweetly, giving him a smile.

After we took Hazel to the hospital, Dean showed up and ushered me away from the police officers before they had a chance to question me. Dean said it was for the best. I haven't thought much about it since.

"We wondered where you ran off to," the man says slowly, his gaze pinning me. "Whoever you are."

He's close to my father's age, with weathered brown eyes and salt and pepper hair that's been cut so close to his head, he's almost bald. It's a style I've never seen in Drakenon. He's dressed head to toe in a black uniform and smells of peppermint and iron. I have to admit, it's all a little intimidating. "Can you come with me to the station?" he continues. "I have some questions about what happened the other night."

His request doesn't sound like a request. It's an order.

I swallow hard. Should I refuse? Pretend it wasn't me? But no, that wouldn't work. I stand out, especially with my different colored eyes. I always have.

"Questions?" I mutter.

"That's right," he says, a glint of something unreadable in his eyes. "That's what detectives do. We ask questions."

What kind of questions? I want to ask, but I don't. So this is why Dean wanted to avoid the police. These humans can't know who I am, they wouldn't understand. I don't know what else to do, so I nod agreeably.

"Yes, that would be fine." My voice is shaky. My hands, too.

I follow him to the black and white car with the flashing lights, grateful they're not flashing at the moment. He opens the door, and I slide into the passenger's seat, buckling the strap like Dean showed me in his car. I'm not sure what I'm going to say or what kind of power this man holds over me, but I take careful breaths before my mind runs away with itself. When the officer gets in and starts driving, my stomach surges and I'm reminded all over again that I *hate* riding in cars.

Actually, I hate almost everything about this realm. Modern conveniences aside, I don't know who I am here. I don't belong. And I absolutely do *not* want to get stuck here. I let out a short breath, remembering what it was like to be trapped in the castle and have other people in control of my life all the time. I eye the police officer at my side, realizing that if anyone can *literally* lock me up in this stifling mortal world, it would be him.

"WHAT'S YOUR NAME?" THE POLICE officer asks. "I'm Detective Sanders."

He's saying something more as he leads me into the station, but I don't hear a word or reply because I'm too distracted by the swarm of police officers occupying the building. It's noisy, with electric ringing sounds and people talking. He leads me into a small barren room and offers me a seat, taking one for himself. I sit down and gather my hands in my lap underneath a small green table that separates us.

Holding a notepad and an odd looking quill, Officer Sanders looks at me expectantly. I don't know what to do or say, but I'm staring at the paper that's unnaturally smooth and marveling at his quill which looks *nothing* like the quills we have back at home. I am so out of my element right now all because I was foolish and left the house in the middle of broad daylight without a plan or without Dean to cover for me.

The man clears his throat and asks for my name for the second time.

"Khali Elliot." My real name pops out, and I immediately wish I'd lied and given him a fake one instead.

"Okay, Khali, can I see your photo identification?" he asks. "Drivers license is preferable, but a student ID would work too."

I'm not sure what he means but I know I don't have anything. I shake my head and when a suspicious expression wrinkles across his features, I'm quick to add, "I don't have anything with me right now. Sorry."

"You went to the coffee shop without your wallet?" He raises an eyebrow.

I shrug. "I forgot it. That's why I was leaving." The lie is quick.

He licks his lips and lets out a little hissing sound but moves on to the next question. "How do you know Hazel Forrester?"

We have the same birthday and we're connected, probably through a spell. When I'm around her my magic goes haywire. "I don't know her," I reply.

"We have video footage of you visiting her in the hospital." His voice is crisp. Certain.

I swallow, my cheeks warming. "Yes," I say, "that was the first time I had a conversation with her." Not a lie. "I wanted to see if she was okay." Also, not a lie.

"And the boy that was with you at the hospital?"

"He's my friend, Dean," I say.

"Does he know her?" Something about the question feels like a trap. I decide to answer as closely to the truth as I can, for Dean's sake since he's not here to defend himself.

"I think so. I don't know the details, but they have a course together at the college." I shrug and smile again, trying to look like a normal human girl. I feel like my speech is wrong, like my face is wrong, like *I'm* all wrong, and he's going to see right through me. "He also wanted to make sure she was all right, considering everything that happened to her."

"She's a minor." He tilts his head. "How would he have known?"

My face grows hot. "She must have called him."

"Hmm… I guess we'll want to bring him in for questioning too." I hold my breath, hoping Dean won't be mad about this. The detective's eyebrows furrow but he moves on. "What about Landon? Did you know him?"

"That was the first time I'd ever seen him before." My voice cracks as the images from that night flash through my mind. My heart rate picks up.

Detective Sanders slides a tall glass of water to me and I take a long drink, trying to calm my nerves. "I know this might be hard for you," he says in a steady tone, "but it's important you answer everything as honestly as you can."

"Okay," I reply, setting the glass back down on the table.

"I'm going to ask you about what happened in the forest."

I nod. Dean had wanted me to get away when the police had arrived, had tried to get me to leave with him. I'd been too shell-shocked to move. And when they'd asked about what had mutilated Hazel's stomach, I'd said something evil, something that I'd killed. How I was going to talk my way out of this, I didn't know.

"Why were you in the forest that night?"

I had just journeyed through the ley line portal underneath the lake when I ended up on the same shore as Hazel, something unexplainable drawing me to save her. "I was on a walk."

He tilts his head. "A walk? In the middle of nowhere, at night, all by yourself?"

"Yes." I squeeze my hands into fists on my lap and keep my face calm. "I do it all the time."

"Even though girls had been going missing, you were going on walks by yourself all the time? Didn't that seem a little dangerous to you?"

I shrug. "I don't like to live my life afraid of other people." I sound like a liar. I *am* a liar!

"All right," he says though tight lips. "And what happened to lead you to Hazel and Landon?"

"I heard a girl screaming so I ran over to see if I could help." Of course I don't elaborate on the true reason Hazel was in trouble. People here don't know about magic. He wouldn't understand that the reaper killed Landon.

"When I got there," I continue, "Landon was hurting her. He wouldn't let her go. He was going to kill her. I fought him off and when he turned on me, I used a rock to knock him out."

The police officer sits back in his seat. "And Landon died of a brain bleed because of it."

I bite my lip. Truthfully, the reaper killed Landon and I killed the reaper.

"Which was self defense," Sanders adds. "And Forrester's story collaborates with yours, even though she wasn't conscious when we arrived on the scene."

"She was bleeding a lot. She passed out right before you arrived." That's another lie. She was gone much earlier.

He gazes off into the distance, going still for a long moment. Something is ticking behind his eyes, more questions, more possible scenarios. "Landon's friends and family don't think he could have done this. They think he was the fall guy for someone else. Was there anyone else there that night?"

Dean. The reaper.

I shake my head. "Only Landon."

But all I can picture is the supernatural reaper and the way he took physical form after he finished Landon off, how I had to fight him, how Dean helped, and the terrifying way it felt to burn the reaper's newly physical form and wash the ashes into the murky lake. Tears spring to my eyes, hot and demanding. I take another drink of water. It's too cold. My teeth hurt. The glass has made a ring of water on the table. I wipe it away and then put the glass back.

"Don't you find it interesting that such a young kid could be responsible for the deaths of three young girls, dating back two years? Of course, we can't know for sure if it was him, considering he's dead and can't confess, but he's the guy everyone wants to blame now."

"I don't know." I force myself to meet his eyes, gritting out my frustration between my teeth. "He was a bad person, right? He did bad things to one girl so who's to say he didn't do bad things to the other girls."

He hums to himself and nods but I can tell he's doing it to placate me. I look away. There's a little square window with bars, and outside, the sun is still shining too bright.

"Are you a student at the college here?"

"Yes," I lie. Again! Why did I do that? I try not to blink as I hold his gaze.

"What are you studying?" He asks it casually, like we're old friends. But the question sends me into a tailspin because I have no idea how to answer it. I wrack my brain to come up with something, remembering that play book Bram lent to me ages ago that I loved so much. *A Midsummer Night's Dream* by William Shakespeare. It had been from this realm because apparently the royal family had access to things the rest of us didn't.

"Shakespeare," I say, praying I pronounced it right. I clear my throat.

"Oh, a literature major? Or theatre?" he asks.

"Theatre." *That* is a word I understand, considering we had a troupe of talented actors back in court.

"Wonderful. They've got a great program. Quite exclusive and I've heard the audition process is brutal. Your eyes probably help you stand out," he continues, "I've never seen anyone with eyes like yours." My face reddens and he clears his throat. "I have a daughter who's into that stuff, too. She just got cast as Lady Macbeth in the high school play." He puffs up his chest, like I should automatically know what he means.

"That's wonderful," I mimic his earlier compliment.

"You must be quite the little actress," he says plainly.

I nod but inside I'm berating myself because it almost feels like he just said I'm quite the little liar. Even though he's dropped a lot of his earlier intimidating attitude, I can feel his skepticism hiding in the subtext of our conversation. We talk for a minute more before he hands me a card and tells me to contact him if I think of anything else. In the back of my mind, all I can wonder is if he's going to ask around about me and realize there is no Khali Elliot at Hayden College or anywhere else for that matter.

"You're free to go," he says, scooting his chair back with a painful screech.

I stand and leave as quickly as possible, hurrying out into the sunlight and gasping for breath the moment I step outside. I don't know the way back to Dean's house from here but I don't care. I need to put distance between me and that building before Detective Sanders figures out exactly how involved I am in all of this. They may believe Landon to be a murderer or they may believe something else.

Maybe Sanders has more questions.

Maybe things aren't adding up as they should.

And maybe it's too easy to blame the crimes on the one person who died that night.

As I walk down the cracked walkway, careful to keep out of the large street with those terrible cars careening past each other, the detectives words come back to me. "You're free to go." I let out a laugh. I don't feel free to go anywhere. Actually, it's quite the opposite, like I'm one mistake closer to losing everything, and "freedom"? Well, that one tops the list.

FIVE
HAZEL

I'M STRIDING DOWN THE CENTER of campus, hundreds of students shuffling past me in a blur of trendy coats and fuzzy scarves, when I spot Dean going into one of the science buildings. I don't go after him, but the sight of him brings back all the hurtful things he's said and done lately. In a moment of indignation, I switch directions. I'm going to skip the rest of my classes for the day. My mind has been so caught up in everything that happened yesterday, I won't be able to concentrate anyway. Besides, what sane person would be able to listen to dry microbiology and chemistry lectures when there are supernatural mysteries going on around them?

Fifteen minutes later, I find myself across the street from Dean's house, leaning against the trunk of a massive maple tree that's lost all of its leaves, and watching for Khali. I can't go any closer, since Dean has a couple cameras and a powerful ward spelled to protect his place. I want to get to her without him knowing, so I'll have to be patient and wait out here. Even if she plans to stay cooped up in his house all day, I'm hoping that she'll glance out one of the windows at some point and see me standing here. If I were her, and I saw me, I'd come out to talk. I can only hope she'd do the same.

Ten minutes go by… twenty minutes… thirty. After an hour of standing around, I'm about to turn into a human popsicle, I'm getting hungry, I feel guilty about skipping class, and basically, I'm not sure how much longer I can handle this. Dean's house is dead. There's been no movement whatsoever and I'm debating what I should do next when I hear footsteps on the sidewalk.

"Hazel?"

Her voice is so unexpectedly welcome that I nearly squeal.

Khali is strolling toward me from the direction of Main Street. The wind blows strands of her dark hair from her braid, creating a web across her face. She brushes it away and I'm struck by how unique her eyes are. I don't think I'll ever get used to looking at a blue and a brown eye on the same person. She's stylish in a shiny black puffer jacket and matching boots, cheeks and nose rosy from the cold. Her hands are buried into her coat pockets, same as mine. If it weren't for the supermodel genetics that make her stand out amongst the crowd, the girl could easily fit right in with the other Hayden students. To think she's a dragon shifter is hard to believe but I know it's true and try not to let what hides beneath her skin make me nervous.

"Hey," I say, stepping forward with a friendly smile. "I'm so glad you're here. I wanted to talk."

She nods once but keeps her distance. "About what happened yesterday?"

"Yes." I take a deep breath, hoping I say the right words. "There's definitely a magical pull between us and I think we should explore it more, but Dean came to my dorm last night and asked me to stay away from you."

"I know." Her face is unreadable.

"So… is it only Dean who wants that or is this something you want, too?"

She looks away, brushing the wayward hair off of her face. "He's just trying to protect us."

"Us?" I scoff bitterly. "More like he's trying to protect you."

She shrugs, but then she looks at me again and something sparks in her eyes, almost like déjà vu or recognition. It's like when you have a dream, forget about it the next morning, but later that afternoon it comes back to you, stronger than ever. It's like that, because I feel it too. The magical link or curse or spell or whatever it is between us is building.

"Don't you feel it? Right now even?" I swallow, hoping I can say this right. "There is energy between us and it's getting stronger."

She is silent for a long moment, staring at the trees lining the street as they rattle against the wind. A few houses down, an elderly man is raking leaves. Further down, hip hop music thumps from the stereo of a car idling in a driveway. I think she's going to deny what I've said, but she finally nods.

"So don't you think we should do something about it?"

She folds her arms over her chest, coat puffing up, and sighs. "I hope I can trust you with this…"

"You can trust me, I swear." I sound too eager, but who cares?

"Okay, okay." Her lips quirk into a small smile. "Whenever we touch, my magic reacts, and last night when I grabbed your arm, it didn't react in a good way."

"What do you mean?" I remember it, how it felt like electricity was exploding through me, but as soon as it happened, it was gone.

She shuffles forward and stands next to me under the tree, still careful to keep her distance, but close enough that I can hear her whisper, "I have four elements: earth, air, water, and fire. You have one, spirit." Her eyes dart around but there's nobody out here except for us. "Last night after I touched you, my earth elemental disappeared for a few hours. Completely gone. That's never happened to me before." Her voice grows hoarse. Scared. And also, angry.

"Earth magic?"

She nods, studying me like I have something to hide. And maybe I do.

My mind instantly jumps to Harmony at the thought of an earth elemental. Harmony used earth to ground me last night, said that I needed the earth magic to counteract my spirit magic being out of control. Could it be when Khali touched me yesterday, the strange bond, or spell, or whatever it is between us, attempted to do the same thing and failed? Maybe it was trying to use her magic to make mine more stable, similar to what Harmony willingly did for me a few hours later, only Khali's backfired and made things worse for me. It's a decent theory but it's also one I decide to keep to myself. I don't want Khali avoiding me, hating me, or worse: hurting me.

Fact is, I don't know her. I don't know all that she's capable of.

She looks innocent enough, looks like she could be a friend, but she's still an unknown variable. I do know she's protective of her magic. I do know she was strong enough to kill that reaper. I've seen Dean as a fire dragon and if Khali is that times three other elements, her power is nothing to be taken lightly. What if she decides I'm a threat that needs to be removed? A little tremor of fear ripples through my body.

"Hazel? Are you even listening to me?" Her voice breaks through my thoughts.

I blink, returning to our conversation. "Sorry, I was thinking and got distracted…" I sound lame but at least I don't sound afraid.

"Thinking about what?" she demands, her tone growing impatient.

"Thinking that we should investigate this more," I say it as a statement but it comes out sounding like a question.

"No, Dean is probably right. We shouldn't be around each other," she goes on. "I don't want my magic to have more problems. I have too much on the line."

I search her face and that's when I realize that I'm not the only one afraid here. There's fear in her eyes, too. I step back. "Fair enough." So I guess it's back to going at this alone. Well, at least I have Harmony on my side. It gives me an idea.

"Maybe we don't have to go our separate ways. We can still help each other. The only thing we have to be careful about is not to get too close so we don't accidentally touch."

She thinks about that for a few seconds and then peers around again like she's worried someone is watching us. The car with the thumping bass is gone and the man raking his leaves is busy wrangling giant black trash bags into his trash cans, oblivious to us. A dog barks from a backyard and the wind picks up, scattering leaves across from the trees.

"Are you okay?" I ask. "You seem… scared."

She clears her throat, her usual stoic mask slipping completely, and the words tumble out of her in a rush. "I got picked up by Detective Sanders this morning who took me to the police station to question me about the night I saved you and I'm pretty sure they don't believe a word of anything I said and the longer I'm in this realm, the more I'm losing my magic."

My mouth forms into an "o" but nothing comes out.

"And to top it off, I need to get out of this pitiful mortal realm and back home so I can help my father and Bram, but I don't have a plan or a way to help them when I get back to Eridas anyway. And Dean is…" her voice trails off as she catches her breath. "Well, let's just say he's not the answer I thought he was going to be."

I feel bad for her and maybe that's why I offer up the idea I had earlier and the only source I have that might be able to help her. "Has Dean introduced you to Harmony?"

"Who's Harmony?"

"I'll take that as a no." I retrieve my book bag from where I left it against the trunk of the maple tree and heave it over my shoulder. "Come on," I say, "if there's anyone who might be able to help you in this *pitiful mortal realm*," I emphasize those three words with a friendly wink, "it's going to be Harmony."

THE BELL CHIMES AS WE walk into The Flowering Chakra. The holiday scent of spicy apple and the blast of artificial heat wraps me up like a warm hug. I smile as I gage Khali's reaction to the store, assuming she's probably never been in a place like it before. Harmony is busy chatting with a customer at the cash register but shoots me a questioning raise of her eyebrow the moment she lays her eyes on my guest. Khali stares right back at the older woman before taking in the matching bookshelves along the back wall, the elegant glass display cases for our more expensive items, mainly jewelry and toning bowls, and the two wooden tables in the center of it all where our more affordable items are laid out. She steps forward and picks up one of the pendulums, running a careful thumb along the diamond-shaped amethyst crystal at the end.

"Let me demonstrate," I say, grabbing an identical pendulum. "You hold the top of the chain between your fingers and let the crystal dangle below."

I lift it up to show her and she follows my example, eyes sparkling with curiosity.

"Now you need to establish a baseline for yes or no." I let out a nervous laugh. "Like, I am going to ask something I already know the answer to." I make sure my hand is still where I hold the silver cord so that the crystal hangs lifeless at the end. "Is my name Hazel?" I ask. "Whichever direction it spins is yes and the other direction is no."

The pendulum gently spins clockwise. I don't know if this is a subconscious thing that I'm controlling or if it's some kind of spiritual energy, but the crystal is definitely spinning. "So now that I know clockwise is yes and counterclockwise is no, I can ask it a question."

Khali scoffs, rolling her eyes. "You believe in this?"

"I didn't believe in dragons for seventeen years but here we are."

She laughs, the kind of laugh that makes her seem like a real person instead of the guarded robot she's been acting like today. I realize it's the first time I've ever heard her laugh because this is a girl, who as far as I can tell, is always serious. I also realize she and I could be friends if given the chance.

"Laughing is a good look on you," I say. "You should do it more often."

"Yeah, yeah. Okay, fine. I'll try it." She rolls her head from side to side, relaxing her shoulders, and then asks if her name is Khali. Her pendulum also spins in a clockwise motion. She looks at me with an eyebrow arched skeptically but with a grin on her face. She's totally having fun with this. "Now what? I just ask it whatever I want?"

I shrug. "Pretty much. I don't take this stuff too seriously but I have also learned not to discount it either."

She hums to herself and then asks with a cheeky grin. "Can I trust Hazel?"

It spins clockwise.

"See!" I laugh. "We're good. We just can't touch each other which is easy enough."

I hold up my pendulum and ask the same question about Khali. When it also spins clockwise, the tiniest pang of relief ignites in my belly. Maybe I do believe this stuff is real, maybe I don't, but right now, I'm going to go with the former.

"Be careful with those," Harmony says, coming to join us by the table. Her customer must have left because it's now the three of us left in the shop. The vibe instantly shifts from playful to serious. "They're not always right," she continues. "You don't want to get dependent on something like that for your answers."

I drop mine back into the basket with the $19.99 tag pasted on front. Khali returns hers as well, eyeing Harmony like she's the one who shouldn't be trusted here, not some rock with a silver string attached.

"Then why do we sell them?" I ask, lips pursing. I totally sound like an accusatory brat without meaning to. I clear my throat. "Sorry."

Harmony lets out a deep breath. "Because they're popular and I got sick of people asking for them so I decided to stock them. When I sell a pendulum, I offer the same warning to everybody and tell them not to get too attached. You should do the same, Hazel."

I'm not sure if she means I shouldn't get attached or I should tell someone that when I sell one of these things. I don't ask for clarification.

"Sure…" my voice trails off and I rub my sweaty palms along the sides of my skinny jeans. My coat is starting to get too hot and I want to take it off but I don't. There's something in the way Khali and Harmony are sizing each other up like predators that makes me think we won't be here long anyway.

"Who are you?" Khali asks. "Better yet, what are you?"

Harmony tilts her head, her white dreads stiff, and the tiniest twinkle of amusement hides behind a guarded expression. "I would ask you the same question but given your eyes, I don't have to."

Khali's face falls in resignation. Does she get that alot? Do a lot of people recognize her by her eyes? There's something here that I'm not catching. It tickles at the back of my mind like a stupid itch I can't scratch.

"Khali, this is my boss and mentor Harmony," I interject, hoping to break the tension. "And Harmony, this is my new friend Khali." Neither says anything at that so I continue on awkwardly, giving Harmony a frustrated look. "I brought Khali here because she needs help with her elemental magic and I thought you might know what to do."

At the same time, both their eyes flash at me in expressions of "what are you doing" and "shut your pie-hole". I'm in on secrets they apparently don't want to share with each other. Oops.

"Are you the one who put wards up for Dean?" Khali asks suddenly, her voice dropping down an octave.

Harmony is quiet for what feels like an eternity before she says a simple, "No."

"But you know him?"

"Yes, I've done a few readings for Dean, sold him a few protection stones and sage, but I've never done anything as powerful as a spell."

"So who helped him put those up?"

"You should ask him that question yourself."

She swallows down her response, folding her arms over her chest, hip jutting out defensively. Oh, for heaven's sake!

"Do you think you could help us?" I turn to Harmony and widen my eyes at her like *come on, throw me a bone here, lady.* "There's something between Khali and I, some kind of magic or something, maybe a spell, and we're trying to figure it out."

Harmony's eyes dart from Khali to me and then back again. "I don't see into the past. That's not my gift."

"So you're an oracle," Khali says. "What kind of oracle? Where do you come from? Are you fae?"

I expect Harmony to laugh at that but she doesn't. She goes around to the other side of the table, busying herself with organizing a display of clearance crystals that already looks perfect, and avoids the question entirely.

I assumed my boss was some kind of witch. The idea that she's actually fae makes my head spin.

"Can't you try something?" I ask her again.

She looks up at us with a shake of her head. "Like I said, I don't see into the past."

"But you could do a reading for Khali, couldn't you?" I ask. "Maybe there's something in her future that could help us now?"

Harmony's face drains of color and I'm so utterly confused by all of this, I don't even know what to say.

"I don't think that's a good idea." Her tone is final, her body language unmoving.

But I've never known Harmony to turn down a reading.

Khali huffs out a growl of frustration. "She doesn't want to help me, Hazel," she says. "Let's just forget about it, okay?"

She strides to the door and before I know what's even happening, before I can muster a response, she's gone.

I look back at Harmony, mouth agape. "What was that about?" I'll be honest, I'm embarrassed. And a little bit mad. "That was so rude! I've been trying to get Khali to trust me and then you go and run her off like that?"

"She's too powerful," Harmony says firmly, holding her hands up in surrender. "She's incredibly dangerous. I can't be around that right now and you shouldn't either." She comes around the table and takes my sweaty hands in her papery ones.

"But she needs our help."

"No. Hazel, listen to me." Her voice is unwavering. "You need to stay away from that girl. Her path isn't something you want to get mixed up in, especially right now."

"But—"

"I promise. You need to trust me on this one."

I blink, her heavy words settling over me. How can I not get mixed up in Khali's path when I know that we're somehow connected?

"Okay?" she says, squeezing my hands. "Promise me?"

"I promise."

Harmony nods once, drops my hands, then goes back to fiddling with the clearance items on the table. My stomach twists and my mind whirls. Harmony doesn't have to *touch* someone to see their future and something about the way she reacted to Khali tells me Harmony saw something just now that she didn't like. Even more than that, she saw something that scared her, something that is dangerous for me.

Before I can question Harmony further, another patron enters the shop and steals her attention. I shift my weight uncomfortably, eyeing the basket of pendulums, wishing something as simple as a crystal attached to a silver cord could answer all my questions.

SIX

KHALI

MY FIRST TIME ALONE ON Hayden's campus, I have to ignore the strange sense that everyone is looking at me. As I stroll along the curving pathway, I try to distinguish one building from the next, but they're all too similar. A gust of icy wind blasts between rows of barren trees, sending students scattering indoors. I tug my arms in close and draw on the tiniest bit of my fire elemental to make the weather bearable. It comes to me quickly, filling me with equal parts warmth and relief. I let out a sigh and unzip the coat, my limbs happy and lose.

The first time I was here was with Dean, the day after the clothes he'd ordered for me arrived in their stack of brown boxes on his doorstep. After dressing in the oddities, he'd brought me with him to show me around the campus and sit in on one of his classes so I could see what his life was like now. It had been exhilarating, one of the most interesting, overwhelming, and exciting experiences of my life. I'd stayed quiet and observed the way the humans lived, part of me wishing I could live that way too, and part of me missing home more than ever.

This time being on campus is different. This time it feels like it's not just my family and friends that are in trouble and running out of time, it's me. Meeting Harmony scared me into action. It was something about the way her cloudy eyes avoided me, the way her tone had an undercurrent of defensive fear, that told me what I needed to know: she doesn't just want to stay out of my future, but she doesn't think I have one at all. I know I might be jumping to conclusions and imagining the worst, but I can't help but think it's why she turned me away.

I start going through the buildings, one by one, hoping to find Dean. I hurry from room to room, peering in the little square windows on each of the doors, no longer caring if I look like a crazy person. But it's no use. This campus is way too big and there are way too many people.

I can't make this happen.

Dejected, I end up outside, walking aimlessly back in the direction of Dean's house. The grounds have quieted down and most of the students have cleared out. My stomach growls with each step and my head pounds for the lack of food but I'm so emotionally and physically drained that I can't go much faster. I should abandon this realm and go to Eridas straight away. But getting myself back to Dean's place means easy food. And heat. And quiet. No cops to question me. No students to laugh at me. No Occultists to chase me. No Hazel to worry me. No Harmony…

There was something supernatural about that lady. The moment I saw her, my elementals sparked to life, rumbling under my skin like boiling water. My dragon was there as well, clawing to break free. Everything about her screamed of Eridas and if I had to guess, I'd say she was some kind of fae, hiding out here instead of dealing with things in her fallen kingdom. Coming through the portal into the human realm meant she has to have some kind of elemental magic. I wonder how long she's been here and how much of that magic she has left. Maybe I shouldn't think too much about the way she treated me because whatever oracle powers she had are rusty now and not to be trusted.

Somehow, I don't think I'm that fortunate.

A prod of awareness nudges me. One of our own is near: a supernatural. Except it doesn't feel dragon or fae or even warlock. It's something new. It may not even be supernatural but it's definitely not human. I stop abruptly and gaze around the area with its sprawling lawn, towering trees, and brick buildings. My eyes draw him out right away.

An unfamiliar young man dressed in crisp black trousers and a matching jacket stands motionless about twenty feet down the sidewalk. His thumbs hang on the edges of his trouser pockets. Golden blonde hair blows gently in the wind, contrasting nicely against his smooth tanned skin. Amber eyes pierce straight through me, stirring something deep inside. He's staring at me as if he knows exactly who I am, like he can see everything about me, every detail, every thought I've ever had, each tear I've ever cried, all of it.

"What are you?" I whisper. I take a step forward, and then another and another until I'm only a few feet away from him. I feel pulled in by him. Dazed.

"You need my help." His statement is dry, almost bored. His voice is all rounded edges and glossy inflections.

Do I need his help? I don't even know what or who he is. I have so many questions but I can't speak even one.

He tilts his head. Something digs around in my brain. I'm powerless against it but I also don't find it frightening. It's odd, like this man has an energetic finger prodding around in there but I can't feel even an ounce of pain or resistance.

"Sorry but I can't go to Eridas," he says, letting out an arduous sigh. "I have no jurisdiction there. My job is to protect *this* realm."

Okay…

"I'll ensure the human police forget all about you." He says it casually, like it's nothing. I blink rapidly, trying to stay focused, trying to speak, to move, anything. It proves to be impossible. More fiddling inside my head. More holding me in with his amber eyes.

"Ahh…" he nods. "Okay. I'll reinforce the wards that I helped Dean place on his house. That's all I can do for now. You have to do the rest on your own."

He turns and walks away.

I blink. He's gone.

My breath speeds as the reality of what just happened pummels me up and down. Whatever that was, it felt like a daydream. Except, I know it was real. And now that he's gone, I can move and speak again. I'm back to myself and more confused than ever.

I sprint back to Dean's place, replaying the strange experience over and over again in my mind as the campus and adjoining neighborhood speed past me. When I throw open the front door to the little cottage, Dean is waiting for me.

"Where have you been?" He strides forward to meet me at the door, his eyes sparking like a freshly stoked fire. "You weren't supposed to leave on your own. We talked about this!"

"I was looking for you," I rush out, "but that's not important right now." I go on to explain what happened with the young man dressed in black. I don't leave a single detail out.

Dean's face softens. "I don't know what he is either, besides some kind of protector for the human realm. He showed up for me shortly after I bought my house. The clothing you described is called a suit, it's a formal thing for humans."

"What did he want?"

"He said I needed wards that would be linked to my magic, that I should refresh them often by walking the perimeter of the house with fire lit in my palm, and then he disappeared just as you described."

"Wow," I breathe.

Dean nods. "My wards work. Nobody can come in here unless I'm okay with it. We have to assume whatever he's done to erase you from the human police force will also work."

The truth of it is so relieving, so incredible, that I nearly scream. "But how can we find him again? Can't we get him to help us more? This is it! This magic could be our answer!"

Dean's face falls. "I'm sorry. But it was like a waking dream for me too. And only happened the one time. I haven't seen him again. And like you said, he won't go to Eridas anyway."

I grumble, hanging my coat on the rack and peeling off the heavy boots. My mind whirls as I pad over to the kitchen and prepare myself thick slices of cheese and apple. I lay them on a plate and find my way over to Dean's couch. I curl up with the snack on my lap and nibble at it. I can't taste a thing.

"Do you think he's a warlock or sorcerer or some kind of witch?" I ask.

Dean relaxes into the other end of the soft leather couch, staring up at the ceiling for a minute or two.

"Probably one of those," he says at last. "Except I've never heard of their kind helping someone without some form of payment in return."

A seed of worry plants itself deep in my gut because Dean is right. I haven't either. So what does that mean? What kind of game are we playing here? I feel so out of sorts, like I haven't been given a set of rules, let alone know who all the players are, but I've been thrust onto the game board anyway and told that if I don't win, everybody loses.

SEVEN
HAZEL

"YOU GUYS ARE REALLY GOING running?" Cora asks, her shiny brown eyes bulging as she sips on her vanilla latte and burrows herself into the monstrous blanket scarf-thingy she's obsessed with. "Seriously? It's like, two degrees out here. There's snow on the forecast."

Macy and I are busy stretching outside of the dormitory entrance, all suited up and ready to go on our morning run. I say "our morning run" like it's something we do daily, but really it's Macy's ritual and today will be my first time tagging along. I tighten the hood of my new sport jacket around my face and try to imagine it's not freezing out here, but the cold air has settled over me like a second skin. The holiday season is right around the corner but, this time, I'm not looking forward to it. I'll be eighteen and will have to deal with whatever this connection to Khali means, which is a problem considering she's more than happy to run away from me. I haven't seen her since she ditched me at The Flowering Chakra and I'm tired of chasing after her. The woman obviously doesn't want my help.

"It's not two degrees." Macy laughs happily. "It's like forty still, and besides, we'll heat up after we get moving." She smiles, her dark blue eyes sparkling like she's a toddler with a lollipop. "You ready?"

"Can we not and say we did?" I joke. Okay, I half-joke. If she gave me an out, I'd probably take it. "Let's go to the Study Life Center instead? We can do one of those classes you love so much. You know? The ones *indoors*."

She rolls her eyes. "They're way too busy on Saturday mornings. I don't want to fight for a spot."

"Right," Cora deadpans. "Because everyone isn't hungover from last night's partying, no, they're all at the Student Life Center."

"You'd be surprised," Macy says, sounding as cheerful as a Disney princess. "Come on!" She takes off, her cute little auburn ponytail bouncing as she bounds away, as if she's in an ad for Tampax or something. Goodness, the girl is the epitome of "morning person" and I wish I could relate, but alas, I do not.

"Wish me luck," I call out to Cora as I follow after our #fitspo friend, trying to muster up half her sunny attitude. The silence from Dean and Khali has been driving me nuts and I figure if running helps other people get "in the zone" maybe it will for me, too.

But again, I am not that girl.

It takes about three minutes for me to realize two things. Number one, I hate running. This isn't a new realization, of course, but a further confirmation of a deep-rooted inner-truth. And number two, I probably *need* to go running everyday with Macy based on how bad I'm huffing and puffing already. I'm like the big bad wolf in the fairytale! The thought makes me giggle to myself.

People joke about the "freshman fifteen," saying how everyone puts on weight when they get to college, and I can attest that it is all too real. Have I gained fifteen pounds? No, but I've definitely added to the junk in my trunk. I refuse to be another girl starving herself at the cafeteria table, so cardio it is! Even if I can't breathe right now and even if I'm crying out to sweet baby Jesus to make it stop.

As we run, I take it all in: my cute friend, the beautiful campus where I get to go to school, the friendly people running past us, and even the few spirits I see ambling about. The spirits leave me alone, it's still like they don't know that I can see them. In fact, it's been like that ever since Harmony "grounded" me with her earth energy. Days later and I still haven't had any more unwanted visitors. Score!

A sweeping feeling of gratitude passes through my entire body and I couldn't stop smiling even if I tried. Despite everything I've been through, I'm overcome with a distinct sense of hope. Perhaps I'm going to be okay.

After awhile, we stop to take a little break because Macy can totally tell that I'm dying. I catch my breath, whip out my phone, and snap a selfie of the two of us.

"I need proof of this experience," I tease. "If we don't post it, does it mean it really happened?"

Macy laughs. "If a tree falls in the forest and nobody is around to hear it, did it really fall?"

"Exactly."

We check out the photo. Macy looks like a ginger goddess, as usual. My face is as red as a tomato and my hair is sticking to my cheek from the disgusting amount of sweat I'm producing, but at least my smile is genuine. This whole endorphins making you happy thing is the real deal.

I message the picture to Mom. **Be proud. I'm running!!! It HURTS.**

Since Mom's an E.R. nurse, she's always harping on about preventive medicine, lifestyle changes, nutrition, and all that granola stuff.

You got this! Love you so much! She immediately texts back.

"You ready to keep going?" Macy asks. The girl is jogging in place! We're on our first break and *she's jogging in place*. I can't help but snort. She's so into her fitness, which I *love* about her, but I feel bad that I'm slowing her down. Also, my side still hurts with that stabby-pain specially reserved for people who suck at running. *As if we don't need another reason to quit!*

"You go ahead," I say. "I think I need to walk for a while."

"I'll walk with you," she replies, like the super awesome friend she is.

"Nah, it's okay." I give her a quick sweaty hug. "I'll work up to doing full runs with you, but for now, I don't want to have you slow down on my account."

She frowns. "Are you sure?"

"Yes." I laugh. "Of course. I'm fine. You go, and I'll walk while mindlessly scrolling social media on my phone. It's a win-win!"

She rolls her eyes before taking off again, her neon-pink Nike tennis shoes creating faint echoes on the pavement. Here one second and gone the next.

I continue down our planned route around campus, walking my heart out like the champion couch-potato I am; meaning to say, I'm walking super slow. It doesn't take long for me to realize that walking our planned five miles is going to take forever and I'll probably turn into a human popsicle if I don't get inside soon.

"Screw this," I mutter, zagging from the paved running path and cutting toward the middle of campus. *I'm taking a shortcut!*

The place is pretty deserted this time of day, which makes me feel a bit like I'm in a Twilight Zone. I'm used to students being everywhere, but considering Saturday is everyone's day off, it makes sense that nobody would be hanging out around locked buildings in forty-degree weather. I'm not too familiar with this section of campus, and the thought of being alone in an unfamiliar place sends me into a tailspin of unease.

Nothing to worry about, Hazel. Stay positive. Look for the good.

So I do. This is the artsy part of Hayden's campus, and since most of my classes are in the sciences, I haven't had the opportunity to check it out. It's quite pretty though, with wide historic-looking stone buildings, towering trees that must be at least a hundred years old, and perfect little patches of grass—sure to be the most amazing hang-out-spots when the weather isn't trying to kill you. The ballet building is here, the theatre, and a tall arts building where people probably get up to all sorts of creative genius.

For a minute, I daydream that I take an art class next semester only to discover an incredible talent I never knew anything about. I'm like one of those child-savants and everyone is shocked at my natural artistic genius. I grow up to make bazillions of dollars, selling my paintings to celebrities and art-enthusiasts the world over. *Ha!* I don't have a creative bone in my body, but a girl can dream, can't she?

A dark shadow swoops around me, fast as a blink.

I jump, my heart hammering as if I'm still running.

Not again.

The black spirit dragon comes to rest only a few feet away, landing gracefully on the sidewalk with the flap of leathery wings. It's massive, beastly, and almost identical to how Dean looked when he shifted for me except for the eyes. That, and the fact that Dean was physical and this creature belongs to the spirit realm—the supernatural one. Dean's eyes were red and fiery, but this dragon stares at me with big pools of watery blue. These are the eyes of intelligence and sorrow.

"Thank you," I whisper, forcing myself not to be afraid of him. "Thank you for helping me fight off the reaper."

He bows his head once in understanding.

My mind jumps back to the night the reaper tried to kill me and this dragon showed up to fight the reaper on my behalf. Since the reaper was still in spirit form, my dragon friend was able to put up a pretty good fight. But he must have been injured because he'd disappeared for a while. *Now he's back!*

Why?

I rub at the prickling sensation along the back of my neck, wishing it wasn't so hard to sort through all the details in my mind. There was so much about the regular human spirit realm I didn't understand, let alone the supernatural one, but remembering that night all again is something I have been trying *not* to do.

The dragon shifts, a flicker of magic crossing over his form in a kaleidoscope of blue. And then, standing before me, is the spirit of a beautiful man. A prince. Is this Dean's dead brother? My heart squeezes. He's too young to be dead. He looks to be about my age, and friendly, maybe even fun, like he could have been my friend had things been different. *What had they said his name was?* I try to remember as I take him in, with his ruffled blonde hair, startling blue eyes with clear laugh lines around the edges, and medieval, princely attire. He smiles—a kind, brilliant, wide-open smile—and I'm momentarily lost for thoughts, except one: his death is a down-right tragedy.

"Owen," I whisper.

Help me, his voice calls through my mind and I freeze. *He can talk to me now, too?* A wave of terror envelops me, remembering the unwanted spirit who'd verbally attacked me before Harmony had grounded me to the earth as a way to help block my out-of-control abilities. I guess it didn't work entirely or Owen wouldn't be here. He must sense my worry because he steps forward and speaks again.

Please, I don't know who else I can turn to.

"What do you need?" I say carefully, my voice cracking, my jaw aching with the cold.

Owen takes another step closer and I catch the scent of a rebellious ocean even though we're nowhere near the sea.

The reapers, he says, *it's the reapers. They're not acting as they should.*

I laugh bitterly. "I think we already established that but Khali killed the one who tried to carve me up after you left."

When I say her name, his face falls. *Khali is in trouble. She needs you. I need you.*

The wind is really starting to get to me now, that and an icy fear I can't seem to shake. "I don't know what you want me to do. She killed the reaper—"

They aren't doing their jobs as they should. Something is wrong with them. They're not supposed to be here. They're supposed to be there.

I shake my head, confused. "What do you mean? What am I supposed to do?"

He stills, his head tilting, as if someone—or something—is calling to him from a far off place, unknown to me. His already pasty face goes even paler and his eyes widen in alarm. The kaleidoscope of blues come back, rippling over his form, returning him to his massive dragon-self, before he takes to the skies.

"Wait!" I call out after the spirit dragon, lost as to what any of this means. "I don't know how to help you!"

But he's gone. Vanished. Almost like he disappeared into an invisible hole.

A portal?

I'm left with more questions and another gust of freezing wind. I shiver and inwardly curse my new athletic jacket, which is doing a crap job at keeping me warm. "Screw this," I huff and take off, back to a steady jog.

The creepy feeling follows me.

Owen spoke not of a reaper but of reapers with an "s." Plural. Not just one, but many. He'd said they're not supposed to be here. He said they weren't doing their job. How am I supposed to help with that? Just the idea that there could be more of them hanging around the human realm makes my insides hurt.

I change directions, but this time it's not toward the dorms. I hustle toward Main Street, and more specifically, The Flowering Chakra. Once again, I need to talk to Harmony, even if it means telling her about Owen. I gave Dean and Khali their chance but it turns out Harmony is still the only reliable ally I've got in this mess. Well, at least the only living one. Too bad Owen flew off as fast as he did, lucky bastard. All I can hope is that Harmony will not only know how to make sense of what he said, but what the heck I'm supposed to do about it.

EIGHT
KHALI

"SHOW ME," I SAY TO Dean the next morning while we eat our breakfast. The meal is called bagels and cream cheese, an odd name, and while it's new and surprisingly tasty, it's nothing compared to the incredible tacos he introduced me to last night. Also, an odd name for a meal. "Show me *exactly* what you're trying to do with this technology so I can help."

"I'm not sure you can help," he says between bites, his tone certain.

I shrug. "Then fine." I set my food down on the plate and stand. "I have to tell you something."

He raises a dark eyebrow.

"I'm leaving this realm and going back to Eridas. Today."

He swallows the last of his bagel, stands, and leans over the table. His eyes are zeroed in on me and my chest tightens with an emotion I can't quite place. "So you can do what?" he questions. "So you can get yourself killed or married off to my brother? I don't see what other options you have but to stay here."

"And lose my magic?" The very thought of it terrifies me. "No way."

"It takes a lot of time to lose it completely," he replies in a careful tone. "That's what I've always been told and I believe it's true. I've been here over two years and I'm still operating at about 80% of my power."

"80% isn't 100%."

"You'll lose it all if you go home and get yourself killed."

I huff. I want to ask him why he cares so much about me being around, but of course I know why, it's the same reason it's always been. It's not *me* he cares about, it's my magic. I have the four elements in my blood and they need me to marry one of the princes and make lots of dragon-elemental babies so they can carry on their royal line. But if Dean doesn't want me to marry Silas, who else is there? Bram would never be accepted as king. Dean has been exiled, but perhaps he thinks he can return someday. He's never made a *real* advance on me but my cheeks flush anyway. I return to the one subject I can't seem to stop thinking about.

"Don't you care about Bram? He needs us to save him." My voice cracks. "And what about my father? Someone has to break the hex."

"Of course I care about Bram," he sighs, exasperated. "I care about Lord Elliot, too. He was my friend and my one link back to my world these past few years." The way he talks about my father makes my heart hurt. "But I want to save *all* of our people," he continues. "And I can't help Bram, or your father, or anyone else for that matter, until I've figured out how to defeat the Occultists. There's no way we can beat the Occultists without technology. Their magic is too strong."

"And how do you know that for certain?"

His eyes narrow. "Think about it, Khali. Come on! The Occultists took over the entirety of the Fae Kingdoms, not just the summer court. Fae have elemental magic as we do, only there are so many more of them and so many varied species. Not just the elves, but the faeries and sirens and all the others." His voice lowers. "You've seen what the Sovereign Occultists have done there, right? They've cursed the elves and killed off all royalty in one swoop." I stand my ground, folding my arms over my chest. He lets out a regretful sigh. "I traveled through the territory as you did, and I wish I could unsee what I saw."

"And what was that?"

A haunted look crosses his face. "A bloodbath. The Occultists nearly wiped everyone out and they didn't even care."

"More reason to stop them sooner rather than later," I challenge.

"Trust me, they won't stop until they've got all of us under their control. You and me? Bram? We'll *all* be dead." He raises his hands, pointing out the large kitchen window to the houses around us. "And you said it yourself, they're coming for the mortal realm next. I agree, we need to stop them. But you don't actually have a plan, and I do."

"Fine," I say. I tuck a loose strand of hair behind my ear, my hand shaking. "Then if you really believe all of that, if you really believe that this human technology is the only way to end them and is worth all of this effort, then you shouldn't have a problem showing me what you plan to do with it."

He closes his eyes for a brief second, letting out a small breath and a miniscule nod. The morning sun filters golden light through the large front windows, accentuating the planes of his face as if he were the statue of a beautiful man and not the living, breathing Dean that has grown into someone I hardly know.

"Fine," he says slowly, as if weighing the word on his tongue and finding it too heavy. "But we have to be careful. It's dangerous. It was one thing to tell you about my plans but it's another to involve you. I don't want you getting hurt."

I grin, pushing down a wave of trepidation. I don't want him to see worry on my face. "What part of my life isn't dangerous?"

He surprises me with a hearty laugh—not bitter or weary or ironic. It's deep, rich, and heartfelt, bringing me right back to the Dean I remember. The one who was always there for his family, who was committed to his studies and his kingdom. He had the most powerful fire elemental magic in the kingdom and yet he didn't have an inflated ego about it. He was good and he was going to be the next king, everybody said so. For ages, Dean was all I could think about. I wanted it to be him and me in the end. But it was like he considered me a little sister, never once giving me a romantic look, until one night when he finally did see me. He'd turned on the charm and I'd fallen for it, kissing him even though it was forbidden. It was my first kiss and it was marvelous, but it wasn't real. It was all a game. Dean used me just as everyone does. I push the thoughts down for the time being, knowing I can't do anything about them now.

"Come on," he says, motioning for me to follow. "I guess it's time to show you the arsenal."

I take a deep breath and follow him down to the basement. It's much like the rest of the house with sleek, clean surfaces. He has a small room with a massive television on one wall, so big it practically takes up the entire space. Even though I'd learned about television on my first day here, I still can't get over how fascinating it is that images of people can move around and speak. I almost wanted to lay across one of the three puffy couches and watch more so

I can forget all my troubles.

He leads me to a massive black and white painting of trees on the back wall. It's floor to ceiling in length and looks so real, I'd swear the painter must be a master, maybe even someone with magical ability in the arts. The scene reminds me of our forests back at home, so much so that I can picture myself there amongst the singing birds, the earthy smells, and the pine forest thick with trees and foliage.

"It's behind this photo," Dean says, lifting the painting from the wall.

"Photo?" I've never heard that word before.

"Yes," he says with a chuckle. "Photography amazed me at first, too. I'll explain that later, but for now…" He motions to an alcove previously hidden behind the photo. It's only a foot in depth with a steel door and a fist-sized lock at the back. There's no keyhole, which doesn't make any sense.

"How do you open it?" I ask.

"With this," he says. "It's a keypad." He points to a square box fixed to the side of the door. The numbers one through nine glow green and Dean presses a sequence of numbers into them. The lock releases with an audible click. He swings the door open and steps inside. The darkness turns to light, as if revealing a hidden treasury.

The space is at least three times bigger than the theatre room. Inside, the floors are the same as those upstairs, made of smooth stone with no seams. Long thin glass rods filled with the brightest white light I've ever seen are affixed to the ceilings. On the walls are rows and rows of shelves with tools I don't recognize. At least, I think they're tools.

"Getting a contractor to build this thing was a piece of work," he says with a note of pride, "but it turned out perfect."

I nod along even though I'm perplexed.

"What is this place?"

"It's my arsenal," he says. He points to some of the tools. "These are guns, drones, bombs, grenades, anything I can get my hands on—which has been pretty easy. The military-grade weapons can be a bit more tricky to track down and I've had to go through some sketchy black market channels to buy them."

"Right…" As if I have any idea what he's talking about.

When I reach out to touch one of the shinier tools, he pulls me away. "Don't do that," he hisses, then steadies his voice. "These are weapons of war. Made to kill. They don't work in Eridas yet, but let me tell you, they certainly work here."

I narrow my eyes, intrigued and a bit nervous. "And what are you doing with them? What do they do?"

He rakes a hand through his dark tresses. "They kill people," he says, his tone conflicted. "In different ways, of course, but the outcome is the same." He sighs. "Honestly, it's a pretty brutal thing—a horrible thing, actually. I wish there was another way…"

"How do they kill?"

"Well, for starters, guns shoot bullets." He points to the long, black sticks with handles and then picks up a box of silver metal tips and hands it to me. I pick one out of the box and study it. It's so small.

"This could kill someone?"

He nods. "Guns shoot those out so fast you can't see them coming. They can blast through skin and bone, like a flying knife."

My stomach twists as the memory of Silas slicing open Owen's throat comes to mind. I quickly push it away. "And drones? Bombs? What are those?"

"Drones are machines that fly and they carry and shoot the guns so that people don't have to do it themselves. Bombs are…" He thinks for a second. "They're like fireballs filled with bullets."

I nod, finally understanding. "So we could send drones out instead of our people?" I try to imagine it, but it's hard. We've always fought with magic and our enormous dragon bodies, deadly weapons in and of themselves.

"We might," he says, "but they're a higher level of tech and I don't know that they'll ever work in Eridas. For now, I'm trying to acquire guns and hand grenades, which are like mini-bombs. If I can get enough of those to work in Eridas, I can take them back to our army and train our men how to use them. When the Occultists attack us, they won't stand a chance."

"Even with their blood magic?"

He shrugs. "I certainly hope so but I don't know. We won't know until we try, but at least it's something more than what we have now."

"And how did you even know about this stuff?" I ask. As far as I knew, everything to do with the human realm was forbidden knowledge.

"We're the royal family," he says with a shrug. "We know things."

His arrogant statement makes me bite my tongue from uttering out a snarky response. My memory flashes to the book I'd picked up in Bram's study that he quickly stole back from me, the one with the tall shiny buildings painted inside. No, not painted, photographed. How much of this mortal realm have they kept to themselves instead of sharing with their people? Probably more than they'd care to admit. Of course the Brightcasters would find a way to be above the rules set forth for our kingdom.

"Right." I twist my lips, thinking. "And why did you have to go? It seems rather odd that a royal prince would be the one to be sent."

"I sent myself. My parents wouldn't listen to me about this idea. They don't believe technology should come to Eridas, not now and not ever, so I took matters into my own hands and found a way to get here myself." *Typical stubborn Brightcaster male.* He grabs one of the guns. "Come on," he says. "Let me show you how to use this thing."

AN HOUR LATER, WE'RE ALONE in the middle of the forest where Dean plans to show me how to work the gun. We drove out of town and hiked even further until we found a safe place. Considering it's broad daylight, we couldn't risk shifting to fly out here. Too bad. My dragon is still too sleepy, and I can't stomach leaving her like that much longer. She needs me.

The sky is a moody gray, light snowflakes dropping to the earth. The forest has a thin layer of white coating everything, barely covering the shades of brown. Autumn has wasted away. Again, it's like home. And again, guilt racks me from head to toe.

"This is the first snowfall of the year," Dean points out. "Next week is Thanksgiving Break, which is a big holiday here, and after that it's only eighteen days until your birthday."

"Hazel's too," I say, studying him. He nods once, those coal eyes growing pensive and guarded. He doesn't fool me. I've seen the tortured way he looks at Hazel. It's the way I have always wished he would look at me. He's not tortured because he wants her; he's tortured because he knows he shouldn't.

A gust of cold brings a smattering of snowflakes to melt against my face, and I burrow deeper into my puffy coat. It's an item of clothing I don't love as much as my velvet cape but Dean says I can't wear the cape without drawing attention to myself. Since I'd rather not deplete my fire elemental, I make myself be grateful for the cumbersome coat. Dean seems to be fine in nothing but his black t-shirt and jeans. It's a testament to how strong of a fire elemental dragon he is if he's been in this realm for over two years and can still draw on his element for warmth without difficulty.

I'll admit it, I'm jealous.

I'm used to being the most powerful dragon. I'm used to everyone looking at me like I'm something to be feared and revered, and always wanted, always useful. Even if they didn't want me to use my magic, they all knew it was there. I miss feeling all that elemental magic bubbling on the surface, eager to be let free, instead of it being so subdued and quiet. I absolutely hate this mortal realm and what it's doing to me. Safe or not, I'd rather be in danger than not be *myself*.

"Whatever this gun thing is supposed to do," I say, letting out a small huff, "it had better be good."

Dean laughs and pulls it from his belt, maneuvers something along the back of the weapon, and points it at the nearby tree stump where he's placed a row of silver cans. The bang is so loud, I squeal and stagger backwards, my breaths coming quick as I recover from the shock. Part of the tree trunk blows apart, splinters flying, and the can is gone. My heart hammers, ears echoing with residual noise.

He lowers the gun. and I reach my hand toward him, adrenaline racing to my fingertips.

"My turn," I say in a rush.

One thing I have learned about power is that it's addictive. It fills you up with a sense of invincibility that is hard to find and even harder to keep. I've been an emotional wreck since being in this realm, so to shoot that gun and have power back in my fingertips is suddenly the only thing I care about right now.

He laughs again. "That's why we're here."

After a safety lecture that seems to go on for ages, he hands over the gun. It fits nicely between my palms but is much heavier than it looks. I point it how

Dean showed me, aim for the can, and pull the trigger. It ignites with a sharp popping sound and pushes me back a step. Sheer power pours over me, thick and wonderful, and I'm reminded of what it feels like to shift, to fly, to fight, *to win.*

"Feels good, right?" he asks with a confident smile.

I nod. "Feels like magic."

And it also feels a little bit wrong, a little bit like cheating, like too much power for one person. If one little bullet can do that to a tree, what could it do to people? The thought makes my teeth hurt. Or maybe that's just the bitter cold.

Could Dean be right? Perhaps if we can get these weapons to work, we can save ourselves. But how much time do we have left to make that happen? The Occultists are gaining strength each day they're left to their own devices. Dean has been at this for two years and he hasn't figured out how to magic the technology yet, and what if he never does? What if none of this will ever work in Eridas? It's a question he's been avoiding, maybe because he put everything on the line to be here. I may have put my life on the line too, but I'm not Dean.

I lift the gun and try again. This time, when I fire, I hit the target.

NINE

HAZEL

BY THE TIME I GET to Main Street, the first snowfall of the year is in full swing. It's beautiful but I'm shivering so bad that I can't appreciate it. Cora was right. I should've stayed back and enjoyed the warmth while I had the chance. A thick coffee aroma wafts from The Roasted Bean, calling me, but I won't be caught dead in there. Landon's parents own the coffee shop and they're the last people I'd want to run into. If they saw me, I'm sure they would recognize me. What would they say? No doubt, they're heartbroken and confused by everything that's happened with their son. The police told me my record could be sealed about what happened, but surely they knew about our date that night? Maybe not. Either way, I'm not going to find out.

I pass right by the shop and make it to Harmony's place, peeking through the glass storefront. No surprises, it's dark inside. I should have known. Since The Flowering Chakra doesn't open until noon, it's still too early for Harmony to be in. I'd hoped to find her stocking shelves or something.

The woman is getting up there in age, which would normally make her a morning person, right? All the old people I know back in Ohio love going to bed early and waking up with the sun. Not Harmony. She told me she hates mornings which is why she doesn't start work until noon and stays open later than most of the other shops and boutiques around town to compensate. Perk of owning your own business, I guess. But she's not here, so…

Now what?

I gaze out at the street. There's a high number of ghosts roaming about today.

Some of them appear normal except for the shimmer of light around them. And others look how they must have when they died. I shiver, but not because of the cold. For now, they are leaving me alone, but how much longer will the grounding spell hold? If Owen could get through to me, who else can? It seems as if my ability is getting stronger every day because I'm seeing the ghosts more and more clearly, like they're suddenly in high-definition when before they had a grainy far-away quality to them. This growing power of mine also explains why I could hear Owen speak. He didn't have trouble with any of the protections Harmony gave me, perhaps because he's from the supernatural spirit realm and not the human one? It's my best guess. His human image still lingers in my mind as do the puzzling words he spoke. I don't know how to help him but I don't want to give up and go back to my dorm, either.

Luckily, I don't have to.

I have Harmony's address from the night she performed her witchy spell in the graveyard. I still have it. I whip out my phone and go to my contacts, finding her address and opening it in the navigation app. It's a forty minute walk. *Nope, not doing that.* I click over to a taxi app and call myself a car. When it arrives a couple minutes later and I slide into the heated interior, I let out a sigh of relief when the artificial warmth wraps me up like a hug.

The snow continues to pour down, and I watch it with equal parts love and hate as we head toward the edge of town. At least snow is pretty, right? Luckily, the driver doesn't try to make small talk as he maneuvers us through the sleepy neighborhoods that surround Hayden College and the town of Westinbrook's main shopping district. I'm not usually anti-social with strangers, but I'm not in the mood today. I'm happy to pay through the app and not say a word. He drops me off at Harmony's address and drives away the second I close the car door behind me.

I stand in her driveway with a knowing smile before jogging up the curving walkway. The cottage is exactly what I expected of someone like Harmony. It's tiny and cozy and perfect, like an image ripped straight from the pages of a storybook and made real. The exterior is comprised of aged wooden logs and polished gray river rocks; the windows even have cute latticed ironwork across them. Tall trees line the entire yard, giving the place privacy, and the property backs up to a thick forest, which I'm guessing is her favorite part given her earth connection. Right now, all I can think about is getting inside and thawing myself out. There are a few lights on so I know she's home and awake.

There's no doorbell, a testament to the fairy-tale character of this place. I knock on the door using the iron knocker inlaid into the oak and wait. She doesn't answer, nor do I hear anything. I try a couple more times before giving up and heading around the back. There's got to be a back entrance, like a kitchen door or something?

When I turn the corner, I freeze, my breath hitching in my lungs. Harmony dances in her yard right next to the forest. Her hands are outstretched and her face points toward the sky. She spins in circles with her eyes closed, as if to welcome the new snow. She's wearing a white flimsy dress and is barefoot. But it's not her dancing or her crazy choice in clothing or the fact that she's barefoot in the snow that has my heart hammering and my brain trying to catch up to my eyes, it's the two large gossamer wings extended out of her back. They are almost see-through and shine iridescent, even without the sunshine.

Wings?

What is she?

She stops, her eyes popping open. They're not the normal water-blues I'm used to. They're still blue but are now animalistic, lacking a pupil, strange and beautiful and a little bit terrifying. They're all those things and staring right at me.

"Sorry," I choke out, turn on soaked-through shoes, and run.

I don't get very far.

"Wait," Harmony calls. And then seconds later, she flies across her yard and lands in front of me. Her wings flap so fast, they practically hum. I stop and hold back a scream. I mean, there's a logical part of me that says this shouldn't be a surprise considering all I've been through, but there's also an even bigger logic that says I've lost my damn mind. *Who am I kidding?* If I can believe in dragons, I can believe in this.

"It's okay," Harmony says calmly. "I won't hurt you, I swear."

My voice is shakes, "Holy crap, you have wings!"

She nods. "I've always had them, but your sight has gotten stronger. You're beginning to see through my glamours."

My mouth hangs open.

"Let's go inside." She smiles. "I'll explain everything."

What else am I going to do? Run away again? I consider it for a moment, but I know I won't be leaving. This may be one of the craziest things I've ever seen but it's also kind of the coolest. *Cooler than a dragon shifter? No, but pretty close!*

She takes me through the back door and into her quaint kitchen, busying herself with making us a pot of tea over the stove. Her skin has a faint blue sheen to it and her eyes are still without pupils. Her hair is the same as usual, long, white dreadlocks. She's also the same build, same height. Her mannerisms haven't changed and neither has her sage smell or ethereal voice. *But* she no longer appears to be an aging lady! How did I not notice that before? It's like she's gone back forty years.

"How old are you?" I blurt. "Sorry, that's probably a rude question. It's just that you're no longer an older-looking woman." Actually, she's a middle-aged goddess. I wouldn't peg her a day over forty. *And those wings! Ah, I can't get over them.* They're gorgeous. They almost look like dragonfly wings, except they're shaped wider like a butterfly's and are the prettiest mix of blues and whites. I want to touch them, but I won't.

She chuckles. "Let's just say I've aged very, very slowly. I'm older than any human."

She leaves the teapot to warm and turns to me. I stand next to the table. I should probably sit but I can't seem to move. She smiles. My eyes widen, and she winks. Her teeth are slightly pointed, two rows of white that could probably rip me to shreds. *Oh good heavens, she's freaking me out.*

"What are you?" I have to hear it from her even though I have a pretty good guess.

"I'm a faerie," she says. "My people hail from the same realm as Dean."

Just as I thought. The second she said the word glamour, it brought back memories of every fantasy novel I've read.

"You know about Dean? Wait, faeries are real? I thought they were supposed to be tiny."

"You're thinking of our cousins, the pixies." She shrugs. "But there are many, many species of faeries, as many as there are types of flowers. And of course I know about Dean. I smelled dragon on him the day he walked into my shop. I suspect he knows what I am too, though we haven't outright talked about our lineage. He keeps coming back for readings so he must believe in what I can do."

"And what's that?"

She pats the knobbly wood table and pulls out a matching chair. "Sit."

I do, and she takes a minute to finish preparing our tea. Her kitchen is painted a happy pastel green, with rows and rows of wooden shelves holding herbs, crystals, and all manner of jars. It's the messier, and witchier, version of The Flowering Chakra. She sits across from me and places our teacups on the table. I take a sip of mine and let the hot lavender and chamomile thaw me from the inside out. The tips of my fingers are like icicles around the piping-hot teacup, and I sigh with relief as they relax.

She takes a drink before clearing her throat. "I'm an oracle," she says. "In fact, I was the most powerful oracle in my kingdom. My skills were highly sought after and well compensated. This was all before the Sovereign Occultists took over, of course. They've taken over everything in Eridas now. Besides the dragons, mind you. Though, the dragons are next."

"The Sovereign Occultists... I've heard Khali and Dean talk about them but I don't know much. Who are they?"

"They're a religious cult of warlocks that have grown in number and power over the centuries. And now they've taken nearly the entire realm for themselves, killing all the royalty and cursing everyone else." Her eyes turn down with the kind of sadness reserved for someone who saw the killing first hand.

My heart pounds. "But why?"

She frowns. "They believe any magic derived from the elements is evil and that their God only wants magic to be from spells and charms and..." her voice cracks, "...blood sacrifice."

I don't know what to say, but it turns out I don't have to say anything because she continues. "Many times I had visions of them coming and the destruction they would cause my people. I helped the faeries do everything we could to stop them but in the end we failed. No matter what path I advised them to take, the ending was always the same." She closes her eyes for a moment, anguish scrunching up her features. "They killed my husband," she says at last. "I *did* have children, but they took them away to be sacrificed for their magic." A fat tear drops down her cheek and my chest squeezes. I can't help it; I cry too.

"I'm so sorry," I say, setting down my cup and wiping away the moisture on my face with the sleeves of my wool sweater.

"I'm lucky to be alive. Not that I feel lucky." She clears her throat. "I got out and am living my life here where my magic lessens every day. My biggest regret is not coming sooner and bringing my family with me."

"You didn't know," I whisper.

She shakes her head. "I did know but I thought I could change it. It's a prideful mistake I'll have to live with for the rest of my life." She takes a deep breath, as if steadying her emotions. "Anyway, this is why you can see me for who I really am now. You, my dear, are getting stronger and I'm getting weaker. It's why I was outside paying tribute to the snowfall. I need the magic the ritual brings me, whatever morsel I can get."

"How can I help you?" I twist my fingers together on my lap.

She smiles. "Your friendship has meant so much to me. You've no idea how good it is to have someone here who knows what I really am."

"But there's got to be something I can do?"

Her strange blue eyes gaze over my shoulder for a long moment, going into that far-away place they go when she's seeing a person's possible "paths." The moment stretches, and I hold my breath, waiting for what feels like a small eternity.

"Your paths are always murky," she finally says, returning to me. "Perhaps it's because I am weaker or perhaps it's because they involve places I struggle to see."

"The spirit realm?"

"Spirit realms," she corrects. "The supernatural one is laid out for Eridas and the human one is for the mortals. You can see both."

That's right, which is still so strange and hard to wrap my mind around. "I think they might be blending together," I say. "How else am I seeing them both at the same time? And how else could that reaper cross over into the human world?"

She nods once. "If that's true, then it must be the Occultists' magic at work and part of their plan."

Before Dean told me everything, he did tell me he wasn't sure if he could trust Harmony and I shouldn't say anything about Owen to her. But Dean is off doing who knows what with Khali and I need to figure this out. *Harmony is all I've got!*

"Tell me about faeries," I say instead, not quite ready to speak about Owen. "Are the myths true?"

"And what are those myths?" Her eyes twinkle—and not in a figurative way; they literally twinkle.

I think back, trying to compile all the knowledge I have on her kind from my years of reading mountains of fantasy books and watching Disney movies as if it were my job. Maybe there's truth in those old stories. "Well, are you allergic to iron? Or is it silver?"

"Elves are allergic to iron. We're allergic to silver."

"And can you tell a lie?" Even as I ask it, I know it's probably a dumb question. She could lie and say she can't. How would I know?

"We cannot lie," she says. "None of us can, but that doesn't mean you can always expect us to tell the truth either."

I raise an eyebrow. "How do you figure that?"

"We're good at omitting and twisting. We're masters of riddled words and half truths."

Well, then.

"But I can trust you, can't I?" I say, biting my lip. "You've helped me so much."

She nods. "Your paths are murky but I still see you as being the answer to our plight. But even if that weren't the case, you can still trust me. I've come to care for you as I would for family."

I swallow, the weight of her words settling over me. "Is that why you're helping me?"

"Yes. I like you." She smiles and another tear slips loose. "You remind me so much of my daughter. She wasn't much younger when she was taken."

"I'm so sorry."

"Me too." She stands and clears our dishes. "Now, tell me why you came here. What has happened?"

I don't know if I should and maybe it's reckless, but I tell her about Owen, and as the story unfolds, she grows pale and fear passes over her face.

"What is it?"

"In a way, I've seen this," she says. "I didn't want it to be true but it makes sense."

Our eyes meet. I can't move. Can't breathe. "Tell me what it means."

"I believe Owen is stuck in a sort of supernatural waiting room, which is the realm that you can see and explains why you usually only see newly dead spirits. There are reapers there who are meant to help spirits pass into the beyond, to the next place that even you can't see…" Her voice trails off as if she's thinking of the loved ones she lost.

"Go on," I whisper, "please."

"Those reapers? They've been magicked by the Occultists."

"To do what, exactly?"

"I'm not certain, but if I had to guess, I'd say they're going to use the reapers to not only wipe out the rest of my kind, but to help bring their blood magic into the mortal realm."

My mind races. "So their magic won't weaken here?"

She shakes her head. "Quite the opposite. It will become stronger. No power on earth would be able to stop them from taking control over every man, woman, and child."

I press the heels of my palms against my eyes and try to think clearly. How is this real? How is this happening? And also, how the heck am I supposed to help? I repeat the final question aloud.

"War is coming between the dragons and the Occultists," Harmony responds. "I'm positive the dragons can't win this without you."

Great. No pressure or anything.

"Then why are you so adamant I stay away from them?"

"Not them," she says with an arched eyebrow, "it's Khali who has something big coming her way that you need to avoid right now."

"Can't we help her change it?"

Her mouth presses into a line. "I already learned that lesson the hard way."

That shuts me up for a second. Only a second.

"Harmony…" I swallow hard. "Can I ask you a favor?"

Her eerie-blue eyes settle on mine, and I take a deep breath. "Just ask," she says. "I already know what it is anyway."

"Can you help me figure out who my father is?"

"I don't see into the past." Her response is too quick. Unnaturally quick.

I lean forward. "But you've seen something in my future about him?"

She looks away. "It's not a good idea…"

"Please." My voice shakes. "I need this. My mom won't tell me anything."

She stills for a minute, thinking it over. "Give me some time," she finally says. "I need to gather some supplies and you need the next few days to… well, you'll find out." A little twinkle lights her eyes mischievously and I'd give anything to read her mind and know exactly what she's talking about.

"A few days for you to prepare a spell or for me to do something else?" I question. "If there's danger coming, I'd appreciate a warning, you know."

Also, Khali deserves a warning too. I'm going to have to figure out how to get that to her without getting too involved.

"No immediate danger is in your path that I can see, but if I say too much, things won't happen the way they're supposed to and the way you'll want them to."

I roll my eyes. "How very convenient for you."

"Don't worry." She winks. Again. I wonder if all faeries do that.

I finally smile and thank her for agreeing to help me. But my insides are messier than ever, my mind whirling with questions. That seems to be happening to me a lot lately.

"Well, I'm flying home for the long weekend coming up." I sigh. "Thanksgiving."

She takes my warm hands in her papery cold ones. "Hazel, this is good. Take this time to think over your request, because once you go down this path, you won't be able to go back."

It's a warning, and it feels like an important one, but I can't help the desperate excitement sparking inside my little-girl heart. I couldn't go back to my old life now even if I tried, and truthfully, I don't want to. I don't want to pretend that my father doesn't matter. I don't want to pretend that my curse will someday magically go away. With everything that's happened to me over the last few weeks, I can't. I need to know where I come from if I'm going to get stronger at this psychic medium thing. And if it does come down to me helping the dragons one day, I'm going to need to harness my spirit magic the way others can harness their elements.

I smile at Harmony, deciding to be brave. "Never going back is exactly what I'm counting on."

TEN
KHALI

THE STILL NIGHT HANGS OVER the fae forest of the Summer Court. Sugary sweet air wraps me in a humid embrace. Compared to the winter landscape of the mortal realm, it's delightful—and it's warm. I gaze out at the lake and sigh. *If only I could stay here.* The surface is as still as a mirror, and I hate that I'll be interrupting it soon to go back to a place I've grown to despise. The mossy trees loom tall around the lake's edges, reflecting dark shadows that crawl toward its center. A chorus of night creatures grows louder by the minute, cicadas and frogs seemingly competing for attention. The moon shines bright and full, casting everything in a bluish tint.

Dean and I share a frustrated look. His is because his plan isn't working and mine is because this means we have to go back to the human realm.

"Let's go," he says, picking up his big black bag of weapons. "We'll try again tomorrow."

We've been sneaking weapons in through the portal at every opportunity and even after a week, nothing is working. The guns don't fire. The bombs don't ignite. The drones don't lift into the air. Dean even uses a special waterproof bag to keep everything dry, but it doesn't matter, it doesn't help.

I inspect the area, inwardly saying goodbye to my realm. Even though this place looks nothing like Drakenon, at least it's still magical. We can only hope the Occultists don't know about this particular portal and spot, or really anyone for that matter, because we need to keep using it. So far, we've yet to encounter any of the fae creatures out here. Even the merwoman from my first passage into the human realm has disappeared. Her absence makes me uneasy but I don't mention her to Dean because *everything* about this makes me uneasy. I don't want Dean to know how I'm feeling, that I hate this, that each time we come here, I'm dying to stay, but I'm also filled with trepidation at the thought.

We wade into the cool lake and slip under the smooth surface, swimming to the other side as fast as possible. It's easy for me with my water elemental, so I haul the bag, but I know it takes a lot of effort for Dean to swim that long. Even though I've done this journey numerous times, it's still jarring to pass through the ley line portal. It feels like my enormous magic is being shoved into a tiny ball. It's painful and shocking and I'm tired of it. I'm tired of it and yet I keep doing it, over and over and over.

We emerge on the other side, Dean gasping for breath. We pull on our fire elementals to fight off the icy sting of the water and the freezing air that pummels us. Luckily, I've found going to Eridas gives my magic a little bit of a recharge, so I have no problems drying myself quickly with my fire and air. But I know it won't be long until that very same magic is weakened again.

The forest here isn't suspended in a permanent summer like it is on the other side of the portal. Ice and snow cover everything in a freezing crust. The darkness only adds to the cold. It's quiet, eerily so. I glance back at the lake. It won't be long until it freezes over. We can fight our way through ice with fire if need be, but what if something happens to our magic and we can't get through? I don't want to imagine the consequences if I got trapped here for too long. I push the thoughts away as I find my boots, coat, and hat, sending them a blast of warmth before sliding them on.

"Are you okay?" Dean steps closer and brushes his heated palm along my cheek. My stomach flips and suddenly, I want to cry. But I don't. Can he see the torment in my face? Can he tell I'm losing weight? Does he notice the dark circles under my eyes? *This place is killing me.* The moon has its same round fullness here but it doesn't provide enough light for me to decipher his expression well enough to guess his thoughts.

"No," my voice cracks. "I'm not okay."

We stand in silence for a long moment before Dean lets out an animated sigh.

"You need to have some fun," he says it matter-of-factly but his smile quirks up at one side. "When was the last time you had a good time?"

I shrug, as if any of that matters. "I can't remember." That's a lie. The last time I truly had a good time was with Owen, but I can't speak of him now or I *will* cry.

"We're flying to the car," Dean says, "and then we're going out."

Flying to the car? My entire being lights up with excitement at the thought. But I have no idea what Dean means by "going out". I shift into my dragon form and take to the skies. He can explain it to me later, right now, I need to fly.

"WE'RE GOING TO A HOUSE party," Dean states as we drive back towards town. Flying was so amazing and it's hard to be back in my human form, sitting in this seat when my wings could be doing the job of carrying me home.

"What's a house party?" The question is obvious.

"It's exactly what it sounds like," He chuckles. "A party at a house."

"But what's a party?"

Dean laughs. "A ball, a feast, a celebration, a—"

"Okay, I get it." I pout, bottom lip jutting out. "You want to go to a party with humans? That sounds like torture and also it doesn't sound like your thing." I know my attitude is terrible but I also don't care. I hated the parties back in Drakenon and from what I remember of Dean, he put up with them but he didn't relish the attention like Silas did or enjoy the festivities like Owen.

"It'll be fun," he says with a knowing smirk. "Humans can be great distractions. They know how to relax and have a good time, especially the ones our age, and especially the ones attending college."

I roll my eyes. "Whatever you say. But you're starting to sound like one of them, you know."

He ignores me. "A few ground rules. Number one, don't drink their alcohol. It's not like our wine back at home and you won't like what it does to your magic."

"I do not enjoy the wine back at home anyway." Nor do I want to think of home, of the castle I miss terribly, of my family, and all the people there who want to control my every move.

"Well, anyway," he continues, "rule number two, no magic."

"That's a given," I scoff.

"Rule number three, if anyone asks, and they will ask, trust me, tell them you're my friend and you're visiting from Canada."

"Canada? What's that?"

"It's another country." He hums to himself. "Kind of like a kingdom."

"So I'm not a student studying theatre, then?" I ask bitterly.

His eyes leave the road for a second to study me but I don't let him in on the joke. He was mad enough about what happened with the police questioning me. We fall into silence for a few minutes until we drive into a neighborhood similar to Dean's, but with houses that don't look nearly as well-kept.

"This is it." He maneuvers the car to a stop and jumps out. I follow his lead as we walk to the one house on the street with all the lights on, odd music pounding inside, and hordes of dancing people lit up through the windows. "Prepare to get hit on, like, a lot."

"They're going to hit me?" I growl, doubly-annoyed.

He chuckles and shakes his head. "It means the guys will want to talk to you, dance with you, and kiss you... among other things."

My eyes widen and my cheeks burn. *Dean knows I can't be kissing anyone!* Kissing me is like signing up for trouble.

"Oh," he goes on, "and be prepared to get a lot of attention about your two different colored eyes. It's a rare thing here, too."

"Noted," I say dryly, as if I didn't already realize that. I internally assess myself, hoping I can fit in. I don't want to stand out among the humans any more than I already have with my odd eyes and lack of knowledge of their customs. My dark brown hair has dried in loose curls that waterfall around my shoulders and down my back, which I'm happy about because I've seen the mortal girls on campus wear it the same way. I left the coat in the car so I'm wearing only my bright red shirt and blue jeans with my new black snow boots. Dean has provided me with the right underclothes for this realm too so I don't have to worry about trying to fit a corset under the tight clothing. Actually, since the different sized tops, pants, skirts, dresses, bras and panties showed up on his doorstep, I've been happy to try everything on. It's much more comfortable than the items I wore into the realm or anything I have back home. Still, I don't know what Dean was hoping for, ordering all those clothes for me. I'm not going to stay here forever. I've already stayed too long. He doesn't know this but if we can't get the weapons working by next week, I'm heading back to Eridas without him.

"You look good," Dean says, as if reading my earlier thoughts about my appearance. "You have nothing to worry about."

I raise an eyebrow. "Thanks. I actually enjoy this new look, even though I find it odd not to have a gown for a ball." I clear my throat. "I mean party."

"House parties are different," he says with a shrug and pushes open the front door. The moment we saunter inside, I stop worrying. I look exactly like the rest of them, except, unlike the women here, I'm not wearing kohl around my eyes or rouge on my lips. My face is bare but that doesn't bother me; I always hated when Faros made me wear that stuff.

The music however? The music is a problem. It assaults my ears with both its lyrics and pounding sounds.

Dean leads me to the center of the room where a mass of bodies dances. Their moves are so different than ours back home... so scandalous! The people are way too close together and some even rub themselves against each other in *very* sexual manners. It's hard not to stare but I feel like I'm imposing on something that should be behind closed doors. Drakenon court has its share of scandals but nothing so out in the open. For a girl who's barely kissed anybody, my face burns and I have to bite my lip from gasping aloud.

"Let's dance." Dean tugs me forward into the throng. "Don't worry, I won't let anyone touch you."

The lights are dim and the music loud but I force myself to relax. Dean is right: I do need to have fun. So for the next few minutes, I pretend I'm not Khali Elliot, wanted fugitive, fiancé to a murderer, and the future queen of Drakenon. Instead I imagine I'm a regular human girl, a college student, studying theatre, dancing at a house party, having a good time. Why shouldn't I enjoy myself for an evening?

Surprisingly, it works.

The music isn't as bad as I'd first thought—in fact, I might even like it. It's easy to dance along with the beat and the lyrics are intense, raw, and vulnerable.

They speak of love and loss, things I know too well. I feel the music burrow down into my soul as I dance. I'm not paying attention to Dean or anyone else around me since my eyes are closed. I smile and dance without overthinking it. Dean has kept true to his word to keep people from touching me so I go on and on for what feels like ages, until sweat glistens from every pore and my limbs start to feel heavy.

And then something shifts in the air, a draw to magic.

A dragon is near.

"It can't be," Dean says, his voice deadly. "He wouldn't dare."

My eyes pop open. My elementals sense it too, but I don't want it to be true.

"No," I whisper.

Dean pulls me close, his lips brushing against my ear. "Do you feel him here?"

I swallow and nod. "Yes."

"I'll kill him." Dean's voice is pure venom. "Where is he?"

We scan the crowd, looking for the source of our anxiety, but we don't see him.

Anger rips across Dean's face, eyes lighting with tiny flames. "We should go," he says through bared teeth. He links his fingers through mine and tugs me after him. We move quickly, weaving in and out of the dancing bodies.

"Brother." The voice calls out behind us, filled with menace and challenge, ego and amusement.

"Silas."

We are at the front door but it's too late to go through it. Hand in hand, we turn to face him. Dean's muscled frame shifts to stand slightly in front of me.

"What are you doing here?" Dean's tone is careful but sharp.

Silas fits in well with the humans. He's dressed casually like we are, his ice-blonde hair tousled and styled to perfection, but those storm-charged lavender eyes, they're unearthly. He doesn't belong here.

Neither do you.

"I should be asking you the same question," he says, his lip quirking, turning his gaze on me. "It's nice to see you again, *Wife.*"

"I'm not your wife," I growl, panic and hatred storming through me.

"Semantics." He shrugs, moving in close. "You will be."

"Never."

He smirks.

It's packed in here but none of the humans seem to notice our heated exchange by the door. They're too wrapped up in the music as it continues to thump loudly through the house. If it weren't for our enhanced dragon genetics, we wouldn't be able to hear each other over the noise.

"What do you want?" Dean presses, eyes narrowing. Dean is still blocking me from his brother, but Silas isn't bothered. He inches closer.

"I want to take my bride home." He says it like he's won a game. My stomach hardens, and I fist my hands into angry balls.

The weapons, they're in the car. But if I had one now...

"She's not going anywhere with you," Dean replies coolly.

"Oh, I'm sorry, were you planning to keep her?" Silas laughs. "No, brother. It's already been decided." He reaches out around Dean to me. I expect him to grab me, but he only trails a light finger down my face. Goosebumps ignite along my skin. His spicy citrus scent wafts over me, and I want to gag. "Khali belongs to me."

Dean flings Silas's hand from my face.

"I belong to no one," I snap.

I look from one brother to the next. Storms churn in Silas's eyes and fire burns behind Dean's. He holds me closer than ever. He wraps one strong arm around me and the other holds my hand in his. Silas glares at the embrace, buzzing with electricity under his skin. I can't see it, but I can sense it's there and growing stronger by the second. We have to get out of here before the brothers erupt into a fight in the middle of all these humans. My respect for them has grown since I've lived among them and I don't want to be responsible for anyone getting hurt.

"Let's go," I say, voice clipped. "We can talk about this somewhere private." I try to stay calm, but inwardly, I'm terrified. My hands shake, my heart races, blood surges through my veins, and my magic? It's dulled. Once again, it's being subdued. But it's also going haywire, which can only mean one thing— one person.

The three of us head for the door, and as we push through and step out into the night, she appears. Hazel. She ambles up the steps to the house, laughing and arm-in-arm with two other girls: a tall dark beauty and a wholesome redhead. Her friends are beautiful and so, so human and Hazel fits right in. If it weren't for our dragon senses, nobody would know she's got spirit magic.

"Oh!" She blurts out, seeing us and nearly stumbling in shiny black boots that reach all the way to her knees. "Hi."

Next to me, I feel Dean freeze mid step.

She runs a hand through dark-blonde hair that is amazingly slick and straight, smoother than my hair has ever been. She looks a million times better than any other time I've seen her and it's not her hair or her dress, it's her eyes. They're less troubled. In fact, her entire demeanor is less burdened. She looks happy.

Guilt wracks through me. *She shouldn't be here!* I sense that her magic is stronger than it's ever been and there's no way Silas won't notice.

"Hi," I reply back, worry simmering through me. Not only worry for her safety, but what if she touches me again? What if she hurts my magic? Now is not the time for something like that to happen.

Her eyes go wide as they flick to Dean, then me, then the arm he's still got around my shoulder and his hand still protectively laced with mine.

"Typical," her tall friend scoffs. "If you'll excuse us." The girl pushes her way past us, knocking into me as she goes. Hazel and her red-headed friend follow, and when Hazel barely brushes up against me, my stomach twists in pain, my magic dimming. Hazel still has her eyes locked on us, her cheeks reddening and concern and pain alight in her eyes. Then her gaze shifts over to Silas and her mouth falls open into a little "o".

"And who are you?" Silas purrs, wrapping her into his stormy gaze. There's an edge to his tone. No doubt, he's sensed her magic. Is he threatened by her? Or does he want to possess her like he's determined to possess me? Whatever it is, alarms of warning sound in my mind.

"She's none of your concern," Dean snaps, his voice thick with warning.

"Rude!" Hazel's remaining friend retorts, dragging her into the party. The door slams and the trio is gone.

Silas's glare roams over us, his mind whirling. "It seems like we have a *lot* of catching up to do, don't we?" His eyes land on me, drinking me in. "Don't worry, Wife, we will have plenty of time to talk later *after* we return home."

The three of us walk down the steps toward the yard and my mind spins with possible ways to get away from him. Movement catches in my peripheral vision. Appearing from the shadows of the darkened yard, several hulking men slink out into the open.

More magic. More dragons.

Silas's men.

These are Dragon Blessed men who have trained in our army and are prepared to do whatever it takes to follow orders. Including Silas, there are nine in total. We're vastly outnumbered.

"They've come to help me bring our runaway-princess home." Silas's voice is a smile.

Dean squeezes my hand and subtly nods toward the car. I think of the weapons stashed away in the back and what we could do with them if we could get to them in time. But can I do that? Can I risk Dean like that? Can I risk all the humans just inside that house?

No. I can't, so I release Dean's hand and put several feet of distance between us.

Silas is triumphant. And me? I need to run, to hide, to fly, anything to get as far from this evil prince as possible. But I'm stuck. My magic is weak. My dragon is asleep and can't be easily roused after Hazel brushed up against me. I can't change the fact that Silas is right here or the inevitable outcome of this encounter should I resist him.

I've been caught.

ELEVEN

HAZEL

MY PHONE ALARM BUZZES, JOLTING me awake. It's five in the freaking morning, exactly what I set it at three measly hours ago. I feel like the walking dead after staying out super late with Cora and Macy but I know if I risk a snooze, ten minutes will turn into hours and I won't make it to the airport in time for my flight. *Turkey waits for no woman!*

I groan and flop out of bed, switching on the light and wincing like a vampire in the sun. *Dang, that hurts.* I shuffle around my room, deciding to stay in my cozy sweatpants and sliding on my beloved Gryffindor hoodie. I can shower and get ready after I get home; who cares that I have a flight and an hour-long car ride with Mom? It's dark and cold outside; I'm not changing yet.

I pile my tangled hair into a top knot, grab my packed suitcase, and make for the door, planning to stop by the shared bathrooms to pee and brush my teeth on my way out.

I clumsily push the rolling suitcase out into the hall ahead of me, running into something blocking the way. Not something—someone. I squeak and stagger back, nearly wetting my pants right then and there.

"What are you doing here?" I hiss, my hand pressing against my rib cage.

Dean looks up at me from sleepy soft eyes. He's camped out on the hard tile, legs bent and arms resting on his knees. His dark hair tumbles across his forehead, casting dark shadows over his unreadable expression.

"I'm making sure you're okay."

I blink, completely stunned. What in the heck? Hours ago when he was with

Khali leaving the party, he gave me the shaft to take care of her and whatever was going on with that blonde supernatural they were with. Whoever that guy was, he had magic in his velvety lavender-gray eyes, but Dean obviously didn't want me around because he didn't introduce me, let alone even say a quick hello to me. Now he's sitting outside my door at five in the morning?

My brows pinch together as I frown. "I don't get it."

He lets out a sigh of relief and gives me a small smile as his eyes travel up and down my bedridden appearance. "What's not to get? I wanted to check on you. It looks like you're doing okay."

My insides flutter to life, hope igniting. *Stupid butterflies!*

"Why didn't you knock?" I whisper, fully-aware there are sleeping people behind these doors. My grip tightens on the handle of my suitcase.

"I didn't want to wake you." He stands and brushes the wrinkles from his clothing. He's wearing the same outfit from last night, his standard dark jeans with the black v-neck top that hugs his delicious muscles.

"Umm—okay."

He motions inside my room. "Can we talk in private?"

I'm still hurt by him. Angry. Confused. And a little afraid. I am so many negative things and I shouldn't give him another moment of my time, but I can't help myself. He might have information that could help me: about my father, about where I come from, about Owen and the reapers and why Harmony says I'm so important to saving their realm. But none of those reasons matter to me right now quite as much as his tousled hair, campfire mixed with rain scent, arresting dark eyes or the way my heart has seized up and started to pound all at the same time the second I saw him.

"You've got five minutes," I say, nodding toward my suitcase. "And then I'm leaving."

He scowls at the suitcase. "Where are you going?"

I laugh and lead him back into my room. "In case you hadn't paid attention, today is the first day of Thanksgiving Break. I'm going home. I'll be back Sunday night." He follows me inside, eyes narrowed on me and only me. I've got all of my favorite fandoms represented beautifully in this little shoe-box of a dorm room but he doesn't care. Then again, this is the guy who doesn't know who The Boy Who Lived is, so he's obviously a lost cause.

"Why are you really here, Dean? You've made it clear you didn't want me around your girlfriend, or fiancé, or whatever you want to call her. Am I supposed to believe you wanted to check on me?"

"Khali is neither my fiancé nor my girlfriend," he says. Something like pain underlines each word. "And she's gone back to our realm. She left earlier tonight."

My stomach twists with worry but the logical part of me wants to know why I should care that Khali left. For someone who acted all friendly when I first met her, Khali sure has given me the cold shoulder ever since. Still… I hope she's okay.

Dean runs a hand through his hair again and I'm beginning to think it's his nervous tic or something. He glances up at the ceiling for a minute, like what he's struggling to say is important.

"What is it?"

"Khali didn't leave by choice. She was taken by a group of dragon shifters working with my brother. She's being forced to return home to our castle and marry him."

I bite my lip. Now I feel bad about thinking mean things. The girl did save my life and now I'm pretty sure I know who that blonde guy at the party was—his brother. Suddenly the tension I felt with the three of them makes sense and I feel stupid for thinking it was ever about me.

"Aren't you going after her?" I ask.

Anguish crosses his features. "I can't. They're taking her to my home and if I so much as step on Drakenon soil right now, I'll be executed. I won't return until I have enough leverage to negotiate my survival."

"That sucks, Dean," I reply. "But what does this have to do with me?"

My insides flare with curiosity and worry. Considering everything I've got going on right now, chances are this development might involve me in one way or another. Khali and I already figured out that our link strengthens my spirit and weakens her elements. Does that mean I'm supposed to continue to stay away from her or am I supposed to help her? Will Dean ask me to go after her? The thought of crossing into the supernatural realm leaves me paralyzed with fear. I can hardly handle the human realm as it is. *No way I can go there!*

"You're being watched," he says at last. "You caught my brother's attention last night."

"And?"

He throws his hands up in the air. "And I can't have his men sniffing around you!"

"Ah, so that's why you suddenly care about me—your sibling rivalry with your brother." I shoot him a wicked glare. I don't know what comes over me, but it's like I want nothing more than to push all his buttons as I continue. "So that blonde hottie was your brother, huh? Nice. Khali is a lucky girl. Did you ever stop to think that maybe she wanted to go?" I waggle my eyebrows. Yes, it's petty and I'm a total brat for saying mean things but something about Dean brings out my snarky side.

"She is most definitely not lucky," he snaps, his body hardening as he leans in close. "Silas murdered Owen! Owen was Khali's best friend and his twin but Silas cares only for his own ambitions." My mouth goes dry, the snark evaporating. "He sensed magic in you last night. Before he left with Khali, he ordered part of his dragon guard to stay here and keep an eye on you. If you display any abilities they might think are useful to him, he's ordered them to kidnap you and take you to him."

My blood runs cold. "He can't do that—"

"He can. You don't know him or what he's capable of." Regret sparks in his eyes. "I do."

I sit with that thought for a minute, and then tuck it away because what am I supposed to do with it? Nothing. All I can do is watch my back and keep working on my own problems. Right now? Right now, I'm going home.

"All right, well, thanks for the warning," I say with a nod. "I've got to go now."

He reaches out to stop me, an emotion I can't place flashing in his eyes and lighting them with the fire I've seen on multiple occasions. This time, I won't let myself be pulled in. "Did you not hear a word I just said? You're in danger. You can't go anywhere."

I rip away from his grip. "I can and I will. Like I said, I'm going home for Thanksgiving. I'll be back Sunday."

"Then I'm coming with you."

That earns him a laugh. "Not happening." The thought of him in my kitchen at home, talking to my mom, sleeping on our couch? No freaking way. "What gives you the right to suddenly care about me? Thanks for the warning about Silas. I'll be careful. I'll watch my back and I won't do anything with the spirit stuff."

"You don't think I care about you?" *Wait, is he stuck on that?*

I laugh. "Not really."

He lets out an exasperated growl. "Well, contrary to what you think, I do care. And you can either take me with you or you can stay here, but I'm not letting you out of my sight until I'm certain the spies are gone. They'll hate being here and won't last more than a few weeks if we're lucky. But if you just up and leave, it will look suspicious. It will look like you got spooked and ran."

"This is ridiculous."

He grabs my suitcase. "Good thing you're packed. You're coming to stay at my house."

"Not happening." I snatch the case back and storm away from him, flinging open my door and racing to the elevator. Sure, it's only a couple flights to the ground floor but I'm not carrying this thing down the stairs with him on my tail.

I wheel the bag behind me and make it in record time, closing the elevator before Dean can get in. He barely misses the door and shoots me an annoyed glare before turning for the nearby staircase. Crap. I hit the ground floor button then whip out my phone and find the taxi app, hoping someone is close by to pick me up.

The lights flicker. The elevator grows cold. Ice cracks all around me as it appears out of nowhere, growing in long clawed edges around the walls. The elevator grinds to stop—between floors. Fear nips up my spine. My eyes water. Hot breath releases into the freezing air. I squeeze my eyes shut, praying this is a dream, that this can't be happening.

I count to ten and open my eyes.

A supernatural reaper hovers inches from me, his cape black as ink, his face unknowable except for two glowing red eyes. Standing next to him, eyes downcast and skin pale as winter, is Landon's ghost. He's dressed exactly how he was the night he died and he's frozen in place, as if bound to this creature. Memories of it all race back to me and I choke back tears.

Is it the same reaper that I thought Khali killed or a new one that's latched on to Landon's spirit?

Get me out of here. The reaper's voice crackles through my mind. *Take me back! I am not meant for this place.*

"Leave me alone," I gasp. "I can't help you."

He leans in close, millimeters from my face, locking me with that glowing stare. He smells like death. I try not to gag. Tears burn my eyes. *Take me back or I'll kill you all!*

He sends a disjointed image to my mind. Men in red robes, chanting in a gutteral foreign language. Women and children, bound in chains and sobbing. Some look like humans and others have supernatural features, but it doesn't matter, they're all bound. They're all tormented. And then, they're all dead.

Blood—so much blood. It's everywhere.

I scream, the curdled cry spewing from my lungs. I scream and scream until the reaper is gone in a wisp of smoke, the ice-cold air leaving with it. Landon's ghost is nowhere to be seen. The elevator starts up again, descending to the ground level and opening with a cheerful ding. The second the doors part Dean is there, pulling me into his arms. I'm sobbing. Inconsolable. What I saw, the suffering, the grotesque images, it had to be what Harmony described happened to her people, to her own family.

And it's what the reaper said he'll do to us if I didn't help him.

"Hazel." Dean's tone is urgent. "Are you okay? What happened?"

But I can't speak it. I can't…

Some of the girls on this floor have woken, rushing out into the hallway to get a better look.

"Yes. I'll go home with you," I whisper, wiping the tears away. I stare at the floor. Luckily, I know Macy and Cora are upstairs in their beds. I can't look at the other girls gaping faces anymore as they stare at me and Dean huddled up by the elevator.

"Just get me out of here."

"Already done."

He ushers me to his car and races us back to his place in no time. I'll have to cancel with Mom. I'll have to lie and say I came down with the flu and can't fly today. She'll be as disappointed as I am, but I can't involve her in whatever's happening. It's too dangerous. It's not only about spirits anymore; it involves so much more. Now there's Khali and the link to think about, there's the

Occultists, there's Silas and his dragon army. There's Landon's ghost.

And there's the reapers.

I can't stop thinking about them because now that I've seen what they're capable of, I can't unsee it. The horrific images repeat over and over in my mind in a cruel loop. My mind begins to numb as fear crashes through my body.

I'll never be the same again.

If Harmony is right and I'm meant to play a part in stopping the Occultists, there's a good chance I won't make it out of this alive. Now that I think of it, she never has said if I will survive this, only that I would play a part in saving Eridas. I'm doubtful it will be a part that ends up with me alive at the end of it. I'm not that powerful. I'm not like *them*.

TWELVE
KHALI

THE SENSATION OF GOING THROUGH the portal is like being submerged in ice water before getting thrown into a fire. One second it presses in on my magic and the next it pulls. My eyes squeeze shut as I breathe through the pain, allowing my water elemental to take over, and willing my body to relax. On either side of me, two of Silas's men hold me in their magicked grips. They're both water elementals too, so this transition is much easier for them than it is for the other dragon shifters who have to swim for their lives to get through the portal. Still, it seems like they all have an extra advantage over me because they weren't in the human realm for long. That and they aren't being taken prisoner!

I keep my eyes wide open, searching through the dark shadowy water for the beautiful merwoman with the moonstone skin and glittering onyx eyes. She showed me where the portal was the first time in exchange for an equal debt to be paid at a later time. But she's nowhere to be found now. I haven't seen her since that night. I wouldn't mind owing her another debt if she could get me out of this situation. She never appears.

When we emerge from the lake and onto the banks of the Summer Fae Forest, Silas summons a cyclone to dry the party. My dripping hair bats around, transforming from wet whips to wild curls, and then the air calms. It's the dead of night, and the sky is alight with twinkling stars. The dewy summer weather from earlier has fallen to cooler stillness. All four of my elementals begin to wake, the magic fizzing under my skin. I should be tired; I'm anything but. I want to shift, to run, to fight, to take any action besides standing here with these two hulking men holding me. Soon my abilities will grow and be superior to anything they could throw at me. I could take them all down. In fact, I *will* take them all down.

"Don't even think about it," Silas says, sauntering close, his silver and black cloak nearly brushing the ground. We size each other up, our gazes stubborn.

Before we passed through the portal, he changed back into his princely clothing—an elaborate cloak of deep teal with silver embroidery stitched around the hems. His tunic, trousers, and boots are all black. He forced me to dress in an ornate gown of silver and teal, with my own pair of black boots. I had to strip off anything that came from the human realm, almost like he wanted to erase it from my history. Matching with Silas makes me want to scream.

He appears to be right at home as he surveys the area, a smug grin on his face. I may be back in Eridas, but I'm not home. Not with him. The corset bites into my rib cage, reminding me of the figurative cage he's going to lock me in with this marriage. I stand up straight and pretend I'm stronger than I feel.

His eyes fall on me, taking me in like I'm the spoils from his very own war effort. "I know what you're planning. Don't be a fool."

"You don't know anything," I challenge.

He doesn't respond but whatever he thinks he's doing here, he's about to be sorely mistaken. I try to pull away from the grip of his men but they don't budge. No matter, it won't be long before my magic is restored well enough to get away from them. Silas smiles, something twisted circling in his quicksilver eyes. They are no longer his normal violet but glow as bright as moons, an indication that he's keeping a lightning storm at his fingertips.

"What are you going to do?" I laugh bitterly. "Electrocute me?"

It's possible, but then again, I have access to the same element. I could fight back.

"If I have to." He nods toward his men. There are five of them left after he left four in the human realm to spy on Dean and Hazel. Each one of these shifters are massive, muscled, and probably power-hungry if they associate themselves with Silas. The biggest of the lot drags me after the group, toward the shadowy forest. I'm momentarily surprised and I can't help but comment.

"I assumed you were going to make us fly out of here while it was still dark and we can blend in." My tone is casual. My worry is not. We shouldn't stay here; who knows what's lurking in the shadows.

No answer.

"Where are we going?" I hiss.

Still, no reply.

The hairs on the back of my neck rise up. Something isn't right.

We enter a clearing surrounded by towering trees. Mossy ropes and thick vines hang down around several canvas tents and a freshly lit fire. The men are quick to disperse into the tents, save for my jailer who still holds tight to my arms. He walks me to one of the tents and throws me inside. I rub at the bruises forming on my upper arms and take in my surroundings with a groan. It's dark but the orange light from the smokey fire dances against the tent walls. I squint and make out a pallet of fur blankets and an open trunk of women's clothing in the corner, but otherwise it's pretty bare in here. At least it's private.

I snap my fingers and a single flame dances atop my thumb. It glows in the darkness and sends a smile to my face. It's tiny, barely there, and weaker than it should be, but it's still enough. Given the right environment, fire grows. I could set this camp aflame and make a run for it.

Footsteps approach, crunching on the fallen leaves.

"That's enough, Princess," Silas says, appearing in the tent opening.

I close my palm to extinguish the flame and look up into his satisfied gaze as he stomps inside. I glare at him. "Get out."

He chuckles and saunters around the small space like it's his. Does he expect us to share it? My hands ball into fists. Never.

"When I look at you," I say, "all I see is your twin brother."

His lip curls as if tasting something rancid. "I'm not here to speak of Owen."

"Owen isn't here to speak for himself because of you," I snap.

"And how does that make you feel, knowing you get to be with me instead?"

Silas steps too close and lifts his hand, catching a piece of my hair between his fingers and yanking me forward until he can dig his fingers into my scalp. It stings. My stomach lurches. Anger washes through me, filling me head to toe with a burning rage. My magic swells a little more. I hold my breath but don't move. I refuse to give him the satisfaction. I will my elements to strengthen faster but nothing happens.

"Do you know why it is forbidden to kiss you before you're married?"

I pause, momentarily flummoxed by his unexpected question. It hardly seems like the time. "We all know the terms of the treaty."

A sinister grin spreads across the smooth planes of his face. Those who don't know him like I do would say it's a charming smile; they'd be drawn in by his stormy eyes and the air of focused confidence with which he carries himself. I know better.

"I'm not talking about the assumption that you would be swayed toward one prince over another, I'm talking about the real reason why."

My eyebrows knit together as I frown. "What game are you playing?"

"I'm done with games." His breath is hot on my face. Sickening. His hand continues to wrap around my hair. If I move, it'll rip. His eyes flick to my lips. Little frenzied streaks of lightning dart across his irises and suddenly I know he's going to kiss me.

"Don't," I whisper.

It's those eyes that tell me he won't listen. They're not filled with surprise like what I saw in Dean's eyes years ago, or alight with drunken wistfulness like in Bram's gaze; they hold something else entirely. They hold ownership. Power. Desire wrapped with the need to possess—to win.

His lips claim mine.

I shove him but he only holds on tighter, greedier. One hand squeezes the hair against my scalp, ripping part of it away in burning pain. The other hand wraps around my torso and pulls me against his body, locking me in a primal claim. I cry out but that only seems to excite him more. He deepens the kiss, a growl rumbling in his throat.

I bite.

He rears back, a small stream of blood dripping down his chin, and smiles like a devil.

"You are not allowed to do that!" I hiss. Tears spring to my eyes. I will not cry. I will not cry. I will not cry.

He laughs. "I'm allowed to do whatever I want."

I shake my head and scurry to the edge of the tent, my back against the cool canvas. "What is going on here? What are you going to do to me?"

"Don't you feel that?" He ignores my questions and runs a thumb along his bloodied lips. "Ahh, I sure do."

"Feel what?" My breaths are short, heart frozen. My thoughts are muddled. He needs to leave.

"Do me a favor, will you?" he asks, drunk on power. "Bring that pathetic little flame back to your fingers, hmm?"

I don't understand why he'd want that, but he doesn't have to ask me twice. A little fire could possibly gain me more space. I snap my fingers, expecting the heat, but it doesn't come. I reach out to my fire element, and I feel it there, but it's quieted down again, almost like how it felt in the mortal human realm.

"That's what I thought," he says. "My turn." He snaps his fingers. I gasp. How is this possible? A flame dances on his thumb. He stares at it with pure adoration.

No, this can't be happening! "But you're not a fire elemental," I croak.

The fire flickers out and is gone. I'm not relieved, I don't trust it. Silas's eyes glow with pride. "No, I'm not," he says. "Don't you see? This is why they put restrictions on who you could kiss. It was never about us. It was always about your power and how to keep it subdued."

"This isn't making any sense. By your logic, a kiss would steal magic. Your father doesn't have your mother's magic."

"That's because he never tried hard enough." He cackles. "Or it's because I'm stronger than he is."

"What are you talking about?" I don't understand anything right now except for the fear swallowing me whole. If Silas has found a way to siphon my magic from me, I'm in way more trouble than I first thought.

"It looks good on you, by the way," he says, raising his blonde eyebrow with glee. "My necklace."

I reach up, my fingers landing on a black cord cinched around my neck. He must have slipped it on while he had me in his grip. I can barely see it since it's so short and ends just above the hollow of my throat. A silver dragon pendant hangs at its end. It's one of Silas's heirlooms. He's worn it for years.

"You put this on me while forcing a kiss," I sneer. "How dare you!"

"Is that how you thank me for a gift?" He's teasing me, enjoying my torment.

"I don't want your gifts." I shove my fingers under the necklace and yank it away. It doesn't budge. I try to pull it over my head, but it's too small. I flip it around to where the cord is tied at the back and start tugging at the thick knot, but that's not working either.

"Don't bother." Silas laughs. "It's been magicked and can't come off unless I remove it."

"What is it?" I growl.

He laughs again. "Are you really so dense? I already told you, it's been magicked using the same spell that grants your kiss to share your elements with me. Only, this method is much more useful, don't you think? Now get some sleep, Princess. We have a long journey home." He strolls from the tent, the flap closing behind him.

I sink onto the pallet of furs, my hands shaking. I use all the strength I have to pull at the necklace, but it won't budge. It's not going anywhere. I tug the pendant up enough to study the dragon etched into the silver, noticing that it glows faintly. This isn't right. This isn't simply dragon elemental magic and it isn't something he did all by himself. Could he be working with a witch? Or worse, one of the Occultists? Who could have helped him do this?

My magic is weak beneath my skin. It's not growing like it was when we first came into the realm. Actually, it's died down since Silas kissed me and placed this cursed thing around my neck. I try to bring some to the surface, but the minute I do, it's almost as if the magic is being funneled to another source. The necklace heats as if being activated. I stop and suck in a breath, hating Silas more than ever.

It's just as he said. Somehow, he's used this necklace to bind my magic and should I use it, it funnels to him instead. So not only has he proved that a kiss can steal from me, but he's put a necklace on me that makes it so I can't even use that magic at all.

"Silas!" I jump up, storming from my tent. "We need to talk about this!"

The second I step outside, the beastly man guarding it tosses me back inside like I weigh no more than a feather.

So Silas has weakened me to strengthen himself and I'm stuck here with him and his most loyal men. There's nothing I can do. *I can't even leave the tent!* For the first time in my life, I truly know what it means to be a prisoner. Even though I thought I knew before, I was never really imprisoned until this very moment. It's more painful than anything I could have imagined. I press my face into the soft furs and for the first time in weeks, I let myself cry.

THIRTEEN
HAZEL

I AWAKE TO THE FAINT woodsy scent of a crackling campfire intermixed with rainstorm. My mind is murky, momentarily suspended in between sleep and wakefulness. I yawn and snuggle in, willing myself to avoid full consciousness for another few minutes. My eyelids are filled with lead and my limbs aren't much use either, held down by life's many stresses… and an arm.

My eyes pop open.

I'm in Dean's guest bedroom and my new digs for the foreseeable future. Dean's familiar body is spooning mine, not that the position itself is familiar—if only I were so lucky. His arm drapes over my torso, holding me flush against the hard planes of his chest. He's fast asleep, breath flowing in and out in a steady rhythm. I carefully roll over to get a better look—usually guarded, all of his defenses are down, and he's a sight to behold. I sigh, enamoured. I don't get it, don't get *him*. Half the time he's trying to protect me and the other half, he's trying to make me go away. He has a deep connection to Khali that's been there for years but does that mean he cares for her beyond friendship? I worry he might and that he's biding his time until he can be with her again.

He stills. "Are you watching me sleep?"

I snort out a laugh and sit up, but I don't deny it either.

"I'm hungry," I announce. "What's for breakfast?"

Dean chuckles. "It's two in the afternoon. You have been sleeping all day."

"Ugh, don't remind me." It all comes back to me—the early morning alarm and how I ended up here. I was an emotional wreck earlier and couldn't stop crying, so he came in and sat with me. He changed the sheets from Khali being here and told me to lie down. It felt weird to take her place but I did it anyway. Eventually, we both fell asleep.

"Sleep is good," he says.

"And *you* have been sleeping with me," I retort with a cheeky grin. My face warms.

He smirks. "Not the kind of sleeping you had in mind?"

"Shut up!" I roll my eyes and make my way down the wooden stairs to his fancy-pants kitchen, Dean following at a distance.

I rummage through the pantry until I find all the ingredients needed for pancakes and get to work. Might as well make myself at home. Dean watches, relaxed and perched against the iceberg-white wall like he's surveying his kingdom. Typical. Now that I know he's an exiled prince, a lot of his mannerisms make sense. He's not what I imagine a prince would look like, all comfortable in a rumpled white cotton v-neck and gray sweat pants hanging low on his hips, but who am I to complain?

I grab what I need from the refrigerator but come up short. "Hmm, where's your mayo?"

He grimaces. "Mayonnaise? I don't have any of that disgusting sauce."

"Too bad," I sing-song. "It's the secret ingredient to fluffy pancakes."

"I'll have to take your word for it."

Twenty minutes later we finish the last of our pancake stack, sans my secret ingredient. It still tasted marvelous. Dean busies himself cleaning up the mess and I take a better look around his house. It's as I remember: traditional on the outside to match the neighborhood, and remodeled bachelor pad on the inside. The floors are made of dark polished concrete and the white walls have a few art pieces here and there. Modern light fixtures and leather furniture complete the space. There's nothing personal about it, so of course it fits Dean like a glove, considering the guy is such an enigma.

"Where's your TV?" I ask, noticing what's missing from the living room.

"It's downstairs," he says from over the sink where he's rinsing the dishes and loading the dishwasher.

"Do you have cable? Satellite? Streaming? What's the set up here?"

He shrugs a shoulder. A splash of the sudsy water rolls down his cheek, unnoticed, and my belly flip-flops. He's too distractingly cute to be my temporary roommate. How am I going to get anything done? With finals coming up, I need to focus because there's no way in hell I'm flunking out. All the supernatural craziness going on needs to be resolved one way or another. I don't know how to balance everything. I feel like I'm walking a tightrope in the middle of a hurricane.

"I barely watch television," he says. "I watch movies sometimes, I guess."

"Hmm, then I *guess* we'll have to see what we can do about that."

I skip across the room and head downstairs, taking the steps two at a time. I'm in a good mood because I'm forcing myself to be. I can't think about what happened this morning, seeing poor Landon's spirit with the reaper, or all the other things beyond my control. All I can do is try to be happy, and if I'm being honest, there's a big part of me that is excited for alone time with Dean.

Another small part of me knows I'm in total denial-mode and that I have important things to be doing, things that could mean life or death! I'm letting fear get the better of me and being a baby about the state of my life. I'm freaked out to the point of running away like a puppy with her tail between her legs. But you know what? I really don't care.

As it turns out, Dean has a fantastic theatre room, complete with three gargantuan couches and the biggest television I've ever seen in real life. Blackout shades hang low over the windows, creating the perfect movie-viewing atmosphere. All of this is here waiting to be enjoyed—and he doesn't use it? What does the man do for fun besides brood and run his hands through his hair?

I find the remote and turn on the TV, hoping it's one of those smart ones that will connect to the WiFi on its own. *Success!* I plop down on one of the huge charcoal couches and wrap myself in the matching throw blanket. If I could imagine what lying on a cloud would feel like, it would be this magnificent piece of furniture, but dang, it's chilly down here. Dean's whole house is too cold, probably because he's his own personal heater, but downstairs is extra freezing.

I continue working with the TV until I get the streaming service to open and scroll through all my options. A little while later, he appears in the doorway and watches me. He's changed his clothes again and this time he's in jeans and a dark green cable knit sweater that looks so soft I want to run my hands over it. His hair is wet from a shower and he smells like heaven, even from all the way down here on the couch I can smell the yummy scent wafting from him.

Oh heavens, I'm in trouble.

"What do you think?" he asks, tilting his head toward the TV. "Will this thing work?"

I snort and snuggle deeper into the blanket, embracing the fluffy goodness. "I think I've found my favorite room in your house."

He shrugs but I can tell he's pleased. "I bought this place because it was furnished, close to campus, and suited my needs. All of this was already here when I moved in."

"I had the same experience with my dorm room," I reply with a cheeky grin. "Who has time for furniture shopping these days anyway? The golden colored, extra long twin and matching desk and dresser set in the freshman dorms are just what I've always wanted. And you know, the mattress was already broken in for me. Bonus."

His mouth twitches, holding back a smile.

I return to the TV screen. "If I'm going to be stuck here with you all weekend instead of at home with Mom," I say, "you'd better believe I'm going to do all the things I would have done there."

When our eyes meet, his are playful, leaving me momentarily breathless. They're rarely anything other than intense. What I would give to see him look at me like that more often. "And what's that?" he asks.

I smirk. "A whole lotta lying around and a whole lotta eating, of course. Which, by the way, you and I are cooking a Thanksgiving dinner tomorrow. Mom and I make ours together every year so I think I can handle it if you promise to be my assistant, but we'll have to go shopping later tonight because the stores will be closed tomorrow."

"You need to stay here." He shakes his head. "You're safer here."

I click my tongue but don't reply. It's not like I'm really going to let him keep me in his house like a prisoner. And he can't manage all those groceries on his own if he's never cooked Thanksgiving before. He'll forget something important, like the marshmallows for the candied yams or the whipped cream for the pumpkin pie. Can't have that.

"Did your mom understand when you told her what happened with the reaper this morning?" he asks carefully. "How did that go?"

Before my nap, Dean left me alone for a few minutes so I could call my mom and cancel our plans. It had been hard, especially with the disappointment in her voice.

"She knows about the spirits but she doesn't know about the reapers. I told her I had the flu and couldn't fly." I release a sad breath and frown. "I hate lying to her but I need her safe. She was understandably upset when I told her I'm not going to be well enough to come home for the break, and since she's working a double shift on Friday, she can't fly here either. Given everything that's going on, it's probably for the best."

"I'm sorry." He folds his arms over his chest and holds my gaze.

"It's okay. I'll see her over winter break anyway. The last day of finals is on my birthday, you know. Then I'll be gone for a month."

There I go again, jumping on the denial-train. Am I really going to be able to leave for a whole month? Doubtful. But a girl can pretend for the sake of her own sanity, can't she?

He frowns, his eyes narrowing as if he's thinking the exact same thoughts. A flash of frustration crosses his face; when he finally speaks, he changes the subject. "I've never had a Thanksgiving dinner."

"Yeah, I figured. You're in for a treat."

He crosses the room to sit next to me, his body sinking into the couch and pressing against my blanket and into me. Hope and excitement rushes through my blood and I mentally swat it away. Don't be an idiot, that's my one goal right now.

"I imagine Thanksgiving is similar to the feasts we had back at home."

"Maybe," I tease. "But I doubt you were so lucky as to experience the amazingness that is frog-eye salad."

He turns on me, his face paling. "I was not."

I laugh. "Don't worry. You'll have to wait and see if it's made with real frog eyes." I'll let him stew over it until tomorrow when he figures out it's just beads of pasta that give the mashmallowy delight its namesake.

Again with the marshmallows!

"I think I can do that." His eyes flit across my face, his gaze lingering on my lips. "Patience is a virtue of mine, but that doesn't mean I always like it."

I swallow, my entire body abuzz with electricity. We're not talking about food anymore, are we? I want to hop up and do a happy dance. I also want to jump on him and make out. But I'm way too nervous to flirt back or make a move and anyway, I'll probably screw up kissing considering I have so much amazing experience. *Not!*

Again, Hazel, don't be an idiot.

"One more day until we get to eat all the things." My voice has risen to an unnaturally high octave. I sound as nervous as I feel. "You'd better wear your fat pants because you're going to need the room to grow."

Did I really just bring up fat-pants at a time like this?

He laughs heartily, little crinkles forming around his eyes, and the romantically charged tension between us dissipates. We spend the rest of the afternoon binge-watching my favorite British baking show, which Dean gets sucked into even more than me. At one point he realizes I'm freezing my butt off and covered in goosebumps.

"Are you okay? Do you want another blanket?"

"Umm—I'm fine," I lie.

Why? Why didn't I just say yes?

He rolls his eyes and pulls me to him, settling us both under the blanket and letting me warm up against his naturally hot body. *Yeah, that's why.* That's also the point I start to struggle to pay attention to the show. Every one of my senses is on fire with this boy but I could stay like this forever if given the choice.

When it's time for a break, I beg him to take me with him to the grocery store and after a good arm twist and a lot of description about what he'd have to find on the shelves by himself, he finally agrees. The store is packed with people and some of the things we need are already picked over. We make due and pile everything into the shopping cart. It's kind of fun, like playing house or something. But also kind of not fun because he and I are both on edge the entire time as we navigate from aisle to aisle, aware that we're probably being watched by his brother's minions, even though we can't identify them.

I think I can feel them there. It's like a prickle on the back of my neck, reminding me of the beginning of a sunburn. But maybe I'm just imagining things?

The second we pull into his three car garage, he visibly relaxes. We put all the food away and then get back to our show for a few hours until we're both too tired to continue to the next episode. We eat a late dinner of milk and cereal and when I finally crawl into bed, about ready to pass out, he leaves for a few minutes, saying he's going to double-check that the fire-elemental wards around his house are strong. I'm glad he has something extra to make this place safe. I know what it means to be on the receiving end of those wards, remembering the horrible burning-alive sensation I experienced when I'd broken in a few weeks ago, and just thinking about it makes me cringe.

Never again.

There's a soft knock on the bedroom door.

"Come in." I'm snuggled into my flannel pajamas, the blankets tucked up to my chin. I sit up when Dean enters. "Everything okay?"

He nods, his eyes roving over me, but he doesn't leave the safety of the doorway. Despite all of our cuddle time today, there's an invisible line between us now that we're going to bed. The nap must not have counted since I was so out of it.

"Nobody can get past the wards unscathed unless they're my guest and welcomed in my home," he says. "So I promise, you'll be safe here with me."

"I feel safe." I swallow hard. *Especially when you're near* is the part I do not add. How would he react? I'm not brave enough to risk rejection, especially when his friendship is finally in my grip.

He runs his hands through his hair, his usual go-to move. I have yet to figure out what causes it. Frustration? Worry? Annoyance? "Goodnight, Hazel." He closes the door and a few seconds later I hear him go into his bedroom.

I release a pent up breath and switch off the lamp, burrowing into the pillows. I know it's all a façade and I'm not *really* safe—not completely. But just for this weekend, I want to pretend. I want to fall asleep with a smile on my face and wake up with one, too. I want to have a normal weekend with the guy I really, really like. I want all the things I've never been able to have before because of my spirit ability that I never asked for in the first place. And yes, I want him to kiss me, and if I'm lucky, he will by Sunday night.

"You stupid girl," I whisper into the dark, "you're going to get your heart broken."

Not to mention, you might get yourself killed.

What was my goal today? Oh, that's right, don't be an idiot. Easier said than done.

FOURTEEN

KHALI

DEEP, DEEP DOWN ALL THE way to my bones, I know someone is watching us; I can feel it like I feel the sunlight on the back of my neck or the crunch of fallen leaves beneath my boots. I glance around subtly, eyes darting about the emerald green forest, certain to discover who it is, but there's nobody. It's the same towering mossy trees and midday sunshine. A few birds fly overhead and squirrels dart in and out of my path, but nothing out of the ordinary.

Silas leads the group, a few steps ahead of us, and the rest of our crew amble along without any clear formation. Since I was burdened with the cursed necklace, nobody treats me as a risk. Why should they? I'm useless. But maybe whoever's been watching us is here to help me. I continue to search through the long shadows of the forest until I eventually hang my head in frustration. *Nothing!* The feeling has been my constant companion for the last few days, always at my back, and always in my thoughts.

I want to scream, "If you're not going to help, then leave me alone!" Of course, I don't.

I hope it's not Dean. He promised me he'd stay behind, but I'm not so sure he actually kept the promise. When Silas took me, Dean and I both knew that should he follow, he'd be asking for death. So assuming it's not Dean, it has to be someone—or something—else, and yet, as we travel toward Drakenon, there's nobody. No creatures. No Fae. No Occultists. No one.

Why is that?

Perhaps that's because the forest creatures are afraid of dragon shifters, and being that we are comprised of five lethal men and myself in the party, it's possible. Or maybe whoever Silas has on his payroll to enact spells for him has also placed some kind of barrier around us, hiding us from the Occultists and the Fae. I'd love to find whoever it was that helped him magic the wretched necklace so I can properly punish them. A good freeze would do the trick. Not that I can control the elements at the moment...

As we travel, I can't help but think of the human play book Bram had lent to me all those weeks ago, *A Midsummer Night's Dream*. It feels like a lifetime has passed since I read the comedic tale of romance gone awry. Even though I thought differently at the time, I had so little to worry over compared to today. I gaze around the enchanted forest, easily imagining Shakespeare's cast of characters fitting in amongst the foliage of bright flowers and towering trees. Every day the forest changes a little more, but it's always beautiful—and always a little frightening to think what could happen to someone out here. I wouldn't mind trading places with one of the heroines of the tale if it meant getting away from Silas; I'd even take the Faeries tricky meddling over this constant dread in the pit of my stomach.

I also can't help but think of Bram.

And my father.

They were counting on me and now what am I going to do? I have nothing to offer. I've ruined everything. I should have left the human realm as soon as I realized Dean wasn't going to be able to help. Instead I stuck around until Silas found me. Of course he was going to find me! I knew he was tracking me and yet I didn't worry about it after I crossed into the mortal realm. I was such a fool. I deserved to be caught.

My fingers trail along the black cord tied around my neck, tugging the necklace taught against my skin. Perhaps I deserve this thing, too. I've been so naive.

I step over a log, and my gown snags on a sharp branch. I rip it free. "Remind me why we're walking again?" I grumble, glaring at Silas. "It seems so dangerous that we'd be walking through this area considering our enemies have taken over it and killed all the royals." Silas doesn't reply. Does he ever? *No.* In fact, every time I've asked Silas about this concern, he's kept his mouth shut. They all have.

"Please." My voice cracks. "Let's fly home tonight. I'm exhausted. As are all of you."

And it's true. My limbs ache with exhaustion and we're all in dire need of a proper bath. At this point, I almost want to get back to the castle so I can regroup. I know the second I get there, Silas plans to marry me, but I'll figure something out. I'll find a way to get out of it—I hope.

"Eager to tie the knot, my queen?" Silas teases, gaze locking in on my face.

I clear my throat. "Never mind. Let's just keep walking and walking and walking so we never have to marry."

He laughs mockingly.

I shouldn't wish to get back to the castle anyway, not without a way to help my father. I can't go home to him empty-handed. Silas stares at me for a long minute, something complicated flashes in his gaze. Pity? I don't want his pity.

"How come we haven't run into any Occultists?" I continue, the accusation coming out hot. "Have you made a deal with them? Is that what this is about?"

His face transforms to disgust and he spits in the dirt. "Never."

Interesting. If I push his buttons on this, perhaps he'll give in and tell me what's going on here.

"I think you did," I say, mustering as much spite into my tone as possible. "I think you don't want to admit to it, but who else would have magicked this necklace for you? You and I both know you'll do anything for power, no matter the cost, no matter who you have to hurt in the process. Isn't that right?"

"No," he snaps. "I would never do *that*."

"So explain to me why we haven't run into any Occultists then."

His jaw clenches. "Because I've outsmarted them."

I laugh. "That's what they want you to think."

"Fine," he growls. "I'll tell you enough to shut you up but nothing more."

I keep my face neutral but inside I'm a ball of triumph.

"We're not flying because we can't fly."

I stop in my tracks, confused. "I've seen several of your men shift since we've been here. Everyone's wings seem to be intact."

"The Occultists have spelled the wind," he says bitterly. "If we fly, we can't control where we'll end up. The wind takes us to them."

My heart squeezes as I picture what that must look like, imagining dragons being swept away by the wind with no way to control the direction they go. "When did this happen?"

"Does it matter? It happened. We lost good men and women since we last saw you, in case you didn't notice."

I swallow hard. "I'm sorry. I didn't know." Now that I think about it, there were more of them when they found me at that fae cottage and I fought them off.

Silas and his crew are all glaring at me now, arms folded over massive chests, sneers pulling at their lips, angry eyes narrowed in on me like I'm the cause of all their troubles. It makes sense considering they wouldn't even be here if it wasn't for me. As much as I dislike them for working with Silas, they're following the orders of their prince, and most of them have left me alone over the last few days. They could have treated me badly but they didn't.

"How many did you lose?" I ask.

"Three," Silas replies. "We're lucky it was only three. It could have been all of us." The frustration rolls off him in waves.

"So let's go get them," I say, surprising myself and everybody else.

The men look around at each other, their expressions guarded.

"I'm serious," I say. "Let's go save our people." I zero in on Silas. "And you can do the right thing for once and save your brother while we're at it."

His expression stills, and I know he's thinking of how Bram betrayed him by helping me get out of Drakenon. But isn't that what this family does to each other? Dean left without telling his brothers why he was leaving. Bram ran away with me. Silas killed Owen. There are so many layers to these relationships and each one is darker than the last.

My eyes narrow. "What aren't you telling me?"

He lets out a stilted breath, and I'm sure he's going to confess an important fact, when something hard snaps around my ankles and suddenly, I'm flying. I scream.

The trees and leaves and roots rush by me in a blur of color. Earthy scents of soil, leaves, and tree bark wrap around me. Fear rattles every one of my emotions, and bile rises to my throat. Below, I hear Silas and his men call out to each other, preparing for battle. But that doesn't last long because soon I'm too far away to hear them at all.

I'm being tossed about like a flimsy piece of paper in a wind storm—passed from tree to tree. My eyes dart every which way, trying to get a sense of who's doing this to me, when I realize it's the trees themselves that are responsible. They reach out with their branches and pass me onward to the next. I have no magic nor strength that could stand a chance against these towering beasts. I've never heard about trees that could move this way and my first thought is the Occultists have magicked them like they did the wind. At least now I know what's been watching us and why I couldn't see anyone.

Fighting proves to be pointless so I let them carry me away.

With Silas's necklace still clinging tight around my throat, I have no chance against the trees or the Occultists. I close my eyes and offer a prayer to the gods, whatever god will listen, and beg for help. I go on like this for I don't know how long, minutes or hours, it's all too intense to tell.

Without warning, I'm dropped to the ground, inertia sending my stomach into a tailspin. I expect pain to follow, but I land on something soft. I release a breath, roll over, and open my eyes to a bed of clovers. They're as thick as a blanket, each as big as a hand, and seem to caress me in a loving embrace.

Around me, the forest is alive with a rainbow of colorful flowers that grow up and around the trees. They glitter in the sunlight. At least there aren't any warlocks to be seen.

I sit up and rub my eyes, then pull a few twigs and leaves from my hair. "What in Eridas is going on here?" I mumble.

"You could say that again," a familiar voice purrs from the trees above. Terek leaps to the ground, landing gracefully on all fours. His catlike features are the same as ever, if not slightly more pronounced. A golden tail loops around his backside and comes to glide down my cheek. I swat it away.

"There, there!" Terek's feline grin spreads across his handsome face. "That's no way to treat an old friend."

"Can I call you that?" I spit back. "Last time I saw you, you ditched me."

"I helped you." He frowns, pouting his pink lips. "Anyway, it seems to me that the forest wants us together. Why do you think that is?"

He stands tall and reaches out a hand. I take it. Five sharp little claws rub against my wrist but don't cut as he pulls me up.

"The trees brought me here on their own?" I question. "They're not spelled?"

He tilts his head and shakes it. "There's been rumors that some of the trees are alive and could move all on their own but I've never seen it until this day. You're special, princess. I would say I'm jealous but that looked like a bumpy ride."

I let out a breath. "Believe me, it was."

So the trees brought me here. These trees must have consciousness and autonomy. The realization is both startling and calming. Startling because it adds another level of danger to this forest, but calming because maybe they hate the Occultists as much as I do.

"I have no idea why they deposited me here with you," I add, looking around at the trees and wishing they could talk. "But I'd like to know the answer."

They don't move, as if nothing ever happened.

Terek raises a golden eyebrow and his blue cat-like eyes sparkle knowingly. "You weren't by any chance headed to the capitol to break your handsome prince free, were you?"

I study him for a long minute. "Maybe."

"Well, I for one have a bone to pick with a certain Occultist. You know the only one who can release a spell is the one who placed it there in the first place? Alas, I'm beginning to be more cat than elf and we can't have that, can we?" He winks.

My mind whirls, the pieces of a plan coming together. "Terek, you genius! You've just given me an idea."

He offers a gentlemanly bow and a strand of his fair hair falls over one eye. As he did when I first met him, he's got his large bow strapped to his back along with a quiver of arrows. He's dressed in the same finely stitched clothing, but it's a little worse for wear these days, as if he's been on the run. He probably has been. And he's just as endearing and sly as when I first met him a few weeks ago.

"Of course I'm a genius." He smiles. "Tell me something I don't know."

"Come on," I say. "Let's go trap ourselves a warlock."

FIFTEEN

HAZEL

I HEAVE MY BACKPACK OVER one shoulder and rinse out the last of the coffee, adding the mug to the dishwasher. It's mostly full so I locate a dishsoap tab and plop it into the machine, then turn it on. It hums to life. Satisfied, I lean against the counter and smile. I still can't believe I'm here. Sure, the circumstances aren't ideal, but that doesn't mean Dean and I didn't just have the best weekend together—because we did. We really did. The only thing that would have made it better would have been a kiss, but no such luck. I wonder if Khali thought the same things when she was here…

"You ready?" Dean asks, joining me in the kitchen. He's wearing a long-sleeved heather gray shirt that looks as soft as a kitten. It's different from his trademark black v-neck and I must say, I'm a fan. I would give anything for it not to be Monday but I also refuse to be locked up in his house by myself. I need to talk to Harmony about my father, not to mention, find a way to talk to Owen again. But I also have to go to my classes because my scholarship and my future as a veterinarian depends on a high GPA. I refuse to hide away in Dean's place forever. At least we have anthropology together this morning.

"Let's go," I sigh. I add my cranberry-colored scarf and hat to my wintery ensemble and head for the front door, the bubble we've been in this weekend officially in deflation mode.

We step out into the dreary morning, Dean without a coat because the man never needs one, and me, wrapped up like the Michelin Man in my layers upon layers of winter gear. It was so weird seeing my clothes hanging up in his guest room closet this morning, especially next to all the stuff Khali left. Yesterday we stopped by my dorm so I could grab a few more essentials and good thing we did because it's been snowing all night and it's still coming down. Dean had his guard up the whole thirty minutes we were gone but nothing happened. If I'm really being watched by dragon shifters, I haven't found any proof, and anyway, it's not like I've *done* anything to alarm the dragons in the last few days.

Give it time, my mind chimes in. I swat the thought away.

"I'm going to walk you to all your classes today," Dean says it casually but I know he's not casual about my safety. I'm so busy traipsing through the crunchy snow, I almost don't hear him.

"Why?" I ask the question I already know the answer to but I'm fishing for a compliment and I know it. I'm such a goner for this guy. I suck on my bottom lip, which reminds me to buy flavored chapstick. You know, just in case…

"Same reason you're staying with me. I need to keep you safe."

I glance around but there's nothing but a whole lot of wet white stuff. There's nobody else out here on his street. Are we sure there are dragon shifters watching me? They can shift into humans so would I be able to tell the difference between one of them and one of us? Probably not.

While there aren't any people out here, there are spirits. There are always spirits, but since the grounding, they've left me alone. A few linger around some of the houses, which is typical. When a preteen ghost with a sour expression on his face turns to stare at me, a chill runs down my spine.

"Hate to break it to you Dean, but I don't think you can keep me safe forever."

"I can try." His response is gruff.

I'd be lying if I said Dean's protectiveness isn't getting my hopes up. Maybe the dragon threat isn't as bad as he says, and this whole staying with him charade is really about getting closer to me. *In my dreams!* He had all weekend to make a move and didn't even try. Not to mention, I know my threats are real. The reaper who tried to carve me up and killed Landon in the process is proof enough that I have a target on my back.

The driveways, sidewalks, and front walks have all been cleared, as has Hayden's campus, so it's not too much of an imposition to walk to class. Except, of course, for the snow that's still coming down and chilling me to the bone. We hurry past students who are just as eager to get out of the cold as I am. When we finally get inside our building, I unwrap my many layers, relishing in the blast of artificial heat. The lecture hall is much warmer than Dean's house, but that also means no excuses for cuddle time.

"Hey, you two lovebirds," Cora sing-songs as she sashays up to us and wraps us both into one of her vanilla-scented hugs.

Macy stands behind her, direct eye-line for Dean and me, giving us two thumbs up. "It's about time." She lifts her eyebrows suggestively. "You know, Dean, you didn't have to be so rude to Hazel at the party last week," she goes on, "playing hard to get is a jerk move."

"Umm—" He doesn't know what to say.

"Treat her right or we'll hurt you," Cora adds into his ear but loud enough for me to hear.

I squeeze my eyes shut, mortified. When Cora lets us go, Dean stumbles back with a bit of a puzzled expression. His gaze locks on mine, and I fake a laugh. "Ha-ha!" My smile is total plastic, and Cora and Macy exchange a weary glance. "Well, my best friends were wondering where I was last night," I say, widening my eyes at Dean. "I had to tell them I was staying at your house. Isn't that right, Babe?"

He catches on quick, smiling one of his rare smiles and wrapping a possessive arm around my waist. My stomach does a little flip-flop. "No worries, *Babe*."

Heat burns my cheeks. We go to find seats together, but Dean stops me. "I'm going to skip class today."

I frown. "Why?"

"There's some things I need to work on for my independent study." He clears his throat and, leaning in, whispers against my ear. "I'm working on some things to try to help my people. I need to figure this out sooner rather than later so I can help Khali, too."

I have no idea what any of that means but I nod and slump into my seat. He's gone in seconds. I wish he'd include me instead of always acting like I'm made out of porcelain and could break at any moment. I went along with it all weekend because, well, cuddles on the couch and playing house together, but I'm regretting that now. I don't want to be left out.

"What was that about?" Cora questions.

Dr. Peters uses that moment to start his lecture, saving me from answering my friend. I have the hardest time paying attention Peters's lecture. I woke up this morning, basically living in an alternate reality, and I don't know what to think. I know what I feel. And I know I'm distracted. I should be focusing on the bigger picture, not caught up in a crush on an unavailable guy like Dean. He's obviously not too distracted, considering he's spending time with me to keep me safe, and then when he has the chance to leave me with the herd, he's off to work on something to help Khali.

As he should be.

And I should be too…

Nervous energy sweeps over me and I'm suddenly eager to get through the day and over to The Flowering Chakra. Anthropology ends without fanfare and I go through my day in a bit of a fog. After my last class ends, I pile on my coat, hat, scarf, and gloves, then hurry toward Harmony's store. I have a shift this afternoon but more than that, she might have answers for me. She asked to give her some time to sort things out and I did. She also said something was going on with Khali that I needed to stay out of, and well, I'm pretty sure I know what that is now that she's been taken back to Eridas against her will.

As I approach the edge of campus, booted footsteps catch up to me and Dean pops into view.

"I'm walking you to work, remember?" His hands are shoved into his jean's pockets and his breath is visible.

"Thanks." And I am grateful.

"Are you okay?" He shoots me a pointed look.

I sigh. "I don't know if another reaper is going to try to possess someone. I don't know if dragon shifter soldiers are watching me right now. And I don't even know the risks I'm taking walking to Main Street in my own town. I want to be safe just as much as you want me to be safe but you can't walk me everywhere forever. I mean, how long are you planning to do this?"

We walk side by side in silence the rest of the way to the shop and stand facing each other under the stoop. Beyond the overhang, fluffy snow falls.

"As long as it takes," he finally answers my earlier question, a muscle in his jaw tightening.

"As long as it takes until what?" I turn to him and our eyes lock.

His lips thin, coal-eyes shifting away.

"Until what, Dean?" I press. "Tell me."

Until he leaves? Until Khali needs him?

"Until there are no more threats to you." He clears his throat. "Or to anybody else."

His eyes fall to my lips and then look away.

"Hello there, Beautifuls!" Harmony calls out as she opens the door to let us inside. Bells chime cheerfully and we turn to face her. "Well, come on in, both of you, hurry up now."

We tread inside, stomping off the snow on the front mat, and she closes the door behind us with a clang. There are no shoppers at the moment but that makes sense considering the craptastic weather. Weird new-agey harp music plays from a nearby speaker. I listen closer and realize it's a rendition of Jingle Bells. I try not to roll my eyes but that proves to be impossible.

"I wondered when you were going to show up." Harmony smiles knowingly. "I've been waiting for you all day." She wags her bony finger at us. "There's something I must show you."

As far as I can tell, her beautiful papery-thin, gossamer wings are on full display but when I glance at Dean, he doesn't seem to notice them. I want to ask if he sees them too, but Harmony said it was my "gift" allowing me to see past her faerie glamour, so he probably doesn't know they're there. Or maybe he knows they're there, but he also knows she's using magic to hide them. Or maybe he knows absolutely nothing about her heritage. Considering he claims to have smelled the "supernatural" on me when I first arrived here, I'm going to guess that last theory isn't a correct one.

She locks the door and hangs the closed sign in the window. A spark of excitement weaves through me.

"Come." She motions for us to follow her into the back room.

"Does this have anything to do with what we talked about last week?" I say, hopeful that I'll finally learn the identity of my father. Harmony is my best chance at this. Mom still won't tell me anything and I checked my birth certificate years ago so I already know his name isn't listed. I don't have any extended family that I can ask about him, just in case Mom was lying about the whole one-night-stand thing.

So it's Harmony's magic or it's giving up, and I'm not ready to give up.

My gaze dances across the items lain out on the table: a bowl of water, a single white rose, a candle, a long black feather, and an ornate, ancient-looking knife. My eyes stay glued to the knife and I swallow hard. *Alrighty then...*

"What's all this?" Dean's tone is sharp. Accusatory.

Harmony sends him a knowing look. "By this point I'm sure you have already figured out what I am, an oracle faerie, just as I know you are a fire-elemental dragon shifter."

Dean's eyes harden but he doesn't respond.

"Let's not keep up the pretences, okay? We're both here to help Hazel."

His hands squeeze into fists and he shifts his body in front of mine. "How can I trust you?"

"You don't have to, Dean," I interject and push past him toward Harmony. "Because I do. She's just as much a part of this as anyone. And we need her help."

He folds his arms over his chest and curls his bottom lip, but doesn't make another move or say another word.

"We're going to try a spell," Harmony says, "a spell that would allow my gift to look backwards instead of forward."

Nervous excitement ignites in my chest, lighting me up like the 4th of July. "So you could see where I come from? Do you think you could see my father?"

"Not just me," she says. "If it works, my gift will flow through you. You'll see it all in your mind's eye."

My inner fireworks show explodes into a cacophony of dread and fear and hope and too many feelings to name. Before I can change my mind, I nod. "Let's do it."

She starts right away, combining the items, putting them all into the bowl. Then she cuts her left palm. Her blood isn't red; it's silver. It drips into the water, spreading like metallic ink.

"Your turn." She hands me the knife.

"Hazel," Dean interrupts. "You don't have to do this. We'll find another way. Blood magic is..." His voice grows hoarse with anger. "It's sacrilege."

Harmony surprises me by agreeing with him. "He's right. It's forbidden in Eridas because it often comes with unseen consequences. I should have told you that to start with. But here the magic is subdued and my hope is that we'll be able to get away unscathed."

Dean snorts in disbelief. "You'd take that risk?"

My mind races, fear creeping into my thoughts and I wonder if it's worth it. But I've already come this far and I can't give up now.

"I need to know."

I take the knife and quickly slice through my palm before I can talk myself out of it. Wincing at the white-hot pain, I pray I didn't just make a huge mistake and squeeze my blood into the bowl anyway. My crimson mixes with her silver.

Harmony grabs my unwounded hand in her wounded one, and I do the same thing back, taking her free hand into mine, blood fresh against our palms. A jolt of something powerful passes through us like an electric current. Magic? I glance at Dean. He's staring at where the blood has landed in the bowl, his face drained of color.

I take a deep breath, close my eyes, and see it all.

My life flashes before my eyes but in reverse, unraveling like a string from a sweater, pulling and pulling until there's no sweater, not a thing, nothing but a mess of string. I am made of all these memories, these things that have happened to me: moments, choices, friendships, enemies, love and hate, days and hours and minutes and seconds all compiled together to make me, me.

They come apart at the seams until there's nothing but an infant.

She's lying with her mother. Crying. She's pink and tiny. She's got barely-there fuzzy blonde hair and her eyes are that dark blue color that babies are born with before they change, in my case to hazel.

She's me.

And that's my mother, only a much younger version.

There's a man. My father?

No, not my father. Not by the way he looks at me.

He's tall. He stands over us while Mom sleeps. His face transforms from disgust into something like pride, so does that mean he actually is my father?

But I don't get that feeling.

I don't know.

Black tendrils of sparkling magic flow from his long white fingertips, surrounding the baby-me and Mom in a cloud of darkness. I stop crying and fall into an immediate sleep. The man takes a vial of something dark red, almost black, from his robes.

Blood.

He speaks in a language I don't understand but I've heard before. It's otherworldly. It's old. Ancient. Evil.

He pulls out a syringe with a long needle at the end.

He places the needle into the vial, filling the entire syringe with blood. Then he finds my foot and injects it, uttering more unsettling words. No hesitation. He does it like it means nothing to him to hurt an innocent child. Like it's nothing, but also like it's everything.

He smiles and vanishes.

The baby's eyes pop open. She screams, so much harder than before.

Mom doesn't wake up.

My infant-self keeps screaming. Screaming and wailing and crying until I'm beet-red. This continues all night and if there is a father somewhere, he doesn't come. That's as far as the memories go before there's nothing left to see.

Sixteen

KHALI

"SO YOU DON'T HAVE ANY magic?" Terek hops over a fallen log with a whimsical bounce. "Nothing at all?" He swoops his tail to swat a luminous fly away without missing a beat.

"Well, I have magic, but it's weak, and if I do try to use it, it goes directly to Silas." I hold up the corded necklace and suppress the immense hatred I feel toward Silas right now. The metal dragon pendant dangles on the cord's end, glinting in the sunlight as if to tease me. "This is the Brightcaster family emblem. I've had to wear it over the years. As it turns out, Silas has had this one spelled to funnel magic to him and it's indestructible. I can't break the string and it's tied too tightly to remove."

Terek clicks his tongue. "How very savage of your little princeling."

"He's not my little princeling," I snap.

Terek winks, his bright blue cat eyes shining in the evening light. "Oh, of course, that would be Bram, wouldn't it?"

"No!"

He chuckles and I bite my tongue. We fall into companionable silence and continue to hike through the forest. The trees are starting to thin. There aren't as many animals either, as if they're put off by whatever has been going on at Highburne. I can sense we're getting closer to it by the way Terek grows quiet, eyes darting about fully alert, and bow and arrow at the ready. It won't be long before we run into friends or foes. Nervous energy simmers in my chest.

Whatever protection Silas had over our party of dragon shifters hasn't stuck around for me and Terek so we've been extra careful to keep our guard up on this excursion toward Highburne. We hike as quickly as possible without drawing extra attention to ourselves, which is easy for Terek because his feline tendencies make him extra quiet. But it's not easy for me, especially without my earth magic to help me feel everything in this forest.

I'm a liability to Terek but he never complains. He's not so bad. Actually, I am beginning to consider him more than an ally, but also, a friend.

Through it all, I can still sense the trees watching over me. I was so concerned by the lingering feeling of being watched when I was with Silas's crew, but now that I know where it's coming from and that the trees are on my side, I'm grateful. I might need them to get me out of a sticky situation again. Terek said he'd heard old stories of the trees autonomy, but that was the first he's ever seen it happen. For all we know, it might never happen again.

The highest-pitched scream I've ever heard careens through the forest, sending a couple of birds flying and my pulse rising. Terek and I freeze, listening intently. The cry comes again: pained, terrified, and screeching. It doesn't sound like any creature I've heard before.

"We should keep going," Terek whispers. "That's not our business."

"But she might need help," I counter.

He shakes his head and pushes on, leading us on no particular path as we climb over some of the lower hanging branches of the forest. The cries continue on and on. My palms begin to sweat.

"We can't," Terek whispers again. "If you want to stay alive, you've got to stay out of others' problems and focus on your own."

I grit my teeth and reply back, "You didn't stay out of my problem when Bram and I faced the Huldra."

"That was different. That wasn't a pixie."

"No, it wasn't," I hiss. "And so what? Why can't we help a pixie?"

"Pixies can't be trusted."

"Who says?"

"Everyone!"

I roll my eyes.

"Pixies can take care of themselves," Terek scoffs. "Believe me."

Are pixies known to be cunning and dangerous? Sure. Are they the most loyal sort in the world? No, not really. But they're also dripping in magic and I know what it feels like to be dripping in magic and *still* needing help. What if Bram hadn't come for me when I'd been lost in the jeweled forest? What if the handsome stranger in the black suit hadn't helped me erase my records from the human police officers? What kind of person would I be if I ignored the fervent cries of a creature in peril?

I can't do it.

I whip around and follow the sound of the crying, ignoring the panic surging within and the voice screaming inside my head that Terek is right and I should stay out of it. He keeps close behind me, grumbling about ogre traps and keeping away from their food if we know what's good for us.

It doesn't take long to spot her and when I do, I can't help but find myself awed.

I've never seen a pixie in person before. She's not much bigger than one of my fingers. Her skin is a pale shade of lavender with what looks to be delicate purple flowers growing out of her shoulders and the top of her head. Royal purple wings jut out of her back, sparkling as they twitch. She belongs in a garden, not caught in a trap.

"Are you okay?" I kneel before her. She's stuck under an intricate, albeit a little haphazard, net of vines that's clearly been designed to catch one of her kind or something just as small.

She blinks up at me, silver eyes rimmed with purple tears. "Please help me?"

I reach out to lift the net.

"I wouldn't do that if I were you." Terek slaps my hand away.

She hisses at Terek, sharp teeth on full display.

He ignores her. "If you move that net, it will put a tracker on you by whatever ogre put that there. Trust me when I say you do not want to interfere with an ogre's food. There is no reasoning with those bloodthirsty brutes. He will hunt you down and kill you."

"Don't listen to him," the pixie squeaks. "That's only a myth! If you don't help me, you're condemning me to death."

"It's not a myth and you know it," Terek seethes. "I've seen it happen with my own eyes. Don't get involved, Khali. Ogres are lethal and their magic is specific to helping them trap, track, catch, kill, and *eat*. Let her pixie friends figure this one out."

"They're not going to come for me. They hate me! You wouldn't understand. Besides, there's no time." Her voice grows frantic.

I thought pixies stuck together but something about her tone makes me believe her.

I don't think. I take action. Grabbing the heavy vined netting, I pry it off the pixie. I expect her to fly away and an ogre to charge through the trees seeking revenge, but neither happens.

The pixie zooms in a circle, a huge smile spreading over her tiny face, and comes to hover in front of me. Golden dust sparkles off of her body as she buzzes about. Her teeth are sharp as razors and would give her a menacing quality if she didn't look so happy.

"You saved me," she gushes. "I owe you one." She flies over and hugs me around my face. I blink and try not to laugh, inhaling her lovely floral scent.

Terek scoffs and steps back. "More than one. You owe her a life because once that ogre finds her she's as good as dead."

The pixie lets me go and hovers just above my eyeline. She gives me a little curtsey midair.

"How can I return the favor?" her wind-chime voice sing-songs.

My hand immediately rises to the necklace. "Can you help me get this thing off? It's magicked with an indestructible cord."

"Indestructible, huh?" her voice chimes.

"Yes," Terek interjects.

She ignores him and grins, her pointy teeth on full display. "I wouldn't be so sure about that."

She swoops in and grabs the cord, getting to work, chomping down on it with vigor. Terek leans against a nearby tree trunk and gazes on skeptically but I can't stop a surge of hope springing to life. *This could be it!*

"Almost got it," she squeaks. She shimmers with pixie dust and continues hacking away at the cord.

Sure enough, with an audible pop, the necklace falls to the ground. My magic immediately swells inside, all four elements bursting beneath my skin. I can feel my dragon there, too. She longs to be let free. More than anything, we want to fly.

"Thank you!" I gush, overwhelmed with my good fortune. "You have no idea what that means to me."

She winks. "My pleasure. Now we're even."

"Are you though?" Terek says dryly.

She blows me a kiss and she flies off, zipping away through the trees, with nothing but a faint gold sparkling of dust behind her.

"I hope you enjoyed that act of heroism," Terek says, "because you're about to pay the price."

Before I can reply, something larger than life booms through the forest.

I look around for the source of the noise. Something rips in the distance and a tree careens through the air before crashing at my feet. Moments later, the ogre appears, letting out a guttural roar that shakes me to my bones. The creature is massive, almost as big as I am when I'm in dragon form, and its arms and legs are nothing but pure muscle. They're also covered in scars. Its bulbous skin gleams in a layer of sweat. It roars again, charging right toward us, two muddy eyes fixed on me and nothing else. Its mouth opens wide, revealing giant yellow teeth the size of boulders. They're stained with blood.

I snatch the broken necklace from the ground and tuck it into my bodice.

"Run!" Terek yells.

We take off. I bring my fire element to the surface and toss fireballs back at the ogre as we jump over fallen logs and duck under branches. My heart hammers against my rib cage and my magic whirls inside me like a cyclone.

Terek shoots me a furious look over his shoulder. "I hope it was worth it."

I smile. I have my magic back. Of course it was worth it.

SEVENTEEN
HAZEL

I'M COVERED IN SWEAT AND panting for air. My body is curled up on the little loveseat in Harmony's back room, surrounded by the purple painted walls and ceiling. Dean and Harmony stand over me, expressions of concern etched into their faces.

"I didn't see him." My voice cracks and disappointment pierces my heart, a physical pain I didn't know I could feel over a man who has never been there for me. Not even when I was an infant. Mom wasn't lying.

I sit up and rub my face, focusing on slowing my breaths in an attempt to relax. "Did you see my father?" I ask Harmony, clinging to one last shred of hope that I missed it somehow.

Her mouth turns down in a frown. "I didn't," she whispers.

I nod and let it sink in. Whoever my father was, I'll never know. I'll never meet him. It's done.

Harmony catches my eye. She's paler than usual. Her white dreadlocked hair is frazzled, like she's been running her fingers through it. Her eyes are that strangely beautiful moonstone color, and her gossamer wings are on full display, but this time I'm not the only one who can see them. Dean stares at her like he knew what she was all along but he's still startled just the same.

"Your glamour is down," he says casually.

I shoot him a little glare and help Harmony to the loveseat next to me. "Are you okay?"

"That took more out of me than I was expecting," she says between several long breaths. "But I'll be okay."

I don't know if I believe she's really fine but I don't say anything.

"I think I know what happened to you, Hazel," she goes on. "Did you see that man, how he injected blood into you when you were a child?"

I nod, the image of it fresh in my mind. I shiver.

"He was casting a spell," she says. "I don't understand all of his language but I do know enough to understand that's what he was doing." She releases a soft moan and reaches to take my hand. Hers is ice cold and quivering.

My eyes water. "What did he do to me?"

Dean kneels in front of us, his recent mask of protection dropping to reveal something I haven't seen on him before: fear. My stomach twists.

"He was binding you to Khali," she says. "We've already figured out that her magic is somehow connected to you but it's more than what we thought—it's worse." She turns to face me. "I believe he connected your life force to hers. It's as if your spirits are tethered together."

"What does that mean?" Dean asks.

Tense silence stretches between the three of us. Khali and I already figured out that we're connected and that when we touch, her magic doesn't respond well. I've never had a negative experience with it but we didn't try that hard and now I'm regretting that my chance is gone.

"It means that if one of you is strong, the other is weak."

"That explains some things," Dean replies, closing his eyes and raking a hand through his hair. His whole body is tense and I can practically feel the stress radiating off of him.

"It's very possible that if one of you were to die," Harmony's voice grows thick, "the other would die, too."

Dean curses. I sit back, realizing the implications. The shock makes its way to my throat like a physical thing and for a second, I can't breathe. Khali isn't here, and not only that, she's in a realm where there is nothing but danger for her. If something were to happen to her and she were to die, it could happen to me, too. And having the pressure of knowing that should something happen to me, she could lose her life as well, is too much for me to handle.

"So you're saying I could drop dead at any moment?" I gasp, tears springing to my eyes.

Harmony nods and squeezes my hand.

"Or," I go on, "the reverse could happen. If I die, she's a goner?" I need her to verify this for me because I still can't believe it. I just can't. How is this possible? How could this happen?

"It's all part of the spell."

I release her hand and fold my arms over my chest, overcome with a sinking feeling of defeat. And here I thought I was—at least marginally—safe. I've been so stupid.

"So how do we break it?" I ask.

Her lips thin. "You would have to find the Occultist who did it and make him break it."

My heart sinks.

"I'm ready to go home now," I say with a shaky voice.

Dean nods and helps me to my feet. I look back at the faerie who is sinking into the little couch, her wings pressed up against the leather. "Harmony, thank you for helping me. But I need you to be honest, are you okay? Because your glamour is down and you don't look like you're doing all right."

"I'll be fine." Her smile is weak but genuine. "This has happened to me before. I just need some extra rest. I can't leave the building right now anyway." She nods toward her wings and winks one of her otherworldly eyes. "But after it gets late enough, and dark enough, I'll go on home. Don't worry about coming to work tomorrow. I'll call you when I'm ready to reopen the shop. It will probably be a few days before I gain my strength back."

"I don't want to leave you." I frown. "It's not right."

"I'll be okay," she says with a lazy smile, eyes fluttering shut. "I'd rather be alone, anyway. You have my cell phone number and you know where I live, so feel free to check up on me tomorrow."

Guilt swallows me whole but what else can I do for her? I'm pretty much useless right now myself. Just like her, I'm overcome with exhaustion. All I can think of is that guest bed in Dean's place and a long, long, long sleep.

Dean makes sure Harmony is comfortable before whisking me back out into the snowy late afternoon. It only takes a few minutes to walk back to his place but those minutes feel like an eternity in this terrible cold, especially with the sun working its way out of the sky. It's the kind of wet cold that can be felt all the way to my bones and it's turning into a deep freeze that makes it hard to breathe. When we finally make it inside his house, I walk into a blast of heat. He's turned up his thermostat to a normal temperature for once. The warmth flows over me like an electric blanket, and I let out a satisfied moan of relief. *Praise Jesus!*

Dean laughs.

"What?" I challenge with a little laugh. But he shakes his head and wanders off.

First thing I do is take a long shower until the hot water and steam thaws me from the inside out. Afterward, I dress in my fuzziest pajamas and thickest socks and pile my wet hair into a messy bun on the top of my head to keep it from dripping everywhere. I'm too tired to deal with a blow dryer, and besides, I left that back at my dorm room. I know it's still early, but I brush my teeth and head for bed, climbing under the covers and falling asleep in about 0.2 seconds.

I dream of the people I love. I see their faces in quick flashes, over and over again. I see them crying and hurting. And then, I see them burning. The man in the robes stands there, watching it all, a satisfied gleam in his eyes as the fire rages. The flames don't touch his robes even though they seem to be emanating from him.

Where am I? I can't help because I'm not there. I scream but they don't hear me. I'm nothing but a shadow, a ghost.

"Hazel!"

I bolt upright. My heart thuds against my rib cage. Dean is here.

"It was just a dream," he says, running a hand along my cheek. "A nightmare."

I sink back into the headboard, gasping. Was it a nightmare or was it the lingering effects of using the blood magic? It felt so real.

The covers are strewn all around me, like I've been kicking at them for hours. I rub my hands against my eyes and try to erase the images from the dream. The acrid smell of burning flesh and heady smoke still hangs close to my senses. My skin is still hot. My eyes still sting from the smoke.

"How long was I out?" I ask, swallowing hard and licking my lips.

"Not long," Dean says. "Maybe an hour."

That might explain why I don't feel any less exhausted than I was before. Only an hour but stuck in a nightmare. The sleepiness clings to me but I refuse to give into it; I'm too scared.

"I'm sorry," I croak, eyes watering. I feel like such a baby.

Dean scoots in closer. His coal eyes burn with worry. There's a line of stubble along his jaw that wasn't there this morning. His raven-black hair hangs around his forehead and pale cheeks, framing his face. The awful smells from the nightmare are replaced by his campy, forested scent. He's so close—the best distraction ever. He's everything in this moment, and I can't help myself from wanting to know what his lips would taste like so I close the distance between us and find out.

I don't care that it's not some picture-perfect, storybook, Hollywood moment. I don't care that my hair is a mess and I'm in the opposite of sexy pajamas. I don't have a lick of makeup on and it's not like we're somewhere romantic with gorgeous lighting and stunning scenery. We never even had a proper date. He didn't give me that "come-hither" look like they do in the movies. And I had to make the first move

It doesn't matter.

None of it matters right now except for his lips on mine and the fact he's kissing me back. I'd worried I wouldn't know what to do and wouldn't know how to be a good kisser, but all that seems to melt away. I sink into his lips and he groans, pulling me close. I crawl onto his lap and wrap my legs around his torso. His arms encircle me, trapping me, protective and strong. He's so warm and burning hotter by the second but that's such a Dean thing anyway. It makes this feel real and I never want it to end.

He deepens the kiss and I'm lost to how close we're becoming. There's a sunrise inside of me. It's rising, brightening at the speed of light. It's so beautiful, the kind of beauty that will be impossible to look directly at soon. I want to bottle it up so I can keep it with me forever.

Somehow my hair tie has come loose. My hair hangs in damp curls around us, and Dean runs one hand through it while the other holds me close. I do the same, enjoying the taught muscles on his back and arms and stomach.

He stills and pulls away.

"You'll be my undoing," he whispers, so quietly I almost don't know if it was real.

But it was.

My heart squeezes. I like the sound of being his undoing. I smile and reach out to bring his soft lips back to mine but he shakes his head and untangles us. Rolling away, he stands at the end of the bed and brushes off his wrinkled clothing. He's too far away.

Outside, darkness covers the windows.

"It stopped snowing," he says before clearing his throat.

"What's wrong?" I ask, refusing to let him change the subject.

"I don't want to burn you," he says, dragging his eyes back to mine.

I frown and sit up. "Is that a metaphor?"

He raises his palms, and I can't help but let out a gasp. Not a metaphor: they're bright red and look like they're going to burst into flames. I think back to the day we had that argument, when he lost control and singed my shirt. I always thought it had to do with anger, but maybe any kind of too-strong emotion causes him to light up. Could positive emotions do it too? I can only hope whatever he just felt was similar to what I felt—which was very, very positive.

"We shouldn't do that again," he says gruffly, his expression filled with longing before fixing into that carefully guarded mask of his.

"But you want to?" The question hangs between us. I've never felt this vulnerable before. I want to push him away, or crawl under the covers. I could transfer schools and change my name. But I simply hold his gaze and wait for him to respond.

"Yes," he sighs. "But what I want is irrelevant."

"No, it's not," I argue. "You're allowed to be happy, Dean."

Something about that sentence changes him. The guilt that overcomes his face is so palpable, it practically fills the room.

"Why is that so hard for you?" I press. "What do you feel guilty about? Khali? Being here instead of with your family? Kissing me? Something else? I don't know but I wish more than anything I could help make it go away."

"I don't know what to say." His voice cracks. He won't look at me.

"Say something!"

He's quiet for a long minute, staring into nothing as if thinking of the perfect thing to say. "Sometimes, it's like the weight of the world is on my shoulders," he confesses. "Actually, the weight of two worlds. And I don't know how to make it stop."

"Dean—"

"I just want you to be safe," he cuts me off. "Goodnight, Hazel." He leaves the room and closes the door before I can get another word in.

I jump up and go after him, not ready to end this conversation, but when I grab the door handle, it's white-hot. I yelp and snatch my hand back before the metal can burn me more. Dean wasn't lying when he said his hands were getting too hot. His footsteps descend the stairs. A few seconds later, the front door opens and shuts. I run over to the window and watch as he strides out into the evening light. He doesn't wear a coat and even from here, I can see his hands are still glowing with the heat of his magic. He shoves them into his pockets. He's heading in the direction of campus, each step more purposeful than the last. I guess he doesn't worry about leaving me in his house alone because of the protection wards he's got up, but that doesn't stop me from worrying about him being out there by himself.

He doesn't want to hurt anyone, not me, and especially not the ones back home that he cares so much about. He's so caught up with taking care of everybody else, that he doesn't stop to realize that at the end of the day, he's the one getting burned.

Maybe that's the saddest part of all of this. And also why I like him so much, because there's so much more to him than I ever thought. When I first met him, I judged him. I believed he was selfish and stuck-up, and probably a playboy type who used people like items to be discarded at his earliest convenience.

Now I know the opposite is true.

A selfish person would choose to be with me if that's what he wanted, even if it hurt his family or his kingdom or whoever else. A selfish person wouldn't run away from his amazing royal life in the first place. He'd have put himself first. But Dean isn't like that. And even though I want him here with me right now and I want him to choose us, I can't be mad.

I flop back down on the bed and breathe in deep, replaying our kiss over and over in my mind in a continuous loop. I want to commit it to memory, even if it is tinged with sadness. I can't let myself forget the way he tasted or the way it felt to be cherished like that for those few minutes because it was probably the best thing that's ever happened to me. That, and I'm pretty sure it will never happen again.

EIGHTEEN
KHALI

MY HEARTBEAT THUNDERS IN MY ears. My side aches and my lungs burn. Terek is so fast it's hard to keep up with him but somehow I manage. Behind me, the ogre grunts with madness, tossing trees and rocks out of his way as if they weigh nothing. We've been running for ages and well into the night. That's our latest problem: darkness. Ogres can see in the dark. We can't. Well, *I* can't. I'm beginning to suspect Terek's cat-like eyes have that advantage. He also has his bow and arrow but it's nothing against the ogre and no matter how many elements I throw back at it, the creature won't let up.

"You have to do something drastic," Terek calls through muffled pants. "We can't go on like this forever."

He's right. Terek was also right when he said this thing would hunt me down and kill me. It's like it has one form of magic and that's to give it the speed and strength needed to catch up to whatever it's tracking. This situation isn't Terek's fault. It's mine.

"Maybe we should split up," I offer between pants.

"No way. We're not doing that again. I learned my lesson the first time."

Despite everything, I smile.

If the forest's watchful trees would help us out, that would be great, but none of the trees move at all and I wonder if those types of autonomous trees are only in certain areas or if they're simply done aiding me. My thoughts are short-lived when a rock smashes into the tree trunk above me, missing my head by a few hairs. I yelp and run faster. Who knew a tiny pixie dinner was so important to such a barbarian? Pixies must be special treats for ogres because this one is mad as hell. He's hard to injure, almost like he's made from stone. And it's become pretty apparent that he's used to destroying things with his bare hands. Who needs elemental magic when you have fists the size of boulders and teeth that can cut through bone?

The Drakenon royals drove all these types of creatures from our lands long ago, save for the merfolk who've been allowed to live in our water sources upon certain conditions. Now I can see why. It seems like every time I meet a new species, I get into more trouble. The High Fae aren't around anymore to make the rules for these forest folk and who knows how the Sovereign Occultists are handling things. They've cursed the remaining elves but perhaps they've left the rest of the species to kill each other off. Shouldn't take too long.

Terek trips and falls into a forward roll before popping back up again. It's slowed his pace and even though the troll is after me, it groans with sickening excitement at Terek's folly. I squint into the darkness and see it careening toward Terek; the glint of an orangish tongue wagging in the moonlight makes my stomach churn. He's going to take a bite out of my friend.

"No way!" I screech, grabbing onto my earth element and bringing it to life like never before. The power of it rises into every inch of my body before exploding out of me. The ground beneath the troll opens up, swallowing the vile monster whole. A plume of dirt puffs into the air. I sweep my hands outward to direct the earth magic to cover him back up, essentially burying him alive.

"Are you okay?" I rush over to Terek who's holding his hand limply, pain etched into his face.

"I think I broke it." He winces. "I'll be fine. We need to keep going."

"The ogre's gone," I say through labored breaths. "I buried him alive. He'll suffocate."

"Didn't you pay attention to your tutors?" Terek shakes his head. "The only way to kill an ogre is to chop off his head. Their necks are the only weak points on their bodies. You buried it but it will claw its way out of there eventually."

I shiver at the thought. And no, I didn't pay that close attention to my tutors but that's mostly because they were focused on preparing me to be a proper lady, not how to kill ogres.

"So you're saying he will keep hunting me until I kill him?" I sigh as a wall of exhaustion hits me.

"Pretty much." Terek shrugs his bony shoulders and turns to look into the forest. The points of his elfin ears catch a shred of moonlight. He's so different from me. And for a second, I don't know if he can make it through the Drakenon wards.

After we get Bram, I want to take him with me, to get him to safety. I hope he'll let me try but that's an idea I keep to myself for now. What if he doesn't want to go? What if he ditches me again? I want to trust him but our friendship is still brand new and vulnerable.

"Alright, let's get out of here." I nod toward his injured wrist. "Know anyone who can help you with that?"

"Actually, I do." He paces ahead. "Follow me."

TEREK IS SILENT AS HE slides between trees and hops over crunchy leaves. It's like he knows exactly where to step in order to keep quiet. I do my best to follow in his exact footsteps. We don't speak as we get closer to whoever is going to fix that wrist of his. Tiredness starts to drag at me, slowing my steps.

"Maybe we should set up camp," I whisper.

"Shh—" Terek holds up a long pointed finger. "Hear that?"

Up ahead, the crackle of a campfire and the distant ring of merry voices echoes between the trees. I nod.

The scent of smoke, roasting nuts, and chicken tantalizes my senses. My stomach rumbles and my mouth waters. We haven't stopped for a meal in hours and our water has since dried up. Firelight dances off the trees, creating long shadows. Terek takes a step forward.

"Do you know them?" I whisper.

He nods.

It's not too much further up the path and there's a chance they'll share their food. I send a little prayer to the Gods that these truly are friends and not foes. I don't think I can handle another battle tonight.

Terek lets out three low whistles in quick succession. The distant laughter cuts off.

"Don't move," he whispers. "I'll be back for you in a few minutes. I need to let them know you're here before they jump to conclusions and try to kill you."

"Well, that's refreshing," I grumble.

Still holding his injured left wrist, he bounds off, leaving me in the middle of the dark and dangerous forest by myself. At least I have my magic back.

I call upon each of my elementals, making sure they're ready should I need to use them. They're all strong, except for water. It's there… but it's weak. Why does this keep happening to me? That same surge of panic hits me as it has every time I've felt that lapse in one of my elements. This time isn't as bad as when I was in the mortal realm and Hazel touched me and I lost earth, but it's pretty close.

I push thoughts of it from my mind to deal with later. I can't let myself give into the fear. There's too much on the line to be giving into something as detrimental as fear.

At least, that's what I tell myself.

Something tickles my nose, and I have the sudden urge to sneeze. I cover my face and muffle the sound as best as I can. My hand comes away with sweet sparkly gold dust on my fingertips. I recognize it immediately as pixie dust. A strange sort of lightness passes through me, lifting all my worries away.

The flowered pixie I saved earlier dances into view on fluttering wings. She's hard to see in this light except for her pointy teeth. They're so white, they practically glow in the darkness as she smiles.

"You followed us here?" I whisper. She must be fast for such a small creature!

"Just in case you needed me," she replies with a soft giggle.

"What's your name?"

"I'm Bellflower Blossom." She holds her tiny index finger to her bow-shaped mouth. "But shhh, the others can't know I'm here. Pixies don't trust elves you know."

She flounces away before I can get another word in, disappearing into the shadows. Seconds later, Terek appears. He's missing his bow and arrows, something I've never seen him without.

"Come on," he says. "It's safe."

"Who is over there?"

"Friends."

They must be if he's willing to leave his weapons with them.

I take a deep breath and follow close behind, trying to wipe away the last of the pixie dust from my fingers and nose before anyone notices. I hope this Bellflower Blossom character can be trusted, but right now I need to focus on whoever is waiting for me by the campfire. The light-hearted feeling she gave me with her golden dust is still going strong so I use it to boost my courage. Whatever's next, I can handle it.

We walk into a clearing where three others wait by the fire. Their stances are defensive and strong. Intimidating.

I recognize the first of the group right away. She's the pretty elf who helped me back in the village when I first met Terek, the one who's slowly turning into a deer with one deer ear and one elf ear, large round brown eyes, and little white spots on her cheeks. She never did give me her name. And, truthfully, she didn't really help me as much as tell me to leave her village. She eyes me with cool indifference, but underneath I can tell she's worried by my presence.

The second is a tall man with elf ears like the others. He's got a warrior's presence to him with armored clothing and a huge sword at his hip. Large curled ram's horns grow out of his forehead, surrounded by curly black hair. He tenses his square jaw, taking me in with a discerning gaze, probably still deciding if I'm welcome in his presence or not.

The third isn't an elf at all, but rather a creature I was told had been hunted to extinction: a centaur. He towers over me, his bronzed muscled chest on full display. My cheeks heat and I can only hope nobody notices me staring. In one hand he holds a long golden spear and in the other a matching shield. His bottom half is that of a black stallion, four hooves planted firmly on the ground. I have no doubt he could inflict some serious damage should the need arise.

I clear my throat. "Hello," I say. "I'm Khali, princess to the Drakenon kingdom."

"Not just any old princess," Terek purrs, his tail wrapping around my shoulder. "She's the future queen."

The girl gives me a sideways glance and then shoots an annoyed glare at

Terek. "How is she going to help us? She's got a whole dragon army after her, in case you forgot."

Terek snickers. "Now probably wouldn't be a good time to tell you about the ogre."

"What?" The horned man growls. "She's got an ogre after her, too?"

The centaur shifts on his hooves but doesn't say anything. I swallow hard, hoping that Terek can smooth this over before they send me away. Or worse.

"Don't worry," Terek says smoothly. "The ogre has been taken care of for the time being. By the time it finds her, you'll probably all be long gone."

His three friends are looking at him like he's grown a second head. Silence hangs over our group, the only sound being that of the crackling fire.

"Anyway," he goes on, "we all have the same goal and in case you didn't know, our Khali here has more magic than the four of us combined. We need her."

"Are the stories true?" The centaur finally speaks. His voice is clear and deep as a moonless sky in summer. It's also wise, like he's seen more than all of us. It reminds me that most of the species here are immortal. There's no telling how old any of them are. I'm definitely the youngest of this lot.

"Well, I can shift into a dragon." I fidget with my hands and then fist them to get myself to stop. "And yes, the stories are true. I have magic in all four elements." My voice is shaky and I hate it.

"Damn," the horned man says, his body relaxing, "that's impressive."

"We already know you're impressive but it also explains why you have that army after you." The girl raises her eyebrows, as if I just proved her point.

The centaur ignores her, gazing at me with a heaviness I've never felt from one stare before. "And you want to stop the Occultists? You'll help us rid them from Eridas?"

The back of my neck prickles. I've always thought a few days ahead, thought of helping Bram or saving my father, thought of ways I could get out of marrying Silas. But these people have been through horrible things at the hands of the Occultists. They don't care who I marry. They don't care about a prince. They care about saving what's left of their people and homes.

And so do I.

"I do," I say, the shakiness to my voice gone.

"Then she's in," he says it like he's the leader. None of the others protest, so maybe he is. "I'm Flannery." He nods toward the girl. "That's Juniper." And toward the man. "And this is Maxx."

"And you obviously all know me," Terek chimes in, batting his eyelashes. The man has no shame.

I hold up my hand for the second time in hello. Flannery gives me a nod and points to the ground next to the fire. "Get something to eat and then sleep. We head into Highburne at first light. After tonight, none of us will be safe."

I blink, letting his words sink in. I'm not sure if it's from the smoke coming off the fire or the worry that's slid its way into my mind, but my eyes start to water. I quickly eat and then busy myself with making a place to sleep out of pine needles and fresh leaves. It probably doesn't matter; something tells me I won't be getting much sleep tonight.

NINETEEN
HAZEL

HARMONY'S HOUSE IS QUIET AND appears to be empty. I knock on the door but as expected, she doesn't answer. My heart sinks. I still had an ounce of hope tucked away that she'd be there and I could go back to leaning on her for strength, but she disappeared a week ago, leaving a note in her shop that she was closed until further notice. I've called and texted but she hasn't replied. We've dropped by her house a few times, just in case, but it's always silent. In my gut I know she's not here. Nobody is. Harmony is gone.

"I'm sorry," Dean says with a frown. "We should go to the library for a few hours and study. You need to get your mind off of this and finals are coming up fast. Besides, we still don't know who's watching us. We should go."

It's true. I don't know who could be watching us.

I glance around the snow-covered property, hoping to see something or someone new, but it's pretty dark out and as far as I can tell, the same empty quiet that it's been all week. There are no signs of a struggle or anything to indicate someone has been here in the last week besides us. I've had the hardest time admitting that Harmony left without telling me where she was going but it's been six days since I've heard from her so what am I supposed to think? It wasn't like she vanished into thin air.

She either left or she was taken.

But there seems to be some preparations done on her part, so she probably left on her own account. First of all, her car isn't in her garage. I know because I've peeked through all the windows multiple times, including the one to the garage. She probably took that little car to wherever she was going. Secondly, her shop has a notification of her absence posted right there for everyone to see.

A whisper of betrayal crawls up my spine.

"Are you okay?" he asks, a note of anger lacing his tone. I know he's mad at her for leaving like she did.

"I keep thinking back to the last time we saw her. She looked so depleted by all that magic. What if something terrible happened to her? I will never forgive myself if that's the case. I keep asking myself over and over why we thought it was okay to leave her alone."

"She said she would call or text you the next day and you were so tired too."

"I never did get that call or text. I never got anything," I grumble.

We stand quietly for a few minutes after that. There's nothing to say.

"Are you sure we can't go in?" I can feel my face twist in desperation. "This isn't like her."

His lips thin into a line and his eyebrows knit together. "How do you know what she's like?" he finally asks. "Did you really know her? I know you want to believe you do, but, Hazel, don't forget what she is. She's a faerie."

"So, what's that supposed to mean?"

He shrugs. "They have a certain reputation for not being the most trustworthy, that's all."

I dig my boot into the stoop, kicking away a layer of snow that ought to have been shovelled away by now. But who would do that? Maybe I'll come back later and clear the driveway and walkways, in case she returns soon. It would be one less thing for her to have to do by herself. I'd ask Dean to do it but he's apparently too good for a faerie.

"I'm sorry," Dean adds. "I didn't mean to upset you. It's not like I distrust her automatically for being a faerie." I huff in interruption and roll my eyes. "It's just that they're known to play games and twist things. I don't want you getting hurt."

I hold my stance, wanting so bad to say that if he didn't want me getting hurt, he shouldn't have pushed me away after our kiss. But I don't say anything. I'm not that brave. He's been so careful to keep his distance from me and to treat me like a friend, or even worse, a sister, but certainly not a lover. We haven't talked about it. *It's fine.* Okay, it's not fine, but telling myself otherwise hurts too much. Lately, it's been easier to focus on Harmony and my frustrations with Dean for not doing more to find her.

"What?" His eyes narrow. "I know there's something you're dying to say."

"Have you ever considered that you're prejudiced against all supernaturals who aren't like you?" I know it's a rude question the second I open my big fat mouth, but I also don't regret it. Sometimes Dean acts like the dragons are the only ones that matter. I know I was singing his praises a week ago, and I still want us to be together, but right now, I can't help it; I'm mad at him.

"No," he replies, exasperated. "That's not it at all. But we've been at this for a week and we both know why we can't go in there uninvited. You're cold—let's get you home."

He's right, it is cold… from his icy heart.

I shiver but don't move. "What if she's hurt in there?" I stand my ground. "What if she needs us? We should go inside and check."

"She wasn't too hurt to put that sign in her shop window, was she? It's in her handwriting, you said so yourself. Her car is gone, we know that. She's not home. And if someone like her disappears, trust me, they will have ways to make sure nobody can follow. Not only that, but you know she has to have wards up protecting her house. Go in there and you will pay the consequences of faerie magic."

I huff, turn on my heels, and stomp down the frosted steps toward where his car is parked on the darkened street. I know he's right about the wards—that I can't go into a supernatural's house uninvited. He won't let me forget I did that once and nearly died from the pain. Harmony is incredibly powerful so there's no telling what kind of protections are around her place. Yeah, yeah, yeah, I get all the reasoning, but that doesn't stop me from knowing deep down that I have to find her.

"Fine," I call back to him. "This doesn't mean I'm going to give up. We're coming back tomorrow after class. And if she's not here, then the day after that and the day after that and every day until she comes home!"

I sound like a brat, but I'm desperate because what I don't tell him is that I'm not only worried about her for her sake, but for mine too. She's my only hope. My lifeline. My sanity. Dean doesn't realize how badly I need Harmony.

Each day of this week my curse has gotten progressively worse. I'm seeing more and more spirits. They linger about, their eyes fixed on me as I go about my day. They send me their images that I try to ignore. Worst of all, a few have been able to speak to me. Those ones follow me, yelling about whatever it is they want, but I don't respond. It's almost like I never met Harmony, never got this necklace, never got her grounding spell or her help. My nightmares are alive, walking, and everywhere I go.

Dean and I head home and I know he's worried about me. My friends are too. They can see something is wrong but I keep it a secret anyway. I don't know why, but I'm scared to acknowledge my problem, like talking about it will make it more real. It's exactly why I'm dead set on finding Harmony and getting her help. She's the only one who understands. Forget about passing my finals; if I don't figure this out soon, college will be the last thing on my mind because I'm sure I'll go crazy. Just thinking about it leaves me exhausted. All I want to do when we get back is crawl into that comfy bed and sleep away my troubles—avoidance at its finest.

WAKE UP, GIRL!

My eyes pop open. Panic prickles over my skin. I'm immobilized, my entire body weighed down by an invisible force. My noise-cancelling headphones have fallen off my ears. The rainstorm music is still trickling out—muffled. I would fix them, but I can't because whatever is paralyzing me isn't letting up. My entire body is glacial cold and I shiver violently. I move my eyes from side to side as they adjust to the near-darkness. Faint light filters through the windows. It's close to dawn. I look straight up and see it.

A reaper hovers several feet above me, levitating in the shadows.

Horror presses down. I try to scream but nothing except for a weak gurgling moan escapes my chapped lips. The reaper doesn't move an inch, but its glowing red eyes peer into me, like it can see through me, see to the deepest parts of my soul. Tears escape down my cheeks. Hot streaks pool in my ears. My heart races faster than ever. My breath explodes in tiny gasps. I can't speak.

Midnight black robes billow around the reaper, brought on by a supernatural wind that sucks the air from the room. It's eyes glow red, just like the one that killed all those girls. The thing that stalked me and killed Landon before trying to kill me. But that creature was killed and something about this one feels different.

Less frantic.

More calculated.

I try to cry out again but my voice is still caught in my throat. Where's Dean? I need help. But even if he burst into the room right now, he wouldn't be able to see what I can see. This is a thing from a realm not meant for Dean's eyes.

The creature dips close, still hovering above me. So close that, if I could move, I could touch it. From beneath the hem of its sleeve, a skeletal finger reaches out and traces its way down my cheek. I shouldn't be able to feel what doesn't have a physical body, but I can. I whimper, the fear so strong it's practically a tangible thing.

Oh, Hazel, a whispery voice echoes through my mind. It reminds me of when the spirits talk to me, but it's also different. Otherworldly. *What am I going to do with you?*

I squeeze my eyes shut and try to brace myself for whatever comes next. Will it possess a human so it can touch me? Will it try to carve me up as some kind of sacrifice? Will it try to assault me, like the previous one?

Open your eyes, Girl, it hisses. *I didn't come all this way to be ignored!*

I do as it asks and stare into the glowing orbs. They're red and hateful and wildly intelligent. The inky blackness surrounding the eyes transforms into a skeleton face and my gut hardens. Ice cracks along the edges of the walls and up onto the ceiling, just like when I was in the elevator. This creature of death has come back for me.

I try to remember what I know about it, gathering the facts quickly into my mind, like they're mouthfuls of air and I'm drowning. The supernatural reaper is meant for the spirits of the supernatural realm and not this human one. It's supposed to help their recently dead move from one plane of existence to the next. But for some reason, it's been trapped in the wrong spirit realm. I can see it because I've got to be some kind of hybrid, there's no other explanation.

My mind races through everything I know about my gift and the human spirit realm. Until recently, I've only been able to see the spirits of recently dead humans. As far as I know, we don't have reapers; we have angels that help guide those spirits to whatever is next.

I know what my brother did to you, its voice hisses through my mind.

The memory cracks like a whip. The searing pain, the terror, the blood. I can see it all so clearly, the way the reaper possessed Landon and took control of his body, enacting some kind of magic to shed Landon of his life and take it for himself. Then he turned on me, trying to trace a symbol into my stomach with the sharp end of a stick as he chanted in an unknown language. Khali saved me before he could get too far. The rest is hazy but I know Dean and Khali burned that reaper to nothing but ash.

It's not a bad idea, the reaper continues. *You have spirit magic and a physical body. If anyone could help us, it would be you.*

I swallow and try to speak, but again, no sound comes out of my mouth. This thing has taken control over me in some way. What if it takes complete control? What if it possesses me? Panic races through my bloodstream. It wants to get back to wherever it came from and needs me to do it. It moves closer.

I swear I can smell death.

It's illness, decay, rotting, fear, blood, panic. It's flowers, tears, laughter, celebration. It's all of that rolled into one, and I can't stand to stare it in the face. I want so badly to close my eyes again but I don't want this thing to reprimand me if I do.

My brother thought he could sacrifice you to undo the spell. He was far too distracted—playing with the humans—he didn't see the truth.

Playing with humans? He must mean possessing men to murder young women and the thought of it makes my eyes burn with tears. The reaper's voice in my mind almost sounds dismissive, as if the murder of innocent people means nothing. Maybe to him it is nothing. What is the value of a human life to a supernatural reaper? What is the value of *my* life?

I want to beg, to plead, but I'm trapped in this frozen coffin. In the room next to mine, Dean sleeps, oblivious to what's happening to me. The wards he's set up must not protect against spirits like this even though he thought they would. All I can do is watch as my end unfolds, because I'm sure that's what this is: the end.

But my brother's demise gave me an idea, the creature goes on. Its eyes continue to stare into mine, words filtering through my brain. The cold has numbed my entire body by this point. *Why use you when I can be you? If I don't do it, one of my other brothers will find you and have the honor. We can't have that now, can we?*

I'm crying. Sobbing silently. There's nothing I can do.

His floating spirit is mere centimeters away.

This will hurt, he says, voice sinister and cutting.

And then he makes his move.

TWENTY
KHALI

FLANNERY LIED. WE DIDN'T LEAVE at dawn; we *arrived* at dawn. It wasn't easy waking up in the pre-morning gloom, but the adrenaline soon kicked in, nervous blood racing through my limbs, loosening them up. Only an hour on foot later and the five of us stand within the edges of the forest surrounding Highburne. We don't speak. We don't move. We wait for Flannery to give the go ahead. Centaurs are excellent guides, sensing everything in the forest before anyone else can.

Our goal today is to catch that Occultist and save Bram—not that I have any idea how that's possible but I'm willing to try anything.

I take in the vastness of the city before me. There are no protective walls anywhere to be seen. The homes clustered together appear to be of much greater wealth than dragon dwellings do if size and style have anything to do with it. It seems a cavalier move on the elves part, to have their homes exposed like this. Foolish. It's no wonder the Occultists were able to infiltrate this kingdom as quickly as they did.

The castle itself lies at the far edge of the city, built into the sheer cliff face of a towering mountain. The mountain must provide excellent defense against enemies, but the castle is so ornate and delicate it's as if it wasn't built with that in mind. It's like it was carved from the gray stone cliff face, with too many turrets and arched bridges to count. In a word, it's gorgeous. But it's also frivolous. Breakable.

Flannery nods for us to follow and a collective wave of nervous energy ripples through our little group. I thought it would be harder for him to maneuver through the dense foliage but he does so with ease. Our group doesn't leave the shadows of the forest. We stick to the edge, moving toward the castle and its mountain home. I keep my magic as close to my fingertips as possible. This morning it's stronger than it has been in ages, as if it's ready to explode out of me. I take that as a good thing and try to let it give me courage.

I notice that Terek, Juniper, and Maxx are all glancing at the castle with equal parts longing and disgust. I don't know their backgrounds, beyond that Terek is on the run from the warlock who attacked us. Juniper must not have royal blood or she wouldn't have been living in that village. And Maxx is a complete mystery. For all I know, one of them is a surviving royal with a secret that could mean death.

Now, wouldn't that be interesting…

Terek pulls a branch aside to help the rest of us around it. I study his wrist, realizing it's no longer broken or sprained. He's completely fine. One of his friends must have healed him after I finally fell asleep last night.

Terek meets my questioning eyes and I nod toward his wrist. He raises his eyebrows in understanding but quickly turns away.

Fine.

I'd love to know who healed him and how they did it. But it's clear they didn't want me to know because they don't fully trust me yet. I tuck my questions on this matter away for later when speaking aloud isn't so dangerous. If someone in this group has healing magic, it would benefit me to figure out who and hopefully gain their trust.

We continue along the forest's edge. Every so often, I glance back at the castle and the sprawl of homes. This was once the capital city of what used to be the Summer Court to the High Fae elves and now it's a fortress of terror where the Occultists take their prisoners to spell them—or worse. The elves have four courts and surrounding territories, one for each season, and *all* of them have been captured by the cult of religious zealots.

What will become of Drakenon when they come for us?

The sunrise is now fully in view, lighting everything in a pinkish morning hue. It's beautiful here but I can't let myself get distracted by the rainbows of wildflowers with their sweet scents, tall trees with their lushly covered branches, or the way the breeze tickles my hair against my cheek.

"It's safe to speak," Flannery says in a low voice.

Terek points back toward the castle and whispers. "They keep the prisoners inside the mountain. I know how to get inside but you have to do exactly as I say."

"How do you know where to go?" I ask.

"Because I broke out of there." His usual charm has vanished—eyes shining with untold horrors. "Why do you think that warlock is after me?"

"The creep who took your prince is the same warlock who put these curses on us," Maxx spits. His grip tightens on the hilt of his sword. "He's the most powerful one they've got in this part of Eridas. He practically runs this forest now. We don't know his name, but Terek recognized him when he came after you."

"And we're going to catch him," Juniper adds. "So don't mess this up."

"From what I remember." I shoot a heated glare at Terek. "The warlock only found us because he was tracking you."

Terek's mouth quirks up on one side. "Sorry about that."

"Remember," Juniper's voice rings with distrust. "We can't kill him outright because our curse will only lift if he purposely lifts it with magic, not death. So be smart." She's looking at me like I can't possibly not mess this up for her. I don't care.

Maybe this warlock is the same one who hexed my father and I can convince him to spare his life. Yes, it's wishful thinking, but my heart races. For the first time in ages, I have hope when I think about my dad. He's been stuck in a perpetual state of torment and I might be close to freeing him from that.

"I won't mess this up." My voice is as bright as my hope. "I have just as much reason to succeed as the rest of you."

Flannery gazes into the distance, flexing his fist around his golden spear. His bronzed muscles glow gold in the sunrise to match the weapon. I've yet to see him put it or the shield down, and I wonder what magic is forged into the metal.

"Why are you here? What's in it for you?" I ask, stepping toward him.

He doesn't move.

"Don't be rude," Juniper hisses.

"It's not rude," I challenge. "It's a fair question."

Flannery's tail whips around his body to swat away a fly. It happens so fast, I nearly jump.

"Everything will be revealed in time." He sets off, once again leading the way without answering my question. I have to grit my teeth to keep from challenging him.

We fall back into silence and before long, we're at the mountain's edge with the castle just beyond. We don't speak anymore, all of us realizing how important silence has become. There are scouts and lookouts all over the castle and if we're caught, we're dead.

Terek is right though; he knows exactly where to go.

He leads us to a stream that bubbles out from the base of the mountain. He points to a boulder about half my size that's right in the center of where the water is coming from. Maxx steps forward and lifts it out as if it weighs nothing, his biceps rolling under his tunic in the process. He quietly sets it to the side. Where the boulder used to be is now a little opening to what appears to be a tunnel.

Flannery is too big to fit through the small opening but it's as if he already knew this would be the case. He stays where he is, nodding us off, his spear and shield ready for action should it come to that. The rest of us glide through the icy water, letting it soak into our boots and clothing, going into the black mouth of the mountain.

It smells of sulfur and dirt and ice—so much different than the tunnels underneath Stonesheath's castle. I will my heartbeat to slow and try not to think of the immense mountain surrounding us. My earth elemental is buzzing at the prospect of what we could do with all this soil and rock.

We have to crouch low and move slowly. The freezing water grows colder the deeper we go into the tunnel. My feet go numb. I draw on the tiniest bit of fire element to warm them but heat floods my entire body so fast and furiously, it's like I've ignited a wildfire within. It's so hot, I almost yelp. I snuff the fire out and suck in a breath. It's so dark here, I'm sure nobody saw anything, but that doesn't stop the worry creeping in. My magic has never been this strong before. What if I make a mistake and ruin this for everyone?

Suddenly, Hazel pops to mind. I wonder what she's doing right now and if she's okay. Can she feel this, too? This massive surge of magic within her own element of spirit? I know we are connected so it's a definite possibility.

The tunnel opens up, leading us to a dry pathway that's carved from the neighboring stone wall. It's a welcomed sight, but I can't help but feel nervous about it. We step from the freezing water and onto the path. Sporadically placed torches bolted to the stone wall light the cavern enough to see what this place is: the prison. Not only can I see that by the iron bars over the cells, which most fae would be allergic to, but I can hear it in the moans of tortured souls and smell it in the decay of unwashed bodies.

And to think, Bram has been here all this time? My guilt is all-consuming, shredding my stomach and twisting my thoughts. I'll be a mess if we don't get him out of this hell. *We have to find him!*

If the earth elemental that should have been Bram's magic actually manifested, he could have gotten out of here. But he's been helpless and stuck, probably tortured and starved, and all because of me. Me, the one who has enough earth magic to bring this place crumbling to the ground. *I shouldn't have waited so long.*

With the tilt of his head, Terek motions for us to follow. We do so carefully, only having to duck into the shadows once when a guard in crimson robes sweeps past us. Doesn't matter that he doesn't see our group, my heartbeat pounds the whole time as if he did. It's not long before Terek leads us down a narrow flight of stairs. It's colder down here, darker, quieter. Water drips from the ceiling and the stale scent of dried blood permeates the air. There's an energy soaked into the stone that feels wrong. Evil.

This must be where the warlock likes to keep his favorite prisoners. If I were able to look into Terek's eyes right now, I'm certain I'd see the haunted man that lies underneath his big personality. This must have been where he was trapped before he escaped. How he manages to portray so much charisma and charm is either a miracle or an act. I like Terek. I hate that he had to endure something like this.

We come to a larger cavern with three more cells. Sulfuric water puddles in the center of the rounded out room, probably by earth magic. It's too perfect to have been done by nature or by hand.

A sharp cry erupts from behind one of the cell doors. We freeze momentarily before scurrying into the shadows. The door doesn't open but the screams continue, deep and excruciating, almost animalistic.

"That's it," a man's voice cackles cheerfully. "Almost there."

The screams continue. My gut twists and acidic bile rises. I don't want to believe it, but somehow, I know it's Bram in there. Panic races through me. What have I done?

"That's the warlock," Terek whispers, voice muffled by the boy's screams. "I'd recognize that sadistic voice anywhere."

My magic burns and quakes, bubbles and zaps. It's wild as a windstorm and needs to get out. So does my dragon.

I can't hold it any longer.

"Isn't he nice?" The warlock's voice echoes through the cavern. "Don't worry, he won't bite." He laughs.

That horrendous laugh sets me off, and I shift, my dragon rippling through me in an instant. Without thought, logic, or feeling, without anything but sheer instinct to protect what is *mine*, I charge the cell door and rip it off its hinges. My dragon is pleased, and I roar with her, ready to avenge our prince.

The dust settles quickly and standing before me is the same warlock who stole Bram from me, the one with eyes that glow like freshly spilled blood. I long to burn him alive, but the image of my father stops me from making a mistake I won't be able to undo. The Occultist doesn't even look alarmed—the bastard! No, he smiles, white teeth gleaming against his porcelain skin, and then steps aside, motioning to his prisoner like this is my welcome present.

The boy lays broken atop a slab of slick, white marble. Blood covers every inch of him and much of the stone beneath. His hair hangs around his face in thick chunks, blackened from dirt and sweat. Slowly, he raises his head. The moment he sees me, his emerald eyes widen with disbelief. He reaches a desperate shaky hand toward me. I expand my wings, ignoring when they brush the edges of the stone walls.

Bram is alive.

TWENTY-ONE
HAZEL

MY BODY IGNORES MY MIND as I stand, leaving any last shred of warmth to the bed. The early morning air, mixed with the supernatural chill, nips at my skin. My sleep shirt brushes softly against my bare thighs and the braid I did last night snakes down my back. My exhale clouds before my eyes and then I suck it in. I pad across the carpeted floor on light toes, staying as silent as the breath I'm holding. I locate the closet and pull on some warmer clothes. Leggings and an oversized sweater. Thick woolen socks, too. The door is silent as I open and close it, slipping out into the hallway. No squeaky hinges here. I hurry down the stairs, slide into my boots and grab my coat on the way out the front door. Lastly, I grab a pair of sunglasses and put them firmly in place.

It's surreal. Like consciously wandering through a dream—a nightmare—but this time it's real and there's no way to wake up. And here I am, a witness to it all, feeling the emotions, experiencing the sensations of my body, but unable to control any of it. This is not me. Not really. This is the reaper in control, and all I can do is watch as he takes my choices away.

Of all the years I've been able to see ghosts, spirits, angels and the like, I've never thought too much about possession. Even when that reaper killed those girls using men's bodies—Landon's body—and I knew it was possible, that it was real, I still didn't think it could happen to me.

But here I am, walking through Dean's neighborhood like a puppet on strings.

It's strange. I want to cry. To scream. To feel the fear and use it to fuel my fight. But none of that is available to me. All I can do is think and watch. Would anybody know? This isn't like *The Exorcist* or a movie where something is clearly wrong with me because my head is spinning around and I'm screaming obscenities in a demonic voice. No. It's just a girl walking down the street. Who would ever know?

I don't know where the reaper is exactly. Is he sitting inside my body, next to my spirit somehow? Is he above me, controlling me from somewhere else? Has he kicked my spirit out and I only get to watch? If this ends, will I even be able to remember it happening? I don't know and I don't know how to stop it.

The snow has mostly melted over the last few days, and for the time being the city has entered that "deep freezer" stage of winter where it's too cold to snow and everything ices over. I wish I could wrap my arms around my torso but I can't. I march in the direction of campus. None of the buildings are open this early but they will be soon. When I left Dean's house, it was almost 7a.m. He'll be awake soon. I pray he goes to check on me soon.

I make it to the running path that borders most of the campus. I never did make it back there. So much for my new healthy habit. But in my defense, I've had a lot going on. *This* is definitely not the way I wanted to return here.

Once I get to the path, I wait. Every few minutes a student runs past. Most are athletic and focused, but a few amble past as if they can hardly breathe and are wondering why they're out here in the cold. I smile and cheerfully wave at each of them. They all wave back. Nobody stops.

And then I see her and wave excitedly. Panic rears up within me. *No. No. No!*

"Hi, Macy!" my voice calls out. *But it's not me!* "I thought I'd find you here."

"Hazel, is that you?"

No!

Of course, she stops.

I give her a big hug. "I'm so happy to see you."

No, I'm not! What does the reaper want with her?

She's stunningly beautiful in this morning light, and I'd give anything to not be here right now. Her cheeks are flushed baby pink and her eyes sparkle. The perfect amount of sweat glistens against her hairline. She catches her breath and smiles, but there's the tiniest bit of suspicion in her smile and I cling to that for life.

Please, don't let the reaper fool you. This isn't me. Would I be out here this early to interrupt your run? No freaking way. You know me better than that! More than anything, I wish she could hear me. Okay, more than anything I wish this reaper wouldn't have possessed me.

"I'll be honest, I'm surprised to see you out here." She eyes me up and down.

I chuckle. "I know." I step in close and put my hand on her shoulder. She eyes it with a furrow in her brow. "Hey, how much longer does it take to get back to the dorms from here?"

"About ten minutes. I'm almost done. Why?"

I frown sheepishly. "There's somewhere I need to go and I was wondering if you'd drive me."

How does the reaper know she has a car? How did he know to wait for her here? The only explanation is that he must have been watching my friends, too.

"Dean can't drive you?" She tilts her head to the side. "Is everything okay?"

"Never better." My voice grows whisper soft, "But Dean can't know about this."

"Umm—"

"Please, you're such a good friend. That's why I came to you first."

We lock gazes and I wonder how much she can see under the dark sunglasses. The silence stretches between us awkwardly, like a horrible game of chicken. Finally, she straightens her shoulders and nods. "All right but we better hurry. We have class at nine."

"Don't worry. We'll be back in plenty of time." My voice is sickly sweet and totally fake. "I promise." I sound like a lunatic.

Give me a break!

It doesn't take long to walk to her cute Jeep that's parked outside of our dorm building and climb inside it's tan leather interior. She blasts the heat even though I suspect she's hot from her run, a courtesy that is totally a Macy thing to do. She is such a great friend, and because of me her kindness is going to end up with her hurt or worse. I'm panicking, trying so hard to regain control of myself, but it's impossible. It's like the reaper has locked me behind a sound and bulletproof window and all I can do is watch.

We turn onto the highway and head toward the part of the woods where

Landon took me the night I almost died. This can't be happening right now.

"Are you sure this is a good idea?" Macy asks.

"Yeah," I say, my voice bright. "My therapist suggested it but I don't want to go without a friend."

What in the world is going on? My therapist? What therapist?

Macy grins. "Oh, I'm so glad you did that."

Except I didn't!

"Me too."

Macy and Cora know I refused to go. They said I was missing an opportunity. I said I didn't want to get thrown into an asylum. She has to remember that, right? She has to know something is wrong here!

I show her exactly where to go and ten minutes later we're pulling off the highway.

"Good thing this Jeep is a 4x4," she laughs, tackling the muddy and frozen side road like it's nothing. "Dad wouldn't let me go off to college without a reliable car."

"Totally!" I laugh. "Dads are great."

Dads are great? This reaper sounds like a commercial, it's so fake!

I can't let anything happen to her. I'd never be able to forgive myself. First there was Landon. Now Harmony has disappeared. Not Macy, too.

We bounce along until we make it to the lake, to the exact same spot Landon took me weeks earlier and where I almost died. It's frozen over now and mounds of snow still sit along much of its edge.

We pull up to a stop and my mind whirls with the implications of this horrible, horrible place.

"I'm really sorry about this but there wasn't a better way." I chuckle, the tone turning nasty. *No!* "Actually, who am I kidding? I'm not sorry. You're a means to an end and none of my concern."

Macy's jaw is hanging open and her cheeks are even pinker than when she was running. "Excuse me?"

I take off my sunglasses and set them on the dashboard, then turn on her.

"What's wrong with your eyes?"

That's when I jump on her. It's so quick she doesn't see it coming. I wrap my hands around her neck and squeeze. She gasps and fights back, all nails and arms and elbows. But I'm unnaturally strong, like stone. She has no chance.

I remember this all too well. It wasn't that long ago that I was the one in her position and Landon was on top of me. I try to close my eyes, to look away, but I can't. I'm forced to watch, horrified, as I strangle my best friend. Her eyes bulge and water before fluttering shut. Her limbs relax. I drop my hands and climb off her.

"Relax," I say aloud with an annoyed sneer.

The reaper is talking to me through me. Bastard!

"She's not dead. She's passed out and will wake up soon and drive off. I'm sure she'll call the police on you but you'll be gone by the time they get here. Trust me, after this, she'll never see you again anyway. They'll all assume you died." My laugh is manic. My head starts to get dizzy. "At least I'm not going to murder her and carve her up like my brother did. I'm too smart for that nonsense."

I climb out of the car, leaving the door open and my bulky coat behind.

As we approach the shore, Landon's ghost appears. Like before, he's forlorn, eyes cast downward, skin pale and ghastly. He doesn't move. I want to cry out to him, want to help.

"That soul is lost but don't worry, once I get home," I say reverently, "this will all be over."

And then I sprint out onto the ice, making it to the center within seconds, never once slipping. It begins to crack. He must be trying to kill me. I'm overcome with nothing but complete and utter terror but it's the strangest thing because I can't feel the terror with quick breaths, or a pounding heart, or sweaty palms. It's all playing out in my mind.

The reaper forces my body to jump up and down, assisting the breaking ice, and smiling like a lunatic the entire time. The hard layer of ice snaps and pops underneath me until it's nothing more than flimsy plastic. *Crack!* Inertia zips up my body. I suck in one last gasp of winter air before I go under.

TWENTY-TWO
KHALI

I WANT TO SCOOP BRAM up and toss him onto my back, to fly the two of us far away and let the others deal with capturing the Occultist. But I know I'm the strongest one here and I can't leave them, even if getting Bram out is my priority. Maxx and Juniper dash forward to help Bram up, carrying him away like a sack of potatoes between them. I turn on the warlock, snarling and grinding my hind legs into the rocky floor. He's going to pay for what he did.

He lifts his palm and a swirl of black magic rolls against his fingertips. I don't know what he plans to do with it nor do I care. I rush him, ramming my nose against his body and pushing him into the wall. I could squish him like a bug if I wanted to, my power is burning brighter than ever before.

Terek steps from the shadows to speak to the Occultist, his cat tail curls around his body and his golden hair flashes in the torchlight. "You're lucky we need you alive," he glares, "or you'd be dead by now."

The warlock grunts a laugh. "You are more stupid than I gave you credit for, coming here. You're not getting out of this mountain twice, Elf."

Terek tries to say something but his voice chokes and he falls to the ground with a moan of pain. I'm aware of him, but I press down harder against the Occultist. My teeth are so close to his neck, I have to stop from slicing it open and letting the life drain free. It's the most tempting instinct my dragon has ever had to resist.

After a few agonized breaths, Terek utters his triumphant reply, "You also underestimated the princess."

That's when I decide enough is enough, calling upon my earth magic and letting it release in a blast of enormous energy. The ground rumbles like angry thunder. Pieces of stone flake off of the ceiling, crumbling as they hit the floor and scatter. I focus the elemental magic onto the stone wall behind us, attuned to every nook and cranny. I can sense where the stone has veins, where it's strongest and it's vulnerabilities lie.

The warlock's eyes widen, and I know he's going to retaliate, so I call wind into the cavern, pulling it from outside. It whips through the tunnels, arriving in seconds. I use it two-fold. First, I bind my prisoner. Wind presses his hands against his sides, and, without those, he can't wield his blood magic. Second, the wind breaks open all the prison cells, ripping the iron completely off the walls. It sounds like we're in the middle of a storm and thunder is rumbling all around us. This is my chance to not only free all the prisoners from the Occultists but to incite a panic for the other warlocks and keep them distracted. If I do this right, they won't realize what really happened until it's too late.

I return to the stone wall, once again zoned in on the mountain. My magic is stronger than it's ever been, almost to the point of losing control, like a wall of water breaking through a dam. I channel all the energy into blasting through the mountain. Rock and soil crumbles out of my way and, still holding onto the warlock, a tunnel begins to form.

In the back of my mind, I'm aware that Terek is yelling and the warlock is attempting to regain control of his hands so he can use his powers. It matters little to me. I don't need my hands to make this work. All I need is my mind. If I stay focused on clearing the way out of this mountain, it'll happen. It doesn't take long before light pierces through the cracks and, with a final push, the mountain opens up.

Instead of flying and risking opening myself to vulnerability, I use a cyclone of wind to carry our entire group out from these bowels of earth and toward the forest. It whips us around like fallen leaves before depositing us at the forest's edge. I allow the wind to calm, noticing my magic protesting. It wants more, wants to keep going, keep building. Not just air or earth, but fire and water. Everything is so strong. I can't think.

Maxx says something but I can't hear him over the torment going on within me. Bram is leaning against Juniper and something about that makes me hate her. Terek and the Occultist are in a physical altercation, rolling around on the ground as they pummel each other. I have to get the warlock's hands back down. Maxx jumps in, beating me to it. I close my eyes and shift back to my human form, hoping I'll have more control there.

Intense agony erupts all over my body. I scream, the elements so much stronger than before. It was like my dragon body, being so large, could handle it. But now it's all stuffed into a much smaller form, I can hardly breathe. I fall to my knees and look for opportunities to release it. I send another blast of air at the warlock, pinning him to the ground. A storm has gathered overhead, and I allow lightning to flash down, careful to keep it away from people; it hits some of the trees, cracking them open and starting fires.

My stomach twists. No! The trees are my friends, too.

Rain begins to pour, so heavy that a flash flood is inevitable. At least it extinguishes the fires. The elements continue to rage on as panic overtakes me. I don't know how to stop this.

"What is she doing?" Juniper yells, her voice almost lost to the wind.

A sound apart from the storm catches my attention. I blink though the rain, momentarily relieved when I find Flannery racing toward us, hooves pelting loudly against the earth. Mud flies up behind him, adding to the effect. I try to focus on watching him instead of responding to my magic. His centaur body is a sight to behold in action, muscles rippling and gold spear ready. His bronzed torso gleams with sweat and his dark curls fan out behind his chiseled face. Arrows arc in his wake, sticking into the ground like pins to a pincushion.

There was something I was supposed to do, an idea I had that I wanted to see to its end. My mind is still so riddled with magic, I'm struggling to find it.

"Run!" Flannery's voice echoes over the stretch of grass and mud.

Behind him, more arrows fly. They're coming from the castle.

I push the arrows away with the wind, sending them back to where they came from.

Terek, Maxx, and the warlock are too busy fighting to hear Flannery or to care. They will soon enough. Behind Flannery, an ogre hurdles toward us at a maddening pace, his giant footsteps making the ground rumble.

Not just any ogre: my ogre.

The beast escaped his underground prison faster than I expected and he's madder than hell. His body is covered in arrows. They stick from his muscles but do little to slow him. He's marred with dirt and blood, willing to kill anything and anyone who gets in his way. When he spots me, he roars. It's a guttural sound that rolls over the landscape like an earthquake.

That gets everyone's attention. Juniper and Bram turn to run as best they can given Bram's condition, but they don't move very fast.

My magic surges, and a calm falls over me. There's no need to run. I channel all the elemental magic that's built up inside me and unleash it on the enemy. Fire and lightning, wind, rain, earth. Everything I have comes bursting forward. The ogre falls to the ground in a matter seconds, unmoving and dead, his neck twisted at an odd angle.

Me and my elements are met with relief, and in an instant, the sky clears. I smile back to my new friends, gasping for breath. They all stare at me with equal parts admiration and fear. Even Flannery has a flabbergasted expression on his face, eyes shining with something akin to respect.

It feels amazing.

The warlock rises to his feet, black magic once again spinning in his hands.

"You just reminded me," I say with a gleeful chuckle, "I know how to bind you."

I bring the air down on him again, stopping his hands from releasing their magic. Then I saunter up to him and pull Silas's cursed necklace from my bodice.

He sneers at me. "You filthy—"

"Shut up." I blast air in his face. He sputters, eyes watering, unable to manage another word. I take the two ends of the cord and tie it firmly around his neck. Whatever has powered this necklace returns immediately, making the cord strong again. The necklace cannot be removed without something like Bellflower Blossom's teeth or perhaps a magicked knife.

I drop all of the air and the warlock slumps to the ground, his robes billowing around him. It's like the energy has been stolen right out of him. He looks so ordinary now. Before this moment, he always appeared ageless to me. Now he looks to be nothing other than a middle-aged bald man and without his power, he could be mistaken for a mortal human.

"How does it feel to be without magic?" I shoot him a haughty glare. It's a rhetorical question. I couldn't care less what he has to say. "Actually, you're not without it."

"What do you mean?" he spits.

"Whatever magic you try to use will go directly to Silas, one of the dragon princes."

His face twists in a sneer of disgust, eyes widening with pure fury.

I return to my friends, eyes roving over Bram to make sure he's okay. He's slumped against Juniper, head lolling to one side. Much of the blood has been washed off from my storm. He's pale as a winter morning, eyes unfocused. We need to get him out of here.

"Who healed Terek?" I look at the elves and the centaur, demanding to know.

They blink and don't answer.

"Heal Bram," I demand. "I know one of you can do it. So do it!"

Again, no answer.

I glare. Are they really my friends? It doesn't look like it to me!

"Come on," I growl. "We have to go and he won't make it very far."

"Not with the Occultist here," Terek whispers at last. "It's a secret for a reason."

I turn back to find the warlock's eyes alight with curiosity. And I get it, whoever has rare healing abilities wants to keep this part of their magic hidden, especially from our enemy, but Bram doesn't have time and we have to get out of here as soon as possible.

"I'm fine," Bram gasps, gaze landing on me. "I'll be fine."

I dig my foot into the ground, wanting to argue more. In the distance, people call out to each other. Occultists? Guards? Doesn't matter. We have to go!

"We're going to Drakenon," I announce, my voice calm and sure. "All of us. We can't stay here where we're fugitives. So let's get there as fast as possible and once we do, our warlock is going to answer for all his crimes. The ones against you and hopefully he can undo the hex against my father, too."

They don't argue, but they don't look too excited about it either. Especially not Flannery. They seem to be communicating with each other with only glances, the kind of thing only those who have a long history together would be able to do. It's obvious Flannery is their leader. Not me.

"You know I'm right," I say to him, "is there anywhere else you'd suggest?"

"There's always the human realm."

The Occultist chuckles.

"No," I snap, "the magic is too stifled there. What if he can't free us from his spells from there? It has to be in Eridas. Besides, my father needs my help."

We size each other up. More arrows rain down around us. I push them away with my mind but there's no doubt we've been spotted. Before they might have been shooting at the ogre. Now we're the target.

"We have to go," Maxx says.

Finally, the centaur gives me a singular nod.

The warlock laughs, but I don't give him the satisfaction of responding. "So you still think it's a hex, then? All right, Princess, let's go see your father. I'd love nothing more than a royal escort into Stoneshearth. Do you know how long I've been trying to get inside those walls? So by all means, take me there yourself. Walk me through the doors so I can kill your people and you can watch."

"I won't be manipulated by your mind games," I spit out the words as doubt creeps in. Maybe this is exactly what he wants? Or he wants me to think that so I do the opposite.

I nod toward the beautiful castle in the distance, knowing that this morning's chaos is starting to sort itself out behind its walls. "Let's go before the rest of them figure out what really happened here today."

"What did happen here today?" Juniper hefts Bram up against her and Maxx scrambles over to help. Bram's head is down again and he looks about ready to pass out.

My magic has settled but it remains stronger than anything I've experienced before. Maybe it will stay this way, but I'm not naive enough to count on that. Juniper asked a great question, one I wish I knew the answer to. Truth is, I don't know how my magic could go from struggling as it was to being immensely powerful. It seemed to come out of nowhere but at least it came at the perfect moment.

Something tells me this has to do with Hazel and our link. What if she needs my help? There's nothing I can do for her, not right now, considering where I am and where I'm headed. I send out a silent prayer that wherever she is, she's okay, and feel a stab of guilt because deep down, I know she's not.

TWENTY-THREE
HAZEL

I SWIM DOWN, DOWN, DOWN, deeper into the biting water. My eyes stay open which might be the worst part of all. The pain is excruciating—a cold stabbing sensation assaulting every inch of my body. The oxygen in my lungs withers away into nothingness. The deeper I go, the more I know this is it for me. This is the end.

Each of my senses is zeroed in on the need to suck in more air. I fight with everything I have left to regain control of my body but it's impossible. My limbs start to go numb, muscles locking up, one by one, useless. I'd always thought there would be a peaceful calm at the end of my life. There's none of that. There's only panic.

The water turns inky black, or maybe that's just my vision. Somehow, my limbs keep moving, pushing me deeper still. The reaper is intent on taking me to the bottom of the lake. I'm not going to survive this.

Brightness flickers further ahead, a glowing rainbow of colors. Is this the light at the end of the tunnel people talk about? It must be…

I continue to swim toward it as the last of my oxygen gives out. Or it gave out a long time ago and none of this is real. Maybe I'm already dead. We're almost to the dancing lights when the last of my consciousness begins to snuff out. Neither myself nor the reaper has control over my body anymore. I'm limp. Water fills my nose, my throat, everything, until there's none of me left.

In a flash, I'm transported to a new place. Bright white light envelops me, brighter than anything I've ever known. The cold is gone. The water, too. I squeeze my eyes shut against the blinding light, and that's when the peace settles in.

So it's not at the end but after the end.

My eyes flutter open. The white light has lessened and after a minute of looking around, I realize I'm not alone. What *is* here? It's like this endless room of white that stretches on for an eternity, but every so often, someone or some*thing* will be projected into the room with me. The more I gaze at one of them, the more in focus they become.

There's Mom working in the Emergency Room. She's filling out charts but her eyes are so tired. It's almost the end of her night shift, and I know she'll be happy to get home soon. All I want is to give her a hug and tell her I love her—but I can't.

I'm a spectator.

I step forward and a whooshing zips past me. I'm suddenly in the hospital with her. I guess that's possible without a body; I'm convinced I'm only a spirit now. I can feel myself, like I'm physically there, but I know it's not true. I reach out toward my mother, touching her shoulder. My hand swipes right through her. Immediately, it's as if she senses me, because she suddenly looks up with a questioning light in her eyes.

"Mom?"

My voice echoes. She doesn't hear me, of course. She pulls out her phone to text me her usual good morning check in. I turn away and walk out of the scene. It hurts too much to know that I won't be able to respond to her and let her know I'm okay.

Fear grows into a tangible thing inside me, like a rock lodged in my chest. My mind whirls with the possibilities of what has happened to me. And yet… there's that same peace there, too. It's an assurance unlike anything I've felt before.

With nothing more than a thought, I'm back in the white room.

I stroll around until I find another scene. It's Cora. She's asleep in her bed, her ebony skin and hair a gorgeous contrast against her white silk pillowcase. She has no idea that her best friends are in trouble, oblivious as she sleeps. I'm sure she'll be awake soon. I don't step into her scene, don't want to face her sadness when she finds out what happened. It never materializes around me like it did with my mom. I look away.

The white room is filled with these portals to the people I care about most in the world. It's strange. I always thought spirits could go wherever they wanted but that doesn't seem to be the case. I can only go where *my* living people are. After that, maybe I could stay somewhere and walk around some more, I don't know. But I can't imagine a place and be transported there—like I can't just think of the Eiffel Tower and be whisked off to Paris, which is sad because I'd always wanted to go to Europe. There's so much I've missed out on.

"Hazel." A voice jars me from my thoughts and I whip around.

Owen stands before me.

He's solid now, not like how I've seen him every other time, as a spirit. They always have a bit of a translucent film to them. Not anymore. And he's not in his dragon form, either. He steps in close and pulls me into a tight hug. I didn't know I needed it, but I'm immediately overcome by emotion and burst into tears.

So it's true, then. I must have died. The reaper must have killed me.

"Shh," he says. "It's okay. It's going to be okay." His low voice reminds me of Dean. My heart breaks even more. I want to go home. But I can't go home and even if I could, I wouldn't be me anymore, so I nod into the flat planes of his chest and let his warm arms hold me for a minute longer before I peel away.

"What is this place? Is this heaven?"

He chuckles bitterly. "Does this feel like heaven to you?"

I shake my head. "No, this is horrible. I don't want to watch everyone I love grieve me and then move on without me."

His blue eyes turn sad. "Yeah, it's not fun."

"So where are we?"

"It's a space meant for waiting," he says. "People come and go—the newly dead, anyway. After a few weeks or months or years of this, when they're finally ready to let it go of the life they lived, the angels take the mortals to the next place and the reapers take the supernaturals."

And that explains why I've seen angels every now and again throughout the years. Those magnificent beings never acknowledged me though, not like how the ghosts do—did.

"And what about you?" I ask the question but think I already know the answer. "Do supernaturals go to heaven?"

"Supernaturals go somewhere different from humans after they're able to make it out of this waiting area. Our reapers are supposed to take us but they're not here anymore. I've been asking anyone in the supernatural realm who will talk to me and apparently it's been years since any supernatural was able to move on."

I swallow and nod, looking out into the whiteness around us. At first glance, I think we're alone, but then I notice several human-like shapes in the distance, as if other spirits are roaming this area too. I know now they're supernatural and mortal ones, being given opportunities to move through time and space to visit the loved ones they left behind until they are taken to the next place.

"So all the supernatural spirits are stuck here because the reapers are in the human realm instead of this waiting area?"

"Seems that way."

I think back to everything I've learned. It makes sense, but it still makes my heart hurt. "I'd hoped it wasn't true."

He nods solemnly. "I haven't figured out how to break whatever spell has caused this." Pain crosses his expression. He wants to leave, wants to move on, and staying here is obviously too hard. "I'd hoped you'd be the one to do it since you're the only living person I've found who can see all of us, but now that you're here, I don't know how that's possible."

"I'm sorry," my voice croaks. "A reaper took possession of my body and drowned me in a lake."

His eyes widen. "He took you to the portal?"

I shrug. "I don't know what you mean."

"He was likely trying to use you to get back to the supernatural realm by using the portal between both realms at the bottom of that lake. But he must have failed or else you'd be there and not here."

My mind spins. "That lake is a portal between the human and supernatural realms?" No wonder it's where that other reaper killed those girls and where he tried to use me as some kind of sacrifice. Suddenly, I'm angry at Dean and Khali for never explaining this to me. I deserved to know. It's probably one of many things they never told me.

Owen nods and his blue eyes lock on me. "It's hard to explain, but yes, it's a portal created by energetic ley lines in the earth. Not everyone can go through a portal. Elemental magic is required. That, and the ability to hold your breath for a good amount of time."

I laugh but it's not funny. Am I being hysterical? All I can think of is the air my lungs were screaming for before they gave out and I woke up here.

Owen shakes his head. "Don't worry," he says, "you'll get used to being dead."

Gee, thanks.

Blackness suddenly edges around my eyeline, and I double over to catch my breath. I feel like I'm going to pass out, like my brain is losing oxygen. Is this a normal part of death?

"Hazel, are you okay?" His hands reach out to steady me.

"I don't know," I pant. "I'm losing my vision."

Owen's excited voice sounds far away, "No, you're not, you're going back!" He holds on tight to me but his physical form is begins to whisk away into nothing but air. "Don't forget what we talked about. You need to help the reapers get back here. It's the only way I can—"

Everything shifts from bright white to endless black.

TWENTY-FOUR

KHALI

AS OUR GROUP DISTANCES OURSELVES further and further away from Highburne Castle, our nerves begin to settle and the importance of staying quiet isn't quite as pressing. Terek and Flannery lead the way, cutting the best path through the forest that will take us in the direction of Drakenon without using the main roads. Maxx, easily the largest in our group, drags the warlock along after us. Now that the spelled necklace is binding him, the Occultist doesn't put up much of a fight. When he's not agile or quick enough to climb over a branch or scoot around a bush, Maxx uses the opportunity to push him around. I wish that could be me, but I'm not letting go of Bram, not for anything.

Bram slumps between me and Juniper, head low and breath shallow. It takes the two of us to help him keep up; his energy is spent. My earlier rainstorm washed away most of his blood and sweat, and where I expected to find scars or wounds, there's nothing. His skin is completely unblemished. But even though they're no longer visible, I know whatever pain was inflicted on him is still festering under the surface. I see it in his glazed over eyes and in the stumbling of his short steps. His clothes are stained and tattered, boots caked in mud, and I wish I could do more for him. I wish I could take it all away. I glare at the warlock's head, tempted to drop a tree on him or shoot another blast of air into his face.

"Hang back," Juniper whispers. "I can't take this anymore."

I don't question her as we slow our steps. Before long, we can hear and see the rest of our group, but we're far enough away that we can talk without being heard.

"I'm going to heal you," Juniper says to Bram, "so hold still."

He doesn't seem to hear her, or if he does, he doesn't care.

My eyes widen. "So it's you? I've never met a healer before."

"Yes," she breathes out an exasperated sigh, "but it doesn't come without its costs so keep it to yourself, okay?"

I nod. "I'll keep your secret."

She raises an eyebrow. "We'll see… Now hold him up, I need to concentrate."

She closes her eyes and places her hands on Bram's chest, splaying out her fingers. They pulse with a faint pink light that grows brighter with each pulse. After a minute, she drops them away. "That's the best I can do. I can only heal physical pain so anything else the warlock did to you I can't fix. I'm sorry."

"Did it help?" I ask.

Bram swallows, and looks at her, not at me. "Yes," he says with a clear voice, "thank you." Their eyes stay locked together for a moment too long and my stomach turns to stone.

I'm jealous. Why am I jealous? Bram isn't—

"There you are." Terek prances into view. "Keep up, will you?" He stops short, those sky blue eyes jumping to me, then Juniper, then Bram, and back again. "So did you do it?"

Juniper nods.

"And you're okay?" He asks the question to Juniper, not to Bram.

"I'll be fine," she cuts him off. She said her magic wasn't without costs and I wonder exactly what that means. Pushing a strand of her bright blonde hair behind her elfin ear, she starts walking again, leaving me and Bram to follow.

He no longer needs someone to slump against and is quick to walk ahead of me. There is something too careful in his movements as he navigates through the foliage. Before coming here he intellectually knew that this place is dangerous, but now he knows it in every other way too. I wish he didn't.

We continue on for a little while longer, everyone seeming to be lost in their own thoughts, until Terek suddenly stops. He's quick to prepare an arrow into his bow and still his entire body. The rest of us follow his lead. A prickling sense that we're being watched rolls over me and it's not like how it was with the trees, it's much worse. I spark fire to my palms, letting it dance there should I need to throw it. Maxx's grip tightens on the warlock, one hand covering his mouth so the man can't scream.

Something snaps. A tree branch?

Terek releases the arrow. A man falls to the ground. Not just any man, an occultist, dressed in familiar crimson robes. The arrow is embedded directly in his windpipe and blood gushes out the sides. He gasps, reaching up, black magic rolling along his palms, but it's short lived. His arms collapse to the earth too and his eyes flutter shut.

"He's dead," Juniper states, letting out a breath. "Are there more?"

Terek is quiet for a minute longer and then he shakes his head. "Not yet, anyway."

We look to Flannery, who doesn't speak, but also shakes his head.

"We need to move faster," Maxx says. "We're being hunted."

"And who's to say we're not walking into a trap?" Juniper shoots me a questioning look. "Am I really supposed to believe your people will let us into Drakenon with open arms? Dragons hate our kind."

"Do you have any better ideas?" I shoot back. "Look around, Juniper. We're not going to make it here much longer. I know they want me back there. I know the Brightcasters need me to cooperate with them. I'll work out a deal for you."

"And what about him?" She points to the warlock. "Like he's really just going to do what you ask. Don't be so naive."

I expected this. I knew it was coming. But now, dealing with it, I wish I had more time. I wish I had a better plan.

But I don't.

I traipse over to where Maxx has the warlock in his grip and ask him to let the man speak. Maxx removes his hand and the warlock lets out a laugh. "There will be more of my brethren here soon enough. You won't get away with this."

I shrug. "Maybe I will, maybe I won't. But I want to make a deal."

His eyes glowed red when his magic was strong but now that his magic is bound, they're muddy brown and depthless. He stares at me for a long while, a slow smile spreading across his pale face. "What kind of a deal?"

"If I take you to Drakenon and you remove all spells against myself, my people, the elves, and anyone else you've harmed," I say, "then I'll let you go."

He laughs.

I hold up a finger, "and you have to promise not to put the spells back."

"And why would I agree to that?"

I eye the pendant around his neck. "Because if you don't, we'll throw you in prison and never take that thing off. You'll die a mortal death but before you do that, you'll live the rest of your days without magic, cold, alone, tortured, and perfectly ordinary."

It's a gamble, a risk, and probably one that won't pay off, but I have to try.

"You'll see to it that I get to go free?" he asks. "Just like that?"

"I'm the next queen, aren't I?" I nod. "I promise on my life, you will walk free."

His eyes twinkle with something akin to justice. "Then shake on it."

I suck in a breath. If we shake on something while in Eridas, it will become a magicked vow. I won't be able to go back on my word and should I somehow find a way to recount it, I'll die. The magic will kill me.

"Don't do it," Maxx cuts in, "don't trust him."

I glance around the group, to Bram with his haunted eyes, to my elfin friends cursed to turn into forest creatures, to Flannery, a leader who has had to hide away from his world. I think of my father, tormented and dying. I think of Hazel back in the human realm, spelled to me against her will. And I think of myself.

I reach out my hand. We shake and when magic sparks between us, all I can think is that this had better not turn out to be a trick.

TWENTY-FIVE
HAZEL

WATER FILLS MY LUNGS. *NO!* The burning pain of drowning returns. My head pounds. I try to cry out but I can't. Everything is water. Everything is death.

Something warm presses against my lips, blowing air. Hands push on my sternum. Too hard. But my body floods with life. I cough up a stream of icy water and roll to my side. My eyes flutter open. I'm lying in the mud, no longer in the lake. It's too bright. I close them again.

"Is she okay?" A shrill panicked voice. Macy's?

I flex my fingers, open and shut. Relief floods me; I've gained control of my body again. The reaper is gone.

"She's alive," another voice says. "But she's in bad shape." *Dean.*

"She needs a hospital."

I cough. Just as I realize I'm numb, feeling returns to my limbs and violent shivers rake over my body. "No," I whimper. I open my eyes again and this time force them to stay open. It hurts. I want to cry.

"Did you hear that?" Macy gasps and kneels next to Dean. She runs a hand along my back. The seriousness of it all comes roaring back to my mind. How the reaper took control, how I hurt Macy, how I went into the water, tried to get through the portal. I died! And Owen was there.

"Take me home." My voice is hoarse. "Please."

Dean picks me up, and I close my eyes again.

I fall in and out of consciousness as he transports me to his house. Macy helps carry me inside, her soft voice talking with Dean's deep one is background music for the swirling darkness behind my eyelids.

We go from warm to cold to warm again.

Somewhere, a faucet runs. It seems to go on forever.

I'm gently laid into a warm bath, still fully clothed. My eyes pop open and I'm suddenly wide awake. I yelp when the water nears my mouth.

"It's okay," Macy coos. "We've got you."

With a deep breath, I make myself relax. It's just a bath; it's unlikely I could drown in this. That's what I tell myself, anyway, even though the memory of drowning won't leave my mind and body; it's like a tattoo and will stay with me forever. I shiver again.

Dean runs heated palms over my arms. It seems impossible that I'd ever be warm again but the water and his perfect hands seem to help. After a good twenty minutes of quiet in the heated water, Dean finds dry clothing and lets Macy get me dressed. She towels me off and carefully checks for frostbite as I put on the new outfit. I can hardly move on my own. My muscles feel like they've run a hundred miles.

"Thank you," I whisper. My voice is raspy and it stings to speak.

"You're lucky," she says. "You don't have any frostbite that I can see." She wipes away a tear. "You could have died."

I don't have the heart to tell her that I *did* die. She wraps me in a thick blanket and helps me walk to my bedroom. "Same goes to you," I whisper. "You could have died, too. I'm so sorry for what I did to you."

"It wasn't you," she says matter-of-factly. "You can't blame yourself."

We sit on my bed, and she curls up next to me. "How do you know?" I ask.

I'm so confused because while Macy knows about my curse, she doesn't know all the details.

Dean gingerly enters the room and sits on the other side of me. They both press in close and their body heat, especially Dean's, is amazing. I lean into him and lay my head on his blazing hot shoulder. He takes my hands in his to warm them up. It feels so good I have to keep myself from moaning.

"After that thing happened with Landon," Macy explains, "Cora and I knew there was something you weren't telling us and no matter how many times we asked, you wouldn't give up, insisting on the story you'd told everyone else."

I bite my lip. "True."

"So they came to me," Dean says, "and they demanded I tell them everything."

I turn to him. Our faces are so close, close enough to touch. And heavens, he smells so good. His eyes flick to my lips for the briefest of seconds and my stomach flips. I want to know just how much he actually told them. He shakes his head once, ever so slightly, and I know to keep my mouth shut. I'm sure he didn't reveal his dragon heritage.

"They already knew about your abilities," he continues. "So, I told them about the reaper and how it was possessing people to hurt those girls. And how it tried to do that to you by using Landon."

"I was a little weirded out when you asked me to give you a ride," Macy admits. "But I didn't put it all together until I saw your black eyes and you attacked me. At that point it was too late." Regret twists her face like she's about to start crying. "I'm so sorry I couldn't help you more."

I'm shocked. "You're the one saying sorry to *me*? No way. I thought for sure you'd hate me. Why didn't you call the police?"

"I woke up just in time to see you go under that ice," she says. "I don't think I've ever been more afraid in my life. I called Dean and he got here in minutes. He jumped right in and pulled you out like it was nothing." She eyes him, questions in her gaze. "How did you do that? And how could you have possibly gotten there that fast? You rode back with me. Where's your car? "

His jaw tenses. "These are questions for later."

Good luck getting any answers out of him, I want to say, but I don't.

I turn to my friend. "You need to leave." I'm frantic again. "You're not safe around me. Neither is Cora. You both need to stay away until I can figure this out."

"No way." She folds her arms over her chest and sets her mouth in a firm line.

"Look at your neck!" I gasp, pointing at the thin, long purple bruises. "There are fingerprints where I choked you. You could have died because of me."

"It's not your fault. I'll wear a turtleneck and won't tell anyone what you did."

"Don't you get it? There could be more reapers out there. Or that same one could come back for me again. I don't know what's going to happen but I do know that they're after *me*. I can't bring you into this. I would never be able to live with myself if something happened to you."

She swallows but there's a compassion in her face that tells me she understands. I can also see a very real fear in her eyes even though she's trying to hide it. She knows I'm right. It's dangerous to be around someone like me. She lets out a little breath and stands.

"Fine," she says softly. "But we're still going to text you and I'm still going to be your friend." She waves her hand around the room. "And whenever this crazy reaper thing is over, you let me know. Cora and I will take you out to dinner to celebrate. A real dinner out, not the dorm cafeteria."

"Deal." I reach out my hand and we shake on it.

She gives me one last lingering look of worry and then leaves quickly, closing the bedroom door behind her. A minute later, I hear her Jeep pull out of the driveway. Dean tugs me against him even tighter. His warm body is everything, and I could stay here all day and pretend like nothing is wrong.

"You can go to class if you need," I offer but my voice is flat.

"No." He shakes his head, pulling me even closer. "I'm not leaving your side again."

"We have finals this week."

"Why are you even thinking about that?" he growls. "It's not important."

I stiffen. I know he's right but I also can't let all my hopes and dreams go. I just can't. "School is the one thing left in my life that's still normal. I *need* that right now."

"Fine," his voice softens. "Take your finals, but other than that, expect to be with me day and night. If you're going home for Christmas break, I'm coming with you. Or you can stay here. I don't care. You choose. But you're not leaving me again."

I deflate against him. My mind wants to take this news and run but I can't, not with the discussion we need to have.

"The reapers are here because the Occultists have spelled them," I blurt out. "So it's true. All of it is true."

Dean stills. "Well, we had our suspicions…"

"I died." My voice sounds far away. "I can't believe I actually died."

He pulls away and sits back. His eyes are a frantic fire, and he runs his hands up and down my arms and face. "Are you sure?"

I nod. "Yes. I was gone and then I came back. Now that I've been there, so many things make sense. I didn't understand the spirit realm very well before."

"What happened?"

"I learned which theories were right. Mainly, when someone dies, they go to sort of a waiting room." I have to admit, I'm a little excited to have this information and talking about it disintegrates some of the fear. "They have these little portals that allow them to visit the friends and family that they loved, which explains how Owen has been able to come into this realm to see you but I haven't seen other supernatural spirits like him here."

"He's been coming to visit me." The way he says it is sad and I wish he could see Owen too. If it were me in his shoes, and my mom was gone, I know I'd give anything to see her.

"But here's the thing: it's just the waiting room he's been in, right? It's not heaven or the afterlife or whatever. Once the spirit is ready to give up checking in on their family, which could take days, months, or even years, they are escorted to the next place. That's the place I don't see, which explains why I've never seen ancient ghosts—it's usually just the newly dead that appear to me."

"And what about the reapers?"

"That's the thing. Owen said that—"

"You *talked* to Owen?" His voice is desperate. "How is he?" There's a hope in his tone too, one I know I'm going to have to squash.

"I more than talked to him," I rush on. "He hugged me. He was physical to me. Do you know he was the one who helped fight off the first reaper who attacked me? It was before the reaper took control of Landon, and that makes sense now because the reaper didn't have a body yet. But anyway," I continue, "what I'm trying to say is, Owen needs our help and now I finally understand why."

I take a deep breath and relax my voice. Dean and I are sitting knee to knee on the bed. I take his hands in mine. He squeezes. "Owen is gone. There's no way he can come back to this life or the body he once had." I pause, considering the best way to put this. "Being on the other side and watching your loved ones move on without you isn't exactly fun."

His face falls. "I can understand that. Being here isn't the same as death but it hasn't been easy for me to know my people are living their lives without me."

"We need to help Owen move on," I say firmly. "There are angels to help the mortals but supernaturals have to be taken by a reaper and there aren't any in that spirit realm waiting room thingy right now."

His mouth quirks up at the edge. He runs a thumb along my hand and my insides turn to mush. "So how do we send the reapers back?"

I sigh. "I wish I knew. We have to figure it out. Nobody is safe until we do."

"And you're sure you're more concerned about finals week?" he challenges.

"I'm not more concerned," I grumble, catching on to his point. "Fine. You're right. I know I can't just pretend nothing is wrong because look where that's gotten me."

"Alright. So we take our tests and every free minute between those, we search for answers. We keep looking for Harmony, we keep our eyes out for other supers, and we research any possible lead that pops up."

"And if that doesn't work?"

Silence. He doesn't have an answer. Or maybe he does, but he knows it's one I won't like. "Okay, deal," I say, squeezing tighter to his hands like they're the only lifeline I have left. At least I don't have to do this thing alone.

TWENTY-SIX

KHALI

I CHECK THAT ALL MY elements are easily accessible. To my immense relief, I find them swirling inside. I'm going to need each of them at full power today. Soon after the display at Highburne, my magic returned to normal and I still haven't been able to bring it back to the same incredible power I felt that day. But this? Having them all strong? This is good enough.

Flannery stands at a distance as our group approaches the wards between the Fae Territory and Drakenon, an unreadable expression on his face. A soft breeze flounces through his chestnut hair. He still holds the golden spear and shield and looks almost godlike with the way the sun is hitting him. He draws me to him. It's not in a romantic kind of way. It's something else entirely, like there's a nourishing energy about him that my magic seeks out.

And there's something else about the centaur that doesn't make sense, but I'm beginning to suspect those golden weapons of his may be the explanation. I'm pretty sure nobody can see him unless *he* allows them to. Our group has been traveling for three days through the fae forest, fighting our way closer and closer to Drakenon, and not once has the warlock looked at Flannery or even acknowledged his presence. Same goes for Bram. It's almost like they don't know he's there. And as for Flannery, he keeps quiet around them, never engaging with me or any of our friends in front of Bram or the Occultist—who still refuses to tell us his name.

"Are you sure you can do this?" Terek says, breaking me from my thoughts about what kind of magic could allow Flannery to stay hidden like he has.

We gaze out at the warded area and grimace. The iridescent wall of fog that we'll have to walk through to get to Drakenon stretches in either direction and as high as the eye can see. There's no going under, around, or over it. We have to go through. They won't be able to do it without me because it takes dragon blood to walk through, but if we all go together, I should be able to create a bubble of elemental energy that will get the group to the other side. It worked with Bram the first time we crossed.

The warlock stands on my other side and shoots me a knowing smirk. "I've been through it myself, in case you're wondering. Take this necklace off me and I'll show you how I managed."

I turn away. I won't speak to him unless I have to; having to keep him close is bad enough. He's playing games again, wanting me to question him, question myself. And more than that, wanting me to take the necklace off so he can use his magic again. I won't be an instrument in his hands.

I glance over to where Maxx, Bram, and Juniper stand whispering in a huddle. "She doesn't think I can do it, does she?" I say to Terek.

"She has her doubts but don't worry about her." He pats me on the back.

Juniper catches me staring and raises a delicate eyebrow, then turns to whisper something to Bram. The tiniest flicker of a smile crosses his mouth and envy burns hot in my chest. I know she's doing it to set me off and seeing Bram smile should make me happy, no matter who puts it there. But Bram has changed and I don't know what to do about it. He barely speaks, hardly lifts his head; it's like he's a broken man, a shell of what he once was.

For some inexplicable reason, Juniper seems to be the only one who can get through to him. I'm jealous that she could heal him when I could not, that he will speak to her, look at her, touch her—when I cannot. Whenever I try to talk to him, he clams up. It seems that in the few short weeks I left him with the Occultist, our relationship was irrevocably damaged. Perhaps it's what I deserve for leaving him behind but my heart hurts regardless.

"Let's go," I say loud enough for everyone to hear. "Hold hands, please. It'll make it easier for me. And once we get to the other side, stick to the plan. We have it for a reason."

Our group lines up. I take the middle. On my right is Bram, Juniper, and Flannery. On my left is Terek, Maxx, and the warlock. The second we clasp hands, I bring my magic to the surface and project it out and around us.

"Hold on to each other," I say. "No matter what, do not let go!"

Then as a group, we charge into the fog. Something purple flashes from the corner of my gaze and I know it's the pixie, coming along for the ride. It's the first I've seen of her in days and something about her makes me feel a little more at ease. She gives me a little wave and hops into the pack I've been carrying before anyone else can see her.

Five minutes later, we arrive on the other side, panting for breath but smiling triumphantly at our success. I quickly count everyone—they're all here. Even the stowaway pixie, who stays hidden in my pack. I send a thank you prayer to the Gods.

"That wasn't so bad," Maxx says. "If you consider feeling like getting your insides ripped out through your throat isn't bad."

Terek laughs, stretching his arms and legs out. "I've felt worse."

He shoots the warlock a disgruntled look and the sunlight reflects against this blue eyes, matching the wide open sky behind him.

In the distance, a snarling and animalistic war call sounds and that same sky fills with small black specks that quickly grow larger: dragons. We huddle in close and ready ourselves for a possible fight. We knew this was a definite possibility and we're prepared to make a deal if we can, and battle if we must.

"They're coming right for us," Juniper says, her stance widening. "They're not slowing down." She holds a knife in one hand and Bram's arm in the other. I grit my teeth.

"They would *never* kill Khali," Bram says softly, eyes turned down to the earth. "Stay close to her." It's the most I've heard from him since he made it clear to me that he was done with me after we rescued him.

"We assumed they'd be waiting for us." Maxx stands in front of Juniper, his stance protective. "Don't act so surprised."

"This was always part of the plan," I remind them.

Flannery stays back, quiet, observant, and most likely, invisible to the incoming army.

A massive dragon lands a few feet away with an earth-shattering crunch. He looms over us, nearly ten feet tall and a wingspan that's twice as wide; he shifts and stands tall in his human form, an expression of both anger and relief playing across his weathered face. I don't know what I expected. A general, maybe? But it's none other than King Titus Brightcaster himself and my breath catches at the sight.

I've always known the king to stick around his castle and let others do the leg work, so seeing him at the border is unnerving. The rest of the dragons follow suit, landing behind their king and shifting. They're all dressed in Drakenon's simplistic military clothing since it's in their dragon forms that they do the most damage. They don't normally have swords or spears, but today they do. They've either been waiting for more than just me or the Occultists. The first thing they do is seize the warlock.

He sneers but doesn't utter a word.

"Khali, it's so nice to see that you've finally returned to us," Titus says, "but I'm afraid I can't play host to this ragtag group of filth you've brought along."

He steps in closer, so proud and sure of himself, and stops in front of Bram. Bram stands tall, pushing the strain from his weeks of torture out of his expression. "Father."

"You have a lot of nerve coming back here." Titus's eyes grow cold. "What were you thinking? That you could take our princess from us? Do you have any idea the havoc you've caused to your family? Guards!"

Three armed men rush forward and seize Bram, causing him to wince and stumble as they pull him away from our group. I grit my teeth from yelling at the king about the complete double standard, considering he allowed Silas to get away with murder!

"Stop! I made Bram take me." That's a lie, but I can't stop it from forming. "I needed a guide, and we can discuss how everything came about later, but right now, we need to get to my father."

"What does *all this*," he circles his fingers at our crew, "have to do with Lord Elliot?" His nose flares as if he's smelled something rotten.

"Everything! Why do you think I left in the first place? I needed to find a cure for the hex."

I point to the Occultist. "He's been bound by that necklace," I say, "for now. He's going to help us unhex my father. He's also going to remove the curse from my friends."

And my own spell to Hazel that the king knows nothing about. All of that in exchange for removing the necklace but the king doesn't have to be let in on that little detail.

"Elves aren't welcomed here." Titus glares.

"They are now."

"And what's in it for us?" He laughs.

I grip my hands into fists and take a deep breath. I've been thinking about this, about how I can save my friends, how I can get them to listen to me about the Occultist, and how I can help my father. What it comes down to is sacrifice. I have to give up the things I want, at least for now, in order to get what we all need.

"I'll marry Silas," I say. The words almost hurt to speak, I hate them so much.

That only makes him laugh again. "You were always going to marry him."

I step in close, whispering so only the two of us can hear, "Was I? Or was I going to tell the court what really happened to Owen? Or maybe I was going to marry him and then undermine him at every turn? You think you can blackmail me into behaving like your little pet but I'll only behave if I get more say in this life you've created for me."

His jaw tenses, mouth pressing into a thin line. Electricity sparks behind his cloudy irises and I know just how angry I've made him. But he also knows I'm right. He needs me more than I need him.

"Fine," he says. "I'll grant them immunity and we'll see what the Occultist can do to help your father, but no more protesting when it comes to Silas. You will be a dutiful wife, just as my Brysta has been to me."

The idea of it makes me sick, especially since Silas is willing to sacrifice my magic to strengthen his own. He's horrible in every single way, but what choice do I have? With the Occultists prone to attacking our kingdom, my father on his deathbed, and my fae friends in need of help, I have to agree. The marriage is inevitable at this point. I'll deal with the consequences later.

"You have a deal, but only if my friends get to stay with us as guests and not prisoners, only if Bram gets to return to court, and only if we use the Occultist to help us before the wedding and not after."

Now for the hard part...

I extend my hand. He eyes it hungrily and is quick to clasp it in his own so we can shake on our agreement. Magic sparks between our palms, setting everything into motion. There's no going back.

Tears spring to my eyes. I'm quick to blink them away. Why do I feel like I just made a terrible bargain? I hope it's not the biggest mistake of my life because I'm bound to it.

"Brysta will be so pleased," he says with a loaded smile. "She's been planning your wedding day and night."

My heart drops.

"I received word that Silas arrived home yesterday. He'll be so happy to see you. And I must say, your timing is impeccable."

"And why is that?" I force the question through my gritted teeth but I already know the answer.

"Wait, what day is it?" Bram speaks loudly, startling us all. "Is it December already?"

That question confuses Titus but he doesn't know all of what his son has been through.

"It's December fifthteenth," I reply, meeting Bram's emerald gaze. His eyes widen and for the first time in days, I think there's a chance he cares about me afterall. Or he's simply grateful that I bargained for his safety.

"That's right," Titus says cheerily to Bram. "Tomorrow is not only Khali's eighteenth birthday but it's the day she'll become your brother's bride."

The warlock's terrible laugh erupts from where the guards hold him. They tighten their grips but it does little to stop him from cackling in that sickly way of his. "Is it the fifteenth already?" His eyes shine with evil intentions. "Time's up, Princess."

A shiver of fear washes over my body, not for fear of a wedding, but for fear of whatever the warlock thinks is going to happen to me tomorrow.

"And why is that?" I hiss.

He smirks. "You'll see."

"Tell me," I demand. "Tell me now."

"What's this?" Titus asks, glaring at us both.

The warlock only smiles, refusing to say another word. I have to turn away, the anger is so strong, like a string about to snap. The worst part of his threats is the unknown.

"What does he mean?" Titus demands.

A king who knows one of his subjects is withholding information from him is one of the most dangerous things in Eridas. I gulp and return my gaze to Titus, pulling my shoulders back in a display of strength. I pray he can't tell that under my dress, my knees have gone weak. "It means we need to act fast. Take us to my father."

TWENTY-SEVEN

HAZEL

I WALK OUT OF MY last final for the semester feeling about ready to drop dead from exhaustion. Dean meets me at the door of my classroom and wraps a protective arm around my shoulders. We make our way back to his place, strolling through the quiet campus. A lot of students have already left for break and a cheerful sense of relief has settled over the place.

This is so strange, being with Dean like this. To think when we met we hated each other, and now we're inseparable. By all outward appearances, anyone would assume we're a serious couple. Fact is, I haven't slept in my dorm in three weeks because I'm always at his house. Outside of classes, we can be seen together constantly. I even started accompanying him to his independent study hours in the evenings. It's boring as heck. I just sit around and study or read while he fiddles with electronics—and magic—but at least I get more time with him.

The spirits are growing stronger and bolder, but when Dean and I are together, they usually tend to leave me alone. It's like they sense his predator dragon energy and steer clear. That part has been great. But yeah, we look like a couple but we're not and I don't think we ever will be. And that's the part that hasn't been so great because it's starting to feel like torture to keep my feelings to myself. It's only one more thing to worry about in my ever-growing list of problems I can't control.

"What's going on in that pretty little head of yours?" he asks.

I suck on my lip. "Just thinking about that Chem test," I lie. "It was hard."

That part isn't a lie.

Ever since the reaper incident on Sunday night, I've been sleeping in Dean's bed because neither of us is willing to let me be alone at night anymore with that reaper—and possibly others—after me. You'd think four nights cuddling under the sheets would have led to another kiss but nope, nothing even close. Meanwhile we haven't been able to find the answers we need to stop the reapers or free Landon from them. I still don't know who my father is. I still don't know how to break this curse with Khali. I'm more lost than ever.

"Well, you did it and I think you should be proud of yourself," Dean says, his tone light and positive. He's trying to brighten my mood. "You survived finals week and your first semester of college. How does it feel?"

I know he's just trying to distract me from all the things I might *not* survive, but I still appreciate it. I shrug, breathing in the crisp air. It snowed earlier and everything is covered in a pretty frosting of gleaming white. "Okay, I guess."

"Are you excited for your birthday tomorrow? December sixteenth and you'll officially be an adult."

Again, there he goes trying to cheer me up.

Once again, I shrug. "I just hope something bad doesn't happen," I confess. "You know what Harmony said about me being connected to Khali and what Khali said about the Occultist saying she would need his help once she turned eighteen. Khali's eighteen tomorrow, too. What if it's a disaster?"

"We can't speculate because we don't have enough information. That Occultist could have been bluffing and Harmony could have been wrong." He doesn't sound like he believes what he's saying. "Fact is, we don't know anything for sure yet. Anyway, you have enough on your mind to worry about."

"That I do," I sigh.

His tone drops an octave, "Let's take it one day at a time, okay? Including tomorrow."

"Okay. At least it's Friday. Mom thinks I'm celebrating my birthday with Cora and Macy tomorrow and then there's the flight on Sunday. I'm supposed to go home for three weeks for the break."

"Have you made a decision about that?" His arm tightens around me and I catch a whiff of his woodsy scent. "Wherever you go, I go."

As much as I would love to leave and bring him with me, it's not going to solve anything.

I release a breath. It sounds like resignation. "I obviously can't do that. What if the reapers follow me? Or Silas's dragon spies? No, I can't risk her safety, plus I need to stay here in case Harmony comes back and so we can keep trying to figure out how to send the reapers back to where they came from."

We've not found a single solid piece of information all week…

"So it's settled."

"Kind of. How am I going to explain this to her? I don't know what to do to make this right."

He doesn't have an answer to that one.

When we make it to his doorstep, he stops before opening it. "I don't know what tomorrow is going to bring," he says, his black eyes shine almost quicksilver as they gaze into mine. His face is more relaxed than I've probably ever seen it. I like this side of him. "I want to celebrate your birthday tonight and make it perfect for you. Don't be mad, okay?"

Mad? How could I be mad about something as sweet as that?

He unlocks the door and we step instead, dropping our stuff in the entry closet. The house is shadowed from both the late afternoon and lack of sunshine this time of year, so I flip on the lights. Rounding the corner, I stop short.

"Surprise! Happy Birthday!"

Cora and Macy jump out from behind the kitchen island, waving their hands around like total idiots. They've decorated the place in a Hawaiian Luau style, complete with paper-mâché flowers hanging from the ceiling, a straw tablecloth over the table, plastic blow-up palm trees, and a couple of fake tiki torches.

Tears spring to my eyes. "You guys!" I rush forward and pull them both into a giant hug.

They're wearing bikinis, grass skirts, and dollar-store leis. They're adorable but more than anything, having them here means the world to me. I've missed them so much lately, and after what happened Monday morning, I feared they wouldn't want to have anything to do with me ever again. I wouldn't blame them.

"Just for tonight," Macy says brightly, "let's have some fun and forget about all the crap going on. Okay?" The bruising around her neck is almost gone and my guilt wants to rear its ugly head but I focus on her kind words instead.

I nod, wiping away the tears.

Cora slaps my butt. "Get upstairs and get dressed. You can't wear a sweater to a luau."

I laugh and scurry to the stairs. A tiny black bikini and grass skirt waits for me on the guest bed. I'm so happy, I don't bother protesting. I'm quick to get changed. I've never worn something so revealing but I'm too excited to let myself feel shy about it.

When I go back downstairs, I catch them whispering.

"What is it?" I ask cautiously.

They turn and smile.

"Damn, you are freaking hot!" Cora laughs, fanning herself. "Girl!"

Macy nods approvingly and laughs. My cheeks burn and I can't even look at Dean, but I can tell he's 100% looking at me which makes me even more embarrassed.

Macy grabs my hand and leads me into the family room.

"What is that?" I squeal.

"Your birthday present!"

They've set up one of those blow-up portable hot tubs right in the middle of Dean's living room. Steam wafts from the water and my jaw practically drops to the ground. Oh my heck, this thing is amazing.

"You're kidding me?" I gape at Dean. "You let them set this up inside your house?"

"I had to do something to keep myself from being on the, what did you call it, Cora? Your 'shit list'?"

Cora smiles proudly even if her cheeks color a bit.

"Actually, the whole thing was his idea." Macy winks at me and suddenly, I'm nervous and all too aware of how much skin I'm showing right now.

"Which reminds me." Cora throws one of the cheapo leis at him. "You can do the honors of laying Hazel since we all know how much you want to."

Oh my God.

"Cora!" Macy slaps her playfully, her pretty blue eyes nearly bulging out her head.

Dean and I exchange a sheepish look and he's totally blushing. Not that

I blame him! My friends don't realize Dean and I are just friends so I never told them about the kiss we shared since it was a one-time thing. Who am I kidding? I didn't share because I didn't want my hopes up any more than they already were.

I push it all from my mind and run for the hot tub. "Last one in is a rotten egg!"

TWO HOURS LATER, WE'VE EXHAUSTED the hot tub and drank the last of the yummy virgin piña coladas. Dean braves the cold, not that it bothers him, and grills us up the juiciest pineapple hamburgers I've ever had the good fortune of eating. We sit around the kitchen table in beach towels, laughing like crazy, eating to our heart's content, and having the time of our lives. I feel like I'm a normal college kid and it means the world to me.

Every so often I'll glance at Dean, noticing that each time I do, he's looking back. Butterflies have set up camp in my stomach and I can't say I mind. Maybe I was wrong about us? Maybe we *are* more than friends.

Before they leave, Cora and Macy gift me more obsidian jewelry. "Because we know you have to wear it every day." That makes me cry again. We hug goodbye and promise to text every day during break. They're both going home tomorrow after a coffee double-date they have planned with some guys they've been hanging out with. I won't see them until mid-January and hopefully Dean and I will have figured out the reaper situation by then and our friendship can go back to normal.

While Dean and I clean up, the room is silent but charged with nervous energy. He uses a hose to drain the water out of the hot tub out into the yard. I do the dishes. I can't get the grin off of my face. It's the happiest I've been since the day we kissed.

"What's that smile for?" he asks, closing the sliding glass door behind him.

"I'm happy." I shut the dishwasher and come around from behind the counter. "Thank you."

I'm still in the teeny bikini, sans the grass skirt. I ditched the towel to deal with the dishes. Dean's in his swim trunks. They hang low on his abdomen and show off his chiseled body perfectly. He's got an incredible athletic physique and I'd be lying if I said I didn't want to run my hands up and down his bare chest. I'm openly staring at this point but I can't even be bothered to be embarrassed about it anymore; it's like the heat of the hot tub has melted away my earlier reservedness. He'd be an idiot if he didn't know how I feel about him by this point. The ball is in his court and we both know it.

He clears his throat. "Did you have fun?"

"It was the best present I've ever received."

He scratches behind his ear sheepishly. "Well, actually, I have one last gift to give you."

"Are you serious?" I laugh. "This surprise party was more than enough."

He shrugs and one of his dark curls falls over his eyes. "It's in your room."

I squeal excitedly and charge up the stairs, taking them two at a time. Sure enough, sitting on the bed of the guest bedroom is another gift—a medium-sized box wrapped in shiny silver paper. Dean stands in the doorway as I rip it open. In the movies, what does a guy get a girl he's interested in? Jewelry or some kind of beautiful, sexy dress he wants her to wear. I'm assuming it'll be something like that but what I find inside the box is so much better.

"This is unreal," I squeal, freaking excited. The box is loaded with Harry Potter swag, specifically with Gryffindor gear. There's a scarf, a flannel pajama set, a set of magnetic bookmarks, and a Crookshanks plushy. Even though it's not his thing, he knows it's my favorite fandom. And at the bottom of the box is a hardback copy of the first book.

"Open it," he says.

I do, and when I see what's inside, I almost drop the book. "This is a signed copy. Dean! Are you crazy?" My heart races. "It's way too much."

He cocks one shoulder as if this is not a big deal. "Money isn't an issue for me since my parents set me up with enough to have whatever I needed here. I figured if anyone should have that book, it's you."

"How did you even find it?"

"I have my ways." He laughs.

"I'm scared to touch it." I carefully pack the items back into the box, leaving the book on top. Of all the things he could have gifted me today, he gifted me time with my friends and items he knew I would cherish. How did I get so lucky?

"There's a card in the back of the book." His voice grows nervous and that makes me nervous, but in the best way.

I open the book from the back and pull out a little blue envelope with my name written across the top in his neat handwriting. I raise my eyebrows at him but he remains as still as a statue. I open it with careful fingers. A folded piece of paper falls into my lap—a letter.

"Did you write this?"

He nods.

I pick it up and read it silently.

Dear Hazel,

I've been struggling to tell you this all week but it's killing me to keep this a secret from you, especially with your birthday coming tomorrow. The truth is, Khali is going to be the next queen of my kingdom. Nobody has any say in that, not even Khali. I always assumed I'd have to marry her one day even though she's a friend and nothing more. When I was exiled and came here, I always planned to go back one day and take my throne, Khali as my wife included.

But then I met you. You challenge me in every way. I feel things I've never felt before when I'm with you. I can't imagine how life could be any fun without you in it. When I pulled you from that water Monday morning and realized I almost lost you, I also realized I couldn't deny my feelings any longer.

I guess what I'm trying to say is that I would give up a kingdom to be with you.

Yours Forever,
Dean

My cheeks burn. This is not at all what I expected to happen tonight. I gaze over at Dean and study him, seeing him in a whole new light. He's still standing in the doorway, hands in the pockets of his swimming trunks, curly black hair hanging in front of his face, and with that unreadable expression he always wears around me.

I finally know what it means.

I place the letter on top of everything else in the box, and standing, move it to the bedside table. Then I go to him, wrapping my arms around his neck and breathing in his rainy scent. His lips are quick to find mine, making everything right with the world. Sure, neither of us knows what's going to happen tomorrow, and our lives seem to be in constant danger. Sometimes it feels like we're waiting for a trainwreck that hasn't happened yet and that's a terrible way to live.

At the end of the day, Dean is right. We can't live our lives worrying about the bad things that could happen. All we can do is try to figure it out, take life as it comes, and make each moment as perfect as two imperfect people can. If I could stay in this moment forever, I would, but tomorrow is coming. I'm powerless to stop it, so instead I pull him closer and deepen the kiss.

TWENTY-EIGHT
KHALI

I PRESS THE KNIFE AGAINST the warlock's neck, not hard enough to cut, but it won't take much pressure to spill his blood. "Help him," I demand. "Remove the hex."

Do as we agreed, is what I want to add, but I don't. Not in front of Titus.

We stand next to my father's bed. He's still in a restless coma. His body is much thinner than I've ever seen it, and his skin is a ghostly shade of white. Mother stands on the other end of the bed, biting her nails and watching us with red-rimmed eyes. Along the back of the dimly lit chambers are Titus, three guards, and my fae friends—except for Flannery. He didn't reveal himself earlier and so he wasn't picked up and flown back with the rest of us. He's somewhere out there in Drakenon. I'm sure he can fend for himself but the whole thing makes me uneasy.

"I mean it," I say, pushing the knife the smallest bit. "This isn't a game!"

"Oh, I assure you, it was most definitely me who helped bring this on your father," the warlock replies, nonplussed. "Unfortunately, it's not a simple little hex."

"Then what is it?"

His lip curls. "It's… magic."

"We already know it's magic!"

"You have to remove this necklace first," the warlock bites back. "I can't do anything without my full powers, now can I?"

Little does he know, I can't remove the necklace, but I know someone who can.

"If I do take it off, do you vow to save my father and remove the curse from these people and any other curses you have cause to us?" I point to my friends and then to myself. "Do you vow not to hurt us ever again?"

Of course, he already did vow it upon a handshake but this is a show for Titus and so we must have a performance.

He shifts to look at me and I hold the knife steady. There's a chilling sheen to his slate colored eyes. "I can't save your father," he says, "because like I said, this is not a hex. It's something far, far worse and not even I can remove it."

Mom shrieks and curls her body against my father's side. Her hair is curled nicely and her gown is pressed, but her eyes, they're tired, discouraged, and filling with tears.

"You're lying." My heart rate speeds up and my breath catches. I press the knife closer against his neck. "I traded my freedom to get you into this castle and now you're telling me you can't help? No way."

He cackles. "Stupid girl."

Maybe I am a stupid girl but a deal is a deal. We shook on it. What's going on?

"What about us?" Juniper steps forward, hands balled into little white fists. "You put this curse on us so now it's time to reverse it."

The warlock clicks his tongue. "Reverse it?" His mouth twitches into a smile. "Sorry, that's not possible."

"You don't get a choice! We had an agreement."

I shoot her a charged look. Now is not the time to speak of the promises we made that would only upset King Titus. From the corner of the cramped room, he eyes us with more interest than is comfortable.

"Let me finish," the warlock sing-songs cruelly. "I can't reverse it, but I can stop it from getting any worse."

"So you mean to tell me I'll be half-kitty cat and half-elf for the rest of my days?" Terek smirks, his tail dancing around his body. "Hmm, can't say that I mind."

"Well, I mind!" Juniper snaps. She points to her one deer ear.

"Take it or leave it," the warlock sounds annoyed and it takes everything in me not to kill him right here and now. "But like I said before, if I'm going to help you, you have to remove the necklace first."

I glare. "Fine."

I knew this was going to have to happen at some point. We all did.

"Back up," he demands, "your knife is not needed any longer."

I remove it but keep it in hand. "We'll see."

"You're really going to trust this guy?" Maxx scoffs. "Unbelievable. He's not going to help anyone but himself. I've been saying this all along!"

I continue to speak to the warlock, ignoring Maxx. "But you're also going to try to help my father, to do everything in your power. I don't care what you have to do so long as you don't hurt anyone else in the process."

I'm hoping to remind him of the bargain we made back in the fae woods even though I can't speak of it here. But he has to know, right? I feel the spark of magic myself, even now!

He tilts his head to one side. "I can try to help but I can't make any promises."

Liar!

The door swings open and Silas strides in. He's fitted into his regular princely attire and cleaned up to perfection. His ice-blonde hair is longer from his time in the forest but instead of cutting it, he's tied it back. The style accentuates his high cheekbones. His velvety eyes light when they land on me, hungry and excited. My stomach churns with hatred.

"There you are." He grins ruefully. "I must say, I'm the tiniest disappointed you came to me. I quite enjoyed the game of cat and mouse we had." He strides in close and whispers in my ear, "Don't ever embarrass me like that again, wife."

"I'm not your wife," I hiss back.

He chuckles low. "Not yet, but what's one more day?" He lingers, breathing me in. "Hmm," he says softly. "Make sure you scrub yourself extra good tonight. Tomorrow is the big day and afterwards I have even bigger plans."

Bile rises to my throat.

He steps away and eyes the scene before him. "Now what have we here? Has my girl gone and caught herself a warlock? How very resourceful of you."

"I freed all the prisoners from the cells, too." I raise my eyebrows, challenging him. "You know, the soldiers that you lost to that wind spell? The ones you were going to leave for dead? Yeah, they're probably on their way home now thanks to me and my friends." His eyes roam my face, a storm of lust and dominance playing in their depths. "So you're welcome."

"Yes, I'd already heard about that. How can I possibly thank you?" he says playfully even though we both know this is not a game.

"You can help me with the warlock," I admit, nodding toward where I've tied Silas's magicked heirloom around the Occultist. "Remove your necklace from his neck so he can undo his spells."

"Hmm…" His lip twitches. "And why would I do that?"

"Because she made a deal with me, Son," Titus says. "Just do as you're told."

A flicker of frustration crosses Silas's face but he does as he's ordered, like always. Well, almost. I push the warlock toward him, and unlike me, Silas is able to untie the cord without magic to stop him. I wonder how much it kills him to take it off someone so powerful.

The warlock steps free of us and a sickly grin spread across his face. His burgundy robes, muddied from our trip, suddenly appear clean again. And as for the warlock, his ageless appearance returns. So I know he has his blood magic back.

"We have a deal," I hiss, pointing the knife at him. I'm still close enough to cut if I need to. "Don't make me regret this."

Maxx scoffs and the room goes silent.

Black cloudy magic forms in the warlock's hands and he chants in that strange, unknown language. The magic grows darker and larger. It swirls about him and then shoots to my friends, flowing into their open mouths in streams as dark as ink.

"Is it supposed to do that?" my mother cries out. I don't turn to look at her.

"I don't know." I bring my own magic to the surface until electricity crackles between my fingertips and around the knife. I step closer to the warlock. "But I swear, if you hurt them, I'll kill you."

"Hush!" The warlock closes his eyes. "I need to concentrate."

Time seems to stretch into eternity as the man relaxes into his powers. Then without notice, the magic bursts out of him, sweeping through every corner of the room. In an instant, it's gone. We all fly back, everyone stumbling to the cold stone floor. Pain shoots up my palm where I accidently cut myself with the knife.

I stand and look around, frantic. The magic is gone—and so is the warlock.

"I told you so," Maxx groans, rolling over onto his stomach and jumping up. He rubs a hand along one of his ram horns, as if it's hurting.

"Where is he?" Titus bellows. His guards rush about the room. "We needed him! We were going to question him about the Occultists and their plans!"

Which is exactly why we never told Titus about the deal we struck with that wretched man.

"You weren't the only one who needed him to stick around," I snap. We were going to let him go *only* after he'd removed all the spells. That was the deal! How did he get out of an agreement forged within Eridas? It shouldn't be possible, not when we shook on it like we did. What about the curse connecting me to Hazel? What about my father's ailment? He promised to help… and now he's gone.

I am such a fool. I never should have struck that deal. He found a way out of it or perhaps the necklace blocked the vow from working on him in the first place. All my friends still have their animalistic features and only time will tell if the spell has been stopped like he said it would or if they'll continue to shift into animals until they lose themselves completely. My heart twists because I doubt the warlock helped, not if he was able to get away as he did without fulfilling everything he said he would.

We've been played.

Father hasn't stirred from where he sleeps fitfully in his bed. Mother still drapes herself across him, crying in despair. The weight of everyone's sadness is too heavy for me to handle. When did everything go so wrong?

I sprint toward the door, dropping the stupid bloodied knife as I go.

"Where are you going?" Silas calls after me.

"It's my last night of freedom," I shoot back. "Tomorrow you can have your say, but for now, leave me alone."

I dart out into the corridor, down the winding staircase, and out into the cold night. I squeeze the wound in my hand the entire time. I should get it patched up but not right now, not with all this emotion raging inside. I can't run away again. I can't go back on my promised handshake with King Titus to marry his son tomorrow. I'm not like the warlock, I don't have a way out.

I find my way to the back garden, one of my favorite places to go when I need space to breathe. It's covered in a layer of hardened snow and the trees are devoid of leaves, but at least the black sky twinkles with stars and the wind is a soft caress against my face. I sit on a stone bench, close my eyes, and cry.

I failed.

I failed to save my father. I failed to save my friends. Owen is dead. Bram is a shadow of who he once was. Dean is still in exile. Hazel is somewhere, probably needing me and in trouble but I was too afraid of her to really help when I had the chance. And now I have to marry Silas, a murderous man who treats me like a possession and who I know will make my life miserable. I'm going to have to be intimate with him, to have his children and stay by his side as he runs our kingdom until the Occultists get us.

And there's nothing I can do about it.

"Are you okay?" Bram's quiet timbre pulls me back to reality. I wipe my eyes of tears and try to slow my breaths. When I look up at him, I force a small smile to my lips.

"No," I admit. "Are you okay?"

"No." He sits next to me. Like Silas, he has been cleaned up from his time in the forest. He smells good, too, like spring rain. I demanded I go straight to my father, so I'm still a mess and in need of some self-care. Maybe a long hot bath will make me feel better, though I doubt it.

"If I tell you something, do you promise not to tell anyone?" he asks.

"Of course." I blink away the last of the tears.

The darkness is like a veil of privacy that also adds a layer of forgiveness between us. This is the first real conversation I've had with Bram since his rescue where he hasn't resisted being around me, let alone talking to me. It's the one good thing about this terrible day.

His voice shakes. "I can't remember what that Occultist did to me." His hand starts to shake too and I so badly want to still it with my own. "I remember being with you and being taken to the mountain, but that's it. The next thing I remember is you saving me and getting us out of there. So as it turns out, I have entire weeks of my memory that are missing."

It explains the lost expression I often see in his eyes. "I'm sorry."

He sighs and rakes both hands through his hair, brushing it off his face. "It's making me crazy. I don't know what he did but I know he did something… unspeakable."

He goes silent but I can feel he wants to say more.

"What is it?"

"I keep missing things," he says.

"What do you mean? What's missing?"

"Time." He clears his throat. "Entire hours will go by and I won't remember them. I'll be doing one thing and then this blackness takes over me and then it's gone and I'm back to being me again. I don't understand."

Worry is a coiled snake around my throat. I don't know how to reply to make him feel better so all I do say is, "I'm sorry."

Again.

I wish he'd told me sooner, wish he'd opened up instead of pushing me away back in the forest. Maybe we could have helped him before the warlock got away? But now it's too little too late.

"It's not your fault," he sighs.

"It kind of is."

He laughs—for real laughs—and it's the second good thing about this day. "Okay, yeah, it kind of is your fault but that's okay. I don't blame you. I never could."

"Well, I thought you did." My voice cracks. "You've been avoiding me."

"Because I'm scared of myself," he admits. "I'm scared of this *thing* that is happening to me. I'm afraid I'm going to do something I can't take back. I keep having these sick dreams and these bad thoughts and… I haven't wanted to be around you because I'm scared I'm going to hurt you."

I swallow down the tiniest bit of fear. "You would never."

"How can you be so sure?" he challenges.

Truthfully, I can't. I should get up now, should leave him here. I should listen to what he's trying to tell me, but I can't. So instead I decide to be brave. I move my unwounded hand along the bench until I find his. His fingers are so cold. I shoot a little bit of warmth into mine using magic and then take his hand fully in mine. He squeezes back and my stomach flips.

"You sought out Juniper." I feel silly for even bringing her up but I can't help it. "Did you not worry you'd endanger her?"

He shakes his head. "There's something about her that feels different than you."

I can't help it; I pull my hand away. He doesn't react.

"Her healing magic?"

"Yeah, it could be that. I don't know. I feel safe with her for some reason."

Maybe it's just her. And not me.

The wound in my hand isn't the only thing that hurts now. I squeeze my hands tight and build a little wall around my heart.

"Everything is going to be okay," I say at last.

I wish I believed it.

TWENTY-NINE
HAZEL

THE PHONE RINGS AT EXACTLY 6:18—the buttcrack of dawn. I bolt awake with a groan and answer it. I know exactly who's calling.

"Hi, Mom." My voice is hoarse from sleep.

"Happy Birthday, baby." Her voice on the other hand, is chipper, which considering it's an hour earlier in Ohio, is downright sadistic. She bursts out into the birthday song, and I have to cover the speaker on my phone to keep from waking Dean.

"On this day, eighteen years ago, at this very moment," Mom carries on, "I pushed with all my might for the final time and out you came, covered in amniotic fluid. You were the cutest baby I'd ever seen. Of course, your head was cone-shaped from the vacuum but it went back to normal. Damn, that thing hurt like hell."

"Oh, my gosh, gross." I press my face into the pillow. "Why do you always have to be so graphic about stuff?"

Mom laughs. "I'm a nurse. It takes a lot to rattle me."

Dean rolls over, nuzzles his stubbly face into the crook of my neck and wraps an arm around my torso. His breath tickles my skin, and I sink deeper into the pillows.

"Well, we're not all nurses and praise the Lord for that."

"Sweetie, do you think vets don't have to deal with blood, guts, and poop? Because trust me, they do."

"Yeah, yeah, so you've said," I retort. "But humans are so much dirtier than animals."

She laughs at that. "Considering some of the things I've seen, I'd have to agree."

Dean's velvety lips press a slow kiss against my collarbone and suddenly I need to get Mom off the phone. At home our annual tradition includes her waking me at my exact birth moment so we can eat birthday cake for breakfast and reminisce about the day I was born. It's not the same over the phone, especially considering I'm all cuddled up with my new boyfriend.

Yup. Last night we made out forever and then agreed to make our relationship official. It didn't go further than some super hot kissing, but considering the state of our living arrangements, I don't know how much longer the only kissing thing will last. We're wearing our pajamas now but trust me when I say our swimsuits left little to the imagination.

"I can't wait to see you tomorrow," she continues. "I miss you so much. We have a lot of catching up to do over the break."

I don't have the heart to tell her I'm not coming home. I still don't know how I'm going to get out of missing another flight or what I'll be able to say to convince her to let me stay here.

"And there's someone here I'd like you to meet."

I gasp. "Mom! Do you have a boyfriend?"

She laughs. "Just wait and see, okay?"

"All right then," I reply. "I'll call you later. I need my beauty sleep, you know, since I'm an old lady now."

"Aww, don't remind me. My baby is all grown up!"

We say our goodbyes and disconnect. I roll over to grin at Dean. He's wide awake and has the same goofy smile as me plastered across his face.

"Well, you're eighteen now." He throws himself under the covers and begins tickling me. "I better make sure you're still in one piece."

I scream with delight and join him under the cocoon of blankets.

THE DAY STARTS OUT NORMAL. Dean and I have an unspoken rule not to talk about the bad things—not today. We eat cereal for breakfast and then curl up in the theatre room to watch a movie. He lets me pick but it doesn't matter; we spend the whole time making out. Being treated like this is the best feeling ever. I've wanted it for so long with him and now that I have him, I can't get enough. But underneath all the bliss, there's this electric current of energy running through me I can't shake because it's new. I've never felt it there before. Part of me thinks I'm imagining the weird feeling and it's fears from my mind manifesting in my body. Another part wonders if something big is coming and I need to get ready.

We hit up my favorite Mexican food place for lunch and then go over to Harmony's to check on her house again. No surprises, but she doesn't answer the door or appear to be there.

I'm prattling on about volunteering for the local animal shelter as we're walking back to the car when Dean stops abruptly. He grabs my hand and pulls me behind him. His stance is protective and fiery power emanates from his body. "They're here."

The trees around us are heavy with fresh snow and a sunny blue sky stretches above. There aren't any footprints in the snow on the lawn and the forest surrounding the house is silent.

"Who's here?"

A low growl sounds from behind us. We turn in a circle but nobody appears. "Silas's men," Dean says under his breath. "They must have decided they're done with just watching you."

I take Dean's hand and squeeze, trying to stay calm. I knew they were supposedly watching us but I never once saw or felt anything out of the ordinary. Dean would know better considering he's a dragon and can sense supernaturals. Besides, I was too distracted with reapers and spirits. I should have paid more attention.

"What do they want?"

"If I had to guess, I'd say they want you."

Four men emerge from behind the trees, practically appearing from thin air. They're young, dressed like regular humans and carry no visible weapons. But their eyes, they glow with magic. And their stances are predatory, ready for a fight.

"Hand her over," one of them calls out. "We won't ask twice."

"She's not yours to take." Dean shifts even further in front of me, like a wall of protection.

"Don't make us fight you," the largest of the men says. He's young enough to be a college student, with a burly mountain man beard and reminds me of a normal guy's guy, the kind you'd see at a Superbowl party or hanging out at the gym. The kind that likes to think he's tough but doesn't act it. And yet, here he is, a dragon shifter, ready to kidnap me. "We will do as we've been commanded and I can promise you won't be able to stop us."

Will Dean end up hurt because of me? Maybe I should turn myself in? But the idea of going anywhere with these men makes me more fearful than ever. My knees grow soft as spaghetti noodles and my breaths come out in short little gasps.

"Give us the girl!" another yells. "Do it, now!"

"Never," Dean snarls, no longer calm.

"What do you want with me?" I call back. Truthfully, I'm hoping to stall but it doesn't matter. They don't answer me, and all at once, they shift.

Glimmering colorful lights pass over their bodies as they turn from men to monstrous dragons with black hides, sharp claws and teeth, and eyes the size of my head. They all look similar, but it's their eyes that differentiate them. Dean's are alive with fire and the other men's are a mix of greens, browns, and blues.

"Run!" Dean yells and then he shifts, too.

Harmony's yard is huge but these creatures are massive and I don't know where to possibly go that could be safe. I start toward the forest but one of the dragons cuts me off, snarling. I scream and turn back. There are four of them but Dean is holding his own, at least for now, but I don't know if he's going to be able to last long.

Making a quick decision, I run for Harmony's back door. I grab a rock from the flowerbed and throw it through the glass pane above the door handle. I reach inside and unlock it, cutting my arm on the glass as I go. I cry out but don't let it deter me. I try to find the deadbolt, but my hands shake like crazy. I can't find it!

"Where do you think you're going?" a man's voice cackles. One of the dragons has shifted back and he's running toward me. Long black hair billows around the face of a handsome African American looking guy. His muscles are so big he looks like he could be a Strong Man weightlifter. His gaze is frenzied and excited as he gains ground.

I finally locate the deadbolt and throw the door open, running inside. I can only hope that whatever protections Harmony has on this place will recognize me as her friend and not kill me like Dean said could happen.

The man follows me inside, undeterred.

I sprint into the kitchen, looking for a knife but there's nothing on the counters. I'm rummaging in the drawers like a maniac when the creep finds me.

"Don't make this harder than it has to be," he says. "Silas wants to—"

He falls to the ground, foaming at the mouth and body seizing. His face turns red and then purple, like he can't breath. The whites of his eyes become bloodshot.

I back away. "Thank you, Harmony," I whisper, because I'm alive and this man is clearly not going to make it. I run around his body and out the back door again so I can check on Dean. I'm careful to stay close to the house, should I need its protections again.

In the yard another man lies on the ground, his body broken at odd angles. By the glossy way his eyes gaze into nothing, I know he's dead. The two dragons left circle Dean, dodging when he blows fire from his enraged mouth. Dean can take them, right? I'm terrified he'll fail. Will they kill him? What will they do to me if they catch me?

Something wet trickles down my right hand. Blood from where I cut it on the glass. It drips from my fingers and into the snow, making little splatters of crimson. Suddenly, I can feel the immense pain of the cut. It's deeper than I first thought. Not fatal, but something that might require stitches. I can squeeze the wound shut with my left hand and try to force the pain away from my mind.

Dean's dragon turns to look at me, stopping when it sees the blood. It's thrown him off his game, and that's when his attackers make their move, ripping into his hide with their teeth. He screeches in agony and bucks to get them off.

"No!" The pain from my cut travels over my entire body, coupled with the need to help Dean. That strange electrical current I've had within me all day zaps to life, covering my entire body in one go.

I run out into the lawn, toward Dean, snow flying everywhere. I have to help. I stumble and fall to my knees, the electricity overpowering me. I close my eyes and try to breathe through the electricity razing my body. Did I get struck by lightning? I don't understand what's happening.

I open my eyes to scream again, only this time, it's a roar that erupts from my mouth. I look down and gasp. I'm not me—I'm a dragon.

What?!

But I'm not like the other dragons. First of all, my hide isn't black. It's white. And I'm a lot smaller. My claws are sharp as blades, two long wings flap behind my back, and my teeth feel long enough to destroy the guys hurting Dean.

I hurl myself forward, catching on to this flying business almost immediately, and barrel toward the group of dragons. They're not fighting anymore, momentarily stunned by the sight of me. I go for the closest enemy, ready to fight to the death if need be. But instead of making contact with the dragon, I glide right through him.

What the...?

I crane my flexible dragon neck to look around.

This doesn't make any sense.

They can see me and I can see them. I try again, but I'm still met with nothing but air. How is that possible?

The two dragons left to fight Dean burst into the air and fly off toward the forest, making their retreat. I can't help but think they're going to the portal but I don't know for sure.

Dean climbs to his feet as I settle to the ground. There's blood in the snow and on his hide, but I think he's okay. I swear if dragons could smile, his would be grinning with an "I told you so" smirk. How am I a dragon that can't touch other dragons? This doesn't make sense. And then I remember who I've seen this happen to before: Owen.

Realization ripples over my body in a violent awakening as I realize the truth of who I am. I'm not like the other dragons. I don't have earth or fire or air or water as my element. What had Khali called it? Spirit.

I'm a spirit dragon—a spirit dragon who can shift into a living girl.

THIRTY
KHALI

MY HEART STRAINS WILD AND frantic. The air whooshes in and out of my lungs too fast to keep up. Little beads of sweat pop up all over my body.

I'm suffocating except I'm not.

I'm drowning but without water.

It's like when Silas roped that necklace around me and shut off my magic; it's like that but worse. The elementals don't feel subdued or sleeping this time, or like they're being syphoned to someone else. They don't feel like anything—because they're gone. I'm empty, void of my essence. And my dragon? She's gone, too. Her loss is the worst part of all of it. She is me and I am her. So who am I now?

I'm sitting in front of a large, gilded mirror while a pack of maids fawn over me like fervent dogs. They seem oblivious to my sudden outburst. Either that, or they don't care. Or maybe they were ordered not to ask. They're here to prepare me for my upcoming nuptials and nothing more. It won't be long now that I'll be walking down the aisle in front of the entire dragon court and swearing myself to Silas. Even though it's a terrible thing, none of that compares to this sudden realization that I'm no longer the Khali I once was.

Out of nowhere, my magic has vanished.

I was sitting here, enduring the maids with their poking and prodding, and the elements were there with me as they always are, and then they left me, draining away into nothingness. My dragon self clawed to stay, but was unable to keep herself from being swept away into that unreachable darkness. It all happened so fast.

I can't... I can't breathe.

"Are you all right?" Faros says, leaning in close.

I look up at her, one of my only friends in this castle, and burst into tears.

"Oh, dear." She wipes my cheek with the soft pad of her thumb as her kind eyes take me in. "It will be okay. Silas isn't so bad. Give it time. You will grow to love him."

I blink back at her. She doesn't know why I'm crying, nor does she understand his true nature and the terrible things he's done. There are so many secrets I've kept from her for fear she'd tell my mother. They're cousins and very close. Mother is the only reason Faros is here and has this employment. It's always kept a distance between us, even though I know Faros has tried to bridge that gap time and again. She loves me. She does. I'm like the daughter she never had. But once again, I decide to keep a secret from her. I can't confess what's really causing my tears, so I nod and suck in a breath.

"You're right," I say. "I'm so sorry."

She smiles cautiously, like she knows I'm withholding something from her, but gets back to fixing my hair. She's left it down and wavy, brushing it for what felt like ages. Now she's braiding tiny, white jeweled flowers into it. Though they aren't the same, they remind me of some of the things I saw in the Jeweled Forest with Bram, and my stomach heaves as the images replay in my mind. The dead who will never leave that place, who will sleep for a century only to wake up with tree trunks growing from their chests. The trees there survive on the blood of those greedy enough to be enticed to take a jewel and I wonder what would have happened if I'd gone there without Bram. I'd probably be sharing the same fate, one worse than death. And now look what's become of Bram—what's become of *me*.

The maids finish with my hair, and then apply rouge to my lips and the perfect amount of kohl around my eyes. It hides the fact that I haven't been sleeping well.

"Now you really mustn't cry," Faros says, brushing her hands off on a linen kerchief. "The black will turn into a mess if you do."

The last thing on my mind is worrying whether my face is pretty enough for my wedding, but I nod along because what is there left to do? Even if I could get away from here, I have no means to survive on my own. I'm stuck. What will Silas do once he discovers his wife is no longer the most powerful elemental dragon shifter in the kingdom? It's the reason why he wants me so badly and without that, I fear I'll end up dead so another queen can take my place. I swallow it down, vowing to keep this secret of mine hidden for as long as I possibly can. Nobody can know. Nobody can be trusted. This loss has to be a result of the spell between me and Hazel and until I can find a way to undo it, I must play my part and play it well.

I stand from my cushioned stool and let them change me into my corset and wedding gown. Once the corset has been cinched to near suffocation, I raise my hands and let them drape the gown onto my frame. They fix it just so and then turn me to face the mirror.

"You are the most beautiful girl in the world," Faros says, meaning every word. They only serve to make me feel worse.

The other maids chatter amongst themselves with delight and envy, agreeing with Faros but taking it a step further. If only they could be me, their wildest dreams could come true. If only they could look like this, be powerful like I am, marry a handsome man like Silas, then nothing could go wrong in their lives. *Little do they know.*

I hardly recognize myself.

The gown is made of a gauzy white lace overlaid atop rich golden silk. The colors bring out the golden undertones in my dark hair, giving it a warm summery quality. Sparkly beaded flower crystals line the bodice, designed exactly to match the ones braided into my hair. The dress itself has been made specially for me and fits snugly around my chest and arms, showing off my curves. It drapes into a flowing waterfall of gold fabric, landing at my feet and belling out behind me.

I have to ball my hands into fists to keep from ripping it off.

Mother enters, stopping short with a gasp when she sees me all done up. She rushes forward and wraps me in her arms. It's so unlike her, I can't help but freeze. "If only your father could see you," she whispers softly against my ear. "He would be so proud."

Would he be proud, though?

"I'm sorry that he can't." My voice cracks. I've failed her, too.

She waves me away and looks about the room, at the furniture, the maids, the fire crackling in the fireplace, the dreary afternoon weather outside, anywhere but at me. She's dressed for the wedding in an elegant gown of deep blue and her hair and makeup are immaculate. She looks so much like me, it's almost like looking in a mirror. Especially with the sadness that lingers like a shadow.

"Well, you got what you wanted, Mother. I'm marrying Silas," I say simply and without malice. I am too tired. I am defeated. She has won.

She turns back to me and swallows hard, more sorrow weighing her down than was already there to begin with. "I never wanted it to be like this," she says, her voice low to keep the others from hearing. "So much has happened…" Her voice trails off. "Come now, let's visit your father's bedside one last time." She's holding back tears. "It's the least we can do given the circumstances."

I suck in a steadying breath and ask the question I've been too afraid to utter until now. "He's lost so much weight since I left. He looks like a ghost. How long has the doctor given him to live?" I know whatever it is, it's not going to be enough.

The idea was that a hex could keep him sleeping indefinitely but starvation would end his life sooner or later. The Occultist said it's not a hex but something much worse. But what could be worse than a spell specially meant to harm? Whatever it is, it's eating him alive before our eyes and we're helpless to stop it.

"Hours," she replies, wiping away a stray tear. "This is the end for him. It's time for us to say goodbye."

"Hours?" I gasp.

This news is so sudden, it feels like a load of bricks being dropped on my head. Tears burn at my eyes. The vast wall that has always existed between my mother and I seems to have crumbled in the wake of our shared tragedy. For all of our differences, we have our love for him in common. It's the one thing he's longed to see and it took his demise to make it happen.

But I *can't* cry with my wedding so close; Silas would be livid to have a bride stained with tears and without my magic, I can't risk his wrath. So I won't cry, not yet. I promise myself I'll be strong. I pick up my skirts and follow her out the door.

It's not far, only one chamber to the next. When we arrive, he isn't alone. Bellflower Blossom flutters above him, sprinkling her pixie dust all over his sleeping body. It glistens in the low light of the afternoon.

"What are you doing?" Mother dashes forward, waving her arms about. "Shoo! Get away!"

"It's okay," I interject and close the door firmly. "She's a friend."

Mother turns on me. "A pixie is your friend?"

Bellflower flies over and extends the tiniest hand. "I am and I mean no harm." Her voice is high and earnest. "I swear it."

Mom eyes me cautiously but I nod. She reaches up and shakes Bellflower's tiny hand.

I clear my throat. "Bellflower's here unofficially, if you know what I mean."

"Nobody has seen me yet." Bellflower spins in a circle, gold pixie dust flying off her. Mom rears back but I don't mind when the smallest bit lands on me. It gives me an instant boost, lifting my spirits fractionally. "I wanted to help Khali's father in this small way."

"What does that do?" Mother asks, pointing to the sparkling dust. It's mostly gone now, as if it's seeped into Father's skin. "Can it really help him?"

"It will make him feel better," Bellflower says, twirling around his body on her flowery wings. "I've never seen anything like this ailment before so I much doubt it will heal him but it can take away some of the pain."

"It's true." I nod, grateful for this small act of kindness. "I've felt it for myself."

Mother's lips tremble. "Thank you."

Bellflower nods and then dashes over to the window. It's open only an inch. "I'll leave you alone," she whispers softly. Then she slips through the window, heaving it shut with her little body, and disappearing into the cloudy sky.

Mom and I gape at each other, the sadness seeping back in. With the brief moment of distraction now gone, we have to face the reality and what we're here to do.

"Are you ready?" Mom asks.

I shake my head.

"Me neither."

She takes my hand in hers and sits at my father's side. I don't know how long we stay. Minutes? Hours? It's a surreal feeling to be saying goodbye to someone who hasn't died yet. But we both know death is on the horizon.

"You need to go back," Mother sighs. "We have a wedding to attend. I expect you to be on your best behavior. Smiles all around, please."

"Ah, there she is," I tease but it feels false. Will I ever be happy again?

As I stand to leave, my father seizes and convulses, body twisting in on itself. Mother grabs his hand in hers. "Paul! Paul, are you okay?"

His skin tone shifts from pale to purple and his chest heaves in violent bursts.

"What's happening?"

His eyes pop open, black from rim to rim, as if his pupils have blown. His scream follows—as wretched as a warcry and equally disturbing.

THIRTY-ONE
HAZEL

A BLACK SHAPE WHOOSHES PAST in my peripheral vision and I stumble back. Reapers swirl around Harmony's house, zeroing in on me like a pack of rabid animals. I count them, trying to stay calm—and failing miserably. There are six in total, and standing at a distance is Landon's ghost. I look to Dean but of course he can't see any of them.

What's wrong? His voice reverberates through my mind, startling me even more. *Hazel, can you hear me? Dragons can communicate telepathically but with you being so different I'm not sure this will work.*

I can hear you, I reply. *Can you hear me?*

Yes.

I'm relieved that I have a way to communicate with him. I don't know what I'd do without that lifeline. *Dean, there are reapers here. Six of them! I don't know what to do.*

Can you get out? You must be in the spirit realm even though I can see you, he responds.

If I shift back to being human, maybe, but I'm not sure how!

What do the reapers want?

Out of nowhere, one veers toward me, slamming my dragon to the cold ground before I can react. Its red eyes peer into me with so much hatred that my blood runs cold.

You killed my brother, it hisses.

I don't say anything back. Not that I don't want to but I can't in this dragon form.

You will pay for what you've done. It extends its bony hand from its black robe and a long scythe appears out of nowhere. *I will end you.*

No! Another reaper sweeps in and knocks the first one off of me. The scythe goes flying and they shoot into the air, fighting each other with their skeletal hands. I scurry backwards across the snow, keeping my eyes on the other reapers as they watch their brothers. The four who remain don't intervene but they do argue amongst themselves as they hover over and around me.

She's the only way back. There's nobody else who has her abilities.

Yes, and how is killing her going to help us?

Our fallen brother tried blood magic on her and it made him physical. Maybe we could do the same.

How is being physical going to change things?

We need to put her through the portal again.

I nearly succeeded and if I could have another go at her I know I'll be able to do it this time. The fourth reaper speaks as he hovers in front of me, closer than any of the others, almost possessively. An intense coldness wafts off of him and suddenly, I know he's the one who possessed me and took me into the lake. Landon floats over to hover closer to the reapers and just as before, he's not a normal human spirit but one trapped by these beasts. His eyes are entirely black and he slumps as if being held under an incredible weight.

Anger burns through my veins. Haven't they done enough to that poor boy? These reapers all look the same, but this one is the creepiest. The very idea of him possessing me again sends me flying into the air. I knock him to the ground and ram my dragon claws into his skeletal frame. He screams but I couldn't care less, he deserves worse. I try to rip him apart with my claws and teeth but he's so much stronger than he looks.

He throws me off in seconds and I hurtle through space, hit a tree, and crash to the ground. My head spins and my vision goes white. I blink rapidly, trying to orient myself. I'm somewhere back in the supernatural spirit realm, the white endless room I was in when I died before. This time, I'm in my dragon form.

Owen appears. "Who are you?" he asks, running at me. Then he shifts into his dragon and asks it again through the telepathic link. *Who are you?*

It's me, Hazel!

That stops him. His blue eyes glow with wonder and he looks me up and down. *You can travel between the physical and spirit realms? You're a dragon?*

I don't know! I don't know how any of this works!

The portals into the human world pop up all at once, just as they did when I was dead and visited my loved ones. In one I can see my mom, sleeping in her bed after a long swing shift. Cora and Macy in another; they're at The Roasted Bean, sitting in a booth and drinking steaming mugs of coffee. They'll be leaving for their flights soon. They're not alone. College-aged men sit next them. The four are laughing together, enjoying themselves. This must be the coffee date Cora mentioned. I can't place the man next to Cora exactly, my mind is a jumbled mess, but I know him somehow.

I'm distracted by the person in the third portal. It's Dean. He's shifted back to his human form and is calling my name as he walks around Harmony's property. His hair is a mess, blood covers his arms, and his face is a mask of panic. The reapers swirl around him, angry and yelling at each other. Landon stands at a distance, anguish stark on his face. Dean can't see or hear any of them and I'm afraid they're going to take their anger out on him.

I step toward the image and stick my dragon face through, about to move into the scene so I can help Dean before the reapers pounce. All at once, the six reapers turn on me.

Do you see that? one says, its voice a guttural cry.

That's it. I see home, another hisses.

All at once, they rush at me. I'm frozen with terror by those glowing red eyes and billowing black robes as they come for me. Owen says something but I can't hear him. When the reapers get to me, they don't actually hit me, instead, they rush right past, pushing me out of their way. In a heap, they move from the human spirit realm and into the supernatural one.

I stumble back into the endless white and watch, stunned, as they vanish, zipping off in all different directions.

A few seconds later, I stand back up and Owen's dragon nuzzles his head into my neck, and it feels like the dragon equivalent of a hug.

You did it, he says, *you must have opened a portal for the reapers to come back.*

I release a breath; the weight lifting off me is tremendous.

That's when an insane amount of that electric energy zaps through me. I rear back from Owen, not wanting to hurt him in the crossfire of whatever this strange lightning feeling is. Before I lose the chance, I jump back through the portal, landing on Harmony's back lawn with a painful thud.

Flat on my back, I blink up into the bright blue sky and hold up my hand. It's just a hand—a human hand, with five fingers. I wiggle them and sigh with relief. Dean's voice echoes from far off, frantically calling my name.

"I'm here!" I call as loud as I can.

He races over in seconds, pulling me to his lap and peppering my face with kisses. "I thought I lost you."

I quickly explain to him what happened. His expression is nothing short of awed.

"So they're gone? You did it?"

I nod.

He hugs me tight and warmth envelops my freezing body. "Of course you did!"

Well, they're not *all* gone. I look across the lawn to find Landon still standing there. His eyes have returned to normal and his entire demeanor is that of an incredible weight lifted. He's no longer imprisoned by those reapers but guilt still rocks me to the core, because I'm reminded that he's dead for having known me. Our eyes meet across the patch of snowy lawn and I'm frozen in place because it's time to answer to him for what has happened.

A break in the clouds shoots a stream of sunlight down on his spirit and he smiles, that genuine playful smile that made me like him in the first place. Someone appears beside him—not just anyone—an angel. His wings are twice the size of his broad frame and the whitest of whites, as if glowing from within. His armor is the exact color of a golden sunset and so beautiful, it's hard to look away. Angels never acknowledge me and this one is no different. He reaches a steady hand to Landon, and when Landon takes it, they both disappear.

I let out a breath, resting my face against Dean's shoulder, and allow the tears to come. We stay like that for a while, I'm not sure how long. We don't speak. Finally the pain of everything melts away enough for me to be able to think clearly.

Something about what happened today is tickling at the back of my mind but I can't quite grasp what it is. Unease settles deep into my bones. I need to remember...

We get up and walk back to his car, arm in arm, bloodied and injured, but at least we're alive. We're both introspective and quiet, and it feels so nice to just *be*. My mind wanders back over seeing my loved ones through the portals. I let out a strangled gasp.

"What's wrong?"

"It's Cora and Macy," I say, tears filling my eyes again. "They're at The Roasted Bean on their coffee date. I assumed the new guys they've been talking about were college students, but they're not, they're two of the dragons! Remember the one with the beard who flew off before the reapers showed up? It was him! I swear, Dean. He knows them somehow. He's there with them right now. Someone else is there too, probably one of the other dragons, I couldn't tell because I only saw the back of his head." I'm rambling, my mind and words going a mile a minute.

Dean's eyes have turned murderous. He throws open the car door. "Then let's go!"

I'm numb as we race through the streets, arriving at The Roasted Bean in a matter of minutes. I hurl myself from the car and run inside, frantically looking around the store and checking all the booths.

They're not here.

"Are you looking for your friends?" It's not the bearded man who speaks.

A man I've never seen before stands from where he sits sipping coffee at one of the tables. He's young, dressed in a crisp black suit, with the lightest amber eyes I've ever seen, so much so that they're almost gold. They stand out against his tanned skin and blonde hair. Something about him seems supernatural but I can't put my finger on what he could be. He doesn't feel like the dragons did.

Dean growls low and glares, pulling me to him. "What are you doing here?" Dean's voice is anything but calm. "Better yet, what are you?"

I have no idea what's going on except that Dean must know this man.

"Today I'm a messenger," the man says, "who has agreed to relay a message to both of you about her friends." When he points to me, my stomach drops. *No...*

"Where are they?" I ask, trying to keep my voice down.

He speaks so coolly, so casually, that around us, none of the other patrons seem to be aware of our altercation. "Since the dragons couldn't make you go come back to Drakenon with them," he says to me, "they found a way to get you to follow instead."

My stomach drops. "What are you saying?"

"They're already through the portal and on their way now. Your friends are with them."

"No!"

"How?" Dean asks.

The young man frowns. "Any mortal can go through as long as they're with someone who has elemental magic. I'm sure getting the humans through was easy."

"Let's go." Dean tugs me back.

"I have one last thing I'm supposed to say." The man's eyes lock onto Dean. "If you hurry, you can save Khali too."

This is a trap.

A trap to get Dean to go back to Drakenon so they can execute him. A trap to make me go there willingly so they can do who knows what to me. But even though it's a trap, it's one I'm going to walk right into if it means saving my friends. They'd do the same for me.

Dean gives the man one last long look. "Why?" he finally asks. "Why are you here?"

"To protect the humans," the man says, "but you already know that."

Dean takes my hand and we hurry back to the car. "We need to pack a few things and then I'll take you there myself," he says as the engine rumbles to life.

I swallow down my protests and nod. There's no way I can get to his kingdom on my own. I've never been to Eridas and only found out about my dragon thing today. We race down the quiet streets, heading toward his house. I grab my phone out of the cup holder where I left it charging earlier.

"I have to call my mom," I say. "I have to tell her I'm not going to be able to fly home tomorrow. I need to make something up. I don't know what but I can't have her worrying about me or filing a missing persons report or something."

Dean nods as I wait for her to answer. I press it to my ear and my hands shake so bad, I nearly drop it.

"Hello?" a familiar ethereal voice answers.

"Harmony?" I sit back, stunned, because I'd recognize that voice anywhere. "What are you doing with my mom's phone? What's going on? Are you okay? Where are you? Are you with her? Why'd you leave me?" The questions are quick to tumble out.

She's silent for a long moment. "We have so much to talk about, my darling Hazel. We can catch up when you get here tomorrow."

"That's the thing," I say, trying not to cry, "I'm not coming. I can't."

"You must!" Her voice is suddenly frantic. "I've seen you here. You must come here, it's the only way."

"No," I challenge, "I can't. I have to go through the portal and help my friends. They were kidnapped."

"Hazel, we need you *here in Ohio*. There are things I have to tell you, things about your past, things about your parents, your father, but I can't without—"

The line goes dead. I call it back but it goes straight to voicemail.

"What happened?"

I tell him everything and by the end, we're sitting in his driveway, frozen with an insurmountable choice. Do we go to Eridas after my friends? Do we go to Ohio to help Mom and Harmony?

It's an impossible decision.

He takes my hand and squeezes. "We're going to figure this out, okay? Together. I'm not going to leave you alone ever again."

I squeeze back but it's not that easy. I don't know what the right choice is to make here. I'm overcome with fear and all the possibilities of what could go wrong, but most of all, I'm afraid time is running out for Cora and Macy. Will they survive in a supernatural world? They're not meant to be there. I should listen to Harmony since she's helped me so many times before. She's always been on my side, that is, until she left me without saying a word.

"What does your gut say?" Dean asks.

That's easy. I can't leave my friends defenseless.

"We're going to Eridas."

THIRTY-TWO
KHALI

FATHER'S SCREAMS CEASE ABRUPTLY, HIS body going limp. He's eerily still and all I can I think is that he's dead and this is it. It's over.

Mother's cry is animalistic, ripping through the room and echoing off the stone walls. She drapes herself across him, clinging on to his body despite all her efforts to prepare for this. I turn away and a strange sort of numbness washes over me. I can't look at him any longer. It's too painful and I'd rather welcome this nothingness than the very real pain of losing my father.

"Paul!" Mother gasps. "Khali, he's awake!"

Despite my immediate disbelief, I turn back and rush over, almost tripping over my gown. Sure enough, Father's eyes are wide open and this time they're not black. Tears spring to my eyes and it takes everything in me to hold them back.

It's real.

This is *really* happening.

Relief washes through me and it's sweeter than anything. He's weak beyond belief but at least he's awake. "You're alive," I whisper and take his hand in mine. It's cool, but I can feel his pulse through the thin papery skin. I bring it to my lips and kiss it softly. My heart is so full. "Despite everything, you're alive."

Mother bursts into tears.

"But how?" I ask.

His chest rises and falls in quick bursts. "Where is it?" His voice is hoarse and the weight of those three words sends a zip of panic through me.

"Where is what?"

"That *thing*." His eyes dart about the room, delirious and searching for whatever this thing is he speaks of.

"There's nothing here, Love," Mother coos. "It's just us."

"No." His voice shakes and he tries to sit up. "It wouldn't let me go. It was in control but I fought it." He looks to me, his eyes frantic. "Khali, you have to stop it."

"Shh—" Mom runs a hand down his face, cupping it with her palm and getting him to look at her. "Relax. Whatever it was, it's gone now. I promise."

But she doesn't know that and neither do I. She shouldn't be making promises even if it is her way to get him to calm down.

"It's gone?" he asks, hope in his breathy voice.

"Yes," she assures him. She grabs the chalice of water from the bedside table and makes him drink. His body is ravaged but he's able to get most of it down. Once he's had enough, his eyes flutter closed, body melting into the bed, and breath slowing to a steady cadence as he falls asleep.

My mind has caught on to what he said about something tormenting him and I remember those terrible black eyes he had before. They were so similar to that boy I saw beside the lake, the human that the reaper had taken possession over and killed. Could it be that the same thing happened to my father? And if so, what could have caused a reaper to leave like that?

For the first time, I wish Hazel was here in Drakenon. She'd probably have the answers.

"I'll call for the doctor," I whisper and Mother nods.

"He'll need rest and hydration before he'll be able to eat anything," she says happily, "but now that he is himself again, there's got to be a chance he'll make it through."

"Yes, there has to be." I squeeze her shoulders.

And I believe it because how could anything else be possible? That would be too cruel.

"Thank you." A peaceful smile spreads across her face. I haven't seen that particular smile on her in ages. "I'll see you at the wedding. I know this is going to be hard for you but you'll get through it. Be strong."

My heart drops, and I leave the room, letting the closest maid know of my father's recovery. She scampers off to fetch the doctor, and I return to my chambers to settle my nerves before the wedding. When I tell Faros of our good fortune, she pulls me into a tight hug.

"See," she says, "it's going to be a good day. You'll see."

I smile and nod along as she prattles on about the court dramas I missed while I was gone. I feign interest and pretend to listen but I can't focus, unable to shake the feeling that something is wrong. It's like an itch I can't scratch; this knowing in the back of my mind that I'm missing something important. It's right in front of my eyes but I can't see it.

I STAND IN FRONT OF a set of intricately carved oak doors, taking deep breaths and trying to calm my jumbled mind. I've been through these doors countless times before, haven't I? All I can do is pray that the Gods will strengthen me as I go through them today. I'm not ready, but they swing open anyway. I glide into the chapel, forcing myself to put one foot in front of the other and walk down the aisle. The orchestra begins to play the traditional marriage song. I tune the melody out.

The guests stand. They're dressed in their finest and watch me with expressions of awe and envy. But it's not me they truly love or hate; it's the Brightcasters. Only the most valued members of court are in attendance. Many of them pretend to be friends to the royals but are actually enemies and would kill to usurp their throne and take it for their own. No matter what family was in charge, I'd still be queen. The treaties say so, the Gods say so, everybody says so.

Everybody except me.

I meet Silas's heavy gaze from across the room. The fake smile slips from my mouth. I can't help it. I don't want to marry him and I especially don't want all that comes with it. He stares at me with nothing save for victory and possession. There's no love there. He's won and he knows it. Behind him is the priest who will officiate the ceremony, and behind the priest, what's left of Silas's immediate family are neatly lined up. His mother has that glazed look in her eyes that I've seen so many times—the look of a woman who gave up on her magic long ago.

Next to her stands the King, his chin held high and jaw set. Bram is beside them, forgiven for his misdeeds because of the agreement I made. They're all dressed in beautiful silky golds that speak of their royal lineage. Bram stares at the floor, unable or unwilling to look at me.

On my side there is only my mother. She's as pretty as ever with much of the burden of my father's illness lifted off her shoulders. She gives me an encouraging smile and a nod as I approach the front of the church.

The sun must have decided to come out because a rainbow of colorful light filters through the stained glass windows and across the centuries old church. Elegant white flowers dripping in gold and silver jewels line the walls and aisle. It's beautiful but it's all wrong. I face Silas, and he takes my warm hands in his cold ones. He's all wrong, too.

The priest begins the ceremony. It's hard for me to listen to my freedom disappear. But what does it matter anyway? I've already lost my magic and my dragon. I have no hope of getting them back if I'm stuck here with a jailer for a husband. Maybe I should tell Silas. Certainly he'll want to help me restore my magic considering it's my only value to him. But then a thought strikes that leaves me reeling: What if it's all still in my blood and even though I can't access it, I can still have elemental dragon shifter children? If that's the case, then this would be a huge win for Silas. He'd never have to worry about struggling to control me. He'd always be stronger.

My palms sweat and my heart skids against my breastbone. I force myself to look at Silas and it's like forcing myself to look at my own death.

It's time to say the vows, and as is tradition, Silas goes first. It's easy for him. There's not one ounce of hesitation as he pledges himself to me. His eyes cage me in as he speaks the few lines. I might be sick. He squeezes my hands and wrists so tight, I'm sure there will be bruises later.

When it's my turn, I can't do it. I can't say the words that will bind me to a man I hate. He killed my best friend. He wants me for nothing more than to secure himself as the next king. He will use me and destroy me and won't care. He'll be unfaithful, taking other lovers and rubbing it in my face, embarrassing me in front of my peers. He'll keep me in a gilded cage, never letting me be free, to be the woman I was meant to be. He'll do all these things and perhaps the worst part is he'll enjoy every bit of it.

I can't do this.

I try to turn away, but I'm unable, like tiny invisible chains are forcing me to stay put. I will my mouth closed, but it opens to speak anyway. The unseen magic created by the deal I made with King Titus sparks to life. I'm powerless to stop it; I have no choice. No, it's not that I don't have a choice; it's that I already made my choice the second I shook hands with the King and agreed to this marriage. After that, there was never going to be an opportunity to turn back. I knew it, but the reality of it still hurts.

I look around, frantic, catching the eyes of Silas's family. Titus is clearly pleased. Brysta appears conflicted but stays quiet as usual. And Bram? Bram looks heartbroken. His bright as summer eyes cling to me as they've never done before. My heart breaks, too. The magic of my agreement forces me to look away before I'm ready.

"I do take thee, Silas Skylen Brightcaster, to be my husband." My voice is clear. Solid. true. "Leaving my father and mother, I will cleave to you, as is the Gods' will, and as is my will as your wife." My voice is one I can hardly call my own. "This is my solemn vow."

My ears ring. My body shakes. The priest speaks again and then Silas guides me to him. Gripping my head between his long fingers, he presses his lips to mine. His spicy citrus smell surrounds me. A soft string of his icy blonde hair brushes against my cheek. One large hand squeezes tighter into my hair until my scalp stings. The other is tight against my waist. This is his victory and his way to lay claim to what is his and only his.

The crowd cheers.

When he pulls away, his blue-lavender stormy eyes are the clearest I've ever seen them. He's always been a tormented man, even as a child, and it's as if he's found peace at long last. He smiles and he's so devastatingly handsome I could cry. It was never supposed to be this way.

"No!" Queen Brysta's cry is sharp as a blade. "Bram, no!"

Horror rakes my body the second I realize what I'm seeing is actually happening and not some terrible nightmare.

Bram has stepped back from King Titus. A knife protrudes from the King's chest, right where his heart should be beating. His eyes are wide with disbelief and his expression tainted by utter betrayal. He tries to speak but all that comes out is a gurgling cough and then an arcing splatter of blood. He falls to his knees first, the marble floor second. His crown clatters and rolls away. Blood pools around him, dark crimson and widening by the second.

Within seconds, he's dead.

The guests are silent for what feels like an eternity before everything erupts into chaos. Brysta drops to her husband, screaming incoherently. Guards rush forward, apprehending Bram. Bram screams in a guttural language and fights against his captors. I've heard this before—it's the same language the Occultist used to perform blood magic. He thrashes out at anyone who comes close, unusually strong, throwing them off with ease. When I try to rush forward to help, Silas holds me back.

"Let me go!" I scream, failing to rip myself from Silas's iron grip.

Bram looks up at me, and I stop short with a horrified gasp. His eyes aren't the normal pretty green I find so captivating, the green from minutes before. They're entirely black. Black like how my father's were. Black like how that human boy's were. Black as midnight. Depthless. Evil. Void.

And that's when I know what's happening.

Silas breaks away, pushing me back, and raises his hand toward his brother. Wind whips into the room, ripping the white flowers from their stems. He directs the wind at Bram, suffocating him. Wind isn't something Bram can fight, not even with this darkness in control. Bram sinks to his knees, his face going red and purple.

"No," I scream. "Stop! It's not him!"

Nobody understands nor can they hear me over the panicked yelling and the shrill scream of the wind. Bram collapses to the ground, about to lose consciousness. The black possessing his eyes leaves, transforming them back to green. He looks around, suddenly confused, scared and alone. He's dying and there's nothing he can do to stop it.

He reminds me of Owen.

I make a snap judgement, knowing it might cost me everything, but I couldn't live with myself if I did nothing. I dive onto Bram and hold him tight against my body. The wind rustles around me, wild and alive with magic. I sputter, unable to breathe. My hair flies everywhere. My eyes water and I have to squeeze them shut. I could let go but I won't. I can't leave Bram defenseless.

This isn't his fault!

The wind stops. I still cling to Bram but open my eyes. The chapel is a mess of strewn flowers and broken glass, and almost everyone is gone including my mother. All that's left is the royal family and a few of their most trusted guards.

"What are you doing?" Silas glares at me. "Get off him! He murdered a royal, a king, he'll die for this!"

"Don't you dare speak to me about murdering royals," I hiss.

"Khali," Silas sneers, coming in close. Lightning snaps between his fingers. "Don't make me forcefully remove you because I will. He just killed my father in front of all the nobility! What else am I supposed to do here?"

"Listen," I say. "Please, just listen to me. That wasn't Bram."

"We all saw it!"

"No," I challenge. "You don't understand. It was the Occultist's blood magic that took over Bram and made him do that. It was a reaper in possession of his mind. I swear to you! Didn't you see his eyes go black? That was the magic! I saw it before. I've seen it *twice* before!"

Silas falls silent, thinking through my claims. All that can be heard are Queen Brysta's sobs over her fallen husband. The guards shift uncomfortably, standing in a circle around us with swords drawn, waiting for their orders. One of the guards is in his dragon form, blocking the door, his razor sharp teeth and knife-like claws on display.

"We'll hold a trial and decide if what you're saying proves to be true," Silas says at last.

"Thank you." And I mean it. I mean it so much that gratitude rings in my ears.

"Now get the hell off of him so my guards can take him to the dungeon where he belongs." Silas's eyes darken and his lip curls. I force myself to release Bram.

The guards converge and he is whisked away in a matter of seconds. As he goes, he catches my gaze and my heart breaks all over again. There's nothing but sorrow and guilt written on his face. Even though what happened wasn't his choice, I know he'll never forgive himself. The oak doors slam and he's gone.

Silas pulls me back to standing next to him and wraps an arm around my side, his large hand spreading over my rib cage. His whisper is close, breath hot against my ear, "Go get yourself cleaned up," he says. "My father's enemies will be thrilled at this new development. We must act fast before they take this opportunity to advance their cause."

"And do what?"

"Congratulations," he says softly. "Turns out this is not only your wedding day but your coronation day. You and I must secure the throne as soon as possible."

I swallow hard, the weight of the world coming down on me all at once.

"That's right," Silas says. His lips are soft against my ear. "It seems that you and I won't have to wait to be crowned King and Queen."

"But—"

"Fight this and your parents will pay," he snaps. "I heard of your father's recovery. Could your mother bear to lose him after all that she's been through?"

I try to step back but he squeezes tighter. He runs his nose along my cheek, breathing me in, and I shiver with fear.

"It's time we take what's rightfully ours."

I close my eyes and will my magic to return. Nothing happens. My anger is white hot and useless. I'd give anything to deny him but I know that's impossible. I'll find a way to fight back, a way to fix this, a way to best my husband. For now, I have to give in. Silas has won.

Throne of Embers

NOT QUITE MIDNIGHT

HIS MASTER DIDN'T GLARE, NOR did he curl his lip. His hands were relaxed, not balled into fists. But his master was angry—very angry. The Occultist was sure, deep down where his blood churned with magic, where bone lay parallel to soul, that his master would never forgive him.

This wasn't simple anger, or disappointment, or frustration... it was red-hot seething hatred. It couldn't be satiated with apologies or excuses, not even if they were true and wholly justified. All that burning hate directed right at the Occultist caused a tremor of fear to rocket down his body—a juvenile reaction. He hadn't felt this way since his long-ago days as an apprentice.

"Master," he said, bowing low and keeping his voice smooth as glass, "the dragon king is dead by his son's own hand. This is cause for celebration."

"And what of Khali?" The master tilted his head, red eyes glowing and burgundy robe pulled so high around his face that it cast shadows over his mouth. "Is the elemental princess still alive?"

They both knew the answer to that question, unfortunately. The Occultist swallowed, nodded once, and then fell to his knees. "I have failed you. I will take my punishment."

Anticipation swept over the crowd. He wasn't alone with his master, not here, not now, not this time. Most of his brethren were in attendance tonight, as many as could be spared. This gathering was important. They needed all that bonded magic in one place—all that blood—if the spell was going to work.

He felt the heaviness of their judgement like he felt the sweat on the back of his neck, like he felt God Himself frowning down at him. Him, the failure, the son with all the favor who still couldn't fulfill the mission.

How could he have been so confident that the spell would work? Khali had been right there. For days, she'd traveled with him, her veins soft as butter, her mortal heart beating behind its flimsy cage, her neck long and elegant, so easy for twisting. He'd had ample opportunities to kill her but he hadn't because her death wasn't supposed to be at his hands. It was supposed to be Bram.

It still was. So why had Bram killed King Titus instead?

Bram. The false prince. The weak link of the Brightcaster family, the one God had given directly to him so he could spell a reaper to the boy's soul and they could be done with the dragons. But Bram failed, Bram was to blame, and one day Bram would die for it. He'd seen the hungry looks the boy had given the princess. He knew of the longing behind those searching eyes and the raspberry flush in those mortal cheeks. Whatever feelings Bram had harbored for the girl, they must have been strong enough to cause him to resist the reaper and turn his task toward another instead. Was the king merely in the wrong place at the wrong time or had the reaper chosen Titus as a second option? No matter. It couldn't be undone now.

As if reading his thoughts, his master interrupted them. "How much can you blame Bram? This is your doing. If you'd been better able to spell the reaper, if your blood had been stronger, you'd have succeeded and Bram would have, too."

He nodded, crestfallen. "Yes."

It was true. All true.

The master held his gaze for another long second, and then like a slap, turned away, his attention leveled on the encircling crowd. Maybe one of the others would be able to succeed where he'd failed. Or maybe it wouldn't take only one warlock, but all of them, collectively, to fulfill destiny.

That's why they were here, wasn't it? That was the purpose of this gathering. It was time to complete the ritual, to mend what the spirit elemental girl had broken, and to bind what was always meant to be bound.

The pale sandstone walls behind them flickered with the firelight. Flames swirled before them in the center of the dias, dancing flashes of deep red, hot orange, and bright blue. Soon the flames would be black with magic.

The Occultist fell back into the circle of his brothers, eager to blend into the sea of robes and pale unaged faces. They all looked the same; only the slightest variations set the warlocks apart from one another. This oneness was ingrained into their blood magic, and when Khali took that from him, reminding him of what it would be to be entirely mortal again, he'd nearly lost his mind. To be one small identical part of this larger whole was lifegiving compared to being a single identity without purpose. That had been torture. Punishment enough. He would not fail again.

Their master initiated the chant, his voice rolling heavy over the landscape, and they all followed in unison, growing louder, voices and faces rising into the night. The stars glistened above, paying tribute. The humid air wrapped around them in a soft embrace. The fire grew taller, wider, darker. The flames transformed from colorful and alive to black and even more vibrant.

This was it. He could feel it in his blood, in the way they were connected, stronger together. He could feel it in the blackness of the raging fire and the silent mirth of the watchful stars. The magic was growing stronger. The reapers, they were drawing closer, closer, closer.

He couldn't see them. No Sovereign Occultist could see them. But he knew they were there.

Perhaps this was what faith was, believing in the unseen things, knowing the unknowable.

Faith and obedience.

First, they would rid the earth of elemental magic—they were nearly there. Second, they would finish the bleeding of the realms, combining the mortal realm with this superior one. And finally? Finally, things would be as they were meant to be, where blood magic created an obedient race and everything and everyone bowed to the one true God.

This was their ultimate task, holy as it was. Squash the evil. Purge the impure. Combine the realms. And then the whole earth would be washed clean.

He would be washed clean—clean and forgiven.

An unknown energy snapped through them, the magic crackling and steaming—a small fire being smothered by an ocean. The shared bond fractured, releasing them from the reapers. The eerie sense of otherness that signaled a reaper was near evaporated quickly, like the thin wisps of smoke coming off of the newly departed fire. Their chanting slowed into a thick silence, like a shared drowning.

A sharp terror ran down the Occultist's body, every muscle coiled tight. A failure now could only mean one thing: the master was growing weak. They would have to strengthen their sovereign bond again, which could put everything they'd accomplished at risk. It put them at risk. Their lives. Their magic. Everything.

They needed a sacrifice.

The master screamed, his guttural voice slicing through the silence. When they all turned to look at him, and not the master, the Occultist felt the crushing weight of his failure all over again. They had trusted him. They had chosen him. And now they hated him.

"I will make this right," he vowed, speaking through clenched teeth. A sense of rightness filled his entire body. "I will sacrifice myself to strengthen the whole."

Somehow, he knew this would happen, that one day he'd volunteer himself over to the blood-bond. But he didn't realize it would happen this way—that it would be tonight—that this breath, this flesh, this moment, would be his last.

His master stepped close and before the Occultist could react, a searing pain pierced his heart straight through. His blood ran hot and then cold. He fell to the pebbled ground, gasping for air. When he tried to beg, there was nothing left in his lungs. The last thing he saw were the red eyes of his master, moving closer. Blood magic took over, filling him with terror and then peace. The two battled within until both drifted away, until he was everything and he was nothing.

Maybe this was forgiveness. Maybe this was mercy. Maybe this was merely the price God wanted him to pay, the price that would cost his life.

ONE
HAZEL

I SWALLOW HARD AND STARE at the icy lake, my boot edging along the crusted snow. My coat is way too thin and the morning air wraps around me like a million frozen fingerprints. Dean insists that once we get through to the other side of the portal, I won't need the extra heavy stuff, so we left it behind. The Summer Forest is just as it sounds: a fae forest stuck in a perpetual state of summer. Even at night it's going to be warm. At least I won't have to worry about freezing to death when I get over there. I'll be too worried about every other little thing I see and hear and smell.

"Are you ready for this?" Dean reaches out and intertwines his fingers with mine. A wave of heat passes through my body. I smile into his fiery eyes and lean in for a simple kiss. The scruff on his chin tickles my face as I breathe in his wonderful smoky rain scent. My already thumping heart picks up a beat. I spent the night tangled in his arms and more than anything, I want to crawl back into that warm bed with him, but I know we can't.

"As ready as I'll ever be," I say, letting out a huff of visible air.

Which is to say, no, I'm not ready, but too bad—we're going in anyway!

Turns out, running away takes careful planning. We couldn't take off immediately, not when there were loose ends to tie up. Believe me, I wanted to go right after leaving the café, my mission to save my friends firmly planted in my mind. But I had to be reasonable because I also didn't want Cora and Macy's families to think something terrible had happened to them. The first thing we did after getting back to Dean's place was have him hack into their school accounts and shoot emails off to their parents. We made up some bogus story about them going with friends on a last minute Christmas vacation to Switzerland—*c'mon Mom and Dad, it's the opportunity of a lifetime*—and promised they'd be in touch as soon as they could. A terrible lie, I know, but it's better than leaving their parents filing a missing person's report. I can only imagine how my mom would react if I disappeared without a trace.

"You want me to carry that?" he asks, nodding toward the backpack I've heaved over my shoulders. I shake my head. His is even bigger.

Dean and I spent the better part of last night packing these backpacks, filling them with weapons, gear, food, and clothing. He added a few guns even though they probably wouldn't work in Eridas, as well as some sharp knives and a bunch of scary crap I have no clue how to use. And then there's his fire elemental magic, the next level of weapon. Thinking about fighting off bad guys makes my stomach feel all hollow and weird.

"Don't worry," I add. "I threw in a few candy bars last night too. You know, just in case chocolate isn't a thing over there."

He smirks. "It's not."

That seems unreasonable. "Well, what can I say? This girl has priorities."

"And you're sure about this?" It's the same question he's been asking since we decided to do this instead of going to Ohio like Harmony wanted.

Before going to sleep last night, he went over and over what I should expect in the days to come. We're going to be traveling through parts of Eridas where it might not be safe to eat the food, especially in the fae forest. We're also not going to talk to anyone we meet along the way, not unless he thinks it's okay. When we get the chance to fly, we will, but that's not always safe outside of Drakenon. And once in Drakenon, I'm not to leave his side. Not once. Trust nobody. And certainly don't fight unless it's in self defense.

Eridas. Drakenon. The Summer Court and the Fae forest…

These are all new to me and belong to this other realm that I apparently belong to as well—considering I'm a freaking dragon shifter! I can hardly believe it but there's no denying it now, not after what happened yesterday. Dean confessed that he wasn't entirely surprised; he smelled dragon on me the moment he met me, which is why he was so hostile at first. He thought I was a spy sent from one of his father's rivals. But he also smelled something else, something he wasn't sure how to describe or where it came from. And what did surprise him? The crazy form my dragon self took: a spirit dragon that seems to belong to both the spirit realm and our physical one. This is not something he's ever heard of and neither of us have any real clue as to what it means or how I'm going to supposedly defeat the Sovereign Occultists—if Harmony is to be believed.

I guess the spirit elemental runs deeper within me than any of us knew.

And I guess Harmony has secrets of her own, considering she called me from my mom's phone yesterday and we haven't been able to reach them since. My phone is now wrapped up in the waterproof backpack or I'd be tempted to pull it out and try again.

I hate this.

I want to make sure Mom's okay and I want to talk to Harmony. But I need to save my friends right now. I know for a fact they're in danger and every second I'm not going after them is a second guilt drums hard against my chest.

They'd have never gotten into this mess if they hadn't met me.

I let out a slow breath and nod to Dean. "Let's go."

Together, we leave the safety of land and run out onto the ice. It gives way almost immediately. My heart nearly explodes as we plunge under the surface. We pop back up and he keeps a tight grip on my hand, pushing the warmth from his fire elemental into my body. It helps. But I'm still terrified. I've never been much of a swimmer and images of the reaper possessing my body and forcing me into this very lake on that awful morning not long ago pierces my mind. We swim out to the middle of the lake, chunky slabs of ice floating around us. I suck in little breaths of freezing air and splashes of what feels like the coldest water on earth.

He kisses me once more. Quick.

"I'm ready," I say. I'm shivering like crazy and he shoots another blast of warmth into my body. He holds my gaze with his. He's so sure, confident and strong. He believes in me and that means the world. We take another deep breath and slide under the surface. Time to swim. Water surrounds everything, me, him, our slick backpacks, our black athletic clothing. We swim into the true blue of it until it grows darker, blacker, riskier. And then, as Dean promised, there's a glow of rainbow lights swirling along the bottom of the lake.

The portal to Eridas.

We kick harder, moving closer, and a thrill of anticipation pushes its way past the fear. *Here we go. Time to be brave.*

Something black floats at my right, catching my attention.

I stop swimming.

A reaper hovers in the water. Otherworldly, dark cloak, red glowing eyes, skeletal.

No!

I want to scream, to tell it to go away, but I can't.

It rushes toward us, and Dean pulls me after him. He can't see the things I see so he has no idea the reaper is beside us. Maybe we should have shifted into our dragon forms before swimming down here because at least then we could have talked to each other. Why didn't we do that? Oh that's right, Dean suggested it, but I'd been too worried about shifting again, not ready to take the leap quite yet.

Stupid, stupid, girl!

Go back, the reaper urges. His voice is different than all the other times I've heard the reapers before. This one is calmer. I'd freed them from whatever spell they were under, hadn't I? I sent them back to their spirit realm. So why was one here?

Go back now! He says again, his raspy voice louder in my mind, no longer so calm.

We keep swimming. The reaper can't touch us now.

At least, I hope it can't.

The Occultists are on the other side of the portal, the reaper says again, his thoughts so clear in my mind that for a flash, I can see what he sees. Men in burgundy robes line the shore, chanting in succession. Their eyes are glowing red, similar to the reapers. Their skin is stark white and they all look the same: bald, ageless. Maybe young. Maybe old. Definitely cultish and creepy. It's one of the strangest things I've ever seen and deep down in my gut, I'm terrified. I cannot face these men.

They'll kill you the second they see you, he says, *that's what they want. You. Dead.*

It's odd, trusting a reaper, but my gut tells me I can. Somehow, I know he's right. He's not trying to hurt me or possess me or use me. He's trying to warn me. And there's something else in his tone, too. Gratitude. Yes, for freeing him from the human spirit realm where he didn't belong.

You must go back, he hisses again, urgency rising.

We're almost to the swirling glow of colors of the portal and the air in my lungs is nearly gone. I tug Dean back with all my force, shaking my head at him when he turns to me with a questioning look on his watery face.

"No!" I scream, my voice muffled by the water and pushing the last of the oxygen from my lungs in a stream of bubbles.

Dean's eyes are wide and confused but he nods once and then swims the two of us to the surface. My lungs are pure fire, panic racing through my veins. An inky darkness edges around my vision. I don't have much time. *It hurts...* We break through the water and I gasp, letting air fill me even though it's agony, like experiencing hell and heaven all at once.

"Are you okay, Hazel?" He holds me above the water, fingers gripping my skin.

"There was a reaper," I say between gasps. "A reaper down there."

"Come on," Dean says, and we swim to the shore and climb out of the lake. He sends another blast of heat through me as soon as we make it to shore. My hands are pressed against my knees as I hunch over, trying to catch my breath and organize my thoughts.

"What happened?" Dean asks, kneeling before me and brushing a loose strand of hair from my eyes. His compassion is a beautiful thing and I'm quick to brush my lips against his before explaining.

"The reaper down there was protecting me from the portal. He told me we couldn't go through. He said the Occultists are on the other side waiting for me." I try not to sob but the tears come anyway and my voice grows thick. "I saw them. He showed me. They're the same men in the robes I saw when Harmony and I did the blood magic. They're evil. And they'll kill us the second we get to the other side of the portal. It's what they want."

Dean is silent. He closes his eyes for a minute and then nods.

"Okay," he says, "so we can't go through this one. We'll have to find another portal."

He's mentioned there are more but I assumed he knew where they were.

"Find?" I ask. "Where's the next closest one?"

He shakes his head and stands, stretching out his back. "I don't know."

I stand too, anxiety snaking its way down my spine. I shake it off before it holds on for dear life. "Well in that case, I guess we're going to Ohio."

"Ohio?"

"If anyone knows where another portal is, it's got to be Harmony, right?"

He lets out a little laugh, even though I know he must be as frustrated as I am. "Right. I guess the faerie called it. She said we needed to come to her first and we're coming to her first after all."

"Well, she can see the future," I sigh, leaning into him. "I should've listened."

As we hike back to the car, a pesky feeling of unease sits low in my stomach. My friends went through that portal only yesterday. Are they okay? Did the occultists get to them when they passed through? Or are they still on their way to Drakenon? Maybe they're already there. It's crazy to hope they're still with the dragons but I do, because if there is anyone worse than those dragon shifters, it's the creepy men lining the lake on the other side of the portal, who apparently, want nothing more than to see me dead.

Once we're back in the car, I retrieve my phone, slide into the passenger seat, blast the heater, and call Mom. It goes directly to voicemail. Why does it keep doing that?

I know it's only been one day and she sometimes works long shifts at the hospital, but this isn't like her. Something is wrong.

I spring from the car because I don't want to shift in a moving car and focus my mind on turning into a dragon. It doesn't work. Nothing happens.

Dean stands with his door open, gaping at me.

"How do you do it?" I ask. "I want to change so I can go through the spirit realm and check on my mom."

He shakes his head once. "I just do it," he says. "It's as natural as a thought coupled with an action. Like choosing to walk."

"It's not so easy for me," I grumble. "I don't know how I managed it the first time."

"Necessity?"

I let out a bitter laugh. "You could say that." Considering I accidentally shifted into a spirit dragon when I was trying to fight off our assailants and save Dean, his theory makes perfect sense. But I can't wait until I'm in mortal danger every time I need to shift.

"I've got to figure this out." I climb back into the car and buckle in. "Let's get to Ohio as fast as we can. I have a bad feeling."

"About what?" He starts the car and pulls onto the two-lane highway, tires crunching over the icy gravel.

Once again, I can't help but laugh. "Umm—how about everything."

TWO
KHALI

I'M A MARRIED WOMAN NOW.

Royal matrimony. Sealed forever. Crowned as Queen. Silas, my king.

I still can't believe this is real.

I press my hands into my stomach and try to breathe. My corset digs into my ribcage. My lungs burn. I need to take this thing off! I rip through material, fingers fumbling to pull lace through the grommets. It slowly releases and my bones ache even more. I drop the dress to my chamber's floor and stumble to the window. My underclothes are loose, which helps, but I need more air. There's latticed iron along the outside of my window but I throw open the panes anyway to let the cold breeze in. It extracts me from the panic until I'm able to relax, breathe, and think.

This new life hasn't quite settled in yet, probably because everything happened so fast. The rushed coronation took place the very same evening as our wedding day, despite the obvious displeasure shown from most of the court. Silas didn't care. He saw to it that we were crowned as quickly as possible before anything could happen to another Brightcaster. Through the whole thing, the chanting and the vows and the hushed reverence and whispers, I didn't smile. Not one time. I couldn't fake it anymore.

The last few days have been a blur of trapped emotions and long stares. I'm boiling over from the silence instead of letting the bitter truth spill from my tongue. I can't stand up to Silas right now. What good would it do? Bram's trial is set to start tomorrow and he can't afford Silas to be in a bad mood. We both know what Silas is capable of. If he can murder his twin brother in cold blood, no doubt he can and will do the same to Bram. And me standing up for Bram? It might just lead to that.

I don't know what to do...

So I stand at the window for ages, staring out into the blanket of fresh white snow that has covered the city below and the rolling hills beyond. I stand and stand and think and think and no matter how long I do it, I still don't have any solutions. For now, Silas has allowed me to stay here in my own chamber. That won't last long. At least he's agreed to give Bram a fair trial, unlike so many others in the king's position who would have struck first and asked questions later—that's if they'd have asked questions at all.

Can anyone be trusted in Eridas? As far as I know my fae friends can, but I've barely seen or spoken to them these last few days. Silas told everyone they're our guests, but it's unmistakable from the distrustful ways people stare at them that they're not welcome. My friends are not going to want to stay here for long if this keeps up. It's probably not the safe haven they were hoping for. The betrayal of that vile Sovereign Occultist still stings as fresh as the day it happened. I've chastised myself over and over for trusting him in the first place, for believing that he would be bound to the same agreements that the rest of us are. Beating myself up about it isn't helpful, but I can't seem to stop, not when there's nobody else to blame.

This is my fault.

Frustrated, I seek my magic as I've done time and time again over the last few days. But it's still absent. And my dragon, my other self, she's still gone. Tears well up in my eyes. The sun sets behind the mountains. The sky turns dark.

Someone knocks and Faros lets herself in, as she's done a thousand times before. Today, however, her face is void of color and her large round eyes can't quite meet mine. Something is wrong. Even with her elegant gown and pretty headdress and perfectly stoic expression, I know it. *I know her.*

"What is it?" My voice trembles.

"Your new chambers..." Her words taper off and I know exactly why she's come here.

I'm not an Elliot anymore. I'm a Brightcaster. Silas and I are expected to move into the King and Queen's chambers. At least they have separate bedrooms. Connected by a sitting room and only two doors, but separate nonetheless. It's a small thing but to me it's everything.

"What about my new chambers?" I push, making her say it.

"They're ready for you," she says, her tired eyes finally looking up to hold mine. There's something else there. Something more.

"What aren't you telling me?" It's a silly question. Once again, I already know.

She squares her shoulders. "It's been three days since the wedding and you still haven't spent the night with your husband."

"Yes, that's true." I hold my breath and fight the bubble of nausea rising into my throat. So far Silas has allowed me to keep my virtue intact, not making me entertain him in his chambers.

"That ends tonight," she finishes with a small smile. "Silas expects you to go to him. Everything is ready."

I squeeze my eyes shut and let out the breath. What am I supposed to do? Fight him off forever? Give in to him even though the very thought of his mouth on my skin makes me want to scratch my own eyes out?

"Fine." My voice sounds so much stronger than I expected. I pause to look out the window one last time. The white snow is a stark line against the black sky. It practically glows under the moonlight. "I'll go now. I might as well get it over with."

"It will be fine," she says, smiling the kind of smile that doesn't reach her eyes. The usual sparkle is gone from them. Even though she's trying to make me feel better about this entire situation, she knows this was never what I wanted. And now I'm stuck. She's quick to dress me, making me beautiful as she's done for years—for a life that might kill me—and now for the very man brandishing the knife.

My hair is brushed into loose curls that waterfall down my back. She finishes with a white silk cape, tying it securely to hide the flimsy lace underclothes beneath. As she escorts me to my new chambers, the drafty hallway makes my flesh prickle. At least I tell myself it's the cold. Only the cold. Admitting to the ocean of fear raging inside feels like admitting to the loss of something I'll never be able to get back. And I don't want to think about that. I've already lost too much.

She ushers me past the set of armed guards waiting at the doors and into the king and queen's chambers. She wraps me up in a quick hug and then is gone before I can collect my thoughts well enough to say goodbye. The huge engraved doors shut me inside with a heavy thud and I spin around.

It's dark in here, but not dark enough. I'm not alone.

Silas stands near the hearth where a crackling fire gently lights up the room. It illuminates the sharp planes of his face and the lightness of his blond hair. He's dressed in loose fitting jet-black linen trousers but no shirt. The black color reminds me of the night outside, his dark cotton contrasting my white silk. The sight of his tanned bare chest makes my throat go dry and my eyes water.

I've been in the royal chambers before to sit with the queen and her ladies but I've never been in this room. It's too private for my liking.

As if reading my thoughts, Silas nods toward one of the doors. "Shall I show you around your new home?"

If I speak, I won't have nice things to say, so I shrug.

He leads the way into the queen's chambers first. The bedroom is double the size of mine, filled with expensive silks and extravagant tapestries, hand carved furniture, and gold-framed paintings of the prettiest spots in Drakenon. I catch sight of a painting of the Jeweled Forest and shiver, wanting to strike that horrid place from my mind forever. There are other smaller rooms attached to this one for bathing and dressing, and then, of course, another room beyond for her to meet with her ladies. Why do I keep thinking of the queen as someone else? It's me. I'm the queen now. Brysta has been moved to another part of the castle to make way for me, and like it or not, here I am.

"It's nice," I manage, my voice straining. Silas doesn't seem to notice because he takes that in stride with a proud expression, as if this ornate room was somehow going to make up for the fact that he murdered his way to get me in here.

There are no reminders of Titus or Brysta; it's as if they've been swept away.

He leads me back into the sitting room. "This space is just for us," he says, clearly enjoying this little tour of ours, "well, and our future children."

He's so confident, so pleased with himself. I want to slap that smirk right off his face. I want nothing more than to get out of these rooms and never ever return. Maybe I can find a way to get back to Hazel and she can help me restore the magic. Or perhaps I need to find that necklace of Silas's and destroy it. Could it have something to do with my magic's disappearance? It seems unlikely but at this point I'm growing desperate.

I need a plan. What's my plan? Realizing I have none leaves me ice cold.

But of a few things I'm certain: I have to find a way to get my magic back, figure out how to punish Silas for what he's done, make sure to save Bram, and put a stop to the Occultists once and for all.

I squeeze my eyes shut for a second, overwhelmed beyond reason.

"Come," Silas says, breaking my thoughts and striding over to the door opposite mine. "Let me show you my room."

My stomach flips. I wonder, does it still smell like King Titus? Could they have erased him so quickly as they did Brysta from my room? He hasn't even been buried yet. His body is in the chapel and won't be laid to rest for three days as his soul is blessed and his people pay their respects. Now there's a smell that will take a while to cleanse, no matter the amount of incense burned. At least elemental magic will be used to help keep his body cold.

The king's room is not much different than the queen's to look at, but it *feels* so vastly different. Suddenly, the energy between Silas and me is charged. Not only with the elemental magic storming behind his lavender eyes, but with something else too. Anticipation prickles off of him. Hatred pours off of me.

Does he mistake the hate for something else? Or maybe he likes it.

He inches closer and I freeze, unable to move. "Don't worry," he says, gently pulling the ribbon that holds my cape together. The silk robe falls to the ground, pooling at my bare ankles. I force myself to stand tall, don't let him see my fear. His eyes rove hungrily over my body. No man has ever seen me like this. "I'll teach you what to do. You'll like it."

He'll teach me because he's been doing this for Gods know how long and plans to continue to keep his mistresses even though he has me. He considers himself above the rules. And it's suddenly clear to me that he's been thinking about the possibility of this night for years. I still can't move. I hate him. I hate him for this. I hate him for Owen. I hate him for stealing what shouldn't be his. When his mouth captures mine, it takes everything within me not to bite him, to push him away, to scream. To cry.

I stand frozen, eyes closed as tight as they can possibly go. I can't force myself to kiss him back. And when his body presses flush against mine and he wraps his warm arms tight around my waist, his hands splayed out across my prickling skin, I don't match his movements. I don't raise my hands. Don't kiss. Don't do anything. My mind is traveling far, far away. My body may have to stay, but I will not. He still doesn't know I've lost my magic. The mere thought hollows out my chest. I am an empty vessel; everything that was me, that is me, has been taken. And Silas, he is going to keep on taking until there is nothing left.

Suddenly I'm met with a blast of cold air.

"You're not even going to try?" he growls angrily.

My eyes pop open.

Silas is several feet back, raking his hand through his pale hair, cheeks flushed and temper rising. He stares at me like I've slapped him. Perhaps doing nothing is worse than a slap to a man like Silas. I can't help it, I feel smug, and it feels good.

"You're my wife," he seethes.

I don't know what to say. If I anger him too much, he might take it out on Bram tomorrow. I want to yell all the hateful things running through my mind but instead, I keep it all locked away and continue to do absolutely nothing.

"What is it?" He glares. "Do you really find me revolting? Do you wish I were Dean? Or pathetic Bram? Or is it Owen you—"

"Don't you dare speak his name!" I hiss, breaking my silence.

He tilts his head. "There she is." The usual smirk-like smile returns to his face. "I'd wondered where you went these last few days. You haven't been acting like yourself."

"And what's that supposed to mean?" I can't help the hellfire crackling through my tone. If I had my magic right now, it would be sizzling in my fingertips.

"It means that I like you with a little bit of sass." He licks his bottom lip, as if remembering the taste of me. "You're more fun that way. You're a challenge that I can't wait to conquer. You remind me of a wild horse that needs taming, you know. And I can't wait to be the one to do it." He wanders off as he finishes, standing over the little bar stand tucked into the corner of the room and pouring himself a glass of wine. He doesn't offer me any, not that I'd take it.

When he turns back, I meet his lazy smile with one of my own. "You might be able to force a claim on my body now that we're married but you will never claim any other part of me, especially my heart."

He slaps his chest like he's been wounded, but it's a mocking gesture. What does he care of love? Or of doing the right thing? He only cares about lust and power and winning.

My heart means nothing to him.

"I will not take a woman who isn't willing," he says coolly. "You will be mine, Khali. The Gods have already decreed it and you've already said your vows."

I swallow. He's right about that.

"So when you're ready—" his expression softens and he winks cruelly "—you'll know where to find me. You're welcome to walk through my door at any time, Wife, but next time you do, be prepared."

"Never."

The candlelight hoods his eyes. "Not never, Khali. Sooner than you think."

And then he begins undressing himself from the waist down, moving toward his bed as if he doesn't care that I'm still watching. Or maybe he does care and this too is part of his game. I catch a quick glimpse of even more bare skin and turn away, cheeks flaming and stomach twisting. As I stumble from his room, his savage laughter follows close behind.

THREE
HAZEL

THE SUN FLASHES ACROSS MY face, stinging my eyes. I lean my forehead against the cool glass and watch the scenery fly by. Outside the car, the forest is thick, a mix of snow and pine, and the sky is robin's egg blue. On the horizon, angry gray storm clouds gather. I blink, catching sight of my reflection. Up close like this, my hazel eyes remind me of my mom's. I've been praying that she's okay and I guess we're about to find out if God is listening. I believe in God, how could I not given my abilities? But I don't know a whole lot about what "God" is and if "He" or "She" is listening. I sure hope so and I also hope something happened with Mom's phone and I'll be hearing from her at any minute. That she's fine.

We're diving to Ohio. There weren't any flights available on such short notice, not to mention, Dean has quite the arsenal of weapons stashed in the trunk of this little black sports car. He offered to try to fly us there himself during the night but was worried his magic would be too depleted from the battle to get us far. So it's his car to the rescue and I sure hope this tiny thing can handle well in the snow. It's only a six hour drive from my school to my house but that's with clear roads and no traffic. The storm on the forecast doesn't look good; it's going to be a bad one. But we're determined to beat it. It's either that or get stuck somewhere between Charleston, which we just passed, and Columbus, our destination. There are a heck of a lot of rural areas and mountain passes between here and there. Two places I'd rather not get stranded in during a blizzard.

"Are you hungry?" Dean asks, his eyes flashing to the dashboard where 4:50PM glows back at us. It's going to be dark soon. And start snowing. My stomach is a mess but I'm not sure if that's from my nerves, being hungry, or the haul of gas station junk food we ate around noon when we hurried out of town. We left soon after getting back to Dean's place, and normally road trip status and alone time with him would excite me, but not today. I'm sick with worry and every minute of this stretch on the freeway seems to feel like an hour.

"I'm okay," I reply. "I don't think I could eat now anyway. Let's just keep going. I want to beat the storm."

He nods and fiddles with the music on the radio, turning the dial until it lands on a more upbeat song. He can probably sense my crappy attitude and wants to cheer me up. Truthfully, I liked the moody stuff we were listening to earlier, it was more in line with my mood, but I keep my mouth shut and hum along.

An hour later and we're in the middle of a full-on whiteout. The sun is long gone, shrouding us in the storm's darkness, and aside from the red taillights of the semi-truck in front of us, all I can see are the white snowflakes shooting into the windshield and flying all around us. The scene reminds me of a Star Trek episode, like we're going at light speed or something. And it feels like we're on a theme park ride and wondering if the semblance of safety is real or if we're about to go flying into the air and crash to our deaths.

The snow piles up on the road so quickly, I have to force myself to look away. I mindlessly scroll social media on my phone instead, but not even the funniest memes can make me feel better. It doesn't take long for Dean's fingers to curl tighter around the steering wheel and his shoulders to grow tense.

"Let's stop," I say, putting down my phone. "I give up. This is too freaky. We can get a room for the night and finish the drive tomorrow."

He keeps staring straight ahead. "Are you sure? We're only a few hours away."

"Yeah." I lean over to get a glimpse of the speedometer. We're only going 40 miles an hour and by the looks of things, we'll be slowing down even more soon. "At this rate we won't get to Mom's house until well after she's gone to work for her night shift. We can make up the time in the morning after the plows have come through."

His tense body deflates like a balloon and a few minutes later, he exits the freeway into a little town called Ripley, West Virginia. It's probably quaint and wonderful, or maybe it's a run-down forgotten town, but I can't tell either way through all the snow. Everything is covered in a blanket of white and the roads are even worse down here off the freeway where the big trucks help to create a path for all the helpless cars in their wake.

There's a motel just off the exit with a vacancy sign flashing, and rather than try to look around for something better, he pulls our car right in.

"This okay?"

"Fine by me."

I wait inside the car while he gets us a room key, and then loads our backpacks onto his back and leads us to room number eight.

"My lucky number." I smile and knock on the door for good luck.

Dean smirks.

"What? I like eight. It's like an infinity symbol. What's not to like about that?"

"I never thought about it." His lips twitch into a smile.

The room is much colder than I was hoping for but I'm sure Dean's extra warm body heat will take care of that in no time. And at least it's clean. There are two queen beds, though I'm sure we'll cuddle up in one, and a simple bathroom at the back. It's in need of a remodel, the place suspended somewhere between the 1970s and the 1980s but I decide to call it retro and be happy we're here and not stuck out on those horrible roads.

"I'll go find us something to eat," Dean offers. "There were a few vending machines back in the lobby. Anything in particular you want?"

Tacos!

But I don't say that. He'd probably get back in the car if I did.

"Anything salty is fine," I supply instead. "I'm going to take a quick shower."

Dean leaves me to it. I rummage around in my backpack, looking for my pajamas, when he knocks on the door less than a minute later. He must have forgotten his wallet or something.

"Miss me already?" I tease, swinging the door wide open. But it's not Dean standing on the other side.

The man is young, my age perhaps, but it's hard to make out his features in the shadows. Behind him the light from the parking lot shines too bright, casting him into a silhouette. He's dressed in a stylish leather jacket with a white t-shirt and dark jeans. His flaxen hair flops perfectly over his smooth forehead, like a male model in a photo shoot. He steps closer and the light from the hotel room illuminates his chiseled face. Amber eyes lock me in.

My stomach drops.

I know him. He's the strange supernatural guy from The Roasted Bean, the one who told us about Cora and Macy. I hurry to push the door closed, a flutter of nerves and shock rippling through my body, but he sticks out a booted foot and stops me.

"Don't worry, Hazel." His voice is beautiful, like a gentle caress. It soothes me and the fear melts away. I'm alarmed, but then I'm not, all at the same time. He's most definitely doing that to me. *So freaky.* "I came to deliver a message."

"Another one?" I choke out.

He nods once. I scan the area for Dean but there's nobody out here but the two of us, the snowy stillness, and the silent night. I don't want this guy coming into our room, no matter the intense way he makes me trust him. Somewhere in the back of my mind, I know I have to be careful and that the feeling I have has more to do with whatever supernatural voodoo he has going on and less to do with my actual feelings.

I've been through enough terror for a lifetime, thank you very much.

I pull the latch on the upper part of the door open so when I step outside and close it, the door stays cracked. I shiver against the cold and tuck my arms into my torso.

"What's your name?" I ask, somehow knowing he's not going to tell me. But to my surprise, he answers.

"I am Elias," he says, tilting his head and letting the name settle over me. "But please, keep that name to yourself."

"Uh, hi." I don't know what to say. I probably sound like an idiot. "So what's the message, Elias?"

He considers me for a moment, his amber eyes intensifying as they bore into mine. "I'm not supposed to meddle in the affairs of the other realm. It is not my job or my place."

"Okay…" And yet, here he is.

"But this realm, this human world, is my concern, and right now, a bunch of crazed lunatics think it's their holy calling to cross over into my realm and take over. You can imagine why that would bother me, yes?"

I raise my eyebrows. "Of course. It bothers me, too."

"So you have to stop them."

"How? I don't know what to do."

"All the portals are jeopardized," he says, cutting my complaint with his sharp tone. "The Occultists currently have members of their cult at every single portal save for the one in Drakenon."

So there's a portal in Drakenon? Good to know…

"And why can't they come through, again? According to you, my human friends were taken through it just fine."

He winces at my barbed tone. "Yes, I have failed Cora and Macy. I would go after them, but I'm forbidden to travel to Eridas."

"So tell me something that could actually help me," I plead. The wind kicks snow at us but I don't even care, this is my chance. "The reapers warned me of the Occultists near Westinbrooke, so it stands to reason they're at other portals too. Give me something I can work with here, Elias. Help me."

"They want to kill you," he sighs.

I scoff. "Ya think."

"They want to kill you because of the spell between you and the dragon princess. If they kill you, they kill her."

"I know, and if they kill her, then I die too."

He shakes his head. "No, you won't. You can go to the spirit realm and back. She can't."

That sends my mind racing. So it turns out this spell between us is most dangerous to Khali? I guess that's kind of nice. Well, except for the fact that I have a bunch of crazies after me because of it. So not nice, after all.

I frown, suddenly unsure of everything. "This is getting weird. How do you know all this? Why do you keep showing up? *Who are you?*"

"As I said, I'm here to protect the humans."

"Okay, fine, but *what* are you?"

He smiles, and something playful flickers across his expression. "You really can't tell? You don't feel it?"

That sets me back. There's definitely something about him that's different and familiar, all at the same time, but I have no idea what it is. "Uh, no, I don't know. Sorry. This is all new to me."

He shakes his head. "My kind are certainly not new to you, Hazel."

"Ummm—"

"No matter. I only came to warn you."

"And how exactly am I supposed to fight the Occultists?" I've barely figured out what I am!

"With the sight."

"The what?"

A door opens and shuts with the clang of metal and the ring of a bell. "I must go," he says, turning and gliding away, just like that. Like our conversation is nothing. He moves quickly, never once looking back. I gape at him, beyond confused at what the heck just happened. Did he follow me here? How? And where's his car?

As he crosses under the streetlamp, something lights up around him. The air is knocked from my lungs—and shock is knocked right on in!

Angel wings stretch out of his back.

They're not the glowing white of the angels I've seen helping humans cross to the other side; those tall guys and gals never look at me and they certainly aren't in physical bodies. Elias's wings are almost white except they're tipped in silvery gray. Even so, they're downright beautiful. Is he a full-blooded angel? Some kind of nephilim crossbreed? I want to run after him and ask. I have so many questions. I shuffle forward, words rushing to the tip of my tongue.

"Hey, You." Dean's velvety voice breaks me from my stare.

I jump and turn to him.

"What are you doing out here? You must be freezing." He holds up two plastic bags full of what must be our vending machine dinner. "Are you alright?" His gaze travels down my face and then flicks out into the parking lot and then back again. "You look like you've seen a ghost."

I bark out a laugh. "Well, I see ghosts everyday so…"

All I want is to point out Elias and his angel wings to Dean, but Elias is gone. And his footsteps, they're gone, too. Dang it! I swear I saw them in the snow. How could they have disappeared already? Vanishing bootprints must be an angel thing. Their rules are different from ours, I already know that considering the things I've seen over the years.

This day keeps getting weirder and weirder.

And scarier…

"What's wrong?" Dean's voice is steeled now, with that protective edge I'm used to. Being on this side of it feels pretty nice, I have to admit.

I push back through the motel room door behind me and smile. "It's okay. Everything's fine. But I have something to tell you."

"Okay?"

"Well, one thing is amazing, but the other's actually pretty terrifying."

Dean follows me inside. "Well, I shouldn't expect anything less."

Thinking about the warning Elias delivered sends my heart racing. I already know I'm going to tell Dean everything except for Elias's name. The guy asked me to keep that to myself and I'm pretty sure betraying an angel is a cosmic no-no.

Dean tosses me my coveted bag of Funions and I rip them open.

"Okay, where should I start…"

FOUR
KHALI

THE AIR CATCHES IN MY lungs the moment Bram appears. My eyes water, tears threatening to break free, but I can't show emotion for another man so I blink them away. I already know what will happen if Silas were to suspect Bram and I have something between us—a death sentence. So I relax my expression as he's dragged into the throne room in chains. He's been beaten, that much is clear. His brown wavy hair is matted around his face and darkened with dried blood. Purple and yellow bruises circle both of his eyes and his limp is unmistakable as he's dragged behind two large jailers.

He's an innocent man. Let him go. I long to scream the words but I don't, not yet. Timing is everything during these tribunals. I've sat through enough to know the farce that they can be. Ultimately the king gets to decide the fate of the accused. I can only hope that somewhere in Silas's cold and ruthless heart is a soft spot for his little brother. He was always pretty nasty toward Bram growing up, so anything could happen today, none of it surprising.

"Be seated," Silas bellows and the members of court comply. We're in the vast throne room, seated along the wood benches that line the sides of the room with a large open space in the middle. At the head sit the thrones, one taller than the other, both carved from dark red oak. I hate them. I sit in mine, trying not to fidget. It's way too hard and being in it means way too much.

Drafty air rolls through the room. I try not to shiver, wishing I had my fire elemental to keep me comfortable. The stone walls feel like they're closing in around us, gray and cold and witness to centuries of court life. I adjust in my gown, attempting to use the fabric to cover more of my legs. This particular dress is too revealing for my taste. It's low cut around the bodice, showing off my breasts. When Faros dressed me in it this morning, she said Silas picked it out.

My eyes zero in on Bram. Nothing else matters except for the boy who stands broken in the center of the room. Not my stupid dress. Not the people seated all around, staring and whispering. Not the dragons stationed at the door, nor the guards, nor the high flames in the candlelit chandelier despite the sunlight streaming through the windows.

He won't meet my eyes. *Why won't he meet my eyes?*

The room is overflowing with the same members of court who attended my wedding and the unexpected coronation that night. Their attire of velvet and lace is rich, much like their enjoyment and anticipation. It's inappropriate and sets a hateful burn in my heart.

Except... they're not all like that.

Many watch Bram with expressions of worry and sadness and horror. And I know beyond the people here, are the thousands all over Drakenon who would never condone such treatment toward one of their princes. Well, that is if they believe he's innocent. Those that don't are undoubtedly calling for his execution.

Everyone grows silent and Silas stands, cocking his head and strolling toward his brother.

"Well, young Bram, what do you have to say for yourself?"

Bram stays silent—the room stays silent. I can't stand it.

"Nothing?" Silas snarls, his voice echoing. "You kill our father and you have nothing to say?"

"I don't remember," Bram says quietly. His tone is thick with guilt. "I don't remember any of it. I blacked out. And I'm so sorry." He peers around for a minute, as if looking for someone who's not here, those green eyes scanning the room, seeking and failing. "Tell Mother I'm sorry."

"She's not here," Silas replies. "She couldn't bear to look at you."

"Yes," is all Bram says to this. My heart twists—this isn't right.

"How does someone black out and do something like that?" Silas questions further but of course he already knows. I've told him about the reapers. I told him and whoever else was left in the room after the murder. Silas is toying with Bram. Does the boy truly not understand what's happened to him?

Bram has nothing more to say and before long the members of court start to murmur among themselves. They begin to speak the most vile words—hateful words—of how Bram should be executed, that Bram was always jealous and never of any use, always worthless, and condemned to hell. This hatred grows and grows, and Silas stands in the midst of it, a playful smile dancing across his lips. Is this all a game to him? Is he enjoying it?

My whole body grows hot, igniting all the way to my bones. I can't let this go on.

"No!" I stand, my voice ringing strong like a bell. It breaks through the noise and the room falls silent again. When eager faces turn to look at me, my knees weaken. "Bram blacked out because an Occultist spelled him to a reaper who made him do things against his will."

Even as I say it, I know it sounds far-fetched. And the complete disbelief that meets me is a force of its own, pressing me down. Silas stares at me through a hooded gaze. I can't tell what he's thinking, but it can't be good. Bram looks as if he's about to be sick. His emerald green eyes are rimmed with red and his face has drained of color.

One of the more outspoken dukes, Duke Kensey, stands. He raises his hand to me and his round belly bounces as he speaks. "Explain how this is possible, Queen Khali."

I swallow. "I don't know how it's possible, but when Bram killed King Titus, his eyes were entirely black. Did you not see it?" A few members of the court nod, their faces softening in understanding. "That's not possible without some kind of magical interference."

"We're supposed to believe that a reaper was involved? We don't even know for sure that they exist," the duke continues. He speaks to me as if I'm an insolent child, not his queen. I'm used to this kind of treatment, but that doesn't make it okay, and it doesn't stop my anger from sparking hot.

"But they do," I snap. "Just because something doesn't have a good explanation doesn't mean it's impossible. Look at who we are, what we can do. How do you explain magic? How do you explain the Dragon Blessing?"

He doesn't have anything to say to that.

The tall oak doors open with a bang and my father appears, making my heart squeeze yet again. He's slow, using a cane to help him walk since his muscles grew weak from being stuck in bed, but the sight of him sends a smile to my face. And dare I say it, hope to my heart. Mother holds onto his arm, her eyes clearer and happier than I've seen in ages. I wonder how long it will be before she starts going back to playing her political games, but then again, she got what she wanted, didn't she? I married her favorite of the Brightcaster brothers and my father is alive.

"What did we miss?" Father asks, his face set in determination. He wears his finest jacket, the maroon one with gold inlay. His hair is much grayer than it was months ago and is combed back into a neat style. Mother's gown matches his jacket. The exhaustion underneath her expression is unmistakable.

"Lord Paul Elliot." Silas motions for them to come sit by us. "Nice of you to join us." But there's something clipped in his tone.

"I can explain why this boy is innocent." My father points to Bram with his cane. "Because the same thing almost happened to me." This is news to most of these people and they lean forward in their creaking benches, dying for an explanation, and of course the next thing to entertain their gossip circles for a while. "When I was last outside of Drakenon on business for King Titus, I was caught by a Sovereign Occultist." The room erupts into gasps, and my father holds up his hand to shush them. He leans against his cane and Mother holds her supportive stance at his side. "I thought he was going to kill me but strangely, he didn't. He cut me, spelled me, and then let me go." The room is so quiet I can hear my heart beating in my ears. "As I traveled home I started to lose bits and pieces of time. I would blackout and end up in places I never intended to be. Entire chunks of time disappeared without any explanation." A haunted tone slips into the cracks of his normally strong voice. "And that's when he started talking to me."

"Who?" Silas asks. The sharpness in his question is unmistakable. Why is he so angry about the truth coming out? Maybe he wanted to execute Bram today. The very thought of it sends bile to my throat. *Evil, evil man.*

"It was a voice in my head," Father continues. "He confessed to being a reaper and told me that the Occultist linked us together. Something was wrong with him... he was off. I don't know how to explain it. He wanted me to do bad things to the people I loved. He wanted me to hurry home and I did, even though I tried not to. I fought it, fought him, and I—" he lets out a resigned breath "—even tried to kill myself. Nothing worked. He brought me back to Drakenon and into this castle anyway."

A tear releases from my eye and splashes hot down my cheek. I don't have the strength to wipe it away.

"Just when the reaper was forcing me to make an attempt at my own daughter's life, I was able to take control over my mind and body again. It nearly cost me everything. I fell into a restless and painful sleep for weeks. I nearly died." A smile flits across his face, accentuating the wrinkles. Many of them are new. "The night the reaper left me was the strangest of all. I didn't have to do anything. He just… left. I felt this tension between us snap, and then this enormous sense of relief came over both of us. It was as if he didn't want to be stuck with me any more than I wanted him. The second he left for good, I woke up, and now I'm here. The reaper is gone and he hasn't come back." Mother hugs Father from the side and he nods, pointing toward Bram. "And I believe the same thing has happened to Bram. Unfortunately Bram wasn't as lucky as I was. His reaper succeeded in completing his murderous task before he was released from the spell."

Bram's face is pale as a ghost, his eyes wide and round. He stares at the ground.

"And how are we supposed to believe they're really gone?" Duke Kensey hollers. "If you've been spelled by an Occultist you should be locked up." The man and his family are but distant acquaintances to me, and if he deserves his title or not, I wouldn't know. But right now? Right now I'd love to strip him of his title and send him away for good. All he's doing is directing suspicion to my father and Bram.

Unfortunately, the court erupts in murmurs of agreement. I can't hold back any longer. I jump off the throne and dash to my dad, pulling him against me and glaring back at the crowd. "Nobody touch him," I growl. "He's fine. He's better. Don't condemn him for something that wasn't his fault."

"Bram could still be dangerous too," the duke goes on, completely ignoring me. He doesn't look at me, doesn't gester to me, as his voice raises higher and higher.

Silas strolls across the room and leans in close to me, his lips brushing soft against my ear. "This is why you should have kept your mouth shut. I was handling it. They didn't need to know about the reapers and now they will use it to say we're unfit for the throne."

"If that was your plan, you should have told me," I whisper back.

I don't know what else to say to him, except that he's right about one thing: the court is outraged. They talk over each other, some yelling, panicking and angry. Others are defending my father and Bram. But everyone, and I mean everyone, is unhappy.

"Enough," Silas shouts and the room fades into reluctant silence again. "We'll make sure Paul Elliot and my brother are kept somewhere they can't hurt anyone."

The court is slow to applaud and my heart is stripped in two.

"That's not fair," I gasp. The pain in my chest swells.

Silas holds up his hand. "It's not going to last forever. They will be carefully monitored and when I decide they can be trusted, they will be. My word is final." He's met with a mix of nods and glares. "But we have a bigger issue to worry about and that is the Occultists. I will do everything in my power to make us stronger and that includes finding allies wherever I can."

Silas is making all these decisions on his own and so quickly. Normally king's have advisors, leaders they must listen to and work together with, but I see none of that here. He's a fool. Truly. And I'm not only going to be seeing it all unfold, I'm going to have to stand at his side and pretend to be a party to it.

The doors open again and my fae friends are escorted into the room. At least they're not in chains. They're dressed in clean riches and groomed better than I've ever seen them. My heart and hands squeeze tighter as I hold onto my father. I haven't seen my friends in days. They look well-rested. Fed. And their smiles seem genuine, if not a little nervous.

"You're not welcome here!" someone jeers and several more clap and cheer.

"Enough," Silas snaps, his voice growing louder than the rest. "Our new fae allies have been around the Occultists far more than we have and we'll welcome our new friends into this kingdom so long as they agree to help us, which they already have."

I don't like this. I don't trust Silas.

What's his endgame? What is he really using my friends for? And of course I don't appreciate the judgemental way so many members of the court are looking at them like they're a problem that needs to be squashed. I don't know if I can take another death on my hands. These fae came to Drakenon because of me; they were offered protection here by King Titus. I can only pray that Silas is true to his word and keeps them safe.

"Now then," Silas says coolly, "let's get ready for a funeral, shall we? We must honor my father and honor him well."

As we walk toward the exit—the royals always get to leave the room first—the energy in the room shifts again. Guards surround us, eyes glued to my father and Bram, their newest prisoners. I hold tight to Father and move along, wanting to get out of here and away from this nightmarish crowd of onlookers.

"You're making a mockery of this kingdom." Duke Kensey lunges forward, pointing his meaty finger at Silas. "You're a foolish child! Not fit for King!"

Silas turns, scowling. Violet lightning zaps from his hand right to the man. It strikes him center in the chest. It's so quick, there's hardly time to react.

He falls, dead before he hits the floor.

The crack of it echoes loud in my ears. The rancid smell of burnt flesh fills the room, making my stomach twist. My heart races through deafening silence and then the cries of fear. I blink, trying to process what I just witnessed. I never saw Titus do *anything* like this.

It's hard to believe.

But I know Silas, so I do believe it.

And Silas? He needs to be stopped. Who else is going to do it if I don't? This is wrong. To strike someone dead for pointing out your failings is the mark of a tyrant. I want to glare at Silas, to say something cutting, or at the very least, go comfort Duke Kensey's horrified family.

I do none of those things.

Instead I stand there and keep calm, because one day I will have a plan, I will enact that plan, and it will end Silas. Until then, I will watch and I will gather information and I will learn everything I need to learn.

"Anyone else have something they'd like to say?" Silas calls back to the crowd, his voice sickly sweet. He ignores the dead man's family who sob next to the smoking body. "I'm not here to be your friend. I'm not here to be manipulated or bullied. I'm King Silas Skylen Brightcaster and what I say is law. You can either support me or you can leave Drakenon. But anyone who speaks ill of me or acts against me *in my kingdom* will not be shown mercy."

The message is clear and nobody rebukes him—nobody dares.

He turns on his polished leather boots and storms from the room, his palms crackling with electricity as he goes.

FIVE
HAZEL

DEAN AND I PARK OUTSIDE of my childhood home, a cute little updated three bedroom rambler built in the 1950s with an added attached garage and a decades' old oak tree taking up most of the yard. An old tire swing hangs from the tallest branch, still and forgotten. The front walk and driveway are covered in a thick layer of fresh snow, but considering Mom should be gone on her nightshift, it isn't the strangest thing to see the snow undisturbed. But what if she's not at work and what if nothing's wrong with her phone? I fumble with the seatbelt.

"That's weird," I say, narrowing my eyes.

"What?"

I point to where the garbage cans are sitting out on the curb, covered in snow. One is tipped on its side.

"Garbage day is Friday." My voice quivers. "It's Monday. Mom would never just let them sit out all weekend like that, especially not during a storm when the city needs space for the plows to come through."

I release a slow breath, trying to calm my nerves. I didn't want to believe something was wrong but of course it is. Is she okay? Is Harmony? Can Harmony really be trusted? Is someone hurt? It's a sharp and painful thought—like a bee's stinger stuck under the skin—the thought may be small but it's everything in this moment. Harmony told me I needed to come to Ohio right away and I didn't listen. That conversation was almost two days ago. A lot can happen in two days.

"Come on." I burst from the car and sprint to the front door, lifting my knees high to get through the heavy snow and trying not to biff it on the icy pavement. Luckily I don't slip. It helps that Dean is right there with me, holding me up. "Door's locked," I grumble. "Follow me."

I lead him over to the garage and enter the code I know by heart. It rumbles open slow as molasses, revealing Mom's little black Toyota sitting inside. Another thing that isn't right; this car shouldn't be here.

"She's definitely not at work."

Dean places a reassuring hand on my shoulder. "Are you okay?"

I shake my head. And I love him for thinking of me, but this isn't the time to soothe my fears. I should be afraid. I should be worried. My only parent is in trouble! My hands start to shake and my breath speeds because I don't know what I'd do if I lost her.

The inner garage door isn't locked—Mom never locks it. I throw open the door and storm into the house, first noticing how very cold it is inside, the air almost the same temperature as outside. Sure, Mom likes to keep the thermostat down to save money but not this much.

I round the corner from the back hallway and run into the living room. I stop short. Mom and Harmony are sprawled across the carpet. Our two cats, Bella and Edward, meow and pace around their bodies. Edward spooks and runs off, but Bella prances over and rubs herself against my ankles, meowing even louder. I'm frozen, all wind having been knocked right out of my lungs at the sight of Mom and Harmony like this. They're laying side by side, as if sleeping.

Sleeping, I tell myself, *they have to be sleeping.*

But what if they're not...

"Mom!" I cry out and fall to my knees between them, going for her first. Her brown curly hair is fanned out around her face and her dainty chin is tilted to the side. I cup her face. She's not cold, not like the room. Her skin is perfectly warm. I lean in close. "She's breathing."

Dean leans over Harmony. "Same here."

I shake Mom and yell for her to wake up and then I say a little prayer, but nothing happens. They're both out cold. "Should we call an ambulance?" My voice sounds miles away.

It's what I was taught growing up. If someone is hurt, you call 911, right? Well, first you go find Mom. But as I glance about the room, taking it all in, I know that's not an option. This situation is beyond what a paramedic or a doctor could diagnose. Not to mention Harmony doesn't have her glamour on anymore. The tips of her wings are visible behind her back and her skin has that baby blue hue to it again.

A silver bowl lays between the two of them. I edge closer. It's filled with a thin layer of a dark liquid.

Blood.

My heart sinks, realizing what this means. Just to be certain, I grab Mom's hands, which are both curled into tight fists. I gently pry them open and sure enough, find the cut across one of her palms. It's a thin line of angry red. Dean lifts Harmony's hand; the same marking lays stark against her blue skin.

"Blood magic," he says, his voice growing dark. "Harmony did it again. She shouldn't have."

"It made her so weak the first time." My voice cracks, remember how she couldn't even stand after she helped me peer into old memories a few weeks ago. "Why would she do that? And why would she come here, of all places? Why get my mom involved in all of this?"

I hate these questions. Every single one.

Dean clears his throat. "Hazel, come on." His frown is so, so sad and I wonder if it's a mirror of my own.

"Come on, what?"

"Look closer." He nods toward my mom but when I don't move, he crawls over and lifts her body, carefully rolling her onto her side. I gasp. Delicate metallic wings hunch together against her back. Her skin is normal. Everything else looks like a regular human. But there's no denying that those wings are anything but normal. "Whatever happened," he says, "it took away her glamour too."

I can't breathe. What's going on? Mom's a faerie, too? But she never said a word to me and I never once suspected anything like this. How could she have kept this from me all this time? It doesn't make sense. Mom and I are all each other has in the world. She knows about me and my curse, or gift, as she likes to call it. So why wouldn't she tell me the truth?

I want to make excuses for her but can't help feeling betrayed. It opens up a chasm of emptiness in my chest, taking away my voice, my thoughts, my everything… and I just sit there. Gutted. Angry. My stomach raw. My throat empty. I have nothing to say.

I feel betrayed to the absolute core but I can't even let myself feel that because Mom is unconscious and needs my help.

"Hazel," Dean asks gently, "what are you thinking?"

I swallow down the heaviness and fight back tears. "Something went wrong." I point to their palms and the bowl. "They were obviously doing something with blood magic and it backfired. They're not dead. They're just… asleep, right? This is some kind of coma?"

"It looks that way." His mouth is thin as he peers around the room, his mind puzzling through something. A plan? I don't know. I hope so, because I've got nothing.

"Do you think they're okay?"

Dean turns back to me with calculating eyes as he considers this for a minute. "I want to say yes but I can't lie to you." He runs a thumb along his lower lip. "I'm sorry, but no, I don't think they're okay, Hazel. I have a bad feeling about this."

My hands shake. I hate that my hands are still shaking. I grit my teeth and try to shake them out. Dean catches them with his own and holds them against his warm chest, a tender move that makes me relax just a little bit. Below us, Harmony sleeps.

"But whatever this means, we'll figure it out and we'll save them." He sounds so sure of himself. I nod numbly, and he releases my hands. "Are you okay?"

I nod again. "I will be."

He glances away and I know he doesn't believe me. "How about I go get your cats a fresh bowl of food and water and then find some towels? Let's get this cleaned up and get them moved into beds and then we'll brainstorm ideas to fix this." He says it like it's important, like it might save them, even though we both know it won't.

He's being so kind and comforting, but he doesn't know what to do. I can tell by the worry in his voice that he has no idea what's going to happen next.

This can't be real. How is this my life?

This is my fault. I should have listened to Harmony and raced to Ohio the second she called. And yet I'm still angry that my mother lied to me for all these years. How did she pull it off? Why did she do it? Did she lie about my father, too? The sucky thing is I might never find out the truth.

Dean leaves and I sit there with Bella in my lap, my eyes searching the family room, my chest rising and falling as the panic rises and falls as well. There's the red brick fireplace and the white mantel with all our pictures lined up in silver frames. There's the big round ticking clock on the wall. The old leather couches that have seen more than a decade of movie nights. The happy little plant in the corner, slightly dusty. The beige carpet, freshly vacuumed, now stained with little drops of blood. I follow the trail of drops until I see it—the glint of metal tucked under Harmony's leg. It's the hilt of her silver dagger. As far as I know, blood magic is strong because it requires a sacrifice of blood, if not more. The one and only time I used it, Harmony had chosen to pay the price for the both of us, and she'd been weaker than ever when it was over. And then? Then she'd disappeared.

Maybe it's my turn to pay for this magic.

Could I wake them if I took a little bit of the pressure off?

Before I can talk myself out of it, I snatch up the dagger and slice the blade across my palm, squeezing a trickle of blood into the bowl to mix with theirs. Bella hisses and darts away just as a zap of prickling magic races through my bloodstream. It stings something fierce—*holy crap*—and I gasp. But I push the pain to the back of my mind and slide the bowl over, grab hold of both their hands, and lie down between them. My vision tunnels, going bright white, then black, then white again.

The air disappears from my lungs, like getting punched right in the stomach. I'm falling fast. It's as if my soul is being syphoned out of my body. When I try to scream, there's no sound. There's nothing. I'm nothing. And then I'm everything and I see it all.

Six

KHALI

AFTER BRAM AND MY PARENTS are escorted from the room, all I can do is stand there. It's like my feet are sinking into the stone floor and at any minute I'll be swallowed up. Anger burns raw in my throat. Hopelessness spreads in my belly. And guilt... guilt is everywhere. Is this my fault? Should I have let Silas handle the tribunal and kept quiet about everything I knew?

No. He can't be trusted.

And from the shocked looks on everyone staring at me, the dead body, and the fae, it's not just me—nobody wants to trust Silas right now. And yet, we all have to. These are my people, they're counting on me to save the day, or at least temper my husband, but I can't. At least, not yet.

Shaking myself free of the intense emotions, I pull my shoulders back and stalk toward my fae friends. I don't care what the people of court think of me doing it. I can't. They probably all hate me or at least find me weak. I hope I haven't lost all my favor with those beyond the castle walls, it's the most vulnerable of our people who need me now more than ever. But what can I do for them until I get my magic back and figure out how to best Silas?

Terek stands relaxed between Maxx and Juniper, his cat-like blue eyes roaming the crowd of onlookers, a tiny smirk on his bronzed face. If I didn't know better, I'd say he was about to hiss at them just to see what they'd do.

"Hello again." I force a smile. "Why don't we get out of here? We need to talk in private."

"As if there's anywhere safe to talk in this place." Juniper rolls her eyes. Her white-blonde hair is tied back into an intricate braid, showcasing her one pointed fae ear and one doe ear. She's prettier today than I've ever seen her. No longer dressed like a warrior, she wears a soft pink gown that could rival even the most beautiful of courtesans.

"I know where we can go," I reply.

Maxx nods at me, his horns reflecting the sunlight streaming in through the windows. More than a few of the men look at him as if they'd love nothing more than to take him out, their stances wide, weapons on display, watchful eyes fixed with animosity. Maxx is huge, muscles bigger than even the biggest of the Dragon Blessed. The elf is a force of nature, to be sure, but I've seen the softer and cautious sides to him. He doesn't worry me in the slightest. Quite the opposite; having him around makes me feel more protected.

Accompanied by two guards, I lead the party to my new chambers where I have my own private sitting room. As I suspected, it's empty. I motion to one of the guards in the hallway outside and tell them not to allow anyone inside. He nods and I lock us inside. Maybe this isn't the safest place to talk but I don't know where else to go. It's not like we can easily sneak off. Times have changed.

"Nice place you got here." Maxx whistles as we make ourselves comfortable in the plush chairs. "Queen Khali," he continues, "has a nice ring to it."

Juniper shrugs, unimpressed, and Terek grins with a questioning raise of his eyebrow.

"Yeah, about that," I groan. "A lot has happened since we got to Drakenon. I'm sorry I haven't had much time to come check in with you. Has everything been okay? Has Silas honored his father's bargain to let you stay here safely?"

"So far." Terek rolls a long lock of his golden hair around one finger. It's normally tied back but today it hangs around his bony shoulders. "He's been nothing but a terrifying gentleman." He flounces into one of the chairs and relaxes into it as if he's right at home.

"He's made it clear that he's not bound by his father's word," Maxx says, standing guard at the door, "so while he's been cordial and has treated us like guests, it's only a matter of time before he turns on us."

"Did you see the way your dragon court looked at us just now? They want us gone or dead," Juniper adds. She ambles over to the window and folds her willowy arms over her chest, staring out at the gardens and the city beyond with a worried grimace.

But I'm still stuck on something Maxx said.

Silas isn't bound by the bargains his father made but does that mean I'm still bound? The magic worked two ways, binding both of us to what we agreed upon. As far as I know, if one of us dies, the magic of the vow isn't suddenly gone. Unfortunately, I'm pretty sure *I'm* still bound to *my* word. I'd agreed to marry Silas but what else had I agreed to? I close my eyes, thinking back through the mess of emotions and craziness of the last week to what exactly happened between Titus and I that day on the Drakenon border.

I agreed to marry Silas, to not fight it, and to have his children. I bend over and grip my stomach, forcing myself to breathe.

He's going to want children.

"Is she okay?" I hear Juniper question, her voice sounding far away.

I straighten. I'm next to one of the tufted chairs and have to grab onto the soft red fabric to keep my knees from buckling. My eyes zero in on the cracking fire in the hearth as my mind whirls. Okay, I can't push Silas away forever, but what if I found another way? What if he was the one to make the choice to end things between us? Or what if something bigger than both of us made the choice for him? Or maybe he could go away…

A sparkling of an idea lights in my mind and I smile faintly at the first shred of hope I've felt in ages.

Terek smacks his lips together, startling me. "Hello there, Queenie, what aren't you telling us?"

I let out a long breath and decide to let these three be my confidantes in at least one thing today. "I've lost my magic," I admit. "Nobody knows."

They offer varying degrees of shock on their faces.

"What do you mean, you lost your magic?" Juniper snaps, her face falling and fear slipping through.

"I mean, on my eighteenth birthday, the same day I had to marry my enemy, it disappeared." I sigh and my eyes water. I'm quick to blink the tears away and continue. "It had been acting strange for a while and then I met the human Hazel and it *really* didn't like her. When I left the human realm I'd hoped that would be the end of the problems but it wasn't. I think the spell must have done something to me." I'm talking in circles. They don't even know what I'm saying!

"Wait, wait, wait." Terek holds up his hands, claws glinting. "Back up, start from the beginning."

I go back to the beginning and tell them everything, answering a million questions as I go, and as we talk the heavy weight of my secrets slowly begin to lift off my body. In one sense, I feel better having friends to share this burden with, but then I have to remind myself just how terrifying this situation is, and the heavy weight of it piles back on.

"We're in deep trouble," Maxx states when I've finished. He leaves his post at the door to start pacing the room. "This is worse than I thought."

"Yeah…"

I brought them here and now I'm powerless to help them stay safe. Our centaur friend is who knows where and the two people we made bargains with, the Occultist and Titus, either died or escaped. Oh, and my husband is a tyrant. Deep trouble about sums it up.

"I'm so sorry."

"Maybe I can help." Juniper strides from her spot by the window and I stand to meet her. Her expression toward me is the softest I've seen. She's always acted like she hates me, and maybe she still does, but now I think she just feels sorry for me. She inches closer and lays cool hands on both my shoulders. "Let me see if there's anything I can heal, alright?" She smiles, and the little spots around her maple colored eyes lift. Her doe-like face falls into concentration, and I pray she can do something for me, anything. She healed Terek's broken wrist and she helped Bram when he was hurt. But I don't feel anything change and after a few tense minutes, she steps back and shakes her head. "I'm sorry," she relents. "It's strange. You're like a vault. I can't break in."

"Thank you for trying."

"So now what?" she asks.

"I can't leave. If I could run away again, I would. But I'm bound by my word to stay here with Silas. But that doesn't mean you all can't leave. The Sovereign Occultists are going to come and when they do I don't want you here. Things could get bad. Very bad."

"Oh believe me," Maxx says, "we know how they can get."

"How they *will* get." Juniper sighs, her eyes growing haunted.

"But we're not leaving." Terek stands and folds me into a tight hug. "We're just going to have to find a way to stop the Occultists together."

His hug feels so good. I didn't know how much I needed it until now. "I need Hazel." My voice cracks. "Or that stupid Occultist to come back and keep his word to us. If I could find a way to get my magic back, all of this would be so much more manageable."

"How exactly are you going to do that?" Maxx asks. It's not a challenge, but a genuine question.

I peel away from Terek. "Do I look like I have a plan?" My eyes fill with tears again and we all go silent. I don't have a plan for my magic, not yet. But I can't stop thinking about the little spark from earlier, about a way I might be able to get Silas to leave me alone.

"Alright," Juniper says at last. "No more feeling sorry for yourself. You may be married to Silas but that also makes you Queen. You have power too. You're walking around acting like you're completely powerless but that can't be true. You have sway over people, even your husband."

"Yeah, right."

"No," she presses. "I'm serious. We all saw it today. People look up to you. Most like you and some revere you." Her words ring true but I have the hardest time believing them. She doesn't know the court like I know them. "And anyway, nobody has to know you've lost your magic. We'll find a way to get it back before they find out it was ever gone. In the meantime, you need to get the court on your side for good, all of them, and especially your husband. And if not your husband, at least the people need to listen to you."

"But why?" I sigh. "What's the point?"

She shakes her head at me. "Are you kidding, Khali? What's the point? The point is that you can get them to take the Occultist problem as seriously as possible, and not only that, you need to convince Silas to let you go find Hazel. You said your magic didn't like her, well that's got to mean something."

"Silas will never let me leave," I challenge. "You could go fetch her, perhaps?"

"No can do," Terek breaks in. "Silas has made it clear to us we're his prisoners, even if we're not locked up right now, we've been ordered not to leave. If we leave, he'll come after us and he won't show mercy."

Mercy—the same word he threw in all our faces earlier and the quality Silas lacks most.

Angry heat prickles all over my body. I know the link with Hazel is all speculation but Silas taking that away from me is too much. And now he's threatening my friends? Of course he is.

"Maybe you could ask him to let you go get her," Juniper tries again. "He obviously likes you."

I laugh. It seems so far-fetched that Silas would let me leave this castle again, let alone travel back to the human realm. I'm not his wife because he cares for me. I'm his wife because he wants to own me. But the word ownership gives me another idea.

"The necklace," I whisper.

"What necklace?"

"You remember. The one I used to subdue the Occultist, the one Silas used on me? I need to find it. What if I can use it on Silas to take his powers? I could blackmail him with it at the very least."

"Sounds dangerous," Maxx interjects, frowning.

"But also kind of fun," Terek purrs as he paces the room. "I'll help you look for the necklace."

"And how are you going to do that?" I scoff.

"Let's just say I like shiny things."

Juniper laughs. "And he has a certain sway with some of our guards."

Terek winks and fans himself, and Maxx rolls his eyes. "Yeah, you could say that again. We've been given a set of rooms together and we're monitored at all times by guards. There's a few who definitely have a soft spot for Terek."

"A few?" I shake my head and laugh.

"Don't look so surprised!" Terek purrs. "I'll ask around. No big deal."

"Okay, but please be careful." I study my friends, so grateful for each one of them. I don't know what I'd do if I didn't have them to talk to and hopefully help me. "All of you. You can't trust people here to be your friends, even if they're attracted to you. We haven't had any fae in our kingdom for a century and the prejudices run deep."

"We're being careful," Maxx assures me and shoots Terek an annoyed look. "At least some of us are."

"Oh, relax." Terek smirks. "I've got everything under control."

"That's what I used to think, too." I pause for a second, looking my new friends up and down. "What can you tell me about magicked items?"

Nobody speaks. "The necklace isn't the only one," I continue, "Flannery has something special with that spear and shield."

"We can't say." Maxx raises a hand. "We've been sworn to secrecy."

"About the spear, yes," Terek adds. "But what I can tell you is this. That necklace probably isn't magicked. It's spelled by a sorcerer. Magicked items are born from the land and are hidden throughout Eridas. There aren't many and it's believed all have been found."

"But..." Juniper bites her lip. "There's no way to know for sure."

That seals my idea and I smile. "So you're saying there's a chance?"

"I HAVE AN IDEA," I GUSH, infusing extra enthusiasm into each word. I sashay across our sitting room and relax next to Silas on the settee. He studies me with equal parts intrigue and skepticism. His blond hair hangs around his face, framing his jaw, and his eyes are alight with electricity. I can guess exactly what he's hoping for and my stomach twists.

"And what idea is that, Wife?" His voice is liquid fire.

I pause for dramatic effect. "We need more magicked items."

He sits back with an exhale. "And why would we need that?"

"To fight the Occultists, obviously." I raise my eyebrows. "And according to my fae friends, they're hidden all over Eridas, especially in the most dangerous of places."

"Yes, well, I already knew that." His voice is growing tired but his eyes say something else; that he's considering what I have to say. He's intrigued. I can work with intrigued.

"What about the Jeweled Forest?" My heart beats frantically as I speak it. "Bram and I traveled through there when I ran away." His eyes flash with jealousy and I hurry to finish. "It's only a day's flight from Stonehearth and if there's any place where a magicked object would be in Drakenon, that would be it."

I long to say more, to ask him about the pendant necklace with the dragon crest. To encourage him to pick up a jewel when he visits the forest. Anything that could help me. But I force myself to keep quiet and let him consider my proposition. If there's one thing I know about Silas, it's that he's willing to take massive risks if it means more power for him to claim. When he agrees to go to the Jeweled Forest a minute of thought later, I'm not the least bit surprised.

SEVEN

HAZEL

I'M SWEPT INTO THE WHITENESS of the supernatural spirit realm, and when I find Harmony and my mother standing aimlessly, I let out a panicked scream. They shouldn't be here! And yet they are and my scream doesn't disturb them. They stand motionless, looking off into the distance, eyes glazed over.

"Mom?" I wave my hand in front of her face.

She doesn't move.

"Harmony?"

Same.

When I reach out to touch them, my hand goes right through their forms as if they're ghosts and my stomach twists into knots. This is so strange—I know they're not dead. I don't understand what's happening. But why can't they see me? I take a deep breath, trying not to let the panic seize control, and stare out into the vastness of bright white. It seems to go on forever.

Something sparkles up ahead, and I'm suddenly struck by the very same image they're watching. It's a scene through a portal, similar to when I could see my loved ones from this place… but also different. There was a sharpness to the scenes before that's lacking here. I edge closer. What exactly am I looking at?

It's a woman—a faerie—walking through a glistening spring meadow at sunrise. She turns, and I'm immediately struck by her youth and flawless beauty. Her skin is perfectly unblemished, her dark curly hair is long, all the way to her butt, and her wide green eyes are oddly familiar. She can't be much older than me. She glides through a field of budding flowers as if they're her best friends. They surround her on all sides, and I try not to gasp by the ridiculous gorgeousness of it all. She stops, twisting the ends of her hair nervously in a gesture that's also familiar to me. Who do I know that does the same thing?

It hits me. I'm looking at a younger version of my mother. Her dainty metallic wings sparkle in the morning sun, the edges of them brushing against the long grass as she strolls. Without thinking, I step forward, reaching my hand out toward the scene, toward this young version of my mother.

Suddenly, I'm pulled forward until I'm no longer in the endless white room but in the spring forest. I look down at my hands. They're not my own. The fingers are slightly longer, nails painted a pretty lavender. This memory of my mother's is no longer a memory. I'm living it now. My heart beats in tandem with hers, and I can feel every emotion she feels, see every color, and smell every scent. My mother's history unfolds before my eyes.

This is the last time I'll have to wait for him and worry if I'll never see him again. A smile spreads across my face as I stroll through the field of wildflowers where we'd agreed to meet at sunrise. This is our place, we made so many memories here, and I'm sad to leave it behind. I let my fingers dance along the tops of the wildflowers instead of where I really want to put them: my belly. I've had to train myself not to cup my hands there and reveal my wonderful secret.

Our child grows within my womb.

I can already feel her kicking, silly little thing that she is. I'm probably imagining the kicks. She's too small to be felt and it's too early for me to know she's a girl. And yet, somehow, I just know she's my daughter and that she's rolling around in there at this very second, as excited for her papa to come back to us as I am to see my husband.

Jamis has been traveling for months and even when he is here; it's hard for him to stay in any one place for long. Most of the faeries hate shifters, especially dragon shifters. Our feuds run centuries deep and although Jamis has nothing to do with them, faeries don't forgive easily. And from what he tells me, Drakenon isn't much better. It's nothing like our sweet kingdom of whimsy and mirth. There are far too many rules and societal obligations.

Him and I? We were never supposed to fall in love.

And yet we did, meeting by chance when he traveled to our Spring Kingdom on behest of his king. And like a roll of thunder impossible to stop, love boomed into our lives and shook our foundations. His family disowned him. His kingdom shunned him, told him he couldn't bring me back. And so he left, choosing to live here, to marry me, and to set up our life. But it was soon apparent that my kingdom wasn't safe for him either.

So he traveled often, in search of a welcoming home for us where both our kinds could be accepted. It was no use. There's nothing here for us in Eridas. And with our child coming, and hybrids being so shunned as they are, we've already decided to leave the realm. As soon as he arrives, we'll be on our way to the nearest portal and venturing into our new life together. My heart hurts just thinking about what it could mean to leave Spring, what it will do to our magicks to flee Eridas, and what it will feel like to never see our extended families again.

But I'll do it. For him, I'll do anything.

I've already concocted the potion that will make my wings retract into my body while I'm in the human realm. Imagining life without flying is hard, but it's not nearly as hard as imagining life without my Jamis, and so I'll do it. I must.

The sun crests the horizon and everything is bathed in that golden reddish hue of early morning. It warms my face, and I breathe in the sweet flowery scent of my home one last time. I'm going to miss it so much. I need to stop thinking about that part. It's too painful.

A speck of black crosses the sun, growing larger as it nears. From this distance, one might mistake him for a bird but I know it's my Jamis. He approaches, his dragon form as majestic as ever. The sight of him sends a blast of excitement mixed with a calm sense of grounding through my entire being and I know we're going to be okay. We're making the right choice.

He lands close and shifts immediately, turning into the man I love smiling down at me with those earthy brown eyes. I could get lost in those eyes—I have many times before. He leans in for a kiss and I give in easily, cherishing his scent and the tender press of his lips. It's been too long.

"Are you ready?" he asks, pressing his forehead to mine. I nod. The plan is to fly to the Spring portal and pass through to the other side. He's already got our new home set up and ready to go, complete with new identities. And I'm going to school to become a nurse, which is a sort of human healer. It's the perfect trade for me. He doesn't need any glamours or potions because shifters look like the *humans when they're not in their dragon form.*

"Do you have the potion you need?"

"It's in here." *I lift the satchel on my arm and he takes it from me.*

"It's safe?"

"The faerie who taught me how to make it can be trusted. It will make my wings retract into my body while I'm in the human realm. And most importantly, it won't harm our baby."

"You're sure?"

"She swore on her life."

That settles it. Faeries don't swear on their lives, not in Eridas, not when to do so could actually mean death. But she did and she's the best in our kingdom, not to mention a dear family friend, so I am confident I can trust her.

I take his hand in mine. "Let's go."

The memory evaporates and I'm back in the endless white room. Harmony and my mother are still there, but this time, they see me. Their eyes become round as saucers and they simultaneously tackle me in a giant hug.

"Hazel, what are you doing here?" Mother asks, her breath hot against my ear.

"Am I too late?" I step back and turn to Harmony.

Harmony shakes her head, dreadlocks bouncing against her shoulders. "No, but you didn't need to come here."

"What do you mean? You called me here."

"I called you to Ohio. But you didn't need to enter into our blood bond." Her voice grows tight. Worried. "We were fine. We are fine."

"Really? Because I found you passed out on the living room floor."

She sighs and runs both hands over her tired face. "This complicates things."

"We had to find out why I lost my magic and retrieve my memories," Mom interjects. "And find out what happened to your father."

I stare at her, her shining eyes and the deep frown. "So someone stole your memories? That's why you didn't tell me the truth?"

"I thought I was a human. Everything I told you about your father being a one night stand? I'm sorry, honey, I honestly thought that was the truth. Harmony knew it wasn't and convinced me to try this magic to return my memories and figure out what's been going on."

It takes a moment for me to digest all of this, I'm shocked and sad and relieved all at the same time.

"And why would Harmony know that you're not human?" I ask, but I think I know.

"You saw the memories?" Mom asks and I nod.

Harmony smiles softly. "Because I was the faerie who helped her, the friend of the family. I taught her how to make the potion to allow her to hide her wings in this realm. Your mother was best friends with the daughter I lost to the Sovereign Occultists. I've been looking for you two for some time. I even performed a spell to get her to come to Westinbrooke, but you're the one who showed up instead."

Mom's face falls. "I'm so sorry to hear about Sariah and the others." She hugs Harmony. "She was my best friend. I can't believe it."

Harmony can't speak.

"This is all a lot to take in." I close my eyes and breathe deep, trying to relax. It's pretty much impossible. Silence falls over us as we think it all through. I open my eyes, ready to speak, when Mom's face jerks up and she screeches. She points and we turn. Fear prickles over my body. It's a reaper. His eyes glow red, his skeleton hands reach toward us, and everything turns cold.

"No!" I yell and position myself in front of Mom and Harmony. "You cannot take them. They're not actually dead."

"Our spirits are here to access memories." Harmony's voice is so much calmer than mine. "Our bodies are fine and waiting for us to return."

The reaper floats toward us, red eyes peering at us from beneath the black cloak, as if seeing into the deepest part of our souls. Finally, he speaks, "I've brought someone to you as my way to express gratitude to Hazel." The reaper pauses. "And apologies for what my kind did to you."

That shocks me, gotta be honest. "Okay..."

A form materializes and I step back as I recognize the man my mother was waiting for: Jamis.

"Dad?" My voice cracks.

He blinks at us, brown eyes mystified and then clearing. He's dressed in medieval type clothing, the same as the other dragons I've seen in visions. He's nothing like I imagined my father to be over the years, to be honest, but I don't even care. He rushes forward and wraps me and Mom into a hug. A lifetime of tears spring to my eyes. He's solid. Real. Flesh and blood. And with his dark blond hair and tannish skin and hazel eyes, he looks like me, way more so than my mom does. I always thought I'd be angry to see him, or at the very least, indifferent. But I'm not. I'm happy. And I'm sad. But mostly I'm overcome with an immense sense of relief.

"You have five minutes." The reaper's scratchy voice cuts through our shared happiness, turning it sour.

Jamis reacts by planting one on mom. To witness her melt into a man's arms like that is something I'd never thought I'd see. Mom doesn't date or do relationships. Growing up, she took care of me and rocked at her job and that was about it. She always said she wasn't interested in letting a man into her life and messing up the good thing she and I had going. Even with her memories wiped, she must have been subconsciously holding on to my father.

She's changed. Even now, I can see it. She remembers their love and is feeling the loss and it's made her a different person.

"What happened to us?" Mother begs the second they seperate. "You're dead. How did that happen?" Her voice cracks, desperate.

He nods once, his mouth turning down at the corners. "What do you remember?"

"Falling in love with you. Getting pregnant with Hazel. Deciding to leave for the human realm and that morning when we met. But then the memory stopped."

He sighs. "I'm glad it stopped. I would never want you to relive what came next."

Mom wipes away the tears.

"We never made it to the human realm that day. We were intercepted by the Occultists. They were a new threat to both of our kingdoms and we never saw them coming, let alone coming for two travelers. They kept us prisoner for months. You really don't remember?"

She shakes her head.

"That's for the best. It was ... terrible. They did horrible things to us. They forced you to take the potion early." His eyes flash to me for a second but he doesn't expound. "Anyway, a few months after Hazel was born, we were able to break out of their prison and make a run for it. When we got to the portal an Occultist was there waiting for us. He took your memory right in front of me. I was able to get you two through the portal but I wasn't so lucky." He swallows hard. "He killed me before I could get to you. I'm so sorry."

Mom and I stare at him, neither one of us knowing what to say. Any words I thought I had have turned to ash on my tongue.

"I watched you from the other side for many years," he says. "I watched you raise Hazel. And then, well, she started seeing me. And that was too hard, too confusing for her. So when Hazel was four years old, I finally went with the reaper and moved on."

I have no memories of seeing him and I wish more than anything that I did. I don't care that it would have been confusing. It would have been better than me growing up believing my dad was a one night stand sperm donor. "You moved on… to heaven?" I ask.

He smiles. "Something like that. And someday, you'll both join me. But not today."

"Time's up," the reapers says, his voice as sharp as his scythe.

"No!" Mom and I gasp.

"It must be this way," his reply slithers over my skin.

"He broke a serious rule to bring me here," Dad relents, his voice losing it's sweet brightness. "I have to go. But don't ever forget how much I love you. Always."

We hug him, and he whispers into my ear, "Hazel, don't be afraid of who you are. You have the sight for a reason."

The sight? He must mean the medium thing, but what if there's more to it?

Before I can ask, he evaporates in our arms. Gone. The reaper, too.

Harmony, Mom, and I all turn to look at each other. Am I at peace with this? Angry? Surprised? I don't even know what to feel. Tears run down Mom's cheeks and that is something I'm definitely pissed off about.

The Occultists ripped my family apart. They spelled me as an infant. They took my mother's memories and killed my father. They want to kill me in order to kill Khali. And now? Now they're going to pay for this.

"Oh honey." Mom pulls me into her arms. "Don't let it make you bitter."

I blink, trying not to let my own tears fall, and suddenly the white room is gone. I'm back in my living room in Ohio, staring up at the ceiling fan.

"Are you okay?" Dean leans over me, his eyes blazing.

I groan and roll to my side. When I see that Harmony and my mom are both blinking and awake, relief floods my body.

"I'm okay," I say, letting out a long slow breath. "But we have a lot to talk about."

Mom's eyes catch mine and she nods once. "Oh yes, we certainly do."

We're shaky and exhausted. It's like waking up from an eons-long dream. What the blood magic did to us is crazy intense. I glance over at Harmony, expecting her to agree, but she's blanched as paper, her breath stilted and eyes pained.

"Are you okay?"

Before she can answer, her eyes roll into the back of her head and she passes out.

EIGHT
KHALI

I COUNT BACKWARDS FROM THREE hundred the moment Silas leaves me in the sitting room. He's gone to discuss the possibility of traveling to the Jeweled Forest with Bram. I can only hope Bram doesn't give too much away about the dangers there. Either way, Silas leaving has given me a chance to search for the spelled necklace.

I can't help but keep wondering about it. Is it a magicked item that was found by one of his ancestors and passed down to him? Terek doesn't think so. A family heirloom can be spelled, which is what Silas has led me to believe, too. Either way, I need to find it in case it can help me get my magic back or help me blackmail my husband.

Since he removed it from the Occultist, I haven't seen it again. He might be keeping it on his person but there's also a good chance it's hidden in his room. Okay, it's a small chance, a careless chance, but I can't stop thinking that maybe it's in there. So here I am, biting my lower lip and staring at the outside of his chamber door. Time slows but I make myself keep counting down until I'm convinced Silas isn't coming back and I'm truly all alone in our royal quarters.

There are always guards stationed in the hallway. Sometimes they will accompany us around the castle; but when we're in our own quarters, we're left alone. This is my chance. It's perfect. Except there's no such thing as perfect around here. If he catches me in his room, what will he do? What will *I* do?

I squash the questions, stroll to the door, and pull it open.

Time to be brave.

It smells like him. Spicy and male, and it makes me want to scream because it ought to smell like all the blood on his hands. Everything about him should be awful to reflect who he is on the inside: he should look awful, smell awful, *be* awful. But at least hating him comes easy to me despite his attractive appearance and alluring scent. Not only do I hate what he's done and his callous nature, I also hate that he got everything he wanted and I got nothing. In another life it would have been Owen and me here. Or Dean.

Or Bram…

I let out a little groan and get to work, rifling through his things, careful not to knock anything out of place. I start with the intricately carved armoire, checking in any hidden areas of the furniture and the pockets of all his clothing. There's nothing. I go to the bookshelf, knowing the bed with the piles of dark bedding are next. Rummaging through the books proves to be fruitless. I was hoping to find a secret compartment in at least one of them but there aren't many to begin with and once again nothing turns up. I pad over to the bed and go for the mattress, heavy with the finest wool Drakenon has to offer. I heave at the edge to see if it's stashed between that and the bedframe.

Again, nothing.

"Hi!" a voice chirps and I startle, dropping the mattress with a thud. Bellflower Blossom pokes her tiny head out from under the bed, a dash of sparkling gold pixie dust catching the sunlight as she moves.

"What are you doing in here?" I gasp at the pixie. I haven't seen her since she helped my father feel better the night he almost died. She said she'd be around, but I'd wondered if she'd decided to take off after all.

"Helping you look for the necklace," her voice chimes happily. She smiles, showing off her razor sharp teeth. "You know I'm in your debt."

"First of all, how do you know I'm looking for the necklace?"

She does a little dance. "I'm a good spy."

I scoff. "Okay. And how long are you in my debt exactly?"

"Until you feel satisfied we're even," she replies. "Or until I decide we are. But for now, I'm quite entertained by you and your friends."

"You helped my father," I whisper. "Thank you."

"It's my pleasure." She does a little curtsy. It makes her look like even more of a flower than before. It's adorable.

"So you listened in on us earlier, did you?" I can't help it; I smile as she nods. She seems so proud of it. "Well, that's great and all but we need to get out of here soon. I've already taken way too long."

I feel as if any moment Silas is going to walk in and catch me!

"Agreed," she says happily. "Let me just finish looking under here." She slides back under the bed. The space is quite small down there so she's perfect for the job.

"Oh by the way," her little voice chimes from under the bed, "you really ought to venture down into the dungeons. You'll never believe what I found today!"

"And what's that?"

"It's probably better if I show you."

I let out sigh and turn, eyes roaming the room one last time to see if I may have missed anything, when I notice something odd about the bookshelf. Why is it inlaid into the wall like that? It's not set apart like all the other furniture. My heart skips. It must be a hidden passage leading into the castle's network of tunnels! This is the King's chambers, it only makes sense that a king would have this kind of direct access.

I rush toward it, excitement building, when the entire bookshelf swings open and Silas steps through. Surprise flashes across his face, followed quickly by suspicion, and then a sort of knowingness, and finally something else entirely. His lavender eyes flit from where I stand, to his bed right behind me, and that something is unmistakable lust.

"I thought you were with Bram?" I blurt out.

He raises an eyebrow. "I was, and then I wasn't…" I shuffle backward. "I see you've finally decided to come to me. I knew leaving you access to my bedroom would prove to be in my benefit."

He doesn't know I was here to snoop. He thinks I'm here to consummate our marriage. And that's worse.

"Yes, but I thought you'd be gone for a while. I didn't expect you so soon."

"Well, it is my room." He smirks, closes the bookcase, and strides toward me while he points. "And my bed." Another step. "And wife." His finger comes to rest against my sternum.

I don't know what to say or do, and I'm frozen because I can't make myself do what would please him right now. I don't want him asking questions or getting angry.

He's only inches from me. He gently runs his fingertip over to my shoulder and then to my hair, pinching the end of a dark curl. His lavender eyes grow dark, the storm clouds gathering, the electricity buzzing underneath his skin. It's lust. But it's also something else.

Satisfaction.

The man was angry with me earlier for not playing along with whatever plan he had for Bram, and now my father and Bram are both in some kind of quarantine situation. I defied him in front of his court, and I've been defying him over and over the last few weeks. But we're here now and clearly he thinks he's won.

He closes the distance and presses his lips to mine. So soft at first. Almost reverent. Not teasing. Not demanding. But asking. It's never been this way before with him.

I turn away.

"Let me ask you, Khali." He sounds hurt. "What are you really doing here?"

I let out a little gasp. I can't think of the right words to say.

He steps back. "You're not looking for this, are you?" He reaches into his pocket and pulls out the necklace. The silver glints in the sunlight as it sways on the black cord.

I want it. I need it. And without thinking of the repercussions, I try to snatch it from him. I'm not fast enough. He holds it away from me as his eyes grow dark. "That's what I was afraid of. I assumed the moment you brought up magicked items you were wondering about this, too. It's not magicked, you know. It really *is* spelled. But I guess they're not so different."

"Yes they are. Magicked means it comes from Eridas's magic itself and spelled means you had some sorcerer do you a favor. If you ask me, the two are quite different."

He laughs. "If you say so."

"Where did you even get that?" I snap. "Who made it for you?" The kind of magic attached to that necklace doesn't come from dragons, not even from fae. It has to be a sorcerer but there aren't any in Drakenon. They're forbidden from our lands.

The questions get a grin out of him and what he says makes no sense. "You really don't remember, do you? Remarkable."

"Remember what?" Something tickles at the back of my mind, something I should know, should *remember*...

He chuckles. "It doesn't matter *now*, does it?"

"I don't know what you're talking about." The memory, it's there, flitting at the back of my mind but it's been caged. "Silas, what aren't you telling me? What do you mean I don't remember where you got the necklace?"

He shrugs. "Maybe I'm not at liberty to say or maybe I just don't want to."

"I'm done with this." I step past him and hurry toward the door. But he catches my wrist and drags me back so fast that I trip. He uses the momentum to push me onto the bed and then he's on me, his lips hot against my neck. His silky hair falls around my face. The scruff on his chin scratches my skin. My heart pounds. My breath catches. Fear is as hot as his breath.

"You know what I told you before," he whispers between his kisses. "If you came back here, you'd better be prepared to act like my wife."

Once again I'm frozen but there's an anger building inside me, seconds from exploding. He takes my silence as a yes and presses himself onto me, his smell overwhelming, his body hot. Part of my body responds in the way my emotions don't want to accept.

But...

But would it be so hard to give in—to give up? He could get what he wants and I could use it to get what I want. If I go along with this and offer my body to him, I'm sure he'll be kinder to me. And maybe he'll be kinder to the people I love. And maybe things will get better.

But then the memory of Owen's dead body flashes through my mind. And the blood. The rain. The cold. All the tears. They ran down my cheeks, tasting of salt on my tongue. And I see it clearly again, all over, the self-justified look Silas had on his face that night. He didn't regret it. It didn't hurt him. And he would do it again—all over again—if he had to.

No. I'm not going to let him win so easily.

I hold my hands against his chest and heave. He doesn't move an inch. I try to say the word "stop" but I can't get it to come out; it's like it's stuck in my throat. So I shake my head, my eyes filling with tears, and begin to cry.

He stops, an angry growl reverberating from his throat as he rolls off of me.

His breath is heavy, eyes electric. "You can't keep pushing me away, Khali. You're my wife, for Gods' sake! You have a duty to me as your husband."

"But—"

"And you have a duty to this kingdom," he continues. "You made vows. You're bound to bear my children and that means *this*."

"I know." My voice is twisted. I can't breathe properly. "But I don't want to."

He jumps up from the bed. "Well, too bad. I don't care about what you want anymore. I care about what I need." There isn't an ounce of compassion in his voice. "And I need to get you pregnant as soon as possible. You saw those people today? They don't want us here. We have to make them accept it. So you need to get yourself together, get over whatever prudish nonsense is going on with you, and let yourself enjoy what I know you'll like if you just give it a chance."

I want to laugh. Or cry again.

"It's not like that. It's not about being a prude and how dare you even say that to me." I run from the bed and make for the door.

"Oh, really? So are you trying to tell me that it's just me, then? That you'd happily sleep with someone else? Maybe Dean? Or is it my other pathetic brother you want? Maybe Bram should be executed but well that doesn't work because then I'd still be competing for your affection with another dead brother."

"Stop," I scream. "You're being cruel!"

"No! I'm being realistic. I'm doing what needs to be done. Nobody else was willing to do it, none of my other brothers. Well, guess what, Princess? I am. I get things done. And you'll see that when the Occultists are gone, because of me, and this castle is filled with another line of Brightcaster Dragon Blessed children, because of me, and you're living in luxury and don't have a care in the world, because of me." He glares, his voice growing dangerously low. "You'll be thanking me."

"I'll never thank you." I wipe away the last of the tears. They've been replaced with a cold hard hatred and I welcome it.

He laughs and I pull open the door. I'm so done with this.

"Hey!" he yells. "Give that back!"

I whip around, my heart leaping with hope. Bellflower Blossom hovers in the center of his room, his spelled necklace wrapped around her arm and she zips toward me with a brazen smile.

"Khali," she squeals. "Catch!"

She tosses it at me with way more force than I would have thought possible for her tiny body. It shoots like a little silver arrow and lands neatly in my hand. Silas roars, and I expect him to come after me but he doesn't. A flash of lightning shoots from his hand and strikes Bellflower. She drops to the ground with a thud, exploding into a pile of glittering pixie dust.

I fall to my knees. "No!"

"Give it to me," Silas seethes, stretching his hand out. "Give me the necklace now."

"How could you?" I choke on my words. "She wasn't bad. She was my friend."

"She was a thief and a pixie and wasn't where she belonged," he scoffs. "What value does she have to us? She got what she deserved."

"You're horrible." My body is numb. The guilt, it's too much. "You didn't even give her a chance."

That only makes him laugh bitterly. "Give the necklace to me," he demands again. "Give it to me now or I'll execute more of your ridiculous fae friends. See if I care about them, Khali. I don't."

I hold out the necklace. So much for having a plan. I really thought if I could destroy it, I could somehow free my magic. Or maybe use it against Silas. But that's stupid isn't it? This necklace isn't the problem. My spell connecting me to Hazel is, and she's not even in this realm. And Silas? Silas isn't easy to outmaneuver.

"That stupid pixie is how you got it off the first time, isn't it?" He laughs but I don't nod or say anything. Why should I give him the satisfaction? "Their teeth are sharper than anything else in Eridas. Did you know that? Well, if you didn't, you do now." He says it like it's no big deal, like we're having a regular old conversation, like he didn't just murder her.

He snags the necklace from me and instead of dropping it into his pocket, he unties the ends and gives me a pitying look. "This is for your own good."

What?

"No!" I scramble back but I'm not fast enough. He's on me, his weight pressing me down, legs straddling me and one hand pinning my arms together. My skull bangs against the doorframe and I cry out.

"Hold still," he sneers.

I feel something snap against my neck and it's over before I can fight him off, his cursed necklace tied tight around my neck, branding me. I don't know how on earth I'm going to get it off a second time now that Bellflower's gone. But then again, does it really matter? My magic is gone anyway. Silas doesn't know and now that this necklace is around my neck, he'll continue to be kept in the dark. Maybe this is for the best right now because I can have an excuse as to why I'm not using my elementals.

Except he used the necklace before to syphon magic from me if I tried to use it. And when he kissed me while I wore this stupid thing, he was able to take my magic by force. Now what is he going to think when he kisses me?

I'm in so much trouble.

He's going to find out the truth sooner rather than later. I can't avoid kissing him forever. I'm not even sure if I can avoid kissing him another week by the level of his threats.

And Gods, it's more than kissing—he wants to get me pregnant!

My stomach twists once again, bile rising. I crawl out from under him and stumble from the room, heading for mine. I don't look back to see his reaction. I want nothing to do with him, want nothing more than to shift into my dragon self and fly far, far away, but instead I'm going to have to settle for emptying my stomach. I got the necklace and all I have to show for it is a pile of pixie dust and another friend's death because of me…

No. Not because of me. Because of Silas.

NINE
HAZEL

"HARMONY?" I SCRAMBLE TO MY knees and lean over her. "Are you okay?"

But it appears she's right back in that endless sleep state again. With her human glamour, she always looked like an older woman. But in her true form, she appears middle aged, even though she told me she's much older than any human walking the earth today. Faeries are practically immortal and age very slowly. But now to look at her, it wouldn't seem that way. Her skin is that same pale blue and her wings are visibly flattened between her back and the carpet. Deep age lines have appeared around her face, eyes, and mouth that I've never seen before.

I glower at Mom. "How much blood magic have you two been doing?"

Mom is completely still, the guilt stretching across her expression. "I didn't know the toll it would take on her. Not until I got my memories back and by then it was already done."

Dean sighs. "Come on. Let's get her into a bed. It might be awhile before she wakes up. Blood magic comes with a dark price and it looks like she's the one who's taken it on for all three of you."

I remember the alarm on Harmony's face when I'd first joined them in the spirit realm. Did she know then that she was going to take this one for all of us? For me, too? She didn't have to do that. Had it been my choice, I would have taken on some of it too. But then again, I wouldn't have known how.

She's clearly too weak from all of this. "What is going to happen to her? Is she going to die?" I brush her hair aside and run my fingers along her cold skin. "Please, wake up," I whisper. But she doesn't.

Dean gathers her into his arms as if she weighs little more than a bag of feathers, and Mom leads him to her bedroom. He lays Harmony across the paisley printed comforter and she tosses to her side, fitfully.

"She's freezing," Mom says, pulling thick covers over Harmony's shivering body.

"She's moving though. That's a good sign, isn't it?" I ask.

"I can help." Dean places his hand on Harmony's arm. "I can give her a boost of heat and then we should turn up the thermostat."

Mom nods at Dean with a grateful smile. "I think she'll be waking up soon." She places the back of her hand on Harmony's cheek. "I had healing magic before I came here. It's mostly gone now. I wish it wasn't."

"That explains your career choice." My voice trails off.

The room falls into silence, and I'm suddenly overcome with this unbelievably awkward feeling and I'm pretty sure they can see it written all over my face. How do I introduce my mom to my boyfriend? Is he my boyfriend? Yes, definitely. But still, it seems such a silly thing, to discuss my relationship status right now considering all the crap we're up against. There are so many more important conversations we need to have.

"Let's let Harmony rest and I'll make us up some hot cocoa," Mom offers. We follow her out and she gets to work while we hover around the little kitchen island.

Just as I'm about to make the introductions, Dean beats me to it. "I'm Dean." He extends his hand and she's quick to shake it. "It's nice to finally meet you. I've heard so many good things."

Mom raises an eyebrow but I can see the twinkle of amusement in her green eyes. She's actually quite pleased to meet Dean which makes me feel better about it. "Let me guess. You are a dragon, too?" She smiles broadly and looks pointedly at me. "I know a dragon when I see one. What is it with our family and falling in love with dragons?"

My cheeks flame and my heart flutters. "Mom!"

Dean clears his throat and changes the subject, asking if he can help her with the cocoa.

"Actually," I interject, "Mom, there's something I've learned about myself that you should know."

Mom turns on me, her face falling. "What is it?"

"Nothing bad!" I think back to Harmony in the bedroom, hopefully in a pleasant dreamland, and wish she could help me explain everything—understand it. "This might take awhile."

We carry our drinks to the table and sit down. Once I get started, I can't help it, I tell her just about everything. I fill her in on the situation with the reapers, to which she was horrified, and then tell her about how I turned into a spirit dragon. That part makes her smile. Now that her memories are back, it's like she's complete again. I never knew she was missing something but now the stark contrast is abundantly clear. She didn't know her past the same as I didn't know my ancestry.

"Like I said," she teases, "our family falls in love with dragons. I fell in love with you, didn't I? From the moment I knew of your existence, I knew you were mine and the love was instant. And to think, you're a spirit dragon? That's remarkable!" She pulls me into a hug and I practically melt into her, the stress of the last four months practically erasing. "I'm so proud of you, honey."

"I should have told you the truth from the beginning. I hope you can understand why I didn't and forgive me."

"I understand why you didn't." She rolls her eyes. "I'd have demanded you return home and wouldn't have taken no for an answer."

"And I wouldn't have blamed you."

Dean leaves us to check on Harmony and comes back with a smile. "She's doing better," he says. "She's starting to warm up. I think she might wake up on her own soon."

"Actually, that reminds me of when we first walked in the house. It had been super cold then too, but the air is almost back to normal now."

Mom nods. "It was the blood magic. It was very… demanding."

The thought of it makes me shiver. "I'm going to go sit with Harmony for a while."

"Good idea," Mom adds. "I'm coming, too."

In the end, we all go in there. I bring a throw blanket and sit on the floor at the edge of the bed. Mom sits in a chair at Harmony's side. Dean hovers by the door, saying he'd rather stand. It's hard not to stare at Harmony, so we all do. We're exhausted, the blood magic and the day catching up with us, but we stay there for what feels like hours.

Eventually, her eyes flutter open, revealing those strange solid white eyes of hers, and I almost scream with excitement. I do jump up and lean over the bed to get a better look. Her eyes remind me to ask Mom why hers are normal and Harmony's are not even close. Maybe faeries are all different. Maybe different *is* normal for them. Mom looks pretty human, excluding the metallic wings sticking out of her back. I've been trying not to stare at them but that's hard!

"Are you okay?" Mom slides in closer, grasping Harmony's hand.

Harmony swallows hard, like she's dangerously close to falling back under the weight of sleep, forcing her eyes to stay open.

"I'm okay," she confirms. I don't believe her. How can I when she looks like she's aged overnight and can hardly breathe?

"You took on the brunt of the blood magic, didn't you?" Dean asks gently, kneeling on the floor beside her.

Harmony doesn't answer but her eyes say it all. She did. Nor does she regret it.

"They're gone," her voice finally croaks.

"Who's gone?" he asks.

She struggles to sit up, and in her wake, a pile of blue ash rests on the white sheets. I gasp, my stomach turning to stone. "My wings," Harmony sighs, her eyes filling with anguish. "They're gone, aren't they? I felt them disintegrate while I was laying there."

She picks at the ash. "And now…"

"I'm so sorry," Mom's voice cracks, "there's nothing left."

Harmony nods. "My magic is gone too. The second I woke up, I knew it had left me. I can't see any paths anymore. I can't feel anything in my blood. It's all empty."

"Blood magic can do that much?" I growl, suddenly angry. "You didn't deserve that. You were helping us."

"Blood magic is costly," Harmony replies softly. "I knew that. The more people involved in a bond of magic, the more powerful it is, but the more sacrifices must be made. Why do you think the Occultists are so powerful? They bring their victims into the bond and then sacrifice them, literally taking all their blood to feed the magic. It's what happened to my family, my children." Her voice catches. "Losing my magic is nothing compared to the pain of losing them."

I don't know what to think or what to say. This is beyond tragic. Harmony knew though; she knew what she was risking. The fact she'd risk that for my mother and I seems extraordinary.

"Why?" I ask. "Why would you sacrifice so much for us? What are we to you?"

Harmony's eyes flash from mine to my mom's and back again. "Because it's my fault."

"What is?"

She turns to my mother and gathers every ounce of strength she has left. "I saw your path before you fled Spring and I didn't warn you. I thought we could change it with the potion. I didn't realize what I'd done until it was too late. I was foolish. It cost you your husband and later it cost me my family." A tear slips down her cheek. "I'm so sorry."

Mom doesn't stop to think. She leans over and wraps Harmony into a tight hug. "It's not your fault. It never was. You are not responsible for what those warlocks did to our people."

Dean and I exchange a look, passing a small smile between us. There's a lot these two need to talk about and we should probably give them their space, but Harmony stops us the moment we start to tiptoe toward the door.

"Wait." Her voice is urgent. "I wanted you to come to Ohio because you needed to learn of your lineage before going into Eridas. Now that you know the truth and that your father is dead, you must go to Eridas. You must stop the Occultists from making it into this side of the portal. You have to destroy their blood magic bond before it's too late."

"Well, that's the plan, except we ran into a bit of a roadblock." Dean and I go on to explain to her what happened with the portal in West Virginia and my warning from the nephilim Elias about all the portals having Occultists stationed on the other side of all of them now.

"I know where you can go." Harmony shakes her head. "It's a lesser known portal only used by a few of the winter fae. Even if the Occultists are waiting there, they won't expect you to go through at this place. You'll have to be careful but it's doable."

"They can't!" Mom interjects. "No way. She's not safe there."

"She's not safe here either," Harmony relents. "Please, we have to let them try. If we don't Eridas will fall and then this realm will follow soon after."

Mom frowns. "There's no other way?"

"No."

Mom deflates. "I don't like it."

"Nobody likes it but we'll be careful," I promise, "and Dean is going with me. He can fight."

Mom points at Dean. "You put her safety first, do you hear me?"

"I always do." And when he says it, I wonder if he always has. I was so angry at him countless times but now I can see why he was pushing me away as an attempt to protect me. And when he brought me close, made me live with him, it was for the same reasons. I want to go to him, to pull him into my arms, and kiss him. But my cheeks flame and I look away. Not in front of my mother.

"And I have weapons," Dean adds. "A trunk full of them."

Harmony laughs bitterly. "Oh boy, you know those will never work in Eridas. No technology, not even the most basic, has ever worked there or will ever work."

"But—"

"I know what you've been trying to do." She cuts him off. "It's a fool's errand, unfortunately. I saw all your paths, Dean, and I can promise you, taking electronics will only slow you down and cause you problems. You have to leave them here. They will never work in Eridas."

"But—"

"Never."

"Why didn't you tell me?"

"You didn't ask, for one. And for two, I needed you to stay in Westinbrooke long enough to meet Hazel."

The room grows hot. Dean is pissed. And frustrated. And probably a million other negative emotions about this. He had told me this work why he got himself exiled from Drakenon in the first place, and now this news? He's not taking it well. But he nods. "Fine."

And then he looks at me, his expression softening. "It wasn't a waste to meet you."

My heart does a little happy dance at that.

"Take some time with your mother." Harmony looks at me, her eyes trying to say something I can't quite read. "Get some rest. I'll give you instructions tomorrow."

I nod, letting it all sink in. A night or two in my childhood home and then what? The future is so unknown that not even Harmony can see it anymore. I can only hope I make it out of this thing alive. Given the pointed look in Harmony's eyes, I wonder if maybe she thinks I won't.

TEN
KHALI

THIS ISN'T MY FIRST VENTURE into the Jeweled Forest. Before I'd been awed by the beauty only to be quickly horrified by the cost. This time, it's all horror, and we haven't even landed yet. This morning when Silas pulled me from slumber, demanding Bram and I accompany his party to the Jeweled Forest, he'd refused to let me stay behind. So now I'm draped across his black scales, clinging to his neck and desperate not to fall off as he flies us through the clouds. I peer over to where Bram is slung across one of Silas's guards. We hold gazes for what feels like ages. His emerald eyes are charged with worry and bow-shaped lips are set into a grim line, but still, he watches me. And I watch him. Eventually, his dragon ride zooms ahead of Silas, breaking our charged stare.

We land in a clearing similar to the one Bram and I used weeks ago. It might even be the same spot but I can't be sure. Either way, the sight of sparkling jewels sends a chill over my entire body. Everything in me is lit up with warning. I hop off Silas's back and brush out my rumpled skirt, pulling my velvety cape tighter around my body. A light dusting of snow coats the ground and ices the jewels on the nearby trees, giving the forest an ethereal aura. I swallow down a bubble of fear and ball my hands into tight fists.

I *really* don't like this.

Silas shifts to his human form, his grin cocky as he surveys the area, eyes alight with excitement. They finally settle on me. "You don't look so thrilled to be here considering this was *your* idea."

It was my idea because I'd hoped he would get his murderous self trapped here, not because I wanted to witness it happen. This place is horrid and one visit was enough for a lifetime.

I shrug and smooth out my expression to one of aloof indifference. "I don't love jewels I can't touch."

Offering this information is pure strategy. I'm sure this crew already knows all about the risk of touching these jewels, but I hope this helps them to trust me more.

Silas laughs and rakes his eyes over my body, resting them on my tight bodice. I pull my cape closed and he chuckles. "You always did like pretty things."

And so does he, which is why I hope the voices here will get to him, that he'll try to take something he shouldn't and get trapped. Rotting away for ages—without fully dying—sounds like the kind of punishment someone deserves for murdering their twin brother in cold blood.

I tug at the dragon pendant tied to my neck and raise an eyebrow. "Do I now?"

It's another bet. I need him to think I hate wearing this. Normally, I would.

"Be good and maybe I'll take it off," he says, lips curling into a hungry smirk. It's full of double meaning and supposed to be flirtatious but it only serves me with disgust. I don't show it. I need to be patient, to string Silas along until I've got him where I want him. So I respond with a simple, "We'll see," and turn away to find Bram watching us with a rueful expression. My stomach dips and shame washes through me.

"Don't look so jealous, brother," Silas quips. "We'll find you a woman soon enough."

Bram says nothing.

Two guards stand at his side. They're the same elemental Dragon Blessed who handled me roughly on our way back from the human realm. I shoot them a glare, hoping they know not to harm Bram, hoping they know that I remember all too clearly how badly they treated me. I'm Queen now, but their loyalty still lies with Silas.

"Oh, calm down," Silas sighs, catching onto my glare at his men. "Bram is supposed to be under lock and key, remember? These guys are just doing their jobs."

"They were doing their jobs when they dragged me through the portal, threw me into a tent with you, and then forced me to continue our journey against my will." And with bruising hands if I tried to protest, is what I don't add. I continue to glare. The men aren't affected.

"Let's get on with it," Bram says, voice already sounding bored. "We're here to search for a magicked item, right? So let's do that."

"Where should we start, Oh Wise One?" Silas laughs.

Bram shifts his gaze away. "I seriously doubt we'll find anything, but let's head to where the forest is the densest. If there's something hidden in here, it's going to be where there's the most danger."

Which is exactly what I was counting on.

But I didn't want Bram and me to have to be here for this part. I sigh, lifting the long hem of my pink skirt as we head out. My leather boots crunch against the snow and I'm careful to keep my eyes pinned right in front of me, as not to get distracted by the glittering jewels and the dazzling temptations they possess. It's not the gems themselves that hold the temptation, because even though they're gorgeous and worth a fortune, I already know the cost of taking them is impossible to pay. No, it's that this entire forest seems to have some kind of numbing effect on my judgement. There's dark magic here, dark and ancient and begging to be unbridled.

I'm struck with a startling thought: what if the forest *is* protecting something? What if there really is a magicked item here and I'm about to lead Silas right to it?

"Do you hear that?" one of the guards yelps, his voice alarmed.

I strain my ears, but I hear nothing save for the breath in my lungs, the heart beating in my chest, and the trickling of winter wind against the glimmering tall trees.

"I can hear it, Sebastian," Silas says. "It sounds like a fae lyre."

The wind kicks up a notch.

"Don't pay it any attention," Bram says, "ignore it. It's dangerous."

"Maybe we should follow it." Sebastian sounds hopeful. He turns away from us and steps toward whatever sound is luring him in. "The strings, they're beautiful."

"No," Bram snaps, grabbing Sebastian's massive bicep. Bram jumps back, hissing and shaking out his hand. It's been burned with what looks like frostbite.

"What did you do?" I gasp, rushing to him as Silas and the other guard grab Sebastian and pin him down. The man must have used his air elemental to zap Bram. Luckily, it's not strong enough for Silas and the other dragon. They hold him back. He's lucky. He might not deserve to be held back if the way he treated me is any indication to his character.

"Snap out of it," Silas growls into Sebastian's ear, "or I'll electrocute you out of it."

Sebastian deflates, his entire body going still. "It's just so—"

"No, whatever you think it is, it's not." Bram scowls. I take his hand in mine, wincing at the patches of red. The skin isn't dead. I let out a sigh of relief. This will heal. "Unless you think something that wants to kill you is beautiful."

Silas shoots me a knowing look.

"When we get back to the castle"—I turn on Bram—"you need to have this looked at." What I don't add is by Juniper. Silas still doesn't know her secret and I can hardly stand to think of what he'd do with her if he knew the truth.

Bram pulls his hand away and puts distance between us. "Come on."

We continue down a path that winds us through the trees. They grow thicker, more alive, more jewels of every color, shape, and size—each begging to be touched. Held. Taken. The blue sky peeks at us from between the trees. It lessens the deeper we go, until there's hardly any blue left through the thick canopy.

That's when the voices start.

"Come to me."

"Help me."

"Where are you?"

They call to us, begging us to free them, offering our wildest dreams in exchange for freedom. We huddle together, the five of us no longer individuals but one united form, slowly winding our way through the dense foliage. Anytime one of us tries to step off, the others pull them in. It happens to each of us at least once. In the back of my mind, I want Silas to go and never come back, but he seems to have control over his faculties better than anyone.

Stubborn dragon.

Every few meters, a living corpse reveals itself. These poor people all seem to hail from different times, but they have one thing in common. They don't decay and they can't move. The trees grow from their flesh, connecting to appendages. Sometimes roots or entire trunks burst from their stomachs or the sides of their heads. I try not to look, try not to vomit or cry or scream.

We continue on.

Something long and white catches my eye. "What's that?" I squint, piecing together what looks like the bones from a forearm and ribcage.

"Skeleton," Bram says. "When the thousand years are up, the body finally decomposes and the souls are released."

"That must be an old soul then," Sebastian deadpans, eyeing the skeleton.

"Maybe this means we're getting closer," Silas says.

Do I hope so? Maybe. Because if he tries to touch it, whatever it is, and the forest may be able to claim him. But what if magicked items don't work like that? What if he's able to take whatever it is? Either way, at least I could get out of here. Because I don't want to be here anymore. My breath is shallow, my hands are shaking, and my heart skips angrily against my ribcage.

And my inner voice, it screams that this isn't right. We aren't meant to be here.

"We need to go," I whisper. "This was a terrible idea."

"No," Silas says, "we're almost there. I can feel it."

That's the problem. I can feel it, too.

We're nearing *something*.

The forest is almost as dark as night, it's become so thick. We continue, huddled close, until we come upon the largest tree I've ever seen. It's gnarled and black, the trunk the size of fifty regular trees, the branches beastly and so intertwined that they outstretch in a roof of black and jewels over our heads.

"There," Silas says breathily, pointing to the center of the trunk. I squint and step forward, trying to understand exactly what it is that I'm seeing.

A long staff is pressed against the trunk. It's embedded with glowing jewels of every color. Jewels that don't simply glitter like all the others. *They glow.*

"A sorcerer's staff," Bram adds. "Unbelievable."

Silas laughs softly, his entire face alive with greed. "Better believe it." He nods at Sebastian who is as equally giddy as he is. "You wanted to be the hero," he says, "go pick it up."

Sebastian's grin falls. "I can't."

Electricity zaps between Silas's fingers. "Do it."

Sebastian gulps and then shuffles forward. It's surreal to see the broad warrior frightened, but he is. When he stops in front of the staff, I expect him to protest, or at least to hesitate, but everything goes quiet and the man seems to become overcome again by the lure of the forest. He speaks, replying to a voice none of us can hear. "Yes," he says hungrily. "Yes, I will." And then, "Mine."

The moment his hands curl around the staff, he releases a blood curdling scream and falls against the tree trunk, convulsions raking his body.

Before we can do anything, the black bark twists and pulses, bursting with life and magic. It wraps him in its woody embrace and sucks him into the tree. Here one second, gone the next.

I scream, nearly falling to my knees.

Bram doesn't move.

The other guard doesn't move.

Silas rolls his shoulders back and sighs, his voice calculated when he says, "Leave the staff."

I have to admit, his admonition wakes me from my stupor. "You're just going to leave it here? You're not going to try to take it?"

Silas turns on me, the smile disappearing from his handsome face. His eyes turn cold. Dead. "You're not going to get rid of me that easily, Wife." His jaw clicks and he steps forward, leaning down close. "But thank you for this." He waves toward the staff. "It's exactly what I needed to find. Aleeryrick will undoubtedly agree to help me now."

"Aleeryrick?" I question. I've never heard the name before. *Or maybe...*

He stands back up and sighs. "No more questions." He spins in a slow circle, taking everything in. The heady magic in the air intensifies, as if to meet his ambition. He turns to me again. "You're going to have to trust me on this one."

ELEVEN
HAZEL

DEAN AND I ARE IN my backyard where I'm attempting, and failing, to shift. The midday sun beats down on my head and the snow beneath my feet is beginning to melt. I unzip my hoodie and tie it around my waist. We've been at this for over an hour already and so far absolutely nothing has happened. I even removed all my obsidian jewelry, which has brought on some ghosty lurkers, but no spirit dragon magic yet. One of those lurkers is Owen. He's in his dragon form, as if to cheer me on. Whatever, it's not working.

"It will be easier in Eridas," Dean assures me. "The magic there is strong, not weak like it is here." He motions around our little yard and shrugs. We have tons of trees lining the old wooden fence and since none of my neighbors have second levels, all that's visible are the varying rooflines. It's given us some great privacy for this activity, too bad nothing is happening.

I sigh and close my eyes, taking a deep breath and letting it out slowly. "I really hope you're right."

The door squeaks open and Harmony's face appears between the frame and the door. Her blue skin is gone, as are her all-white eyes and her younger faerie glamour. Still no gossamer wings, either, not that anyone expected them to grow back. Hiding the rest of her faerie appearance was her and Mom's mission this morning and I guess whatever they were up to, it worked. I skip over to her and gather her papery hands in mine.

"You're not blue anymore. How are you feeling?"

"I'm alright." But there's a crackle of sadness in her tone and regret behind her eyes that tells me she's actually *anything* but alright.

"I've been trying so freaking hard to shift," I complain, changing the subject, "but it's not working."

She nods once, white dreadlocks stiff contrast against her bright blue sweater. "I heard, and Dean is right, it will be easier in Eridas than it is here. I believe you were able to before because you had so much at stake and were fighting for your life. You don't have that right now."

"I really hope you guys are right about this." Something she said gives me pause. "Wait, can you see it? Can you see me being able to shift in Eridas?"

She squeezes my hands and leads me to the outdoor loveseat. It's under the porch so even though it's ice-cube cold, it's not wet or anything. "We must discuss the plan."

"You didn't answer my question." I point out as we settle into the padded seats. Dean towers over us with a look of sheer concentration on his face. I raise a brow at him and eye one of the chairs, but he just crosses his arms over his chest. He can be such an alpha-male sometimes.

Harmony frowns. "My elemental magic hasn't come back. I believe it was sacrificed to the blood magic. I'm lucky to be alive."

"I'm so sorry."

She shrugs. "I can't see your paths anymore or anyone's for that matter. But I saw them before this happened and still believe you'll be able to shift in Eridas. What's important now is how to get you to safety once you cross over."

"So you do know of a portal we can use?" Dean asks.

"I do." Harmony nods, her lips twisting as she considers her next statement. "But it's an extremely dangerous portal. You'll be catapulted into an open field right in the middle of the Winter Kingdom, which is now the center of the Occultist's territory." Just the thought sends a shiver up my spine that has nothing to do with the crappy weather. "You'll have to seek shelter and perform a spell once you're on the other side that will take you to safety."

Dean nods. "We can do that."

"We can?" This is news to me.

"You can," Harmony confirms.

"We're not witches though. But... I guess neither are you. So how did you do it?"

"There are many elemental spells." Harmony smiles softly and her eyes fill with memories. "It's different magic than sorcery. Would you like to learn?"

I nod enthusiastically. I want to learn anything and everything I can about magic, especially the kinds I can access.

We spend the rest of the day talking through everything, going over the landscape of the Winter Kingdom, discussing the spell we're to perform, and the plan to get to Drakenon from there. That's when I'll bust my friends free. Harmony still insists I'll be battling the Occultists before I head home. That's the part I'm having trouble coming to terms with. Truth is, I don't know how I could possibly stop those guys. I'm a spirit elemental dragon. I'm not filled with fire like Dean. Or four elements like Khali. I don't have control over my abilities and I've only shifted once.

Everyone may think I'm going to save them all, but right now, I'm only concerned with saving my friends and getting the heck out of there.

It stays on my mind all through dinner, and as we're cleaning up, I still can't stop thinking about it. My arms are elbow deep in a sink full of bubbles because our old dishwasher is broken again, when Mom comes to my side.

"Are you sure about this?" Her voice is as earnest as her expression.

"Saving my friends? Yes. The rest of it? No."

"Yeah, me either." Her voice trails off.

"There's a 'but' in there, isn't there?" I tease. "Spit it out."

"What if the Sovereign Occultists succeed." She massages her bottom lip between worried teeth as she considers her fears. "It won't only be Eridas that's in trouble, it'll be this world. I can glamour myself and Harmony and keep us safe for now. You can be safe here, too. But for how long?" She closes her eyes and a tear slips loose. "I don't want to lose you."

"So what you're saying is if I'm not successful in everything, not just freeing my college friends but eradicating the most powerful cult of warlocks Eridas has ever known, then we all might lose everything and die terrible deaths."

Mom lets out a laugh. Dean appears behind me and begins to massage my neck. I try to let myself relax, to melt into his touch, but it's difficult. "We've known this for a while, Hazel."

"I know. But why has it been so hard for me to accept?"

"Because you don't believe in yourself," Harmony joins in the conversation from where she's resting at the dining table. She stares at me with complete determination in her watery eyes. "But you must. And if it's any consolation, we believe in you, and I've *seen* you succeed."

I fake a smile and lie through my teeth. "Don't worry, I'm going to figure this out. And before you know it, we'll all be back together."

Mom's eyes gleam. "Maybe even by Christmas."

I laugh, the very idea ridiculous. "At the very least, New Years." I wink.

"Why don't you two go to a movie or something?" Mom suggests. "Go enjoy a night out before your big trip tomorrow."

A huge smile lifts my cheeks. "That sounds amazing, thanks, Mom." I dry my hands on the towel and turn into Dean's arms. "And actually, I have something else in mind instead of a movie." I grin up at him. "Are you game?"

"Game?"

"Yes, pun intended."

He doesn't get the joke but he will! "Always." His dark eyes twinkle with little sparks of orange. And a half hour later as we're walking into the town arcade, those sparks turn red.

"What is this place?" Dean asks, eyeing the digging games, flashing lights, and screaming children. It's a lot to take in, but for me, all I feel is happy and excited.

"That's exactly why I brought you here." I wrap my arms around his torso. "I figured you've never been somewhere like this." I point to the skee-ball. "We'll come back to the arcade games later. Right now, you and I have a date with the laser tag room."

His eyebrows raise. "Laser tag? Is that what it sounds like, because it sounds intense."

"It's exactly like it sounds and it is awesome. Come on!"

I tug him after me, pay for our wristbands, and before we know it, we're on the blue team getting briefed by a bored looking teenager. The other players are a mix of families and highschoolers, nobody I recognize, not that I wouldn't mind showing off my hot boyfriend to all the kids who bullied me growing up.

The worker opens the door and we race into the laser tag room, heavy plastic vests with fake guns attached bouncing against our rib cages. We find a good hiding spot behind a paint splattered pillar and huddle together in the darkness.

The blacklight makes Dean's teeth glow crazy white as he smiles down at me. "This is actually pretty cool."

"Just you wait."

The countdown ends—three, two, one—and we're off. The techno music is head-pounding, kids are running everywhere, and we're shooting like complete maniacs, half taking this seriously and half laughing our heads off. We shoot our lasers, Dean with practiced skill, me like a girl who knows her way around a video game, and in the end, Dean and I lead the blue team to victory.

"Let's play again!" Dean laughs.

So we do. We play three more times, and then spend another two hours in the arcade, collecting a bazillion tickets that only buy us a bunch of stupid crappy toys and random hard candies at the prize counter. It's glorious. And it's also the most I've ever seen Dean relax and let himself have fun. It's kind of hard to imagine the scary, mean, threatening guy I first met back in August. It's also kind of hard to imagine this guy is an exiled prince, the kind that comes from an intense royal family and a whole dragon society.

That part I try not to think about too much, because when I do, I can't help but wonder what will happen if his people decide they want him back. Where will that leave me? Hybrids aren't welcome in Eridas, right? No way they'll think I'm good enough for a full-blooded dragon prince. It's one thing to be his girlfriend in the human realm and laser tag partner for a fun date night. But what happens down the road? Dean and I belong to two separate worlds and I want to live in this one, however great Eridas might be. What if Dean gets back to Drakenon and feels the same way about *his* home?

My heart hurts just thinking about it.

TWELVE
KHALI

EARLY THE NEXT MORNING, I join my parents for breakfast in their chambers. Father doesn't eat much, picking at the food, then going back to rest on his bed. I follow him and sit on the edge, running my hand along the oak footboard. He's still a little pale and has a long ways to go in getting his full strength back. He hadn't used his muscles or eaten properly in weeks while he was sick. "Don't you worry about me, Khali," he says adamantly. "At least I'm not stuck in some dark corner of the castle somewhere. I'll be fine here."

"I'm taking good care of him," Mother adds, coming to stand at his side. She cups her hand to his forehead and smiles gratefully. "He hasn't had a fever since he woke up and it broke."

"I still worry…" My voice trails off.

"Don't," he presses, "not about me anyway."

Mother shoots him a warning look, the kind I'm usually on the receiving end of, that gives me pause.

"I'm tired," Father is quick to supply.

"Fine." I slip off the bed and give them both a hug, finishing with a kiss on Father's cheek. "But I promise I'll be visiting as often as I can. I'm sure it won't be long until life will go back to normal."

I leave before they can see how hard it is for me to believe my own lie. But also, I leave because it's hard to be around them.

I don't feel like myself anymore and I don't wish to tell them just how unhappy I am in my marriage. What good would that do any of us? They can't help me now. Nobody can, not really. And besides, I don't want to get them involved in this mess any more than they already are. I know father would want me to confide in him. I suspect he can sense something is wrong with me and that he's worried. But at least for now, I vow to keep it all locked inside.

The same feelings come up around Faros. She's still my lady's maid and we have a history that will never be erased, but it's hard to consider her the kind of friend I could confide in. It's not like how it was before, and certainly not like how it was with Owen. I never had a friend like him before his death and worry I never will again. Things simply aren't what they used to be. I've been through so much and can no longer tolerate idle chat about court gossip and affairs and what fashion will be in style next. I know it's not Faros's fault—she hasn't been through what I've been through—but the fact still remains that there aren't very many people in this castle who I can relate to right now.

As I exit their chambers and find myself in the stone hallway I know so well, with the light streaming through the windows, with the dragon army practicing drills outside, and my old room only next door, all I want to do is find Bram. It's startling, this pull I have to him, but I can't deny it. I want to make sure he's okay after what happened yesterday in the Jeweled Forest. And I want to be near him, simply to talk to him, to see him, be with him, even though I shouldn't.

The hallway is quiet, it's still quite early. Something is different.

My guards.

They're not here. Silas has had at least two on me whenever I'm outside of the queen's chambers but now they're nowhere to be seen.

This is my chance to explore the tunnels more, except the entrance Owen and I used leads to a dead end now and the only other one I know of is behind Silas's bookshelf—no way I'm going there. And once again, it's Bram's face that flits across my mind.

Is he locked in his room right now, same as my father? If anyone sees me going to him alone we'll become the center of gossip. One thing I've learned about this place is that if people have the opportunity to spread the lastest news, they will. But the guards aren't here right now and I have no doubt that won't last. I have to do something with my sudden freedom.

I'm safe to do as I want.

Except...

Except I don't have magic anymore.

Except my husband has spies everywhere.

Except there is an Occultist on the loose somewhere, possibly still in Drakenon, and even if Silas has swept that fact under the rug, I still know it. But he knows the truth. So why isn't he being more careful? There's got to me something more going on here—something I'm not seeing. *Something secret.*

Does it have to do with what Bellflower Blossom was trying to tell me? Is it something to do with the sorcerer's staff and that strange name, Aleeryrick?

No matter what, it's my job to figure it out, to stop Silas from hurting more people, and to figure out a way to save this kingdom from the Sovereign Occultists. I may not be able to control my set of circumstances but I certainly can work toward those goals. The warlocks are coming for us; they have to be. It's only a matter of time before they show up for battle and if we're not prepared we will die. So I'll make allies and convince them to get ready, to take this seriously. And I'll spy on Silas, find a way to figure out what he's up to, and hopefully, even restore my own magic in the process.

I let out a breath and turn on my heels, striding fast, trying not to let a million doubts follow at my heels.

Enough of that. Juniper was right. Stop feeling sorry for yourself.

As I walk to Bram's chamber, I notice the way the few people awake at this hour look at me, both the servants and the courtesans. It's the way they looked at Queen Brysta, like I have something important to say, like I should be admired and sought out. I run my hand over my loose curls and try not to fidget with them. Faros met me early today and managed to create a perfect crown braid around the top of my head and secured sparkly ruby pins into the braid all before the sun had completely risen. Add the matching dress of glossy red, cut tight around the waist and low around the bodice, and I look exactly how a Queen of Drakenon should look. Silas's awful necklace holds tight around my neck but Faros layered strings of pearls over it to cover it up.

I don't feel like a queen on the inside but I look it and right now, that's all that matters. Nobody stops to question why I'm alone or where I'm going.

Maybe Juniper is right about that too and it's time I start acting like a queen, because apparently I can get a lot more done with this attitude. Would a queen fear walking into her brother-in-law's chambers to check on his health? Of course not.

I walk right past the sleepy guard stationed outside of his door, noting it's a different man from the one who survived the Jeweled Forest, and waltz in like I'm an expected guest. I don't know if Bram will be sleeping or eating breakfast, but I'm not surprised to find him the same as I've always found him in these chambers over the years, in his library with his nose stuck in a book. The pink color in his cheeks is strong and his hair is the same usual curly shag around his face which I suddenly find so endearing. I used to think he was messy and unkempt, boring and too serious, but now I don't think any of those things. When he catches me staring, there's still that haunted expression behind his eyes, but he smiles and for a second it's as if all the bad things never happened, like we're back to doing our weekly visits.

But no. This isn't mandatory and it won't be weekly. *And ... I want to be here.* And besides, this is nothing like all the other visits. It can't be. I'm married.

"Hi," I say brightly, closing the library door behind me. It's just the two of us now. Another thing that never happened with our previous visits. Does he notice it, too? Does he care? And does it make his heart beat wildly like it does mine?

I stand frozen, chest rising and falling with heavy breaths, as I realize just how much I've changed. Him, too.

"Hi," he replies slowly, his voice like molten honey, and then he does the last thing I expect him to do. He stands, strides right over to me, and pulls me into a full-bodied hug. He smells earthy and wonderful, feels stronger and taller than I remember. Relief floods my system.

The contact is like a soothing balm and creates the first moment of clarity I've had in days.

I want Bram to be safe. I want him to be happy. And I care about him far more than I ever thought I did. He's so much more than a friend to me now. *I like him.* I might even love him. But it's too late to tell him these things and certainly too dangerous to act on them, so I peel myself out of his arms and step back, clearing my throat.

"How are you?" I ask. "Is everything okay now? Do you feel better? I wanted to ask you yesterday but…"

He searches my eyes like a dying man searching for life. I can't help but admire the vibrant green of his irises and I have to look away before he sees too much truth in me.

He can't know. He can't know. He can't know.

"I'm okay," he finally answers. "Devastated about my father, among other things." He swallows and his cheeks redden. "But I'm okay."

"Yeah... devastated is a good word for it." I let out a long sigh and grasp his hand in mine, holding on tight. "I'm so sorry."

"You're sorry?" He shakes his head. "No, Khali, this is my fault. If I hadn't killed my father, you'd not be queen yet and I thought maybe we could find a way to annul the wedding before the coronation but now everything has gotten so—"

"Stop," I hiss. He's already said too much.

Panic rises in my chest and I have to force myself from speaking too loudly. "You have to stop. This is treasonous and if one word of it got to your brother, you'd be dead, just like Owen, or exiled like Dean. You can't ever speak like this again."

His mouth thins into a peckish line.

"Do you promise?" When he doesn't immediately reply I can't help it, I have to push the matter. I squeeze his hand even harder. "Seriously, Bram, I mean it. I need you to promise."

"Fine." He squeezes back. "I won't speak of it again after I say this one thing."

"Bram..."

He holds up his free hand, fisting the air as he speaks. "The reaper had me and I didn't know it because I couldn't see it. But I could hear him sometimes. I thought it was my thoughts but I couldn't control them and that scared me. I don't know how to explain it."

"Bram, what happened wasn't your fault."

"But I need you to understand something." He steps closer and takes my other hand, pulling both of them against the planes of his chest. His hands are so soft and warm and envelop mine so perfectly, like they were made to rest there. And his chest, it's so hard, with a heart pounding underneath. "The reaper didn't want me to kill my father. It wanted me to kill you."

I swallow hard, letting the revelation sink in. I don't know what to say.

"That's why I was trying to distance myself from you and why I was hoping Juniper could heal me. I've never wanted to hurt you but then I'd get these images or these thoughts and I knew something was wrong. When I killed my father, it was only because I made the creature direct his hate toward whoever was standing closest to me in that moment." His voice cracks, pain breaking through. "That moment when I was going to kill you." His hands start to shake. "It could have been anyone. My mother. Silas. The Priest. Anyone could have died that day but it happened to be my father who was closest to me. Once it took over my mind, I blacked out. I don't remember everything. Only the start of it and the end when I was being dragged from the room and you were yelling about the reapers and my father was surrounded by a pool of his own blood."

"I'm sorry." A tear splashes down my cheek. "I should have figured out what was going on sooner. I could have helped you. I made so many mistakes."

"Listen to me, Khali," he whispers. I look up to focus on him. We're standing so close now. "I hate that my father is dead and that you're married to my brother. I hate that he's the king now, but I can't regret that you're still alive. I could never regret that. If I had to choose, you'd be the last one to get hurt."

"What are you saying?" I whisper back.

His smile quirks. "I thought it was obvious."

My heart skips and his confession settles over me. "But you've never seemed interested in me," I blurt. "Or seemed to care."

He's silent for a long minute. We're closer than ever now and still holding hands. His thumb gently caresses the back of my hand and my knees grow weak. "I couldn't be honest but that doesn't mean I haven't loved you since I could remember, because I have. But then we all grew up and I wasn't Dragon Blessed and my brothers were. There was absolutely zero chance for us."

"You loved me?" That word, love, it means everything. And I want to say it back so bad that it's like a physical thing squeezing my chest, this overpowering desire to reciprocate his feelings.

"I still do," he whispers. "I love you."

It's everything... but it's forbidden.

"Bram don't." It hurts to stop him but I can't do this. It's too dangerous. My eyes burn. My heart rips in two. "We can't."

"Everyone thought I was resentful because I didn't have magic but really it was because I knew I'd never get to have you." He swallows, searching my face. "Can I have you now? Just this once. And then I'll fade into the background and we'll go back to the way things were before."

I should run away. *I need to go.* But my feet and my heart aren't listening to my mind and before I know it I'm inching forward and letting him wrap me into his arms. Our lips are so close but we don't close the gap, not yet. We just look at each other, everything revealing itself without words. He smells like life, like florals and sandalwood and earth and everything that is so, so alive—*I am so, so alive.*

He kisses me.

And it's gone. The fear and confusion and anger. All the bad things evaporate into nothing but him. Only him and me and this one moment in my life that makes sense. I could stay here forever and he could too. I know it because I deepen the kiss and he moans and we're up against the wall now and I suddenly understand so many things I didn't understand before about why people do careless things for love.

But then someone is knocking on the door and we're flying apart and I'm wiping my mouth and Bram's cussing with frustration and I get it.

Again, I understand.

Juniper strides through the door. Juniper ... and Silas.

My breath catches, and I straighten my spine, smiling absentmindedly like I haven't a care in the world. But all I can think is if Silas saw us what he would do and why is he with Juniper? What is he going to do next? Silas's piercing gaze zeros in on me before shooting to his brother and back to me again.

No. He can't know. Not for sure. Stay calm.

"Hello, Silas," Bram says, his voice as smooth and relaxed as ever. He wanders over to his bookshelf and straightens a few volumes before turning back to us.

"What is she doing here?"

Bram shrugs. "Khali came to check on me, worried that the Jeweled Forest may have brought the reaper back, but nothing has changed. I'm fine. Is that what you two are doing here as well?" He looks away, staring out the window with a frown. "You already know I'll never forgive myself for what happened to our father. Feel free to keep me locked up in here as long as you'd like. I deserve it."

"Oh, no." Silas smiles coolly. "Give the courtesans enough time and they'll have someone else to gossip about and you can go back to whatever it is you do around here." He waves at the bookshelves like they're filled with things for children. His blond hair is tied back and his clothing is tailored to perfection. He looks amazing, like a king should look, but there's zero comparison to my stunning Bram. "I couldn't help but notice the sweet little relationship you have with our little fae elf friend here," he says to Bram. His tone is meant to sound playful, but to me, it's anything but.

Juniper smiles, her big brown doe-eyes softening when they reach Bram's fallen expression. She doesn't look at me.

"And I also couldn't help but wonder if you two ought to become more than friends," Silas continues, his words turning wicked and proud. He raises his eyebrows suggestively and smirks. "It would smooth things over with some of the courtesans, I think, to have some kind of alliance. And anyway, you're not a eunuch, are you? You ought to enjoy yourself. So I asked Juniper if she'd do us all a favor and give you a chance. Luckily, she has agreed to date you."

Bram's face burns bright red. I can't tell if this is something Juniper wants or simply something Silas wants and is demanding of her. She's become my friend, sure, but I've sensed her desire to be close to Bram. Not that I blame her.

But it can't be about diplomacy and court politics. Silas is lying about something and this must be part of his scheme.

Everyone is still as the implications set in, my heart twisting under Silas's cruelty.

"Great idea," Bram says at last. He strides to Juniper, then gives her a little bow and a soft kiss to her hand. My eyes water and all I can think of is what we were doing just minutes before. "I would be a lucky man. Anyone would."

She smiles faintly and arches a perfect brow. "We'll see. You haven't won me over yet."

Everyone laughs, though it's stilted, and Silas pats Bram on the back. "Don't screw this one up, huh? It's about time you're useful for something around here."

He turns to me, a violence in his movements I can't trust. "Khali, I'll escort you back to your room. Wouldn't want anyone to think you were in here alone, would we?"

"No." My voice croaks and I hate myself for it. Why aren't I stronger?

"Don't let it happen again." The threat is clear.

"Of course, not." My smile is sickly-sweet as I go to him, threading his arm with mine.

As he escorts me from the room, I catch Bram's eyes. They're filled with so much pain and I can only imagine they're an exact mirror of my own. And then it's Juniper I see and she's studying my neckline. Her face falls as she spots Silas's necklace underneath all the pearls. Just as well. This way she can tell Maxx and Terek to call off the search. I smile sadly at her and she frowns back. What did we really think was going to happen? Did we really think we could change things? That we'd beat Silas?

No. I'm a caged animal—locked in with a monster—and so are they.

THIRTEEN
HAZEL

"SO WHAT DID YOU LEARN?" Dean asks as I skim through the article on my phone.

"Well, in 1862, part of the Sioux Indian tribe, called the "Dakotas" got into a conflict with the United States government along the Minnesota River. It was a bad winter and the tribe was starving to death." I skip ahead. "It looks like some agents of the government had promised to give the tribe payments but they were late or never turned up at all." I click my tongue. "Geeze, this is horrible."

"What?"

"It escalated to the point of an all out bloodbath. Settlers and their families were attacked and murdered and then thirty-eight Dakotas were sentenced to hanging. Yuck—it was the largest mass execution in US history."

"That's pretty bad." Dean maneuvers our shiny new rental car that we picked up after our flight into a parking spot and kills the engine. I peer up at the weathered brick building with its mounds of snow on the roof and I'm reminded of our own little Main Street in Westinbrooke.

"It was not a great moment, that's for sure," I say. "And not something I remember learning about in history class as a kid."

"It also explains why there's a ley line portal here."

"Yup." I let out a breath. "Welcome to Minnesota."

Dean says that ley lines are energetic pathways that run all over the earth. In the areas of intense emotional events, the land will hang onto that energy forever. If there also happens to be a ley line in the same spot? Bam! Portal.

Which is exactly how Dean and I have ended up flying to freezing Mankato, Minnesota, only five days before Christmas. Harmony said she'd never been to the portal herself but knew it was here, and we should go to where the hangings took place to look for it.

"Remind me again why people live here?" I ask as soon as we get out of the car, only half joking as I bury myself into my fur-lined coat. We pop open the trunk and I heave the backpack on my shoulder. It hangs heavy, filled with everything we could possibly need for our trip to Eridas. "It's only thirteen degrees out here today," I add, "but with the wind-chill factor it's so much worse."

I borrowed this particular coat from Mom before we left. The woman hates the cold even more than I do and I knew I'd need something extra warm for where we were headed. Nothing screams bitter cold like the Winter Court! Dang, if only the Summer thing had worked out but I guess you can't win them all.

"Get used to it," Dean teases but immediately wraps an arm around me and shoots some of his elemental warmth into my limbs. I relax into it, my body melting. *Ahh, that's nice.*

"Heaven," I sigh.

Dean kisses my cheek. "The Winter Kingdom is in a perpetual state of icy winter and besides that, the Occultists have taken over, so it won't be a very safe place for either of us. We're going to have to be extra careful and move quickly to the Drakenon border."

"Good thing Harmony's got contacts for us, right?" I think back on the plan she gave us to find them, worried it won't work, but trusting that it will.

"Yes, of course," Dean says. "But either way, we can't stay for long."

"I hope it'll be the pretty blue skies and sparkling icicles kind of winter weather," I muse, trying not to let my nerves get the better of me and staying on the topic that doesn't freak me the freak out. "And not the 'colder than a freezer and blocks out the sun' kind of winter."

Dean laughs, shaking his head.

Mankato is a cute little town on the farthest outskirts of Saint Paul, Minnesota. We're near the river where there are fully grown trees everywhere and quaint historic buildings. This close to Christmas, it's dripping in holiday charm. I half expect a gaggle of carolers to come barreling around the corner. I peer at the different colored brick buildings stacked right next to each other with their welcoming stoops and neat awnings, and I almost wish we could stay here until this evening and see what it looks like lit up with Christmas lights.

Almost.

My friends are counting on me. Not just my friends—everyone. We need to keep moving.

"Reconciliation Park is this way," Dean says and we hurry across the road, ice melt crunching under our boots as we try to beat the flashing crosswalk sign before it changes to a red hand. All the info we could get from the locals at the airport is that the mass hanging took place near where the park was built in the 70s, but nobody was sure if it was the *exact* spot. As we step into the small park, we spot a memorial monument erected in dark stone and rush over.

My eyes rove across the script. It's a prayer to the tribes of the area, to the north, south, east, and west, to the Great Spirit and Mother Earth. The words are so heartfelt, but also sad, and I know that they're going to stay with me long after I leave this place.

"Wow. That's a nice tribute," Dean says softly.

"I can't pretend to understand all that went on here," I say, "but yes, it is."

Together we press our hands against the icy stone; maybe it will somehow transport us through the portal. Nothing happens. We peel away from it and wander around the park, which is actually pretty small, but loaded with something everywhere you look: the memorial monument, a few statues, a water fountain feature, a green area that's currently covered with snow, and a short path that leads to a river overlook. In the middle of a cold day like this, nobody else is milling about. I imagine this place will get busy when the Christmas lights come on though.

"I don't know, Dean. There's nothing even remotely similar to the other portal around here." The sparkling swirl of colors would be unmistakable, and even if regular human eyes couldn't see it, we would be able to. "I mean, I'm sure Harmony was right that this was the event that created the portal, but do you think it's really right here? Maybe it's nearby or somewhere else along the river."

"Maybe. Wherever it is, we'll find it," Dean assures me.

I eye the flash of sparkling river water with trepidation. "You don't think it's under the water, do you?"

"Could be." He furrows his brow, worry crossing his features. "Some portals are."

The thought of jumping into a lake is bad enough, but it's colder here than it is in West Virginia, and rivers have currents. Strong ones. We may very likely end up dead if we even attempted to swim in that kind of water, even with Dean's fire to keep us from freezing. It's not like we can shift into our dragon forms out here in public and I'm obviously not able to do that right now anyway. Harmony told us her contacts in the Winter Court might be able to help me learn to control my abilities. The plan is to dodge the Occultists, find Harmony's friends, learn as much as I can about my magic in as short of a period as I can, then go to Drakenon, and convince them to not only spare Dean's life, but to let my friends go, oh and then we're all supposed to defeat the Occultists together.

No big deal.

I shake my head, focus returning to the matter at hand. *One problem at a time, Hazel.* "We're not water elementals. It's too risky to go near moving water like that. If the portal is under there, we're going to have to find another way into Eridas."

Dean pulls me into a hug and I relax against this chest. "We'll find a way. Let's keep looking around, okay?"

I nod and gaze around again, this time focusing on the few spirits mingling about the park instead of the scenery. Ever since my birthday, I haven't had any problems with the spirits bothering me. Maybe they know what I truly am now and they're afraid of me. Or maybe I have more control over this gift when before it was a curse always spiralling out of control. I can't say one way or the other, but I'm hopeful and trying super hard not to get too excited about it or too comfortable.

We amble around the park, Dean sending me blasts of heat every few minutes, which I know isn't the best idea. He needs to get back to Eridas to restore his fire elemental magic and shouldn't be using it for my comfort, not when we might need it for a better reason. But I can see the worry growing on his face and if this is one way he can ease the tension, then I'm going to let him have it. We end up walking down a side path shrouded with trees on both sides. The leaves are long gone and the branches stick out in a chaotic pattern. No streams of sunlight bursting through; it's too cloudy today.

A Dakota warrior stands in the middle of the path, his presence unlike anything I've experienced. It stops me dead in my tracks, and a frosty chill runs through me that has nothing to do with the weather.

"What is it?" Dean asks. But I'm lost for words.

This spirit is so unlike the other spirits I'm used to seeing. There's no way he's from this modern age, which means he hasn't crossed over from the spirit realm to whatever next place waits for him. Ancient ghosts are incredibly rare. Even Westinbrooke, with its civil war history, didn't have anyone sticking around to haunt it—at least not that I saw. It's like he stepped out of a black and white photo from the past, brought to life in living color. His layered clothing is made from thick wool in every color of the rainbow and tan elk hide. Large feathers stick out the back of his headdress, and long dark braids cascade down his back. Around his neck hang more feathers, beads too, and in his right hand, rests a wooden staff with intricate carvings and more feathers adorning the top. He's magnificent, and terrifying—and staring right at me.

Dean steps forward and the ghost slams his staff into the path to block him. It's not as if Dean couldn't just walk right through him, but I pull him back anyway. "Stop."

Dean stills. "What do you see?"

"A Dakota warrior." I swallow hard. "I think he's protecting something."

"The portal?" Dean whispers and I nod. Maybe the portal, maybe not, but this man is definitely protecting *something*.

The Dakota warrior begins speaking in a language I can't even begin to understand, his voice sharp angles and deep resonance.

"Can you help us?" I ask him as soon as he pauses.

He slams his staff into the ground, harder this time, and I scramble back. I'll take that as a big fat *NO and get the hell off this land right now, white woman!*

"It must mean the portal is nearby," Dean states and I shush him. He can't see what I'm seeing. I don't want him to mess this up, not when we're so close.

I try to connect again, this time keeping my mouth sealed and reaching under my coat to remove one of the obsidian necklaces. I keep the one Cora and Macy gave me for my birthday hidden and hold out the string of black round beads.

Harmony gifted me it all those weeks ago and I hate to part with it but this is a worthy enough cause. I don't know if it's possible, but if anyone can pass an item from this world into the spirit one, it would be me, wouldn't it?

I bow my head and peer up at the warrior, hoping he can sense that I come in peace. Am I being disrespectful for looking in his eyes? Should I look down instead? Is the small gift enough? Am I being pretentious to even offer it? Maybe I should try to learn how to ask for help in his language and come back later? The questions race through my mind and I feel foolish and inadequate, trying to understand something that is so far beyond my comfort zone and life experience.

But his stony face softens, the flicker of a smile turning the corner of his lips, and he reaches out for the necklace. It works. One second it's dangling from my fingers in the mortal realm and the next he's holding it in the spirit realm. I smile, too.

Dean growls under his breath and squeezes tighter where he's holding my other hand with his. He may not be able to see what I can, but we're in this together, and thank heavens for that because my knees are starting to grow weak. I need to do this right.

The Dakota warrior runs his thumb along the black beads before depositing them into an inner pocket. Then he slams his staff into the earth again and this time, the sound of it takes on an echoing quality—unearthly. Dean tightens next to me, pulling me close. The sky flashes, turning pitch black for a second and then lighting in a swirl of sparking color. It surrounds us, spinning faster and faster as it goes, like a tornado of pinks and red, blues and greens, yellows and oranges. My hair whips around my head. Dean hugs me to his body. It grows even colder. Impossibly cold.

"Do you see this?" I pant.

"Yes," Dean says into my ear, his voice tight.

The Dakota warrior is unaffected. He slams his staff into the path one last time and then he's gone… and we're gone too. The world flashes dark again—bright white, so bright, before returning to normal. We blink.

"We're here," Dean whispers.

Eridas. The Fae's Winter Kingdom.

It's far more beautiful than I'd imagined. And far more deadly, too.

FOURTEEN
KHALI

I STARE AIMLESSLY AT THE smoke as it billows from the fire, a misshapen line of gray streaking the blue sky. It takes me back to Owen's funeral and the pain of his death stings all over again. The recent blanket of white snow reflects the bright midday sun and I try not to squint or look uncomfortable—or worse, disinterested. To appear anything other than sad during King Titus's funeral wouldn't be wise. And in a way, I am sad. He wasn't always kind to me but he was an important part of Drakenon and loved by the Brightcaster bloodline. He did a lot in recent years to make life better for the non-Dragon Blessed. And his absence will change history—he will be missed. But it's Owen who occupies my thoughts right now. He was my best friend, and I wonder what he'd say about me and Bram? What he'd make of everything that's happened with Silas. I wish I could talk to him. I'd give anything for one more conversation with my favorite person.

We're all outside, eyes glazed by the funeral pyre as it slowly burns. These kinds of goodbyes aren't easy, and Silas and Bram are visibly upset; but it's Brysta who makes my heart hurt. She loved her husband. I always wondered if maybe she didn't, or maybe he did something to her to make her so compliant to his wishes, but the raw pain on her face is unmistakable and I'm certain that she really did love him. Maybe that's why she didn't fight him more on his stance toward her magic and toward my future. Perhaps she was happy to go along with whatever he wanted because of how much she cared about him. Or it could be that she actually agreed with all of his staunch opinions. It is the way things are done, after all.

She catches me watching her and stares right back. The one brown and one blue of her eyes is hard for me to look at. I don't want to be like her. I never wanted this life, never asked for it. Does she see the resistance etched across my face? Letting her grieve in peace, I offer a kind smile and then turn back to the crackling fire even though the breeze has shifted directions and the smoke burns my eyes. I let them water, a few rogue tears falling down my face. It looks better this way.

The formal part of the funeral is long over and after a while, most people leave, couples arm in arm, long gowns brushing the snow and mud. Bram is escorted back to his chambers, Juniper at his side. I don't look at him, not even once. It's too hard knowing that we can't be together. I stand by Silas for what feels like hours, shivering under my cloak, legs aching, toes pinching in my boots, stomach growling, but I don't dare complain. He's going to be extra emotional after this and I don't want him to take any negative feelings out on me. For now his expression shifts from stoic and cold, to broken and angry. I'm not sure what to expect from him next.

The ground shakes and my knees buckle. Silas catches me before I hit the ground. Someone screams, her voice echoing across the open field. Confusion is a hot knife slicing right through my center. Are the Occultists here? Is it an elemental doing this? Something booms and crashes, and on the horizon, trees split and fall, making way for a shrouded figure emerging from the forest. Silas is yelling and his guards are circling in around us. Brysta bursts into tears which is so unlike the normally composed woman. This day is going to break her down even more than she already is.

I turn back to Silas. "What's happening?" He grips my hand in his; mine are shaking. We need to get back to the castle but...

"I can't shift."

His eyes flash to the necklace and I think maybe this is my chance to get it off but he frowns and returns to watching the field. His hands are now crackling with power. I squeal and jump away to avoid the shock. A horde of our men and women surround us, shifting into dragons. They're quicker than I expected, quicker than I remember. They must have been training more since I left. Many of them take to the skies, black scales reflecting the sun, and a few charge forward on foot, animalistic warcries booming. The rest stay behind as our protectors.

The figure continues to stride toward us. Is that all? *One* person is creating all this power?

I don't know what I expected, maybe a swarm of Occultists in their red robes and with black magic swirling about them. But no. It's only one man—one man who is most definitely *not* an Occultist. He's far enough away that I can't make out his features exactly, but he's not wearing red, his eyes aren't glowing, and he has hair, which none of the Occultists do. It's long and white, coupled with a long white beard. He's got a staff in one hand and is dressed in a silver reflective cloak, the likes of which I've never seen before.

Silas stills, his face forming an unreadable mask. He stares for a long hard minute. One of the dragons swoops in, claws outstretched, but all the man does is nudge the staff toward the dragon and the creature goes careening away, slamming into the ground. I'm not sure what's happening here but fear slips into my thoughts and I wonder if this is the end of Drakenon and by an enemy we never even knew we had.

Except... do I know him? Something about this old man is vaguely familiar.

The staff glints in the sun and my stomach drops *because I definitely know that staff!*

"That's enough," Silas belts at the dragons. "Call off the attack." When they don't immediately, he responds with a barked, "Now!"

They must relay the orders through the telepathic link we have in our dragon forms because they're quick to back off. Silas returns to holding my hand, squeezing. I wince and he pulls me forward. We cross through the line of dragons, toward the wizened man who glides across the snowy field like he's here to save us all.

Either that, or kill us.

By the time we meet in the middle, I'm holding my breath. Something doesn't feel right. I can't quite place what it is, save for a knowningness deep in my gut. I study the old man, his deep brown eyes and the hard line of his thin mouth, his white hair and beard and aged skin. He looks powerful and there's a magic unknown to me here. Different and powerful. *But wait, am I sure I don't know it?* That sense that I should know creeps into my awareness again.

None of that scares me as much as the staff in his hand does—the same one we left in the Jeweled Forest.

"Aleeryrick." Silas smiles. "I hoped you would come. I didn't know if you'd take me up on my offer."

The man bows to Silas. "Of course, Your Majesty." His grip tightens on the staff, like it's the greatest of treasures. "I am at your disposal."

Then he peers at me and my entire body goes cold. "Ah, nice to see you Queen Khali." He holds out his hand to shake mine and so I do. When our fingers touch, crackling magic travels up my arm and into the necklace at my throat. I stumble back, yanking my hand from his.

"What are you?" I don't trust him.

Silas smirks. "Aleeryrick is a sorcerer. And he's come to save us all."

I blink, trying to take this information in. This must be the sorcerer who magicked Silas's necklace. And now Silas thinks this man is going to save us? No, that can't be right. Nothing about this man or his magic feels like it's going to save us, in fact, it feels quite the opposite. His presence comes with an emptiness in my chest, a burning in my gut, and an animalistic desire to either run away or destroy him.

"Nice to meet you," I say to the man, forcing a queenly smile.

It makes Aleeryrick laugh, a knowing and terrible laugh. I still hate it—hate him and fear him—and I need to figure out why.

FIFTEEN
HAZEL

WHATEVER SLAMMED INTO MY BACK knocked away both my backpack and my breath. I blink up, expecting the blanket of clouds from before, but they're replaced with endless blue. I roll to my side to find Dean—thank goodness. We've landed in the middle of a glistening field of snow that's hard as rock, as if it's been frozen for ages. Perhaps it has! It's the bright white of untouched snow but with the softest of blues glowing from within. Is this actually ice? A glacier? No, I don't think so because—

"Come on," Dean whispers, jumping right into action while I'm still busy marveling at our new surroundings. He grabs my hand and tugs me up after him and toward a bunch of boulders that look like small jagged mountains. Some are solid white, some gray, and a few are clear blue ice. They're all taller than us and instead of being rounded off, they're covered in razor sharp edges. I don't have much time to consider why Dean's so intent on hiding us right away until we're crouching behind a boulder. He lifts a finger to his mouth and points back out to where we were.

Of course...

Across the ice field a line of men stand along a river. It's not just any river; it sparkles like it's made of countless diamonds. And these aren't just any men; they're dressed in long burgundy robes with wet hems that brush the snow. They face away from us. Raising their hands, they chant in their guttural language. My heart races, burning fear exploding through my veins.

"Occultists," I breathe, the word barely a whisper on my lips. To see them in person, to know that they're real and they're right here, makes me want to go back through the portal and never return. Except, where is the portal? I look all around, fingertips clinging to the rock, desperately trying to find that rainbow color again, but it's gone. It's clear blue sky and jagged rocks and white snow and nothing else...

So the angel Elias was right that there would be more occultists at the portals. When we found the Dakota warrior and he brought us through, I'd been so awed and distracted that I'd almost forgotten about the very real threat waiting for me on the other side. It's a good thing Dean is better suited for this stuff or I'd have been dead within minutes of arriving.

"No matter what, I can't let the Occultists capture us because they will kill us," Dean whispers. "Especially you."

I nod and attempt to steady my ragged breath. "What's the plan again?" I know we have one, Dean and Harmony talked it through a million times, but my brain is sort of fritzing out.

"We have to get out of here." His voice is so quiet I have to strain my ears to hear him and something about that freaks me out even more. What was I thinking coming to Eridas? I'm not ready for this. I thought I was, I'm not.

I'm so not!

"But first," he whispers. "I want to know what they're doing."

Umm—what!? Shouldn't we be running for our lives?

But we stay and watch for a minute more, trying to understand what the Occultists are up to. This whole area is essentially on a giant slab of ice or snow with the pointy boulders on one side and the river on the other. A group of gray tents are erected near where the warlocks chant. There are no trees to be seen. It's so different from the cute little city of Mankato, so barren and cold.

So freaking cold...

I shiver and Dean runs his hands down my arms, flooding me with warmth. Already I can tell his magic is stronger here than in my world. And speaking of magic...

I can feel mine, actually *feel* it alive within me. Before it was this thing I cognitively knew was a part of me, but I couldn't physically feel it. Well, I did a little on my birthday. Now I couldn't not feel it if I tried—it's like an electric current buzzing under my skin. I'm not sure what to do with it. At the moment

I don't see any supernatural spirits but that doesn't mean things won't change soon. I only hope that whatever happens with this spirit elemental, I'll be able to handle it.

I count the men on the river banks—thirteen. Are they trying to get through the portal? That's what Elias had said and Harmony confirmed, but how exactly are they going about it? I'm so naive to the ways of magic.

A woman screams, a wail so charged with terror, the sound magnifies my fear tenfold.

"What's that?" I whisper so low that it hurts my throat.

My question is immediately answered. A girl is dragged from a nearby tent by two more men. She looks young, younger than me for sure. Her skin is icy white and her hair is the brightest cotton-candy blue I've ever seen. Even from all the way across the field, I can tell the color is like that of a precious gem. I catch a glimpse of pointy ears and bite my lip.

"Elf," Dean whispers. "One of the High Fae."

"What are they going to do to her?"

All at once, black tendrils of magic shoot from all thirteen of the Occultists' palms. The elf falls to her knees, screams wildly, begging for mercy, and just when I'm about ready to run out there and fight for her, she goes limp. The black magic transforms, going from the darkest of dark, to blood red. My stomach turns. It is blood. *Her* blood. And it flows into the Occultists' hands. They chant louder, happier, jovial, as if welcoming the new blood.

"They sacrificed her," Dean seethes, gritting his teeth. "They can't go through portals, probably not even with an elemental to accompany them, so they're trying to steal her magic for themselves. Either that, or they're using her magic to make whatever spell they're working stronger."

"Do you think it will work?"

"Maybe. Give them enough time and enough blood to grow the bond and it's possible."

I think of the bond and how Harmony had taken on the sacrifice of it for herself the few times we'd used ours. In this case, it looks like the warlocks are using an unwilling third-party sacrifice by entering them into the bond and then stealing away all of her power. What will happen to the elf? Will she lose her powers like Harmony?

No. She is gone.

The cult has surrounded the girl now, who I'm sure is already dead because her body is so limp and broken. They chant for a minute more and then utter silence descends. The only sounds are the rumble of the river, the soft breeze as it scatters bits of snow across the white field, and my heartbeat reverberating in my ears. The group steps away from the girl and all that's left are her simple clothes. Her body has turned to a sparkly pink ash, similar to what happened with Harmony's wings. My stomach hardens, bile burning its way up my throat.

This is what happened to Harmony's family. I saw it, the reaper showed me, but now that it's confirmed with my own eyes I can't help but think this will one day happen to me and maybe the people I love. My heart aches for the young elf girl and for a split second, I imagine Dean in her place. Tears well up and blur my vision.

Something dark swooshes above, racing toward the scene. A reaper. My heart clenches. Is the reaper here for the girl or is he here because the Occultists are binding the reapers to them again? I don't think I want to know. But I must know. I need to figure out the truth.

Even though they can't see the reaper, the Occultists must sense it, because they turn in our direction. One points directly to where we're standing.

"Time to go," Dean growls.

He takes my hand and points behind us. The rocks aren't so tightly packed together and we'll be able to navigate through them—but with an Occultist on our tail? Because I swear that guy just saw us.

I look back and the warlock is storming toward us, red eyes glowing bright.

I squeal and we take off. This might turn into a bit of a maze and we may get lost, but I'm not ready to shift yet and we have to get away. Maybe Dean could shift and carry me on his back? But with the sun bright and centered in the blue sky and enemies after us, it seems too risky to take to the skies.

Sometimes the unknown danger is a better choice than the known one.

We're quiet and quick, maneuvering through the spiraling boulders and mounds of ice. They glisten in the sunlight, catching little rainbow rays that add to the beauty of this place. It's a cruel beauty—a sharpness that looks like it could kill you but first it wants you to admire it. We continue on like this for a while, sometimes having to turn back and take a different route. Each time that happens, I swear we're going to run into an Occultist, but we never do. I don't voice my fears as Dean leads the way.

We turn a corner and a face stares out from one of the ice spires. I stumble backwards and hold my hands to my mouth.

"What?" Dean whispers. He ducks next to me in a fighter's stance.

I point to the face.

"I don't see it."

But it's still there, as if frozen in time and ice. I look closer, studying the green eyes and the pointed ears. Is this a spirit? My imagination? I take a deep breath. "It's a spirit trapped in the ice... I think."

"There's so much about this place we don't know." Dean's voice is dark. "This court was never very forthcoming with the dragons. It might be a spirit trapped in there or it might be something else." A haunted expression takes over his normally pensive face. "Let's hurry. Don't touch anything."

This isn't the first time he's told me not to touch anything while I'm here in Eridas but now I'm beginning to understand why. About an hour later, we pass more frozen faces, more that Dean can't see, and a few that he can, until we reach the other side of this horrid landmark. I'm happy to be free of it, hoping to erase it from my mind as soon as possible. My stomach is a mess, curdled with fear, and my chest feels like it's an empty cavity, my heart frozen back with those people.

Holy crap, I really hate this place.

We're not met with another field of white or sparkling river, nor are there any more warlocks. This time, it's a forest and perhaps the most beautiful one I've ever seen. I have to keep myself from gasping aloud. It's fully in bloom, unlike the winter forests of my world. Flowers of all shapes and sizes and colors that seem to be made from ice and the leaves on the trees are every shade of green with a frosty layer, giving them a pastel quality. The trees are tall and generous, like they've been growing here for a century or more. Maybe they have. They remind me of the California Redwoods, not quite as big but close, and definitely magicked for year-round winter weather.

Icicles hang off many of the branches, longer than my entire body and probably deadly sharp from the way the end points are little more than a needle. It's all so fantastic and terrifying and exactly what a magical realm should look like if

I have all the books and movies I've consumed to compare it to. I immediately fall in love with this enchanted forest but I'm equally terrified, too. At least Dean's hand is still in mine. At least I'm not alone out here. There's a clear path leading into the forest that's made entirely from glistening ice crystals.

Oh, boy... this is not what I had in mind.

"Remember not to touch anything," Dean speaks of the warning again and I nod. "And don't talk to anyone, don't eat or drink anything, and stick with me. We can't get separated."

Our backpacks are still slung over our shoulders, so at least we have that. Food from home. Change of clothes. Matches. Water. Chocolate. We're going to be okay. We have to be.

"Here goes nothing." I say it sarcastically but the truth is, for the first time since arriving in Eridas, I actually feel like I'm on an adventure, like I'm the hero of one of my favorite books. A determined smile pulls at my lips and all I can hope for is that I'm actually the hero and not the geeky sidekick who ends up getting killed off in the second act.

SIXTEEN
KHALI

"THIS HAS GOT TO BE the strangest dinner I've ever experienced in my twenty years at Stonehearth's Castle." Silas laughs and takes another bite of his food, slouching across his chair like he hasn't a care in the world.

"Strange would be one way to put it," I reply.

We're at the head of the room, long tables and at least a hundred members of court stretch out before us. I fidget in Queen Brysta's old throne-like chair and try not to glower at Silas's half-witted comments. The food is much the same, buttery and rich, well seasoned and heavy. The smells of spicy meat, yeasty breads, and hearty vegetables permeate the room. Outside the black sky is sprinkled with stars.

Oh how I long to fly among them...

I study the people instead, with their buzzing background chatter, fake smiles, and questioning eyes. And it hits me again that these are *my* people. Who else is going to protect them but their queen? The energy of the room is charged with speculation and fear. Many of the guests are the same as always but my fae friends have joined the funeral dinner tonight. I can already tell that while most people here still don't believe they belong, many are starting to get used to them, and a few seem excited by the prospect of fae at their dinner table.

Juniper sits next to Bram, a perfect match to his good looks. Her hair is down and so blonde and smooth that it reflects the candlelight. Terek and Maxx are seated farther down, flirting with a few of the courtesans who respond with both scandalized and seduced expressions. But it's none of these people that are getting to me.

They're not Aleeryrick.

The wizened sorcerer sits on my other side, magicked staff from the Jeweled Forest leaning against the table while he tackles his dinner like he hasn't eaten in ages. Who knows, maybe he hasn't. The immense magic wafting off of him is so suffocating that I can hardly eat a single bite. Not only does it remind me of the magic I've lost, but it seems to invade my space, and it especially likes Silas's necklace. The thing is freezing cold again, any colder it would burn my throat. I breathe through the sting of it, trying to focus on the conversations going on around me, especially the ones including Aleeryrick and especially not those between or about Bram and Juniper. I don't want to hear them flirting, even if it's for show.

To see them together hurts me but the idea that something real may come out of it absolutely breaks me. Even though Bram and I can never be together. Even though I've already decided I'll never be alone in a room with him again. Even though I know he deserves to be happy and Juniper is beautiful and spirited and can offer him all her attention. All that, and it still leaves my heart scattered across this castle like broken glass.

Bram is drawn to Juniper because of her healing abilities, but what if it turns into more? What if it turns into lust? Love? Marriage. I'll have to witness every stage of their relationship.

By this point I'm staring at the couple and Bram catches me, his eyes growing pensive. I can't look away. But then Juniper turns to me too and I force myself to refocus on my food.

Juniper isn't so bad. This isn't her fault. Gods, I wish she'd been able to help Bellflower Blossom. I'd love to see my feisty pixie friend here too and my heart still hurts every time I think about her. Silas didn't even care when he murdered her, it was like she meant nothing to him. More than anything I'd love to yell at Silas and embarrass him in front of everyone here, but I daren't. My fae friends might mean as little to him as Bellflower Blossom did. Not to mention, my parents aren't far away. He could blackmail me with them anytime he wants, just like his father did.

I scoff to myself. It seems Bram's been allowed to show his face lately but my father still hasn't. Not that I care to have my father embedded in this mess; he's safer in his chamber. But his absence is one more strike against Silas, and proof that he'll manipulate people and situations to better suit him, and cares little for the benefit of others.

"How are you enjoying your roasted beef, Your Majesty?" Aleeryrick asks, raising a bushy eyebrow. A ruthless glint flashes in his muddy eyes as he studies me. "You've barely touched it. Has something stolen your appetite?"

The necklace burns even colder. He knows it's him, doesn't he? He knows how much he scares me and this is his way of letting me know that he's fine with frightening me. He has no problem with it at all, in fact, he enjoys it.

"I can't eat when I'm sad," I respond.

"And what are you sad about?" His mouth thins.

"King Titus's death and the funeral, of course."

His eyes narrow. "Of course."

Dinner continues, stilted, uncomfortable, with surface level conversation and everything I want to say left brewing underneath. It goes by too slow and once it's finally over, Silas asks Aleeryrick to join him in his parlor. He doesn't ask me; in fact, he encourages me to visit my parents.

So I smile and agree with Silas like the sweet little wife he wants me to be, but I don't seek out my parents. After the guards and Faros have walked me back to my chamber, I close myself inside, and hurry through to press my ear to the door leading into our shared sitting room. It's quiet; nobody's there. I creep in and find the room empty so I go to Silas's room next, also empty, then his own private parlor, but still nobody is there. Knowing what I have to do, I sneak to the bookshelf. It's already open a crack so I slide it back a little more and slip inside.

I haven't been in these tunnels since Bram and I ran away from Drakenon weeks ago and I've been wanting to pursue what Bellflower said. So much has happened in the last few months but the tunnels feel the same. Now they're an old friend I'm not sure I can trust anymore. They're low and winding, some built into the castle, like this one, but many run underneath the castle itself and out into the town or beyond the village wall. I am convinced I don't know them all. Owen and I were fantastic at journeying through them but the one I'm sneaking through at the moment is entirely new to me.

And it's also pitch black. I don't have elements at my disposal like so many times before. I can't just light a flame in my hand. It hurts my heart to know that my favorite part of myself, the thing that made me me, has disappeared.

Don't give up, Khali, I tell myself.

I'm forced to use my hands to navigate my way down the dark tunnel, hoping I don't injure myself or run into someone or worse. The risk is worth it if I can find Silas and that creepy sorcerer. I don't know how to get my magic back yet, but putting one foot in front of the other is better than not taking any steps at all. So I wind my way farther and farther through the tunnel, and when I nearly miss a step, I catch my breath and find stairs. Down, down, down I go as my heart thunders in my ears and my limbs shake. I've never been so vulnerable in my entire life but I keep going. My eyes stay open despite the darkness and I listen attentively despite the sound of my heartbeat thudding in my ears.

Finally, I hear voices ahead. The unmistakable smooth timbre of Silas's demanding drawl and the gravelly tone of Aleeryrick's intonations. I let out a sigh of relief and I freeze, the relief evaporating because now what?

I sneak closer until I'm at the opening to a room forged from the stone like a man-made cave and lit by torches on the walls. And then I see them.

"What can I do to get you to undo my father's bargain?" Silas asks.

"Your father and his father and many before that have kept me hidden away," Aleeryrick says bluntly. "They told me I'd prefer it that way but in actuality they wanted their secret hidden. It was always better that the bordering wards were shrouded in mystery, it gave them more of an edge over the other dragon clans."

"So you want prestige?" Silas asks with a sly smile. "Done. Live here. Work at my right hand. I would be happy to welcome you into my family."

The sorcerer scoffs and there's a stretch of silence. "Have you collected the assets?"

"All but one," Silas replies, "but it will be here soon."

"Soon had better mean within days," Aleeryrick snaps. "The Occultists are close to taking down the border. I can feel it."

"Your magic is superior to theirs," Silas is quick to placate. "But yes, she'll be here soon."

She?

The sorcerer clicks his tongue but says nothing more.

"So what about if I have a daughter…" Silas seems nervous. "How can we negotiate a better deal on her behalf?"

Confusion wraps around me in a vice at this question and my breath catches.

The sorcerer laughs. "Maybe we should ask your wife about it?"

I shudder.

"She doesn't remember and she doesn't need to," Silas growls.

"Really? Because I'd like to enlighten her."

"No."

Something snags me—an unseen hand. I cry out as I'm dragged forward from the darkness and into the light of the caverned room. The sorcerer gazes at me like he knew I was listening in on them all along. I come to a halt a mere foot away from them. I still can't move. It must be his magic that pulled me in here, that's binding me now. Silas's stormy eyes are round and anger thins his mouth.

"Khali," Aleeryrick purrs. "It's so nice of you to join us."

"No," Silas snaps again. "She doesn't need to know. And you made a bargain with my father. You break it now and you break all of it."

The sorcerer only shrugs and says, "Sorry, Silas, but I don't see it that way. You know how bargains work, don't you? It doesn't matter that your father is dead. It still holds."

And then I'm surrounded by bright white. I shield my eyes as my memories, the ones I didn't even know had been taken from me, come flooding back like scorching water being dumped over my body.

It was a few years ago, right before Dean was exiled. There had been a tournament to join the king's army and I had entered myself under an alias and tried to win it. But things had gone wrong, *really wrong*. My powers were so much stronger than anyone had anticipated and I'd revealed myself in a way that undermined the throne.

King Titus was beyond furious. He'd dragged me, along with Dean, Owen and Silas, north to see Aleeryrick. It was there that Titus and the sorcerer made a bargain to erase the memories of my show of power from myself and from all the people of Drakenon, except for the few others who were in the room that day. In exchange, if I ever had a daughter, she would become Aleeryrick's apprentice. I'd fought against the bargain, tried to get away from the spell, but everything had gone blank the moment my memories had been stripped from me. We'd returned to the castle and that was that.

It's not until this very moment that I remember what happened to me—remember how my memories and choices had been violated.

But Owen? Silas? Dean? *They all knew...*

It was shortly after that experience that Dean was exiled. And then Owen had asked me to sneak out with him so I could train and get stronger. He'd risked everything to help me. And Silas? He'd gone right along with keeping me from knowing the truth of my abilities, even at the expense of my future daughter, someone he wanted to father.

"I remember it all now… and the looks on your faces." My voice is hollow. Titus, satisfied. Aleeryrick triumphant. And Owen? He'd been horrified, while Dean was sickened, Silas was unfeeling, and Bram wasn't even there at all.

"Khali—" Silas warns.

I blink and the whiteness and hot pain of the memories clears, making way for savage anger.

"How could you!" I snarl at the sorcerer, pointing at his smug expression. "You can't have her."

The vile man raises a white eyebrow. "I can and I will."

"Over my dead body," I hiss. "That wasn't King Titus's child to bargain away."

"And besides," Silas adds more calmly. "You don't have a deal anymore now that you've returned her memories. You broke your side of the bargain."

"Titus never said I couldn't return the memories." Aleeryrick smiles ruefully. "He only said that I had to take them away in the first place, which I did."

"You disgust me," I snarl.

He slams the staff into the dirt floor and the gems embedded into the wood light up like how they were in the Jeweled Forest. "You two act like an apprenticeship with me won't be an honor to your future child. Believe me, it will. Don't you want the most powerful child in all of Eridas to be yours?"

"No," Silas and I say in unison.

I gape at Silas, expecting to see the same outrage on his face as mine. But outrage isn't what I find there. It's fear and intimidation and jealousy. My mouth goes dry. Silas doesn't want anyone to be more powerful than him, not even his own child. What would he do to her? Would he hurt her? The answer is yes, I know it deep down. *I know it.* Lust for power can damage a soul, and Silas is the prime example.

"It's no matter," Aleeryrick sighs. "What's done is done and can't be undone. And anyway, you have to worry about the Occultists now, don't you? They're close." He turns to me, eyes narrowing and expression becoming accusatory. "And you, my dear, don't actually have the magic needed to stop them."

Silas gazes at me with a question in his eyes but I don't know what to say or what to do. I stand there, hopeless, because the sorcerer is right.

"What do you mean?" Silas questions.

Rather than let Aleeryrick explain, I decide to confess. "My magic and my dragon disappeared on my eighteenth birthday." I lock eyes with Silas and let out a bitter laugh as I step forward, our faces inches apart. The drafty room grows unimaginably still. "I wonder, Dear Husband, if you'd known you were about to wed a girl who was no longer Dragon Blessed, would you have gone through with it?"

For once in his life, Silas can't think of anything to say.

SEVENTEEN
HAZEL

AS SOON AS NIGHT FALLS, we find a clearing of trees and get to work building the altar. Every few minutes I turn and peer into the darkness because that prickling feeling that someone might be watching us refuses to go away. The Occultists are looking for us—I can feel it like I can feel the bitter air nipping at my skin.

We don't speak a word, moving as quietly as we can. The plan is to pay homage to the four directions, as well as Father Sky and Mother Earth, and the elements. In doing so, our spell will hopefully spark to life. Dean piles round, icy rocks on top of each other like Harmony had instructed. Once he's done, I start with the elemental items—the dash of water, the long thin feather for air, the little flame of fire, the handful of earth; and for spirit—a piece of charcoal that once Dean lights with his magic, smokes and crackles. I stare at the items atop the stones and turn to Dean.

He clasps my hand and I speak, my voice barely above a whisper. The words feel silly at first, foreign and ridiculous, but I push through because I need to get it right.

"North, South, East, and West. New beginnings with the rising sun. Peaceful endings with the dusk. Mother Earth and Father Sky, Ancestral spirits, and all the elements, I ask thee to lead me to my closest family."

Family...

What a loaded word. I've only ever considered my mom to be my family. I don't have any *real* family here in this strange place, but Harmony says Faeries are one big clan and my blood is half fae so I'll belong and I'm theirs. I hope they see it that way. I'm also half dragon, a hybrid, different, grown up in the human realm. What if they turn me away? Or what if the spell doesn't even work in the first place? I quickly banish the thoughts. Harmony promised. We can trust her. Right now, I need to stay focused, to believe this will lead me to the help we desperately need.

We didn't come to this kingdom without a plan and I have to cling to that. The locator spell is ancient magic, linked to the elements, and only works for those who don't wish ill on those they're trying to find.

And my heart? It beats wildly, begging to find that help—help for me, for them, for all of us.

The smoke billows and grows, forming a long line of whitish gray, with little sparkles of magic. They remind me of stars. We watch, mesmerized, until it veers off in a strange direction, taking on a life of its own.

"This is it," Dean says. "Let's go."

He releases my hand, steps back, and shifts into his dragon form so suddenly, I don't have time to voice my fears. In fact, I don't have time to react other than grab our backpacks, climb on his scaly back, and hold on tight around his neck.

This is the plan. It's going to be okay. Breathe. Just breathe, Hazel.

He jumps into the air, wings flapping, and follows the smoke. It's so dark out, I'm surprised he can even see the smoke anymore. I keep losing sight of it myself. But that slight starry sparkle is visible to my human eyes and Dean said his eyesight is better in dragon form. They have night vision. I wonder if I will too.

I catch sight of something in the forest below us, making chase. A flash of deep red. *An Occultist!* My heart thunders and I call out to Dean, who flies even faster—impossibly fast.

The warlock is losing ground. He won't be able to keep up, not with someone as fast as Dean.

The icy wind slices past and I burrow into his back, pressing my face against his warm skin, finding his scales to be surprisingly soft compared to how they appear. I think of how Harmony told me about the spell before we left the house. It started with more history—her history. Her backstory got more and more tragic. Honestly, it was hard for me to keep it together, but I'm glad I did,

I'm glad I trusted her, because so far her plan is working.

Before she left Eridas, after she lost everything and everyone she loved, she fled from the Spring Court to the Winter Court. The court hadn't fallen to the Occultists yet and they welcomed her and any other fae refugees with open arms. But did that mean they listened to her warnings? Unfortunately not.

She didn't get too far into the specifics of what happened, only that she'd had to go into hiding with a bunch of others when the Occultists came sacrificing anyone linked to elemental magic that they could find. They didn't limit the deaths to the High Fae as they'd done with other courts. No, here it was anyone and everyone, all kinds of creatures, not just the ruling class. She'd barely gotten out alive and had escaped to Summer, begging them too to heed her warnings. They'd set up a lot more precautions by then but not enough to make her feel safe, so when the Autumn Court fell, she left. By the time the Occultists arrived in Summer and had started their slaughter, she'd already gone through the portal and had her new life set up with the humans. Hers is a tragedy, a story of losing love and home, of becoming a refugee in an entirely different world, completely alone. And I can't help but wonder if we will end up the same way.

Harmony kept her secrets from me—she knew what happened to my father for one thing—but I understand her better now and why she did the things she did. Her life experiences taught her to pay closer attention to visions of the future, to stop trying to change things but to instead use her gifts to keep those she loves safe by any means possible. She's cautious about what she does, says, and when she says them. *Perfect timing,* she'd said to us last night, *is its own kind of magic, and is often more powerful than anything else in this world.*

From the way Dean follows the camouflaged smoke in the darkness of night, the locator spell must be working. A rush of nervous excitement takes over my body and I get the craziest temptation to look down. But I refuse, squeezing my eyes closed instead. We're going so fast that the Occultist doesn't have a chance of keeping up. Does he? I brave a look behind me but there is no forest. We're high in the clouds! My stomach just about drops out of my butt at that moment because *oh my heck!* This flying thing would be different if I was in my dragon form; I wouldn't be quite so freaked out. I vow here and now to try to shift again soon. I've got to get the hang of it and Harmony was right, Eridas is connecting with my magic in a way I've never felt before. It calls to it like an old friend, so natural and easy.

But this flying on Dean's back thing? Oh, this is terrifying. Almost as terrifying as going to see a bunch of fae who may hate me or may love me. But I need help and definitely need someone to train me. Harmony said the Winter Court was known for having spirit magic, far more so than any of the other kingdoms in Eridas. If there's going to be someone out there who can help me with this magic, they're probably here in this frosted world.

We race after the smoke, dropping out of the clouds and zooming right down toward a snowy forest so thick I can't imagine sunlight can make it through the branches, let alone us. The Occultist from before is long gone.

Dean speeds forward, going headlong right into the thicket of branches and I'm sure we're going to crash. Smoke may not be solid but we sure are! I squeeze tight and hold back a scream as we zip through the trees.

Wait.

Through the trees? But I didn't feel a single thing. It doesn't make logical sense. Then again, magic rarely does.

There is no forest here.

None at all.

In the darkness I can make out the outline of a village, complete with sprawling farm fields and even an old stone chapel covered in ice. This place must be surrounded by magic to make it appear as a dense forest to disguise what it truly is.

"Amazing," I murmur. And then I smile—*we freaking made it!* My smile is quickly replaced with a slice of white-hot worry *because we freaking made it* and now what? What if we're not welcomed here like we're hoping?

Dean lands in a wide open space between two homes, quiet and stealthy in his maneuvering. He crouches and I vault off his back. He shifts, smiling and pulling me into a hug. "Wow," he whispers, "That was exhilarating."

"Was it now?" a gruff voice barks from across the darkened field. We startle and turn to find a man glaring back at us as he traipses through the snow. It's pretty dark out here and he's cloaked so I don't get much of a look at him, plus I'm too distracted by the spear with the super sharp pointed end he's got a few inches from Dean's face. *Oh, crap!*

"Please," I gasp, "wait."

"We're here in peace," Dean says carefully, his voice low and even. If needed, he could wreak fire elemental havoc on this dude which would not be a good way to introduce ourselves.

"You're not welcome here," the man snaps.

I squint, trying to make out his features, but it's impossible in this light. He towers over us, his hood casting his face in shadows. But what I can tell is that this guy is broad shouldered, insanely huge, and seething mad if his fighter's stance and gritted teeth are anything to go by. Oh and the scary-sharp spear isn't too fun either!

I see all that *and* I see something else—*someone else*. Off to his right stands the ghost of a woman. She is tall and gorgeous, with bright smiling eyes, pink skin, and long flowing red hair. She nods, sending me a series of images so quickly it's like she's downloading her entire life story directly into my mind. My breath catches—she's this man's beloved wife. He lost her to the Occultists and even though the reapers are back in the supernatural spirit realm, she hasn't moved on, she won't until he's ready to let her go. Until then she refuses to leave him.

And now she wants to help me.

"Please," I try again, forcing myself to be brave. "I have a message from Penelope."

He stills, his voice growing dangerous. "What did you just say?"

I still can't see him well enough to make out his features and I have to swallow the frog that jumps in my throat. I really freaking hope I didn't sign our death certificates.

EIGHTEEN
KHALI

A FINGER TRAILS DOWN MY back and I roll toward it. My eyelids strain to open because the heaviness of sleep is too much. The glorious unconsciousness from moments before presses down and I give into it, surrendering myself to be swept away. I want to sleep, to forget everything that's happened lately. But then the finger from before becomes an arm, rocking my body in tight against another. It's so warm—*he's* so warm. I burrow against his lean chest, relaxing into him. I'm so tired; I need to sleep. I'm back in the Summer Forest with Bram and we're laying in a bed of pine needles and he's protecting me. He's—

"I need you." His voice is soft velvet against my ear.

But it's not Bram's voice.

Silas is the one holding me now. And I'm not in the forest. I'm in my new bed.

I jolt awake.

He presses a kiss to my shoulder, then to my cheek, his lips brushing the corner of my mouth.

I rear back. "What are you doing in here?"

"What do you think?" he murmurs, moving in and pressing another kiss to my shoulder. I push him off and scramble to sit up.

"You can't sneak into my bed in the middle of the night." He shushes me with another kiss. "What did you think was going to happen?" I pull back even farther.

A long strand of blond hair falls across his eyes but he doesn't brush it away.

It's too dark to see much but I know he's staring at me. He doesn't answer my question.

"And another thing," I continue, "this sorcerer friend of yours thinks he's got free reign to our future daughter, if we ever have a baby. When were you going to tell me about this?"

"*When* we have a baby." He tries to sound endearing but really he just sounds like the arrogant boy I've always known. "And he doesn't get free reign. Our first daughter would be his apprentice but you know Brightcasters rarely have girls so it's unlikely to ever happen."

Wait—*that's* his excuse?

"You believe that? This is a sorcerer we're talking about. If I get pregnant, he'll probably spell me to have a girl."

Silas shrugs.

"Ugh, I'm serious. Get out." I ball the blanket into my fist and hold it over my chest. My nightgown is too thin for comfort. "This is supposed to be my safe space. It's my bedroom and you can't just come in here whenever you'd like. You weren't invited."

"How many times have you gone into my room uninvited?" He chuckles low.

"This is different." And it is different. "You woke me up by kissing me!"

He waves me off. "I have a proposition for you."

I know I shouldn't hear him out but there's something about the way he says it that leaves me curious. "What?"

He sits closer until his knees are pressed against mine through the silken blanket. He likes being close to me, likes pushing my buttons and making me uncomfortable.

"Give me a child," he says, "a son. Secure our bloodline, and I'll not only do whatever it takes to help you get your magic back, but I'll give you your freedom too."

"Freedom?" I scoff. "What does that word even mean to someone like you?"

"It means you can do as you please around the castle. You can fly, shift, use your magic, I don't care. You can be who you've always wanted to be."

I pause, rolling the proposition around in my head. "Why? Why do you want a baby so bad?"

His eyes flick across my body. "More reasons than one."

My stomach hardens. Even if his bargain is enticing, I can't imagine going through with it. Not with him. "I should be able to do all those things anyway and you know it. Flying, being myself, using my magic, it's all part of my birthright as Dragon Blessed!"

"Correction, you were Dragon Blessed." He talks like this is all one big game to him. "And yet I'm the one with the power to help you or stop you."

And I hate him for it.

I grit my teeth. "I don't believe you. You won't let me do as I please. That's a lie."

He scoffs. "Well, you can't touch Bram or any other man if that's what you were hoping for."

"It wasn't." But the mere thought of being with Bram sends warmth curling through my entire body.

Silas smiles and the whites of his teeth and eyes glow in the dark. Any other girl would kill to be in this position but I know better than to trust the snake.

"Good girl," he whispers.

He acts as if I'm as physically attracted to him as he is to me. But he's got it all wrong. The thought of being with him makes me want to claw my eyes out or vomit or a million other terrible things. I hate him. I truly do. That hate isn't going to magically turn into love or even lust just because he's good looking and an expert flirt. He can't bribe me into having children with him, even if his promises prove to be true.

"You know you want to." He edges closer.

But I don't. I really don't. Even if this is my duty as queen, even if I'm bound by oath, and eventually, I'm not going to be able to say no anymore. This standoff can't last forever, not with a man like Silas.

"What about the sorcerer?" I ask. "We can't have a child and risk it being a girl. You need to find a way to get rid of Aleeryrick before I could ever agree to this."

"Hmm, you and I think more alike than you realize." He runs a finger along my bare knee. "We're good for each other, you know."

"And why's that?"

"We're powerful. We're intellectually matched. And guess what?" He leans forward and whispers. "I hate that sorcerer too, but unlike you, I know how to play the long game."

"And what game is that?"

He cups my chin. He's so close now. He smells of citrus tonight, and of an impending storm. "I have a plan to get what we need from him and then get rid of him for good."

"How very Silas Brightcaster of you."

He laughs and lets me go.

"I'm not making this deal. You can leave now."

He tilts his head at me, unconvinced. "And what about your magic? How does it just disappear overnight like that? Poof! There's something you're not telling me."

My body grows cold. I don't want to tell him about Hazel because somehow I know if he believes she's standing in our way, he'll find her and kill her without a second thought. So instead I tug on the necklace. "Don't you think this is making things worse?" I hold it up. My eyes have finally adjusted to the darkness enough that I can make out the glint of the dragon engraved on the silver. My bad human eyes are one more reminder of the dragon self that I've lost. "You have this thing on me. Aleeryrick made it, didn't he?"

It's a guess, but I know Silas had someone make it for him and he swore it wasn't an Occultist back when I challenged him on it in the Summer Forest. This is the best explanation. Silas reaches for my face, and I think he's going to try to kiss me again, which I'm not going to allow. I tense, lips sealed. "Just hold on, will you?" He grabs hold of the necklace, not me, and leans in closer. The cord strains against my neck.

"One kiss on the lips," he says. "One kiss and I'll take it off."

I turn my head away. "No."

I expect him to be angry or to laugh, what I don't expect is for him to remove the necklace anyway. It falls from my skin and I gasp, leaning back against the bed frame, rubbing my neck.

"Consider this a measure of my good faith," he says, "and my trust in you to do the right thing."

My hands clench into fists against my chest because what does he know of doing the right thing?

"Thank you." I force myself to say, voice hoarse. I don't know what this means except that Silas is trying to buy my trust and at least for tonight, he's not going to force me to try and make a child with him.

"But remember I can put this back on you anytime I need." He squeezes the silver pendant into his palm. His voice turns to liquid silver. "It's mine. Don't try to take it from me again or more than a useless pixie will get hurt."

He wants me to trust him, to sleep with him, to go along with his plans, but he doesn't want me to ever forget that he can control me. Not only me, this kingdom. "What a cruel thing to bring up right now. She was my friend."

"Sometimes cruelty gets things done."

"And sometimes so does kindness."

He shrugs. "Maybe, but I prefer guarantees. Speaking of which," he continues. "You and I are going to have to work together whether you like it or not. And I'm not just talking about children, I'm talking about the Occultists and Aleeryrick. They think we're a weak kingdom but we're two of the last ones standing for a reason. I intend to take it all."

"Take it all? What does that mean?"

But I think I already know...

He pauses for a second, his eyes filling with lust and greed. He wants to tell me something but it's as if he's trying to talk himself out of it.

"Tell me, Silas," I say, "you know I'll figure it out soon anyway. Wouldn't you rather be the one to tell me what you're planning?"

That does the trick.

"Drakenon will conquer all of Eridas and I will rule..." His eyes grow hungry. "And you, Wife, will be at my side."

Silence stretches between us. I want to say the right thing, the cunning thing, but I can't speak anything other than the truth. "I always knew you were a greedy bastard but this is too far."

"You'll understand one day," he sighs. "Besides, if we don't take care of Eridas then the Occultists will eradicate it."

"Nothing will ever be enough for you."

"The Sovereign Occultists did the dirty work but I'm going to finish the job. And you'll see, Khali, when all is said and done, *that I was right.*"

"Right? You're talking about reigning over the fae kingdoms."

"Their royal lines are all dead," he replies simply, "and it only makes sense that we step in and rule. We'll be fair to them and it will be for the best. The Gods want this, Khali, I can feel it."

This is crazy. He's talking about the very thing that has made the Occultists evil. I let out a slow breath. "Let's say you're right and we are meant to rule over Eridas, which I don't agree with, by the way, how do you actually think you're going to pull that off?"

He leans in and plants a quick kiss on my forehead. "Have you ever known me to not have a plan?" He gets up then, climbing from the bed. "If I'm going to trust you, it's your turn to trust me." He leaves my room without a backwards glance or another word. But he's right, he's never been someone to not have a plan, and that's exactly what scares me the most. That and the fact that he seems to think I'm going to help him accomplish his selfish goals.

My fingers trace the space where the necklace used to be and I suddenly feel more lost than ever. Silas brought up Bellflower Blossom which reminds me of what she told me before she died; that there's something in the dungeons, something Silas is hiding. Whatever it is, I need to get back to the tunnels, find my way to those dungeons, and figure out Silas's secret.

NINETEEN
HAZEL

"TELL ME! TELL ME HOW you know her name," the man growls, prodding his spear at me now instead of Dean. Dean growls, moving his weight to shield me.

My throat goes dry but I force her name out anyway. "Penelope wants me to give you a message. And she wants to make sure you're okay."

He juts his head back and the hood of his black cloak falls. The moonlight catches the planes of his face, his pointed elf ears, his graying black hair tied back in a knot. "How dare you speak her name? What do you know? Who are you?" With each question his spear gets closer and closer. Dean tenses and I know it won't be long until there are fireballs in his palms. I have to stop this.

I raise my hands, deciding to be as honest as possible. "My name is Hazel Forrester. I'm a hybrid between a dragon shifter and a faerie. I was born with the spirit element and can see some of the people in the spirit realm. Your deceased wife is here right now."

The spear wobbles and he lowers it ever so slightly. Nobody speaks. A gust of wind kicks up snow, in the distance an owl hoots. The cold wraps itself around me but I don't dare move. "C'mon then," he says at last, his voice still guarded. "What's the message from my Penelope?"

I can tell he doesn't quite believe me but he wants to. He won't let himself, which is understandable for anyone. I probably look like a crazy girl, what with my black jeans and puffer coat, hair pulled back in a basic ponytail. I'm not from here, that much is clear. Either way, I must prove myself to him right here and now or else things are going to get bad real fast.

I clear my throat. "She wants you to know it's not your fault that she died and you need to stop blaming yourself."

His mouth hardens. "I'm not going to listen to this crap."

The woman sends another image to my mind and then I hear her voice telling me exactly what to say.

"She says that whenever you see an ice butterfly, she wants you to think of her. She knows you already do, but she wants you to know that she knows."

An ice butterfly is exactly what it sounds like from the image she's showing me, all crystalline and fluttery. I'd love to see one in real life but considering this memory is rather spectacular, I'll take it.

The elf steps back, his face clearing of anger and filling with something else entirely: grief, despair, hope... "You really can see her, can't you? How does she look? Is she okay?"

I nod and study the woman hovering next to him. She smiles. "Yes, I can and she's okay. If they're not able to move on because of something bad in their lifetime, I can usually see that by how they appear to me. But she looks great. She really does. She's beautiful, for starters. Super tall. Rosy cheeks against pink skin. Deep brown eyes. Long red hair. It's so pretty, the color of a candied apple."

"What's a candied apple?"

"Oh sorry." I smile. "This is my first time in Eridas since I was a baby. I grew up in the human realm and it's something they do there. They take like this liquid sugary stuff, it's bright red candy, and they pour it—"

"Hazel," Dean cuts me off.

"You're from the human realm?" The man's voice turns sour once again. "Well, I guess that explains your attire. But then you better have a good reason for why in the hell you'd come here?" He raises the spear. *Oh crap on a cracker, I overshared!*

Dean growls.

I can hear Penelope and the sass in her voice. It makes me smile. I repeat what she says word for word. "Your wife says to tell you, Gregory, cut it out, leave the poor girl alone. It's not like you aren't a refugee yourself now. You have no right to judge her..." My voice trails off and my cheeks warm.

583

"You know my name?"

"Your wife does," Dean interjects. "Hazel's already explained."

Desperation washes over me. We need help—refuge. We need to be welcomed here. The gusty wind builds and I begin to shiver. Dean immediately grabs my hand to warm me.

"Please? What do I have to do to convince you?" I beg. "Penelope showed me everything. You met when you were children, you and your father used to travel to trade with Spring where she lived. You fell in love with her and when you were old enough, you went back on your own and convinced her to marry you. You lived here in Winter. You never had any children, though you both wanted them, and maybe given enough time it would have happened, but the Occultists came and took her away. You blame yourself but she doesn't want you to do that anymore. She says they caught almost everyone and you couldn't have known they'd get her too. She's so glad you're alive and wants you to be happy."

"I think I've heard enough." Gregory's voice is hollow. He's closer now, close enough that I can see tears have welled up in his wide eyes. "I believe you. Follow me."

He turns and traipses toward one of the little houses, throwing open a door like he's taking out all his sadness on the poor rusty hinges. "It's been empty for a while. Sorry about the dust. You can stay here tonight and in the morning we can work out what to do about you. The others aren't going to like this, you know."

Relief settles over me. This is a start. "But you believe me about Penelope?"

He sighs. "Unfortunately, I do. And you can tell Penelope to stop telling me what to do. If I want to go on blaming myself for the rest of my life then I damn well can do as I please."

Penelope stands behind him and she laughs, throwing her head back, her red curls dancing as her body shakes.

"She's laughing at you, like full body laughing."

He shrugs, the corner of his burly mouth slipping into a smile. "Yeah, I'm not surprised. That girl always had the loudest laugh. It was annoying." She shoots him a mocking look. "But cute. I loved it. I loved her. Still do."

Dean and I study the small one-roomed cottage, taking in the dust and mildew, the sparse furniture and tiny windows. Gregory throws the door closed, locking us in. Not that I'm worried: what's a lock going to do against a couple of dragons? He probably already knows the lock isn't worth much. Maybe the lock isn't to keep us in but to keep others out? I shiver at the thought. Not to mention, it's nearly as cold in here as it is outside but Dean makes quick work of the fireplace and before long we're toasty and at least the wind is gone.

Penelope still hangs out in the corner, watching me with curious eyes. I set down my backpack and let out a strangled breath. "Why are you still here?" I ask her. "In the supernatural spirit realm, I mean. Why haven't you moved on to the next place?"

At first I couldn't move on, she sighs, her voice filtering through my mind. I still find it strange that the spirits can talk to me now, it's going to take some getting used to.

But she's also… different.

She's so real compared to the spirits I see in the human realm and all I can think is the magic of Eridas must have something to do with that, too.

None of us could move on for a long time because the reapers were gone and the Occultists… She pauses for a while and I almost expect her to disappear, but then she looks back at me, brown eyes shining. *Anyway, now that the reapers are back, I suppose I'm still not ready to go. I need Gregory to stop blaming himself before I can leave him.*

I scoff but offer her a grin and a raised eyebrow. "Well, I don't think that's going to happen. He seems way too stubborn."

She shrugs, her white gown glinting under an unseen light. *Oh he is, but so am I. If I have to wait for him to pass on before I go, that's just as well. Honestly, I'd rather go to whatever is next with him than without him.*

I nod, because I get it. It would be hard for me too. But I also think it would be too hard to stick around watching people live a life when you can't have one of your own. "You don't know what's next?"

No. Do you?

I shake my head. "Heaven, maybe? I don't know. I hope it's good."

She full body laughs again. *Same!*

"How am I going to win these people over?" I ask.

Same as you did Gregory, she replies. *Help them communicate with whoever is still waiting around for them. They'll love you for it.*

"I don't think you could call that winning Gregory over."

She raises a delicate eyebrow. *Oh no? Because I would. If he didn't like you, you wouldn't be here right now. You'd have your memories wiped clean and would be off wandering around Winter until the Occultists found you. You probably wouldn't even be able to remember your own name.*

My face falls and my body goes cold. The very idea that someone could magic me to forget who I am makes me want to get out of here. My family has been through enough of that kind of tampering, thank you very much! "Well, I guess that means you trust me if you're telling me all this."

She shrugs a round shoulder. *Who else is going to help me?*

"What's wrong?" Dean asks, his stance growing protective. "What is the spirit saying?"

It's okay, Penelope says, *you can tell him.*

So I repeat what she said about Gregory's magic.

He's worried, I can see it in the way his black eyes spark with flames and the room warms by another few degrees. "It's a rare magic and obviously useful, probably the same thing used to protect this little village from the outside world and keep it hidden."

"She says I can win these people over by doing the same thing I just did for Gregory."

"And you can." Dean wraps me in a warm hug and presses a kiss to my forehead "But if it doesn't work, I'll get you out of here before they can hurt us."

He sounds so confident but I know he's not. How can he be? If someone wipes our memory, we're as good as dead.

But it turns out that Penelope is right.

The next morning Gregory takes us around the enchanting stone village to meet a myriad of fae: elves, faeries, pixies, a few guarded centaurs, and a handful of creatures that I have no clue what they are and I'm too polite to ask. We introduce ourselves over and over again as I work my magic on anyone who has a hanger-on in the spirit realm. Turns out a lot of these people lost loved ones to the Occultists. It doesn't take long for news of us to spread and Dean and I are welcomed into the community.

After many hours of this, I'm emotionally exhausted and physically worn down, but I don't stop until everyone has their chance. We go from house to house, Gregory at our side. Finally, on the way out of the last house, I confide in Gregory about why we've come here. "We needed a place to hide out for a few days. But there's more…"

He looks at me sideways, the lines around his eyes deepening. "Out with it," he says gruffly.

"I need to train with someone who has spirit magic. That's why Harmony sent me here, she said the Winter Court was known for it."

"Harmony?" He stops abruptly, his brown eyes widening and his mouth turning up at the corners into a happy grin. It's the lightest I've seen him all day. Dean and I exchange an optimistic glance. "You know Harmony? Why didn't you say something earlier?"

And then, he does something I never expected. He pulls me into a barrel hug, lifting me off the ground as I squeak.

"You should have started with that!" He laughs.

Well, I guess we're idiots because that sure would have been easier than a day spent communing with the dead. But then again, it was worth the hard work to see the looks on people's faces when they realized I was for real.

"Knowing you're friends of Harmony means you're friends of ours. A lot of us knew Harmony when she lived in our court. And let me tell you something about that faerie, to know her is to love her."

I grin, thinking back on all that she's done for me. "I would have to agree with that statement."

"Everyone is going to be pleased to hear she's still alive. We assumed she'd died like so many others."

We talk about Harmony for a while and about all their good times together. This carries on as we walk from one end of the village, to the other, back toward the little hovel Dean and I are camping out in.

I squint, noticing a quaint stone cottage on the far edge of the community.

"We never visited there. Do you think they'll want to meet me?"

"I'm sure, but actually, I think Opal is the one you want to meet." Gregory forges ahead, passing our place and continuing to the cottage. "She's the other fae with spirit elemental."

"And by other one, you mean besides you?" Dean questions.

Gregory hums to himself. "Well, what I can do is linked to spirit, but it's nothing like what Hazel can do, or Opal for that matter." He points around the village. "All of this is protected because of her. She's the one who can keep us hidden. We'd be lost without her," his voice grows weary, "or more likely dead."

Our boots crunch against the snow as we head over. Nobody speaks. Finally, I can't help but ask. "What can she do?"

"It's something to do with memories and vision but I don't know all the details and I don't ask. Not my business. The little girl is... sweet. But she's also... a lot."

Girl? A little girl can do all that?

"This is where I'll leave you." He stops about a hundred yards from the house. "Good luck."

Umm, okay?

Dean and I cross the field, approaching the cottage with nerves flying.

"You sure about this?" he questions. He's always asking me that lately and I have to laugh.

"What?"

"Nothing, you're cute."

He frowns at that.

I shake out my hands and then ball them into fists to keep from fidgeting. "Yup, we gotta do this. We didn't come all this way for nothing."

I stare up at the cottage. It's adorable and made of stone and log, reminding me of a smaller version of Harmony's house back in West Virginia. The trees around the cottage twist in unearthly angles, spiraling in and around themselves. Sparkly white ice is crystallized across every surface, tiny snowflakes that don't melt when you touch them, not even for Dean. The flowers are like how they were back in the forest, a mix of beautiful pastels that look like they've been magicked to stay alive in the cold. We make it to the front door and knock.

It swings open right away.

Okay, first of all, this girl doesn't look like someone to worry about. Not at all. If she were human, I'd say she couldn't be more than thirteen or fourteen years old, but I know age works differently for the fae. She's an elf, with cute pointy ears and gold and silver earrings pierced up and down each one. Her skin is deep brown, eyes are sky blue, hair long and stick straight and white as the snow surrounding us. She's dressed in a midnight blue velvet dress and matching cape with silver embroidery around the edges. In a word, she's stunning.

She jumps forward, crushing me into a hug. It's so unexpected, I nearly fall backward.

"I'm so glad you're here," her wispy voice gushes. "I heard them talking about you in the village this morning when I went to get some eggs. Another spirit elemental! Finally! I've always been the only one, you know. Well, besides Gregory, but that man isn't exactly the most chatty with me if you know what I mean."

"Umm, hi." I peel myself out of her arms and smile brightly. "I'm Hazel and this is Dean."

Dean raises a hand.

"You're gorgeous." She gives him a wink and then another one to me. "Lucky girl. Of course it would be a girl that would bring him back out of hiding. You're the exiled prince aren't you? You are. I can tell."

Dean stiffens but doesn't move. She's the first fae to point out who he is and if she knows, it stands to reason others here might recognize him too. I wonder why nobody else said anything. Maybe they didn't know *what* to say.

"I was wondering if you could help me train." I take a deep breath and get right to the point. "I have spirit magic and can see the other realms but I can also turn into a spirit dragon, which is new for me. I don't really know what I'm doing but I have to figure it out like, yesterday."

She laughs. "Right. Well, we can start that part tomorrow." She pulls us inside her home as she keeps babbling. Her house is as cute as she is, small and cozy, with warm colors decorating the space. I catch a whiff of sage and immediately think of Harmony. "Today I want you to tell me all about the humans. You grew up in their realm, right? What's it like out there? I've never left this little bubble, you know? I have to stay and keep everyone safe. Can't leave." She lets out a breath. "Nobody else can do it. It's all on me." She grins again. "But I secretly love the attention."

I don't even know what to say, not that I can get a word in. Maybe *this* is why Gregory didn't want to join us. Not because there's something to fear about the girl but because she's got a huge personality for someone as quiet and broody as Gregory.

"I'll help you, Hazel," she babbles on, "but only if we talk first, okay? I have so many questions. I mean, you're from Spring I hear but grew up in the human realm which is wow, just wow. I'm not kidding, when I say I have questions, I mean I have a million and one questions. Maybe more!"

That makes me laugh. "You and me both."

TWENTY
KHALI

"SOMETHING ISN'T RIGHT," I WHISPER, leaning over the back of the couch between Terek and Maxx. We're in the queen's sitting room attempting to enjoy an afternoon tea service. Mother and Faros forced me to invite a handful of the higher ranking ladies and socialites to tea but I insisted on inviting my friends along as well. The food is as garish as the decor, with little cakes in every color, and the conversation is as fake as most of the company, but at least I have Terek's playful anecdotes to entertain me and get my mind off of everything. Thoughts of the arrival of the sorcerer and unraveling of my hidden memories pester me constantly. "I need to know why Aleeryrick is really here."

Terek looks at me sidelong underneath his dark lashes and raises an eyebrow. "Well, isn't that the understatement of the century?"

I need to go back to my seat soon but I can't help myself and lean in farther, quieting my voice even more. "Did something happen?"

The four other ladies are busy chatting with my mother but that doesn't mean some of them might not be trying to eavesdrop.

"Most people we've met aren't happy we're here," Maxx says. He takes an awkward sip of tea. His hand is twice the size of the delicate teacup and I almost laugh.

Mother shoots me a scandalized glare and I kind of want to slap her but she's right and I should sit down and be the good queen she taught me to be, but why? I'm so tired of the games. This is my life and she already got what she wanted, didn't she? I blame this sudden need to glare back at her on our old feelings. Or maybe on the fact that she's beginning to return to her old self now that father is doing better. Her and Faros insisted that only ladies be invited but I'm queen, aren't I? There's not a lot I can control at the moment but inviting my male friends is one of them.

"Why didn't Juniper come?" I ask. I thought for sure she'd take me up on the invitation considering she actually *is* a female and looks the part of a lady.

Maxx grumbles and sets his teacup down, folding his arms over his chest and leaning back in his chair.

"Let's just say Juniper has been spending a lot of time with the little princeling." Terek waggles his eyebrows and my heart sinks.

"Oh." I don't have to ask, I know he means Bram.

"I don't know who's more upset about it, you or Maxx?" He grins.

I turn to my horned friend. "You like Juniper?"

His tanned skin turns the sweetest shade of pink and before he can answer, one of the more troublesome ladies pipes in from across the room.

"Are you enjoying your stay here at Stoneshearth?" The woman directs her question to Terek and Maxx. I take that as my cue to return to my chair.

The woman is older, closer to my mother's age, and I don't know her too well, though I've seen her flit about Queen Brysta often. I wonder if she even cares about the previous queen now that I've taken her place. Her name is Duchess Dasha. She's married to one of the more ambitious dukes in the kingdom and her daughter is the fifteen year old girl I saw kissing Silas before I ran away.

I give the woman a disinterested glower. I don't know if Silas is still having an affair with her daughter and I honestly don't want to know. Actually, I take that back. I hope they're still involved. Someone needs to keep him busy and *she* actually wants him.

Maxx and Terek answer the duchess's question in predictable fashion, complimenting the staff and the accommodations, but there's a resentful undertone to the direction of the conversation that worries me. Something is off but it's more than just hateful looks and snide comments. Most of the court aren't happy to have the fae here and they're even more upset by the sorcerer, but it's not these people that any of us need to be worried about.

It's Silas and his ambitions and his plan that are the problems.

Why would he be so welcoming to the fae? He never made the bargain to keep them around and well taken care of, that was all Titus. So what's Silas's endgame? Who's going to get hurt? Because someone always does…

"We've been talking with the king," Terek responds to some underhanded comment from Duchess Dasha about foreigners in the court. "He's invited us to bring anyone we know back home out of hiding to live in Drakenon."

I cough into my teacup. They all turn to look at me and I motion for them to carry on.

"Of course, that would take great time and a whole lot of convincing," Maxx adds with a sarcastic laugh. "Most of the fae don't trust dragons any better than the Occultists."

Terek clears his throat and the room falls into a moment of stunned silence. To compare us to them is a low blow.

But… I understand. Our peoples have been contentious for over a century.

"Well, I for one believe our king to be generous and wise." Dasha smiles through her thin lips and I'm pretty sure she's lying through her teeth.

"Generous is one way to put it," I whisper into my teacup but nobody hears.

My friends are smart enough to know they can't bring any more fae here, not with the Occultists closing in, and not with a king nobody can trust. I haven't told them that Silas is bound and determined to not only destroy the warlocks but to take over all of Eridas when he's done. There are so many things I want to warn them about but I can't with all these listening ears. So instead I ask Dasha, "Wouldn't that be nice to have so many more fae friends in our castle? They are such fun."

It forces another nod of agreement from the lady and I smile. *Liar.*

I inspect my friends. "But you ought to hold off moving anyone until you are sure they would be happy here." Happy is a synonym for safe.

"Oh but you must be missing them terribly," my mother interjects. She straightens her shoulders and brushes back a strand of dark hair. I eye her warily, hoping she's not back to her usual scheming.

"We do." Maxx nods.

"So why don't you leave and go back to them?" Duchess Dasha asks, sweet as vinegar.

"That's enough." I shoot her the kind of look that says she better be careful. Everyone stills. "I'm not feeling well," I cut off the conversation right there. "I'm going to take a walk alone to get some fresh air. Perhaps we can do this again another time?"

I stand, brush out my coral colored skirt, and hasten for the door. I don't give them time to argue or respond.

"Would you like me to join you?" my mother asks but it's more of a statement since it's not customary for queens to walk outside alone. Not that I'll be alone, I'm sure a guard will keep watch over me. They always do.

"Not today, Mother." I stroll through the door and out into the hallway. Really, I'm hoping my friends will follow me, but they don't...

Something is wrong. Something is wrong. Something is wrong, the mantra echoes through my mind.

I need to get out of this castle, out of these stuffy rooms and echoing corridors. I haven't even been able to search for the dungeons yet, but I can go outside, can't I? There are no rules against that.

I don't have my cloak on me but I don't care. I pass a few people on my way out of the castle who give me little bows and curious glances but I pay them no attention. It's fresh air I need and nothing else. My breath starts to come out in little bursts and the walls begin to close in around me.

The winter air jolts me awake, snapping me from my worried thoughts, and I suck in a deep breath. Relief sweeps through my body. I head around the back of the castle to the gardens, my favorite spot. Not too far behind, the guards linger—ever watchful.

The garden is quiet this time of year, which I appreciate. In the warmer months it's always filled with people milling about, showing off their gowns, gossiping, admiring the floral smells and array of flowers. Last time I was here was with Bram, just over a week ago, but it feels like an eternity with everything that's happened.

I enter the labyrinth. The hedges are sparse but I know the maze well and it gives me something to do. The snow is hard and icy. It crunches easily under my boots. The guards wait at the entrance.

A few minutes into my walk, the sound of another's footsteps stop me short. I'm not alone.

Maybe the guards decided to follow after all?

Goosebumps crawl up my arms. I hold my tongue and stay as still as possible, listening. There are voices, two male, one female, but they're quiet, whispered, hurried. I can't tell exactly who they are or what they're talking about.

I take another step forward, so softly, and cringe when the snow crunches under my shoes. The voices fall silent.

I continue walking. This is ridiculous. I shouldn't feel afraid in my own garden. This is my favorite place and I'm queen now and I'll walk through this maze if I please. I don't need to skulk around and hide in the shadows.

"Who's there?" I demand. "Show yourselves."

"Khali?"

Bram steps out from around a nearby corner, Juniper on his arm. Her rosy cheeks and pretty blonde hair make my stomach twist but I force a happy smile anyway.

"It's nice to see you." I say. "Both of you." I clear my throat. "Together."

Now I'm the liar. What am I even saying?

Bram frowns and stares at me like I've hurt him and Juniper looks at me like she's been caught. "This isn't what you think it is," he blurts.

"Who were you talking to just now? I heard another man's voice."

Bram opens his mouth to reply but Juniper beats him to it. "Nobody else," she says sharply. "Just us."

Bram pales and then stares at me hard, like he wants me to say something, to challenge them. But what? Do I accuse Juniper of lying to me? Do I tell the truth, that I hate to see them together? I'm lost for words entirely because I'm sure, certain even, that they're keeping a secret.

"We'll be on our way," Bram says, giving me a sad smile. "Take care of yourself, Khali." Just as he passes, he whispers low into my ear. "Things aren't what they seem."

"Right." My voice is clipped.

And then I brush past them, pushing through the maze and as far away from the couple as I can get. My eyes water and my heart thuds angrily. Why are they lying? And who were they talking to?

I wanted to confess Silas's plans to them, like I've wanted to with Terek and Maxx. They all need to know that Silas is bent on taking over Eridas. I hate being the only one carrying this weight.

After a few minutes, I reach the center of the maze. I turn around in a circle, looking up at the sky. Some of the dragons are out training again, they swoop and spin, black specks in a sea of blue.

A man clears his throat.

I turn with a gasp to find I'm no longer alone. I don't know this man well. Growing up I was sheltered from most of the court, especially the people who had jobs to do and weren't interested with the frivolities of court life. This man, he's one of them. I only know of him, because everyone does.

General Cardos.

A fierce dragon shifter and earth elemental, and the head of the Drakenon Army—one of the most powerful positions in the kingdom.

"You were the one talking with Bram and Juniper, weren't you?" I say, keeping my voice low.

The general doesn't look at me. He stares up at the sky, hands pulling on his lapel, and clears his throat. "Yes," he answers, voice clear and honest.

Why didn't Bram just tell me that? Maybe it's stupid, but it hurts to know he's chosen Juniper as his confidant and not me.

"You were King Titus's right hand man," I continue. "And now you're Silas's…"

"Yes." His tone is flat. I can't read him, not even a little bit.

I study his profile, the salt and pepper hair, the broad shoulders, the relaxed way he crosses the expanse and sits down on the bench. I stare at him, right in his mossy green eyes. "What was the conversation with Bram about?"

He doesn't answer. Instead, he stares right back, and my limbs start to shake.

Is he loyal to Silas? My heart speeds because somehow I think he is not. Why else would he be sneaking around in here talking with Bram? Or maybe it's me he doesn't trust? But then again, I could be jumping to conclusions. I fold my arms over my chest, warding off the shivers.

"Do you know what Silas plans to do?"

His expression turns haunted. "Yes, I do."

"You know that he wants to take over all of Eridas?" I whisper, my voice barely a breath above the slight breeze.

He winces slightly and nods.

"And do you know how he plans to do that?"

The silence grows between us and he finally answers. "That, I don't know yet. It's what I'm trying to find out. He's been in talks with the merpeople but I don't know about what exactly. Perhaps it's the portal they are sworn to protect."

I freeze. "The portal to the human realm?"

His lips thin and he nods once. The news is so great, I'm forced to sit down next to him and collect my bearings.

"Do you know his plan?" General Cardos asks. "Why else could he be talking with the merpeople?"

The merpeople scare me to death and I hate that they're another piece in the puzzle. I turn and hold his gaze. "Not yet. But so we're clear, I don't agree with my husband's desire to take over Eridas. I don't think dragons should rule over fae or anyone else. I have to warn you he'll do anything to get his way, hurt anyone, kill anyone. Do you understand what I'm saying?"

He laughs, his stoic facade breaking the whispered silence. "Believe me, I know."

I wonder how much King Titus told this man. Titus was strict and backwards in a lot of ways but he wasn't a tyrant. He'd never have done the things Silas is doing. But then again, he knew the truth about Owen's murder and tried to hide it. Titus may be dead, but he's to blame for a lot of what's happening now.

"You better watch your back." My voice is hollow.

His mouth hardens. "Yes. And you need to take the same advice."

I don't know if it's a warning or a threat but he strides away, shifting into his dragon and taking to the sky before I can ask. His dragon joins the other black specks that cut ruthlessly into the sprinkling of gray clouds against the blue.

I know I should be feeling many things in this moment, but all I can feel is a deep, deep jealousy of those dragons because I'm still stuck down here in the center of the hedge maze.

TWENTY-ONE
HAZEL

"ARE YOU READY?" OPAL ASKS, soft pink lips grinning from where she's perched on a bench made entirely of ice. She pats the open space next to her and I join her, trying to ignore the sharp cold of it. The padding of my pillowy black coat doesn't really help all that much.

I gaze out to the horizon, to the sun rising over the snowy field and the way it paints the sky blazing pink. If hope was a color, it would be this. And if someone would have told me a few months ago that I'd be learning how to control my abilities from an elf, I'd have laughed and said they were crazy. And yet here I am, sitting at the edge of a magically hidden supernatural village with a young fae elf who looks like she's about thirteen years old, but who is probably much older, and desperate for her to help me.

"I'm ready." I clear my throat and smile. "So where do we start?"

A dimple forms on her dark brown cheek and her blue eyes sparkle against the sunlight. "Why don't you tell me about what you do know about your magic?"

This still feels crazy to even think that I have magic, but here I am! And since Opal's the only one here with the spirit element, I've got to bite the bullet and at least try. I tell her about what I see, in both the human spirit realm and the supernatural one, and what I think it means.

She stops me. "But you said your mother is a faerie and your father is a dragon shifter, so why would you be so connected to humans?"

"Maybe because I grew up in the human realm? Maybe a distant ancestor was human? Or it could be something to do with the spell the Occultists put on me? I don't know."

"You're under a spell?"

I let out a long sigh. "An Occultist linked me to the dragon princess, Khali. Our magic reacts when we're around each other, she grows weaker and I grow stronger. And from what I understand, if I die, she will die. I can't help but wonder if the spell is what's making me who I am with all this"—I wave my hands around—"giving me access to multiple spirit realms and stuff."

She ponders on that for a bit. "It is curious. Maybe it is the spell that's given you that access or maybe the explanation is simpler than that. I think it's more likely that you have human blood in you. Could be a grandparent or some ancestor who's a full-blooded human. It's rare but it happens."

I nod but it's not like I have any clue. These realms are separate but it's not like it's impossible to crossover. People who have no business falling in love with each other do it all the time. I like the idea of one of my ancestors being a regular old human.

She smiles and twists a long strand of bright white hair around her finger. "Go on." She's got rings lined up on all her fingers, piercings up and down her pointed ears, and an energy about her that is so much more mature than she looks. It's different but definitely cool.

We spend most of the morning talking through everything that's on my mind. I'm anxious for action but I force myself to be patient—not an easy task. Finally she asks me to meditate, something I don't think I've ever done with any real effort.

"Clear your mind," she says, like it's the simplest thing in the world.

Yeah, right.

It's still hard to believe that I'm here. Lucky for us, the ghost of Penelope had been the first of many keys to unlock the doors Dean and I needed to be allowed to stay in this adorable snowy sanctuary. Pretty much all I did yesterday was connect these fae who'd passed on and relayed messages. Some people didn't have their loved ones show up, but at least I could offer them the peace of knowing their person must have moved on to a better place. And then last night Opal and I had talked well past nightfall, becoming instant friends. We'd gotten up first thing in the morning to practice my magic, when she'd insisted I'd be stronger from rest.

"Do you see anything?" Opal interrupts. "Or perhaps feel anything interesting?"

"Uhhh…" My face reddens and my eyes pop open. "Sorry, I sort of got busy thinking about other things and forgot what I was supposed to be doing."

Opal rolls her eyes and giggles sweetly, and I'm suddenly so grateful that she is the one training me and not any of the others. She's kind but more importantly she's not intimidating. So many of the others are intimidating, older, war-torn, hardened… set in their ways. Opal is the opposite of those things. She's relaxed and fun, smart but doesn't take herself too seriously. Kind of like me.

"Sorry," I sigh. "I woke up this morning super worried about my friends and family. I've got to do what I came to do. I need to train and learn to grow my spirit abilities so that I can confidently shift again. I believe you about this meditation stuff, and about this realm being easier to work in than the human one, but my mind is struggling to catch up."

"I'm going to ask you something and you have to promise not to take it personally."

"Umm—okay." *This doesn't sound good.*

"Have you always struggled with self confidence?"

And now I feel like I'm talking to a therapist. "Well shoot, you don't hold back, do you? Yeah, I guess I've always had a hard time with it."

She clasps my hands into hers and stares me down with an arched eyebrow. "Forget about your past for a minute and give yourself credit for where you are." She motions around the village, with its frosted and enchanted coating over everything. "You're in Eridas. You're safe here with me. You are powerful and special. It's time for you to step into your destiny."

My eyes sting. "You're right. And I'm ready. I truly want to work my magic the way I see the other elementals working theirs, like Dean with his fire."

I glance over to where he watches us from a distance.

"And you can."

"But…"

"You're scared?"

I nod. "Yeah, I am. What if I fail? What if I can't control it? Or I hurt myself or others? Not everyone's magic works in the same way. Harmony was a seer…"

"Was?"

I blink rapidly, holding back tears. "Umm, yeah, Harmony kind of got herself into trouble. She's okay now. Safe. But her magic is gone. Wings, too. She sacrificed everything to help me."

Opal sits with that information for a long time, thoughts whirling behind her blue eyes. "What's done is done and what will be will be. You can only control right now, and right now, you need to give yourself a chance. Like I said, you're strong here in Eridas. If you meditate, you will connect with the land and your magic will grow."

I smile softly. "Okay, you're right. Sorry, I'm not great at doing something that feels like doing nothing, but *I know* it's not nothing."

"It will help you," she assures me. "There's so much magic in Eridas, more than you've ever had access to before. It's always helped me to clear my mind and let the stillness boost my magic."

"And your magic is?" I hold my breath.

She stares off into the distance for a while, as if trying to decide if she can trust me. A slow smile creeps across her face. "I can do two things. Mine is also connected to spirit. I don't see spirits as you do and I can't go to the other realm and talk to them. It's nothing like that."

"Then what's it like?"

"First of all, I can visit the past."

I tilt my head. "You're a time traveler?"

She snorts. "No, that's not real. I can see memories, that's all. Not many understand it."

Actually, I think I do because it reminds me of what Harmony did with blood magic.

"So try to explain it?" My voice is earnest and I want so badly for her to trust me. Maybe she wants the same thing. "Because I want to understand. Truly, I do."

"When I'm sleeping and sometimes when I'm awake, I leave my body and my mind is transported to someone else's life. I'm able to see their memories, but it's not like I just see them, I live them."

"That actually makes perfect sense," I say. "I've had that happen to me a few times. Once with a girl who died who showed her memories to me of what happened and again looking back at my mom's past to try to figure out some things we needed to know."

Her eyes go wide. "How did you do it?"

I hope that she doesn't judge me. "The first time the spirit showed me the things herself and the other times, well, we used magic."

Opal's smile falls. "Blood magic?"

I nod once.

"And I take it Harmony took the sacrifice to do that?"

"We all used our blood but…" I choke up.

I don't know what to say but I don't have to. "That's why you said she'd gotten herself into trouble. I remember her from when I was a small child but I barely have any memories left of her. Well, I guess I could go look." She shakes her head. "Is she okay?"

"Yeah, like I said, she's okay. She's alive at least." I don't have the courage to say the rest but I find it anyway. "She lost her wings, her magic, and she aged."

Opal nods in understanding.

"And what's the other thing you can do?" I ask. But I think I already know.

"The glamour over this place? That's all me. Gregory has spelled people to forget about us if they got too close. And I have a spell that uses my magic to glamour this place to an earlier memory of what it once was—an uninhabitable forest."

"Wow." It's the only word I've got!

Over the last two days I've sometimes wondered if these fae feel an extra level of security because they have magic and a way to protect themselves. Or maybe it's that I have an extra layer of fear, worrying that I'm not strong enough and my magic won't be what I hope. Either way, I feel bad for Opal. I always thought my gift was a curse, but I prefer it to being trapped in other people's memories every time I go to sleep at night. I hated it the few times I've experienced it. And I'd hate to be stuck in one village for the rest of my life because people were counting on me to protect them.

"We're going to figure this out together," Opal says brightly, clapping her thin hands together. "My magic is connected to the spirit element just as yours is. If I can clear my mind, push out all the chatter, the pictures, the fear, the worries, I can control my gift. I can choose where I go, what I see, how long I'm in there for. What if it's the same for you? What if we get you centered and calm and trusting yourself, then maybe you wouldn't be so scared to shift again and maybe you'd actually be able to be in control of your gift?"

I laugh but smile, too. "That sounds like a great idea to me." Maybe it's all closer than I realize, maybe I do just need to trust. "My gift was spiraling out of control and then I turned eighteen and something happened to me. My magic got stronger but so did I. These last few days I've felt way more in control and I've never felt that way before. Being in Eridas has only helped, almost like this part of me has been set free."

She squeezes my hands and lets go. "Things become natural and automatic. Same as your lungs know how to breathe air without you putting any effort in."

"Geez, you're so freaking wise, for being what? Thirteen? Fourteen?"

She laughs and shrugs. "Sixteen. But I've been in a world at war for as long as I can remember so the only peace I've been able to count on is the peace I find inside of myself."

"This is exactly what I'm talking about! You're like a Greek philosopher."

"What's a Greek philosopher?"

"Umm—ages ago there were super smart and wise people who said a lot of super smart and wise things and humans still talk about them centuries later. I'm not kidding, there's whole classes dedicated to these dudes."

She rolls her eyes but I can tell she's pleased with the compliment. What must her life be like, stuck here in this tiny village? Maybe being able to travel through memories is what makes her feel alive. Maybe it isn't so bad, after all. Maybe she's traveled through my memories? That thought gives me pause. Wow, if anyone can understand what I've been through, it's this girl.

"So let's try again, okay? This time, I really want you to focus on clearing your mind. Your dragon self, remember that she's already a part of you and always has been. Same with your spirit elemental. The only difference is now you're accepting of them, you're welcoming them, loving them, instead of pushing them away."

I nod, hoping she's right. She sounds right.

"Maybe this was always meant to be easy but you were the one making it hard."

"There you go again!" I pull her into a side hug. "You should write a self help book. We could call it, Spirit Magic: A Self Love Story." I laugh at myself.

"Self help?"

"Human stuff. We'll talk about that later." I wink. "Right now I need to meditate."

I breathe in the crisp air, close my eyes tight, and push out all the little thoughts, one by one. I have to block out memories, they come at me automatically, good ones like kissing Dean, bad ones like evil spirits I've seen. I get to the point where instead of trying to push them out, I let them come and then pass right by me, like feathers on the wind. I relax more and more, until nothing has any meaning. I'm just me.

Here.

Slowly, I'm surrounded by the white snow and then I'm surrounded by the white room of the spirit realm—on and on it goes. This time when I see a reaper settle next to me, I don't allow fear to enter. It can't hurt me anymore. It never wanted to.

"What happened to you?" I take in its red glowing eyes and stare at them, mesmerized. "Did the Occultists spell you?"

Yes, it hisses, *they spelled us to the human spirit realm. We were willing to do anything to be released.*

"Why did they spell you there?" The question echoes around me.

Because they wanted to go there and were attempting to use us as a bridge. They want to bring all the realms together. They want to make everything one.

"So they can rule over it all, right?" It's what we've known for a while. This is total confirmation.

"Can they do that to you again?" I ask. "Spell you?"

They're trying but it's not working, not since you set us free. Not since you're alive.

A chill runs over my entire body and I'm filled with a million more questions. It's like as soon as I get one answered, more multiply.

His raspy voice turns impatient. *I've got a lot of work to do.* He zips away, and I'm once again alone in the white room.

It makes sense he'd have work to do considering the reapers were parted from their duties for so long. Still, I'm bugged that he left so quickly. There must be a lot of supernatural spirits that need to be moved to their appropriate destinations. I wish I could see whatever that destination is, could know with absolute certainty that whatever comes next is something good, something worth looking forward to, but for whatever reason, that knowledge must not be meant for me.

Every time I've been in this realm before I've been afraid. The human version and the supernatural one look the same and I'm still not sure how to differentiate between the two. Or maybe I really am a bridge somehow? Maybe that's why the Occultists want me so bad. I breathe it all in, letting myself accept the fact that there might not *ever* be someone who will be able to give me all the answers.

I'll find as many as I can on my own, even if deep down, I know I have to be okay with not knowing everything about the spirit realms or the spirit elemental magic. The control freak within me hates the idea but the bigger part of me, the real part, is actually okay with it.

I'm not afraid anymore.

I'm not afraid.

And with that final thought, I allow it to happen. I don't force it. I don't resist. I simply allow it to pour over me, the truth that I can trust myself, that it's *safe* for me to be powerful. And all at once, I go from being Hazel the girl, to Hazel the little white spirit dragon with the great big life mission.

TWENTY-TWO

KHALI

IF THE KING HAS A secret passage from his room, it would stand to reason that the queen would have one as well. But I've been trying to find another way to the tunnels for days and so far I've failed. I can't keep sneaking into Silas's room without getting caught. Beyond our royal chambers, there are too many eyes on me, which means I can't go to the old entrance Owen and I used to use, even though much of that particular tunnel was blocked.

So sneaking through Silas's room seems to be my only option.

After breakfast, I dress in a simple white a-line gown and cover it with a matching cloak, then I wait until Silas is gone for the day. With one solid breath to bolster my courage, I slip through the shared family room and into his empty bedroom, going right for the bookcase. I slide my fingers along its edge until I find the hidden latch to unlock it. I'm more prepared this time with a lit candle to guide my way through the narrow tunnel and down the steep stairs. The darkness is thick but my eyes adjust quickly with the aid of candlelight.

When I get to Silas's underground study, I set down my candle and check the door. It doesn't open. If I had magic, I would try to break the lock. Bellflower Blossom wanted me to see something down here and whatever it is, it stands to reason it could be behind this door. I stop for a quick listen but there's nothing. I press my hands to the cool oak and I am met with a sharp zap. I scramble back, stifling a broken sob. Electricity burns through my body.

My palms are burned.

I hurry on, angry with myself for being foolish, with Silas for the ward, with everything.

The goal now is to get out of the castle altogether, not to run away but to go to the lake. I want to cool my hands off but also if Silas has been talking with the merpeople, they probably still have sentries near the surface for anyone requesting an audience. As the queen, and someone they've used as a pawn in the past, I'm eager to know what's going on. I don't know if they'll confess anything but maybe they'll talk. At this point, some information is better than none. I'm beginning to suspect Silas is rounding up as many fae species as he can to help take down the Occultists but knowing him, probably as part of his strategy to overpower their fractured kingdoms. He's playing nice right now, but he's not a nice man. He'll hurt them. Not if he has to, when he has to. It's only a matter of time.

The tunnels here are unfamiliar so I'm careful to memorize each turn so I don't get lost on the way back. Finally, I recognize a fork in the road, marked by a series of deep etches in the wall. It's the path Bram and I used to escape all those weeks ago. I'm slow, walking on soft footsteps, flickering light barely illuminating a few feet in front of me at a time. The walls are stone and dripping water. The ground is cold hard dirt, with puddled mud every few turns. Sometimes I hear people talking through the walls, or footsteps up ahead. Those are the moments when I hold my breath and move forward only an inch at a time.

Finally, just when I'm beginning to think I'll be lost down here forever, the little metal door to the outer wall appears before me like an answer to a prayer. I open it, pushing against the brushes that hide it, and scramble out onto the rolling fields of white snow. Glinting in the distance is the vast lake, mostly iced over from the winter. I tuck my hair into my cloak and hope that the white of my outfit blends in well enough with the snow. Dragons patrol these areas from above, but they're not looking for someone in a white cloak, they're looking for burgundy robes, they're looking for magic, for things in the sky, for things that don't belong.

I hurry to the lake's edge, my breath billowing out ahead of me as I run. The lake is enormous and so much deeper than meets the eye. The water elemental dragons have no problem training in here from time to time because of the treaty with the merpeople, but I've always hated the water. I was taken prisoner as a child by the merpeople. They used me as a pawn and even though things worked out okay in the end, I've never been able to get over my fear of them or their watery home.

Even the merwoman from the Summer Forest, the one who helped me find the portal there, terrified me. Her sharp luminescent scales and haunted milky eyes brought me right back to my worst childhood memories. Not to mention, she asked that I would repay the favor with an equal debt. I haven't seen her since and don't know that I will again on this dragon land, far away from that Summer lake. I may never have to pay that debt, though that seems like wishful thinking.

I trudge along the shoreline, nervous energy keeping me from stepping out onto the ice. As a child my elementals revealed themselves enough that I could breathe underwater but I can't do that right now. I notice a circle of blue up ahead and hurry to inspect it. It looks like someone took heat to the ice and forged a hole, which might have been the case, or maybe Silas used his lightning to bore the hole himself.

My palms still sting, but holding a bit of snow in each hand will have to suffice.

I daren't get too close to the lake but I hope if I stand near, someone will come to speak to me. The wind picks up, tossing my hood off my face and blowing my dark hair behind me. I hurry to fix it, trying not to shiver. The hole of water ripples. At first I think it's from the wind, but then a young man's head lifts through the surface. His skin is covered in pale blue scales. His eyes are acrid yellow, hair too, and he smiles with pointed teeth. I almost expect those to be yellow too, but they're stark white.

"Queen Khali." His voice is deeper than his apparent age. It sends a chill down my body. "Stay where you are. I'll let them know you're here."

And then he's gone.

I wrap my arms in on myself and stay put, making sure I'm not too close to the water that an arm could reach out and pull me in. A few minutes later the glassy surface ripples again and two new faces appear—a man and a woman. They're older and wearing identical crowns made of silvery gemstones and black pearls.

I step back and stand tall, recognizing them instantly.

They are Queen Talis and King Sentin, the monarchs of the community of merpeople, and the two people who stole me away as a child. Despite trying to block those memories, they now tug at me and I feel as if I'm being dragged underwater all over again.

I suck in a quick breath and bow low, forcing myself to be stronger than my fear.

"Queen Khali," Talis says, "we heard about your marriage and subsequent coronation." Her voice is dangerous, an ax cutting through steel. "Congratulations."

"Thank you."

"Yes," King Sentin adds stoically, "we look forward to working with you and Silas."

"My husband feels the same way," I lie and smile. "He sent me here to see if everything is in order."

It's a gamble, pretending I know why he came here earlier. But according to the general he did. And according to the general, these people are protecting a portal.

Talis cocks her head. Her eyes are deep purple and shine unnaturally in the sunlight. I don't think she comes to the surface very often. "Is that so? And what exactly does he want from us now?"

"I don't know what you mean."

"He already knows our terms but he didn't agree to them," she continues. "Perhaps you see reason? We can't very well turn over the portal to a sorcerer without adequate payment."

My stomach flips and I blink. *This* isn't at all what I expected.

"Yes." Sentin grins, his pointed teeth look like they could easily slice my flesh into ribbons. "And Khali, we've spoken with our cousin in Summer. We know that you owe her. She agrees our demands would satisfy the debt as well as what your husband has asked for."

"What demands?" I blurt out, then immediately chastise myself for revealing too much.

They exchange a bemused look, likely catching on that my husband and I aren't actually talking to each other about this *at all*.

"We want to return to land," Talis hisses.

"But you're merpeople." I frown, genuinely confused. "You can't."

"Some of us could if the treaty was amended," Sentin juts in. "Our ancestors walked on land but they're also the fools who agreed to keep our people locked underwater. We want to change the terms of our treaty. In exchange we'll give Silas what he wants and we'll consider your debt to our cousin in Summer forgiven."

My heart thuds in my chest. "I don't have the authority to change the treaty." I step back, my stomach turning to a lump. This isn't good, especially knowing that Silas is trying to get access to the portal. "I'm sorry. That's not why I came here."

"So you came here only to demand answers? You wanted to know why Silas has asked for our help." Sentin's tone turns abrasive. "And what of your debt? It's time to pay it."

"I don't owe *you* that debt," I challenge. "It was an agreement I made with someone else." I'm quick to lose my temper and immediately regret it. What was I thinking, coming here alone? These people don't care about me. They used me once and would use me again if they could.

"We're one and the same." Talis rises slightly from the water, her fin long and slimy green, reminding me of a giant snake. "Unlike the dragons who have so many clans, merpeople people are one. We live in unison. We work in unison. We can communicate with each other through magic, no matter where we live. Do wrong to one of us and do wrong to all of us."

"I'm sorry." I shake my head. "I mean no disrespect. I shouldn't have come here."

As I turn to leave, a loud crack violates the quiet morning. The ice is breaking. Water splashes on shore, some of it hitting me, like wanting fingers. I whip around. Long ropes of seaweed fly toward me. A net!

I don't react fast enough. The icy net covers me, ropes digging into my skin, dragging me toward the water. I claw at the snow but it's too slick and my palms are still burned. I scream, crying out for help, my voice ripe with panic. I can't shift into my dragon to get out of the net. I'll drown. They don't know that I no longer have water elemental magic.

"Please," I beg. "You'll kill me within minutes. I can't go in the water!"

They don't listen. I'm sliding, closer, closer, closer. And I know, the moment I hit that water, I'll be dragged under. Sure as I know that the sky is blue and the snow is white and that the blue water will turn inky black down below, I know I am going to die.

TWENTY-THREE
HAZEL

I GAPE DOWN AT MYSELF, stunned by what I see and what I am. I don't know if I'll ever get used to this. My white scales glisten in the sunlight, blending in seamlessly with the snow. I stretch out my claws, marveling at the shiny pink tips. I take one of them to the ice bench, sure it's sharp enough to slice into it, but it slides right through. I'm in the spirit realm, then, unable to touch the physical even though they can see me and I can see them. I roll my shoulders back and my wings roll with them. Wings… I remember what it felt like to fly, how easy and natural it was for me. I want to do it again.

Opal observes calmly on the far side of the ice-bench, smiling at me with a knowing twinkle in her eye. I inch toward her and she stands, reaching out to pat my head, but like before, it slides right through me. "Amazing," she whispers. "This is unlike anything I've ever heard of before."

I peer around, noticing others watching in the distance, expressions of confusion and awe. Dean stands across the field, observing from the stoop of the little house we've been staying in, his arms folded over his chest, a giant smile on his normally unreadable face. He's giving me space to do this, but he's not willing to let me out of his sight, which is actually pretty sweet.

I turn back to Opal, wishing I could speak to her right now and explain that when I'm a spirit dragon, I'm in two places at once. But then again, I'm pretty sure she's already figured that part out. My eyes adjust and on top of the physical world are the spirit realms, both the supernatural and the human. Everything is layered on top of each other and they call out to me, begging to be explored. I could go. Right now, I know I could go.

But... my wings twitch. The urge to lift off and soar into the wide open sky grasps me again, stronger this time. The temptation of it is so unbearable, I have to force myself to stay put. I don't know how far the magicked border around this little village goes and I need to keep control. I would never forgive myself if I put these people in danger. They're already taking a huge risk by letting Dean and me stay here.

Stop thinking about flying.

Focus on something else.

"Clear your mind," Opal says again. "You can do this. *You're* in control."

And I try, but the light of the spirit realm, it grows and grows, brighter, whiter, wider—so so beautiful. Before I can stop myself, I step toward it, and then I'm no longer in two places at once. The living world is gone and I'm wholly in the spirit realm—nor am I alone. I gaze at the people here, realizing I'm in the supernatural spirit realm. A few of the dead people I saw yesterday are here again, eager to reconnect with their family again, they surround me, some talking, some sending images. Elves and faeries, mostly. There's a gorgeous centaur, with bright azure eyes, black hair and body, who stands far back, ever watchful and guarded. A few pixies dash past, chasing after each other, oblivious to me.

A black dragon flies in and I already know by his blue eyes and the swift movements that it's Owen. He lands right in front of me, nuzzling his head against me in a sort of hug, and the others leave us.

It's good to see you again, he says through the dragon link. *You have no idea how happy am I to see you've shifted again. I've been waiting and waiting for you to come talk to me.*

I smile to myself. *And where have you been? I haven't seen you in a while.*

He releases me and stretches his wings out. They're so strong, so real, so *here*. I almost can't believe that he's dead. It's different when spirits visit me in the other realms; they don't have this solidness to them. It's hard for me to understand why I get to be here with a link back to real life and they don't, but then there are so many things I don't understand, so what else is new?

I've been watching Khali. I'm worried about her. Owen's voice is strained and almost accusatory.

Dean and I are worried about her, too.

Could have fooled me... His tone turns sour.

What? What do you think we're doing in Eridas? Ever since Silas took her away we've been trying to find the safest way to get to her. Well, and Cora and Macy, but Owen doesn't have to know that.

Well you're not trying hard enough. A low growl rumbles through his body.

I'm stunned. Is he kidding me? This is the first time I've ever had Owen be rude toward me and I don't appreciate it. I don't know how to respond with only words so without much thought, I shift into my regular self and fold my arms over my chest. He can talk to me face to face if he's going to have an attitude.

He shifts too, but it's not a crappy attitude I find staring back at me, it's fear. His hair is a wild mess around bloodshot eyes.

"Owen, what's going on?"

"Look for yourself." He points into the white vastness and an image appears.

It's Khali. She's on a shoreline, caught in a net, screaming for her life. Someone is pulling her toward the water. Are those mermaids? They don't look like the pretty versions human idolize, these are terrifying, with pale sickly scaled skin, unearthly eyes, and razor sharp teeth. Khali screams again, her eyes wide with horror and rimmed in red.

"She's in trouble," Owen presses. "She's lost her magic. She lost it the day she turned eighteen. And now the merpeople are going to drown her!"

My chest burns hot and then cold. I want to help her, to save her, but I'm also wondering... how is it that my magic grew and hers was lost on the same day? It must be the spell. I've finally found myself and I don't want to let that go. But another part of me, the bigger part, wants to fix her magic and save her from the scary mermaids. We're connected. I have to help.

"Go to her." Owen points at the image. "You can walk right through that and go to her now. You don't have to stay in this village."

I nod and fill my lungs with a long, slow breath. He's right, of course. I know this is true, that this is part of my abilities. Like spirits, I can basically teleport from this realm to the people I love. So why am I so afraid? I could check on Mom and Harmony. I could go to Cora and Macy and make sure they're okay. Just the thought of them and more images pop up around me. I glimpse Harmony and my mother in our kitchen, cooking breakfast. They have false smiles and worry in their eyes. I could go to them, tell them I'm okay, and then come right back here.

But what if it doesn't work? What if I got stuck there?

No, I shouldn't risk it.

I turn away from the vision of them to find the one of Cora and Macy. I cry out, the image of my friends sending me reeling. They're asleep and alone in a barren and dark stone room, laying on tiny straw beds, dressed in tattered gowns. Relief hits me because at least they're not dead, but it's short lived and quickly followed by guilt. Are they locked up in that room? How much do they know about where they are? I want so badly to go to them and ask a million questions, to make sure they're okay, to get them out of there and back home.

But again, what if I can't come back? Or what if I can only travel through the portals like the other living dragons and faeries. What if it's not that easy like it seems to be for the spirits? Owen is right, I have to go to Khali, she's in mortal danger.

She needs me *now*.

My voice cracks. "What if I fail?"

"You need to do the right thing," Owen snaps, running his hands through his sandy hair and staring at me with the clearest blue eyes I've ever seen. "Go. Go help her now."

"Okay." I suck in a breath. "But I can't leave Dean here. And I'm training. I'm not prepared to deal with the dragons and whatever comes next."

"Don't you get it?" Owen growls. "Dean can't go to Drakenon! He'll be executed on sight. And my people are running out of time—all of them, especially Khali! *They* don't have the luxury of waiting."

He opens his mouth to speak again, but a flash of black swoops between us and cuts him off. The reaper is so fast and swift that we barely scramble out of the way.

"No," Owen growls, turning on the reaper. "I'm not ready yet. I haven't said goodbye. I haven't made sure they're safe—"

The reaper stretches out a bony hand toward Owen anyway. "It's your time, Boy."

"No!" I scream and dive on top of Owen, dragging him away from the reaper.

The white room disappears in a flash and we're right back to where I was in

Winter. This time, Owen is with me, but he's taken on that ghost quality again. I'm the only one who can see him.

I'm solid, back to me, and my heart is racing. I pant and little puffs of steam flit into the cold morning air.

"Are you okay?" Opal asks. Her eyes are wide pools of blue and her dark complexion has gone pale.

"Yes," I groan, but really, I'm not. And Khali, she most definitely *isn't* okay. I might already be too late as it is. I shoot Owen's spirit a charged look and a nod before turning back to Opal.

I spot Dean across the field, still watching all of this. He's abandoned his spot on the porch and is jogging toward us.

"I'm okay," I whisper to Opal. "But I have to leave you. Today. Right now."

Her face falls. "So soon? Are you sure? There was more I wanted to do."

I nod and rest my hands on my knees, still trying to catch my breath. "Me too but I'm sure. I have people that need my help right now."

Owen nudges me, his expression growing even more impatient. "Not to mention a dragon spirit who's going to haunt my butt until I do what he wants."

Owen laughs and growls at the same time and the sound cracks through some of my fear.

Opal stares at me like I've lost my mind, but she nods anyway. "Well alright then," she says brightly, pulling me into a quick hug. "Let's go tell Dean."

Owen shoots me another annoyed glare. "There's no time for that."

I know he's getting impatient. I hope that Khali is okay, that she's fighting the merpeople off, but he's right. I can't keep thinking about this, about her, I have to go. *Now!*

I look back to Dean and wonder if I should leave him here where he'll be safe. Drakenon isn't going to be kind to him. What if they kill him like Owen says they will? What if they don't even give us a chance to try to get him pardoned for his stupid "crime"? But deep in my gut I know that if I ditch Dean right now, he might find a way to follow, but he may never forgive me for leaving him. There's no reasoning with that boy when he's got his mind made up about something; he and I have that stubborn trait in common.

He catches up to us across the snowy field and wraps me into his warm arms. "You did it," his breath tickles my ears. "Good job. I'm so proud of you."

"Well I hope it's good enough," I groan.

"It will be."

"It has to be now." I step back and give him a cheesy smile. "Cause guess what? Your dead brother is insisting I go to Drakenon *right this second*. He says our friends are out of time. They need me. Khali's in big trouble with the mermaids."

His expression turns stony.

Owen is busy pacing behind us. His blond hair is a disheveled mess and he looks about ready to explode. *Okay, Dude, I get it.*

"And this next part is going to be hard for you to understand." My voice wobbles and I have to force myself to hold his gaze. I breathe in his smoky rain scent, take in his coal fire eyes, his warmth and goodness, and try to cage it in my memory. "But I need to go alone."

"What?" Dean hisses. "No way!"

"I can go directly to Khali using my gift and Owen will be there with me."

"What the hell is Owen going to be able to do for you? No way, Hazel. It's too dangerous. You don't know these people. You don't know how ruthless they can be."

"Which is exactly why you can't come," I beg. "They exiled you!"

"Don't do this," Dean pleads. He's gripping my wrists so tight. His eyes are so wide, so pleading and desperate. My heart aches but I have to do this. I have to. For him.

"I love you," I whisper the words for the first time. This wasn't the situation I imagined saying them in but I can't go without telling him how I feel. "I love you so much and I'm doing this because I love you."

He's speechless and my heart breaks a little.

"But I really have to go, Khali is running out of time. I have to find her. Please, don't follow."

I rip myself away from him and shift, immediately jumping into the spirit realm. Owen is already there. He shifts too. Praying I'm doing the right thing, I follow the dragon into the unknown.

TWENTY-FOUR
KHALI

THE TINGY WHOOSH OF A blade slicing through the air precedes a quick snap. The net goes limp and I scramble to push the heavy wet net away. The merpeople yell but I can't focus enough to listen to what they're saying. A strong hand grabs hold of my upper arm and heaves me to my feet.

Flannery, my centaur friend, holds me against his hard chest. In his hand, the golden spear glints. My heart leaps with gratitude. "Where have you been?"

"No time," he says gruffly. "Jump on my back and hold tight to me and the spear. We have to go."

I don't quite understand but I do as he says, climbing onto his horse back and reaching my arms around his broad shoulders and wrapping one hand around the spear. He holds on to it as well, never once letting go as he charges through the snow and away from the lake, toward the neighboring forest. Bits of snow and mud fly all around us and the merpeople are still yelling in the distance. It won't be long until the dragon army is here, demanding answers. Once we're in the cover of trees, Flannery slows to a stop and I climb off his back.

"You saved my life." I'm on the verge of crying. I throw my arms around him for a hug. "Thank you. I owe you."

And then it all comes tumbling out right along with the stupid tears. I confess to my magic being lost, to my hopelessness, and explain how everything went wrong after we parted ways with him at the border. I cry as I talk about our hostage Occultist betraying us and the wedding to Silas and Bram killing his father and finally about how the merpeople would have drowned me if he hadn't shown up. Flannery watches me in that steady way of his until I'm finally done. I wipe away the tears and apologize.

"No need to apologize," he offers simply. "You've been carrying a lot on your shoulders."

I nod and release a cathartic laugh. "I just don't get it. How did the Occultist get away from us? We had a deal. Everything should have worked out."

"You can't make deals with the Occultists." His voice goes flat. "I tried to warn you. Their blood magic ties them to a bond that nothing else can break."

I let out a shaky breath and gaze up into the pine trees heavy with snow. Flannery is bare chested just as the day I met him, but he doesn't seem to mind, he doesn't even shiver. His blood must run hotter than mine because I'm freezing.

"I've been traveling to new places and learning about the Sovereign Occultists for years," he says. "But it wasn't until a recent conversation where I learned that not only does their blood magic make them strong because they offer so many sacrifices to it, but there's so much more that goes into it. A strong blood bond like that is powerful enough to resist other kinds of magic, even the agreement you two made."

I stomp my boot into the snow, angry. "Okay, so how do we stop them?"

"Break the bond."

I roll my eyes. "Okay, but it seems like nothing can break it."

"Something must."

"And what would that be?"

Flannery frowns. "If only I knew."

"So, okay… what else is their magic capable of? Let's start there."

He shakes his head and grimaces. "I'm afraid it's capable of far more than we realized. It's cursed the fae who are left to slowly turn into animals, which I don't have to remind you about."

And it's linked me to Hazel somehow… but I don't want to explain that right now. "And it caused the reapers to attach to my father and Bram, leading to King Titus's death."

"Yes."

"We have to stop them."

"Yes," he says again. "And soon because they're working on bringing

Drakenon's borders down entirely so not only will their strongest be able to pass through but their weakest too. All of them are planning to invade you. They've been at the ley line portals trying to get through there as well but it hasn't worked, they simply don't have the right kind of magic, so now they've refocused on Drakenon. And what do you think they'll do to you if they catch you, Khali?"

"They'll kill me." I swallow the hard lump in my throat. It's still hoarse from screaming earlier. "And they'll use my death to strengthen their bond even further."

"Exactly. But you're the most powerful elemental alive in Eridas right now. It could make them strong enough to do anything, strong enough to pass through the ley line portals, strong enough to regain control of the reapers. Khali, if they do get through before you figure out what's going on with your magic, you can't let them find you."

"But my magic is gone, remember? What good am I to them?"

"Are you certain of your magic's disappearance?" He questions, raising his eyebrows. "Or is it spelled away to make you *think* it's gone so that you're extra weak when they come for you."

I blink, the truth of his words settling in. "You're brilliant, do you know that?"

He laughs, the sound hearty and solid. "So I've been told."

"How do you know they've spelled my magic?" I never told him about Hazel.

"The Occultist talked about it when he was with us, remember?"

I let out a breath. "Okay, so how do I get my magic back?"

"Unfortunately I don't have any ideas." He ponders each and every word. The breeze catches his hair and blows it off his shoulders, making him appear even more intense. "You'll have to figure that one out for yourself. But here." He hands me the golden spear. When my fingers wrap around it, I have to swallow down a gulp of panic. "This spear is one of the last magicked objects left in Eridas. It was forged by my people centuries ago, passed down from chief to chief, and is magicked with the gift of invisibility. It will help you survive the coming battle."

"I knew it!" I laugh, feeling the heaviness of the spear and marveling at its beauty and power. "I knew Bram and that Occultist couldn't see you when we were traveling."

"It only makes you invisible to those you don't want to be visible to at the time." He shrugs. "I didn't want them to see me, so as long as I held it, they didn't."

I switch the golden spear from hand to hand, admiring the intricate detail of carved vines and flowers. It's heavier than it looks. "Which is why you had me hold onto it too when we ran from the merpeople. Are you sure you don't need this?" I can't imagine how hard it must be for him to part with something so special.

"Of course I need it." He smiles and his eyes sparkle knowingly. "But you need it more. And besides, you must promise to return it to me when this is all over."

"If I'm not dead," I grumble.

"I have faith in you." He stares straight on, meaning what he says, and something about his words boost me up.

"Thank you. And yes, I promise."

The weight of his incredible gift presses down on me. I'm grateful, but I'm also scared I won't be able to live up to his expectations. I have to find a way to get to Hazel because I'm sure now that she's the only one who can help me get my magic back. It's that damned spell linking us together. I need to break it.

Well, that and I have one other idea of what I need to break...

"There are very few of my kind left," he says, cutting off my thoughts. "My wife and child are hiding in the Winter Kingdom. They're safe for now but I fear for them every day. I haven't been to see them in many years."

His confession cuts me to the core.

"Are you sure you don't want this back?" I frown at the spear. "You could use it to go to them and take them somewhere safer."

"There is nowhere in Eridas safer for them than where they are." He shakes his head, and then his demeanor lightens. "I already told you." His smile quirks. "I'll get the spear back when this is all over and you've defeated the Occultists. But until then, you must be brave."

I want to make a self-deprecating joke but instead I just say thank you again. This is the nicest gift anyone has ever given me and despite everything working against me, his confidence in me gives me the boost I've been needing. Before

I can talk myself out of it, I rush forward and wrap him in yet another tight hug. He hugs me back and I can't help but smile against his warm chest. His heartbeat thumps against my ear. His hind legs kick at the dirt. And he feels— so solid—so real. And he believes in me. The stakes just got higher but I also just got stronger thanks to Flannery. I'm not going to fail him. I'm not going to fail anyone. At least, that's what I'll keep telling myself.

TWENTY-FIVE
HAZEL

I FOLLOW OWEN THROUGH THE white light and into the portal that will lead us to Khali. Time seems to slow, fraying at the edges, and then speeding up as I'm transported from the spirit realm to the castle. I'm back to me, no longer a dragon, standing in a room of stormy gray stone and detailed dark wood carving all the accents.

Wait… this isn't the lake where we saw Khali needing our help. So why on earth did I pop up here? And where did Owen go?

The rugs are plush and the furniture velvet and everything is medieval looking, like something from a European museum. It's actually pretty neat—too bad I'm freaking the freak out! I feel like I'm in a storybook and should be dressed in a princess gown, but instead I'm in head to toe black with tight jeans, fitted puffer jacket, and snow boots. I'm so wholly out of place, it reminds me of when I went to a Halloween party in middle school dressed up like the Wicked Witch of the West, complete with green body paint. Yeah, I'd missed the memo that dressing up wasn't cool anymore. Fun times.

I gaze around, looking for Owen, but he's still gone. Unease crashes over me. *What the heck? Where is he? And where is Khali? Does this mean she's okay? Does it mean this is actually where she was last or something else?*

I suck in a gulp of stuffy air and muster up the courage to find Khali. All I can figure is I must have lost time because it's no longer a bright morning sun casting through the windows at the back of the room. In fact, it's a dark starry night that greets me. I hope she's okay, but right now, I need to make a decision.

There are three doors—three choices.

One on either side of the room and one on the far end. I'm reminded of a gameshow and I've got to pick the right door to get my prize: door number one, two, or three, which is it?

"Okay, here goes nothing," I whisper and go for door number one on the side of the room.

The cool brass handle presses into my palm and I push it open, peering into the room. I don't find Khali. Actually, I don't find anyone. The room is empty except for a large four-poster bed, as intricately carved as the other wood accents, and wardrobe, and a bookshelf. But it smells decidedly male in here and I know at once this isn't where I'm going to find Khali.

"Nevermind." I turn on my heels but run right into a hard male chest and stumble back. He catches me by the forearms.

"Ah." The boy smiles proudly. "I've been wondering when you were going to show up."

My voice catches and panic zips down my body. "Silas."

He's almost as I remember him, with memorizing eyes, a winning smile, and white blond hair. But his clothes are completely different. Gone are his casual human clothes from that night at the party and in their place are the kind of clothes that match this place. I don't know what they're called, but they're exactly what a medieval prince would wear. Again, he's out of a storybook and I'm out of place.

"Like what you see?" he laughs.

"I'm sorry," I mumble. "I was looking for Khali."

"My wife is busy at the moment." His voice goes sour.

When he calls her his wife, my heart hurts. "Busy? Does that mean you saved her?" I can only hope that she was rescued from those freaky mermaids.

He frowns for a second. "She's fine. I just had dinner with her." He tightens his hands on my forearms and shoves me forward. I trip over my own feet and he hauls me against him, marching me farther into the bedroom.

"What are you doing?" I gasp.

"You need to come with me."

"Where?"

"Well, we have options." He chuckles low. "I could kill you now or I could deliver you to the sorcerer and he can kill you later. Hmm…"

"If you kill me, you'll kill Khali."

That stops him for a second, a mark of frustrating realization passing over his pretty features. "Didn't she tell you about the spell?"

He's silent and I let out a laugh. "You don't know."

He shoves me against the wall. My wrists sting and I brace myself for another impact. I'm suddenly certain he's going to hurt me. He fiddles with the bookshelf until it opens, revealing a secret passage into a dark tunnel. It looks so cool, reminding me of a million fantasy books I've read, but being in the situation myself, being forced to go into that dark tunnel with a bad guy and no light? Yeah, not so cool.

I cry out for help and he covers my mouth with one hand and twists my arms behind my back with his other hand. He's taller and larger than me on every count, and when I try to bite him or shove back, I don't get anywhere. It seems to make him even more excited.

"Come now." His voice is pure metal. "Don't you want to see your friends? What were their names again? Oh, I forgot, I don't care enough for mortal humans to remember their names. But I do appreciate that bringing them here got you to follow."

I go limp, thinking of Cora and Macy, and stop fighting. I let him lead me through the cold darkness. I can't see a thing. He must know these tunnels well though because he has no trouble navigating the turns and steep stairs. He holds on to me the entire time. My magic churns within, but it's weakened from traveling through the spirit realm, and anyway, it's not like I'm going to shift right now, not when he's taking me to see my friends. He says Khali is fine so she must have gotten away from the mermaids and this is my chance to help Cora and Macy. I hope they're okay and don't hate me. I'd probably hate me if I were in their shoes. My life is so insanely complicated and those complications have put them in this position.

Silas said he was considering killing me. Now that he knows what it will do to Khali, I'm praying he believes me and doesn't follow through with it. Still, I can't know for sure, so my heart is racing a million miles a minute, my palms are sweating, and I'm pretty sure I'm like two seconds away from having a full-blown panic attack.

We come upon a torch hooked into the wall, and what little light it's fire gives soothes my panic just a enough for me to get ahold of my wits.

"I'm going to let go of your mouth now," he says against my ear. "If you scream, nobody will hear you."

Somehow, I believe him.

I do as he says, keeping the panic inside when he lifts his hand from my mouth and grabs the torch off the wall. He carries it, still holding my wrists, and the deeper we go, the darker and colder it gets. We pass a few doors and eventually Silas leads me into one of them, using a key to let us in. As we stride inside, I force myself to go willingly even though it's still too dark to make out anything. The air is damp and the cold is a deep freeze, even with my coat on. It looks like I haven't escaped winter even though I left the Winter Kingdom. Why couldn't this dragon castle have been the one stuck in eternal summer or spring? Heck, I'd even take autumn at this point. After this crap is all over, and assuming I make it out alive, I'm going on a beach vacation!

We continue to walk for a while and then eventually a brighter torchlight flickers up ahead. My eyes adjust. We're in some kind of dungeon. *Oh, crap!*

"You locked them all the way down here?" My eyes water and anger burns deep.

"I needed to keep the fact they were here from making it to the court gossip," he replies simply, not the least bit defensive. "They don't know about my recent escapades into the human realm and I'd rather like to keep it that way. I don't need my army deserting me right when they're actually going to be needed to do something for once in their pathetic little lives."

I hold back my tongue and all I can think is that this guy is awful and his people probably hate having to deal with his snotty attitude and selfish ways.

When we find them, at least they are together, at least they're clothed and have beds and blankets—at least they're okay. But their dresses are dirty and thin, their eyes are tired and worn, and when they see Silas, they scramble back. When they look closer and realize I'm here too, they blink with surprise and confusion and relief and pain.

I rush forward, my hands gripping the barred window on the door that locks them in. Silas stands right behind me, hands on my shoulders.

"Are you okay?" Tears run down my cheeks.

"Hazel? Is that really you?" Macy asks in that sweet soft voice of hers.

Cora sighs with relief. "Please tell us you came here to save us?"

"Yes!" I gush. "Of course I'm here to save you!"

Silas barks out a laugh and uses that moment to open the door and throw me into the cell. He slams the door shut with a clang just as the three of us run at it.

A wind forces us back, slamming us to the far wall. The air is cold and choking, piercing my lungs. *I can't breathe!* I scramble to locate my own magic and inner dragon but she's not there. Where is she? Is this it for me? Is he going to kill us after all that?

But the wind stops abruptly and we all gasp and sputter for breath.

"You will stay here," he growls through the bars, "until I am ready for you."

"You can't hold me!" I threaten.

He smirks. "Elemental magic won't work with that necklace on."

And then he's gone.

Necklace? My fingers fumble to my neck and locate a cord. It's tied tightly enough that I can't get it off. A pendant rests at its end but it's too close to my skin for me to see it.

"It's a dragon," Cora says. "Of course it is. Because nothing makes sense anymore and apparently dragons are real."

"I can't get it off," I growl. "I think it's magicked to stay tied." My eyes fill with tears again and I drop my head into my freezing cold hands. This isn't what I came here for; it wasn't supposed to happen this way. I left Dean. Owen is missing. Khali doesn't even know I'm here or was coming. Nobody knows we're down here.

"Hey." Macy scooches in closer and rests her head on my shoulder. "It's okay, Babe. Don't cry."

"It's... not... okay," I mutter between sobs. "This is my fault."

"Yeah, it's not okay." Cora lays her head on my other shoulder. "But we'll figure it out. Don't worry too much."

Her tone doesn't match her words in the slightest and I know she's just as worried as I am, if not more so. I wonder how long they've been down here. Have they been treated okay? Are they hungry? I wish I had food but I lost my backpack when I left it back in Winter.

A wave of exhaustion greets me and suddenly all I want to do is sleep. And what do you know? There aren't just two beds in here, there are three. Silas was waiting for me to show up and I played right into his plan.

Stupid!

I crawl to the bed and climb under the heavy blankets, not even bothering to remove my puffer jacket. It's too cold to take it off anyway. "I just need a nap," I whisper to my friends. "Getting here took everything out of me. Let me sleep for an hour and then we can come up with a plan."

They exchange nervous glances but I'm way too tired to ponder their meaning. No way can I think another coherent though, let alone hold a conversation right now. It's all too much. My eyes flutter closed and I drift off within seconds, only to be met with nightmares.

TWENTY-SIX
KHALI

I CAN'T SLEEP. I LAY on my too-soft bed, staring at the shadowed ceiling, my mind racing as I categorize the events of the day. It appears that the merpeople went back to their watery home after I ran off this morning because I haven't heard a word about it. I hope nobody else saw me, which seems too good to be true, and I worry that Silas already knows what I did. But at dinner tonight, he didn't mention it.

After Flannery gifted me the spear, getting back into the castle proved easy—being invisible made sure of that. But finding a place to hide the magicked item? Not so easy. I couldn't disappear for long without an alarm being raised so I had to find a place for it. Right now it's stashed under my bed but I know that I can't leave it there. One maid or another cleans every nook and cranny of the room almost daily, and besides, I don't want this spear near Silas. My parents are still being watched and I'm not sure that I can trust my mother right now, so I can't take it there. My fae friends already don't feel safe here so hiding the spear with them could put them in even more danger.

I peel myself from the bed and retrieve the golden artifact, enjoying the weight of it in my hands and deciding that Bram is the best choice to look after it. He's the type to have stacks of books and relics in his chamber, not to mention he has a huge locked chest in his study. He might even be able to hide it in plain sight. Part of me doesn't want to see him after catching him and Juniper with secrets. That hurt me. But a bigger part of me wants to see him more than anything.

Using the item's magic to shield me, I steal through the castle's corridors, sneaking past the guards, and slipping into his chambers. He's reading, as usual. His nose is in a huge book and he's so engrossed in the text that he doesn't care about the way his hair is standing on end, probably from running his hands through it one too many times. Nor does he seem to notice the fire burning in his hearth is nothing more than a pile of glowing embers. A small oil lamp glows from the table beside him, lighting the planes of his face and the gold of my spear.

I'm invisible but I let my guard down, revealing myself.

At first, he doesn't move or seem to notice me. But then his voice comes out in a scratchy whisper. "I didn't think I'd ever see you in here again."

I step forward and lay the spear at his feet. "It's a gift from a friend and I need a place to hide it."

He doesn't seem surprised by the magicked item itself, more awed than anything. He takes it into his hands, examining it, turning it as the light catches every angle.

"Careful. The tip is sharper than it looks. Can you hide it for me?"

His eyes flash to mine. "Of course."

He stands and strides to his bookshelf, opening a book at random, but it's not random because there's a little brass skeleton key inside. He uses it to unlock the trunk. He pulls out a silvery blanket and turns on me with a sheepish smile. "After I walk you back to your room, I'll return the spear here and wrap it in this blanket. This chest has been warded and can only be opened with this key"—he holds it up— "so your spear will be safe here. You're the only other person who knows where to find the key and I promise not to tell anyone of what you've entrusted to me."

He worries his bottom lip between his teeth. "Thank you for trusting me."

We stand staring at each other for a long moment, the space between us is small but right now it feels impassable. "What secret are you keeping from me? I have to ask."

He stills. "It's not my secret to tell."

"Bram—"

"I shook on it, I'm sorry." He grimaces. "But I promise it's to protect us from Silas and you'll know about it soon anyway."

I have nothing to say. I want to trust him, and actually, I do trust him more than anyone. But I can't help from feeling left out, rejected, my heart a little bruised.

And then, I think I know. "Is it the portal? The one the merpeople guard?"

"So you know…"

"Walk me back," I say. "I'm ready to be done with this conversation."

But he doesn't make a move. He just continues to stare at me, the emotions behind his eyes charged with wanting. It's the same wanting I feel low in my stomach.

"We can't," is all I say and he understands, the burning expression on his face fading into coolness. And that makes it even harder, makes me want to go to him, to kiss him again, to not go back to my rooms but to stay here with him tonight instead.

But I was right and I've been right. We can't. I'd rather hurt him than do something that would end up killing him. I didn't have a choice in this, not really. I've already decided I wasn't going to endanger him, I've already risked that with the spear and I won't do more.

"How was your day?" he asks, startling me with the typical question.

Truth be told, after hiding the spear under my bed, the day felt pointless. This? Taking care of Bram's safety, asking him for help, being with him, even seeing just him and breathing the same air as him? This feels like purpose.

"Well, getting this spear was quite the story."

He raises an eyebrow but I don't elaborate.

"I had to entertain more ladies in the queen's rooms in the afternoon," I sigh sarcastically. "So that was fun."

I don't mention that I had to suffer through dinner with Silas that evening as he discussed war strategy with his army generals. I'd looked the part of a doting wife and said all the right things, but a deep sadness had fallen over me like a dark cloud. Maybe because I didn't know how I was going to get my magic back and was starting to believe I never would. Maybe because Flannery's spear made this so real, and I was feeling a little guilty for accepting it in the first place. Or maybe because Aleeryrick was popping up everywhere Silas was lately and I hated that King Titus bargained my first daughter away to be that man's apprentice. Everything had become such a mess and each time I tried to make a plan or move forward, I had failed. Again and again, I was failing.

"Are you doing okay?" Bram steps closer. Too close. My mind flashes back to the kiss we shared in this very spot and I'm overwhelmed with impatience.

"I'm fine." It's not true.

He must see it because he frowns. Then he picks up the spear, disappearing from view. I suck in a breath, and when his hand brushes my cheek, I hold it.

"Nobody can see us, Khali."

And that's all it takes for him to save me.

Our lips collide—a fervent prayer—and every ounce of fear and sadness and frustration is washed clean with passion and love and *choice*. We stay like that until we're panting and burning for more but it's time for me to get back because if we keep going we won't be able to stop.

True to his word, he uses the magicked spear to escort me back, stealing more kisses along the way. When I slip inside my room and he leaves, I plop down on the rumpled bed, and go back to staring at the dark ceiling, but this time, I don't feel so awful anymore.

It doesn't last long.

I should sleep and give myself a break, but I couldn't even manage to. Tears bubble, hot and demanding. A heaviness presses in on my chest and I can't help but cry, trying to breathe through the pain. I love Bram. I do. I don't care if he's not Dragon Blessed or if he's not my husband or not the best mate for me. I can't change whom my heart wants. And that realization is a wound to my soul. Our relationship is only the top of a mountain of problems I'm facing. I squeeze my eyes closed and pray to the Gods. *I need help. I can't keep doing this. Please.*

Muffled shouts snap me out of prayers and I bolt upright. The noise is coming from Silas's room. It's dangerous for me to go check it out but I can't help myself. I spring from the bed and tiptoe into our shared family room, pressing my ear to his bedroom door.

"You're wrong." Silas's voice is prickly. "I did the right thing. If I hadn't done it, Drakenon would've been doomed to fall to the Occultists because you'd never had agreed to my plan."

There's a moment of silence before something slams to the ground. "No!"

More silence.

Then a quieter "I'm sorry" from Silas, two words I don't think I've ever heard him say. He clears his throat and a quick sob escapes followed by another sorry.

What in the world is going on in there?

"Queen Khali." The voice is deadpanned but it makes me jump and spin around. My response catches in my throat and my breath evaporates as I stare up at the sorcerer. "Spying on your husband, are you?" He holds his magicked wooden staff in one hand and I can't help but stare. It glows brighter than ever before. Colors of green, blue, red, and yellow swirl within the wood and the inlaid gemstones pulse. It's mesmerizing but also terrifying, and I take a step back, pressing myself into the hard door.

I don't have a chance to answer him. The door swings open and I stumble into Silas's arms.

"Khali?" he questions, voice throaty. "What are you doing awake?"

I turn to him. His eyes are bloodshot. He's obviously been crying.

"You woke me up with your yelling," I lie. "Who were you talking to in there?"

Silas sighs and steers me to one of the chairs in our shared sitting room. He deflates into the chair next to mine and Aleeryrick joins us, as if none of this is odd, as if we do this all the time.

"Did it work?" Aleeryrick asks Silas. His face is unreadable behind his white beard and steely eyes.

Silas nods.

"So that's all of them." He smiles, satisfied.

"All of what?" I ask. Worry unravels in my stomach.

"All the elementals," Silas says. He releases a slow breath, running his hands through tangled hair. "Khali, you heard me talking to Owen and my father. They appeared to me in spirit form."

I blink, disbelieving. "How?"

"I found a way to harness spirit magic," he says, a little flicker of pride dancing on his upturned lips. But there's a restless sadness in his eyes still. So he had to face the twin he murdered and the king he replaced? Good. I hope they haunt him for the rest of his miserable life.

"So you have all the elementals now?" I can't believe this. "All of the elements for what purpose? I don't understand. And how could you get spirit? And fire is nearly as rare as spirit is."

Does this mean he's like how I was? Or is he talking about something else? These questions stir in my mind, an ocean, each drop unable to separate from the rest.

Silas turns away from me, refusing to answer, and my stomach hardens. I look to Aleeryrick and his staff. I haven't forgotten that Silas told me he has a plan to trick the sorcerer and the very thought of it makes me sick.

"What's going on there?" I point to the staff. "Why does it look like that?"

Silas shakes his head. "That sorcerer's staff is what's going on here, Khali."

"This is how your kingdom is going to beat the Occultists," Aleeryrick adds. "The blood magic is strong, and the bond grows stronger every day, but this magic"—he slams the end of the staff into the rug—"is far more powerful. Combining all the elements together makes us unstoppable."

I scoff. "And what's in it for you? Why would you help us? Is this all for the staff?"

Silas drops his gaze and Aleeryrick smiles ruefully. "You'll see." He turns back to Silas. "The army is ready?"

Silas nods. "They're in position."

"And everyone else?"

"Yes."

"Good. We can begin." His muddy brown eyes glisten. "By this time tomorrow we will have succeeded."

"I still don't understand," I whisper, but nobody is talking to me or listening. I'm a spectator now and that is all.

Silas reaches out and grips the staff that Aleeryrick still holds tight. A new color appears, mixing in with the others—a bright and relentless white. It must be the spirit magic Silas somehow managed to procure. I rack my brain, trying to focus on what I could be missing, but my palms are sweaty and my heart is racing and I can only stare at the magic staff as the colors grow brighter, shifting, twirling, blending together and then spreading apart.

"Do you feel that?" Aleeryrick asks Silas. "Feel all that magic?"

Silas nods. His eyes are no longer bloodshot, they're clear and sure.

Aleeryrick glances at me. "Do you want to experience this kind of power?"

So badly. More than they could ever know. Maybe it would bring my magic back. Or maybe it would make me like them...

I stand, shake my head, and edge back toward my bedroom door.

"The wards will be gone by morning." Silas gazes up at me. The colored light from the staff reflects off his face and hair, and his eyes, they're darker than normal. Excited. Nervous. Prepared. "Get some sleep. Tomorrow is the big day."

TWENTY-SEVEN

HAZEL

MY EYES FLUTTER OPEN AND I bolt up with a gasp, everything coming back to me. I have no way to tell what time of day it is or how long I've been asleep. The torchlight from the tunnel outside the room still flickers through the barred window. Cora and Macy are fast asleep. I climb from the bed and pad toward the door, peering out into the hallway. There's nobody there.

"Don't bother." Cora's quiet voice startles me. "There's never anybody there except sometimes the hot boy king or that creepy old dude."

"Creepy old dude?"

"I don't know who he is," Cora continues, "but he looks like a wizard or something. Carries a wooden glowy staff with him and has a white beard and everything."

"How stereotypical." We both laugh softly but it rings false. "I'm so sorry."

Macy sits up on her bed and gazes over at me through bleary eyes. "Hazel, are you going to tell us why we're here? We were kidnapped and taken by dragons. If I had been alone, I would have for sure thought I'd gone crazy." Her voice cracks like she's about to cry. "Sometimes I still think I'm crazy."

I go to her and wrap her into the biggest and tightest hug I can. "I'm so sorry." I say it again. I could say it a million times and it would never make up for what has happened to them. But what I can do is explain and so I do. I answer all their questions and they readily believe every word I say. Considering where we are right now, I'm not surprised. If I'd told them all this back at Westinbrooke, I don't know if they'd have believed me. Probably not.

But now they're—we're—living it. And unfortunately, they may be living it for a while. I just hope that they can survive this place. Now that Silas has got me here, what use does he have for them? He may kill them and get rid of the evidence.

"I'm going to get you out of here," I finish with a promise. "We're all going home. But right now we need to figure out a way to get this necklace off. If I can't use my spirit magic then I can't get out of this room, but if I can, then I can travel through the spirit realm and go find help."

They blink at me, as if they're caught in a dream. Maybe we all are.

It's strange but I haven't felt an ounce of my spirit magic since Silas put this thing on me. It's everything I'd hoped the obsidian necklaces would do. This thing really works. A few months ago I would have done anything to get my hands on this necklace, but now that I have it, I'd do anything to get it off. I don't feel the electric pulse I've had ever since I turned eighteen when my dragon self manifested and I definitely don't see any spirits. It's not as if I see them all the time but I feel it deep in my soul that they're gone from me. I am completely shut off from the spirit realm. Is this what it's like to be normal? It's what I've always wanted but now that it's here, I kind of hate it. I'm too empty.

Cora and Macy take turns trying to undo the knotted cord but it's impossible—the necklace doesn't want to budge. We don't have anything sharp to cut it off but even if we did I don't think it would work.

"It's hopeless," I declare. I try to calm my breathing but I'm starting to hyperventilate. This wasn't supposed to happen. And Dean? Dean is going to come after me. I'm sure of it. *I know him.* He doesn't have any idea where to find me all the way down here. He'll be executed.

The room goes ice cold. A little snap sounds and the necklace falls to the ground. "What the...?"

Macy and Cora stare at the necklace, dumbfounded. "How?" Macy asks.

But I'm not staring at the necklace anymore, it's the three spirits standing in front of me who've caught my attention. One is Owen. Another is a reaper, his scythe shining like liquid silver and balancing between skeletal fingers. And the third spirit is an old version of the Brightcaster boys, most resembling Silas.

"Sorry that took so long," Owen says in an annoyed tone. "I had to find a reaper who would agree to cut that thing off of you." He points to the necklace and my mouth drops open. "Hazel, I'd like you to meet my father, King Titus Brightcaster."

The man doesn't say anything, he just stares at me like I'm some sort of deformed creature. This guy is unnerving and totally intimidating. He's tall with impossibly broad shoulders and long blondish hair. His eyes are bluish purple and dance with untapped electricity. He wears kingly attire and even a golden crown on his head.

"Woah…" is about all I can manage to say.

"Hazel, what's going on?" Cora asks, "What do you see?" But I can't answer her, not now, not yet.

At the back of my mind, I still wonder if I should fear the reaper. But they're not my problem anymore. They're here to help, not to harm.

Owen turns on the reaper. "I'm almost ready. Soon, I promise."

The reaper hisses and disappears in a cloud of black smoke.

"Come on," Owen says, reaching out to me. "We're running out of time."

"Time for what?"

"Time to save Khali," the king says, his deep rich voice catching me off guard. "And the rest of my family. Silas is…" His voice trails off. "He's dangerous. And so are the others."

I swallow. "The others?"

"The wards have been down for hours. The Occultists are almost here."

A fear unlike anything I've ever known crawls over my skin with icy fingers.

This is happening.

I turn back to my friends, hoping they'll understand. "I'll be back, I promise, but for now you're much safer down here."

"What's going on?" Cora demands again. Macy stands frozen, tears in her eyes.

"We need to go, Hazel," Owen says, voice growing more urgent.

"Some really bad guys are here," I say. "And I have to go stop them before they kill everyone." My friends' eyes go wide and their faces pale. "Step back, okay? I'm going to shift."

I don't think I can hurt them considering my spirit dragon is part of two realms and they'll be able to see me but not touch me—still, I can't risk it. Macy and Cora press themselves against the far wall and I shift into my dragon form. I'm small enough to fit in here but just barely. The last thing I see are the mystified expressions on my best friend's faces before I'm hurling myself from this dingy prison cell and into the relentless white of the supernatural spirit realm.

This time traveling through the spirit realm isn't nearly as exhausting as the first time. Maybe because I'm already getting the hang of it or maybe because I'm not going far, but time doesn't slow like it did earlier. I follow Owen and Titus through the white and to the image of Khali. She's pacing in her room, dressed in the type of a-line green princess gown that I'd expect for Drakenon. Her hair is pulled back into braids on the top of her head. She's dripping in red rubies and her eyes are painted with some kind of smudgy eyeliner. She's beautiful, but she's sad.

I have to help her.

I jump through the image, landing in the physical room beside her. I'm panting, like I've finished running a mile, but at least I'm in my human form.

"Hazel?" Khali gasps and wraps me into a tight hug. She's shaking and thinner than I remember her. "I'm so glad you're here!"

She's never hugged me before. Actually, she's stayed away from me, since touching me has hurt her in the past. But I hug her back and my magic doesn't react.

"Where's Dean? He's not here, is he? Silas will kill him!"

"No, he's not here. He's somewhere safe for now. What about you? Are you okay?"

"Yeah," she sighs. "No."

"What's going on?"

She releases a heavy breath. "Well, the wards are down meaning the Occultists are going to be here any minute. Silas has a plan to stop them but I'm pretty sure it's going to create an even bigger problem. I have to get to Bram. He has something I need… " Her voice trails off.

"I know all about the wards. Owen and Titus told me."

"Owen and Titus? You saw them?" She stops short, gaping at me.

"Yeah, but we can talk about that later. Where's Silas?" I take in the room, and yeah, she's the queen alright. This room is gorgeous, but that also means her vile husband could be near. "I don't want that jerk to catch me and lock me up again."

Her face pales as she releases me from the hug and steps back. "He locked you up? When?"

"Last night," I say. "He's got some of my friends down there too."

"Oh no." She starts to pace again. "Your friends are down there? For how long?"

"Maybe a week."

"That must be what Bellflower Blossom was talking about."

"I don't know—"

"And *that's* how he got the spirit magic. He took it from you."

"He did," I growl, "but I'm fine now. I got it back." I swallow down the fear about what I'm about to tell her. She needs to know. "Khali, you need to know the truth about the spell between us." Her eyes hold mine. "If I die, you will die too. That's why they did it. They're trying to kill you. They thought they'd hold me prisoner as a baby and keep me until I was eighteen when they could sacrifice me, but my mom got us out and raised me in the human world."

"Well, that explains a lot…"

"We have to stop the Occultists," I say, "and I think we have to do it together."

Her pretty round face sets into a look of sheer determination. "Okay, but first we need to go get my weapon from Bram."

I raise a brow. "And what might that be?"

She smiles for the first time since I've found her, her unusual eyes twinkling. "A really sharp spear with magical powers."

I can't help it, I smile too. "Sign me up! Let's go get it."

TWENTY-EIGHT
KHALI

"THE SPEAR ISN'T HERE." MY panic is a frantic punch in my gut as I look around Bram's library, skeleton key in my hand and empty chest at my feet. He's not here either. "No, no, no, this can't be happening."

"Hey, it's okay," Hazel says. She tries to sound calm but worry slips in the cracks between her words. "We'll figure something out."

"This *was* my something." I fall to my knees and rest my head against the edge of the wooden chest. Just last night Bram had locked Flannery's spear in here for me. Did he take it? And if he took it, why would he break his promise to me?

"We can fight without it." Hazel sounds confident but she doesn't know about my lost magic or exactly why the Occultists want to sacrifice me. "Come on. It's going to be okay. We need to go out there though." She points to the window and I stand on shaky legs to peer out. Beyond the city wall, lines of black lethal dragons are readying to fight. "That's where the action is going to be so that's where we need to be."

My throat goes dry. *No, no, no!* How am I supposed to fight? I need to tell her the truth. "Hazel, there's something you should know—"

A chorus of dragons roar, interrupting me. It's not just the dragon army preparing themselves for battle anymore. I squint, making out Aleeryrick and Silas among the crowd. There are others with him too. I catch the sun shining off Juniper's blonde hair and Maxx's ram horns. Someone turns and I'm sure it's Terek's face glancing back up at the castle. They're all dressed in armor.

They're here because I brought them here.

"What is it?" Hazel asks.

"It doesn't matter right now. You're right. Whatever is going on, it's not happening in this castle." I thought perhaps Silas would keep his guards on me or lock me up in my chamber, knowing that my magic is gone, but he hasn't. In fact, I haven't seen him all morning. Everyone who can fight has joined the battlefield. And now it's our turn.

Nerves wash over Hazel's face and I give her a stiff nod and speak the words we're both probably thinking but afraid to say. "Okay, let's go."

I LEAD HAZEL THROUGH THE tunnels. She tells me this is where Silas has been keeping her human friends and where she spent the night. It immediately makes sense as to why Silas was able to talk to Owen and Titus last night and why Aleeryrick asked him to pass some of the spirit magic onto the staff—the necklace.

"Did he put a necklace on you?" I already know the answer.

"Yes!" Her voice grows angry. "It took my magic away."

"It didn't just take it away," I say, wishing I didn't have to tell her the rest. "Anytime you tried to use your magic, it was syphoned right to Silas."

She shakes her head and fists her palms. "Son of a—"

"I'm sorry, I know, he's horrible." I peer at her over the flicker of the oil lamp's small flame. "But when this is all over, I promise to help get you and your friends home."

"Thank you." She sucks her bottom lip between her teeth and thinks for a while. "I hope you can make good on that promise, Khali."

"Believe me, so do I." What am I doing? I shouldn't be making promises. Truth is, I'm probably not going to survive this. If she knew I didn't have magic, she wouldn't be putting her trust in me right now.

We continue on through the narrow tunnel, the little flame as our guide through the darkness, and fall into silence. My mind returns to when I hugged Hazel earlier. I'd hoped that it would trigger something within me, that maybe my elementals would return, but nothing happened.

Nothing.

I'm certain that whatever the Occultists did to spell us together as babies meant that when we turned eighteen she'd fully develop her powers but I'd lose mine. Now they just need to kill one of us, right? I shudder to think what that would mean.

She tells me about her parentage and even though we're both Dragon Blessed, we're not closely related. All I can think is that the warlocks had to find a dragon child who was born on the same day I was for their spell to work and they caught wind of Hazel's mother's pregnancy and somehow spelled her to give birth the day I was born.

As we walk, she confides in me more about being half faerie and half dragon, and explains how her dragon actually manifests in between realms.

"Your gift sounds very unique," I supply. "Don't take it for granted, okay? Promise me you'll work hard on developing it."

She looks at me sideways but agrees.

I hate that my four elements are nowhere to be found. But despite the openness of her eyes and the honesty in this conversation, I keep my secret locked up tight.

It's killing me.

It's probably literally going to kill me very soon, but if I told her the truth now she wouldn't want to go out there with me. None of them would want me there for the battle. I can't have that. I need to be part of this, I need to fight, to do something. I won't stand down any longer. The Occultists have taken nearly everything from me. If we can defeat them, we can defeat their spells as well. It's the only way I'm going to get my magic back. I have to try.

With each step forward, I've realized something about myself. I always thought I needed to get away from this place, to fly and to be free on my own. I thought I needed freedom to be happy and I wanted to avoid my duties as Drakenon's future queen. But it turns out, what I thought wasn't actually true. To be happy I need to help the people I love and do the right thing. Standing up for myself has never been a problem, but what about all the other people who need someone to stand up for them? What about the fae who are left to hide away? And Bellflower Blossom who died for nothing? What about Bram and people like him who aren't Dragon Blessed?

I'll die today to save my people if I have to… and I'm at peace with that.

Because I'd rather die than live as a coward. It's an odd feeling, knowing this will likely be my final day of life. I wonder if Owen will be there for me on the other side and what King Titus will have to say about my choices. I can only hope Bram and my parents and so many others will make it out of this fight alive. And I hope that they can have a better life, without a tyrant for a king, and without the zealous warlocks bent on destroying them.

We finally make it to the end of the tunnel and step out from the hidden trapdoor in the wall, scrambling through the thicket of bushes and blinking against the midday sun. I'm hit with a caress of gentle wind. It brushes the hair from my face, almost to tell me that everything is going to be okay.

I know it won't, but still, I allow myself to hope.

I squint and look around. Most of the snow has melted. The ground is rock hard in some places and muddy in others. The smell of fresh winter and metal armor and bridled fear dance on the breeze.

"This isn't going to be easy, is it?" Hazel sighs.

"I'm afraid not."

"Hmm..."

"Stay away from Silas," I say quickly, grabbing onto her hand. "And don't touch the sorcerer's staff. There's something dark going on there with those two. You shouldn't get any more involved than you already are. Let's just focus on keeping as many people alive as we can and fight off the Occultists."

"Easier said than done, right?" She chuckles with self-deprecation and rolls her eyes. "But sure, I'll do my best."

Bootsteps squash against mud to our right and we turn to find several of the Dragon Blessed army approaching. Some are already shifted into fearsome dragons but most are still men and women, dressed in heavy leathers. They're the same leathers Hazel and I stole to put over our clothes on the way out of the tunnel. No guards were left in the castle. It was easy.

Was it too easy?

"Queen Khali," a man says, "Silas has requested you to join him."

A sinking feeling comes over me because yes, it was far too easy. Maybe Silas wanted me to follow him down here. What if this is a trap?

I glance at Hazel, holding her gaze for a long second, wishing I could speak to her through the dragon link. "Stay here."

"Both of you," the man adds, his voice clipped.

"Well, then…" Hazel sighs. A strand of her wheat colored hair catches in her mouth and she pushes it back up into her hair tie. "Let's get this over with."

We follow the army men and women over to King Silas. As we approach, I look to Terek, Maxx, and Juniper, who all seem excited by the prospect of a fight. These are people who've probably trained for something like this, or maybe they're just ready to get vengeance on the Occultists. They're dressed the part, with swords and bows in their hands, and determination on their faces.

One by one, they see me, and they startle. They know it isn't safe for me to be here. Terek opens his mouth to say something but Maxx pulls him back. Juniper just stares, her face draining of color.

And Silas? The man is beautiful in his battle clothes, there's no denying it. He looks every part a dragon king, with his blond hair tied back and a small crown perched on his head. The black battle leathers look good against his muscled arms and legs and he stands like he has everything to gain. But the way he watches us approach is anything but beautiful. It's terrifying. And I want to look away but I don't.

"I see you've found my prisoner." Silas's electric eyes land on Hazel.

"Keeping her locked away is a mistake. She's an asset to this fight," I challenge.

He frowns at that, and then his eyes linger on her neckline. "Where's the necklace?"

"Destroyed," she growls back, shoulders tensing.

"I made it myself," Aleeryrick says, stepping forward. The sorcerer looks older in this light but then again he's immortal so there's no telling how old he really must be. The magicked staff glows beneath his palm and his brown eyes narrow on Hazel. "It can't be destroyed. It's impossible."

"Not with a reaper's scythe it isn't," Hazel barks back.

The group falls silent for a tense moment. I worry about what they'll do but Aleeryrick only smiles curiously and Silas laughs like this is an amazing new development.

Not what I expected.

"What do you think?" Silas turns to Aleeryrick. "Can we still do it?"

Aleeryrick's hand tightens on his staff. "We can."

"They're here!" someone yells.

It happens so fast. Black tendrils of smoky magic curl around us out of seemingly nowhere the very same moment a line of endless Occultists appear on the horizon. Within seconds, people start to fall, their bodies being eaten alive by the smoke. Blood seeps from their eyes and mouths in a gruesome scene. Chaos erupts.

"Charge!" a man yells and the dragons shift, taking off in flight toward the enemies. Earth rattles, wind roars, water from the nearby lakes shoots through the air, a fire burns—all the elements are at play here, meaning all the best of the Dragon Blessed are fighting. It's an amazing sight to behold. The black smoke retreats just as quickly as it came and I think that maybe we will stand a chance to beat them.

Hazel grabs my hand. "Ready to shift?"

She thinks we're going to charge in there and take them on together. She still doesn't know my problem. I take a step back, my mouth dropping open and a soft "I can't" tumbles from my lips. She stares at me, dumbfounded.

"Now," Silas says. He grabs hold of Aleeryrick's staff and the pulsing colors swirl through it like they did last night. The men slam the end of the staff into the hard ground, and when they do, all my friends fall.

Juniper falls.

Terek falls.

Maxx falls.

Hazel falls.

"What?" I scream, rushing forward to yell at Silas. "What are you doing to them?"

But he doesn't answer. I whip my head around, frantic, and that's when I notice my friends aren't the only ones who have fallen. Many of the dragons are on the ground too.

And color, like the black smoky magic only in color, is seeping from them and traveling to the staff. Browns, greens, reds, oranges—every color is joining the staff, power radiating off it.

"What's going on?" I scream at Silas again.

Still holding one hand on the staff, he pulls a pouch from his pocket and dumps a plume of sparking gold dust on the staff.

"The pixie dust I promised," he says to Aleeryrick.

My heart drops to my stomach as guilt and anger take over. He got that from Bellflower Blossom! He killed her for it! I shove at the men, careful to stay away from touching the staff. They don't budge but at least my angry shoving seems to get their attention. "What are you doing?" I scream again, pointing to all the bodies writhing in the snow and mud. "You're killing them!"

"Then so be it!" Silas glares back at me. "This is what it takes to beat the Occultists, to take their magic as our own."

As our own? "No!"

"All this elemental magic in one magical object," Silas continues, his voice growing mad with power. "It's worth the sacrifice."

"It's not your sacrifice to make!" I scream but my words fall on deaf ears.

Aleeryrick laughs. "Yes, it's quite perfect." He eyes Silas with glee. "And you still think you're going to betray me. Didn't you ever wonder if I'd be the one to betray you?"

Silas blinks, the madness clearing from his eyes. "Wait…"

Aleeryrick shoves Silas off the staff and he falls to the ground, immediately convulsing like all the others. An electric blue color floats from his body, joining the staff. The crown atop his head pops off and rolls to rest against my leather boots.

"You can join me, Khali," Aleeryrick speaks with a casual tone though I know he's anything but casual, "or you can die."

I'm speechless.

"Just as well," he cackles. "This way I'll take what they wanted."

I can only stand there. Stunned and angry and not knowing what to do. He must take that as a no because he shrugs and nudges the staff toward me. That's all it takes, a simple nudge. Searing pain envelopes my entire being from the inside out, so terrible that I can't even scream, my throat won't let me. My limbs go numb. I hit the ground with a thud and my vision goes from white to black to white again.

And then there's nothing else.

TWENTY-NINE
HAZEL

MY BREATH HITCHES, JOLTING ME awake. I'm in a vast white room—the spirit realm. My heart pounds. My ears ring. Something about being here this time feels different. I'm more solid somehow, but also the opposite of that, like my body is weightless.

Isn't there somewhere I'm supposed to be right now?

I blink and gaze around, noticing the images of my loved ones floating in space. I reach out toward the scene of Harmony and my mother decorating a tall and skinny Christmas tree. Mom's wings are back, they glisten silver in the light of the multicolored lights as she hangs a vintage ornament. She was waiting until I got home from school so we could go to the tree farm and decorate it together, but that was before everything changed. I can't believe I'm going to miss Christmas but even more startling is that I forgot about it entirely over the last few days. How does someone like me, someone obsessed with the holidays, forget about it?

I'm trying to remember—to put all the pieces together—but my mind is foggy.

I catch sight of another image, one that makes me scream and rush forward, until I'm no longer in the white room. I'm standing on a patch of white snow, reaching out for Dean. He's bloodied and bruised, his black hair hanging around this face, as he struggles to stand. On each side, two Occultists hold onto him, keeping him up right.

"No! Dean, why did you follow me?" I cry.

And then I remember it all—and how I got here.

Nobody hears me. And the Occultists, they look eerily similar and ageless, with glowing lustful red eyes and deep burgundy robes caked in water and mud along the bottoms. Their hoods cover sickly white bald heads and they chant together, their voices somehow rearing a black smoky magic that rumbles and pulses along the ground.

"Dean?" My voice squeaks. Tears burn my eyes. "Can you hear me?"

But I already know that he can't. And when I put my hand out to touch him, my fingers pass right through him. I scream again and look out over the expanse of the field, spotting the sorcerer with the staff, and my own body laying there among the carnage.

I'm not using my spirit magic right now. This isn't a normal shift and travel between realms. This is death.

I've died.

My lungs pulse, holding back a scream, but the battle scene around me is replaced with the white room before a sound escapes my throat.

This time I'm not alone.

Owen is here and King Titus, too. And also so many others. Too many. People I don't know on a name basis but who I recognize from the battlefield, dressed in the dark leathers that the Dragon Blessed wore into battle.

I find Khali standing aimlessly and my heart plummets. "No," I whisper. My death must have meant hers, too. *Unless...*

"Where are we?"

Her question interrupts my thoughts and I meet her fearful eyes with a simple nod of my head. I wish I could lie to her but I can't. "This is the spirit realm."

Her face pales. "Does that mean...?"

"I'm afraid so, for me too." My voice breaks as I try to get the words out. "I'm so sorry."

I pull her into a hug and she's solid to me, real, and even though we're dead and we've failed, we're still in this together. My heart aches for everything and everyone we're about to leave behind. Knowing what I know, being who I am, I've had a lot of time to think about death. And I know this: I'm not going to stick around this waiting place. I want to move on. I can't be the ghost who won't let go of the life she lost, sad or angry or desperate to send a message to the living. I already know my mom won't be able to see me, nobody will, so why would I want to see her pain? And there's nothing I can do to help Dean without a body. All I can wish for is that everyone I love survives this attack and goes on to live wonderful lives, and one day when it's their time, I'll meet them on the other side.

It's strange, I already can't wait for that reunion but I also want it to be a long time away.

I'm crying. I didn't even realize it at first but the tears are unstoppable, hot and wet and burning. It feels like someone has stuck a dagger in my heart which they just keep twisting and twisting. This hurts so bad. It wasn't supposed to be this way.

"Khali?" a deep voice comes between us, filled with confusion and regret but also love and joy. Khali and I turn to find Owen standing before us. He's so, so beautiful. He's dressed in his princely attire again and has a mischievous glint in his bright eyes but also something else, something only reserved for Khali, something unmistakable—love.

In an instant she's out of my arms and burrowed into his, sobbing. They hug for a while and whisper to each other in hushed tones. I hear "I'm sorry" and "my fault" and "I love you" and "it's going to be okay" but then Khali suddenly steps back and says forcefully, "no."

"I am not leaving," she says vehemently, "I can't give up."

"But you're dead." Owen's sky blue eyes are sad and pleading. "You can't go back. Believe me, I've tried. It doesn't work that way."

She shakes her head again, settling into denial like the stubborn girl that she is. I guess it takes one to know one.

"I knew I was most likely going to die today," she says, "but not like this, not so quickly, and not before I made a difference. We have to stop the Occultists first. And now we have to stop Aleeryrick and Silas."

"Silas is dead, too."

Shock races across her expression and she's left without words.

"You saw it happen."

Her hand covers her mouth. "But I didn't realize that's what was happening."

King Titus pops in out of nowhere, startling us all. His eyes are frantic and overbearing as he looks around the white room, witnessing the growing number of people who have appeared here. He grabs Khali and hugs her hard against this broad chest. She sputters with surprise. "I'm so sorry," he says. "This is my fault. I should have never made you marry Silas or trusted the sorcerer in the first place."

He lets her go and stares into her eyes, like whatever he has to say next is of utmost importance. "But there's still a chance for you. And if you go back, all your vows and bonds and spells will be broken. You will start fresh."

"What?" Her voice cracks with disbelief. "How can I go back though?"

"Bram," he says simply, his face filling with pride.

"And Juniper." One of the fae steps forward, a handsome one with golden blond hair, catlike eyes, and an easy smile. "Maxx just disappeared," he says, his voice excited. "And Juniper isn't here which might mean what I think it means."

I don't quite understand any of it but his words light Khali's eyes and she jumps from Titus's arms and into the fae's. "Terek! Are you saying there's a chance?"

"I think so!"

"A chance for what?"

They turn on me. "Juniper is a healer," she gushes. "She might be able to bring us back."

My eyes practically pop out of my head as hope burns bright in my chest. "But if I'm dead, then you're dead. The Occultists or that sorcerer should already have your magic."

"Not if I died first," she muses, "the spell only works if they kill you first, remember?"

"Listen to me, girls," Titus says gruffly, taking both our hands between his large rough ones. It's strange, but also comforting. "This is important. Don't forget what I'm about to tell you."

We nod, all ears.

"The Occultist's blood bond works through sacrifice, strengthening their bond each time someone dies, but it also leaves them weaker because if their master is killed, then they will all die." He grins. "Don't you see? By spelling you two, they revealed their weakness."

"How do you know this?" Khali questions.

"We've been able to visit them because of Dean," Owen adds, "we can go visit our living family and he's with them now. He's with the master. They're going to sacrifice him to the bond once they get to the portal the mermaids are protecting."

"I love my son," Titus says, "I love all my sons. I have failed them. But you might have a chance to save Dean. He needs you."

Owen interjects. "It was only in death that we learned the truth of the blood bond but now we know—we know the truth—and so do you. They never could have anticipated this."

I nod, because they're both right. And I'm determined to save Dean, to save us, and everyone I possibly can.

"Juniper is close," Khali says, her eyes fluttering shut and then opening again, landing on Owen. "I have to leave you."

Something light and feathery tugs at my conscience, and Owen and Khali hurry to say their goodbyes. The edges of my vision start to fade to black and my body grows heavier and heavier, but I don't give into the fear. Rather, I fall into the void. I'm being given another chance. It feels exactly like a miracle.

THIRTY
KHALI

IT'S ALEERYRICK'S BLOOD CURDLING SCREAMS that wake me before anything else. "What have you done?" he bellows. My eyes flutter open. "Now you're all going to die!" He screams again, vengeful and determined. Fuzzy thoughts cling to my mind but his words wake me. I scamper to my feet, the haze of death clearing in seconds.

"Bram…" His name is a balm, soft on my lips, and my heart speeds to find him. Standing with Flannery's golden spear in one hand, Bram is covered in dirt and sweat and blood. His emerald eyes are zeroed in on the wizard with complete determination, his jaw set in a sharp line. I gasp. At their feet are the two broken ends of the Jeweled Forest staff. All the color and magic that was being held there has vanished.

"You okay?" Juniper asks. I almost forgot she was at my side but I nod. She's holding my hand and I didn't even realize it. She squeezes it once and then runs over to where Hazel is sprawled out. Thank the Gods for Bram and Juniper. Bram for being brave and smart. And Juniper for her healing magic, which must have saved her first and now she's saving each of us, one by one, attempting to heal us before we're fully lost.

But the sorcerer's staff is broken so whatever it was meant to do, it failed. The black smoke from the Sovereign Occultists has also vanished but I'm certain that won't last much longer. The charge of the magic still lingers in the air. They'll realize whatever was stopping them has failed and come back at us, and with more force than the first time. I blink across the expanse of the field and see them, still lined up, still chanting, still very much alive.

No. I won't let them win.

Aleeryrick yells again and raises his fist to Bram, his arm readying to swing. I lunge forward. Magic bursts through my body, the four elementals filling every last crevice, and tears spring to my eyes. Titus was right! My magic has returned because all vows and spells were broken when I passed through death and joined the spirit realm. I've returned stronger than ever.

I use air to send a gust of wind to push Aleeryrick away from Bram, flattening him to the ground. "You will pay for this!" I use the earth elemental to have the mud around him suck at his limbs and pull him under. *I will bury this traitor alive if I have to!* His eyes flash to mine, fear crossing his features. *Good—he should be afraid.* I'm not going to let him get away with this. He thought he could take my first daughter, thought he could work with Silas to steal our magic, then turn on us.

"Please," he gasps, as if I can be swayed to take mercy on him. I can't.

A savage anger burns molten within me, hotter even than my fire elemental rising to the surface. Fireballs flicker to my fingers and grow into flames, taller and taller and taller. And hot, hotter than anything I've ever felt before. Aleeryrick is half under the earth but the fire wants to take a crack at him, too. And who am I to stop it? The rage is all encompassing. Maybe I should stop the anger; maybe I should take pity on the man. But I don't. Immortal doesn't mean he can't be killed, just that he won't die of old age. Well, I think he's lived long enough.

"Please stop!" he begs.

"You claim to have lived more than a century," I snarl. "That your magic kept others from entering Drakenon."

"I can explain."

"Your time is up!"

"No!" he bellows, squeezes his eyes shut, softening his expression, and then... he completely disappears.

I blink, confused. He's gone? "What? How? Where is he!"

The staff still lays broken beside where he was and I direct the fire at that instead, burning it until it is nothing more than ash. It hisses and resists, but my magic is too much for it.

"I need to find that sorcerer!" I scream, the anger still raging inside me.

"We have other things to worry about," Bram's voice is sure and soothing, quick to temper my flame. He steps forward and pulls me into a hug, kissing the top of my head. I melt into him.

My Bram. Thank Gods my Bram is alive.

We survey the battlefield. So many are dead. Silas, included—he still hasn't gotten up from where he lays sprawled out and bloodied. Juniper runs from person to person but steers clear of the young king. Maybe I should direct her back to him, maybe I should have pity on Silas, forgive him, but I don't. Seeing Owen on the other side and saying goodbye didn't give me the peace I thought it would. It only made me sad. His death was unnecessary. So much of what has happened shouldn't have happened. But it was at Silas's hand and there are more who would have died because of him. My fae friends, some of the dragons, Silas was in on this with Aleeryrick and he was willing to sacrifice even more lives to get the power he wanted—the Occultist's power.

Being king of Drakenon wasn't enough for him and it never would have been.

He was willing to kill whoever necessary for his selfish ambitions. I don't know what kind of fate Silas will meet on the other side, or who he'll have to answer to, but I'm not going to stop righteous judgement from happening. He deserves the death he got, the betrayal he walked into. He chose it with his actions.

And Bram is right. I have other things to worry about right now. Namely the plume of crawling black smoke that is billowing toward us and the hordes of Occultists floating in our direction from the other end of the field. Their chanting grows louder with every passing second. Whatever break in the battle this was, it's over.

"Keep going," I yell to Juniper. "Bring back as many as you can!"

Then I turn, frantic to find Hazel, but she's already beat me to it. She's awake again, human again, and charging right back toward the Occultists, her blonde hair streaming behind her, her legs pumping her forward.

"Come on!" she yells at me. "They have Dean!"

My heart seizes. *No, please not Dean, too…*

Bram releases me from the hug. "You can do this," he says. He's so sure. His face, his eyes, everything about him is positive that I'm capable of success. He believes in me, more than I believe in myself, and that gives me the strength to do what needs to be done.

"Keep using that!" I point to the spear. "Stay hidden!"

Then I shift, my dragon form taking over like a second skin, and vault into the air, flying after Hazel. I catch up to her and she shifts as well. Her white dragon is half the size of mine, and not quite solid, but she's fast. And she's able to be in multiple realms at once, to see this place and the spirit realm, and for a moment I wish I could see it, too.

But I have my own magic to wield—magic I'll never take for granted. Not ever.

The battle begins with a roar, louder than I expected, and the action moves fast. My body takes over, knowing exactly what to do. I blow fire when I can and use my other elements to cut down the enemy. They're quick to dodge me and fire back with their black magic. It hits me a few times, sucking the life out of me before I can get away. I'm growing weaker with each hit but I don't let it deter me. And I'm not alone in that. The expanse of snowy field transforms into sheer hellfire and magic and black death and powerful elementals—and best of all, dragons.

We're everywhere.

These are *my people* and I love them. I'll fight to the death for them. And I'll never ever *ever* run away from them again. As I fight alongside them, defending who I can, letting them defend me, roaring with sadness and anger when one goes down, and triumph when one of ours takes one of theirs, I realize this is exactly where I am meant to be. We call to each other through our dragon link, our thoughts instantly communicated to the group, and it turns us into a ruthless and united force. It's our own kind of bond, and it's not made of blood sacrifice. It's made of centuries old magic, of friends and family, of being who we were born to be. And now, finally, I get to be one of them. I get to lead. To prove myself. To do all the things I've dreamed of doing.

The fae join us. Terek shoots arrows. Maxx cuts through the enemies. Juniper heals the fallen, as many as she can get to in time. Over the crest of a nearby hill, others charge toward us. Not dragons. Fae of all kinds, here to fight, led by a gorgeous bronzed centaur—Flannery. They send out a battle cry as they come at the warlocks from behind.

With their help, we're surrounding the warlocks on all sides. They seem to be moving toward the lake's edge, to get at the portal no doubt. The merpeople appear, cracking through the ice, spears at the ready. They snarl and hiss, determined to defend their territory. It's the warlocks against every other kind they have wronged and maybe, just maybe, we can win this.

I catch sight of Hazel. She's right near Dean, so close to breaking him free from the two warlocks who hold him. I screech and fly forward to help, dodging black magic as I zip through the frosty air. I blast the men who hold Dean with a torrent of ice and they lose their grip, trying to fight off the impenetrable cold. That one small moment of freedom is all Dean needs. He shifts into a roaring dragon and pours judgement upon their heads, lighting them like torches. They fall and he cuts away from the warlocks, quick to team up with Hazel.

The two of them take on the world together, moving in tandem, as if they are of the same mind. He shoots fireballs and rips the enemy apart with his teeth, and she's right there with him. I'm not entirely sure what she's doing, but she must be doing something with her spirit elemental as she sweeps through the crowd, because there's a determination leading her little white dragon body, something that speaks of ancient magic.

I don't have time to wonder about it, I have to keep moving. Keep fighting. It's kill or be killed. There are simply so many warlocks, countless more than I ever thought possible. And they just keep coming. They don't fight with swords or fists, it's that black magic, and it's growing more and more with each passing second. I knew the Sovereign Occultists had years to build their cult, decades, maybe longer, but I never knew it was this big. Maybe that's a good thing that I didn't know because if I had, I would've had a lot more fear coming into this fight.

Bram is out here with the spear and even though part of me wants to make him go back, he's too vulnerable, I have to trust in the magicked spear to keep him alive. Flannery brandishes a mighty sword. He seems comfortable with the weapon, crazed by the fight—by revenge—as he screams a gutteral battle cry and charges into a horde of the evil men, cutting each opponent down in seconds. His bare muscles move in a strange kind of grace as he fights, it's dazzling. I wish I could fight like that.

But then… he falls too.

Juniper sees it happen at the same time I do. I swoop toward him and she sprints forward, falling to her knees at his side. She puts her hands out to heal him. I shift back to my human form so I can talk to her.

"Is he okay?"

"He's not waking up," her voice is strained. She keeps her hands pressed to him while life gushes from the wound at his abdomen. "The blood should be stopping by now. The wound should be healing itself." Her eyes grow frantic. "Why isn't it working?"

Flannery's eyes flutter open, staring into nothing as if they're trying to focus but they can't. "Tell them…" he whispers, "tell them I love them."

Then his entire body slackens.

He's gone.

The black plumes of the Occultists' blood magic crash over us, swallowing us whole. I can feel their bond coiling through me, heavy and powerful. It's stronger than I ever could have imagined, a condensed magic unlike anything I've experienced in my life. Juniper is here with me in this magic, both of us lost to it. I reach out to her but find nothing. I'm alone and all I can see is inky, endless black. My lifeforce is sucked away as my body weakens. I crumple to the ground—it too, is an endless darkness. One thought centers in my mind: there's no coming back from death this time.

THIRTY-ONE
HAZEL

MY WINGS CARRY ME AS if I'm weightless, the inertia of flight creating an awesome sense of purpose. It's indescribable! If I wasn't in the middle of an epic battle that could be straight from a fantasy TV show, I would be able to appreciate it more. As it is, I'm just trying to keep Dean alive. My thoughts are all my own but my body is still new to me, this dragon self who feels like an old friend. I'm untouchable when I'm her—nothing can hurt me. No magic. No enemy. It's the most freeing feeling I've ever experienced.

I'm straddling two realms like it's my natural state of being. I can see the physical world and the spirit realm at once, but that also means I can't touch either of them, almost like I'm a ghost, visible to all.

They can't touch me. And *that* is the only good thing about this because there is blood, so much blood, everywhere. And there are cries and screams. And the smell of burning flesh and blood and sweat and magic and snow and mud and so many things I can't even begin to describe.

I follow close as Dean charges after the enemy, attacking without hesitation. I swoop in and around him, awed as he fully awakens to his powers in a way he's never shown me before. He's ruthless, leaving no warlock alive in his wake of raw power, claws and teeth and fire.

Why did you leave me? His accusatory voice juts through my mind. It's the question he asks me again and again since we reunited. And I don't know what to say… This dragon communication is far more amazing and capable than what humans can do. I can hear the dragons calling out to each other as they work to bring the enemy down, but I can also clearly hear all my own thoughts, and Dean and I can speak to each other without others listening in if we want.

But now, because of this shared intelligence, I have to answer to Dean. I can't keep putting this off.

I didn't want you to get hurt, I relent. *I still don't.*

That wasn't your decision to make. I was prepared to see this through to the end.

Well, I see you followed me anyway, didn't you? And let me guess, that's how you got caught. The village wasn't compromised too, was it?

Suddenly I imagine hordes of Occultists converging on the cute little Winter village and my gut turns. I don't know what I would do if the hidden fae village was found out and people were hurt.

They're fine, Dean responds. *I left the village to come after you the second you took off, but many of the fae demanded to come with me. The Occultists caught me at the border. The other fae got away, thank Gods.*

They were going to sacrifice you, weren't they? As I ask the question, I know without any doubts that this is true and my heart aches at the possibility.

Yes. Eventually.

Dean follows his answer by cutting down another warlock. The man bellows in pain, his eyes crazed and glowing red as he drops to the ground. His body changes, ages, and within seconds he's dead. I watch as a reaper appears and overtakes on him, dragging him away to whatever hell is waiting. This is how it is with each warlock, whether the death is easy or hard, the reapers are here, swarming, ready to take them. It's nothing like so many others I've seen, where the reapers give the dead time to decide they're ready to move on. Not anymore. They just act, grabbing hold of them in the spirit realm and disappearing into a portal of black.

So in a way, I guess they are making it through portals, just not the kind of portals they were hoping for. Karma, right? They deserve it.

When I think the battle is starting to sway toward the dragons' favor, the thick black magic from the warlocks multiplies tenfold. The men chant together, loud and clear, in that ancient language that makes my toes curl. The black wraps around the entire battlefield, like a cloud of death. Dean, Khali, the fae, all the other dragons, everyone is lost to the darkness.

And we've played right into their plan.

They wanted this, sacrificed many of their own for this, because now we're all in one place. They'll suck the life from all of us and that will be the end of it, the royals, the army, everyone will be dead. The rest of Drakenon will have no choice but to surrender.

I continue to fly, the black magic unable to hurt me in this form, horrified that I have to watch these people die and I can't stop it. I blink, looking for Dean, but he's gone. I can't see anyone anymore, it's too thick. *Dean? Khali? Where are you?* Nobody replies. The communication is gone. All of it. I roar, the noise rolling over the too-quiet field.

This can't be happening. No!

If my dragon could cry, she would be crying right now, but she can't. And the only people I can see are the ones popping up in the spirit realm, dragons and warlocks. I can't save them if they end up there. I don't have Juniper's power. I don't know where their bodies are.

The reapers hover around, waiting for more warlocks.

One turns to me. *What do you see?* he asks. *You have the sight.*

I shake my head.

We can't see mortal realms, he continues, *not unless we possess a mortal body. We can only sense you and feel what you feel. That is how we find you.*

How are the warlocks doing this? another one asks, swooping in. His voice is a slippery hiss. But I'm not afraid of him or any of them anymore. They don't feel scary, they feel wise and even compassionate.

I gaze from side to side, trying to make sense of what they're asking me. *There's black magic,* I think through the dragon link, hoping they can understand.

What does it look like? a third reaper says, coming in closer than the rest. *Describe it.*

It's black, swirling, cloudy, kind of like smoke and magic. I don't know.

Look closer, he presses, *use your spiritual eyes, see what we see.*

He reaches a skeletal hand out and places it on my dragon shoulder and suddenly, the fear and anger and pain, everything clears and I can focus in on exactly what he's talking about.

It's not just black magic. It's so much more.

And I understand that the reapers were the key to everything all along.

For a while I thought they were the problem, but they were only being used for evil by the Sovereign Occultists. The warlocks wanted so desperately to cross the portals and when they couldn't do it by manipulating elemental magic, they forced a spell on the reapers to try to take their abilities for themselves. The only problem was the reapers were never meant to travel from the Eridas spirit realm to the human realm and the ability never transferred to the warlocks, it simply pushed the reapers to where they didn't belong. So that's why they became sick. They're not sick anymore. They're here to help me. Not just me, countless others. All the supernaturals. All the fae, the dragons, the merpeople, anyone who belongs to Eridas also belongs to them after death.

But the Occultists? They *are* sick. They *are* evil. And it is of their own choosing. The magicked bond they share is forged by blood magic, by countless unwilling sacrifices. It's made them powerful but King Titus is right, it's also made them too dependent on each other and vulnerable. I can't only feel the weighty magic of the blood bond coming from the Sovereign Occultists as they work in tandem to destroy, I can see it.

It's the sight my father tried to tell me about!

The black smoky magic in the physical world is how it manifests to the eyes, but to my spirit eyes, it's far more than smoke. It's alive and intelligent… but it's also dead in a way. It's a thing riling against itself, rotting and grotesque. The more it grows, the sicker it becomes, sick with power, sick with death, sick with tainted magic.

Today, I will end it, even if it means I end, too. This isn't a power I want to see in my human world, let alone in Eridas. It has to go.

Where does it lead? a reaper asks. *Show us. Take us to the master.*

I study the magic, trying to make sense of what they're asking. At first it's as I saw it before, a black pulsing smoke, but then it's as I see it with the spirit eyes, sparkling and interconnected, but also broken, the magic full of fissures. It rolls in on itself, leading back to one direction—the source. Could that be the master? I take flight again, following the direction in which the magic is sucking the life from the fallen and syphoning to the blood bond. The reapers follow close behind me, nipping at my wings.

They may not be able to see everything that I can see but they can see me. And that will have to be enough.

I force myself to ignore fallen dragons and fae on the battlefield, pushing onward until the black magic converges to a single point, like the eye of a hurricane. And there stands the master.

He's not what I expected.

He's not as ageless as the others, as well built or tall.

He is older and smaller, and his face is deformed on one side, the bone concave. Still, he has those glowing red eyes, those endless orbs dripping with death. He stands with his legs and hands apart as the others around him chant. They surround him on all sides in a wall of protection. From his outstretched hands flows the black magic, and right back into his hands flows the sparkling intelligence. It's like he's feeding this entire thing and being fed by it, too.

And that, that right there, *that's* the blood bond.

Kill him, a reaper hisses, *kill him quickly. Show no mercy.*

A shock of pure terror runs through me. I'm supposed to kill him? How? I can't touch him in this dragon form.

"Ah," the master speaks, voice low and reverent. "The spirit elemental is near." He smiles. "We've been waiting for you."

I can't fight him. I'll die.

But I have to try. I'm almost out of time as it is. Dean needs me. Khali. My mom. Harmony. This is it, this is my destiny. I might die, but if I die, he's going down with me.

And with that thought, I shift.

I'm human. Vulnerable flesh and blood. And I'm standing a mere foot away from the master.

"There you are."

He lunges.

Something metallic flashes to my right. As I'm taking the leap to dodge him, a reaper tosses me his scythe. I expect it to be heavy. It's not. It barely weighs anything—the ethereal made manifest. The blade arcs effortlessly as I swing it forward with all my strength and cut right through the master's frail neck.

There's no time for him to react. His body falls the same moment I turn away, screaming as hot blood sprays.

The same reaper swings into action, immediately taking his spirit away. I use the scythe, hacking away at the black magic. I don't know what makes me do it. Fear? Anger? Hope? The black magic screams and sizzles, dying almost as fast as it sprang to life.

The smoke and haze clears. I'm surrounded by the men in robes. They're ageing, dying with the loss of the blood bond, their bodies decaying instantly until there is nothing left but brittle skeletons littering the muddy snow. My stomach roils and bile rises in my throat. I turn away and run, glorious satisfaction lifting a smile to my face, lifting my heart, too. With my spirit eyes, the reapers are attacking the warlock's spirits, taking them away with swift vengeance. There's no coming back from this. It's over for them.

The smoke clears and I search the battlefield. There's so much death. Bodies are everywhere. The snow is red with blood. I try to find Dean and Khali, but I can't make them out amongst the carnage. What if I'm too late? What if they're already dead?

THIRTY-TWO
KHALI

TIME, THOUGHTS, PEOPLE, MY BREATH, my heart—it all moves in slow motion. The deadly smoke magic clears away and I'm left to see who is still alive and who didn't make it. Juniper is faster than me, up and moving, quick to heal whoever she can. I'm sure it's going to be impossible for so many to come back from this, they'd have been dead too long, wounded beyond even what her healing magic can repair. We're bound to have casualties and I can't bear to look just yet.

Flannery is dead.

I crawl over to him, taking his strong lifeless hand in my own and kissing it once. "I'll tell them," I whisper, my voice growing ragged. "I'll tell them that you love them." His long hair is matted and bloodied, and his warm eyes stare off into an unseen distance. Flannery's sacrifice meant his death. His family is waiting for a father who will never return home and my heart aches as I realize the repercussions of their loss. The centaurs have been said to be extinct. To lose this incredible unique man is a terrible blow to all of Eridas.

I rest his hands against his chest and softly push his eyelids closed. Then I muster up the courage to look around. The warlocks are nothing but bone and dust among fallen robes, but they're not the only ones who are gone. Bellflower Blossom already died because of this mess. Silas is dead and so many of the people he hurt along the way are never coming back. And now there are more, so many more. I force myself to wipe away the blurry tears threatening to fall and stand on weak legs. I need to be strong. The ones who are left, they will need me to be strong for them, to lead them into something better—they deserve better. The wind brushes against my cheeks as I survey the battlefield, glad to see that more people and dragons are getting up. At the lake, the merpeople are wailing over the death of their Queen.

I will have to reward them for helping. Despite everything, they did their duty and protected the portal below the lake. They want to walk on land again. Silas and his ancestors wouldn't grant that but maybe I will find a way to make that happen and keep my people safe.

I turn away and a flash of bright blond hair catches my eye. Juniper is draped over a body, her sobbing voice high and desperate. My heart breaks all over again—what if it's Bram? I run after her, tripping on my own boots as I go.

But it's not Bram I find in her arms.

It's Maxx.

I pull her against me as she sobs. "He's g-gone. And I-I never got to t-tell him how m-much I loved him."

"I'm so sorry." It's all I can say.

She caresses his face, his horns, his arms… all lifeless.

Across the field, I spot Hazel and Dean and Terek, and my heart swells with relief. And then it's Bram standing just feet away from me, bloodied and bruised, but very much alive. And it's my turn to burst into tears.

I let Juniper go and run to him, no longer caring who sees the love on my face. It's Bram—he's it for me. Blood and dirt mar his beautiful face. He staggers with a pained limp, the spear dragging behind him. Our gazes collide and his hold me in their emerald focus. He's always been so focused, this man of books and intellect and observance and sacrifice. I watched him grow from a pensive boy into a loyal man and I feel blessed to see him for who he really is.

When I reach him, he drops the spear, no longer invisible to anyone he wishes. We're truly exposed now but I don't care. I wrap my arms around his shoulders, my fingers trailing along his curled hair, and stand on my toes, pressing my lips to his.

He doesn't hold back.

He returns the kiss, deepening it. Others must be watching but none of that matters right now. It will soon, very soon, but right now, all that matters is this exact moment, this kiss, and this perfect boy.

"DO WE REALLY HAVE TO do this?" My voice, my spirit, my thoughts—everything is heavy, and sad, and relieved, and exhausted, and delighted and simply ready to be *done*.

"The remaining court demands an audience," Faros says, hovering over me as she brushes my hair into long loose curls. I stare at myself in the mirror, every bit of me feeling numb. My eyes are red around the rims, proof of the sadness in my heart. I hate my eyes in this moment, I hate the two colors and what they're going to do to me just as they have always done to me. Because this is it, isn't it? This is the moment the court demands I remarry someone other than Bram. Because they can't imagine someone save for a Dragon Blessed as their king, and they'll want a king. They'll demand one right away.

I won't do it. I'll refuse.

"Are you going to be okay?" Faros asks. She stares down at me, worried.

I shrug. "No… but does it matter?"

"To me it does."

"But what about the rest of them?"

She doesn't have an answer to that.

It took hours to clean up everything after the battle yesterday. The dead were carefully wrapped up in linen and we're planning to begin funerals tomorrow. There were simply too many pyres to build to have them right away. And I refused to have mass funerals. I want each and every fae and dragon that fell to receive a proper send off into the afterlife.

The bloodied snow was washed away and once all was said and done, everyone went home, hardly believing what had happened. There should have been feelings of celebration, because we'd finally won, but how could we celebrate when so many were dead? Impossible. What little was left of the Occultists was burned immediately and we at least praised the Gods for that.

The clean up? The death? I could handle all that. It was hard, but I was stronger than I knew. It was *okay*.

But this right now? This demand to present myself to the court? This, I can't handle this. I'm not strong enough anymore to deny my feelings for Bram or let someone else choose my future.

I'm back to being scrubbed and primped, dressed up like a pretty doll, a crown placed atop my head, as if everything in my life didn't just change forever. The metal digs into my scalp as Faros adjusts the silver, rubies and emeralds and diamonds sparkling against the morning sunlight. I glare at the crown because I don't know if I want it anymore. I mean, I do, I want to be Queen, but as *myself*. The cost of being Drakenon's Queen as the woman others want me to be has always been so high.

But…

But maybe this time, things could be different.

No matter what, I don't want to be a queen to someone who isn't Bram. Because I love him. I do. And now what? I'd give up my crown for him but I also don't want another person like Silas to reign. So then I'm stuck, aren't I?

I haven't even seen him since our passionate kiss on the battlefield. He took the magicked spear after that and disappeared, hiding it again until we can return it to Flannery's wife. He said he took it from the chest in the first place because he was bringing it to me, but I'd already left my chambers by the time he arrived. That's when he knew he had to take it to the battlefield himself. I'm so glad it worked out that way, that he had it, that he used it when we all needed it most. My heart shudders to think of what would have happened if he hadn't been there to break the sorcerer's staff.

I long to see Bram again, to go to him right now. And my heart aches with what he must think now that Dean is back.

Oh, Dean…

I won't let them kill Dean. No way. And now that he's here maybe he'll want to be king but I saw the way Hazel looked at him and I can't take that from her. I don't think he would want to do that either. It's obvious they're in love. Would he give up love to be king?

Maybe… but I don't think so. Actually, it's the other way around. That man would give up just about anything to be with Hazel.

"You are stunning." My mother lets herself into my room. She's Lady Alivia Elliot by the looks of it, taking on that air of sophistication and poise that she has used so well to her advantage over the years. "Come on," she says, reaching out to pull me from where I'm slumped on the chair. "I'm going with you."

I don't bother to say anything in return.

My gown is fitted, golden with red adornments and as beautiful as anything else in a queen's wardrobe. My hair is a pile of perfect curls cascading down my back. Faros put all the right makeup on my face to hide the puffiness from crying and lack of sleep. I look the part of Drakenon's Queen but I don't feel it. I don't feel much of anything.

"Snap out of it." Mother places her arm through mine as we walk down the castle's long empty corridor. "If we're going to pull this off, you can't go in there moping."

"What?"

Before she can answer me, we're swept into the throne room.

It's not a room I've spent a lot of time in since the coronation. But today must mean business because it's filled with every surviving member of the dragon court and they're all looking at me like I'm the most wonderful creature on earth.

What?

Their respect is the second biggest relief to killing off the Occultists. I can breathe, finally. I can breathe. The peace that is met with it rings through me like a church bell, filling every crevice of my soul. Maybe everything is going to be okay, after all.

They bow and curtsy to me.

Hazel is here with her two human friends. The fae are here, too. Everyone watches me, like they know what is about to happen, like they're excited for the show.

And in the back stands Bram, leaning against the far wall, eyes locked on me and filled with pride.

When I take my seat in the throne up front, I don't choose the smaller one next to the king's. I choose the bigger one, the one normally reserved for a Brightcaster King, and take it for my own.

The energy in the room shifts, growing charged.

The doors swing open. Dean strides in, dressed head to toe in the princely attire I remember so well. I expect whispers to erupt, as that's how these things usually go, but today they don't. Or maybe some of these people will yell and try to get their word in, demanding his execution, but nobody does. It's quiet, calm, again it's like everyone has a shared understanding except for me.

What is going on here? My eyes narrow and my spine goes stick straight.

Dean reaches the front of the room to stand before me. His black hair hangs across his molten fire eyes and a little smile flickers at the corner of his lips.

Seriously, what is going on here?

Could it be…

He motions to the members of court, to all the people I grew up with, many of whom are my friends. "We gathered this morning before you were asked to come here," Dean says coolly, "and we all agreed on one thing."

My heart pounds. Is he going to ask me to marry him? I don't think I could handle that. But I also… don't think he will ask such a thing of me. For so long Dean was all I wanted but now I wouldn't be able to accept him, not with Bram in the back, watching me like I'm the only person in the room—the only girl in the world. His green eyes have so much love in their depths. I risk a glance at him, my heart dancing when he runs a hand through his disheveled brown hair, a stray strand letting loose, and he smirks reassuringly. All I want is to go over there and fix his hair and bring those knowing lips down on my own.

"And what's that you agreed on?" I force myself to refocus on Dean.

"That you should be our queen."

I laugh, not quite impressed. "I already am your queen."

"Let me rephrase." His smile hitches at the corner and turns into a full-blown grin, a rare sight for the broody Dean I know so well. "That you should be the sovereign queen, the ruler of Drakenon, in your own right. *You* and nobody else."

My face drains, lips popping open. "Me alone? Which means… "

"That you're going to start your own royal line with whomever you choose? That your husband, whoever that may be"—he winks knowingly—"will be your partner and not your ruler. Yes, that's exactly what I mean."

I blink, dumbfounded. One by one, the members of the court stand and bow, calling out "Gods save the queen."

Nobody protests. Not even one.

I stand, finding my words one at a time. My dragon leaps joyfully alongside my elements. "Thank you." My voice cracks and tears fill my eyes. "I promise. I will not let you down. I will do my best to be the queen you deserve. I'll take care of us and put the needs of the kingdom before my own. We will learn and grow stronger from our past mistakes and become the best version of Drakenon we can be."

I've walked forward by this point to be among my people. I turn to gaze back at the thrones. I never did like them. How they're raised above everyone else. How one throne sits higher than the other. That's not the kind of monarch I want to be.

The decision comes easy.

I draw the fire to my palms and throw it at the thrones, smiling wide as they catch the flames. That gets more than a few gasps but I don't let it stop me. The thrones burn quick, embers rising into the room. I use my magic to fling open the windows, releasing the smoke. And then I call on my water elemental to extinguish the flames. There's nothing left of the thrones besides ash and embers which is just as well. It's time for something new.

I turn back to the crowd, letting the steam rise behind me.

"I am not above you. I am your queen, but I am here to love you and guide you, not to lord over you. I want to be a part of this kingdom but most of all I want us all to be one. United."

They stare at me, shocked, but also eager. They must want the same thing.

"We're one," I say. "We're Drakenon."

"We're Drakenon!" They call out in unison and the room erupts into rapturous applause.

I catch Bram's eye from where he still lingers in the back of the room and return his knowing smile. No matter what happens next, he's the man I'm going to marry. He will be my husband. And this time, it'll be my choice—the right choice. And the best part is that I have no doubt he'll choose me back, not because of my status or my magic or what I can do for him, but because he loves me.

And that is its own kind of magic.

ONE YEAR LATER
HAZEL

"ARE YOU READY TO GO?" I hitch my backpack over my shoulder and wink at Dean. "This isn't too much luggage, is it?" I'm standing at the entrance to Dean's house with my little roller bag at my feet. It's packed full of everything I could possibly need to visit Stoneshearth, excluding the medieval gowns I'll wear once we get there. I seriously can't wait for that part. Dressing up like a storybook princess is super fun and I'm about to do it for a whole week.

He raises an incredulous eyebrow at me. "Yeah, I'm ready. What do you have in that thing?" He points to the suitcase.

"I've packed presents for Khali and Bram, mainly in the form of chocolate and books. Maybe a plushie or two... or three."

He laughs and zips the suitcase and backpack into his massive waterproof duffle bag. That thing is ridiculous, but he can lift it up like it weighs nothing. Mom is going to meet us at the portal in an hour and then once we get through the freezing cold water—always the worst part—we'll be on our way to Drakenon. I could just jump through the spirit realm and skip the water but I don't know, I kind of like doing it all together. It's sort of our own little Polar Bear Plunge.

"So what books are you bringing Khali this time?" He eyes me with feigned interest. I know he doesn't really care about the books, fiction isn't his thing, but I love him for humoring me.

I got her hooked on Harry Potter when we visited over the summer and it turns out she actually appreciates the amazingness that is my all time favorite book series. Sometimes when she gets a break and can visit me, I'm going to whisk her away to Universal Studios and blow her mind. For now though, we'll work our way through the rest of the best fandoms one at a time. The girl is busy, what with being queen and all, but she loves reading for entertainment as much as I do, so it's fun to share that common interest. "Next I'm getting her into Twilight—Go Team Edward!" I mumble to myself. "Actually, I was Team Jacob until the weird baby thing happened and then I didn't really know what to think."

"I have no idea what any of that means."

"Don't worry!" I pull him into a hug and plop a kiss on his cheek. "When we get back, we'll have a movie marathon, and you'll know exactly what this Edward versus Jacob rivalry is all about. Prepare to be entertained!"

"Twilight has movies, too?" He doesn't sound so excited.

I laugh because he has no idea the amount of eye-rolls that are in his future and this is going to be so much fun.

"You're sure you want to go?" he asks, "We really can just do the entire Christmas break in Ohio, or split it between here and there. No homework for a month. It sounds pretty good to me."

Yeah, right. I know he wants to go visit his home just as much as I do.

"And miss the opportunity to experience Yule in Drakenon?" I pout. "No freaking way! We'll be back to my Mom's place by the 24th, and Harmony is going to join us there, so we can have the best of both worlds."

And it really is the best of both worlds.

Dean and I are still attending college and living in the human world, but we travel to Eridas often. Usually it's to hang out in the Fae Forest and work on our magic. It's nice to get that little recharge. But sometimes we travel over to Drakenon to see his old friends, his mom and brother, and of course Khali. I tend to fly with him, even though I could go through the spirit realm portals. It just depends on the mood I'm in but I don't love how the portals lose time and the whole day is just "poof" when I travel those long distances. I'd rather experience the thrill of flight as a dragon and have Dean at my side.

Dean kisses me softly before opening the front door. "Let's go to our other home."

We shuffle out into the icy morning air and wait for Macy to arrive. She should be here any minute. Good thing she's agreed to give us a ride. A hired driver might question why we want to be dropped off on the side of a forested highway in the middle of winter.

"Oh shoot!" I pull my phone out of my back pocket and frown. "I forgot to put this away." We can't take any electronics with us to Eridas because they'll get fried.

"I'll go put it in my safe with my computer and phone."

"Thanks, Babe."

He takes it and runs back inside, leaving me to wait on the front stoop. The wind picks up a notch and then settles into complete silence. Eerily, so.

"Wait a second." My eyes narrow as I take in the mysterious man sauntering up the drive. "I know you."

It's the angel Elias. He looks the same as that night he appeared to me at that seedy motel. His blond hair is pushed back off his chiseled face and his amber eyes are so bright, they almost look like fake contacts. He wears a tan wool trench coat—no wings visible today—and his hands are hooked into deep pockets.

If I wasn't head over heels in love with Dean, I'd be all sorts of swoony right now.

"And I gotta be honest," I say as I go out to greet him. "I never thought I was going to see you again."

His smiles hitches. "I'm here to thank you."

"Well, you're welcome, but please don't warn me of some new threat. I don't think I can take on another battle anytime soon."

"There will always be threats to the humans." His voice is surprisingly playful. "Good thing too, or I'd be out of a job."

This makes me laugh. I get to see the angels doing their tasks sometimes, but they're not like the reapers and they don't talk to me. Elias is different though. He's got to be some kind of hybrid because his wings aren't brilliant white, he's not freakishly tall, and well, he's flesh and blood and bone standing right in front of me.

"So what are you doing here?"

"I told you, I came to thank you."

"Is that really all?"

He sighs. "I have to leave this place. I'm being transferred to another," his voice tapers off. "Well, anyway, I came to let you know that you won't be seeing me again. I need you to promise you'll keep the spirit realms protected as best as you can."

"Well, yeah, sure, but nothing has happened in a year."

He nods once. "And I hope it stays that way but the thing about supernaturals is they can get… greedy. There may come a time that you will have to take action again and I need you to promise me that you won't hesitate to protect the humans."

"Okay, this is weird, but fine. Sure."

He's acting strange, like he doesn't want to leave, and I wonder if this man has been watching me and the other supernaturals around here more than he's willing to let on. But he's an angel and he said himself he's not allowed to travel to Eridas, that his job is limited to humans, so I guess it makes sense. Maybe this meeting really is just his way of bidding me goodbye.

"Can I give you a hug?" I ask. "You look like you need a hug."

His eyebrows shoot up and his mouth turns down. "No." He steps back, adamant. "I'm leaving now."

And then he disappears into thin air.

Well, okay then.

"Who were you talking to?" Dean returns. No way I'm going to keep this from him. So I tell him the whole thing, still keeping Elias's name to myself, and by the end, Dean is as confused as I am, if not a little nervous. "Well, he's right that supers get greedy and it's smart to be on the lookout."

We don't talk about it again.

Before long we're with my mom and the three of us are flying over the Summer Forest on our way to Drakenon. I can't wait to tackle Khali in a huge hug. We've become good friends now and dang, is that woman rocking it as queen or what?! Seriously it's like she was born for diplomacy and grace and all the things a monarch should be. Not to mention she's all shacked up with the hottie Bram now. Those two are so adorably cute together that it's borderline gross. Like I thought Dean and I were a little too much PDA at times but those two can't keep their hands off each other. No doubt there will be a wedding and then little dragon babies running around the castle soon. And thank heavens for that because I don't know what I'd have done if Dean had chosen that life over the one he has with me.

And I love my life.

I love school. Him. My friends. We brought Cora and Macy home as soon as we could after the battle. It was difficult at first for them to process things and move on, especially since their parents were pissed that they "went on vacation without permission", but eventually everything went back to normal between all of us. Macy declared her major as exercise science and wants to become a personal trainer and Cora has decided on a double major with political science and business, she even has a boyfriend now and it's been fun to watch her fall in love this year. She's always been such a tough cookie but Julian brings out her soft side. They're super cute.

Mom went back to work as a nurse, and now that she knows who she is, she's able to use her own glamour to cover her wings out in public, but she's also able to help people heal. Her ability is a lot like Juniper's, though it's quite tempered from all her time in the human realm. It's pretty telling that she was able to figure out her calling in life, even before the memories returned. She visits me in Westinbrooke and travels to Eridas a lot now so she can grow her abilities. I don't mind because I love spending time with her. She keeps talking about moving down here and I bet within the next year she lands a job and can make it happen. Who wouldn't want to hire an amazing nurse like her?

And fortunately for me, Harmony came back to Westinbrooke and reopened The Flowering Chakra. She doesn't do readings anymore because she can't, but I do medium readings and enjoy the time I get in the shop. And I *love* working with her. She's the perfect mentor for me. I never thought I'd be able to embrace my gift and stop calling it a curse, but I have. I'm able to help people move on after death, both on this side of the veil and the other, which is kind of remarkable. I keep saying I still want to go to vet school, but more and more often, I'm feeling like that might change. At least I have time to figure it out since I'm only nineteen. So much can happen in a year or two, or even a month or two, so who knows what's next for me. All in all, things are magical—as cheesy as that is to say. I don't know what the future holds, but I know I get to have Dean in it, I know I get to live between all the realms that I love, and that's enough for me.

Mom is slower than Dean and I, so we don't make it to Stonehearth until well after dark. The sky sparkles with stars and the castle below is lit up with candles in every window. More dragons join us as we veer toward the roof, calling out happy greetings through the telepathic link. We land and shift, Dean dropping the duffle bag at our feet, just as Brysta, Khali, and Bram burst through the doors.

"You're here!" Khali squeals and runs toward us, hugging us both and planting a friendly kiss on Dean's cheek. "Oh, I'm so glad you made it. You're going to love Yule!"

We're ushered inside and laden with gifts and food and so many welcomed greetings. It's the first night of what is going to be a week-long celebration and I seriously can't wait. My dragon is stronger here, my magic and my family too. I love this place!

Growing up, I always felt like I didn't belong anywhere. I struggled to make friends and never fit in. I didn't know my ancestry and certainly didn't have control over my gift. But now that's all changed. I've been able to say goodbye to my dad and make peace with my past. I have my mom and Dean, and now Khali and so many others who love me.

I have my home in West Virginia, the spirit realms to explore, and now this magical place to call my own. I realize now that I was never meant to fit into one kind of place or only connect with one type of people. Harmony once told me I was a bridge and at first I didn't understand what that meant or why it was a good thing but now I get it and I'm thrilled to be the bridge between all these amazing people and places.

"Are you happy?" Dean whispers low into my ear and laces his fingers with mine. His touch still sends a flutter of butterflies in my chest.

"Yes," I respond first with the words and second with a kiss. In fact, I never thought this kind of happiness could exist.

"Are you happy?" I ask the question right back.

His eyes bore into mine, dancing flames lighting up around the coal irises, and he smiles. "Thank you," he whispers.

"For what?"

He nods toward where his brother and mother are sitting on the nearby sofa, laughing at something so loudly that tears stream down the older woman's elegant face. Khali stands at the window nearby, not gazing out longingly, but with peace on her face. My mom stands at her side, chatting with her about the upcoming festivities.

"For putting my family back together," he says softly, his lips a brush against mine as he speaks. "At least, as much as possible."

I kiss him again. Just once. Quick. "We did that. Both of us. All of us, actually. But you're welcome."

Now that we know what we've got and how fleeting life can be, we won't ever take it for granted again. Not even for a second.

THE END

ACKNOWLEDGMENTS

THANK YOU FOR READING. I appreciate your support. If you enjoyed this book, please consider leaving a written review and telling your friends. I can't do this without you.

Thank you to my husband for always supporting me, to my cover designer Artscandare, my paperback formatter Molly Phipps, my editor Kate Foster, and my proofreaders Sarah Mostaghel, Ailene Kubricky, and Kate Anderson. Thank you to all the readers, friends, and family who continue to champion my books—I LOVE YOU ALL!

ABOUT THE AUTHOR

NINA WALKER is a *USA Today* Bestselling author. She lives near the beautiful red mountains of southern Utah with her family. She writes across multiple genres and loves metaphysical magic systems, forbidden love interests, and unexpected plot twists. She takes pride in publishing books that both teens and adults can enjoy. You can learn more at **WWW.NINAWALKERBOOKS.COM** or find her on social media to join in on the fun!

Made in United States
North Haven, CT
23 March 2024